PENGUIN BOOKS

# THE BOOK OF DAVE

Will Self has earned his reputation through a body of innovative work: there's nobody quite like him writing today. He is the author of four previous novels, four collections of short stories, three novellas and four non-fiction works. As a journalist he has contributed to a plethora of publications over the years; he is also a regular broadcaster on television and radio. He lives in London with his wife and four children.

# *The Book of Dave*

## A Revelation of the Recent Past and the Distant Future

WILL SELF

PENGUIN BOOKS

PENGUIN BOOKS

Published by the Penguin Group
Penguin Books Ltd, 80 Strand, London WC2R 0RL, England
Penguin Group (USA) Inc., 375 Hudson Street, New York, New York 10014, USA
Penguin Group (Canada), 90 Eglinton Avenue East, Suite 700, Toronto, Ontario, Canada M4P 2Y3
(a division of Pearson Penguin Canada Inc.)
Penguin Ireland, 25 St Stephen's Green, Dublin 2, Ireland
(a division of Penguin Books Ltd)
Penguin Group (Australia), 250 Camberwell Road, Camberwell, Victoria 3124, Australia
(a division of Pearson Australia Group Pty Ltd)
Penguin Books India Pvt Ltd, 11 Community Centre, Panchsheel Park, New Delhi – 110 017, India
Penguin Group (NZ), 67 Apollo Drive, Rosedale, North Shore 0632, New Zealand
(a division of Pearson New Zealand Ltd)
Penguin Books (South Africa) (Pty) Ltd, 24 Sturdee Avenue, Rosebank, Johannesburg 2196, South Africa

Penguin Books Ltd, Registered Offices: 80 Strand, London WC2R 0RL, England

www.penguin.com

First published by Viking 2006
Published in Penguin Books 2007
8



Printed in England by Clays Ltd, St Ives plc



ISBN: 978-0-141-01454-8

www.greenpenguin.co.uk

*For Luther*
*and with thanks to*
*Harry Harris and Nick Papadimitriou*

I like to think how easily Nature will absorb London as she absorbed the mastodon, setting her spiders to spin the winding sheet and her worms to fill in the graves, and her grass to cover it pitifully up, adding flowers – as an unknown hand added them to the grave of Nero.

Edward Thomas, *The South Country*

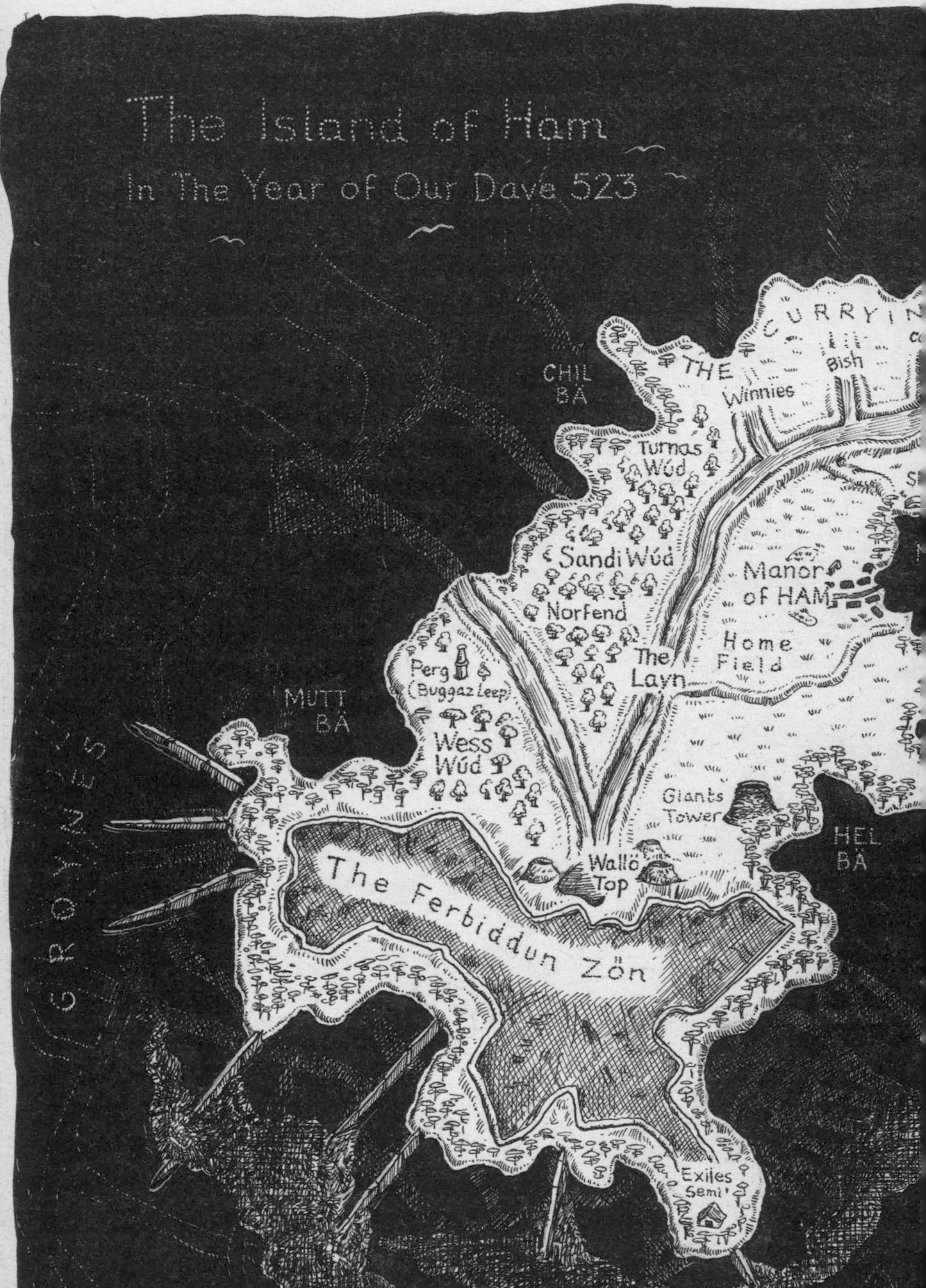
The Island of Ham
In The Year of Our Dave 523
CHIL BA
THE
Winnies
Bish
Tumas Wúd
Sandi Wúd
Norfend
Manor of HAM
Home Field
The Layn
Perg (Buggaz Leep)
MUTT BA
Wess Wúd
Giants Tower
HEL BA
Wallö Top
The Ferbiddun Zön
GROYNES
Exiles Semi

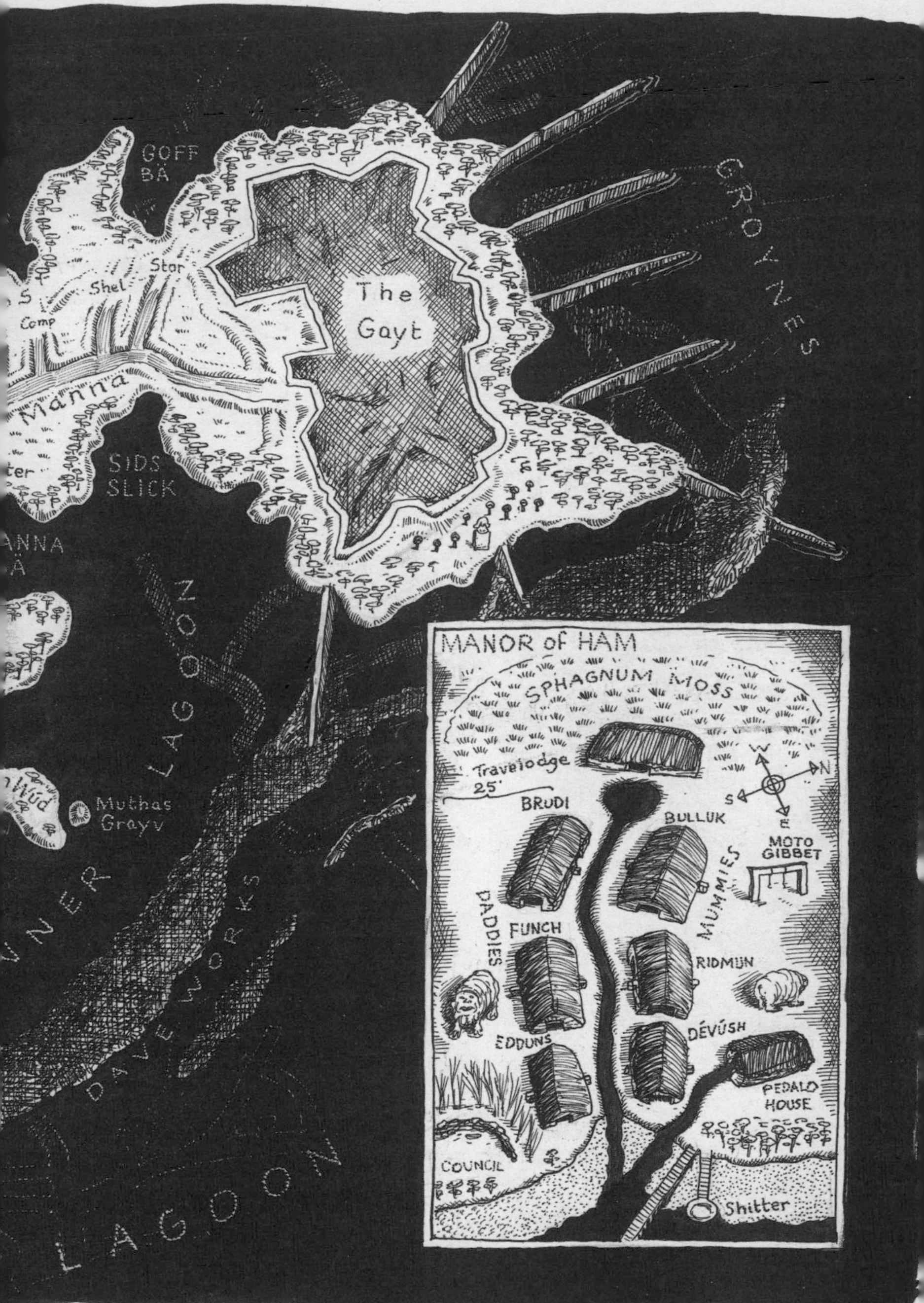
GOFF
BÄ
Stor
Shel
Comp
The Gayt
Manna
SIDS
SLICK
GROYNES
Muthas
Grayv
LAGOON
DAVE WORKS
LAGOON
MANOR of HAM
SPHAGNUM MOSS
Travelodge
25'
W
N
S
E
BRUDI
BULLUK
MOTO
GIBBET
MUMMIES
DADDIES
FUNCH
RIDMUN
EDDUNS
DÉVÚSH
PEDALO
HOUSE
COUNCIL
Shitter

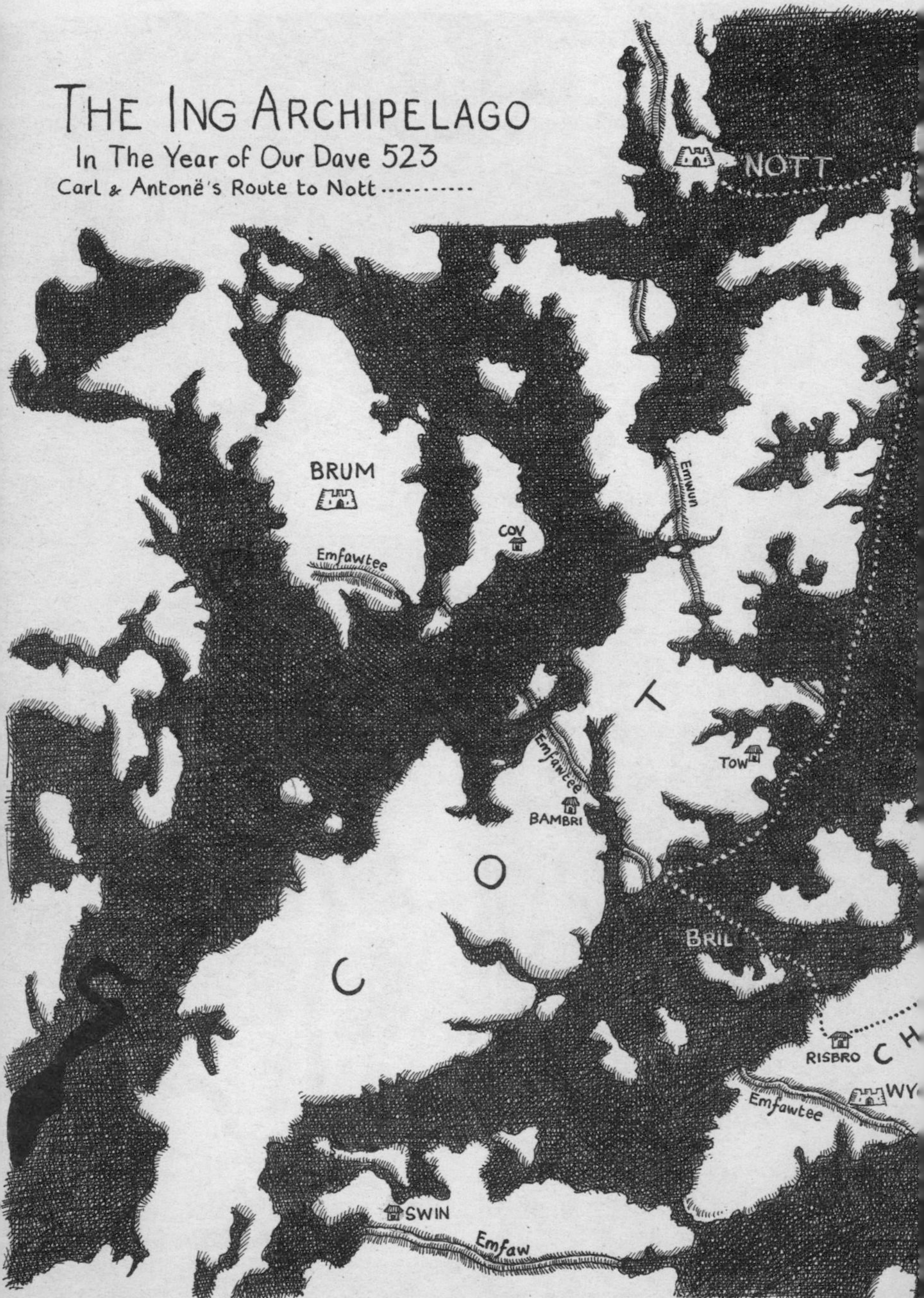
THE ING ARCHIPELAGO
In The Year of Our Dave 523
Carl & Antonë's Route to Nott
NOTT
BRUM
COV
Emfawtee
Emwun
T
O
C
TOW
BAMBRI
BRIL
RISBRO
CH
WY
SWIN
Emfaw

NEW LONDON 523 AD
Not to Scale
Emtwenny 5
The Wheel
Canary Wharf
The Dome
The Tower
NatWest Tower
Bedlam
Charing X
St Paul's Shelter
Trafalgar Square
Whitehall Palace
Royal Parks
Marble Arch
PARK LANE
STEVE
Emwun
LÚT
HEMÚ
BARN
NIMAR
HAM
SENTRUL STAC

# *Contents*

I

# *The Hack's Party*

JUN 523 AD*

Carl Dévúsh, spindle-shanked, bleach-blond, lampburnt, twelve years old, kicked up buff puffs of sand with his bare feet as he scampered along the path from the manor. Although it was still early in the first tariff, the foglamp had already bored through the cloud and boiled the dew off the island. As he gained height and looked back over his shoulder, Carl saw first the homely notch of Manna Bä, then the shrub-choked slopes of the Gayt rising up beyond it. The sea mist had retreated offshore, where it hovered, a white-grey bank merging with the blue screen above. Wot if Eye woz up vair, Carl thought, up vair lyke ve Flyin I? He put himself in this lofty perspective and saw Ham, floating like a water beetle, thrusting out angled legs of grey stone deep into the placid waters of its ultramarine lagoon. The waters intensified the beetle island's myriad greens: its golden wheatie crop, its purple, blue and mauve flowering buddyspike, its yellowy banks of pricklebush and its feathery stands of fireweed. The whole lustrous shell was picked out by a palisade of blisterweed, the lacy umbels of which trimmed the entire shoreline.

The real island was quite as vivified as any toyist vision, the southeast-facing undulation of land audibly hummed. Bees, drugged by the heat, lay down in the flowers, ants reclined on beds of leaf mould, flying rats gave a liquid coo-burble – then stoppered up. To

* Dating is from the purported discovery of the Book of Dave.

the south a few gulls soared above the denser greenery of the Ferbiddun Zön.

The little kids who'd left the manor with Carl had run on ahead, up the slope towards the Layn, the avenue of trees that formed the spine of Ham. These thick-trunked, stunted crinkleleafs bordered the cultivated land with a dark, shimmering froth. Carl saw brown legs, tan T-shirts and mops of curly hair flashing among the trunks as the young Hamsters scattered into the woodland. Reedy whoops of joy reached Carl's ears, and he wished he could go with them into Norfend, galumphing through the undergrowth, sloshing into the boggy hollows to flush out the motos, then herd them towards their wallows.

Up from the manor in a line behind Carl came the older lads – those between ten and fourteen years old – whose graft it was to oversee the motos' wallowing, before assigning the beasts their day's toil. Despite everything, Carl remained the acknowledged gaffer of this group, and, as he swerved off the path along one of the linchets dividing the rips, the other eight followed suit, so that the whole party were walking abreast, following the bands of wheatie as they rolled up the rise.

Carl remembered how this ground had been in buddout, each rip mounded with a mixture of moto dung, seaweed, birdshit and roof straw. The motos had deftly laid their own fresh dung, but the other ingredients had to be dug from the byres, scraped from the rocks and gathered from the shore by the older girls and opares. Next the mummies laboriously dragged truckle after truckle of the mixture up from the manor, before spreading and digging it into the earth with their mattocks. There were no wheels on Ham – save for symbols of them – and therefore no cars or vans either, so the Hamsterwomen tilled the long rips themselves – a team of six yoked to the island's sole plough, with its heavy irony share. Now the ripening wheatie stood as high as his knees, and it looked as if it would be a good crop this year – not that Carl would necessarily be there to see the mummies grind it under the autumn foglamp, their bare breasts nuzzling the hot stone of their querns as they bent sweatily to the graft.

– Ware2, guv, said Billi Brudi, catching Carl's eye as they reached the linchet bordering the next rip and together stepped over it.

– 2 Nú Lundun, Carl replied.

– Ware2, guv, Sam Brudi chipped in – and his brother Billi chimed up:

– 2 Nú Lundun.

Then Gari Edduns uttered the salutation, and Peet Bulluk made the response – and so it went along the line. Between them the nine lads represented all the six families of Ham, the Brudis, Funches, Edduns, Bulluks, Ridmuns and Dévúshes. Good, solid Ingish names – all from the Book, all established on Ham from time out of mind, as rooted as smoothbark and crinkleleaf.

At the top of the slope the land formed a sharp ridge, which fell away in narrow terraces to the waters of Hel Bä. On a knoll on the far side of the water stood one of the five old round towers the Hamsters called giants' gaffs, foglight flashing from its chipped wall. Carl's companions, having reached the edge of the home field, followed the dyke up to the Layn, then walked south along it for three hundred paces, to where a stand of pines guarded the moto wallows. Carl parted from the group and took one of the terraces that curled round the bay to the foot of the tower. Here, in the crete rubble, a few dwarfish apple trees had taken root. He found a level flag and sat down.

Twigs stubbed him through his coarse T-shirt. Brown and white butterflies flip-flopped over a stand of fireweed. Bees came doodling down from the bank of pricklebush that rose up, barring the way to the Ferbiddun Zön. Carl tracked the sticky-arsed stopovers as they wavered down to the water's edge, where squishprims, dry-vys and heaps of other blooms grew between the hefty, hairy stalks of the blisterweed. A stone's throw into the bay the submarine reef of seaweed and Daveworks eddied and swirled in the sluggish swell. Carl could see the bright, red shells of the crabs that teemed on the reef, and in the muddy shallows of the lagoon little gangs of rusty sprats flickered.

Carl leaned his head against a bar of old irony and stared at the delicate tracery of lichen that covered the crete at his feet – living on dead, dead on deader. A low clattering buzz roused him, and, peering at one of the apple trees, he saw that its trunk was mobbed with a dense cluster of golden flies, which spread and agitated their wings the better to suck up the bigwatt rays of the now fully risen foglamp. To leave all this – how would it be possible – this life mummy that cuddled him so?

Carl had been to this spot maybe two or three times with Salli Brudi – and that was forbidden. They'd get a cuff from their daddies and a bigger clump from the Driver if they were found out. The last time she'd whipped off her cloakyfing and wound it around her pretty ginger head like a turban. As she bent low, the neck of her T-shirt gaped open, showing her tiny titties; yet Carl understood there was no chellish vanity in this – Salli was too young. She held a Davework in her hand: it was the size of a baby's finger, a flat black sliver with a faint-cut mark.

– Wot chew fink, Carl, she asked him, reel aw toyist?

Carl took the Davework from her; his thumb traced the edge, once jagged but now smoothed by its millennia-long meander through the lagoon since the MadeinChina. He looked closely at the mark for the shapes of phonics.

– C eer, Sal, he said, beckoning her closer, iss an éd, C ve eer, an vose lyns muss B . . . Eye dunno . . . sowns aw sumffing . . . mebë.

– So toyist? She was disappointed.

– Toyist, deffo. He flung it decisively away from them, and it whirred like a sickseed for a few moments before falling into the grass.

Carl started up – what was the point in such dumb imaginings?

Cockslip an bumrub, nodditankijelli snuggul. Sal Brudi ul B up ve duff soon enuff bì wunnuvose ugli öl shitters . . . No, he best forget it, forget her – and get up to the wallows. Whatever might happen in the next few days, this tariff he had graft to do, important graft.

When Carl arrived the other lads were milling between the seven conical wallows, darting among the motos to kiss and cuddle them. Peet was guiding Boysi by his jonckheeres up the steep steps of the highest wallow.

– Ul luv í ven yer inní, Boysi, he was saying, U no U will, yeah, U no U will.

Boysi turned his big pink muzzle, and his little blue eyes, buried in their fleshfolds, twinkled with recognition. Carwl! Carwl! the moto lowed, Carwl, wawwow wiv mee, wawwow wiv mee!

Carl let out a peal of laughter – it was impossible to stay gloomy for long when the motos were being wallowed. Boysi's dam, Gorj, was already half submerged in the next wallow along, snorting and funnelling her lips to squirt the weedy-green water over her wallow mates. Hands of humans and hands of motos shot above the earthen parapet, flinging screenwasher arcs of droplets as they mucked about.

– Eye carn, Boysi, Carl cried, Eye gotta fynd Runti, iss iz turn, iss iz big dä.

– F slorwa, f slorwa! Hack cummin, Hack cummin! the beast chanted as he heaved himself up the last two steps to the top of the wallow, then plunged in, dragging Peet with him. Other motos took up this cry:

– F slorwa, f slorwa, Hack cummin, Hack cummin!

While Carl doubted any of them truly understood what the slaughter was, the motos knew it was connected with the visitors who were due.

Even the littlest mopeds such as Chukki and Bunni were alive to what visitors brought with them. After the Hack's party arrived, at least half the lads who mushed the motos would be sick with the pedalo fever, so the beasts would be free to cruise as they wished, clear along the underwood to the curryings, and even into the zones, where they'd thieve the gulls' eggs and stuff themselves with shrooms. Motos were soppy things, yet, sorry as they might be for their young mushers, being shot of them was a buzz. Day by day they could be relied on to do as told: Rootaht vat rat coloni, grubbup vis unnerwood, gé shottuv vat notweed. However, left to their own devices, they'd soon be babyishly dry-humping, which could well lead to motorage. Then they'd run amok, trampling down the walls of their own wallows, or even crash into the Hamsters' gaffs. Each year one or two of the friskier males would have to be gelded.

Carl stood watching as first one moto, then the next, was coaxed up and eased over into a wallow, until all seven were occupied. The other motos waited their turn, snuffling and licking each other's buttocks and flanks. Each elevated pool of muddy water was just broad enough to hold one of the creatures. Once in, they used their webbed feet and hands to turn in a tight circle, ducking their little mushers.

By now the bank of sea mist had pulled still further away from the island, far enough for Carl to make out the outcropping of the gull roost at Nimar, five clicks away at the very tip of the long spit that extended from the northern island of Barn. It was around this promontory that the Hack's pedalo would come with its load of sick fares bound for Ham, the isle of the Driven-by-Dave.

Carl thought about the Beastlyman, the tongueless exile who lived at Nimar. On summer days such as this, he could be seen from the highest point of Ham, skipping among the rocks – or, rather, the gulls he disturbed could be seen, flapping aloft and eluding his clumsy, hungry grasp. Last summer Carl had been taken for the first time on a fowling expedition over to Nimar, and, while the other Hamstermen snared prettybeaks and grabbed oilgulls from their nests, he'd guarded the pedalo at its mooring. It was typical that the youngest birder should be left like this, to suffer the repeated attacks of the bonkergulls, who, determined to protect their nests, dived at Carl again and again, trying to plant their sharp beaks in his head.

None of the dads had bothered to tell Carl from whom he was guarding the pedalo, so when the Beastlyman crept up and Carl was confronted by an emaciated figure, clad in a long filthy cloakyfing, its beard and hair matted with dirt, its hands cracked and broken, he was totally freaked out. They'd stared at one another for a long time, with only a few feet separating them. Oilgulls that had escaped the hands of Carl's mates screamed overhead. The Beastlyman opened his mouth and tried to give voice as well, and Carl saw in the dark cave the red root where his tongue had once been, uselessly writhing in the gargling gale of the dad's madness. Carl said, Ware2, guv, but the Beastlyman only flinched as if struck by the greeting, then scrabbled round on the rocks and scrambled away.

When the dads returned to the pedalo, the corpses of many birds stuck by the neck into their tight leather belts, their beards damp with sweat, Carl told them what – or who – he had seen.

– So Uve clokked ve Beestlimun, av U, Carl, said his stepdad, Fred. Eyem glad, yeah, coz thass wottul áppen 2 U if U go on fukkinabaht in ve zön wiv Tonë!

Fukka Funch, never one to miss the opportunity for a crude jape, thrust his bacon schnozz in Carl's face and did a Beastlyman shtick, gargling and spitting until Fred snapped:

– Thass enuff!

His half-brother Bert broke in on Carl's reverie, asking:

– Djoo wan me 2 cumman gé Runti wiv U?

– Nah, nah, he stuttered, vis iss tween me an ím an Dave. U an ve lads betta gé ve wallowin dun an pack ve uvvers orf. Runti – eez mì mayt. Av U ló sed yer tartars 2 Runti? he called to the wallowing motos.

– Goo-bì, Wunti, goo-bì! they lisped in response.

– Catch U lò bakkat ve manna, Carl called to the other lads, then he started down off the crest of the hill and into the woodland.

The first few paces Carl took were between well-spaced, carefully pruned apple trees, the turf beneath them moto mown. The warm air was fruitylicious and butterfly rustled. As he went further down into the Wess Wúd, the orchard gave way to smoothbark trees, some of which had been allowed to grow straight and true, while others were cut back to near their mossy green roots, so that they erupted in a clatter of withies. He bore to the right, crashing through the brack and keeping the winking jewels of Mutt Bä at a constant distance below him.

Carl had a pretty good idea where Runti would be waiting for him. The moto loved to graze in the deep thicket of rhodies and whippystalk that choked the Perg, the long barrier of brick and crete that divided the Wess Wúd from Norfend. There were odd hollows and man-made terraces here, full of strange flowers and shrubs that the Hamsters had no names for, since they were too rare and peculiar to be of any use. However, the Perg was an ancient name, and Effi, Carl's nan, had told him that it too had once been regarded as a zone forbidden to the Hamsters. She had cradled the little lad in her bony arms and said, Nó bì Dave, luv, nah, ee wooden giv a toss abaht such fings, but ferbiddun bì olda gods, yeah. Her fleshy nose twitched in his hair. Bì Jeebus an Ali.

Carl found Runti a little way inside the Perg. The big moto had his front paws up on a lump of crete and was cropping on a plant with glossy, serrated leaves. The fodder was caught up in his muzzle as if he had a spiky beard, and Carl couldn't help but laugh at the sight. Runti stopped munching and his mouth fell open, showing his lolling pink tongue and his peg teeth braided with vegetative threads.

– Cawl? he lisped. Ithatoo?

– Yeah, iss me, Runti. Iss me.

The boy struggled through the barbed boughs of a stunted tree and came right up to the moto so that he could hug his head – a head so large that, even pressing his tank against the jowls, Carl could only just join his hands in the rough bristles at the back of the moto's neck. They stood like that for some time, the moto's blubbery eyes squished against the lad's chest, his veggie breath rasping on Carl's shirt.

– Iss tym, Runti, Carl cooed, tym fer yer slorta, yeah? Ve Acks partë ul B eer vis tariff or ve nex, an Eye gotta tayk yer bak 2 ve manna.

– Slorwa, the moto said wonderingly, slorwa.

– Thass rì, Runti, slorta. Weel uze yaw meet 2 feed ve Ack an iz dads, yer oyl fer vair woonz, an yul be wiv Dave á lars, yeah.

– In Nú Lundun.

– Yeah, thass rì, Carl said, kissing Runti delightedly, in Nú Lundun. It mattered not what doubts the lad had, for, in this article at least, the creature's simple faith and his own scepticism were at one.

They took all morning to get back to the manor. Carl led Runti round the northern end of the Perg, then up and down the bumps and dips of Sandi Wúd. He'd played here with Runti all of his life. When he'd been a tiny boy, the moto had minded him – and when he grew older, he had minded the moto. They revisited all of their favourite haunts: the big hollow crinkleleaf that stood at the edge of the curryings, the ridged bark of which was perfect for scratching moto hide; the boggy slough in Turnas Wúd, where Runti could wallow; the grove of silverbarks in the heart of the wood, where they stopped so that Carl could tear off A4 strips and feed them to Runti on the palm of his hand.

They ambled on with Carl's arm slung around Runti's neck, or, when the undergrowth grew thick, he'd tailgate so he could grab the moto's cock and balls. Feeling his touch, Runti gently squeezed his mighty haunches together, lisping:

– Thath ware.

– Yeah, Carl answered him, thass ware.

And he recalled the great beast's final mating: his feet crunching on the frosted leaf fall, his hot breath clouding the sharp kipper air, while Runti's hands scrabbled to gain purchase on the barrel back of old Gorj. Such tiny genitals the motos had – they could never have mated without human help. Surely this alone proved that men and motos were meant to be together? Together on Ham – and together for eternity in New London. How could the Driver ever doubt it?

Towards the beginning of the second tariff, boy and moto trudged back up to the Layn, crossed over it and broke through the last tattered curtain of leaves. Below them they could see the gaffs of the manor, its bay and the easterly cape of the island. From behind this – just that moment emerging – came the prow of the Hack's pedalo, a sharp black wedge against the brilliant sea. Carl could make out five pedalers on each side of the vessel, and deep in its well the heads of at least fifteen more fares. Yes, it was a big enough party this year. An weel mayk em elfy wyl vey mayk us sikk, Carl muttered. He turned to the moto and kissed it on its snub nose. Cummon, luv, iss time 2 go 2 Dave. Then they ambled off down the hill.

The six gaffs of the Hamsters' little manor were set in two rows of three, on each side of an evian stream that was rich in irony. At the western end a seventh – used as a travelodge – was built above the spring itself. Pod-shaped, the gaffs hunkered down into the land, their rough reddish sides hugged by the greensward, their lumpy thatched roofs lashed down by crude ropes. For hundreds of years – perhaps even since the dawn of the Knowledge itself, for the gaffs were known to be very ancient – they had gone by the names of the six clans of Ham. To the south of the stream, running from east to west, were the Edduns, Funch and Brudi gaffs; while on the north side were the Dévúsh, the Ridmun and the Bulluk. The Breakup had not changed this, although the dads now occupied the gaffs to the south of the stream, and the mummies those to the north. That the Hamsters should cleave so to this redundant nomenclature was only one of the reasons why their Driver was now insisting that the unsanitary manor – with its dwellings shared by kith and kine – be demolished and a new one built.

On a frayed patch of ground a few paces from the Ridmun gaff, Fred Ridmun, the Guvnor of Ham, together with three of the other dads, had knocked together a gibbet big enough to hang the moto from once its throat had been cut. In late autumn, when several motos were slaughtered, such a gibbet would have been far larger, and all the Hamstermen would have spent a blob or more building it. However, for this, the midsummer's feast for the Hack's party, only one moto was to be slain.

This was Runti, who now lay on his side, slack flesh squidging from under him, his tank slopping, his arse bubbling. His legs were lashed with some of the better imported rope, a length of which was also slung over the top beam of the gibbet. At the moto's head knelt Carl, together with his stepdad, Fred. Carl held a small knife that was hidden in the dense wattles of the beast's throat. Fred was tall like all of the Ridmun clan, his hair lanky, his beard a lustrous, curly brown, his eyes a stony grey, his lips sickle-sharp and sickle-curved. He was a dävine dad, so he called over the slaughter run:

– Leev on rì smiffeeld, leffpoltreeavenoo, leffchartaowse . . . rìfarringdunlayn . . .

His stepson stroked Runti's stubbly brow as the run and its points were called.

– Tym 2 go nah, Runti, he said.

– Nó hwurtin, the moto lisped.

– Nah, nó hurtin, yul ardli feel í.

This was true, because at that very instant Carl pressed the knife deep into the beast's neck and a maroon tide pulsed out on to the bare earth. Púlupp! Fred cried to Fukka Funch, Sid Brudi and Ozzi Bulluk. The three dads began hauling on the end of the rope; it came taut, and the moto's bleeding body was dragged jerkily towards the wooden frame, leaving an old irony stain in its wake. Giss an and! Fukka shouted to the gang of Chilmen who were standing a way off, looking on both enthralled and horrified.

Reluctantly the Hack's pedalers detached themselves from the group, strolled over and grabbed the rope. All eight dads gathered as much purchase as they could and pulled. Their muscles knotted, their backs creaked, the gibbet groaned. First Runti's hindquarters, then his sagging tank lifted from the ground. Carl stayed by his head, whispering endearments:

Iss orlrì, luvvi, doan wurri, ear we go, nó long nah, ittul B bé-er wen ure up on ve fingi.

– Itun hwurtin, Cwarl. Eye hwurtin sum, the moto protested, and one of his large hands sought out his musher's smaller one.

– Onli a lyttul, Runti, onli a lyttul, an itull soon B ovah an yul ave a nyce kip.

– Mwy nek hwurtin, Cwarl, ish hwurtin.

The moto's whole body – which was the length of one and a half men and considerably bulkier – was now part-resting on his crumpled neck. Then, with a great heave and a shout from the hauliers, the moto cleared the ground and swung free, a fat, fleshy pendulum spraying pink mist.

While all this had been going on, the Driver was coming along the bay from his semi, his back stiff, his bright orange trainers glaring as the hem of his black robe rose and fell, his mirror flashing in the foglight, the sign of the wheel embroidered on his breast commanding attention. Now he came up to the Hack's party and turned his back on them. The Hack, Mister Greaves, was staring full into Runti's dying face.

– Ware2, guv, he said to the Driver in a cursory fashion.

– To New London, came the answer in Arpee with considerably more solemnity.

– Iss awlways a fyn fing 2 C a moto slorta, said Mister Greaves, grabbing the loose stuff of his long T-shirt with both hands so that it stretched over his pot tank.

– Maybe, the Driver snapped. At any rate, it's a practice the Hamsters wouldn't wish to forgo.

Carl looked up into the Driver's mirror and saw there cold black eyes under high, white, gull's-wing eyebrows. The lad bent back to stroking Runti's muzzle, murmuring:

– Vare-vare, vare-vare, Runti, soon ovah, soon ovah . . .

– Why should they forgo it, Reervú? said Mister Greaves, setting his jaw and thrusting out his long, wispy ginger beard. His nose was bulbous, his brows beetled, his cheeks were tenderized with old pox scars – yet he fronted up well. Still, the Driver had got to him – so much so that he had shifted to Arpee as he bit and nibbled his curry-stung lips.

– Because the moto is real, not toyist . . . The Driver's voice was low, but his enunciation was perfectly clear. Even in chitchat he sounded like a zealot . . . and only toyist beasts may be scoffed.

– Come off it, Dad. Mister Greaves was up for a bit of bother, and the dads, who'd by now finished lashing Runti to the gibbet, came up to hear them. The moto is a sacred creature, ordained as such by the Book!

– On one reading perhaps. The Driver hooked his hands into the side vents of his robe, mimicking Mister Greaves's posture. However, on the true one – as higher authorities would tell you, if you listened clearly – it is an abomination.

The Chilmen – both the Hack's pedalers and the sick fares – certainly looked disposed to agree with the Driver. Carl recognized two of the older pedalers – they'd been in the party on previous summers – while the rest of them, some twenty dads in all, had never visited Ham before. In the lad's eyes fares and pedalers alike were a motley crew, their awkward bones an ill fit for their scrawny hides. Their blue caps, yellow tops and red jeans were garish – babyish even – and naturally most of them bore fresh pox scars or weeping goitres. The Chilmen stood as close to the Hack as their rank allowed and stared at the moto with frank disgust.

– Í lúks lyke an abominowotsit 2 me, said a slight man, whose bald head was cloven by a fresh trepanning wound. Í az ve eyes ovva ooman, ve teef, ve cok an balls 2. Iss feet ar lyke ands wiv pads uv flesh mell-éd intavem, but iss muzzle iz lyke a burgakynes an iss bodi iz lyke vat uv an idëus bäcön . . . Í duz me fukkin éd in.

– Me 2! Yeah, me 2! the other Chilmen cried.

Carl continued to cradle Runti's upside-down head in his arms, heedless of the blood coursing down his neck and blotting out his T-shirt. With one hand he held an earflap closed, with the other he stroked the moto's bulging jonckheeres. He went on whispering into the beast's free ear, Vare-vare, Runti, vare-vare, mì sweet . . . but it seemed doubtful that the moto could hear him, for his baby-blue eyes were rolled back in their sockets, while his breath came in a laboured squeak and his blood continued to pulse. Then Runti gave a final convulsive shudder, arching his long back, snapping the ropes. Before, the dying creature had lisped in an undertone; now a single clear statement issued from his already bluing lips: Eye thleepy nah! Gonna B wiv Dave! Then he went completely slack. Carl stepped back from the gibbet, letting go of Runti's head, and plodded away, his face averted so the dads couldn't see his tears. He wished it were Changeover day with all his heart.

– Bluddë el! the cloven-headed Chilman said wondrously, iss trew, ven – vat vey speek!

Hmm, yes, the Driver answered him, but only with the voice of a child just weaned; they have no more reason than any toyist beast.

– Be that as it may, said Mister Greaves, pulling his shirt still tighter around his tank, I've been Hack here at Ham for twenty-five years now and I've learned to love the moto well enough. I'd advise you, dads of my party, to love this fine beast too. His flesh will preserve you, his fat will grease you, and once it's extracted his oil will – as you well know – prove the most effective of remedies for whatever ails you. Is this not why you've been allowed to come here, to this most distant and yet dävine island of our Lawd's? Nah – he slewed angrily into Mokni – pissoff ve ló-uv U – go an kip in yer gaff. Yaw oasts av wurk 2 do – rispek vem.

The Chilmen scattered in obedience, heading up the stream to the travelodge and disappearing one after another into its dark doorway, their faces still white with astonishment.

The Driver addressed the Hack:

– Mister Greaves, come and have a cuppa at my gaff; there's matters we must talk over before tonight's do.

– And tomorrow's Council. Greaves looked over at Carl as he said this.

– Yes, and tomorrow's Council. Shall we go?

They walked away, the Driver taking his first few paces backwards before spinning on his heel; yet neither – in the mirror or directly – gave the slaughtered moto so much as a backward glance.

Once the off-islanders were all gone, the Hamstermen set to work with a vengeance. From an oilcloth bundle Fred Ridmun drew out a hooked knife the length of his forearm. Fukka Funch dragged a large piece of oilcloth beneath Runti's dangling head. Carl put his weight on the dead moto's arms. Ozzi Bulluk pulled the rope that kept one of its hind feet lashed to the gibbet as tightly as possible, splaying the moto's legs. Its genitals, tank and ribs were all thrown into prominence. Taking a deep breath and crying out, Stikk í 2 im, Dave! Fred thrust the knife into the notch beneath the rib cage and, sawing vigorously, yanked it up. Hide and flesh parted with a loud popping sound, and Runti's guts flumped down in a tangled mass on to the cloth. Fukka moved in at once with a shorter knife and, feeling around in the moto's abdominal cavity, cut the intestines away. Behind him came Carl with a pail of sea water, which he sloshed up into the gory hole, slooshing out any shit or half-digested fodder. Carl was laughing as he barged Fukka out of the way, and instead of clumping him the dad laughed as well. It mattered not how old or how dävine you were – butchering a moto was always a joyous occasion so far as the Hamsters were concerned.

The mummies and opares now came out from where they'd been waiting in a huddle behind the Brudi gaff. Hitching up their cloakyfings, they crossed the stream and came towards the slaughter site. All that morning the Hamsters' huge irony kettle had been simmering over a fire a few paces away from the gibbet. Now the women went to this, formed a chain, poured pails of boiling water and passed them, hand to hand, to Carl, who attached them to a rope and winched them up so that they could be tipped over the carcass. Once it was well and truly scalded, the dads dragged over boards and trestles to make up the skinning table. This was assembled immediately under the scaffold and the dead moto lowered down on to it.

Next the daddies lined up along one side of the table and the mummies along the other. Short, broad-bladed knives were taken out from another cherished bundle and distributed among them. Then the company set to, scraping the thick bristles from the hide. Carl was too young to take part in this work; nevertheless he loitered near by and even risked smiling at his mum, Caff. She smiled back while the others chose not to notice this exchange.

For twelve long years the Driver had sought to snuff out such intercourse between the sexes; however there were some of the Hamsters' rituals that he could neither proscribe nor modify. When the Hack's party came and the moto was slain, the dads and mums spoke to one another with warm vitality, exchanging news, opinions and especially gossip about the strangers, their remarks shooting back and forth across the table as rapidly as their knives scraped at the hide. Had the Hack accepted the rent? What illnesses or deformities did the Chilmen have? Was there any news of Chil, or even of the world beyond? What business did the Hack have with their Driver? And most importantly: what had been brought to trade? Was there fresh seed? Woolly? Fags? Booze even?

The foglamp beat down on them out of a blue screen that tinted at the southern horizon, the sea pitter-purled against shingle, the gulls cawed over the Gayt, the flying rats coo-burbled from the top of the home field, the sweat stood out on the grafters' brows, and the mummies – with the Driver gone – risked loosening their cloakyfings. When free-flowing, the Hamsters' chitchat had the intimacy of thought, so when the old moto-skinning rap started up it was like a mummy humming to her sprog.

– Allö, mö-ö, cum 2 feed us, cum 2 eel us, the mummies called.

And the daddies responded:

– Tara, öl mayt, gissa cuddul B4 U dì.

Summoning himself as if from a dream, Fred wiped the sweat from his reddened brow and fixed the company with his flinty gaze. The mums and dads left off singing, downed tools and looked over towards the Driver's gaff, but, seeing the smoky ribbon that coiled from his chimney, they began singing again – if anything a little louder. Fred shrugged and joined in with them.

By the time the moto's hide had been scraped, its carcass skinned, and its blubber flensed and set out in a number of pots for trying out, the slaughter site was crawling with flies, and blood had crusted on the sward. Fred and Ozzi had expertly disjointed the moto's limbs and hacked off its hams, shins, feet and hands. Runti's head had been severed and borne off by the mummies to make the headcheese for the Hack's cake. His tank had been cut away from his guts and hung up to dry; it would be used to store his own oil. Fukka Funch had set up a second trestle table and was skilfully fashioning smaller cuts from the chunks of carcass and trimming off the side meat to be smoked. He then reserved the spare ribs and the tank meat – for these would be curried and barrelled. He cut out the heart, liver and kidneys from their viscous basketry and slithered them across the bloody boards into the hands of the waiting mummies. A smoky, meaty smell began to hang in a pall over the manor as the blubber started to simmer.

The other kids had returned from the woodland, and, as it was daddytime, the opares fed them with odd scraps of flesh, quickly fried up with handfuls of herbs. Then they were packed off with a tot of moto gubbins to ward away the pedalo fever. Fred retrieved the moto's slack bladder from Fukka's table, washed it in a pail, found its opening, inflated it with a few breaths and tied it off with a length of sinew. He tossed the whitish sphere towards the little kids, and Ad Brudi – who although only seven was a head taller than the others – grabbed it and ran off down to the shore. The whole pack followed after him, hooting and yelling as they batted it between them. They ran around the bay, and, as they passed the Driver's semi, he loomed in the doorway, a tall and threatening figure. The other kids wormed their way through the blisterweed, but he managed to catch hold of Ad and took the bladder from him. Shaking it, the Driver held it up to the screen, then returned it to Ad and sent him back towards the dads.

At the slaughter site Ad handed the bladder to Fred.

– Ve Driver sez í aint rì fer ve kids 2 B larkin abaht.

– So B í, the Guvnor said grimly, and he tied the bladder to the side of the gibbet, where it wobbled in the breeze.

Carl had no idea how Antonë Böm had arrived in the manor without being noticed, but he looked up from currying the meats to find that the teacher was standing right by his shoulder.

– Ware2, guv, Böm said.

– 2 Nú Lundun, Carl replied.

A smirk played upon Antonë's fat wet lips. He compressed them and emitted the buzzing noise that signified his abstraction from the workaday toil of the Hamsters. His spectacles flashed the foglamp in Carl's eyes, his prematurely white beard lay lank on his bulbous chin. His cheeks were heavily scarred with the pox, his jeans were full – but his tank fuller. His soft, plump hands, with their tiny, recessed nails, dwelt on his swelling hips. Carl blanked him and concentrated on rubbing coarse seacurry into the moto meat.

– So, Böm asked after a while, az Runti bin chekked?

– Sluffoffs ovah vare. Carl jerked a thumb at the skin that lay at Fukka's feet, buzzing with flies. Böm ambled over and began to sort through the greasy folds. At once Fred was by his side.

– Ware2, guv, he snapped.

– 2 Nú Lundun, Böm cooed. Eyem juss lookin fer ve mark.

– No bovver, Tonë, said Fred, refusing to be mollified. U no azwellaz me vat Runti woz reel enuff; úve seen iz mark a fouwzan tymes.

– Stil, we muss chekk í, iss ve way, innit. Böm carried on examining the moto skin.

– Iss nó yer graft, Tonë, an djoo no í!

Fred grabbed the skin, so that the two men held it stretched between them. The foglight streamed through the membrane, perfectly illuminating the phonics C-A-L-B-I-O-T-E-C-H. Looking from the Guvnor's angry face to his mentor's quizzical one, Carl felt his riven mind part still more.

– C! Fred spat in the dirt. Reel enuff fer U, Tonë, reel enuff?

~

Late in the third tariff, when the headlight was close to dipping, Antonë Böm sat writing in his journal. His tiny, one-roomed semi lay two hundred paces beyond the Driver's on the shore of the inlet known as Sid's Slick. The room was bare, the brick walls unpainted. The tiny table was dwarfed by his plump form, and his plump form was overseen by the dark shadow the letric threw on the walls, a shadow that shifted uneasily in a draught. It had been a long tariff – the Driver had called over with great zeal. He had led the Hamstermen and the Chilmen in at least twenty runs and their points. The Hamsters – as was their way – had been cowed, as gluttonous for this spiritual sustenance as they were for the feast to come. The Hack's party, as in previous years, had been overawed by such Dävinanity in this peculiar place at the very edge of the Lawyer's dominion. Yet the Driver was clever enough to be politic – his battle for the fares of the Hamsters was a protracted one; and when the tariff had rolled on, the headlight had been switched on and the dashboard shone out over the placid lagoon, he faded away to his own gaff, so that Runti's flesh could be eaten and the sick dads of Chil anointed with moto oil.

Later still, old raps were sung in the island's Mokni, Effi Dévúsh making the call and the whole population – mummies, daddies, boilers, opares and kids – the response. Then the dancing commenced. In the margins of the firelight, where the shadows flickered and the darkness took on substance, Böm saw the gaunt form of Luvvie Joolee, the Exile, who had crept up to observe the festivities. She must by now, he thought, know what awaits Carl and me at first tariff. He tried to catch her eye but to no avail, for the tragic old boiler ignored him.

The last thing Böm noticed before he left were the wide eyes of the Chilmen, glazed by moto-oily gluttony, as they watched the increasingly abandoned gyrations of the Hamsters, pissed on the booze they'd brought, fags dangling from their sloppy lips. He guessed what the Chilmen were thinking: what a contrast there was between piety and licentiousness! The Chilmen cast surreptitious glances at the opares – who had undone their cloakyfings most immodestly. No doubt the pedalers and sick fares alike were wondering if they could afford the childsupport.

Böm could not rest – his lumpy sofabed held no appeal for him. In the morning the Guvnor and the Hack would deliberate everything before the Council. Who knew what else might come out concerning him and Carl? The Hamsters could not forbear from speaking when spoken to, and who could guess what Caff might say if she were examined? Böm had no illusions about what awaited him if he were returned to London. It was the curse of his speculative mind that had brought him to Ham in the first place, and the Inspectors had long memories while the PCO's Examiners possessed the harshest of powers. He sighed, dipped his biro in the inkwell and scratched on into the night.

Carl Dévúsh couldn't sleep either. When he finally went to his bed in the Funch gaff, and threw himself on to the rough palliasse in among the hurly-burly of his mates' limbs, their dream cries and night farts beset him. His mind stirred and turned. He recalled the bizarre garb of the Chilmen, their red jeans and ornate leather trainers. Every word the off-islanders spoke betrayed an unsettling incomprehension of all that was certain to Carl: the firm ground of Ham itself. To go out into the world of these fares, what would that be like? Besides, from what Antonë had told him, the strange ways of the Chilmen were as nothing compared to those of Londoners. It wasn't the threat of the PCO and its Inspectors that bothered Carl – such things were too remote – but the loss of his home, his beautiful island.

Towards first tariff, Carl crept out from the box bed, slapped across the yok flags, unlatched the door and went out into the greying gloom. He followed the same route he had the day before, back across the home field, over the ridge and around Hel Bä until he reached the old tower. Dave had switched off the headlight, but Carl had no need of it to find his way. He could have walked the whole island – saving the zones – in his sleep. Once at the tower, he walked under the heavy lintel, ignoring the buddyspikes growing out of the stonework that tore at his face. It wasn't strictly forbidden to enter the five towers of Ham, although it wasn't altogether allowed. Nevertheless the children had all been in before, frightening each other with tales of how the giants would get them. Sitting down in the remains of a fireplace, Carl looked up through the open roof of the tower to the screen. The dashboard still shone up there, the arrangements of lights the same as those he had been taught to recognize by Caff when he was a little fare, sitting on her lap on the ground outside the Ridmun gaff, his head nestling in the hollow of her neck.

– Vass ve édlite, she'd said, ven iss on fulbeem we C ve lites ahtside, yeah, ve streetlites uv Nú Lundun. An ven iss dipped, we C ve dashbawd, rì, mì lyttul luv?

– Owzabaht Dave, Mummi, vairs ee?

– Ees sittin infruntuv uz, luv, but we carn C im coz ees invizzibull.

– But ee can C uz, carn ee, Mummi?

– O yeah, mì luv, ee can C uz, ee sees uz in iz mirra. Ees lookin awl ve tym – lookin in ve mirra á uz, an lookin froo ve screen 4 ve Loss Boy. An uppabuv im, mì luv, uppabuv im vairs ve Flyin I, an ee sees all ve wurl.

Yet now, seven years later, huddling in the fireplace at the giants' tower, Carl doubted that Dave saw anything at all in his mirror – let alone him.

~

Midway through the first tariff of the following day, when the foglamp was already high over the Gayt, the dads of Ham gathered for the Council. While the Council wall was right by the manor, stands of willowstalk and blisterweed hid their deliberations from the prying eyes of mummies, opares and kids. The dads looked instead to the bay, where, through the sole gap in the vegetation, the Hack's pedalo could be seen, drawn up on the shore. Although there were only twelve dads and granddads now, Fred had told Carl that in his own youth twenty dads had deliberated, while a generation before that there had been more than thirty – all pitching in to argue and dispute the business of the community.

In those days the Council had been a babel, but in the years since the Driver came among them order had been imposed on the noisy little assembly. This was never more noticeable than during midsummer, when for a full month the Hack's party was in residence. Then the Council conducted itself with great solemnity, the better to impress the visitors. On the first day after the Hack had arrived it was customary for him to judge those wrongdoers who had committed crimes in the intervening year deemed too serious to be dealt with by the Guvnor. However, there were hardly ever any of these – theft and violence were all but unknown among the dads, while tittle-tattle, bubbling and other instances of bad faith were dealt with by Fred. A simple oath upon the Book was always sufficient to discover the truth, while a ticket of a few quid served for most offences.

The Driver had not intervened directly in the running of the Council – he was too wily for that. Yet the time the dads had to spend in the Shelter – a whole tariff each day, two every seventh – had brought a dävine rigour to everything they undertook. There was this dampener on the little assembly, and there were also the first symptoms of the pedalo fever: noses were clogged up, throats were sore, eyes watered. Some of the dads were gripped by an ague so severe that their newly bartered fags shook from their fingers and fell to the beaten earth. That the Council had to judge the most serious crime on the island in thirteen years weighed heavily upon all of them, not least because until thirteen years previously the concept – let alone the actuality – of flying had been unknown on Ham.

The Hack sat on the highest part of the circular wall. He gathered his bubbery carcoat about his hunched back in tight pleats. His full side whiskers – an anomaly among the Hamstermen, who grew their beards from the chins alone – gave him a magisterial air. Fred Ridmun stood before him, his official baseball cap in one hand, his cudgel in the other, while Carl and Antonë sat on the ground at his feet.

– Mì sun, Fred said, az bin gó á bì Tonë Böm, guv, ee nevah wooduv dun viss stuff wivaht Böm.

– U shor abaht vat? The Hack drew meditatively on his fag. Iz reel dad dun stuff lyke viss innal, innit?

– But wurs, Fred answered. Far wurs.

– Wot cood B wurs van diggin in ve zön, eh? Eye no wot sumuv U ló bleev in yer arts. Eye no U stil fink vat ve Búk woz fown ere on Am. U granddads iz öl enuff 2 remembah ve Geezer? There was a low murmur of assent. B4 King Dave vair woz enni numbah uv pissi lyttul playsez wot ad a clame 2 B ve craydul uv ar faif, innit? Another murmur. But ve Kings granddad, ee chaynjd all vat. Ee ad a revelashun vat ve Búk woz fahnd in Lundun, aint vat ve troof?

– Iss ve troof, the ailing Hamsters muttered.

– Iss nó juss ure zön wich iz ferbiddun – all ve zöns on Chil iz juss ve saym. Ven U need brik aw crete aw yok aw grint U gé í from ve edj. But U avent ve skil uv wurkin wiv ironi, an U av no Inspektur 2 soopavys such diggins. Nah vis bloke – he stabbed a finger at Böm – oo cums ear a refewjee, ee dares 2 muck abaht in ve zön. Wot else az ee dun, eh?

– Nah, nah, Mistah Greaves, Fred said, nó a bí-uv-í, we aint gó no uvva bovva wiv Tonë, ees juss lyke wunnuv us.

The dads gave affirmative grunts, and Fukka Funch spoke up, saying:

– Ee sayvd mì Bellas lyf.

– Izzat so? The Hack addressed himself only to Fred.

– Í iz, Tonë iz a grayt jeepee, an im bein kweer ve wimmin av lé im be á summuv vair birfs.

Mister Greaves shifted into the more sonorous cadences of Arpee, and Antonë Böm realized he meant there to be no further inquisition:

– None the less, flying counts against this man more than giving life counts for him. Flying takes away faith, and without faith we have nothing, no runs, no points, no intercom, no New London.

– No Nú Lundun, the dads chanted.

Greaves turned to Böm:

– Is there anything you can lay before this Council concerning your behaviour that could possibly justify it in the mirror of Dave? Do you want to tell us why you took young Carl Dévúsh into the zone and why you dug and delved in there?

Antonë Böm looked up at Greaves. He knew something of the Hack's status in the Bouncy Castle of Chil. He knew that, while Greaves may have paid hard dosh for the privilege of becoming his Lawd's subcontractor, nevertheless he had always been a sincere protector of the Hamsters. It would do the Hack's cause no good to be seen to go against the Driver – and beyond him the PCO.

– No, Böm said at last, I have nothing to say on my own account. So far as Carl is concerned, he's but a lad, he came with me unwittingly, and I sought to dissuade him. He had no idea of my purpose.

The Hack took a deep drag on his fag and blew out a plume of smoke.

– I care not one whit, he said, the lad's crime is the same as yours, flying, and I am not fit to sit in judgement on either of you. You will have to go to London, to the PCO. The Examiners have taken it upon themselves to try all flyers, and I cannot stand in their way. Dave have mercy on your fares!

– Dave av mursee, the dads echoed.

– W-will we aff 2 go viss mumf wiv ure partë? Carl couldn't prevent himself from blurting out – then he cowered in anticipation of a slap.

Greaves, however, remained calm, and his voice chimed with a note of sympathy:

– No, lad, you're too young this year. Next year, when I return, you'll be dad enough. Until then you and Böm will remain here, but mark me, if either of you meddle in the zone from now until then, or if you bother the Driver in any way, it will count still more severely against you when you arrive in London. Remember your own dad, Carl Dévúsh, remember what happened to him.

# 2
# *Trapping a Flyer*

December 2001

Hunched low over the wheel, foglamps piercing the miasma, Dave Rudman powered his cab through the chicane at the bottom of Park Lane. The cabbie's furious thoughts shot through the windscreen and ricocheted off the unfeeling world. Achilles was up on his plinth *with his tiny bronze cock*, his black shield fending off the hair-styling wand of the Hilton, *where all my heartache began*. Solid clouds hung overhead *lunging up fresh blood*. The gates to Hyde Park, erected for the Queen Mother, looked *like bent paperclips* in the gloom, the lion and unicorn on their Warner Brothers escutcheon were prancing cartoon characters. Evil be to him who thinks of it, said the Unicorn, and the Lion replied, *Eeee, whassup, Doc?*

Stuttering by them, Rudman's Faredar picked up a Burberry bundle trapped on the heel of grass that was cut off from the central reservation by the taut, tarmac tendon of Achilles Way. *Stupid plonker*. The cab's wipers went 'eek-eek'. The bundle was trying to roll over the Y-shaped crash barrier – all that prevented him from being mown down by the four lanes of traffic, traffic that came whipping past the war memorial where bronze corpses lay beneath concrete howitzers. *Tatty coaches full of carrot-crunchers up for the Xmas wallet-fuck*, pale-skinned, rust-grazed Transit vans with England flags taped across their back windows, *boogaloo bruvvers in Seven Series BMWs, throw-cushion specialists in skateboard-sized Smart cars, Conan-the-fucking-Barbarian motorcycle couriers*, warped flat-bed trucks piled high with scrap metal, one-eyed old Routemaster buses

– the whole stinky caravan of London wholesale-to-retail, five credit-worthy days before Christmas was intent on crushing this bit of *Yank, wannabe roadkill* . . . So Dave slewed the Fairway over to the nearside lane and waited to see whether he'd make it.

He did. He came puffing up to the driver-side window. 'Sir, sir, excuse me, sir . . .' *Sir, sir?! Is he fucking insane?* 'Thank you for stopping.' *He's going to ask me if I know which theatre The King and I is playing at. Stupid cunt.* 'Could you take me to . . .' The Yank drew a piece of paper from his trench-coat pocket and consulted it. 'Mill Hill . . .' He said the two words slowly and distinctly, as if they might be difficult for Dave to comprehend. 'If that's . . . that's not kinduv of beyond your range?' *My range, what does he think I am, some fucking wild boar?* Dave pictured beastly London cabs, rolling in the roadway, shaking their metal shoulders to rid themselves of railings hurled by Hoorays starved of sport.

'Get in, please.' Dave bent his arm out of the window and opened the door, then he shrugged back inside and hit the meter. The bundle bowled in, a grateful blob of wet gaberdine that wafted a gentle stench of some male fragrance *advertised by chest-waxing ponces in underpants*. Dave Rudman shifted the cab into drive and shuddered off up the nearside lane, expertly swerving to avoid a coach that lurched out of its bay. Then he rubbed his sore nostrils with a wad of tissue as shapeless as snot. *Day-and-fucking-Night-Nurse . . . that's what you need in this job. Open the hatch and through it comes another slant-eyed virus at 120 mph.*

The fare sat in the middle of the back seat, knees akimbo, potbelly exposed by the open flaps of his trench coat, both hands on the safety handles set in the rear doors of the cab *as if he's in a rickshaw costing twenty-five-fucking-grand*. 'When I say range, cabbie,' said the fare, leaning forward to push his fat face through the open hatch, 'I mean, I've heard of your famous Knowledge, but I figure that maybe Mill Hill is a bit beyond it . . . beyond the area you have to cover.' *He's a talker, this one, he wants to talk, he goes to whores and when they try to plate him he says he'd rather talk, 'coz the only thing he wants in their mouths is comforting words. He'll start on fucking Afghanistan in two minutes flat. He's gonna go all Tora Bora on me . . .*

'That's right, it is a little beyond the six-mile radius from Charing Cross, which is the theoretical limit of the London streets we have to learn.'

'Theoretical?' *He doesn't expect to hear this word out of my lower-class lips, lips he sees flapping in the rearview. He's putting together a photofit of me from lips, chin and the back of my head. He ain't fooled by the baseball cap – and he likes that I'm going bald, as a fatty it gives him the drop.* 'Yeah' – *put him still more at his ease, this cunt could be an earner* – 'theoretical, because in practice we also have to know a fair bit of the suburbs, which would cover Mill Hill as well.'

'Uh huh.' The fare was satisfied, he'd marked his card, he'd shown Dave he wasn't just another dumb tourist who thinks London is *a nine-hundred-square-mile souvenir T-shirt, decorated with tit-helmeted coppers, red phone boxes, Mohican-sporters, tiara-jockeys and black-bloody-cabs*. The fare looked to the left at the avenue of plane trees running up to Speakers' Corner. He looked to the right at the tiny road-cleaning machine bumping along the gutter, its circular electric brushes polishing the York stone molars. He was lost, momentarily, in a reverie provoked by a pair of backpacking lovers, wet-weather freaks, who were leaning up against the lip of a fountain, her thighs imprisoned in his. He was thinking about his family – and Afghanistan.

'Kinduv weird being in Europe.'

'I imagine you'd rather be at home, what with all this business –'

'In Afghanistan, you bet I would. Sure, it's crazy to think you're any more at risk here, or your family's any more at risk if you're not there, but still –'

'You'd rather be with them.' *And so would I, in a small clean family hotel on Gloucester Place, seventy quid a night, walking tour of Bloomsbury inclusive. Two big, burger-stuffed kids, plenty of metalwork in their mouths, Mom in a beige trouser suit. I want his family so I can slot them into the gap left by my own.*

'I'd booked the flight before 9/11, I figured it would be giving like succour to the enemy if I didn't come over.'

'Gotcha.'

'Eek-eek' the wipers went; the cab braked, then heeled over to join the other rusty hulks cruising around Marble Arch, a reef of Nash that loomed up out of the silty drizzle. 'I tell you something, cabbie.' *Tell me everything, you dumb motherfucker, pour it all out.* 'I didn't vote for Bush, but I reckon he's handling this OK, and it wasn't the Twin Towers that set me against these Taliban fellows – though heavens to Betsy it was a terrible thing – but I knew these were dreadful people when they blew up those two ancient statues of the Buddha, you know the ones?'

'Yes.' *Fellows? Heavens to Betsy!?*

'Any folk who could destroy a thing of ancient beauty so brutally . . . well, nothing they could do would surprise me after that . . . and the way they treat their women too.'

*So far as I'm concerned the way they treat their women is the best thing going for those fuckers . . . keep those bints in line, I say . . . you take my ex, she's only gone and slapped a fucking restraining order on me, now that'd never 'appen in Kabul, I'd have 'er trussed up in one of them black cloaky things before she could say CSA . . .* 'I couldn't agree with you more. Very sad business.' *'Coz they should go a bit bloody further – take the kids offa them – no kids, no bloody power over us . . .*

Past the Odeon, with its egg-box roof, the cab squealed to a halt at some lights and the meter – which had been ticking away with generous increments – slowed to a trickle of pence. After fifteen years of cabbing Dave Rudman was so finely attuned to the meter that he could minutely calibrate it with his own outgoings. At the beginning of each day a spreadsheet popped up behind his heavy eyelids, and as he drove, picking up and dropping off, ranking up and driving again – so the figures were instantly calculated to inform him whether he was ahead or behind, if he could pay for his diesel, his insurance, his cab repayments, his food, his fags, his booze, his prescriptions, his child support and his divorce lawyer. At 8 p.m., when the second tariff band comes in, the figures alter accordingly; at 10 p.m., when the third starts, they change again. *But they all oughta be the bloody same: 6 to 2, 2 to 10, 10 to 6. That way, you know what you're getting – punters inall. In the future the tariffs will be equal, oh, yeah.* Time, distance and money – the three dimensions of Dave Rudman's universe. Up above it all was the Flying Eye, Russ Kane *trying to make a joke out of a fucking lorry what's shed its load at the Robin Hood Roundabout . . .*

Dave Rudman hardly ever used to go into the dozen or so cabbies' shelters that were still scattered about Central London. However, nowadays he was so skint he needed the cheap and greasy fuel the old biddies who ran them pumped out. They were weird little structures, the shelters, like antediluvian cricket pavilions of green wood, which the city had grown up around. Inside, the cabbies sat jawing and noshing at a table covered with a plastic cloth. So many cabbies, their faces dissipated by the life – like those of prematurely aged peasants, worn out by their bigoted credo. Dave didn't want to talk about the lost boy, but last week, in the shelter in Grosvenor Gardens, when *some pillock* of a cabbie, seeing Dave's face, horsey with depression, stupidly asked what was eating him, Dave spilled. Then the other cabbie quipped: 'A woman is like a hurricane: when they pitch up they're wet and wild, and when they bugger off they take your house and your car.'

Michelle hadn't only taken Dave's house; she'd got a bigger, flasher one. She'd even got a new daddy for Dave's boy – *and how fucking sick is that?* As for this Cohen cow who was milking Dave, *she must 'ave a fucking meter in her desk drawer and every time I bell her she pops it on and it goes up and up, fifty quid at a time, a wunner for a letter. Then there's the brief she gets to stand up on his hind legs in the judge's chambers for a grand a pop – but I bet she gets a kick-back, though. Cow. Lawyers – they're all scum.*

As the cab crawled up the Edgware Road, the fare looked bemused by the shiny pavements thronged by Arabs. Arabs sitting behind the plate-glass windows of Maroush supping fruit juices and smoking shishas, Arabs stopping at kiosks to buy their newspapers full of squashed-fly print. Their women flapped along behind them, *tagged and bagged, but under their chadors they're tricked out like fucking tarts in silk undies, they are. It gives 'em a big turn-on . . . And my ex, with her little job up in Hampstead, wrapping up thongs in fucking tissue paper . . . She's just the same . . . They're all the same . . .* 'Where to in Mill Hill exactly, guv?'

'Oh . . . sure . . . OK . . .' The fare did some uncrumpling. 'It's right next to somewhere called Wills Grove, but it doesn't have a name of its own, it's like a lane.'

'I know it.'

'You know it?'

'I know it – it's by the school.'

'That's right. I'm going to see a man who works at the National Research Institute – it's business – that's why I'm here. I work for CalBioTech – you may have heard of us. We're one of the organizations developing human genome patents . . .' When Dave didn't respond, the fare continued on another tack: 'I must say, I'm very impressed by how well you know London. Very impressed. In Denver, where I live, you can't get a driver who knows downtown – let alone the 'burbs.'

Dave Rudman had been to New York once, dragged there resisting by his ex-wife, a drogue behind her jet. The human ant heap was bad enough – but worse was the disorientation. Even with the grid system, *I didn't know the runs, I didn't know the points . . . I was fucking ignorant . . . I'll happily let America alone, mate, 'coz my Knowledge is all here. There are plenty of fucking thickos right here –*

*I don't need to go across the pond and learn your lot. Not that I'm even bothering with these ones, I've done it now, I've said my piece, an' I'll tell you what the real knowledge is fer nuffing! Women and their fucking wiles, kids and how the loss of them can drive a man fucking mad, money and how the getting of it breaks your bloody back!* The obsolete Apricot computer sat in the garage of his parents' house on Heath View. It squatted there on an old steamer trunk, beside two of his father's defunct one-armed bandits, their innards exposed, once glossy oranges and lemons waxed by the twilight. In a rare moment of clarity – an oblique glance through the quarterlight of his mind – Dave Rudman remembered the long shifts in his Gospel Oak flat. The tapping and the transcribing, the laying down of His Law. Then his eyes tracked back to the misty windscreen, and the figure hunched over the keyboard hadn't been him at all – only some other monk or monkey.

'Well, we aim to please, sir. Most London cabbies see themselves as ambassadors for the city, part driver, part tour guide.' Dave slowed the cab before the junction with Sussex Gardens, allowing a Hispanic woman wearing a fur-trimmed denim jacket to shepherd her great shelf of bosom across the road. He sensed the fare's approbation like a sunlamp on his bald spot. 'Now to the right here, sir, almost all the property between here and Baker Street is owned by the Portman family; not a lot of people realize how much of London is concentrated in the hands of a very few, very rich people.'

'That's very inner-resting.'

'I'm glad you think so, sir, and this road we're driving up, you may've noticed that it's very straight for a London road, that's because it's the old Roman Watling Street.'

'You don't say.' *I do fucking say. I fucking know. I know it all – I hold it all. If all of this were swamped, taken out by a huge fucking flood, who'd be able to tell you what it was like? Not the fucking Mayor or the Prime Minister – that's for sure. But me, an 'umble cabbie.*

'Yes, if we were here seventeen hundred years ago, we might've seen a legion marching off to Chester, on its way up north to duff up a bunch of blue-painted savages.'

The cab, its wipers 'eek-eeking', pulled away from the lights and scraped by the concrete barnacles of the Hilton tucked beneath the Marylebone Flyover. It was late lunchtime on a wet December day, so the shop windows were lighting up. Dave tried to imagine who – who he knew – might be the type to have pitched up in a room there, for no other reason but *to smoke crack with brasses from the Bayswater Road and rape the minibar*. From some dark rank in his memory a recollection pulled away: *Superb Sid, Sid Gold . . . picked 'im up last year outside the Old Curiosity Shop . . . He was looking pretty fucking flush, pretty pleased with 'imself. Bespoke fucking whistle, cashmere overcoat, the whole bit. He wouldn't've done me any favours if I'd reminded 'im of the perm he used to sport at school. He became a brief, didn't 'e, criminal fucking brief – in both senses. Gave me his card. Ponce. Still, he's the type I'm gonna need because that Cohen cow ain't gonna come through. If I'm gonna see the boy again, I'm gonna have to get some dirt on that cunt Devenish. There has to be some . . . there always is . . . all you gotta do is dig.*

'My oldest son would be fascinated by this stuff,' said the fare, who'd relaxed now they were trundling past Little Venice and up through Maida Vale. 'He's a history geek . . . gets it from his dad, I guess.' The fare looked about him at the five-storey Tudorbethan apartment blocks, and, as if taking comfort in their solidity, unglued his hands from the handles and at last eased himself back in the seat.

Dave hit the intercom button – a plastic nubbin incised with a hieroglyphic head: 'Yeah, I always think of Watling Street as a sorta time tunnel, connecting the past with the present.' *What's the point in knowing there's a time tunnel there if you've got no one to go down it with? Now I understand that I learned this city to hold in my mind for a while – then lose it to my boy. Without him it's starting to disappear – like a fucking mirage.*

'It must be busy for you now . . . before Christmas?' The fare was uncomfortable with Dave's extravagant image, *but thass alright, he's paying to feel superior as well as be driven. Superior in knowledge, superior in wealth, he don't need some hack to tell him he's neither.*

'Yeah, busy enough, I'm out in the begging box all hours.'

'Begging box . . . ? Oh, I get it.'

'But come New Year town'll be dead as a doornail. We call it the kipper season.'

'I'm sorry?'

''Coz it's flat – nuffing 'appening 'til the spring.' *When the Ideal-fucking-Home-Show hits town, more ponces than you can shake a roll-neck at. Then the headscarf-and-sleeveless-anorak mob up for the Flower Show, Chelsea Bridge crammed with shuttle buses and off-roaders that've never even slid off the fuckin' gravel drive. Benny used to clear out to Tenerife on the banana boat for the kipper season. Said he could live out there all winter for five bob a day, come back when the trade picked up again.*

They passed Fratelli's, a glass-container bistro below the deck of the new Marriott, then the cab flipped up on to the Kilburn High Road. The *shitty little shopping centre* at Kilburn Square teemed with *bat-eared London Irish kids exchanging benefit money for synthetic-furred animals with glued-on eyes. Cheapo chavs . . . baggy fucking tracksuits . . . flapping their skinny arms.* Still, Dave felt at home here – he'd reached the right circle of the city, the one where he more or less belonged. Built up over centuries in concentric rings, like the trunk of a gargantuan tree, London districts derived their character from their ring: Kilburn, Shepherd's Bush, Balham, Catford – all of them grown from the same barky bricks and pithy masonry.

The rain had died away to a cellulite pucker of drizzle on the brown puddles, and there was an oily gloss on everything. The wipers 'eeked' to a standstill. Dave tried to make the lights at Willesden Lane and failed. He pulled up short in the yellow net of lines thrown across the junction and applied the handbrake with its wooden stair creak. The Kilburn State Ballroom leaned over them, posters peeling away from its *diarrhoea tiling. Fucking Taigs, dumb Paddies, with their hurdy-gurdy show bands and their leaky-eyed, pissed-up, violent lovelessness, worshipping a sexless cow with her chest hacked open.* The fare was looking through the speckled windows at the old navvies, flannel trews lashed round Guinness bellies, who came tottering out of Paddy Power's shredding their slips and chucking them in the air so they created localized snowfalls, off-white Christmases of loss.

'We call this County Kilburn,' Dave said, and, when the fare looked uncomprehending, he enlarged, 'because a lot of the Irish live here.'

'Oh . . . sure . . . OK.'

'Lovely people.' *I wouldn't be here at all if it weren't for you, my son. No pick-ups and precious few drop-offs either. Who wants some son of the sod blowing Bushmills chunks on the upholstery while he blabs about his poor old mammy? Not me. Still, I ought to go and see my poor old mammy, she worries about Carl. It's on the way back into town, I could even look in at the Five Bells and have a drink . . . No, make me fuzzy with the pills . . . Fucking bejazus! What if the PCO pulled me in for a medical?*

Dave didn't want to see his poor old mammy anyway. Didn't want to see her sitting in the worn-out armchair by the window, scrupulously marking her pupils' projects even though it was the start of a two-week holiday or, worse, diligently preparing for a child-centred Christmas that the central grandchild wouldn't be attending. Folding paper serviettes decorated with prancing reindeer, checking cracker availability, climbing up the tiny aluminium stepladder to get the box of decorations down from the equally tiny loft. *Mum never liked Michelle – hated her, more like. Funny, when I feel Mum's hatred I stop hating 'chelle.* They would sit there, over mugs of instant coffee in the kitchen, listening to the old man snooze next door in front of the racing: 'They're on the home straight now, past the last furlong marker . . . and it's Tenderfoot, Tenderfoot . . . all the way from Little Darling . . .' The unspoken lay on the tablecloth between mother and son, among blue Tupperware, the *Hendon Advertiser* and a pile of dog-eared exercise books.

If Dave offered his mother the opportunity, she'd vouchsafe some of her ailments – the hot flushes, the sweats, the cramps and pains . . . *She's in her mid sixties, but it's like she's still on the fucking blob!* He deliberately framed the most disgusting thoughts – hating mummies was what he excelled at, and this – he dimly comprehended – was because *I'm such a fucking mummy's boy . . .*

The cab trundled under the railway bridge at Brondesbury and began to strain up Shoot Up Hill. *Pile of shit, rip-off on wheels. That's the trouble with cabs – they're all fucking ringers, they're all pretending to be cabs but none of them are the real thing. Benny's old FX4 was so underpowered it could hardly make it up the ramp from the Euston rank. He told me he once had to ask some fatties to climb out and walk 'til he made it to the level. This Fairway is bearable, so why would I lay out thirty grand for a TX? For a bigger windscreen so I can see more of this bollocks? A wheelchair ramp so I can pick up spazzes? I'd be in hock to the finance company and having to work still bloody harder to keep those fat fuckers in time-share villas in fucking Marbella . . .*

'I must say, cabbie,' said the fare, 'the reputation of these vehicles doesn't do them justice, they are most exceptionally comfortable.' *Comfortable for who? You try getting your porky trotters down under this dash, it's like putting your legs in a coffin, mate, a vibrating bloody coffin. It fits tighter than a ridged dick in a ribbed condom. I swear, I've got out of this thing at the end of a day's work and fallen straight fucking over.* 'I'm glad you're enjoying the ride, sir, we like to say that this is the finest custom-built taxi in the world. Its unique twenty-five-foot turning circle makes it ideal for London's crowded streets, and helps to ensure that the licensed trade stays in business.' *I'd give it up tomorrow and drive a fucking Renault Espace for Addison Lee if it wasn't for the ghost of old Benny urging me on, and my own dumb pride.*

The cab growled over the brow of Shoot Up Hill and on along Cricklewood Broadway. This was another ring of the city. Outside the grocer's there were stacks of plantains and boxes of sweet potatoes under flapping plastic – garish, alien vegetables infesting the lacklustre suburb. Outside the pound shops West Africans flicked amber worry beads and peered at displays of washing-up brushes. A big pub hove into view, the Crown, engraved glass, double bow windows, free-standing sign. It looked impressive, *but it's only been made over to look like what it once was. Inside are fifteen kinds of piss on electronic tap, a video jukebox and a bunch of slappers giving the come-on to farting salesmen full of refried cheer.*

'And what's this county called, then?' the fare asked.

'County yourself bloody lucky you don't live here, sir,' Dave said, then laughed to show he wasn't serious. *Not that I'm racial or anything, it's only that if I'm perfectly honest, at the end of this particular bloody awful day, I can't stand the fucking shvartzers . . . Can't stand their tight, furry curls, their chocolate skin, their blubbery lips . . . their dreadful fucking driving . . .* Shvartzers. Hard to think of Big End, whom Dave had known since he was a teenager, as a shvartzer. *But it's better to say shvartzer than coon or nigger, innit? Afro-Caribbean's plain stupid, 'coz they aren't all that. If Benny were still alive he'd be amazed to see black, black cabbies, fucking blown away. Black, black cabbies and diesel dykes inall. Not that there are anything like as many blacks as there were Jews – thank fucking God. Benny said that in the sixties most cabbies were Jewish. What the fuck's 'appened to 'em? Disappeared to Emerson Park, Redbridge and fucking Stanmore, living out their days behind double glazing, under the watchful eyes of lawyer daughters and doctor sons. Hung up their ski jackets and fur boots, quit the patch leaving only their bloody shtoopid shlang behind 'em.*

The cab bundled on past bed shops and a new Matalan, before finally ridding itself of the endless parade of commerce and entering authentic suburbia, the great shrubbery of three-bedroom, inter-war semis that defined London more than any mere black cab or Big

Ben ever could. The road fell away towards the North Circular, splitting into three tongues, one poking through the arch of a still higher flyover, while the two others lolled down to the ground. The VDU façades of PC World and Computer Warehouse glared at each other across six lanes. The cab passed between them, then was aloft, buffeted by wind, spattered by grit, slapped by waste paper. To the east seagulls soared above the sea-greenery of Hampstead. *Like a kid's snowstorm toy, the little cab shaken up.* Dave remembered *the little kid crying, huge pink finger marks on his naked bum.* And what he had whimpered: *Not hurting Dad . . . not hurting* . . . as he confused the pain and the action that had caused it.

Dave had been driving for so many years he hardly ever thought about the actual graft of turning the wheel – except for when he did, and then it was a torment. *When Carl was little and I felt like this, I'd find a call box and pull over. I was working nights. 'Do you want to speak to Daddy? Daddy's on the phone?'* The sound of two-year-old breathing rasping the mouthpiece, then his voice, piping yet oddly distinct:

*'Daddy?'*

*'Hiyah, Runty, how's it going, mate?'*

*'Mummy, issa ghost.'*

The ghost drove on up the Broadway past the uglified slab of the Connaught Business Centre and on through Colindale, turning right down Colindale Avenue by the Newspaper Library, where ageing amateur genealogists sifted the dusty old doings of their ancestors between their arthritic fingers. The copper roof of the National Institute for Medical Research at Mill Hill shone in a single faint beam from the setting sun. 'That's NIMR, isn't it?' said the fare, but Dave didn't hear him, he was aiming for it, tacking the cab this way and that: under the M1 at Bunns Lane, then up Flower Lane to Mill Hill Circus. He wasn't using any knowledge to get to his destination – simply a homing instinct. *Now it's Carl that's the ghost* . . . First they stopped meeting in the flesh, then the phone calls got shorter and shorter, a few muffled phrases: 'Yeah, Dad, alright, yeah,' a few muffled phrases that eventually deteriorated into text messages: 'Eye not CU . . . Eye 8 B4 . . . Eye luv U 2 . . .' A staccato script of letters and digits beamed from an alternative world. Then they ceased communicating altogether and began to liaise in dreams or nightmares.

It wasn't until he turned off Wells Lane and bumped up the rough track between Mill Hill School and its sports fields that Dave realized he hadn't replied to the fare. He thought of remedying the deficiency, but it was too late for anything save a hearty 'Well, here you are, sir, up on the heights. If it were only a little earlier I'd suggest you take a stroll after your meeting. You can see most of the northwest of London from here, and right into the city centre.' The fare only grunted, examined his crumpled paper, then sang out, 'This is it!' as they drew level with a prosperous cantonment. The Burberry bundle tugged up his briefcase and piled out of the door. Standing by the driver's window, he sorted through the pigskin wallet he'd drawn from an inside pocket in the irritating, dilatory way of a foreigner, examining each note as if he weren't quite sure if it had any value at all – let alone its face one. Dave saw his tip dwindle to nothing. Americans who were used to London tipped well; newcomers seldom bothered – they certainly didn't understand that twenty per cent was considered perfectly acceptable for a black cab. *Still, twenty-five notes on the meter, and who knows if* . . . 'You wouldn't like me to wait would you, sir? I can turn the meter off if you're not going to be more than an hour.' The fare consulted his watch before replying, 'No, thank you, I'm gonna be a good deal longer.' He handed over the money, a tenner and a twenty, then hesitated while Dave combed the coin in his bag, finger waves pitter-purling on metal shingle, then, 'Keep the change, cabbie.'

'Thank you very much, sir, much obliged to you!' *Consider yerself at home! Consider yerself one of the fa-mi-ly! We've taken t'you so strong!*

*It's clear! We're! Going to get along!'* In the jaundiced eye of his own self-contempt Dave saw himself leaping from the cab to hoe down in the dirty puddles, skipping and splashing, his sleeves up to his elbows, tugging the peak of his cap in lieu of a forelock.

Once the ex-fare had turned and walked off under the homely glow of a solitary streetlight, Dave bumped the cab on over the top of the hill and down to the Ridgeway. He made a right and parked up opposite the Institute. There were seven storeys of big, metal-framed windows – including dormers – and all were brightly lit. From the open transoms came the hum of purposive machinery. When Dave was a boy, hidden in the estate off Bittacy Hill gasping on a fag, and waiting for the rest of his class to return from their run up to the top of the Ridgeway so he could rejoin the race at a believably low ranking, the word was that the cure for cancer was on the point of discovery under the Institute's green copper roof. Then he'd glimpsed white-coated lab assistants doing things with racks of test tubes, but now the lower windows were equipped with reflective glass, and Dave had found out that if he moved towards the fence CCTV cameras tracked him, each one equipped with its own little 'eek' of a wiper. Inside, the biomedical boffins had given up on the cancer cure – just as they themselves had given up smoking. Instead the American's colleagues were splicing genes, humanizing antibodies and growing ferny little forests of stem cells. The occasional puppy's eye was dissected, the live animal pinioned in a savage clamp. White girls with dreadlocks, maddened by the deficiencies of their vegan diets, would come up here and try to kill the boffins. *It's a bitch save dog world* . . .

Dave Rudman switched off the engine and got out of the cab. He was a large man with broad shoulders rounded by occupational hunching. He had the standard issue potbelly of the sedentary forty-year-old, and his unfit jeans hung low on his sagging rear. His features were handsome enough and taken at a glance they gave an impression of strength and sensuality: broad, full-lipped mouth;

prominent, fine-bridged nose; firm, dimpled chin. Sadly, up close this wavered, then dissolved. His dark eyes were too bulbous and too close set. His complexion was worked over by the leather-puncher of old acne scars. His thin, veined ears stuck out. When he took off his cap he revealed that his hair – which anyway had been nondescript – was gone, leaving behind a lumpy skull, full of odd depressions and queer mounds. Where his hairline used to be were several rows of little craters, as if a minuscule crop had been lifted. His two front teeth niggled at each other, one bony knee trying to cross over the other. Given a measure of content it was a face that might have cohered; now, standing in the damp dusk of winter's day on the bluffs above London, Dave Rudman's face was disorganized by pain, his features driven apart from one another by an antagonism so powerful that it pitted ear against eye, cheek against nose, chin against the world. Five days' stubble gave him a cartoon muzzle.

Desperate Dave limped to the fence and climbed over it into the playground of a little breeze block of a nursery. Threading his way between shoulder-high slides and swings, he gained a second fence and hoisted himself over that. He hardly seemed conscious of his progress, lifting each heavy denim leg over the chainlink as if it were a prosthesis, until he stood unsteadily, looking out over the darkening valley strung with the fairy lights of street lamps. Rudman sank to his knees – a sudden plunge. His hands – big, soft and hairy – drove into the muddy surface; he grabbed at the soil, lifting clutches of it up, squeezing the morass between his fingers. 'You fucking bitch!' he blubbered. 'You fucking bitch, you've taken . . . you've taken . . . ev-ery-thing!'

'We're fathers first,' said the group leader. 'We're loving dads,' responded the nine men who sat in a loose circle of plastic chairs.

'Iss juss a formality,' Gary Finch whispered to Dave, 'don't take it serious.'

'Good,' said Keith Greaves, the group leader, 'I'm glad we got that straight.' His gaze ranged around the circle, from Dan Brooke in his adman's Armani, to Finch and Rudman in their jeans and tracksuit tops. 'It doesn't matter who we are or where we come from – the only important thing here at Fathers First is that we're dads who want to care for our kids.' There was a throaty mutter of assent. Dave looked away from the men's faces to the tiny gold features of the figurines on the swimming trophies in the glass cabinet that took up a whole wall of the institutional room. 'Now!' Greaves gave a motivational thigh-slap and hunched forward. His white shirt was savagely pressed, his jeans sharply creased, everything about him shouted defiance of lone male neglect. 'Is there any particular issue that a dad wants to raise with the group this evening?'

A skinny man in a leather jacket with a wispy beard raised a tentative finger. 'Access,' he croaked.

'Good, Steve,' said Greaves, his thin lips curling, 'we can all identify with that, now, what's the problem?' Steve began slowly and in measured tones to complain: he'd seen the court welfare reporter, he'd punctiliously attended meetings with the Children and Family Court Advisory and Support Service, he'd honestly reported his earnings to the Child Support Agency, but 'Babs, she dicks me around.' His voice began to rise: 'I turn up on a Wednesday afternoon to pick the girls up from school and she's already got them' – a low rumble of identification from the dads – 'she sends them to her mother's on my weekends' – another rumble – 'they go to her place in new clothes I've bought them, then the clothes never come back to my place' – more rumbling, and, egged on by it, Steve began to rant, 'she's got the house, she's got the car, she's even got another fucking bloke! Now she wants to stop my girls having any relationship with me at all, I can't stand it, I –' Dave

Rudman looked at the faces paled by resentment, the eyes bright with anger. *How's this going to help?* Adding his own can of pain to this slopping tank of loss?

~

*Forward Regent's Park Road. Forward Finchley Road. Left Temple Fortune Lane. Bear left Meadway Crescent. Bear left Meadway. Right Hampstead Way* . . . Driving by the Heath Extension, looking over the mock meadows, Dave remembered childhood forays up here with his brother, Noel: jumping their bikes over the hillocks and dells in North End Woods, dismounting to battle with other kids, their weaponry sticks and acorns, then charging through the undergrowth – sloshing into the boggy hollows. Finally they would freewheel towards home down Wildwood Road, past the big houses with their glossy privet hedges, cooling Jags and Rollers ticking in the driveways. *Right Wildwood Road. Left North End Way. Comply Jack Straws Castle . . . Comply . . . comply with your fucking restraining order, you dickhead! If you do it again and they catch you, you'll be in a fucking sweat box!* Dave's headlights washed over a gaggle of seven-year-olds who were tumbling out of the new-old coaching inn. They were batting a white balloon between them. A tall figure loomed behind them in the doorway and lifted a hand to remonstrate, while gesturing with the other to the busy traffic only feet away. Dave drove on. *Right West Heath Road. Left Branch Hill. Right and comply Frognal* . . . The Fairway wallowed over the speed bumps. Nowadays, when the stress built up, he found himself doing this, calling over the route while he drove it, just as he did in his days as a Knowledge boy, puttering around the city on his moped . . . *Left Arkwright Road. Right Fitzjohn's Avenue* . . . It helped to keep his wheels on the ground, stop the cab from taking off *like fucking Chitty Chitty bloody Bang Bang. Left Lyndhurst Road. Right Haverstock Hill* . . . which he roared down, his Faredar off. He couldn't afford to pick up a fare up here on the borders of the forbidden zone. It could be anyone – and they might tell someone. *Forward Chalk Farm Road. Points at the beginning: Mill Hill School, St Joseph's College, The Rising Sun. Points at the end: None, it's all fucking pointless, innit* . . . Dave sighed, hit the window switches, lit a B & H, switched on his 'For Hire' sign and aimed for the West End. If he was lucky he'd get the after-work crowd, then still be back down in town for something to eat before the theatre burst.

On Shaftesbury Avenue three women extended from the kerb in a chain of linked arms. *Whadda they fink they're doin' – fording a river?* Dave picked them up. They were on their way back to Chelmsford, and Shirley had some cava in her thermos – this much he gathered. They'd loved *Mamma Mia!*, although not as much as they'd hoped. They did a chorus of 'Waterloo' and two of 'Fernando', drumming on the seats with their fists until he asked them to stop. Nicely. The cab heaved itself off of Primrose Street and squealed down the ramp into the bowels of Liverpool Street Station. The Essex housewives squealed as well, their glassy eyes running up the polished flanks of the new block. At the bottom the tiling reverted to public convenience and oofing they helped each other out, paid what was on the meter and tipped him with their tipsy adoration, '30544, we'll be looking out for yoo-hoo!' Confusing the cab's number with his own, confusing the cab with him. But everyone did that – even Dave.

Dave circled the wheel and pulled back up the ramp. Before he had time to drive round to the rank, he got a fare. *Bit dodgy but it was quiet up West, not enough Yanks, not enough shoppers* . . . The lights up Regent Street flashed mostly at themselves.

The new fare was tipsy as well . . . *a City getter* . . . one Lobb in the gutter, the other on top of his big shiny case, the boxy kind suits use for overnighters. His camelhair overcoat was open, his jacket was undone, his blue-and-white check shirt was unbuttoned at the collar, *his eggy-puke tie* yanked down. He lunged in the back without asking, because he was *pissed and yakking on his mobile.* Dave remained stationary, pointedly not hitting the meter. 'Where to, guv?'

'I don't fucking care where that tranche is, Beaky, put it in the other account, mix it up, shift it round – 'eathrow –' he flung through the glass panel and then resumed: 'It's not a case of coverin' up, man, it's getting things done. I get things done – you get things done, the whole whatsit moves . . . moves forward.' Dave could hear Beaky pecking to get in from the ether, until he flicked the shift into drive and the cab lurched off through the unmanned police check and round the corner into London Wall.

The fare couldn't stop talking as Dave threaded the cab down through the dark fabric of the City to the Embankment. He got out his laptop and began linking it up to his mobile with a pigtail of cable, until this proved beyond him, so he just read stuff off it to Beaky. Not that Dave was paying much attention, but this getter – young, *ferret face, lock of mousy hair on a voddie-sweat brow, fake signet ring* – didn't care if he listened or not. The driver was only another part of the cab's equipment for him, like the reading light or the fan heater. Dave obliged him – he had his own thoughts for company.

*Fifteen up West, fiver from those old girls, airport run'll score me thirty or forty. Rank up in the feeder park and 'ave a snack at Doug Sherry's, run back into town – if I'm lucky – and I'll call it a night.* Globular old lamp-posts with fat fish curled round them stood along the Embankment, while above the drooling Thames cast-iron lions sucked their dummies. The Millennium Wheel slowly revolved on the South Bank, its people-pods ever threatening to dip into the silty wash. Dave hugged the river, zoning out as the cab puttered up through Olympia, until they hit the Cromwell Road, where life-sized mannequins of business-class travellers advertised inter-continental seat-beds. *Not real, toyist . . .*

*Not toys, son,* Dave's father said, *machines for entertainment.* They were in the lounge bar of the Green Man out at Enfield Lock; nicotine was smeared on Paul Rudman's hair and fingers like toxic pollen. The week's take for the slot machines was racked out on the table in little pewter columns. Vince Bittern, the ex-Old Bill who ran the boozer, wasn't too bothered with exact calculation. He put his flabby forearm down the middle of the table and curled it round a rough half of the stacks. *Orlright, Paul?* he demanded. *No bother, mate, no bother,* Dave's father acquiesced, lifting his wine glass of Bells to his wet lips so that the rim rattled on his denture. Dave sat in the corner, his face *cherried-up with shame – Dad was so weak, so bloody hopeless . . .*

*Not toys,* Dave told Carl, who was sitting on the tip seat immediately behind him, sighting back along the road, asking interminable questions – a tyrannical seven-year-old inquisitor. *They're real, son.* The boy howled with anger, *Nooooo, stop it! Stop lying! They're not real, they're toyist.*

*Toyist*. Dave had taken the child's coinage for his own. On good days only obvious fake things were toyist, like the giant spine stuck on a chiropractor's in Old Street, or the big plug sunk into the wall of a block on Foubert's Place. But on bad days almost everything could be toyist: the Bloomberg VDU on the corner of North End Road was an outsized Game Boy, the flaring torch outside the new Marriott Hotel at Gloucester Road a lit match. The buildings themselves were so many CD towers and hair-styling wands, while people walked the street with the jerky motion of puppets, visible strings lifting styrofoam cups to their painted lips.

The fare was still at it when the cab reached the Hammersmith Flyover: 'I don't fucking care.' Beaky was still on the receiving end. 'I know how to value a company, mate, an' I tellya everything counts, bloody everything. We look at everything – we wanna drive down the asking price, we can dig as deep as we like . . . Yeah, yeah, I know they've sold a million bloody episodes to Taiwan, and I know they look kosher, but I've heard things concerning that

Devenish –' *Devenish?! What the fuck, it can't be, think back, episodes . . . asking price – it figures.* 'He's flash as it goes, lives in a fuck-off gaff up in Hampstead, spreads his money round like Lurpak . . . You can't tell me, Beaky, that it's all off the back of *Bluey* – or whatever that stupid kids' show is called. Someone's buying into Channel Devenish, and I wanna make certain it ain't the cunt who's selling it . . . I know, I know, mate, do the necessary, use who you want, put it on my research account.'

By the time they were rolling up the Great West Road and Dave had the cab in overdrive for the first time in over a week, he'd undergone an attitude change – from surly serf to willing servant. The fare was slumped in the back seat, phone cast to one side, laptop to the other. The perspiration of bumptiousness and liquor had curdled into thick, fearful sweat on his hollow temples and tight forehead. 'Y'know what, mate?' he served up through the hatch.

'What?'

'I can't stand flying, can't bloody stand it.'

'Nor me, nor me.' *Ah, poor iddle kiddie, iddums scaredums?*

'Yeah, puts the kibosh on my whole bloody day.'

'Where're you off to, then, guv?' *Keep him talking, I want his card.*

'New York.'

The cab was rollicking along the Chiswick flyover past fifteen-storey corporate conservatories. *What's through the arched window tonight? Another bank of blinking screens, another coffee machine, another yucca, another Polish cleaner? There are more Poles in Ealing than fucking Cracow – at least that's what they say.* 'Eye of the storm, then . . . do us a favour willya and see if you can persuade a few of 'em to come back this way.'

'Business bad, issit?'

'Bad, I tell you it's fucking diabolical.' *Diabolical, he'll like that, he finks e's a leading actor an' 'e wants the rest of us to be supporting ones.*

'Yeah, well, it's not been too clever in my line either.' And so it went on, the two men bantering as the taxi canted down off the flyover, then bumbled along the motorway. *Heston Services. Moto 1 and 32. Since when has this been a Moto Services? Used to be Granada – I think. Moto? Moto? Bloody stupid name for a motorway services. Bloody stupid logo as well* . . . A man, lying back, arms behind his head, a sort of crown on his head, an atomic swirl of lines in the region of his supine belly *like 'e's bin fucking gutted.*

All the way up to the second Heathrow exit Dave sought a way to get the man's card out of him, but after years of minding his own business intrusiveness didn't come easily. The rain started up again as they hit the motorway spur. 'That's all I need,' said the fare; 'must make it ten times worse for those bastards in the cockpit.'

'Yeah,' Dave drawled, 'specially if their wipers ain't working.' The fare laughed gratefully – the cockney chitchat made it possible for him to let go of his nerves, get back in character.

Toyist Heathrow, a confusion of *up-ended Rotadexes and fax-machine terminals*. The cab pulled up to the drop-off at Terminal 3. The fare got out and stood in the damp sodium night of jet screech and taxi mutter adjusting his suit and overcoat, getting out his wallet. He gave a tenner's tip; Dave thanked him, then said, 'Receipt?' And when the fare took it and thanked him in turn, Dave went on, 'Giss yer card, mate.'

'What?'

'Give us your business card: the radio circuit I'm on are doing a raffle-type thingy for our customers. If your card gets drawn you get two hundred quid's worth of free travel in the new year.' The fare dug his card out and passed it over. Dave thanked him, wished him a merry Christmas and flicked the shift into drive. *''Course I'm not on the fucking radio circuit, am I, haven't been for years, I'd rather be a straightforward musher than bother with that malarkey.* He looked at the card: the lettering meant nothing to him – CB & EFN INVESTMENT STRATEGIES, STEPHEN BRICE, CEO EUROPE – but he was one step closer to nailing Devenish now, *pulling him off of Michelle with his wet dick gleaming in the dark, rolling the wanker over and grinding a boot into his fucking smug face.*

Dave drove back out through the long, fume-filled tunnel under the runway, pulled round the roundabout and up on to the peripheral road, where there were hotels so large other hotels could have checked into them. He turned into the cul-de-sac that ran behind the police station to the taxi feeder parks. He pulled into the first one and parked up; it was a quarter full – not at all heavy for a mid evening in late December. Doug Sherry's, the taxi drivers' café, looked cheery enough, *if you think any joint full of these mugs can be cheery*. The windows and eaves were draped with tinsel, and when he'd locked up the cab and strolled into the lobby, there was a Christmas tree propped by the bins full of the drivers' free rags: *Taxi*, *Call Sign*, *London Taxi Times* and *HALT*. Tacked to the bare brick wall was a laminated poster showing a *cheeky chappy cabbie's* grinning mug. '233 Sexual Assaults and 45 Rapes' the caption read, 'So What's He Got to Laugh About?'

Dave took his place in the queue for the serving counters and checked out his peers. *Fat, thick, racist, ugly, rotten wankers. In their dumb fucking zip-up jackets carrying their stupid little change bags, giving it this, giving it that, and saying fuck all.* Dave didn't like many cabbies at all, but he reserved his special derision for the estimated half of London licensed taxi drivers who did nothing else but work the airport. *With their stupid bloody gang names* . . . The Quality Street Gang, the Lavender Hill Mob . . . *and their stupider nicknames* . . . The Farmer, Gentleman Jim, Last Chancer, Musher Freddy . . . *Sitting out here ranked up for half their fucking lives, tootling up West with a fare, then putting their lights out and tootling back again. Too bloody scared to ply for hire like a real cabbie, too fucking fond of their fishing and their golf, their cards and their sweepstakes. Fancy themselves part of some stupid elite, following the 'cabbies' code', when half of them are faces on the fiddle, putting foil over their computer discs before they go into the feeder park to bilk a few quid, or going down on to the terminals to steal fares, pretending they're picking someone up on the radio if they get pulled. Makes me sick.*

And always had, which is why Dave avoided the airport as much as he could. This evening he was *bilked by a fucking pork chop* that looked succulent under the bright lights of the servery, but, once he'd borne it over to one of the blue melamine tables, turned out to be dry and solid. Meat to murder with. He wouldn't have minded plunging it like an ice axe into the red neck of the cabbie who stood feet away, leaning his elbows on a table, sticking his fat arse in the air and slamming down dominoes with Caribbean vigour. He might have done, if the back hadn't turned to reveal a face he knew: 'Wot you doin' aht 'ere ven, Tufty?' the other cabbie asked and Dave grunted, 'Nuffing, I 'appens to trap a flyer.' *Yeah, a flyer, a fucking 'eretic . . . some scumbag who's lost his faith in London.*

Dave's eyes wavered over to the wood-panelled wall that was hung with photographs of dead cabbies: 'Sid Greenglass, always early, now he's late, 1935–1986', 'Chancer Ross with the one that didn't get away, 1944–1998' (this one featured a rod, a reel and two fishy faces), 'The Maida Vale Marauder, Terry Groves, 1941–1997'. Their lives seemed shorter than average, fifties and sixties mostly. It could have been the selection that was made when the new café was built and the photos transferred over from General Roy's – but Dave doubted it. Cabbing was always an unhealthy occupation, sitting on the shuddering seat, all the dreadful humours gathering in your belly and legs as the stress flowed in through ears and eyes and hands on the steering wheel. *Piles – that's what you get from all that sitting . . . piles . . . that's why they're such arseholes. Cabbies aren't anything much anyway – they think they're professionals, but they aren't. They're mostly ex-something else, ex-coppers, ex-army, ex-crims, ex-bloody-boxers – and then they end up here on the wall at the airport, ex-fucking everything.*

A screen was wedged high up in the corner of the dining area showing the lane movements in the second feeder park. This was bigger than the one outside the café, thirty lanes wide, each one with thirty-odd cabs lined up in it. When a driver had inched his way through both these cattle pens a screen told him which terminal he was to go down to. On a good day it could take a couple of hours, on a slow one a lot longer. Then there was no guarantee you'd get a fare into the middle of London; you might just get a transit passenger, marooned for the night, who wanted to go to the Holiday Inn at the end of the motorway spur. Or worse still – because at least with a run under five miles you didn't have to rank up again – you'd get a full load of Southall grannies, saris flying, all with *bundles of shmatte from Pakkiland*, all needing your capable assistance, who'd scrape the *poor old Fairway up and down the speed bumps* to No. 47, Acacia Avenue, then pay the meter and *not a bloody penny more*. Two hours waiting, twenty minutes driving, twenty minutes portering *and all for eight bloody quid, you're better off flipping Big Macs*.

Dave abandoned the pork chop long before he had to pull over to the second feeder park. Better to sit in the darkness of the cab – polluted with air freshener, tangy with diesel and rank with old cigarette smoke – than bear the hateful company of his own kind. The cab – he'd spent half his adult life in it. *It's not juss a motor – it's almost fucking human* . . . He thought pointedly and with great fervour of the sleeping pills by his bed and the bottle of Scotch alongside them. He rasped his stubble with a quick-bitten thumb. When his turn came, it was a relief: he drove across the road, divvied up his ticket and joined the next metal anaconda worming its way towards the money prey. Eventually he got to the front and the screen flashed up 'No. 47304, Terminal 2'.

Down at the Terminal 2 rank passengers were being expelled by the sliding doors, sucked out of the warm nowhere and into the wet, cold here of wintertime London. Shuttle buses grunted like great pigs; armed police strutted, submachine-gun necklaces on their Kevlar décolletage. In front of Dave travellers mashed their over-stuffed cases into a cab, while the driver ignored them. *When I was a butter boy, I'd've been out on the road, bouncing like a puppy . . . Can I help you? Let me slot this in here, I'll be careful, we can put that one up front . . . Not now, oh no.*

Finally it was Dave's turn. He checked his watch: he'd been at Heathrow for an hour and three quarters. *City getter would've made a grand in that time, that fucking brief of mine would've scalped half that, and I've got nothing to show for it . . . Still, at least we're into the third tariff band.* His passenger shook herself free from the damp queue and stepped towards the cab; Dave handed his docket to the dispatcher, who said, 'North London, mate, Belsize Park, good for you?' Dave grunted, 'Not bad.' And the cab rocked a little as the woman got in; she only had a single, wheeled flight bag, the handle of which she'd already deftly stowed. 'Where to, love?' Dave asked, and she answered, 'England's Lane, please, just off Haverstock Hill?' Like so many fares she was querying his competence, wanting Dave's reassurance that he knew exactly where this was, but he didn't bother to give it, only put the cab in gear and grumbled off out of the terminal.

Thrumming back through the airport tunnel, Dave looked in the rearview mirror. The fare was a stringy brunette in her late forties, thick dark hair scraped back over sallow flesh, *bony as a fucking skull.* When she turned to look at the scale model of Concorde, Dave saw the tendons in her thin neck, exposed by the open neck of her blouse. She wore no make-up and a series of distinct grooves ran down her long top lip. The pashmina with the embroidered hem, the naked fingers that played with it, the bifocals on a chain, the myopic eyes blinking in the gloom: all said to Dave *spinnie or lezzer, one or other*, and either way not an object of desire – not that he had any available; nor one of pity – not that he had any of this either. He took out his slunk of Mansize and crunched the dried snot in his pitted nose.

The cab paused at the traffic lights under the M4 flyover, then accelerated up the slip road. Dr Jane Bernal slid her tired frame to the side of the seat and leant against the rain-dappled window. After the paranoia of the flight and the bucketing descent into Heathrow, even this chilly vibration was a comfort. Could it be mere culture shock *or is London dirtier, darker, sadder and madder than when I left it? I thought Carla was a screamingly tedious hostess, and the Brunswick Opera Festival worse than dull. Yet, now I'm home, Canada suddenly looks beautiful to me, the frozen lake, the bold tartans of the opera goers' jackets, their bright cheeks, their flaxen hair . . . The minute I cleared immigration and saw the drivers lined up by the rail like undertakers I wanted to be back there. Back, if necessary, with Carla, squirming my way out of her serpentine grasp. She promised . . . she promised we could have a great time anyway, even if I wanted to keep things platonic. But she wouldn't let me alone for a second. Not a bloody second.*

Still, at least Carla had been importuning in an immaculate split-level house surrounded by clean, crisp snow. There had been glasses of good wine on the glossy white rug in front of the circular, bronze fireplace. *Everything clean and untainted. As I walked from the terminal to the cab rank, I stepped on sticky gum and there was spit everywhere. The people's faces were so closed up . . . so angry. Now this cab driver, all I can see of him in the mirror is a pair of bloodshot eyes. He's exhausted, his hands shake even though they're clamped to the wheel . . . Is he drunk? Withdrawing from drink or drugs – or worse? He mutters to himself, his voice is peculiar . . . breathless – almost squeaking. He aspirates flat swear words, cunts and fucks, mixed in with what? Is it religious stuff – talk of a book, a prophet? He's going to turn to me and say he has special telepathy or a divine hot line – but how could a schizophrenic drive a London cab? He's too old for a flamboyant psychotic breakdown, surely?*

On the Chiswick flyover, Jane Bernal, despite herself, fastened her seatbelt. She did it as unobtrusively as possible, pulling the strap gently, terrified it might snag, or that the crazed cabbie would swivel round, taking his eyes off the road, and berate her for her lack of faith. *Crazy indeed, to've flown across the Atlantic, the whole cabin still humming with anxiety after the Twin Towers, each locked in his or her own miserable fears of being one of the holy martyrs' Chosen Ones, and to now find myself more frightened on the ground.* But as the cab shimmied on into the wet city, Dr Bernal allowed her professional detachment to come to the fore. *He's ill*, she thought as he turned off at Chiswick Lane and worked his way through Shepherd's Bush to the A40. *He's ill and he doesn't even know it.*

She'd seen men like this – and they were almost always men – in her consulting room at Heath Hospital: punctilious managers who couldn't comprehend why it was that they had to check the cooker five hundred times in succession; big-fisted brawlers who assumed foetal positions on the floor; fiery entrepreneurs doused by overwhelming uncertainty. Men of this stripe went mad the same way that they got cancers or arteriosclerosis: blindly, ignorantly, the absent fathers of their own, growing maladies – 'I'm just a little short of breath', 'They're only very quiet voices' – until the skin of their denial was stretched so taut it ripped apart.

She tried to strike up a conversation with the cabbie as they turned up Lisson Grove. 'Have you got any special plans for the holiday?'

'Very low-key, love, dead quiet, me and my old people, maybe my sister and her lot,' he began plausibly enough, then trailed off into 'I'll haveta slaughter the fucking meter . . . Can't afford it . . . Serve it up to that fucking cunt of a lawyer,' under his laboured breath.

Jane tried again as they belted past the zoo. 'Will you be working much?'

'Maybe,' he sighed. 'I might go out if I can be bothered,' running down into 'If you go into the forbidden zone and start diggin' abaht . . . well . . . what can you expect?'

As the cab chuffed up Primrose Hill, its headlights and foglamps carving a tunnel through the darkness, Jane decided she ought to do more. The man was driving a runaway train – and the points were welded up ahead. *My own Christmas, well, not so bad. On the day I'll go out to Hertfordshire and see Mother. Amazing, her resilience, her good humour. My God! It would be vaguely insulting if it weren't such a relief, only she could ingratiate herself with the staff in that dreadful home, charm them into caring for her, giving her treats, petting her. For the rest, silence or good music, not much food, a lot of solitude. Walks on the Heath, the time to think while others . . . well, often fall apart. Not so bad, not so bad at all. Being queer and self-sufficient is the best present at this season.*

The cab gargled round the bend by the Washington pub and into England's Lane. 'Which one, love?' he snapped.

'Up here on the left, please, driver, by that shop, Dolce Vita.' Jane summoned herself, grasped the handle of the bag, backed out of the door pulling it after her. On the pavement she sorted through her purse and put three cashpoint-ironed twenties together with one of her cards. *Best be straightforward, the only approach that ever works*. 'Here's a little extra,' she said, crumpling the bundle into his waiting palm, 'and also my card – don't be put off by the title, I think I might be able to help you.'

'Ta, love.' He didn't even look at it. 'Receipt?'

'No, thank you' – he made to drive away – 'and merry Christmas, driver.' But the cab was ten yards off already, hidden by a net curtain of drizzle and moving with the heavy inertia of a bad dream.

Dave Rudman looked at the card half an hour later. After he'd parked the cab up in Agincourt Road, Gospel Oak. After he'd clamped on the steering lock and taken out the radio. After he'd unlocked the door and pushed the chewed-up pile of loan offers and credit-card teasers across the sad mat. After he'd padded up the bare stairs and into the barer bedroom. After he'd dumped his coin holder and his cash bag on the table by the window and stripped to his rancid pants. After he'd swigged from the bottle, swallowed the pills and slumped across the unmade bed. He looked at it in the glow from the street lamp and read DR JANE BERNAL, FRCPSYCH, CONSULTANT, PSYCHIATRY DEPARTMENT, HEATH HOSPITAL. He contemplated the oblong of pasteboard for long seconds, then he shredded it deliberately with his sore fingers, a tatter of quick and cuticle. Then he threw the wad towards the radiator and heard it disintegrate with his hurting ears, each little piece falling to the dusty carpet. Then he twisted and fell across the bed, and, raising one hand above his head, slowly and methodically began to bludgeon it into the pillows, as if it were a peg and his fist an unfeeling mallet.

# 3
# *The Geezer*

SEP 509–10 AD

When Symun Dévúsh had been a little boy, his mummy, Effi, often came to him and took him from his moto. She led him away so it was just the two of them, all snugglewise and cuddleup. The other mummies thought this strange – and said so – but Effi was their knee woman and a rapper like her mummy Sharún before her. Drivers came and went while the knee woman remained, a power to be reckoned with on the island of Ham. Effi told little Symun the old legends of Ham, from before the Breakup and the Book that had ordained it, legends that, she maintained, went back to the MadeinChina, when the world had been created out of the maelstrom.

Am iz shaypd lyke a feetus, she intoned, coz í iz 1. According to Effi, Ham was the aborted child of the Mutha, an ancient warrior queen of the giants, who leaped from island to island across the archipelago of Ing, pursued by her treacherous enemies. Fearing herself about to be caught, the Mutha sucked seawater into her vagina as an abortifacient, then squatted in the Great Lagoon and voided herself of Ham. When her pursuers saw the foetus, they were terrified, because it was an abomination – part moto and part human – and so they fled. The Mutha stayed and revived the corpse of her child, revived it so successfully that it grew and grew until it became an island. And on this island a second race of smaller giants sprang up, who, over years, then decades and finally centuries, gradually separated themselves into the two species of men and motos. Í woz so slo, Effi said, vat vares awlways a bí uv moto inna

Amster, anna bí uv Amster inna moto. Together they cultivated Ham, establishing the fields for wheatie and the orchards for fruit, the woodlands for moto foraging and the saltings for samphire. These giants were prodigious climbers – for at that time there were many more stacks in the Great Lagoon and they were far higher. The islanders of Ham were thus rich in seafowl and moto oil, and their home was a veritable Arcadia. The giants used brick, crete and yok from the zones to build their castles, the five towers, which guarded the island from covetous invaders. They also built the groynes to protect Ham's coastline from the eroding sea. They planted the blisterweed that grew along the shoreline. An vay uzed vair bare bluddë ands 2 do í, Effi said, closing her own bony fist and shaking it in front of the little boy's wondering eyes. Vay wur vat bluddë strong an ard.

Sadly, with each successive generation the giants grew smaller in stature, their arts declined, and their ambitions shrank. Where once they had been frantic rappers, spinning word pictures of great solidity and duration out of the island's mist, now all poetry deserted them. Where once they could lift huge rocks and uproot mighty trees, now they could barely summon the strength to cultivate their meagre fields. They became subjects of the island – rather than its lawds and luvvies. In time the Lawyer of Chil's Hack came among them, supplanting their native mushers and replacing them with the Drivers of the PCO, brought from London in the far north.

The mushers had been ordinary Hamsters – dads with kiddies of their own. The Drivers were queers – men who had no desire to father children. Such a strange inclination, which, if known at all on Ham, was suppressed, made these dävines still more alien and imposing to the simple peasants.

If little Sy was disposed to give any credence to his mother's tales, then it was only a semi-belief. For every fourth day Change-over would come, and he'd be sent across the stream with his cousins to stop at the daddies' gaffs. Here a rigid Dävinanity held sway: the runs and the points were ceaselessly called over whenever the dads were not at work or amusing themselves with the opares. For little Symun – as much as for the other kids, who were not so exposed to the ancient lore – their mummies' influence was eclipsed entirely. It was as if when they were with their daddies the kids were other people altogether, with different natures, different likes, different fares even. Yet none more so than Symun, because, while the other kids ran to their daddies at Changeover, he had no dad of his own. Peet Dévúsh had fallen from the Sentrul Stac to his death before his only son was born, so Symun was the lad of all the dads, making him still more of a daddies' boy when he was under their care and control.

Although the last Driver to be dropped off on Ham had been picked up five years before Symun was born, his influence remained strong among the dads. The most dävine among them would not talk or look at the womenfolk, and avowed that they did not even recognize the mummies of their own kids. Had these fanatics prevailed, they would have wrapped all the mummies up in their cloakyfings from top to toe. If the dads were to be believed – especially the two or three of them who could read – the Book was all the understanding any Hamster needed of anything. The Book stood outside of the seasons and of the years. What Dave had described he had also foretold, and what he had seen in his own era would come again – for it had never truly gone. Dave's New London was all around them, trapped in the zones and the reef, a hidden yet still tangible world. Just as the roots of the herb pilewort resembled piles and so were good for the treatment of this malady, so the Daveworks were tiny pictures and fragmented legends of a transcendent city of Dave – Dave the Dad and Carl the Lost Boy – that had been deposited there, by Dave, at the MadeinChina. The problem for the Hamsters was not to build a New London but only to prove themselves worthy of realizing it by their Knowledge.

In the time of the last Driver all Daveworks had been rejected as toyist, and the practice of garlanding the gaffs, wayside shrines, the island's pedalo – and indeed themselves – with the plastic amulets had been forbidden. The mummies – who were, of course, denied the rituals of the Shelter – continued to believe in the ancient lore. Their Knowledge was of the Mutha, not Chelle, and of the lost Ham, rather than the Lost Boy. Denied their kids for half of each blob, they cleaved to the motos, and they looked to the knee woman and her anointing for their absolution.

As the years passed the less dävine of the dads allowed their faith, once more, to become softened by their temperate and isolate home. Even the Guvnor, Dave Brudi, began to speculate on such things. In his own youth he had travelled to Chil, and he told Symun that the giants' ruins were greater in their density here on Ham than in any other part of Ing; and, try as he might, he could not help but give credence to the legend that this was because the Book had been found, as he put it, rì ear on Am.

Symun Dévúsh grew to dadhood. He was a charismatic young bloke, attractive to both sexes – taller than his peers, finer boned, more open of countenance. His fingers were quick and dextrous, his eyes blue and dancing. His light beard was golden and curly, while the Hamsters' barnets were mostly a lank, dun brown. If there had been any reflective surface on Ham besides still water and dull irony, Symun might have been vain; as it was, he was aware of his appeal to others, without knowing precisely what it consisted of. Although he was popular with his posse and a good holder of the Book, there could never be any question of Symun reaching the first cab of the Shelter. He was an orphan, his mummy the knee woman. This meant that, unlike his best mate, Fred Ridmun, he was destined to be always a waver-upper, never the fare.

The autumn he and Fred turned fourteen, the two lads changed over for the last time and took their permanent place in the dads' gaffs. Then a peculiar thing happened to Sy. While he was still growing up he had never thought to question any of the kids about what they felt at Changeover – mummytime was for mummies, daddytime for daddies. He knew that, like him, they left their mummyselves on the east bank of the stream and that even their most recent memories of cuddleup and snuggledown were as half-remembered dreams.

Yet, when he changed over for the last time Symun Dévúsh took his mummyself with him – not entire but enough of it for him to feel marked out from the other Hamstermen. Unlike Fred, Sy couldn't prevent himself from looking at the mummies and kids when he saw them together – he even had eyes for the old boilers. Fred noticed it and teased him, saying, If U wanna lookit byrds, vares plenny uv opares on vis syde uv ve streem. Although Sy became more circumspect, Effi noticed his gaze as well, and when she returned it, Sy saw in turn that she knew what had happened, she understood what she had done by seeding his fertile imagination with such potent lore. She smiled at him often and strangely. However, he couldn't detect much love in these smiles, only fear.

~

– Eyem gonna go onna bí! Symun called to the rest of the gang, C if vairs anyfing bettah ovah vair!

And Fred called back:

– Yeah, orlrì, but nó 2 fa.

– Eye ear yer, Symun called back, while to himself he said, Sillë gí.

He shouldered his mattock and pushed his way between two banks of pricklebush that scratched him through his shirt. It was an overcast day in SEP and a year since Symun's Changeover. Foggy rags snagged at the soaking foliage and the screenwasher was on. This was good weather for gathering building material, the soil loose and yielding. If they found a pile of brickwork, beat back the undergrowth, then wedged and wielded their mattocks efficiently, the morta would crumble away and the individual bricks tumble from the earth – Dave's bounty for the young dads of Ham.

At Council that first tariff the five young dads had asked if they could go to the edge of the Ferbiddun Zön and fetch some brick to repair the pedalo gaff. It took most of the rest of the tariff for consensus to emerge, for each of the nine older dads had a view, and they all had tremendous affection for the sound of their own voices. There were moto gibbets to be built, fowling equipment to be repaired, the pedalo needed caulking – however, eventually permission was given. It mattered that it was Fred Ridmun's idea. The whole community understood that despite Fred's youth he would be the new Guvnor once Dave Brudi was dead, and the way the old dad retched and hawked blood that couldn't be far off. It was an important liberty for the five to be alone together for a shift. In the next year duty would bear down still more heavily upon them. Caff Funch, old Benni's daughter, was already knocked up by Fred – more of them would become dads soon enough. Meanwhile the older generation was passing into the shadows. Ham, as was the way every thirty years or so, stood on the cusp.

The posse had worked hard and soon amassed sufficient brick, so Sy's desire to press further into the zone wasn't governed by any necessity. The impulse puzzled him – he felt the place's aura as strongly as any of his companions did – perhaps even more. He had been among the most enthusiastic of the Hamsters when the bounds of the zone had been beaten that buddout. He had lashed at the sawleaf and fireweed with such frenzy that the granddads had muttered among themselves: Eye rekkun ees earin Dave on iz interkom. Now, the impulse to go further in, further than he had ever ventured before, was provoked as much by the need to be alone with his secret mummyness as by any thought of what he might find there.

Beyond the clearing in which Symun found himself the true zone began. The yellow-flowering pricklebush was the plant of the zone margin; in the interior it ceded to glossy-leafed rhodies that clambered over the hypogean brickwork, cracking it with their woody roots. These dense shrubs had enormous white flowers, exuding a heady aroma that kept the insects away from the zone. In turn, there was nothing for the landfowl to eat – not that there were many of these on Ham anyway, certainly compared to Chil or the rest of Ing. Only handfuls of toms and bobs nested on the island, together with the ubiquitous flying rats.

An occasional green ringneck whirred over Symun's head, and he could hear, higher up in the clouds, the unceasing lament of the gulls. At ground level the zone was eerily quiet – even the voices of his mates, scant paces away, sounded muffled and distant. The motos also found rhodies unpalatable, while in the very heart of the zone there were Utrees poisonous to them. The granddads also claimed that the rats – which the motos kept down elsewhere on Ham – had colonies deep in the zone, vast and labyrinthine nests from which they would emerge to gnaw to the bone any Hamster fool enough to breach taboo. Symun doubted this – what could such rat colonies live on? There was no wheatie hereabouts, and, while gulls nested on the rocky bluffs of the eastern shore, even massed rats were no match for aggressive oilgulls and blackwings. Besides, posses of Hamstermen often went along these bluffs, netting prettybeaks in season; if there were rats there he would have seen them for himself. No, the rat colonies were intended to frighten off anyone brave or foolhardy enough to penetrate too far into the zone; they were part of the mystique of the place.

As if the zone needed any more mystique – to Symun it was thickly permeated by Dave's prophecies of the world that had been and the world that would come again. He pushed on past the thicket, feeling the waxy rhodie leaves cool and damp on his exposed arms. The cries of his companions came again as Symun shouldered his way on into the zone, but he ignored them. Another ringneck flew whirring overhead in a greenish blur – and he took this to be a good omen, an excuse to push on still further.

After another hundred paces Symun sat down on a mound and lowered his head between his knees. He breathed deeply, inhaling the atmosphere of the place, its brooding silence redolent of ancient abandonment. Muttering to himself he scrabbled in the mud: Vare ass 2 B sum, vare awlways iz, awl U gotta do iz dig. Sure enough, he soon exposed a corner of brickwork encrusted with a rough rind of morta. Holding his mattock close to its blade, slowly and deliberately Symun bludgeoned the earth, until the beginnings of a substantial course were revealed. London bricks: the very stuff of Dave, created by Him, the material that old London had been built from and out of which New London was rising once more – or so Mister Greaves assured them. When the Hamstermen dug up courses of these sacred artefacts from the undergrowth, most were too cracked and weathered to be of use. However, if they broke off the outer layer there were almost always one or two inside that retained their vivid redness, their sharp edges and their incised legend: LONDON BRICK.

Here, alone, deep in the Ferbiddun Zön for the first time in his life, Symun Dévúsh allowed what had, up until now, been only stray intuitions and inchoate thoughts to coalesce. How could it be, he wondered, that his mummy's account of Ham and that of the dävine dads were both true? Where the other Hamstermen remained credulous, he sensed a profound jibing between the old natural religion of the island and the doctrine of the Book. What was the truth? The answer – if there were one – must lie here.

Then Symun heard a rustling in the bushes behind him and leaped to his feet, staring wildly about at the rhodies. Scuttling into his fevered mind came all the sharp-toothed fears that infested the zone, protecting its secrets. Symun's curiosity vanished, swallowed up by terror – he'd been crazy to stray this far in, he must get out. His throat constricted, his breath bulged in his lungs, he felt himself losing consciousness. Then, a blunt, pink muzzle parted the glossy leaves and he was staring straight into the baby-blue eyes of Champ.

– Thy-mun, sing-songed the moto, Thy-mun, wanna wawwow wiv me?

Symun let out a peal of delighted laughter and lunged forward to embrace the beast's great bristly head. It was like this, still hugging, that the two of them emerged from the thick undergrowth of the zone a few units later. Man and moto, together under the suspicious eyes of the other young Hamstermen, who were resting on their mattocks, the pile of newly mined bricks at their bare feet.

– U bin a wyle, Sy, said Fred Ridmun, his narrow grey eyes piercing under his ragged fringe.

– An nuffing much 2 show 4 í neevah, put in Ozzi Bulluk, who stood with his brawny red arms held loosely at his sides. As ever Ozzi looked ready for a fight. If any Hamster was too long alone it caused disquiet – and to seek solitude within the zone was more subversive than eccentric.

~

At first tariff of the next day the Council of Ham assembled. It was a breezy autumnal day, the clouds scudding across the screen, the foglamp casting an ever-mutating pattern on the tawny land. Wrapped in their cloakyfings, the four granddads propped themselves upon the highest piles of bricks. These greybeards were all bent and pained, racked by all the cracked bones and wrenched muscles they'd acquired in a lifetime of risky endeavour. The four older dads took their positions sitting on lower piles, while the seven of their lads who were of an age to join in deliberations lay at their feet, sprawled on the turf by a smouldering fire. It was only three months since the Hack's party had left the island and there were still a few fags and plenty of gum to go round, so the granddads puffed and squinted out from the drifting smoke with benign, abstracted expressions.

– Yeah, wen we wuz vair vay layd anifyng we wannid on uz, said Ozmun Bulluk, who was standing in for Dave Brudi and so led the discussion. Eye tel U wot, vo, vey wuz ryte moodë if we gayv vair opares ve wunceovah. Ozmun settled back on his pile, stroking his thick, reddish-brown beard with an equally hairy hand. He was a heavy-set dad, quick to anger like all the Bulluks. When he was shouting – which was often – spittle flecked his beard. Yet he cooled as fast as he heated – and for a granddad was unusually tolerant.

– Meenin? his son, Ozzi, queried.

– Meenin booze, fagz, anifyng á awl. Eye diddun fancee vair byrds much ennëway, dodji if U ask me, awl spillinahtuv vair cloff dressis.

– W-w-wots cloff? stuttered Sid Brudi, one wiry finger twining his ginger hair, his freckled face full of stupid awe.

– Yeah, wel, nah yer Lundun cloff iz prittë bluddë smart, Eyel grant yer, said Ozmun, settling into his yarn. Seams í cums from viss bush, rì, iss a froot aw sumffing, sorta wyte bawl uv fluff, wych cums in bì ferry from dahn souf. Ennë wä, vey gé a bit uv vis geer an sorta teese í aht, lyke cardin vool, rì?

– O Dave! Symun suddenly exclaimed. U gonna go on lyke vis awl fukkin day! He spat his gum out and stood up. Ow mennë tymes av Eye erred all vis bollox abaht Chil – iss gotta B a fouzand aw maw. Eyev erred abaht vair cloff, Eyev erred abaht vair traynors an vair barnets, an vair beefansemis an vair fukkin opares. Wot Eye wanna no iz, wy didunchew ask em abaht fishin aw farmin, or sumffing – anifyng vat myte B an urna eer on Am!

The other dads coughed and stared pointedly at the ground. They waited for Ozmun to administer a drubbing – which he duly did, leaning down from his pile and striking Symun hard with his cudgel. Symun shook more with the effort of repressing his fury than with the pain. He groped for his discarded gum, stuck it back in his cheek, then sat cross-legged, staring out through the blisterweed at the lagoon, with its glaucous tinge of subsurface algae.

– Sorrë, Dad, he said to Ozmun, Eye juss sorta lost í.

– Vass orlrì, Ozmun replied, í appuns.

Then he resumed his account of the voyage the Hamstermen had made to Wyc, to the Bouncy Castle of the Lawyer of Chil – a journey that had taken place over thirty years before, when Ozmun was himself a young dad of twenty-three. This was the last time the Hamstermen had visited Chil as a group. Isolated individuals had been taken away by the Hack, either because of wrongdoing, or because they were opares fancied by one of his party. However, these emigrants never sent back any news of the outside world; for that the Hamsters had to depend on the Chilmen, and they were usually too ill and too overawed by the strangeness of the island to be effective informers.

Over the years that he had been Hack, Mister Greaves himself had been reluctant to remedy the islanders' deficiency. His own view was a conflicted one. To begin with he considered that the business of the island, ensuring its continuing productivity of moto oil and seafowl feathers, would be impaired if the Hamsters understood the commercial value of their products. However, latterly, as the value of these products declined in the rest of Ing, and Mister Greaves found himself having to subsidize his own tenants some years, he inclined to the view that the Hamsters' ignorance was a large part of what made them the happy, healthful, seemingly naturally dävine folk they were.

Furthermore, the Hamsters' hunger for information was difficult to assuage, so utterly ignorant were they of the world beyond their shores. The last King of Ing of whom Ozmun and his contemporaries had heard was David I, who was on the throne at London in the time of their own granddads. Try as he might, Mister Greaves could not convince them that this monarch was long dead, for the meter was not well calibrated within them. As for the last Driver, while he had spent seventeen years among the Hamsters, his vocation had been to awaken them to the world to come, not enlighten them as to their place in this one.

So this decades-old visit to Chil, which had lasted a scant few blobs, remained the most comprehensive picture the Hamstermen had of the lands beyond. In the intervening years, at Council after Council, its tapestry had been picked over and over again, until in some parts it was worn threadbare, while in others it had been fancifully embroidered. Although not much, for the Hamstermen had encountered a peculiar fact about themselves when they tied their pedalo up to the landing stage at Wyc, and, doffing their caps, shuffled into the awesome presence of their Lawd. This was, that while when they left their own island they had spoken in their usual, competitive babble, by the time they came to address the Lawyer of Chil they found that they spoke in complete unison: twelve dads with a single, polyphonic voice. This curious unanimity – born, perhaps, of the intense harmoniousness of their secluded lives – extended to their vivid impressions of this outer world, so that they also recalled it as one, in a sole, unanimous remembering.

Every glancing detail and minute observation culled from the Hamstermen's sojourn on Chil was already seared into Symun – and he found it torture to listen yet again, as Ozmun called over this lore in his sing-song voice: the fine stitching of cotton shirts and the scissoring of hair, the curious motion of wheeled vehicles, and the equally peculiar burdening of jeejees and burgakine. Even decades later the amazement that had prevented the Hamstermen from getting to the nub of it all was still evident. For theirs was a word picture of only the surface of these remarkable things: the chaps with their shooters and railings on the Bouncy Castle ramparts, the ocean-going ferries in the harbour, the beefansemis that clustered about it. Symun cherished a desire to read, so he considered it foolish of the granddads not to have attempted to set down their account, so that it might be read in the same manner as the Book. He sighed and, gathering his legs under him, got up. Eyem ahtuví, U ló, he said to no one in particular.

Symun strolled away from the Council ground, slid between the shitter and the Edduns gaff, then sauntered up the stream through the heart of the manor. Down by the Council wall the dads could hear the mummies singing: We R ve Amster gurls, we ware R air in curls . . . When Symun appeared they fell silent. It was daddytime, with two days to go until Changeover. The opares were minding the babies and toddlers in the dads' gaffs; the older kids were out with the motos. The bare earth surrounding the walls of the gaffs was beaten and churned by the hurrying feet of the mummies as they worked. Symun stood and, since there were no dads to observe him doing so, watched them intently.

Shell Brudi and Bella Funch sat on the ground grinding flour in the quern set between them. Their legs were outstretched and each bent forward in turn to grasp the wooden rod and pull the heavy top stone for half of its rotation. The air was white with wheatie dust, and sweat stood out on their brows. Shell's sister, Liz, was nursing her newborn baby as she sat in the lea of the Brudi gaff. The infant, a girl, was only a day old and had been anointed with moto oil by Effi that tariff. If she survived the next two blobs without dying of lockjaw, she would then receive both a name and the wheel of Dave.

Effi herself stood at a trestle table braiding the tops of some crybulbs together, so that they could be hung up in the rafters for the kipper. On the table were piles of herbs: jack-by-hedge, comforty, blacktartdog and piss-a-bed. Two other mummies were carding wool, two more were spinning thread. Another posse were changing the thatch on the Bulluk gaff. Three mummies carried bundles of dried pricklebush on their backs and clambered up and down the curved walls, depositing them on the eaves, while one remained aloft so she could lash them down. Nearer to Symun, at another trestle table set up between the Ridmun and Dévúsh gaffs, stood Caff Ridmun, who was dyeing cloth in a tub. Caff, with her withered leg, who leaned heavily so as to favour the sound one. Caff, whom he loved – much as he had once loved his mummy, and still loved Champ, his moto. Caff, who as an opare had been courted, then wed, by Fred Ridmun. Yet, now Caff was knocked up, Fred had no more eyes for her than any daddy did for a mummy. He had paid her childsupport, so he would lie with her again in the mummies' gaff once the baby was weaned – but he would seldom, if ever, speak to her. When she was on the blob Caff would wear a red rag on her cloakyfing – and at that time her old man would not come near her at all.

Symun burned with his desire for Caff – or was it that strange mummyself left inside of him after his final Changeover that wanted not only to lie with her but also to be with her, look at her and talk with her? He could not say; he knew only a desperate motorage as he stared at her slim shoulders and the thick brown plait that trailed from her headdress. If she felt his gaze on her, Caff made no response. She went on pummelling the cloth, gently shoving her full, round tank against the tabletop. Eventually Symun turned and walked away along the shore in the direction of the Shelter.

Fred Ridmun had a few words of the Book; Bill Edduns and Sid Brudi also. Symun Dévúsh had some as well. The granddads didn't set any great store on reading. Fukka Funch, who had no words at all, held more of the Knowledge than any of the other young men, and it was often he who led the calling over in the Shelter. There may not have been a Driver on Ham for five years, although Mister

Greaves had promised them another, yet it was universally – if tacitly – understood that for any Hamsterman to have too many words would be a usurpation of that role. In the meantime, the Guvnor needed only enough words to mark out the sections of the Book: where a run began and where it ended, the order of the points, the headings for the Doctrines and Covenants, the instructions set out in the Letter to Carl. This was sufficient, for the dads' collective memory furnished the rest.

When old Dave Brudi knew that he was dying he called Fred Ridmun to him in the Brudi gaff and handed over his Guvnor's cap and the Council cudgel. The screen was tinting earlier and earlier in the second tariff, while the final darkness was fast approaching, for the old Guvnor as well. Passing by the door on cold mornings, when the ground was irony hard and his breath misty, Symun saw his mate bent low over the old granddad's sofabed and heard Dave grunting:

– Iss nó nó, iss no-*t*, no-*t*. Ve Búk iz awl in Arpee, C. Vese wurds wiv *ough* in em – vair trikki. Sumtyms vair *off* sahnds lyke coff, uvvatyms vair *ow* sahnds lyke plow. Nah less ear yer kee wurds, mì sun.

It was a testament to the departing Guvnor's bearing and fortitude that he had enough strength at the end to instruct Fred in these phonics, for, by the time the kipper season came, Dave was dead and buried in the little graveyard behind the Shelter, where the wheels on top of the headstones spun crazily in the mournful winds.

Symun made a point of always being the last to leave the Shelter after the dads had called over the runs and points. He helped Fred to tidy up the tincans, swab the table and straighten its cover, then put the Hamstermen's sole copy of the Book away in the micro. Fred was usually preoccupied – the office of Guvnor brought heavy responsibilities and only modest rewards. He was entitled to an extra tank of moto oil from every slain beast, an extra rip of land in the home field, and an extra share of both feathers and seafowl whenever the pedalo went out to the Sentrul Stac or Nimar. In turn he had to be the first to make the leap on to the rocks when the dads were birding, and he had to be first up the stack – a dizzying, dangerous ascent. He also had to settle all disputes on the island, thus making himself the focus of much resentment. When the Hack came, it was Fred who would have to negotiate with him, bartering the Hamsters' produce for the rent, and this too was a thankless task.

Fred thought it a bit odd the way Symun would open the Book whenever they were alone together and, pointing to this or that word, ask him to read it out; yet not very, for Symun had never been like the other Hamstermen. Where they adapted themselves to the rhythms of their island, its seasons and its tides, he jibed against them. Where they found certainty in the Book and its Knowledge, he was always questioning, his dancing eyes piercing to the core of things.

As autumn progressed, the island's multitudinous greens changed to a cascade of copper finery, which then faded to tawny browns, dull silvers and mossy blacks. The equinoctial gale rose one night and come lampon the trees were bare, their branches making thin cracks in the clear, kipper screen. The mums retreated to the mummies' gaffs, where they wove rough bubbery with the woolly the Hack had brought that summer. The dads also retreated to their own gaffs, where they turned this coarse stuff into cloakyfings, jeans, T-shirts and jackets; for just as weaving was mummies' graft, so was tailoring daddies'. The motos were brought into the byres that took up half of each gaff, and the kids hunkered down with them for warmth. So the Hamsters drew in upon themselves in their little manor. All the Hamsters save one, for Sy Dévúsh began to spend more and more time in that peculiar state, so unfamiliar to his fellows, of being alone.

All that kipper Symun haunted the foreshore. The blisterweed lay on the ground, hollow, papery reeds that crunched harmlessly beneath his feet. The tide was never that high or low on Ham – even at dipped and full beam it only rose a matter of a few steps. This moderation was seemingly in harmony with the temperate clime of the isle. When the tide was out at the curryings on the north coast of Ham, Symun could gain the shallows, then wade unobserved, either to the east, under the Gayt, or to the west beneath the bluffs of the Ferbiddun Zön. Here, on the most isolated promontory of Ham, facing due south, stood the Exile's pathetic semi. Often Symun would see Luvvie Joolee wandering up and down one of the groynes, her gaunt face set, her eyes fixed on distant and unattainable prospects.

In buddout and summer Symun would have been with other Hamstermen, out netting prettybeaks, or else gathering the mussels that clung to the weedy flanks of the groynes. The mummies came on to the foreshore as well, if there were particular herbs they needed, or a dead seadog had been washed up. And all the Hamsters went there from time to time to gather fresh Daveworks, although this task was mostly left to the children, who, it was believed, benefited from it. Every Hamster had his or her Daveworks, strung on to lengths of thread. Now that the Driver was long gone, the dads would tell theirs as they sat in the Shelter and called over the runs and the points. The mums wore theirs as necklaces. Daveworks were also nailed to the lintels of the Hamsters' gaffs and garlanded their motos. Field strips were marked out by poles from which Daveworks dangled, serving both to scare off the birds and to sanctify the crops. Certain groves in the woods, because they were the site of an ancient calamity, had become shrines, adorned with posies, scrawled messages and Daveworks. Here the Hamsters came to speak to Dave through the intercom.

Real Daveworks were most prized, because they bore phonics and were therefore fragments of the Book. Toyist Daveworks, if they were particularly fine and realistic, were also kept by some, in the belief that sooner or later Dave himself would come to redeem them for that which they depicted. Daveworks came in many shapes: there were straight ones and bent ones, T-shaped and H-shaped, circular and square, spherical and triangular. These were all designated accordingly: strayts, bentuns, tees, aytchez, sirkúls, skwares, bawls and trys. Most were too convoluted to be given a name; even the term 'plastic' – for a great many Daveworks bore these phonics, or at least some – could not serve to differentiate them, for as it was written in the Book, plastic was only the vital clay from which the world had been moulded.

What the Hamsters did know was that the supply of Daveworks was inexhaustible, continual proof of the immanence of Dave. They were more common on the southern coast, where whole reefs lay offshore. After a storm fresh Daveworks would be freed and come floating in to lodge in the sand and shingle. The Hamsters could simply have waded out to the reef and gathered as many as they wanted, if the crabs in their thousands hadn't deterred them. Not because of their claws – which could deliver at most a nip – but because their presence suggested that the reef was toyist. Dävwurks cum in Daves oan tym, said Effi Dévúsh, nó Rs.

Symun's expeditions in search of Daveworks were quite different. He sought only real Daveworks, and he looked for them with great single-mindedness. He was searching for those that bore discernible words, and when he found one that duplicated those already in his collection, he discarded it. For there were many bearing the phonics M-A-D-E, H-O-N-G or .-C-O-M; and quite a few that had E-N-G-L-A-N-D and C-H-I-N-A. 'England' he knew to be Dave's term for Ingerland, but of .COM there was no mention in the Book – at least not in the runs he knew. Symun kept his Daveworks in the hollow trunk of a dead groovebark on the fringes of the Ferbiddun Zön.

With the alphabet he had gleaned from Fred, Symun was able to decipher his Daveworks. By matching the words he had himself found to those words he could see on those rare occasions he could handle the Book, he came to be able to read. Symun was intelligent, formidably so, and while the first few phrases had cost him whole tariffs of frustration, once he had cracked the code entire rants of the Book leaped off the page at him.

Naturally Symun was familiar with the Book; all Hamstermen were. Its runs and points were called over by them in unison, in the Shelter. Its doctrines and covenants were constantly on their lips as they disciplined their mummies, opares and boilers. Its Ware2, guvs were what they welcomed one another with, and its farewells to the Lost Boy were their valedictions. Yet much of what they recited was gibberish to them – deprived, as they were, of the good offices of a Driver. Now that Symun could read he could provide his own interpretation: he could see how the Book explained Ham, its shape, its isolation, its peculiar character. This was the true revelation: the island, which had for all his life been an immutable given, now became fluidly legible. Then he knew what he must do. He understood what his mummy had implied but dared not openly state: he should use the Book to penetrate the mysteries of the Ferbiddun Zön.

~

The Hamsters were sowing the kipper wheatie. First the mummies went on their hands and knees rooting out the weeds; the daddies came after them, casting the seed along the rips. It was mummy-time, so babies in swaddling were propped up in the furrows; they bawled but no one paid them any mind. The Hamsters worked as one, the dads chatted a little among themselves while the mummies were silent. A sadness lay over the whole community. Caff Ridmun's baby had been born a month before, in due course it was anointed by Effi, and then, eight days later, after the most excruciating suffering, the mite had died. Unnamed and unblessed by Dave, its little corpse had been buried without a wheelstone in the waste ground beyond the graveyard.

It was a fresh, breezy day. Mountainous clouds passed over Ham, dark grey at their flat bases, brilliant white at their lumpy peaks. To the south the Sentrul Stac rose from the choppy sea, its crenellated sides streaked white and brown with gull shit; while beyond it the far islands of Surrë were a bright green streak along the horizon. Beams of foglight fell on the land and on the white-capped waves, yet there was a damp tang to the air – there would be screenwash before nightfall. Frogwash, the Hamsters called it, because they believed that at this time of the year the showers were sticky with spawn. The crinkleleafs and smoothbarks above the home field quickened with buds, and their limbs tossed in the breeze. The land birds had begun to return at the new headlight, and as they worked the Hamstermen hailed them, Orlrì, Bob! Orlrì, Jen! Orlrì, Tom! while the kids ran at them with flails, scaring them away from the newly sown seed.

Gari Funch had finished his changebag of seed and gone up into the trees to relieve himself when he saw Symun Dévúsh coming along the Layn from the moto wallows. Later on, Gari said there was an aura about Symun that struck him as soon as he saw the other young dad. His mates teased him about it, saying, Ure lyke awl ve Funchis, Fukka, so shortarsed anifyngs up in ve air 2 U! Yet he stuck to his recollection of Symun floating above the ground, with a wisp of mist wrapped around him like a cloakyfing, while his jeans and T-shirt were rent.

– Ware2, guv? Gari had hailed him, and then, as Symun wafted closer, he said, Orlrì, mayt?

Symun only looked straight through him, his blue eyes glassy. Gari stepped forward and made to take his shoulder, but Symun twisted away and blurted:

– Bakkoff! Eyem nó Symun no maw, Eyem ve Geezer nah, Eyev ung aht wiv Dave, C, an ees toll me ve troof.

– W-wotcher meen? Gari spluttered.

– Lyke Eye say, Eye bin in ve Zön, Eye bin 2 ve playce vair ee berried ve Búk, an ee cum 2 me, an ee giv me anuvvah Búk – yeah, a nú 1 – an we cauled í ovah togevvah, yeah, an ee toll me 2 cum an tell U ló abaht í, rì.

– Bluddyel.

– Bluddyel iz abaht ve syze uv í, mayt, coz iss awl chaynj fer nah. Dave sez weev gó ve rong end uv ve stikk – ee doan wannus livin lyke vis, nó torkin wiv ar mummies, treetin em lyke shit an vat. Iss ve saym wiv ve Nú Lundun stuff, ee sez iss awl bollox, ee doan give a toss abaht bildin Nú Lundun, aw ve Pee-See-bleedin-Oh. Ee sez we shood liv az bess we can an nó wurri, if we wanner do fings diffrent iss fyn bì im . . .

There was much more of this, all spoken in a rush by Symun, his voice strangely breathy and high-pitched. If this was blasphemous to Gari, it was also beguiling. All his life Dave had been present to him yet invisible, untouchable and unreachable; now here was Sy – who Gari knew as well as he knew himself – claiming to have spoken with Dave and saying that he'd received a second Book, which did away with all of the tiresome strictures inhibiting the Hamsters' natural inclinations. Gari wasn't the most credulous of the Hamsters, but, even if he'd been disposed to challenge Symun, he was forestalled by the Geezer, who began to spout whole chunks of the new Book. They were beautiful to Gari's ears: sonorous, ringing – incontrovertibly the words of Dave. Gari felt his bowlegs buckling beneath him, and he collapsed to the ground. Worming forwards in the muddy lane, he reached out and touched Symun's foot – now reassuringly earthbound – with a trembling hand. Orlrì, ven, Geezer, he said faintly.

Geezers had been a part of the religious life of Ham for as far back as the chain of linked individual memories reached. These were charismatic dads – and occasionally mums – touched by the Word of Dave, who sprang on to the stage afforded by the island

and strutted there for a few months or even years. Certain brick-built hovels on the margins of the Gayt were known as the 'Geezers' gaffs', and among the Hamsters the feeling was that the Geezers had been present in the time of the giants – or even before. Naturally, whenever a Driver had been among them, all talk of the Geezers was suppressed, yet the receptivity of the Hamsters to such things remained high, so that when Symun came down through the home field spouting revelation the daddies and mummies cast away their tools and followed him to the Shelter. The screen itself responded to Symun's new calling; Dave's demister powered up and swept the clouds up into higher and higher masses, which teetered, then dispersed with supernatural rapidity, leaving the foglamp blazing down on the green isle.

– Yeah, rì, Symun began, U ló av sussed Eyev bin angin aht in ve Zön. Bú wotchoo doan no iss Eyev bin ailed bì Dave, C, an Eyem iz fare. Ee gayv me iz sekkun Búk. An ee sat wiv me wyl Eye red ve öl fing – coz Eye can dú fonix nah – an ee mayd me tayk í awl on bord so az Eye can caul í ovah, rì?

– So caul í ovah, ven, clevah clogs! shouted out Symun's uncle, Fil Edduns, from the back of the little throng. His sister, Effi, may have been the repository of the old folkways, but Fil was the most rigidly dävist of the daddies. Despite the long years that Ham had been beyond the PCO's writ, he still looked to London in all things spiritual.

If Fil had been hoping to expose Symun and to put paid to this new Geezer, he was utterly vanquished. The granddad stood, kneading the mulberry birthmark that stained the left side of his face, while the Knowledge flowed out of his nephew: a flood of eloquence that slaked his audience's thirst for poetry. While Symun spoke, skipping from verse to verse of the new book – so az Eye can stikk í strayt 2 yer – a remarkable thing happened.

The older lads who'd been away on the other side of the island tending the motos came fanning down from the woodland, their charges plodding at their heels, and joined the congregation. It was said years later, when the boilers met together in secret, away from the ears of the new Driver, and recalled this time of delirious heterodoxy, that even the birds fluttered from the trees to hear Sy Dévúsh preach. Perching here and there on the shoulders of the Hamsters, or the broad backs of the recumbent motos, they twittered their assent to his words. The only Hamsters who were absent were the infants, still propped in their furrows at the top of the home field; their reedy cries could be heard piercing Symun's calling over with their own message of eternal need.

There was no mystery as to why the Hamsters heeded the Geezer: the message he brought them from Dave was highly congenial. Henceforth they should regard Ham and all its fruits as theirs and theirs alone.

– Dave sez stikk í 2 ve Ack, stikk í 2 ve Loyah uv Chil inall – loyahs, vare awl skum. Vay swyp arf uv awl we mayk, an weave nuffing 2 shew 4 í. Stikk í 2 Nú Lundun ëvun. Iss nó abaht bildin nuffing but Am – Am iz 4 U an U iz 4 Am. An ee sez ve mummies can dú wottevah vay lyke. If Ewe wanna B wiv a dad, fayre enuff, iss no bovvah, juss dú í. Ee tayks bakk all vat guff abaht mummitym an dadditym, ve Braykup an ve Chaynjova. Ve kids shúd B wiv vair mums an vair dads awluv ve tym. Í aint dahn 2 ve granddads 2 decyd awl vat stuff, iss dahn 2 awluv uz in R arts.

Many of the Hamstermen spoke with Dave on the intercom – such was the effect of their calling over. It was an angry voice, a harsh voice – a voice that drowned out their memories of the mummytime. Now, in turn, Symun's words shouted that voice down. Furthermore, if the granddads were inclined to dispute with the Geezer, they were silenced by their own uneasy acknowledgement that he was only restating the true status quo of the community, long disrupted by Dävinanity and now triumphantly reasserted.

The original Book was spurned by the Geezer in its entirety:

– Dave sed ee roat í wen ee woz off iz rokkah, vass wy iss fulluv awl vat mad shit – runs an poynts an stuff. U doan aff 2 dú awl vat 2 luv Dave – awl we gotta dú iz luv eech uvvah. Ee sez weer awl Carl – weer awl iz lads, an if we luv eech uvvah iss lyke luvvin im.

Concerning the whereabouts of the miraculous, second Book, the Geezer was equally emphatic:

– Dave túk í bakk, he told those who asked. Ee borrered me í, an ven ee túk í bakkoffuv me. Iss nó 4 uz ló 2 reed, we shúd B reedin uvvah stuff, maykin R oan búks ëvun.

Those Hamsters disposed to follow the new teaching took this to heart and began, under Symun's tutelage, to learn their phonics. However, they didn't believe what he said about the second Book, for the Geezer never went anywhere without his changingbag.

~

The two young Hamsters lay a pace apart from one another. Beyond their bare and horny feet the curryings spread away into lapping water. Here and there the green tendrils of samphire twitched in the breeze, and small mounds of pebbles showed where the mummies had piled up the shingle to blanch the kale. A small flock of oyster-catchers picked at the seaweed frilling the tide line, their black and white plumage sharp strokes on the bobbled ground. From where the couple lay, on the east side of the spit, there was nothing to seaward save for the islet of Hìtop in the far distance, which, having no colony of seafowl, the Hamstermen never visited. Symun Dévúsh and Caff Ridmun had never known the confinement of landscape; only in the dark core of their gaffs or the deepest thickets of the woodland were they ever parted from the sea's effortless superfluity.

The legends spoke of giants in former times, yet each generation of these isolates were giant to one another, looming large and pale against the island's arboreal backdrop. When carnal love struck a

Hamster, he or she tossed in its fiery embrace. So Symun groaned in his motorage, Eye wan yaw sex, and reached towards Caff again and again, while she slapped him away again and again. Givví a ress, willya! she cried, Freds yer best bluddë mayt. Symun had already made his seductive speeches and spoken of how, under the new dispensation, all were free to do as they wished: Í doan má-er vat ewe an Fred woz wed coz í wurnt 4 reel. He'd even insinuated that if it had been his and her baby who'd been anointed by Effi, the child would have lived.

Caff was in turmoil. It was true, she had no great feeling for Fred – she barely even knew him, and, while some of the daddies had got to know their wives since the Geezer came among them, Fred was not one of their number. Caff couldn't deny that she found Symun attractive, and the older mummies and boilers told her there would be great honour in lying with the Geezer, yet still she slapped him away. He wouldn't give up – he pursued her, over the fields, through the underbrush, along the foreshore guarded by its umbelliferous sentinels, until at last, here, in the blue of noon, he reached for her and she didn't slap him away. His hand pulled up the hem of her cloakyfing, then lay brown on her white thigh; it lingered, then advanced, his fingers gliding over pinky-brown moles, their tips caressing the golden down. Soon they were married – Caff leaned back against the shingle bank, her thighs imprisoned in his.

~

Effi Dévúsh took all the new opportunities the Geezer's reign provided to discourse with the dads. She seemed intent on vitally reconnecting them with the ancient lore. Yet towards his person and his teaching she remained aloof and even openly critical. As buddout swelled into summer the Hamsters laboured with a curious fervour. The notion that they alone were entitled to all the fruits of Ham possessed them – and some of the younger dads even spoke wildly of sinking the Hack's pedalo with bricks when he arrived for his midsummer visit. At the same time the promiscuity of the daddies and mummies became desperate and frenzied. At night the little manor was busy with flitting figures; then, when the foglamp was switched on, they stumbled back to their own gaffs. Effi stalked among them uttering prophecies of doom.

One morning, before the foglamp was on, Effi managed to catch her son as he returned from performing his necessary offices in the Shelter. Effi grabbed his arm in a nasty grip.

– Givovah, Mum! He shrugged her off, saying, Wass yaw problum?

– U bluddë R! She was breathing heavily, the taut tendons in her neck exposed by a flap of her cloakyfing. U fink Eye dunno wot vis iz awl abaht?

– Wotcher meen? The Geezer was highly aggrieved. Eye onlë dun wotchew toll me 2.

– Eye toll U! Eye toll U! Eye aint eevun spoakin 2 U 4 bluddë yeers! Nah Uve adda crakkat Caff Ridmun U gonna avta tayk ve consikwencis. U fink yul gé away wiv í coz yaw so fukkin smart, but U wont, ve Acks gonna B ear juss lyke ee iz evri summer, an awl vem uz kepp shtum R gonna fukk U ovah.

Rather than remonstrate with him further – because she knew he desired even this commerce with her – Effi flapped away to the mummies' gaffs. Symun took himself off to the Ferbiddun Zön to brood. This wild, overgrown place held no terror for him now that his revelation was complete. Symun could read the Book, so he could read the zone; all the island of Ham was legible to him. He understood its origin – and he felt certain he knew its future as well.

~

Ever since the day when the Geezer had preached outside the Shelter, Fred Ridmun had been preparing for this eventuality. He had made no public objection to his friend's teaching, nor did he foment discontent, yet neither was he among Symun's disciples. For blobs Fred had been engaged on a simple yet momentous job of carpentry: first chopping, then shaping, and finally whittling a seasoned smoothbark bough, so as to contrive the sturdy lines of a miniature pedalo. His task was undertaken in the tangled core of the Perg, far from the prying eyes of the other Hamsters and foraging motos.

At first tariff on the day after his best friend had first lain with his wife, Fred took the clay bottle he had earmarked from the brick dresser in the Funch gaff. He also took a small tank of moto oil and some twine. From a hidden nook in the Shelter itself, he retrieved a missive he had laboriously composed. He slipped across the home field through the spectral dawn, over the brow of the hill between the moto wallows, then down into the Wess Wúd. At the Perg, he retrieved his odd craft and hoisted it over his shoulder. He walked on through the dips and hollows of Sandi Wúd, hardly conscious of his progress, lifting his legs over the trunks of fallen trees as if they belonged to another.

On the very spit of land where he'd been betrayed, Fred Ridmun mated earthenware and wood. The bottle sat snugly in the hollow he'd carved out of the deck. He rolled up the ragged sheet of A4 – a blank endpage torn from the Book itself – then inserted it in the neck. He stoppered the bottle and wound the oiled twine around its neck, pulling each loop tight. Then he lashed the bottle to the pedalo with strips of moto hide. He erected a little mast whittled from a sapling in a notch forward of the cargo, then rigged a diminutive sail of precious London cloth.

Pulling the keel of the pedalo over the shingle, the scraping sound merging with the rattle of the waves, Fred was aware that he was doing something that had been done before in times of distress. When, in the era of his great-great-grandparents, the pox had carried off half the island's population, just such a vessel had been dispatched to Chil. There was every chance that the prevailing currents would fail him, or that the little craft would become waterlogged and sink. However, if it was spotted by a Chilman, recovered and the bottle opened, and if the message was understood, then taken on to its intended recipient, the crude phonics Fred had scrawled could brook no misinterpretation: FLIAR ON AM. DAD SEZ EE IZ DAVE. CUM NAH PLEEZ KWIK MISTAH GREEVS. Fred Ridmun pushed the pedalo off and sat back on his haunches. A thin smile cut through his sharp features as the wind caught the patch of sail and the craft began to slap up and over the waves, heading due northeast. It was a providential course – for him.

Two nights later the equinoctial headlight rose over the big lagoon, and it was an earthy blood-red in colour. In the far distance sheet lightning slashed across the Surrë hills. The restive Hamsters gathered outside their gaffs. They soon became terrified, because, as if these portents weren't bad enough, when it was barely above the horizon the headlight began to be blotted out by a black crescent that moved slowly but inexorably across its flyspeckled surface. Effi Dévúsh cried out in the crowd that huddled in the streambed, saying:

– Iss a syne orlrì, me luvs, issa bluddë syne! Iss ve édlyt uv Dave, thass fer sure. Ees pú í on, an nah ees turned í off. An U wanna no wy?

There was a groaned chorus of whys from the other Hamsters.

– Eyel tell U wy – ees turned í off so as ee can run that fukkin fliar dahn!

She swivelled to confront her son, who, unnoticed by the others, had come among them, and now stood in their midst, his face covered with thick, fearful sweat and dark with dreadful incomprehension.

# 4
# *The Family of Man*

June 1987

'Orlright, put 'em on full,' Dave Rudman called to Kemal the mechanic. The headlights flared in the gloom of the railway arch. 'Orlright, orlright' – Dave was blinded for several seconds, until earthy Victorian brickwork swam back from the blood-red aureoles and artificial mauve sundogs – 'now try dipped.' The lights flared again but with less intensity. 'Full again . . . and DIPPED.' Kemal turned the lights off and came out from the cab shaking his tousled head; Dave stepped towards him, his face dark with incomprehension. 'Beats me,' he said, 'if it's not the bulbs.'

'Could be the alternator,' said Kemal, patting down the pockets of his oily overalls for his cigarettes.

'Yeah, yeah,' Dave laughed, 'it's always the alternator, innit? I dunno why I'm bothering, it ain't like I'm doing nights.'

Dave was renting from Ali Baba on the half-flat for eighty quid a week, and the night driver he shared the cab with was *a fucking animal*. Dave had given him the nickname Mister Hyde. Strictly speaking Dave didn't have to return the cab to the garage in Bethnal Green until eight, although he usually had it back an hour earlier. Early, clean and filled up – even though only the last was his responsibility. This particular evening Dr Jekyll had prevailed on Kemal to examine the headlights, which he'd noticed weren't working when he went through the Blackwall Tunnel.

Mister Hyde showed no such consideration. After the night shift the cab was always filthy: the ashtrays full, the driver's compartment rattling with discarded soft-drink cans. One morning when he picked the cab up, Dave found a used condom glued to the back seat by spunk and hair. Hyde was also nicking diesel, a couple of quid every fill-up. It was pathetic criminality, because ever since *the Big-fucking-Bang* the year before, the City Boys had been hellbent on booting the Footsie right back up again. If you got a getter, they'd double up on the meter, maybe treble it. Dave had whole days of cream fares splurging across town. He harvested tourists as if they were wheat and he was driving a *fucking combine 'arvester*. While Mister Hyde didn't even keep up with his rent, which was *fucking stupid . . . You never owe a Turk. Never.*

Ali came out from a glassed-off office – a heavy man with iron-filing hair who walked on the balls of his feet. His top lip bulged as if he had a moustache growing inside of it. 'Your man,' he said, showing Dave peg teeth, ''e juss rang, 'e ain't gonna be in.'

'Oh, yeah.'

'Yeah, you wan' the cab?' Ali jabbed a tripod of fingers at the old Fairway. It was a gambler's gesture: twist, fold, hit me again.

'Um . . . well . . . yeah . . . why not? Ta.'

'My plezzure.' Ali stalked off again. Kemal tootled smoke and a high-pitched note. Dave realized the mechanic was giggling – but at whom?

~

At around seven thirty, after he'd dropped off the cab, Dave Rudman was in the habit of stopping by the Old Globe in Stepney for a drink with his mates. By day Dave kept a lid on it, but, after a few beers and a *row or five of barley*, he was ready for anything. The quiet pub funnelled into the noisy bedlam of a dance club. They went up west to the Wag or Camden Palace, or out to the sticks, where innocuous doors turned out to be fissures leading to subterranean reservoirs of sweat. At the end of a shift Dave got out of the cab *feeling like a fucking cripple*, so he liked the dancercise, but it was mostly home alone, or, even if accompanied by a damp, drunk girl, alone again by morning, a cooling depression in the pillow beside him.

~

The girlfriend Dave had when he was a teenager in Finchley went off to university. Some of the lads he'd been at school with went as well, and most of the others got management trainee positions and were issued with middle-class uniforms. Dropping out was passé – dropping in was cool. Into business, into the City, into property, into lifestyle. Everyone wanted mobility – on a graph. Dave Rudman should have been with them but he baulked. He didn't want to go away to work, or study, or even score cheap hash abroad. All Dave's peers wanted to get out of London – at least for a bit – while Dave wanted to go deeper in. Lun-dun – how could such leaden syllables be so magical? He craved London like an identity. He wanted to be a Londoner – not an assistant manager on twelve grand a year, married to Karen, who liked *Spandau-fucking-Ballet*.

There were only four years between the three Rudman kids, Samantha, David and Noel. They stuck together. On summer mornings they'd set off down the steep slope of Ossulton Way, carrying Tupperware containers of sandwiches in their dad's old army rucksack. Sam had five bob for Tizer and crisps. In the shoe-box house they left behind them was the senseless slaughter of a one-sided row, their father a sitting duck in the weedy pond of his hangover, their mother railing against him. In front of the children lay the valley of the Mutton Brook, and beyond it the hills of Hampstead and Highgate rose up, a mass of shrubbery, studded with the red-tiled roofs of detached villas.

It would take them hours to reach the Heath, dawdling along the avenues of the Hampstead Garden Suburb, sweet with the smell of warm tar, fresh-cut grass and clipped privet. Dave and Noel pelted each other with the orange buckshot of rowan berries and tore satisfying slabs of bark from the silver birches. Serious Samantha – her mother's daughter – sought out the gaps in the net curtains and scrutinized the interiors of rooms, noting three-piece suites, Sanderson's wallpaper, television cabinets – all the aspirational durables.

When they reached North End Woods Dave and Noel would run and whoop, while Sam acquired her first detached home, with a hollow oak for a kitchen and a fallen beech for a living room. Noel always wanted to play cowboys and Indians; Dave had a more unusual kind of make-believe. He saw his grandfather's cab nosing through the bracken. With its goggling headlights, bonnet muzzle and toothy bumper, it was like a cartoon beast. He waved it down, and together cab and boy cruised the hummocks and dells, picking up and dropping off imaginary passengers.

They were close, the Rudman kids, too close. They clung together on the cold margins of their parents' marriage, and when the opportunity came along both oldest and youngest fled. Sam into a career, then marriage to Howard, whom she had met, dancing to 'Chirpy-Chirpy Cheep-Cheep', at the Maccabi Youth Club in West Hampstead. She was nineteen and unashamedly, anachronistically, married him for his money.

Noel fled to Aberystwyth. The family had once had a couple of mournful B & B holidays there, and Dave supposed that his younger brother imagined staying for good would be a permanent holiday. It didn't turn out that way. Dave knew they'd all regret this falling apart, yet there was nothing he could do. The Rudmans weren't the sort to make an effort, to keep up. They weren't – in the idiom of the time – people people.

After Dave dropped out of college he did eighteen months as a driver-labourer for a builder's up in Stoke Newington. He loved the rattle-bang of the three-ton flat-bed truck as it whacked over the London potholes; he loved the peculiar groan of the dinky tipper as he deftly piloted it up a pair of planks, to offload stock bricks and clayey soil into a skip. He loved everything to do with driving – driving made him feel free. It was easy, it was simple, it was open to all. The minute you got in a vehicle and turned the ignition the world was revved up with possibilities. Which would he rather have, a driving licence or an HND? *No fucking contest . . .* So he put his application into the Public Carriage Office on Penton Street and began puttering about the cavernous city on his moped, committing its concrete gulches and York stone wadis to memory.

Annette Rudman had nothing but contempt for her father. On Sunday afternoons, when his black cab came puttering down Heath View, she behaved as if it were a loan shark arriving to collect her in lieu of the interest. *Fought you'd escape, didja? Fought you'd get away from the East End, my girl? Fought you'd become a teacher and move out to the bloody sticks? No chance, my love . . . no chance at all* . . . Even though Benny was nothing but friendly, his daughter would put him in his place with her Received Pronunciation and her cultivated vocabulary. She made him drink endless cups of tea – and when he asked for the toilet, directed him to the lavatory.

But little Dave loved Benny – loved his patter and his natty threads – pressed grey slacks, tweed caps with elasticated sides, zip-up suede jackets and mirror-shiny shoes. He loved the way his grandfather exuded his Knowledge, a comprehensive understanding not only of the London streets – but what went on in them as well. After thirty-odd years behind the wheel, Benny Cohen gave the distinct impression that he'd been plying for a hire for a couple of millennia. As he drove his grandson through the city, he regaled him with a steady stream of anecdotes and facts, a spiel that spilled from the corner of his mouth and blew over his shoulder braided with cigarette smoke.

As he drove down from Vallance Road to the Old Globe, Dave reflected on how his grandfather had stayed on. A remnant of the

Jewish ghetto in the East End, living out his days in a small flat on the inter-war LCC estate off the Bethnal Green Road. Now he was surrounded by a rising tide of Bengalis. 'Not that I mind them; they're mostly well behaved. Still, their food smells fucking awful.' Benny's food didn't smell of anything at all, the slow worm noodles and watery chicken soup he slurped down at Bloom's in Whitechapel, under an enlarged photographic mural of the old Brick Lane Market without a brown face in sight.

Benny was still alive – but only just. He stopped at home behind nets distempered with nicotine and chuffed on his oxygen mask, lifting it now and again to insinuate a Woodbine beneath his walrus moustache. Benny's left leg had been amputated below the knee, and there was talk of the right hopping along too. When Dave went to see him, his grandfather waggled the stump at him like a gesturing hand, turning it out to express bemusement, karate-chopping for finality. Prised from his cab – which, although it stank of cigarette fumes, was always beautifully clean – the old man took on the appearance of a smoked oyster on Tubby Isaacs's stall, then a soused whelk, until finally – most unkosher this – he dwindled to a pickled winkle.

In the Old Globe Mrs Hedges the landlady was berating two of Dave's mates, Fucker Finch and Norbert Davis. 'I'm not bein' funny,' said the withered Chow of a woman, 'but the trouble wiv you lot is that you all 'ad a crack at 'er an' none of yer is prepared to take the consequences, see.' Thick slap was plastered on her pouched cheeks, wind-chime earrings dragged deep slits in her earlobes. Dave sidled up to the bar. On the optic were bottles of Martell, Archers, and Jack Daniel's. On beer mats stood an outsized wine glass full of promotional lighters and a cubic ice bucket advertising Gordon's Gin. 'Usual, luv?' asked Mrs Hedges. Dave grunted affirmatively and she threw her weight on the pump so hard her bingo wings flapped. Fucker said, 'Orlright, then, geezer,' and he and Norbert rolled their eyes at him. Norbert – who was known as Big End, on account of the ridiculousness of his given name and by reason of racial stereotyping – said, 'My round, Tufty,' his deep voice shouting through the wall of his chest.

Mrs Hedges resumed, 'Believe you me, there's four blokes 'as come in the pub an' she's slept wiv all of 'em once. I told 'er old man "she wuz not 'erself", but 'e don' lissen, 'e went absolutely fucking ballistic, 'e cut 'er up an' that – which is a bit ironical seein' as she does it to 'erself anyways!' Mrs Hedges fell silent, then relayed Dave's pint to him, a brown torch with a creamy flame. 'Cheers,' Dave said, and the other two grunted affirmatively. Behind the bar lay a drift of Quavers packets, crisp notation rustling in silence. Big End's fluorescent jacket – he was a site chippie – lay on a nearby banquette like a crumpled drunk. 'I woz absolutely ragarsed last night,' Big End said, 'fucking mullered.'

'No kiddin',' Dave responded, bitter-mouthed.

'Wossup wiv you, Tufty?' Fucker put in. 'You're a bit down in the mouf.'

Tufty was Dave's cabbing nickname. It referred both to the unsmarmable sprig of hair at the back of his broad neck, and a cartoon squirrel that had fronted a 1960s road-safety campaign. Gary Finch – aka Fucker – was a cabbie as well; he and Dave had done the Knowledge at the same time, then they'd been butter boys together, wangling nights with cabs fronted by Gorgeous George at Nationwide Taxi Garages. 'Mister Hyde 'as pulled a stroke,' Dave explained. ''E's not in tonight, so Ali said I could 'ave the cab.'

'Result, no?' Fucker wiped a smear of lager from his full lips; with his curly mop, fat tummy and stubby legs, he was like a stationary bowling ball in the alley of the bar.

'Yeah, s'pose, still, I was looking forward to hoisting a few with you, an' then –'

'On to Browns, then a club, then a shebeen, then before I know it I'm rolling in at five in the fucking morning and the boiler's giving it this.' Fucker made an emu glove puppet of his hand and pecked at his own neck and head.

'Nick-nick.' Dave felt for him, but he thought also of Gary's wife, as rotund as her husband and with an extra ball stuffed up her jumper, due to fall out in a few weeks. Dave knew Debbie – and he knew Gary's mum and dad as well. They'd been a bit of a surrogate family for him. Dave wondered at the way things were panning out – the young couple had fallen out with both their families. Instead of cheeky cockney consanguinity, the mother-to-be was isolated in their flat in Edmonton, while Gary, well . . . *Fucker by name . . .*

'As soon as she fell pregnant,' Mrs Hedges coincidentally resumed, ''e done 'is nut an' cut 'er up again – she 'ad t'go fer a tonic from the doctor.' Big End tutted sympathetically. *What am I doing here?* Dave said to himself with Received Pronunciation, as Mrs Hedges's Hs fell at the floor by his feet and Ts stopped up his companions' throats. *This isn't me, it's an act* . . . because Dave hadn't dropped his Hs – he'd flung them away from himself, ninja stars that stuck quivering in the smoky bacon Victorian woodwork. *There's no going back now, no three-point turn out of here. All that Knowledge, the city crumpled up in my head* . . . He could envision it, the streets superimposed on the whorls of his cerebellum *and I'm holding on to it*. He downed the last of his pint and thudded the glass on to the bar. He snatched up his keys and swivelled to leave, his badge – which he wore on a leather thong around his neck – swinging into Fucker. 'Oi!' The tubby little man howled, clutched his mop of curls and fell against the bar. Dave, shocked, made to grab him before he fell, whereupon Finch reared up laughing, 'Adjoo there, mate! Adjoo there!' When he saw how shocked Dave was, he stopped and asked, 'You fucking off already?'

'May as well,' Dave said, addressing them all. 'I ain't gonna get a fare in 'ere am I, but if I start now I'll catch the theatre burst – might clear a wunner before midnight.'

'Well,' Big End put in, 'meet me down the club if you knock off.' As he bashed out through the door, Dave heard the fresh conversation resume behind him.

'She was pretty big by then?'

'Fucking big.'

'Is it John's?'

''Course it is . . .'

Outside in the Mile End Road, Dave unlocked the cab and stood for a moment looking west to where the buildings of the City stacked up. There were new blocks at Aldgate and down towards the Tower of London; a thicket of cranes sprouted over the old Broad Street Station, and above it all reared the black, glassy stack of the NatWest Tower. Another course of London was being laid on top of the last, millions of tons of steel, concrete, brick and stone, weighing down on the present, pressing it into the past.

While here, in the East End, magenta buddleia spears and coils of fluffy rosebay willowherb sprang from between the sheets of corrugated iron that fenced off the bombsite behind the pub. Benny had once told Dave that during the war sand had been gouged from the top of Hampstead Heath and poured into bags that were then piled in front of the hospitals and government ministries. When the ack-ack ceased and the barrage balloons were winched down, the pulverized terraces of the East End were swept up, loaded on to trucks, and dumped in the hollows and dips where the sand had been dug. Round and round it went, London's auto-cannibalism. It made Dave feel queasy to be standing suspended over such deep time, on the taut cable of a summer evening. He lowered himself into the cab and, starting the engine, felt better immediately, and better still when within seconds his Faredar peeped and he netted a commuter heading for Fenchurch Street. Go west, young man.

It was the tempo of the times – the years themselves were in a rush, the decades even, struggling to attain the next era. The matt-black chrysalis of the 1980s was splitting and, with stop-action rapidity, out came a vast moth, unfurling sticky, tinted-glass wings.

In the layer cake of Olympia – jammy carpet tiling, spongy exhibition space – Michelle Brodie struggled to keep up with her idea of who she ought to be. Almost all those who laboured to get Olympia ready for the opening of Business Computing '87 knew Michelle by sight – she was hard to miss, with her fiery plume of auburn hair and her trim figure in its neat, scarlet suit. Hurrying here, rushing there, her heels clicking and a comet tail of gaseous regard streaming behind her.

The fabricators weren't working hard enough on the stand. Michelle wasn't in charge of this – any more than she was in charge of the account overall – *if it's a success Manning takes the credit, and if it bombs it'll be my fault.* Manning, the Exhibitions Executive, *that fat wanker with his white socks and cheap loafers, his greased-back hair and C&A suit . . . thinks he's God's fucking gift*, had made his obligatory pass at Michelle within days of his appointment. *Since he's been brought in over me, he thinks he has the right to climb on top of me.* Although by the standards of the passes that had been made at Michelle – and there were many at this time – Clive Manning's was low key. His fish-belly hand lounged towards her coppery tights while he burbled of 'forward planning', then, when she flinched, it flopped away while he continued uttering banalities about 'feedback'.

*What if I'd let him? Pork-pie breath on my shoulder, greasy hair in my eye, little dick digging at me down below . . .* The grim vision goaded Michelle on past fabricators who were bolting steel frames and hammering together wooden partitions, speedily erecting a model city inside the cavernous exhibition hall; a new London, shiny, two-dimensional, every façade commercially artful. The workmen, scenting her perfume, turned to stare, wet tongues lolling on their yellow teeth, while women looked daggers at her, searching for chinks in her beautiful armour – the hint of a sag or a blemish.

At her clients' area Michelle talked to the foreman, a dependable Irishman, older, his wedding band emphatic on his veined hand. *I remind him of his daughter or niece – he can't respect me 'cause I'm not a virgin – but he doesn't dream of fucking me.* She showed him the revised drawing: the stand was to be in the shape of a giant desktop computer, with the staff answering queries through the screen. Prospects would be ushered in to look at its shiny innards. It was her idea.

~

Michelle's mate Sandra took the call at her desk in the Shell Centre, while forking grated carrot from a plastic container and peering myopically at the drizzly window. 'Not at lunch, San?' Michelle said.

'Issat you,' 'chelle? No, rain's come on, his nibs got me a salad. What's up?'

'I was going to call *him*, but I'm in a café with that Rachel from work and I swear she knows.' Michelle risked a glance over her shoulder: Rachel was sizing up a builder at the next table, whose flesh-coloured dust mask disfigured his neck like a goitre.

'Yeah,' Sandra laughed, 'she knows she's a scheming little cow, that's what she knows.'

'I dunno, San, I'm bloody nervy today, it's . . . it's like something's gonna happen, I dunno what – just something.' Michelle's eyes flicked outside to the Hammersmith Road, where a black cab shook with mechanical ague.

'Are you meant to be seeing him?'

'Yeah, later, I don't know where, though, he'll leave me a message at home – lissen, I gotta go.'

'What?'

But Michelle had hung up. She went back to her seat opposite Rachel. The builders at the next table rose, four big bodies moving in dusty puffs. From the kerfuffle a meaty arm tossed the *Sun* between the two young women. 'Paper for yer, luv,' he said, giving Michelle a gappy grin. She picked it up: it was open at the horoscopes and she read: 'PISCES. It has been a long, rough and lonely road emotionally. However, with the sun in Cancer and a new moon to boot, this will be a week of amazing highs and the realization that at last your darkest days are over.' *Snip-snip . . . He's gonna leave her . . . Snip-snip, he's gonna cut her out of his life . . . Snip-snip.*

Michelle unlocked the front door and took the stairs at a run. Fiddling with her flat key on the top landing, she felt her nostrils prickling with dust – then the Yale clicked. Without bothering to shut the door, she lunged for the answer-phone. It peeped, hissed, crackled: ''chelle, it's Mum here.' *As if I don't know your voice.* 'I was wonderin' if you were coming by Friday . . .' *so you can put me down with sly digs* '. . . 'cause I'm going down the market an' if you are I'll get a whole chicken instead of pieces.' *A thigh or two for her, a leg for Ronnie, gross.* 'Anyway, love, gissa call, there's a good girl, love, Mum.' *She thinks she's writing a bloody letter.* 'Peep!' 'Alright, 'chelle? A load of us are going down Gossips tonight.' *That's desperate.* 'We'll be in the wine bar before that . . .' *getting pissed enough to take on anything in trousers – and it's only Thursday* '. . . so see ya there, unless you're getting shagged by wossisface, ta-ra.' *I should keep my big mouth shut. Shut.* 'Peep!' 'Hilton on Park Lane . . .' *His voice!* '. . . eight o'clock in the lobby, don't be late.' 'Peep!'

Michelle kicked off the black heels, she shrugged off the red jacket, she sloughed off the tight red skirt, she tore off the white cotton blouse. In her bra, tights and knickers, she raced into the bathroom, her head a whirl of transportation schedules. *I don't want to rush, it'll be sweaty on the tube, I don't want to sweat. No sweat, he doesn't want sweat – he doesn't want real, he wants a fantasy girl . . . Weird thing is . . . I wannabe that for him.* Crouching in the bath, Michelle used the rubber Y of the shower fitment to sluice away Olympia and Manning. She pushed the heel of her hand down through her pubic hair, then gouged out her vagina with the bar of lavender soap . . . *Dirty girl. Dirty, dirty girl.* On the mat, she twisted in front of the full-length mirror, checking for stubble under arms and between thighs. *I wonder if Mrs Thatcher ever does this? Or Chris Evert? They must do.* Michelle flipped her mane forward and vigorously stroked it with the saddle brush. A hiss of spray to stop the frizz and Michelle flipped it back. Deodorant was sprayed under arms still damp from their douche. Perfume was dabbed at ear and neck and crotch. In the bedroom she pulled multicoloured handfuls of silk and cotton scraps from her drawer, and strewed them like blossom on the counterpane of her bed. *Why bother? He doesn't want this – I don't want this. He wants in – I want him in as fast as possible.*

Michelle Brodie had always been a fashion victor, triumphing over each season's army of styles, colours and cloths with her own inimitable Look. Aged sixteen, trolling through Crystal Palace on her way to her Saturday job, she'd been spotted by Ben Bendicks, a photographer so famous that even Michelle had heard of him. He came at her out of the shiny fourth dimension that was folded into *Vogue* and *Harpers*. They were deep in Sarf London, deep and high up – to the south lay the North Downs, a bright, green streak on the horizon. All this airy calm was annihilated by the Yank car flung against the kerb, the man in the iridescent silk shirt and wraparound shades shouting, 'You've got it girl! You've got the Look!' She was wearing a midi-length black skirt and a white blouse. *Some Look.* Still, Bendicks conjured up her exhibitionism with his own. A spread-legged year followed – not that he ever laid a hand on her – as Michelle posed in front of paper flats, morphing to the rat-a-tat-tat of his shutter. The freckles on her face and hands were airbrushed out, and she learned to think of nothing so as to achieve the allure of a Zen garden. Bendicks got her on hoardings as the Face of Fermata – *the* designer label of that year.

To begin with Michelle kept the modelling a secret, convinced her mother would freak out. When, inevitably, Cath did find out, she egged her on – the money was so good for them, after always having to scrimp towards bare adequacy. Michelle liked to think that it was she who'd drawn back. Much later she would say, 'It was crap, like going out with a big latex head jammed on my own.' She disavowed such caricatured regard. The truth was less heroic: Bendicks had used her up. She wasn't that photogenic anyway – she'd had her year, 1979, and her look was fossilized within it, crushed in a layer of fashionable sediment. So she retrieved her freckles and went to college. She dressed down and got her HND in Business Studies. She had boyfriends who were musicians; their greasy hair stained the tummy of her old teddy bear, brought from home to cosify a shared flat on the Wandsworth Road. The recognition factor faded until it was merely a subliminal thing that made every tenth person who passed her by in the street – and every third who met her face to face – feel certain they'd encountered her before. It was a villagey regard, quite tolerable. Michelle depended on the approbation of her good looks more than she could ever admit – that they weren't quite good enough gnawed at her.

Michelle put on a tan suede dress, calf-length, silk-lined, low on the back, high on the breast. She slung on a cream linen jacket and slipped into high-heeled sandals. She put a tiny diamond stud in each ear lobe and, after having turned back the cuffs, a chunky ethnic bracelet on each wrist . . . *the salesgirl said they were from Malawi, I say Malaysia.* On the radio a middle-aged smoothie was braking drivetime with his soft-shoe voice. The Flying Eye was summoned up, banking high over the North Circular: 'Lorry lost its load at the Welsh Harp' – an atmospheric crackle – 'tailbacks all the way back to Staples Corner . . .' Michelle snatched up her bag and rasped the door to. Glancing at her watch, she saw it was *Seven fifteen! I can still make it.*

'It's just a bloody toy of that Prince Albert,' Dave's fare expounded; 'it's not a real football team.' Dave had picked him up underneath the glass portico of the new Lloyd's Building and the getter hadn't stopped yapping since. 'I tellya that Hoddle's a fucking mercenary. He said he'd take a pay cut to go to a good European club – now he's taking a million quid to piss off to Monaco.' The fare was leaning right forward on the seat, shifting from one plump buttock to the other as the cab cornered, yet keeping his muzzle right in the conversational trough.

'Well, y'know how it is, guv, 'oddle is a born-again, so 'e's only followin' 'is inner voice.'

'Yeah, right!' the fare snorted. 'Just like Ian Rush. God said, "Pick up three mil' to go to Juventus" and Rushy replied, "Hallelujah!"' The fare waggled outstretched fingers like a nigger minstrel.

Dave was on a run, leapfrogging from fare to fare, using their pinstriped backs to propel himself across town. The bliss of driving when the only goal was money – and money was everywhere – was still with him a year into the job. Besides, he'd long since learned that just as he had to throw away his Hs, so he had to gather up the beautiful game. Dave didn't give a shit about football any more, but his mates demanded football talk, the fares demanded it, the world – itself just a bladder in space – demanded it. Dave thought the fare was *a racist cunt*, but his appearances before the PCO had taught him *not to rise to anything. Don't rise to it. The Examiner tells you to leave the minute you've got your bum on the seat – do what he says. If he tells you you're not fit to be examined 'coz you've got a cold, say, 'Yes, sir' and leave. Never argue. Always talk football.*

He'd enjoyed the appearances – and done well. The Knowledge was vast – yet circumscribed. The Examiners drove to the heart of it: they asked you for a run and its points. If you got them right, the number of days before your next appearance was halved – if not you were knocked back. Dave had two fifty-sixes, six twenty-eights, four fourteens. Then he took his driving test, and got his precious badge.

~

Michelle saw him standing right at the back of the lobby by glass cases full of headscarves and Rolexes. He was looking endearingly distracted, *his face empty like when he comes.* She headed for him, with each pace the air-conditioning whispering the sweat off of her. *Not that he minds. I-love-every-thing-a-bout-you!* he'd shouted into her neck at the climax of their last rendezvous. Now, he rose into her embrace. 'Why here?' Michelle spoke into his ear, while trapping his hand in hers and dragging it between their bellies. Her nail snagged his wedding band – he winced and they broke. 'You won't believe it,' he flustered, 'but a client of my dad's did a runner from here this morning. He's asked me to come and check the room, then settle the bill. So . . . well . . . I thought.'

Michelle felt a trickle of desire descend her inner thigh as the lift urged them up. The bell tinged for the eleventh floor, and he dragged her out. The carpet shushed their feet as they staggered, pawing at each other, past a maid unloading haircare from a steel cart. The key fob clattered against the door as he fiddled for the lock, then they fell into its cigar-stunk interior. A corridor led them down to a harsh light box. The drapes had been pulled open and the sun setting over the jungly canopy of Hyde Park shone directly in on a scene of animal debauchery. *Dogs and ducks have been fighting in here* was Michelle's first thought, for there were bloody claw marks on the white sheet, and a pillow had been slashed open . . . *fighting over chocolate* . . . because there were hundreds of tinfoil scraps strewn on the carpet . . . *to the death*, because there was an evil atmosphere in the room – not only cigars had been extinguished in here but hope as well.

'Guy's a druggie,' he said. 'I didn't think it'd be this bad, though, sorry.' He slumped against a stark armoire, on top of which empty spirits miniatures played chess.

'It's OK, don't worry, it doesn't bother me.' To show how little it bothered her she took his hand and used it to pull up the back of her suede dress. He peered through the red mist of her hair at the rear view of her in an opposing full-length mirror. 'Come on.' Michelle's tongue licked the pulse in his neck. 'Come on . . .' Her hand, groping at his hip, felt a wad of stuff and he recoiled, his hand going to his pocket to half withdraw a rolled-up nappy. 'Jesus,' he softly exclaimed, 'oh, Jesus . . . I . . . I . . .' He shrank away from her. 'I can't, Michelle.'

'Whaddya mean?' *You know what he means, you stupid cow.*

'I can't.' His shaky hands had lost their magic, while the nappy poking from his pocket was the ear of a rabbit conjured up by conscience. For three seconds Michelle teetered between self-righteousness and self-pity, before falling to the right, into the briny.

~

*Come on, you Spu-urs! Come on, you Yids!* Dave had sunk into a memory of White Hart Lane, where little Dave and big Benny bawled with the mob, urging on the Tottenham players, who spun, dipped and slid on the viridescent stage . . . *Yids shouting 'Yids' – you gotta hand it to us – getting in the dig before the yocks did.* 'Anywhere here – no, there!' The fare cut in on Dave's reverie. They were bumbling up Hill Street in Mayfair, swarthy types in lilac shirts were debouching from townhouses stamped with brass plates. *Jet-set pikeys who live in gaffs so stuffed with glass-topped furniture they look like fucking department stores*. 'Here?' Dave slotted the Fairway in between two Daimlers.

'It'll do.' The fare had become all business again . . . *Obviously I wasn't quite chummy enough for him.*

'Seven-eighty, guv.' The fare handed over a tenner, and there was a moment during which Dave's long face looked at him, a graven image before which it was customary to lay quantifiable offerings. Then at last: 'Keep the change, cabbie.'

Michelle hadn't even noticed the doormen on her way in, borne as she was on hot draughts of desire. Now that she was clammy and unpleasantly weak at the knees they loomed in the plate glass, stripping her of her Hilton get-up, exposing the naked girl from Streatham. One of them was going to *click his fingers, say, 'Weren't you the girl in that ad'* or worse *'What you been up to, girl, no slappers allowed in 'ere, I'm gonna call the Old Bill. Steve, grab this one!'* Instead the doorman only opened the door with a white-gloved hand and said, 'Do you require a cab, miss?'

Dave had been scanning the *Standard* on the rank outside the Hilton for about five minutes before the waver-upper in the gold-frogged frockcoat did his bit. *What'll it be, some Yank div wanting a diesel trot along Rotten Row?* But it was a young woman perhaps a year or two younger than himself, a beautiful young woman *if you like the freckled Irish type and I can't say I do*. She wore a tan suede dress, tight at the breast, flared from the thigh. She carried a linen jacket slung over one arm and a handbag that matched the dress. Her flaming hair crackled on her bare shoulders. *She isn't wearing a bra*. The waver-upper had the door of the cab open, and she shoved herself inside. Dave took in her pale face, her vacant eyes, her bit-upon lip. *She's 'ad a blow*. When he asked her, 'Where to?' she didn't reply for several seconds, and he had to say it again and louder. 'Where to, luv?'

'Soho,' she replied, sounding desperate. Dave fingered the meter and drove – which was what he did best.

Michelle sat stiffly on the sweaty yet dusty upholstery. The insides of black cabs had a peculiar ambience of extreme enclosure. This – they seemed to say – is the real interior of London; your sick office buildings, stuffy houses – even your deep-bore tube tunnels – are mere lean-tos, open to the elements. It's only when you're in one of us that you're utterly contained. The cab's thumping engine pounded the shocked Michelle deep inside herself to where her mother, Cath, betrayed for the twentieth time by feckless, freckled Dermot Brodie, sobbed and sorted through the tokens of her girlhood, yellowing communion cards and postcards from Lourdes. Cath Brodie keened and plucked at her British Home Stores cardigan, as if intent on exposing her own wounded heart, so as to let it fall, beating, on to the leatherette pouffe where the lost trick of her innocence was fanned out.

No matter that somehow she got over it and, when Dermot was finally gone, made a life for herself complete with boyfriends like Ron, Cath still hugged her betrayal, loving it more than anything or anyone else. To be Cath's only child was to be her closest ally, *her Siamese-fucking-twin*. They were tied to the same stake, consumed by the same fiery male lust. The only way to escape this awful complicity was for Michelle to practise . . . *secrecy . . . that's what I called it . . . They were only little lies . . . white ones. I'm going out with Janey – when it was Avril; I'm staying at Paula's – when it was Sharon. All kids lie to their parents at that age – but I lied more. But if I hadn't've lied I wouldn't've had any life of my own at all! She'd've dragged me down with her. I had to . . . I had to. But if she knew I'd been seeing a married man she wouldn't know what to do first – kill me or kill herself.* Michelle's fabricators went to work in the cab and speedily erected a plausible mockup of the flat on Streatham High Road, its sharp-cornered rooms and stippled walls, its fussy matriarch presiding from the suite over the TV, the coffee table, the cabinet full of dolls in national dress – all of which stank of ammonia. *Dolly daughters who couldn't do wrong if they tried . . . whose knickers can't be removed because they're sewn on.*

Dave sensed the bruised silence at the back of his neck, but he drove on, feeding the wheel through his large hands as they orbited Berkeley Square. He glanced in the rearview a couple of times, but the fare wasn't actually crying. If she'd been crying, he would have reached for a tissue from the box he kept underneath the dash and offered it to her, saying lightheartedly *all part of the service*. Yet she didn't cry, only sat, white-faced and desperate.

The traffic was easing as the curtains went up at the Lyric on Shaftesbury Avenue, the Comedy Theatre on Panton Street and the Garrick on Charing Cross Road, where provincial audiences began merrily to consider . . . *when did you last see your trousers?* Dave dropped the fare outside Gossips in Dean Street and said, 'A little early for dancing, isn't it, luv?' Luv was on a par with guv, both tip-getters, both evoking a happier age of honest amity and sturdy deference; yet for once he meant it, the fare looked so luvlorn.

'I'm meeting some mates in the wine bar,' she mumbled, as if giving an alibi along with her fiver. 'Keep the change.'

'You sure?'

'Sure.' She teetered on the heel of her sandal, recovered herself and was gone into the glass-fronted wine box, which welcomed her with a gush of chatter. Dave didn't put the 'For Hire' sign on. *I'll eat now, then work when the theatre's out*. He drove over to the little yard behind Gerrard Street – a tarmac cranny that only those with the Knowledge knew was there at all – parked up and strolled round to the Celestial Empire, his change bag banging his thigh with a 'cash-cash' sound.

Three glasses of house white and Michelle was tipsy enough to tell her friends what had happened; four glasses and she felt drunk enough to regret having done so. All of them judged her in their different ways, all of them lapped up her shame and misery like a catholicon that cured them of their own. Not that any of them said anything mean – they soothed, patted and combed the victim's hair with their sympathetic bicker, while from concealed speakers George Michael politely implored, 'I want your sex . . .'

Sandra, who filed her nails to a point out of boredom and sensibly wore brown skirts that camouflaged her wide hips against the null terrain of London. Bubbly, blonde Betty, whose electric-blue chenille top hid red, self-inflicted wounds. Pale and interesting Jane, who stood in Shepherd's Bush, propping up a domestic fantasy: the pretence that her husband Rick went out to work, when he stole her purse and went out to score. Sandra judged Michelle with the prerogative of a first officer, for whom her captain's decisions are always foolhardy. Betty felt that her follies were permitted by reason of her vulnerability, whereas Michelle – who was tough and self-reliant – should know better. Jane was quite straightforwardly contemptuous: her husband might be a lying abuser, faithful only because he was impotent, but he was a husband and, importantly, he was hers.

*They really care*, Michelle thought, looking from Sandra's spaniel waves to Betty's poodle curls. However, her belly gurgled the opposite: there was justice in their poorly concealed *schadenfreude*, for, while all vain, pretty young women require at least one who is less so, to offset their own allure, she'd greedily insisted on three.

~

In the Celestial Empire, Dave Rudman ate barbecued pork and crispy pork rice, washing it down with a pot of green tea. He wedged the *Standard* under the lip of his plate and read about the Public Carriage Office, who were ruthlessly failing black cabs for their annual test, picking up on such tiny infractions as under-inflated tyres and 'lacklustre' bodywork. *Not been getting their kick-back, the wankers.*

After he'd paid, Dave strolled back round to the cab. He had no clear plan beyond working the theatre crowd for a couple of hours. It could be *a doddle*, hacking the cab on an evening like this. There were the right on–off rainy conditions to get *nervous nellies'* umbrellas up and their arms out. He was throbbing back down Shaftesbury Avenue when he saw her again – the girl from the Hilton. She wasn't exactly hailing him, but she did have an arm out to steady herself as she bent down to retrieve a lost sandal. Dave slewed the cab into the kerb and called through the offside window: 'Cab, luv?'

Michelle had decided to go home after snorting the line of cocaine in the toilet with Jane that was meant to make her go on to Gossips. She had only taken coke once before – and as soon as the powder crinkled up her face she regretted it; for it chopped her into two Michelles, idiot drunk and calculating fool, lashed together in *a freckled skin bag*. She felt awful, she wanted *revenge on that wanker, I'll call his hippy-dippy posh wife and tell her what he's been up to while she sits at home with baby* . . . The intensity of this shook her, so she didn't make any excuses – she just left. The walk down Dean Street didn't clear her head; it thickened it with the sight of crotchless panties on plastic dummies, stared at by City types with eager-beaver faces. *I should go in that open door and up those stairs . . . The pimp could put a new sign under the buzzer: 'Busty redhead new on scene, likes to be abused . . .'*

When the cab squealed to a halt beside her, she crawled into the back, grateful for respite, even though *two cabs in one evening, it's insane . . . I can't afford it*. The cocaine was making tiny little calculations for her, white beads on a sparking synaptic abacus, so that when Dave said, 'Where to, luv?' Michelle replied, 'Olympia, then on to Danebury Road, it's off the Fulham Palace Road.'

Dave drove in silence and snatched occasional glances in the rearview at the fare slumped in the corner of the back seat. They trundled down Haymarket and along Pall Mall, past the mock temple of the Athenaeum, with its golden statue of Athene, poised on the pediment, dispensing wisdom to a Clubland frieze. They swerved into the Mall and bumbled under the blank white eyes of Victoria – who hefted her orb, as if about to rise and pitch it from her stubby shoulder. They roared up Constitution Hill, around Hyde Park Corner and down Knightsbridge. Quite unexpectedly Michelle spoke: 'D'you mind going that way?' She waved her hand towards Edinburgh Gate. 'I want to – I want to see the statue.'

'The one under Bowater House? The Epstein – Pan chasing the Family of Man?' Dave lapsed into his mother's pedagogic manner. *Bloody 'ell*, Michelle sniggered to herself, *it's Fred Housego*, then said: 'Er, yeah, that's the one, but I thought he was the Devil.'

'I love this statue,' Dave remarked, because they were by it, shuddering through the arch, past the oil-dark goat legs of Pan. Michelle looked up at his fig-leaf scrotum. He was pursuing the primordial couple with their kids and pets. Their hard faces were flattened against the future, the whole bronze gaggle pelting full tilt from the swamp of Belgravia towards the greying greenery of the Park.

Rolling up the South Carriage Drive . . . *a fine brougham, milady* . . . Dave imagined there was now some complicity between them – although he had no idea what in. The glass partition had been slid open, he wanted to talk about the statue, but Michelle had slumped back in the corner, her eyes vacant and her coral pink nails worrying at the neck of her dress.

When they got to Olympia and Dave pulled up on the empty rank alongside the overground station, Michelle got unsteadily out of the cab. 'Can you wait?' she asked. 'I'll leave my bag.' When Dave saw the security guard disputing with her, he decided to intervene. *What must she think of me in my sweaty T-shirt with my spotty nose and mucked up, thinning hair?* Michelle saw a tall, commanding figure. 'The young lady needs to pick something up from the stand she's working on,' Dave said, and to back this up Michelle produced her exhibitor's badge in its plastic sheath. 'Strictly speaking no one's allowed in, mate,' the guard said, already unlocking the door.

'We'll only be a few minutes,' Dave replied, ushering Michelle in. He darted back to lock the cab, before following on behind.

Padding along the shadowy defiles between the half-built stands, slapping the rubber treads of the stairways, their complicity grew – they were children infiltrating a school by night and the cardboard cut-outs of winsome computer salesmen were caricatures of derided teachers. On Level 5, at her clients' stand, Michelle found the ring-binders of plans and specifications where she'd left them in a steel cabinet, and Dave took them from her.

Back in the cab, he homed in unerringly on Danebury Road, using the North End Road as a flight path into the heart of Fulham. IVERS MARMA, OCKINGS, ETERKIN'S CUSTARD: the revenants of Victorian advertisements remained, haunting the pitted redbrick shopfronts. Feeling the city wheel about the cab – a widening gyre of miles and years – Dave thought, *I'm never going to be this connected to anything ever again . . . I'm falling.*

~

In the small hours of the following morning it dawned on Michelle that she should be able to locate that precise point where drink, drugs and anger were mixed inside her in exactly the right parts to simulate lust. It was mostly anger. The flaming thought of what devastation it would wreak on *him* if he were to know that within hours of leaving the Hilton she was *fucking someone else* heated Michelle up enough, so that when the cab finally turned into Danebury Road and jounced to a halt outside No. 43, she slid herself off the greasy seat and said, 'You couldn't help me with these, could you?'

*Confessions of a bloody lucky cab driver* . . . Dave plodded up the stairs, the binders under each arm. He knew a cabbie called Stan who liked to be stood upon. *That's how he got his moniker: Stood-upon-Stan.* If he got an overweight woman fare and she looked biddable, he'd strike up a conversation and eventually make the peculiar proposition: 'If you'll stand on me for a few minutes, luv – juss stand on me chest in yer stockinged feet – nuffin' kinky – I'll waive the fare.' *Nothing kinky! That's fucking kinky* . . . Yet according to Stan lots of them would. Apart from this oddity, although Dave had heard a few stories about the allure of the cabbie to women of a certain age, he mostly discounted them. He no more thought of trying it on with a fare than he considered picking up a black guy heading south. *No offence, mate,* he'd mutter to an archetypally good black man as he swept past, *too many fucking nose bleeds. 'None taken,'* replied Nelson Mandela, and bent back to pulverizing the York stone kerb with his prison mallet.

In the strongly perfumed interior of Michelle's flat – with its framed film posters, draped silk scarves and potted geraniums – events took a queer course. She slopped warm vodka and flat tonic into tumblers, which they then drank on a tiny rooftop terrace. They sat awkwardly on metal chairs, looking at the green belt of gardens three storeys below. Then the alcohol got her dander up again and Michelle said, 'I asked you up here to fuck me.' *I never speak like this, never* . . . 'Don't you want to?'

'Oh . . . well . . .' *Oh? Well . . . ?!* 'I dunno.' She stood and pulled him back inside. She turned and, lifting up her hair, snapped 'Zip!' Dave unzipped the suede dress and she stepped out of it. As he'd suspected she was naked underneath – but it was a flat declaration, this nudity, not a form of allure; and just as her command had imposed a marital note on this encounter between strangers, so her sudden, bare body had an accent of familiarity. She brushed his lips with the back of her freckled hand. If Dave found her sexy at all, it was because there was no intimacy between them. He wanted – while not being able to conceive of such a thing – an entire society in which women were kept this way: strange, distant screens of taut skin, on to which the most preposterous imaginings might be projected.

Their sex was conducted right there on the living-room floor, assisted by cushions grabbed from chairs and the sofa. Through her haze Michelle was pleased that Dave wasn't repellent, although since it wasn't him who she was fucking, but the other she was fucking over, it hardly mattered. With *him* there was no need to worry about any uncalled-for embryo – *he's had the 'snip-snip'* – and so for vital moments, as she gagged on the cabbie's shoulder, Michelle forgot who it was who was bearing down on her. As for Dave, he muttered, 'You on the pill, luv?', took her silence for acquiescence, then approached Michelle as he would call over a run: *leave on left tit, comply throat, comply mouth, left shoulder, right hip, forward cunt* . . . The junctions of her body were well signed, and his Knowledge was sufficient to hold her.

Yet in the friction of their final lunge there was an anticipation of more than arrival. Their jerking bodies prefigured the bondage of shackled partners. They both sensed this and struggled to avoid it – backpedalling into the present. Dave came in desperation . . . while the mere cessation of bucking was Michelle's end.

Rising groggily from the carpet, eluding his helping hands, Michelle staggered down the three stairs to the bathroom and locked herself in with a desperate 'click'. Crouching in the bath, carpet-burned bottom cooled by the enamel, she shook her ginger head with disgust as she sluiced Rudman out of her. 'Are you alright in there . . . Michelle?' *At least he knows my name* . . . She tried to smile ruefully into the mirror over the sink, but her reflection only looked ashamed. Bitterly ashamed – and worried *No condom . . . no fucking protection*. When Dave left, he gave her a cab receipt with his phone number scrawled across it. That night, in bed, he marvelled at her musk still strong on his belly and balls. He never expected her to call . . . *she thinks she's well out of my league* . . . and for seven months she didn't.

Dave Rudman was sharing a semi-detached house with two mates that year. It was near the Metal Box Company building in Palmers Green. They were all cabbies who'd got to know each other doing the Knowledge. It forged a bond – this open university of bitumen. They did tutorials in dingy bedsits or else the painfully tidy front rooms of their parents' houses – calling over the points and the runs for night after night. Fear of getting any police record kept them mostly sober. Dave Quinn, Phil Eddings, Tufty Rudman, Gary 'Fucker' Finch. Musketeers on mopeds – that's how they thought of themselves. And when they weren't out doing the Knowledge, they worked together for a dodgy contract-cleaning outfit run by Quinn's Uncle Gerry, which operated out of Barking.

They cleaned hospitals, care homes and offices – or rather they didn't. Dave Quinn showed them the fiddle on their first night: 'See this.' He'd climbed up on a ladder and was pointing at a dingy patch on the off-white wall near the ceiling. 'Thass a tester, that is, yer leave a little bit of the wall uncleaned to show the 'ole floor's been done, right? Except' – he scampered down the aluminium ladder, snapped it shut, hung it on his shoulder, picked up a bucket slopping dirty water, and with the others in his wake, ran up the stairs to the next floor – 'that's not 'ow we do it 'ere.' He yanked the ladder open and, still carrying the bucket, ascended. 'You got yer little bit of card, see, like a stencil, right.' He held this up to the wall. 'Then you dobs a sloosh of yer dirty water on it, an' Bob's yer fuckin' uncle, a tester!' He cackled his maniacal laugh, a pocket version of his Irish uncle, his full lips twisting into cupidity.

Dave didn't like it – this dirtying of a tiny patch instead of cleaning a broad expanse – but he got used to it, it was a liberty *but not a diabolical one*. They were little guys, weren't they? Dave and his mates – and little guys had to take what they could. Uncle Gerry knew the score, the environmental services managers he gave kickbacks to knew the score. Everyone knew the score . . . *except for the boring straight-goers*. Besides, Dave liked the all-night-shift poker games they played in the empty offices. The hundreds of desks, personalized with a photo cube or a jokey sign – 'THE BOSS IS IN . . . YOUR FACE' – now depersonalized entirely, swivel chairs pushed back, papers abandoned, calculators cast aside, their daytime inhabitants tucked up in bed, *in the sticks*.

Walking the echoing corridors, creeping down the emergency stairs to check on the security guard, then finally hitting the streets as dawn silvered the glassy peaks of the city; this, Dave had imagined, was the topsy-turvy world he'd inhabit when he got his badge. *I'll choose my own hours and my own patch . . . I'll be free of the hamster wheel these desk jockeys swivel in, free of the need to kowtow to some finger-fucking, expense-account-padding wanker, in from his carport in the sticks, who finks 'e's Robert-fucking-Maxwell 'coz 'e drives a company bloody Ford Sierra*. And if he felt a little wonky when he got on his Honda later that morning, he could always neck a wrap of whizz and let the two-stroke of his young heart yank him forward.

The Palmers Green gaff was a parody of domesticity: T-shirts in the sink, ashtrays in the fridge, the pot plants weedy specimens of *Cannabis sativa*. The lads worked different shifts and rarely collided at a social hour – if they did mayhem ensued. One would rustle up girls, another drugs, a third booze. The partying was frenetic and loud, neighbours despaired – the garden made their eyes sore. They came round to complain and were met by Phil Eddings, whose suede head and skull face were enough to terrify anyone. On one much recounted occasion, the neighbour visited an apparition: Big End, who'd let some giggly girls, high on mushrooms, anoint him with their foundation. He came to the front door looking like Baron Samedi, his happy face masked with Caucasian flesh tones, his big naked torso sweaty and black.

Towards Christmas of that year the partying died down. The lads were cramming in as many shifts as they could; Dave Quinn and Tufty Rudman had switched to renting full-flat so they could mush whenever they wanted. Ever since Black Monday in October, it'd got a lot tougher to get the getters. Quartering the Square Mile – up Lothbury, down Houndsditch – Dave Rudman wondered *Where 'av all the little chancers in their striped blazers got to?* Still, Christmas Day and New Year's Eve should double up their money. The plan was to put enough doubloons in the war chest so they could take off in January. *Just like Benny and his mob used to . . . Las Palmas . . . shtupping grateful golf widows.*

*Poor Fucker* was working as hard – but every penny he made went into soft furnishings and white goods, kandy-striped kiddy klothes and presents. 'Fer me fuckin' bird. I tell you lot,' he told them over a spliff sucked down in front of the news, lithe Palestinian boys lobbing rocks at Uzi-toting Israelis, asymmetrical warfare among the Semites, 'don't fucking go there, keep your rain hat on 'cept when she's on the blob. That's bin my bloody downfall.' He laughed bitterly. *Women, eh . . . they're like beautiful flowers . . . luring you in, then once you've dumped your pollen before you know it they're fat old boilers with fucking 'taches. Still – a kid's a cute thing . . .* Dave tiptoed into a nursery and began playing with his secret mummyness. *I'd call my little chap Champ . . .*

Fucker had borrowed the money from Mann & Overton in the Holloway Road to get his own cab. To make the payments he had been forced to suffer the indignity of a full *Evening Standard* livery job. 'Makes me eyes funny looking at it,' he moaned, and the other lads, standing on the kerb, squinting at the newsprint plastered all over the new vehicle, laughed until they felt sick. 'Your sherbert looks like sumfing you got from the chip shop,' Phil Eddings quipped. 'Yeah, and you're the fucking wally!' Dave Rudman added.

One afternoon in December, Dave ranked up at King's Cross and went for a tea in the grimy booking hall. The place still stank with all the evil fumes of the fire the previous month, when thirty punters had been incinerated on the tube escalator. The night it happened, Dave had been at Victoria when the radio began to spit out the news in sizzling horror gobs. The cabbies got out of their vehicles and huddled together, shifting from one foot to the other, as if sensing the Hades beneath their feet. Now, standing under the barrel ceiling of this other terminus, looking at the *junky scum and Jock chancers fresh off the InterCity*, Dave felt sudden and unaccustomed depression: a premonitory sadness that took him back to the cab, back to Palmers Green and into his daytime bed.

When the bell woke him from his couvade, hours later, Dave wanted to ignore it. He had a cookie of sputum lodged in his throat . . . *gotta pack in the fags*. He felt like he was skiving off school . . . *It might be an inspector from the PCO, or Ali from the garage come to check out why I'm not on the fucking road* . . . So he pulled his jeans and T-shirt back on and tramped down the narrow stairs. When he swung the door open, there she was, her beautiful mouth pulled hard down at one side, as if sneering at her own good looks. Michelle was seven months pregnant, and there was no question in his mind of not letting her in.

~

They were married four weeks later, in a registry office on Burnt Oak Broadway. The cab was tricked out for the wedding in frills and bows. Gary Finch drove while Dave and Michelle sat in the back. They were both being taken for a ride.

# 5

## *The Exile*

### OCT 523 AD

Luvvie Joolee Blunt lived in a two-room semi that had been built from the finest courses of London brick she could afford. Her dosh was of no use on Ham, and it was through an arrangement the Lawyer of Chil had made with Mister Greaves's predecessor that the Hamsters who were prepared to assist her were remitted in trade goods. Many a tincan and irony blade owed its presence on the island to her mournful requirements. Unable to fend for herself in any way, a distracted – and to the Hamsters' way of thinking – half-mad old boiler, she whiled her days away reading a breviary of the Book, embroidering oddments of cloth and staring out to sea. She had requested that her dwelling be erected as far from the manor as possible, and on the southern shore, so that she would not be reminded of the cruel expediency that had led to her long incarceration on Ham.

To the opares who came to cook her food, empty her slops and launder her peculiar garments – once garishly bright, now long since faded – Luvvie Joolee was not merely peculiar but incomprehensible. Her clipped Arpee, her abrupt gestures, her constant talk of a city that remained continually present to her yet was utterly unknown to them, struck them as craziness. She had allowed the stands of blisterweed to grow right up to the small yard of her dwelling, so fearful was she of the motos; and she remained within this poisonous thicket, growing older and more distracted by the year.

The Hamsters were hard pressed to say exactly how long she

had resided on the island – for the concept of ordinal time was not strong in them. Carl's grandmother, Effi, had told him that she was a young mum when Luvvie Joolee landed on Ham, and they must be roughly the same age. Everyone knew why Luvvie Joolee had been exiled. She and her husband, the Lawyer of Blunt, had fallen foul of the PCO by living together, with their children, under the same roof. Their loathsome conduct was bandied about the town in decauxs and standards, until a gang of their own kinsmen took the law into their hands. They removed her to the docks and bundled her aboard a southbound ferry. For a time she was held in the Bouncy Castle at Chil, then, when her whereabouts became known to her husband, she was dispatched still further to Ham.

Effi Dévúsh also told Carl that during the early years of her exile Luvvie Joolee had appeared often in the village, ranting and raving about the injustices done to her, and trying to rouse the Hamsters in rebellion against the Lawyer of Chil. Eventually the old Hack, Mister Hurst, had made it clear to her that were she to continue, he would have no alternative but to return her to London for formal judgement. Understanding that this would mean torture, and very likely breaking upon the wheel, henceforth Luvvie Joolee withdrew into her troubled seclusion. When Antonë Böm arrived on Ham, under a cloud of a similar hue, he sought to gain her confidence. He knew members of her circle in the capital by repute, and was able to chitchat with her in the manner to which she had been accustomed. However, the highborn luvvie had little trust in a mere teacher and so rebuffed him.

Carl Dévúsh and Antonë Böm had been summoned to Luvvie Joolee's toxic bower by a note entrusted to an opare. They came creeping along under the bluffs of the Ferbiddun Zön, slipping and scraping over the groynes thick with seaweed and barnacles. Crabs scuttled away, while overhead was the relentless cawing of the gulls. They squeezed gingerly between the stalks of the blisterweed, which even now, browned and hollowed, still had the capacity to wound. Böm tapped diffidently on the rough-hewn door and a voice from inside rasped, Cummon in. Inside the whitewashed austerity of the little semi, the unshuttered windows, covered with stretched moto hide, admitted a pinkish light. The sharp odour of human faeces – unknown in the Hamsters' gaffs – assailed the visitors.

Siddahn, boy! the old boiler snapped, and so disoriented was Carl that it took him seconds to realize she was addressing him. Ve stoowal! she snapped again, and, casting about, he saw the one she meant and collapsed on to it. Luvvie Joolee – her short, tattered tunic exposing white arms and legs worming with purplish veins – leaned against one wall while the teach remained standing in the middle of the room. Seeing her close up for the first time, Carl was struck by how closely the Luvvie resembled the Driver: both had long, concave faces, with brows and chins sharp as the rim of a plate. The boiler's face was like a mask. She had no eyebrows, and her downy, white hair was cut to within a finger's breadth of her bumpy scalp. Thick slap was plastered on her gaunt cheeks. She wore heavy, angular earrings carved from a dark wood Carl couldn't identify – and these had dragged deep slits in her earlobes. As tall as the Driver, she looked down on both Carl and Böm, her black eyes lambent in deep sockets. To Carl she had the otherworldliness of all those who came from off the island.

Staring at the earthen floor of the room, so as to avoid the fanatic eyes of the Exile, Carl was seized by a peculiar irony contrivance, which had many spinning flywheels and a slowly turning knurled cylinder. These were obscurely connected to a white disc, the rim of which was inscribed with figures: 1, 2, 3 and so on.

– Wassermattah, boy? Luvvie Joolee rasped. Aynt chew evah seen a meeta B4? Her Mokni was fluent, her manner lucid. Despite her eccentric appearance there was no trace of madness.

– N-no, mum, Carl stuttered.

– Mum! she snorted. Mum! Eye tellya, boy, vat vare iz ve diffrunz

Btween U chavs an reel folk. Tym, munny, distunz. She pointed at the dial: Daves tym – nó Rs. Daves munny – nó yaws, Daves distunz – iz root 2 Nú Lundun! Then she rounded on Böm: Djoo bleev in Dave, ven, Böm? she spat out.

– Enuff, the teach replied.

– Djoo bleev in iz cummagayn, djoo bleev in iz mirrakulz, djoo bleev in Nú Lundun?

– Yeah, enuff. Carl had never seen Böm so tongue-tied.

– So ow cum ve Dryva sez U 2 iz fliars? Djoo bleev, boy? she said, rounding on Carl again.

– Yeah, L-Luvvie, he stammered.

– Luvvie! she spat. Wotevah, ve pawtunt fing iz djoo bleev, Eye carnt B doin wiv fliars. Eye carnt B doin wiv vose oo aynt lé Dave inter vair arts. Eye tellya boaf vat Dryva issa nastë bituv wurk. E aynt no trú bleevah. E aynt got Dave in iz art. Dave vat iz gentul, Dave wot luvs us jussaz if we woz awl ve Loss Boy. The old boiler's face took on an expression both wistful and profound. Transfigured by her Dävinanity, she was, Carl understood, almost beautiful.

– Eye bleev vat, Böm said in a hushed undertone.

– Wel ve Dryva doan, an eel shaft ve 2 uv U B4 U gettof Am, so Eyem gonna affta elp U. U bin cummin 2 ang aht 4 yeers nah, Böm, but Eye aynt toal U nuffing, rì?

– Nuffing much, Böm conceded with a rueful nod of his head.

The old boiler bent down from her great height and shuffled into the corner of the room where a pile of cloth scraps lay in a heap. As she rooted among them, Luvvie Joolee continued: Wot Eye aynt nevah toal U iz vat Mistah Greaves brungus maw van juss trayd plastik, ee brungus vese inall. She held up a bundle tightly wound with twine. Lettuce, she announced, lettuce from Lundun, ees a frend, Mistah Greaves, nó an allì but a mayt. She unwrapped the bundle, and Carl gazed wonderingly upon the sheaves of onion-skin-thin leaves that sprang from it, each one covered with spindly phonics. Siddahn, Luvvie Joolee commanded Böm, siddahn on ve flaw. Eyem gonna reed U wot me öl mukkas in Lundun av bin sayin abaht ve PCO an vat. U 2 needta no.

~

It was with the motos that Carl was able to be himself and accept his secret mummyself. The motos gathered together in a rank in a woodland clearing under the screenwash, their backs shiny with moisture. When the shower ceased their bristles caught the bigwatt like jewels. The motos were always prepared to admit him to their cuddling and nuzzling. Unlike the Hamsters, the motos maintained an exact knowledge of who was whose mum and dad, going back for many generations. Old Champ, who had been the minder of Carl's dad, Symun, when he was a young boy, would hunker down before the lad and in his sing-slurp voice intone the moto lineage: Ven Darlin an Shoogar ad Hunnë, an Hunnë an Gorj ad Boythë, an Boythë an Poppit ad Wunti, an Wunti an Thweetë ad me. That there were only a handful of names for all the motos that were, had been and ever would be on Ham did not confuse the beast. In recounting who he was, old Champ's baby-blue eyes took on a strange luminousness that they never ordinarily possessed.

Those dävine dads most in sway to the Driver were apt to dismiss such evidence of moto wisdom, asserting that the nicety of their intimate relations was a mere mechanical contrivance. Yet Carl had seen for himself that when a moto was put to mate with another he or she deemed unsuitable, a frightful motorage ensued; and his grandmother Effi told him it was the motos who mysteriously instructed their human keepers in their own management. Vares no Am wivaht ve motos, she had often said, no Am, juss barran lan.

During the blobs since the departure of the Hack's pedalo in JUL, while the Hamsters turned their attention to preparations for the kipper, Carl went increasingly to the motos. He sought out the rank that trundled over the harvested fields depositing dung, and, with old Champ's agreement, cut out a moped – usually Sweetë or Tyga – to accompany him on his forays. Despite the dads' objections, Carl's half-brother, Bert Ridmun, also accompanied him on trips along the ragged shoreline of the Gayt, where the rotten stumps of crinkleleafs subsided into the lagoon. In this unusual seclusion, Carl encouraged Bert to join him in riding the moto, as they were wont to do when kiddies. While the older beasts would have bridled at such treatment, the moped docilely accepted it, even allowing Carl to spur him a few paces into the sea. Here, half swimming, half wading, the moped conveyed the lad through the placid waters of the lagoon.

~

One day, towards the end of the second tariff, they were both being taken for a ride by Tyga. When they'd gone a few hundred paces round the headland, the two lads saw that the entire population were gathered in front of the Shelter. The daddies, mummies and opares were listening, rapt, to one of the Driver's spontaneous effusions, while, despite the cuffs of their dads, the younger kids were playing tag. One or two motos cropped the turf, their muzzles gooey with forage.

Carl and Bert slid off Tyga's back, and, drawing nearer, they heard the Driver's angry voice rising high over the bowed heads of the Hamsters. He stood facing the low wooden hut, his back to his audience, his eyes on his mirror. His deep voice shouted through the wall of his chest:

– It's not enough! Your Knowledge is not enough! I have never reviled the motos, my fares, yet, in those passages of the Book that describe the moto, it is clear that Dave didn't mean these . . . creatures but conveyances of the kind that I have seen in the streets of New London. I know your attachment to these beasts and how you have depended on them; nevertheless you must understand that their oil is no longer in demand elsewhere in Ing; there are diverse other fuels, beeswax, tallow and suchlike, with which to conjure letric. In accepting the oil in place of dosh-rent, my Lawd's Hack is supporting you as if you were the meanest foundlings!

The Driver paused and ran a hawkish eye over the congregation; there wasn't even a mutter of dissent, so he resumed:

– Since I came among you and abolished the vile practice of anointing, many more of your infants have survived!

This was manifestly the case, for the evidence was right behind him, a gaggle of infants and toddlers that exceeded in number all the other Hamsters.

– You all know, the Driver continued, his voice dropping still lower, that you will have to change if the island is to support these greater numbers. Mister Greaves is prepared to pay for more bubbery and London bricks if you increase your industry. He is prepared to pay for the feathers of seafowl as well; however he will no longer offer you a good price for the oil of these . . . these . . . toyist beasts!

At this the Hamsters let out a great groan, but the Driver, feeling the rhythm of his own rhetoric, was not to be halted:

– Yes, yes, toyist beasts, with their infantile slubberish and gross bodies. You muss free yawselves from your chavveri, he said, beginning to slide, for emphasis, into Mokni. U awl no viss, U muss taykup ve nú wä aw Nú Lundun wil nevah B bilt. U muss follo ve Búk aw U wil afta leev Am – U no viss. He suddenly broke off, having seen Carl and Bert trying unobtrusively to join the back of the throng.

The Driver had the ability to incorporate chance phenomena – the cry of a bird, the shape of a cloud, even the breaking of a large wave on the reef – into his calling over, which mightily impressed the Hamsters. So it was now; he stretched out his hand and clawed at Carl:

– U C viss 1! They all turned to stare. Yeah, yeah, ve 1 oo därs 2 enta ve Ferbiddun Zön an digabaht vare! U no viss! Ve 1 oo wil B fahnd a fliar bì ve PeeSeeO an broak! U no viss! Innit vat ee iz rì palli wiv vese beests? Innit vat ee cuddlsup wiv em? Innit vat ee iz vair bumchum?! But ee aynt ve onlë 1! Losing all composure, the Driver swivelled to confront them directly: U awl dú í! U awl ewes ve moto 2 gé off wiv eechuvva, mummies an daddies boaf! Iss dis-sgusstyn! Remembah ve Braykup! Stikk 2 ve Chaynjova! Caulova ve Búk – 4 wivaht í U R awl fliars!

Carl could no longer bear the Driver's hateful rant. Although the Hamstermen made no move to grab him, he ran away in case they did. He feinted towards the startled motos, swerved and darted off behind the Shelter. Then he scampered full tilt up the home field towards the Layn, and kept on going down the far side into Nor-fend, crunching fallen leaves, snapping branches, sloshing through puddles, until at last he slid to a halt in a boggy slough and collapsed in a huddle of quaking limbs. He was alone now with his secret mummyself – he wouldn't cry, even though his tank was tight with misery.

Carl had only been lying like this for a few units when he felt a soft, familiar hand on his head and registered the calm tones that almost always accompanied it.

– We nú viss woz cummin, Carl, said Antonë Böm, hunkering down beside him, í woz onlë a matta uv wen. Carl looked up and his mentor's eyeglasses reflected his own thin face back at him.

– B-but iss sew unfayre on ve motos.

– Eye no vat. Böm helped Carl out of the boggy patch, and they seated themselves on drier ground. He cleared his throat and shifted to Arpee, gaining, he felt, in clarity of expression what he lost in intimacy: Unfair also on the Hamsters, whose simple dävness is used so badly. The Driver's calling over is designed to make them affirm a truth, while removing from them any responsibility for what it entails. It makes of them, um, um – he searched for the requisite analogy – nought save woollies and the Driver their gaffer. Böm began to grope in the inside pockets of his carcoat, eventually drawing out a blisterpack.

– We carnt stä eer, Carl said, struggling to his feet, vayl cummun fyndus.

– I don't think so. Now the Driver has begun he'll continue for a full tariff or more. Think on it, Carl. Ever since the Hack's party left, the Driver has called over more and more. A day no longer passes without his haling the three cabs. The dads can't get any work done – if he keeps on like this Ham will be unable to support itself through the kipper.

– An wot abaht ve motos? Carl insisted.

– The motos, ah, yes . . . Böm tore off a chaw of gum and stuck it in his mouth. Um, well, the Hamsters could no more slaughter their motos than they could walk over the sea to Chil, he chuckled, or build New London here and now. It'll never happen.

Carl was unmoved by this levity. Vey no, he said.

– What do you mean? Böm said, recovering himself.

– Ve dads, ve Dryva – vey no wee bin anginaht wiv ve Xeyel.

– Hmm, indeed, well, I saw young Sid Brudi scampering off when we came back along to Hel Bä the other day. I surmised it wasn't the first time he'd followed us. Still, how could they know what we were speaking of?

– Eye dunno. Vey wanna shuttusup. Bert erred Fred an ve uvvah dads tawkin.

– Well, then, said Böm, chewing meditatively on this, it appears that our takeaway is ready, my lad. When we add this to what Luvvie Joolee has told us concerning her old man and his allies in London, it drives us to a single conclusion: we must find a way to leave Ham at once. We will travel to the last place our pursuers will think of: to London, and there make common cause with the Blunt dissenters. A simple petition will enable us to discover the fate of your dad. Mayhap these two endeavours, so curiously enmeshed, will serve to put a spoke in the Wheel.

Banging hard, then pushing open the heavy door of the Funch gaff, Carl was assailed by a dreadful caterwauling. His Uncle Gari, who was known familiarly as Fukka, was seated in front of a roaring fire, stripped naked save for a bubbery cockpiece; his paps were roseate with gingery hairs, his skin shone with sweat, and he had a squalling infant propped on each of his bandy legs, while his blunt hands grasped their chubby shoulders. The kids' curly mops bounced as Fukka joggled them unmercifully. Ranged along the sloping walls of the gaff were the opares, while sitting on the yok floor, crammed in between the box beds, and even atop the dresser, were a gaggle of little Hamsters. The entire juvenile population of Ham was there: it was the last tariff before Changeover, and Fukka liked to give them a good send-off. Many of the kids had the distinctive Funch face – full-lipped, broad-nosed, pop-eyed. The other Hamsters said that the Funches looked like motos, something that Fukka didn't mind in the least. Unlike his father, Burny, Fukka was almost untouched by the rigours of Dävinanity. He had a simple and straightforward nature – as close to the earth as his wide frame; and, although it was now dangerous to speak of such things, the time of the Geezer had affected him deeply.

All the kids held a vessel of some sort, a clay pot or earthenware ewer for the older ones, a wooden bowl or tincup for the youngsters. They were all beating upon them with spoons and sticks in time to Fukka's crazy jouncing, while with one discordant voice – at once bass and booming, cracked and reedy – they belted out a string of nonsense: Makk-daar-nal, makk-daar-nal, kennukkëfrichikkin anapeetsa-hut! Makk-daar-nal, makk-daar-nal, kennuckëfrichikkin anapeetsa-hut! When Carl's pale face appeared in the firelight, far from moderating their racket the rambunctious crew redoubled it: Makk-daar-nal, makk-daar-nal, kennukkëfrichikkin anapeetsa-hut! Makk-daar-nal, makk-daar-nal, kennuckëfrichikkin anapeetsa-hut! Ending in a rat-a-tat-tat of beats and a great shout of laughter.

Ha, ha! Fukka let the infants slide from his legs to the flags and opened his arms to embrace his nephew. Ve lairë yung git! he cried. Cummeer! They hugged, and Carl breathed in his uncle's oily smell. If the Funches were the offspring of motos and humans, and – as Effi Dévúsh maintained – motos were themselves monstrous products of the union of still other beasts and the gigantic settlers of Ham, then perhaps this explained why his uncle's clan were so congenial to Carl. For the Funches were notably affectionate for Hamsters, kissing and petting their kids in a way that the others didn't.

– Wassup, ven? Fukka asked, when Carl was seated on a stool beside him, a tincan of booze in his hand.

– Iss ve Dryva, Carl replied, anna granddads. Nah ve Dryvas göinnon lyke vat Eye fink ees gonna gé me an Tonë bangdupp. Carnt U sä sumffing, Nunkul?

Fukka cast a plump red hand about him at the tumultuous scene in the house. From the rafters hung bunches of dried herbage. The curry bubbled over the fire, stirred by one of the opares, while a couple of the lads were mending a fowling rope that was uncoiled on the table. Clokk viss, Carl, Fukka said. Í doan matta wot Eye fink, coz ve granddads doan giv a munkees abaht ve Funches, nor ve Bulluks neevah. Weer inturnal Xeyels Rsels, juss lyke Luvvie Joolee aw, Dayv sayv us – he sketched a wheel on his chest and Carl did the same – ve Beestlimun. Eye gotta famlee 2 feed, if Eye speek aht abaht U weer fukked. Nah, Carl, U gotta tek yer charnsez. Fukka shook his great russet mop with a pained expression on his face, as if the whole peculiar weight of Ham had him in a headlock.

Then, summoning himself, Fukka reached out to the opare at

the kettle and, grabbing her by her cloakyfing, pulled her down on to his lap. He began to jounce her as he had the infants before, and tried to get the rap going: Makk-daar-nal, makk-daar-nal! While a number of the little kids joined in, the rest remained silent, their eyes averted; and although such a sight – the swollen cockpiece battering at the opare's thin behind again and again – was so familiar as to be commonplace, nonetheless Carl felt queasy, averted his eyes, then made his excuses and left.

When, on the following morning, Carl returned from the shitter to see the Council assembled on its wall, he knew what was coming. The granddads sat, swaddled in their bubbery carcoats like melancholy auks. The Driver stood among them, his black robe lying slack in the misty air. The weedy stench of a calm sea blanketed the dads, and while Ozzi Bulluk and Gari Funch chewed their gum stubbornly, spitting from time to time on the turf between their feet, the others were silent. Cummeer! Fred Ridmun called to Carl. We wanna tawk wiv U. The Driver gestured to Bill Edduns, and, ever the willing fony, he dashed off along the shoreline towards Böm's semi no doubt to fetch him too for summary judgement.

When they'd returned, and Carl and Böm were seated at the dads' feet, the Driver presented his back to the Guvnor and made his suit:

– These two flyers have been seen consorting with the Exile, and doubtless they've also continued to enter the Ferbiddun Zön. I lay it before the Council that the two of them should henceforth be confined to the manor.

– Yeah, yeah – Carl didn't know where such boldness came from – but wot if Eye sed Eye woz gonna mayk ve furs jump onta ve stac, wot ven?

There was a rumble of disquiet from the men.

– Wotjoosayin? said Fred Ridmun, leaning forward to examine his stepson.

– Eyem sayin vat wen me an Bert wozzup eest yesterdä vare woz stil fowl landin an tekkin off from ve stac, yeah. Nó lots but vey iz angin on. U sez – Carl stood to confront the Driver – vat weave gotta gé maw fevvers an vat, well U no ve wayuvit, doanchew?

For the first time in many tariffs the Driver was bereft of words. He stood, white-faced and shaking, making no pretence of observing his fares in his mirror, for he did indeed know the Hamsters' way. Any dad might volunteer to make the first leap on to the Sentrul Stac in place of the Guvnor. This entailed privileges: the right to wear a baseball cap and to carry a lighter. Certain allotments of moto oil, booze and fags were also forthcoming. To molest a dad who had made the leap, fixed the cradle ropes and survived was unthinkable.

At last Fred Ridmun spoke:

– Iss troo wot ee sez, if ee mayks ve leep ee carnt B bangedup, innit.

– Issit? The discomfited Driver lapsed into Mokni.

– Ittis! the Hamsters chorused, and the Driver, bested, strode away to the Shelter.

Although Carl had outwitted the Driver, there remained the question of when a party should be dispatched to the Sentrul Stac. It was late in the season, and the Hamstermen were neither confident pedalers, nor could they swim. In former times they may have prided themselves on their bold ascents, not just of the Sentrul Stac but also of the other, lesser stacks that stood in the sluggish waters of the great lagoon. Most years the Sentrul Stac boasted the largest blackwing colony, although oilgulls also shared the pinnacle, taking the lower galleries. The fowling party would pitch camp on the summit and on successive nights harvest the birds there and on the other stacks. In former times, when the stacks had been more numerous and the Hamstermen more intrepid, they had stayed out on them throughout the breeding season, their vessel carrying several loads back to the shore. However, in the past few generations the birding had, increasingly, become a symbolic activity – a means of inducting the lads into the mysteries of dadhood, rather than a serious part of the island's economy. In the time of the Driver this tendency towards emasculation had increased, almost as if the imminent erection of the New London that he called over had sapped the will of the Hamstermen to maintain their own more laborious paradise.

~

So it took a full blob of lengthy debate and preparation before the day dawned when the party was readied for departure. First the pedalo was dragged out from its shed and every seam caulked anew, each dad working on his allotted portion of the vessel. Next the fowling ropes were oiled and coiled, the cradle repaired and lashed to the pedalo's gunnels; finally the supplies – chiefly takeaway, tanks of moto gubbins and evian – were stowed.

While all this was under way, Carl and Antonë had little opportunity to talk alone, for they were constantly observed by the other islanders. Böm assumed that Carl had volunteered because he hoped to use the pedalo to effect their escape and was learning how to handle it. When they did manage to grab a few words in private he was disabused of this notion: Nah, Carl said, lookit ve syz uvit. Vares no way we cúd andle it. Nah, Eyem gonna distrak vem, an wyle Eyem gon Ure gonna gé ve stuff togevver 4 ve trip. In answer to Böm's quite reasonable inquiry as to how they were going to cross the five clicks of open water separating Ham from Barn, Carl had a single word: Motos. Antonë, weer gonna swim wiv ve motos.

The Sentrul Stac reared from the waters of the great lagoon about five clicks due southeast of Manna Bä. Its jagged peak was thus the opposite pole of the Hamsters' diminutive world to the rubble of Nimar in the northwest. Effi Dévúsh's legends told of how this stack – and the three further to the east, as well as the four smaller ones grouped around it – were the stepping stones that the Mutha and her giant company had thrown down in the waters so as to cross between Ham and the scattering of uninhabited islands to the south.

Those Hamsters more under the influence of the Driver were inclined to view the stacks as natural features, left behind during the MadeinChina, when the sea had broken into the lagoon and washed away the land. From the moment when he first rounded the Gayt and saw the great lagoon, Antonë Böm had entertained a different hypothesis concerning these curious features and longed to visit them. Each year that he'd remained on the island, he had asked to be allowed on a fowling expedition. The Hamstermen would never take him: fowling was too dävine and too dangerous a pursuit for off-islanders to be allowed to participate. To climb the stacks was the most daddyish of all the rituals in a daddyish world. If a mummy or an opare so much as looked at the cradles or ropes when an expedition was being organized, it would have to be aborted.

This was to be Carl's first time out to the stacks, although he'd sat at the feet of the Council for enough fowling seasons to know what to expect. Sat at the dads' feet and listened in minute detail while they mulled over the nature of their adversary. For, to the Hamstermen, the Sentrul Stac itself had a brooding personality. It was like a rocky pine cone – a series of open chambers, all set in tiers, one upon the other, rising up sheer out of the waves to the height of forty men. At the top of the stack there was a platform forty paces across; this was thick with shrubbery, as were the cavities below. All the stacks had this coating of vegetation; where the lagoon washed at their bases, hanks of seaweed clung to the crete, while above the waterline clumps of buddyspike furred their contours. In the summer, they tinged the air with their flowers, so that a bluish nimbus formed about the summits of the stacks. Now they were gone, and the Sentrul Stac was a grim snaggle, streaked white and black with birdshit.

The Hamstermen maintained that their forefathers had deliberately seeded the birdshit with buddyspike to provide handholds; however, this shrubbery was only shallowly rooted, and it was a foolhardy fowler who relied on it to support him. The first Hamster off the pedalo and on to the stack was charged with climbing to the summit, where he would tie one end of the rope he carried to an irony stanchion buried in the crete; the other end he would let down to his companions, so that they might lash on the cradle. It was also the first bloke's task to descend the rope and dispatch the sentinel blackwing. The Hamstermen would arrive at the allotted stack by night, when the blackwings were all asleep save for the one bird charged with guarding them. If this one could be prevented from uttering a warning cry, then the rest would remain oblivious as the birders swung their cradle from one nest to the next, twisting their necks with the same easy rhythm they employed ashore when casting seed or scything the wheatie crop. If the stack jumper failed in his task, the whole colony would lift off and mob the invaders. With their wingspan as great as a man's outstretched arms, and their sharp, downward-curving beaks, the blackwings were fearful aggressors. Many a Hamsterman had fallen to his death from the stacks, the blood from his ruptured eyes spreading slick on the heaving swell. Carl's own granddad, Peet Dévúsh, had fallen from the Sentrul Stac and died. This was the curse upon the Dévúsh line – for the Hamsters believed that if a bloke was sufficiently dävine the choppa would come. This was a great host of seafowl, flying in such close formation that the falling man could be caught on their backs, then lifted up and set safely back on the stack once more.

Shuvoff, mì luvs! Fred Ridmun cried, and under a bigwatt screen the prow of the Ham pedalo flattened a stand of blisterweed, grated on shingle, then hit the water, sending up a plume of emerald spray. The dads pushed the stern of the craft, their bare, moto-oiled feet slithering on the mat of vegetation, while the lads splashed thigh-deep in the wavelets, yanking on the prow. In the effort of their final push was a dread anticipation – but then came the mysterious moment when the dead weight of the beached pedalo was transformed into the live motion of being afloat. There was a clamour of shouting and more bellowed instructions from the Guvnor as the dads and lads unshipped the long pedals and took their places. The mummies came out from their gaffs and commenced an eerie ululating. The motos had been led down from their wallows especially to participate in the leave-taking – and they sent up a frightful bellowing.

Then there came a shout from the bow, Reef up! There was the swish of seaweed and the patter of Daveworks against the hull. Ship pedals! the Guvnor cried, and they all waited, frozen in their frail shell, as the screen wheeled around them and the reef grated beneath them. Then they were over, the pedals dipped to the water, and the pedalo sped offshore.

Seated in the bows with the other lads, Carl turned back and saw the green wall of the island stretch into a band, then a ribbon, and eventually shrink until it was but a green cap set on the massive furrowed brow of the sea. The Hamsters on the shore were reduced to an agitation of waving arms, while some way apart from them, in front of his semi, Carl could make out the Driver, a black stroke on the ledger of the land. Even from this distance Carl could sense that the Driver's savage gaze was upon him, doubtless willing him to mistime his leap on to the stack, to fall and release his final flying breaths as bubbles in the briny.

Carl grabbed Fred Funch's belt and leaned forward over the gnarled stempost. Fred let his head dangle down so that the bow wave tangled with his hair. Using both hands, he picked out the Daveworks that had lodged in the seams of the boat's timbers as they ran over the reef. Dragging him back up, Carl sat, tense and expectant, as Fred sorted the plastic shards into the appropriate categories: reel, toyist, reel, toyist, reel, toyist . . . The others amplified these words into a chant with which to punctuate the rhythm of their pedalling. The pedalo, slewing in the current, shook itself like a leviathan breaching for air and picked up speed. Carl picked up one of the Daveworks, biggish, bone-white and the size of his own middle finger. The way its two smooth sides met at a sharp right angle recalled to him the corners of Luvvie Joolee's white-washed room. It was the stillest place Carl had ever been in: stiller than the Shelter, the doors of which were always open to the breeze; stiller than the blackened interiors of the Hamsters' gaffs, which were ever eddying with smoke, milling with people and motos; stiller even than the deepest thicket in Norfend, where a leaf fragment spun or a scuttlebug trundled.

Carl fingered the broken jagged top of the Davework and looked back towards the island, now wholly encompassed by the ragged edge of the sea. How small it was, and how vast were the waters; if they chose to – if they could will such a thing – they might simply stretch a little and swamp it for ever. The Davework was real: it had a single, enigmatic figure 7 incised in it. Carl recalled the one moving thing in Luvvie Joolee's chamber besides its inhabitant's grooved lips. As she had droned on about the PCO, her husband's sectaries, the politicking of the Guilds – matters of which Carl could not even begin to frame a comprehension – he had watched the dial of the meter. A black stick was pegged to its centre, and when the Exile began the stick was aimed at a 6; when she finished at 7.

The Sentrul Stac mounted from the waves as the Hamstermen's pedalo drew closer. While from the island it gleamed in the foglight, near to it had a dark and impenetrable appearance. The shaggy, shit-spattered greenery merged with glossy seaweed at the point where the swell washed its flanks. The mephitic fumes of the birdshit enveloped them. There were also strange hanks and even coils of a nacreous substance Carl couldn't identify encrusting the base.

– Wossvose? he asked his stepdad, who had shipped his pedal and come forward.

– Vem? Fred laughed. Vemiz oystahs, mì sun, oystahs. Gúd eatin, yeah, we av em on fowlin trips, but we nevah taykem bak oam.

– Y nó?

– Coz vey iz lyttul creetchus an U gotta suckemup alyve, innit.

– Vare 2 taystë 4 ve mummies Bsydes, put in Fukka Funch, an vay lookabit lyke cunt, wooden wannem gettin ennë Ideers!

There was a shout of laughter from the other dads. The separation from Ham was having a paradoxical effect on them: they were all craven in the face of the mighty sea and the sweeping wind, yet dävine and pagan alike felt the dead weight of the Driver's hand lift from them, and this led to ribaldry and defiance. That psychic melding that had occurred a generation before on the voyage to Chil half happened again, and the Hamstermen experienced a complete accord with one another, sniggering and jibing, slapping and teasing the lads.

Fred Ridmun brought them to order, and they pedalled the vessel in below Blakk Stac, which stood about half a click from the Sentrul Stac. Here, in a patch of dead water, they could wait out the hours until darkness, when it would be time for Carl to make the leap.

– Vat Dryva, said Sid Brudi, chewing meditatively on a piece of curried moto as the pedalo rocked gently on the swell, ee stopsus wurkin awl ve tyme, ven sez ee wansus 2 B maw produktiv.

– Yeah, his brother Dave chimed in, maw produktiv but ee wansus 2 getridov ve motos. Iss nó rì.

Carl looked from one thin, green-eyed Brudi to the other. He thought of Salli, and unbidden a memory came to him, of the two of them assisting motos to mate. Salli smëaring Gorj's folds with moto oil, while he, crouching beneath Runti's great sagging tank, guided his tiny cock in.

– Wotevah U fink abaht ve Dryva, said Fred Ridmun, breaking in on Carl's reverie, ee az ve faredar, ee nose ve runs an ve poynts. U ló ardlee no nuffink. Nuffink. We ad bettah caul sumovah nah 4 Daves lukk, yeah?

This appeal to the Hamstermen's religious instincts had the desired result: they put aside their takeaway and, gathering themselves into two cabs – one at the stern, one in the bow – they began to call over. Carl was joined by Fred and four other dads. Äteen! cried Bill Edduns, and Fukka Funch – who had the knowledge of this one – commenced: Leev on leff Marryleebo, leff alsop playce, leff baykastree, forrad pormanskware . . . The arcane words drifted over the waves, and some inquisitive oilgulls came spiralling down from their nests on the Blakk Stac. The fowl floated alongside the pedalo and called over their own rasping Knowledge.

It wasn't until lampoff that the Guvnor halted the calling over. The Hamstermen stowed their gear and took to their pedals. Slowly, the pedalo came out from behind the Blakk Stac and crept over the booze-dark swell, silvered at its peaks by a dipped headlight. Hunched in the bow, wrapped in his cloakyfing, Carl felt little fear. Ever since the pedalo had cast off, in this more compact version of Ham, this floating islet, he felt once again the tight and affectionate enclosure of his early childhood. Whether the jump killed him or not, he was at least accepted.

Where the long skeins of oysters scraped at the sea there were streaks of phosphorescence. A milky deliquescence of birdshit hung in the water at the base of the Sentrul Stac. High above the pedalo in the purpled darkness, the Hamstermen sensed the sleeping blackwings – not so many as there had been earlier in the season, but, from the comings and goings through the long second tariff, they knew there to be thousands. A remorseless coo-burbling was caught by the breeze and flung down to them.

– Ears ve roap. Fred hung the heavy, moto-oiled hank around Carl's neck and shoulder. U jump, U grab, U clyme. Wunce U R up on ve Stac, ve clymin iz eezee enuff slongas U doan slippup. Upontop yul fynd ve stayk eezee enuff 2.

– Eye no, Dad, Eye no, Carl broke in. U toll me 10fowzan tymes awlreddy.

The pedalo nosed in closer and closer, until Carl could make out the first ledge, a man's height above the top of the highest swell. When the bow was only three paces away, he rose. Fukka grabbed the seat of his jeans, and Carl buckled his belt over the hank of rope. His arms were grasped firmly by the Guvnor so that Carl could place his right foot on the stempost. Carl relaxed his legs as the pedalo nosed still closer. Dave B wiv U! came the whispered invocation from the dads, and then, as the pedalo reached the top of a wave, feeling his centre of gravity shift to the point of no return, Carl flung himself into the darkness.

~

Two days later, when, with the tinting screen, the pedalo came wallowing round the eastern cape of Ham and headed for Manna Bä, the anxiety among the waiting mummies had reached a dangerous level. They knew there had been no injuries on the trip, because kids had been dispatched each morning to the giant's gaff on the margin of the Gayt, from where the top of the Sentrul Stac could be clearly seen. If one of the fowling party had been injured, the dads would have scraped away some of the cap of shit on the summit. Yet this did not discount the possibility of a fatality, for there was no point in giving any warning of such a dread eventuality. If a dad had died on the expedition, then the mourning would be both extreme and protracted. As the pedalo drew closer, the mummies made ready to rend their cloakyfings and beat their brows. A widow would swoon and feign death herself for the first blob. She would take no food and accept only water trickled through a sphagnum sponge. She would soil herself and lie prostrate. The exigencies of tending her – together with the funeral calling over for the dead dad – would paralyse the working life of the community; so, in part, the Hamsters' worry was not simply for the loss of a beloved but also a fearful anticipation of these privations.

Bert Ridmun waded out into the chilly water to hail the returnees: Orlrì?! And when his dad's voice boomed back, Orlrì! a whoop went up from the Hamsters on the shore. Another few units and they saw that the gunnels of the vessel were within a hand's breadth of the waterline, so overloaded was it with blackwings. Carl was standing up in the bow, a triumphant grin on his face. As the keel grounded on the sandy shingle, he leaped into the waiting arms of the Hamsterwomen, who petted and caressed him with many tender cries. Salli Brudi was with them, and she had a special intensity as she brushed his cracked lips with the back of her freckled hand. Looking up from the unaccustomed cuddle, Carl was confronted by the mirror: in it were the hooked beak and mad yellow eyes of the Driver. The old crow glared hatred at the lad. Nevertheless, he understood the situation well enough: in the Hamsters' minds such bounty drove out any thoughts of Breakup for the moment. The Driver turned and stalked away towards the Shelter.

To be replaced, on the fringes of the crowd unloading the pedalo, by the rubicund face of Antonë Böm, who came forward at once to assist. He was greeted with much warmth by the fowlers. Orlrì, Ant, they said clapping him on the shoulder, looki vis 1, and they thrust into his arms the floppy carcass of a blackwing. However, there was little time for chitchat since the fowl had to be unloaded and stored in the fridges for the night. At first tariff the serious business of dividing the catch, plucking, gutting and currying them would begin.

The following evening there would be a Dave's curry – the last of the year. Fred Ridmun would offer up half his own share, together with half that of the stack jumper, for the consumption of the rest. A further quarter portion of the Guvnor's would be snuck away to the Gayt and placed before the monumental bronze head that lay near the southern shore. Despite the calling over of the

Driver, most Hamsters remained convinced that this enigmatic, bearded visage was that of Dave himself. The quantifiable offering was significant, for, as exact as they were in all aspects of their property – according ownership to the last peck of wheatie and drip of oil – so their cohesion was preserved by gifting. Power resided not among those who retained their bounty but among those who divested themselves of it.

Eased by the hottest cupasoup the opares could provide, his aching limbs massaged with oil, his curry-cracked feet bathed, Carl sat in front of the fire in the Brudi gaff and absorbed the warm fug. He had recounted his jump and the scramble up the stack. He had frightened the little ones with his vivid enactment of his near-fall, as he leaned low to grab the sentinel blackwing and his hands slipped on the rope. He told how he had hung from a buddyspike root for long units and the memory ghost had visited him, so that he saw the Sentrul Stac sheathed in golden glass, and through this translucent skin appeared beautiful angels, clad in jeans and jackets of the finest cut. They were playing upon curious plastic instruments and their silent airs were kaleidoscopes of imagery on sparkling mirrors.

The Guvnor looked on approvingly, for this too was the way of it: the stack jumper's tale was a vital addition to the story the community told of itself, one of humans spitting in the indifferent face of Nature. After Carl had recounted it in this gaff, he would sally forth and retell it in all the others, until the entire manor was buzzing with his accomplishment.

Pausing, flushed with this approbation, and preparing to dive under the stone lintel of the Funch gaff, Carl saw a pale flash at the end of the manor. For an instant he wanted to ignore the signal, but what then? He sloshed down the sodden bank of the stream. Screenwash was falling, softening the night, and his feet were numb. Antonë Böm was waiting for him at the seaward end of the Dévúsh gaff, his broad back propped against the mossy brick. It was so dark that Carl could only make out his mentor's beard, wavering like a moth.

– Eyev bin bizzë, he said without any preamble, Eye gó ve geer awl stashed up bì ve wallos. Takeaway, oil an evian – awl Eye cúd nik wivaht bein sussed. We gotta go nah, Carl, rì nah.

– But Eye onlee juss gó bak, innit. Eye onlee juss toal mì storë an vat . . . As Carl trailed off, Böm's hand tightened on his arm, his face came up close, the lenses of his spectacles were two owlish discs.

– Carl, he said simply, we go nah aw nevah. Nah aw nevah.

The night pressed in on them, a nightjar chirred, the sea snatched at the shoreline. Carl felt the whole of his life slipping away – perhaps it would have been better to have fallen from the Stac? He had a sudden image of his body lying in the milky waves, the gulls pecking at his bloody face.

~

When Fred Ridmun, early to rise, opened the heavy door of the gaff to admit the foglight to its dark interior, he first noticed that Dave's demister had powered up, leaving a bright autumnal day. Then, tracking the bigwatt from the doorway, he saw lying in its exact oblong the copy of the Book that was held by the Guvnor. It was open on the table, a handful of Daveworks scattered on its thick yellow A4s. He let out a cry that woke the rest of the dads. For Fred Ridmun knew immediately what this meant: it was the Hamster way that a traveller departing on a journey off the island left the Book thus, and therefore his stepson must be gone.

Tyga and Sweetë, old Runti's mopeds, had been easy to drive. They always foraged in the woodlands immediately beyond the wallows. Hunnë and Champ, Pippin's mopeds, were a trickier proposition. Carl left Antonë with half the rank and the changingbags, while he ventured down into Sandi Wúd. Foglight streamed between the trees, while up above them piled brilliant white clouds, their undersides glowing mauve and orange. New leaf fall swished beneath Carl's feet, and, despite his haste to find the motos, he was still awed by the beauty of his homeland.

At last, Carl found the two motos on the shoreline below the thick undergrowth of Turnas Wúd. They were sunk deep in a slough covered with dead brack and leaves. He roused them by gently stroking their jonckheeres, then brought them fully to consciousness by whispering his plan into their floppy ears. He knew that any resistance on their part would thus be forestalled, for motos would accept any idea – no matter how unusual – as simply an aspect of the new world they'd awoken to. Weer goin onna big wallo, he cooed, me an U 2, an Ant an Tyga an Sweetë. Biggist wallo evah, gonna B luvverlë – yul C.

Hunnë drew her legs up beneath her bulk, rolled sideways on to her slopping tank and then hefted first her front and then her rear end upright. Champ followed suit, with much snorting and gobbling, until he too was on all fours. Wegonna wawwow, Cawl? he asked. Thass rì, said Carl, grabbing a handful of each beast's wattles, and with expert tugs moved them off along the coast towards Mutt Bä. Although the big creatures were still only half awake, they were as surefooted as ever, their long fingers and toes neatly grasping the tree roots that snaked underfoot. Their shuddery breathing smoked the air, and their hot, damp withers gently steamed. Carl buried his hands deeper in the clammy neck folds. Nothing else in the world gave him a feeling of such secure content, and even if he had to leave Ham then at least he'd be taking with him its unique natives. Surely, with four motos to accompany them, the journey to London could not prove too arduous?

He settled Tyga and Sweetë at Mutt Bä, then returned to the wallows, where he found Böm pacing nervously and casting fearful looks towards the manor. Fyahs iz smoakin, he said, vey muss B up, we gotta moovit, Carl. Then all was a pell-mell descent through the woods back down to the shore, Tyga and Sweetë jogging, tanks and changingbags bouncing against their thick necks. The two humans struggled to keep up with them, and Carl was frantic that when the two halves of the rank met up their nuzzling would dislodge the loads.

As it was, Carl and Antonë slithered between the last few trees to find not only the motos butting and bumping but a far more disturbing sight: the Driver. His beard and hair were in wild disarray, his robe was hitched up above his legs, and he wasn't even wearing his mirror. He was brandishing a staff. Oi, U! he screamed as he clapped eyes on them. U – U! He was quite beside himself, swishing the heavy staff back and forth in the air, turning to confront first the motos, then the escapees. Wot djoo fink yaw doin? he managed to say at last. Böm backed off, placing a stand of blisterweed between himself and the hysterical man of Dave, but Carl was suddenly enraged. He ran over and grabbed Tyga's ear, then drove the moto off the rank. Sorlrì, Tyga, he told him, weer juss goin 4 vat big wallo lyke Eye sed. They advanced together on the Driver.

Carl knew that, despite his long stay on Ham, the Driver had never lost his initial revulsion for the motos; now, in this charged moment, Tyga's gaping jaws and peg teeth struck terror into him. Dropping his staff, the Driver reared back, tripped, then fell headlong to the ground, where he lay motionless. Wassamatter wivim, Cawl? Issë urtë? Tyga goggled at the black stain of the Driver's robe on the carpet of leaves. Antonë knelt and lifted up the Driver's head. Ees it a brik, he said, ees aht cold. Nah we reelë gotta moovit. Swiftly the two men stripped and coated themselves with a slather of moto oil.

Carl had splashed in the shallows with the motos, yet he had no idea if the beasts would consent to bear him and Antonë into open water. The rank was orderly if excitable as he led them down to the shoreline. Only Sweetë moaned:

– Eye wanna fowidj, lemme fowidj.

– Plennë uv fowidj ovah vare, Carl told her, pointing to the distance, where the rocks of Nimar rose up above the waves. Cummon nah.

He coaxed Tyga a few paces into the sea, then, grasping a handful of neck wattle, swung himself on to the moto's broad back. Behind him Antonë followed suit with Champ. Cummon nah! Carl urged Tyga on, and, feeling the rising water buoy up his body, the moto began to paddle strongly. Eye thwimmin! Eye thwimmin! he lisped. Looking back, Carl saw the two other motos enter the water after Antonë and Champ. As they came out of the bay, then scraped across the reef, the waves began to break over Tyga's back, and Carl was instantly soaked. His anger had drained away with the advancing sea to be replaced by a naked terror. Yet, looking back at the shore, he saw the Driver still lying prone, final confirmation – if any were needed – that there was no going back.

# 6

## *The Skip Tracer*

April 2002

When Michelle came out of the lawyers' offices, which were sunk in the isthmus of nineteenth-century stonework separating Savile Row from Vigo Street, her logical course would have been to take a cab. She had become a cab-hailing type of bird – she had the money, she had the gym-toned wing to fling in the air, she was even dressed for it in a fashionable mac like a shiny red bell tent. Her hair had recently been dyed its natural colour – only more so. Yet she couldn't hail a cab; if an orange TAXI sign had shone out from the London downpour she'd have turned tail and flapped away. The likelihood that it was driven by her ex-husband, Dave, was infinitesimal, still the Law of Sod said it would be him, echo-locating her by bouncing a screech of anger off the buildings and picking it up with his bat ears. He was that mad.

'I honestly think he's mad,' Michelle had said to the lawyer, whose name was Blair. 'There's already a restraining order to prevent him coming near to the house.' She felt comfortable with the 'honestly'; it sounded right for this dark wood panelling and thick, turquoise carpet.

'But he's breached it, yes?' Blair took notes on a yellow legal pad with a gold propelling pencil. He was leaning far back in his leather swivel chair and had to stretch to reach the notepad. This emphasized his petiteness.

'Well . . . yeah . . . I mean pretty drastically so far as I can see. My . . . partner and I saw him in the garden, at night, but he ran off.'

'And this was in December?'

'Yeah.' *Yeah? You sound like trailer-park trash.*

'You didn't report it to the police?' Blair raised one plucked eyebrow on his sallow forehead.

'That's what Fischbein – the other lawyer – asked us. We were so shocked, it'd never happened before.' Michelle took a sip of coffee: it was tepid, and she put the bone-china cup down next to a plate of refined shortbread. 'When he broke the order again we did call the police, but there was nothing we could get him for, because . . . because . . . my son . . . he wouldn't . . .' Michelle gulped down hot tears with more tepid coffee. *I'm gonna start crying now* . . . the thought of being offered a tissue by Blair – who'd asked her to call him 'Mitchell' – nauseated her. Not that Blair made any move to dispense tissues; he remained recumbent and tapped his unnaturally small teeth with the tip of his pencil. Michelle controlled herself and went on: 'My son wouldn't say anything against his father – that's what he told me. Still, he doesn't want his dad turning up like that, outside his new school. It upsets him . . . his dad acts . . . I dunno, crazy, but Carl's very loyal . . . He's angry with both of us.'

Then it came pouring out of her, the whole sorry, stereotypical tale. Yet even as Michelle recounted the clouts Dave Rudman had aimed at her and the crockery he'd hurled, the way the volume of the rows had risen into a vacuous silence, followed by the lawyers' letters and the fruitless mediation, she was aware that this was precisely what Mitchell Blair required. He might have spent hours extracting this evidence from her; instead it came bagged, tagged and slammed down on his Moroccan leather desktop. The gold pencil raced across the narrow feint to keep pace with her.

When Michelle had finished – or at any rate ceased, for there could be no end to such a litany – Blair cleared his throat: 'Erhem.' 'Ms Brodie,' he said, 'may I summarize?' He smiled. 'Your ex-husband was physically and mentally abusive within the marriage.

You divorced on those grounds and your only son, Carl, initially stayed with you at the family home. Your husband moved to a rented flat near by. To begin with they had normal contact, alternate weekends and Wednesday visits, half school holidays when Mr Rudman's . . . ah, work, permitted. During this time he, ah, behaved himself well enough. Then, when last year you began a relationship with Mr Devenish, and you and your son moved in with him to a new house in Hampstead, your ex-husband became abusive again. Increasingly so. He turned up at your house and banged on the door; he also made threats which led to . . . Mr Fischbein obtaining a non-molestation order through the County Court, although your son continued to have contact with his father.'

'Carl's old enough to go to see his father by himself. I didn't want to stop them seeing each other.'

'Quite so. But now the situation has changed again, your ex-husband's behaviour is highly erratic, and you feel that –'

'I dunno what I feel, but I'm worried about what Dave might do. Fischbein said it was difficult to get a further injunction unless Dave had been arrested – I don't want to wait for that to happen, I don'tthinkitsrightthat –' Michelle's words tumbled out, Blair caught them in his plump hands, set them down in the opulent solemnity of the office. The air was stilled by leather-bound precedents – they might have been anywhere, or even in another, quieter era.

'What Mr Fischbein says of the Family Division at County Court may well be true, but, given the right approach' – Blair paused to emphasize that such an approach was a Blair speciality – 'it is entirely possible to obtain a total exclusion order from the Principal Registry in the High Court. If this is breached, a power of arrest is automatically invoked carrying a committal warrant for six months' imprisonment. As to visitation rights, if you insist on these continuing, there can be supervised access.'

'Me?' Michelle was nonplussed. 'If *I* insist?'

'That's right, but you may regard it as in your best interests for any contact between your son and your ex-husband to be stopped at once.'

Michelle had sat through years of deliberations with lawyers, mediators, court welfare officers and Child Support Agency assessors: 'your best interests' was not a phrase she had heard during all this time; 'the child's best interests' certainly; there had also been much talk of 'the relationship's interests', as if it were an entity in its own right; but her own, unalloyed, selfish interests had never been alluded to. 'I'm sorry . . . Mister Blair.'

'Mitchell.' He smiled again with the titchy gnashers.

'I'm not used to what I want being talked about so . . . so . . .'

'Bluntly, Ms Brodie? If you retain me I act in *your* interests. There's a lot of nonsense talked in family law, and I'm not in the habit of contributing to it. If you require an order against your ex-husband with more' – he tapped them with the pencil – 'teeth, that is something I can arrange. The law – like any other art – is one of the possible.'

~

Glancing over her shoulder as she joined the parade of rainwear heading west along Oxford Street, Michelle saw schools of snorting black cabs, pods of red bus leviathans, and beyond it all the towering stack of Centrepoint rising up from the swell of masonry. A single sunbeam fingering its way through the dirty clouds picked out its concrete summit. She shuddered. Where was it now, the internal warmth of that long-maintained secret? The secret that had sutured up the bloody gash of Carl's birth, that had annulled every awful moment of her marriage to Dave Rudman, the secret that justified any number of Blairy bills whirling down like A4 snowflakes on to Cal Devenish's desk?

Michelle shuffled on past the cut-and-shut architecture of Oxford Street – the top storeys of Loire chateaux cemented to provincial car showrooms. In Selfridges she lost herself in the Food Hall among others of her kind: trim, middle-aged, nouveau riche women, anatomizing the ideal snack under lights of operating-theatre strength. This, surely, was what had been meant for her all along? The Queen Anne house in Hampstead, the coffee breaks with interior designers, and the trip home from the West End where she'd been visiting her expensive lawyer, bearing no malice but instead a glossy paper bag, inside it a bottle of L'Occitane Lavender Body Cream.

The mineshaft of the Northern Line gave way, once Michelle had been winched up through the heavy hill, to the pithead of Hampstead. She walked up Heath Street, which was shining under April sun after a low-pressure hosing. The shop windows were clotted with affluence – the pavements busy with the economically unproductive. Halfway up the hill Michelle passed Liberation, the lingerie shop she owned in partnership with her new friend Peter Prince. The window was thronged with knickers: flesh pink, organdie and eau-de-Nil scraps, worth, weight for weight, more than currency and *hardly flying out of the place.*

Two flights of stairs curled up from each side to the glossy maroon front door of Beech House. Twelve twelve-paned windows looked down on the narrow lane below – a gross of affluence. Michelle was still thinking about pants. *Dave didn't take them off when he came to bed . . . disgusting paisley Y-fronts with white piping . . . I couldn't bear to touch them, if he guided my hand there I yanked it away. I could do it with him after exactly three glasses of wine, but his prick always felt small inside me, like a pip I could squeeze out . . . Then later, when the rows got violent, I lost all feeling in my tits . . . That GP said I should do a regular self-examination for lumps . . . Sod the fucking lumps – with Dave pawing me my tits were numb . . . numb with disgust . . .*

The way that Beech House had been freshly tricked out could have been wholly deduced from the lacquered Chinese box full of decorative walking sticks that stood beside the front door. Michelle looked across the hall to where a door opened on to a kitchen fitted with slate worktops, quarry-tiled floor and oaken units. *To be fair, he was always lying down in the hollow Cal had left in my bed . . . When Cal came back and we made love for the first time after so many years I thought I'd be embarrassed – him seeing what having a kid had done to me . . . my floppy white belly, my stretch marks. It wasn't like that at all* . . . Shucking off her shiny mac, Michelle hugged her own baby-soft cashmere shoulders. *Being naked in the daylight with him . . . it made me as young as a child . . . He felt like a father as much as a lover when he took off my dress* . . . Sweat prickled her brow as she sheathed her umbrella in the box. *My father and Carl's. Then afterwards we slept so sweetly, such sweet dreams . . .*

In the humming silence of the mid-afternoon house, redolent of beeswax, Michelle Brodie stared hungrily at the television in the kitchen: a packet of humdrum delights. From outside in the road she heard a tinkling 'Byeee!' and could imagine the girl in the brindled uniform of an exclusive Highgate school, her glossy mane and chocolate shoes. But before she could move towards the kettle and the television, Michelle sensed a presence in the house, faint – but threatening. She rushed into the drawing room to find Cal bedded down in the Eames chair, the pink and black patchwork of the *Financial Times* spread on his slow-rising chest.

Michelle woke him up with a cup of Earl Grey. She told him about Blair and the letter he was going to send to her ex – he made the right noises, but his mind was in two other places. 'I can't face another day like today,' he sighed when it was his turn. 'There are consultants and accountants all over the offices like flies on a fucking corpse . . . and . . . and I told Saskia I'd go to find Daisy . . .' Michelle switched her grimace into a smirk of sympathy. If Cal noticed this, he chose not to remark on it; he understood. Daisy stank.

Cal Devenish – former writer, former hell raiser, now the emollient yet forceful face of Channel Devenish – was exhausted. The production company he'd taken over six years ago was being sold to an American media conglomerate. The business had been a wrinkled little thing when Cal got it; now it was a taut balloon of gassy cash. Devenish had developed a series of hit programmes: *Tumour Swap*, *TWOC Rally*, *Whorecam* – and especially *Blackie*, a kids' show featuring a depressed spaniel that had been globally syndicated. As well as being a shrewd purveyor of eyetrash to the myopic, Cal was also a panellist on arts review shows and current events forums, a wag and a wit. He'd skilfully blended his waning creativity with orange foundation cream, then slapped it all over his face so that it didn't shine under the studio lights. He bestrode the steadily narrowing gulf between high culture and low entertainment like a credible, shrinking colossus. Even if he managed to flog Channel Devenish – and this was by no means in the bag – he was still going to have to do a management workout, three years in the shafts of corporate carters, while maintaining his public profile – because they wanted that as well.

Devenish's career change had come with his recovery from addiction to cocaine, alcohol and commercial sex. Not that he pursued this recovery actively any more. There had been the predictable treatment centre, a Jenga of gables in the Greenbelt, where counsellors nutty as walnuts cracked other nutters with their shells. After that he did therapy for a while – both individual and group – so that he might irrigate his costive immaturity. Then he took to the gym, which tempered his skinny limbs, and acquired a goatee like a neat hairy portcullis, which, oddly, gave him gravitas. Now Cal worked all the hours he could, and when he wasn't working he was dealing with his troublesome daughter or moping around the house, never saying – although clearly thinking . . . *what the fuck have I got myself into with this woman and her mad bloody ex-husband. Her sulky son . . . where will it all end?*

They didn't fight, though. They never raised their voices. They had a great deal of compatible secrecy – which would serve as intimacy for a while. As they were working their way gingerly through this minefield of mutuality, the front door opened, then explosively slammed, the fanlight rattled, the stairs reverberated, and Carl's bedroom door provided the final report that an adolescent was in the house. Michelle became acutely aware of him . . . *my sweety, my honey* . . . sitting up there on the end of his bed, disdaining the pastel-painted work unit, complete with personal computer, ignoring the framed posters of Tintin book covers on the candy-striped walls, instead pawing yet again through the box of kiddy stuff that he'd brought with him from Gospel Oak. Shabby memorabilia of a time before he moved up in the world: an incredibly battered Hulk; some broken Beyblades; a toy London cab driven by a faceless plastic cabbie. Stuck through the window of the cab was a shard of plastic the size of Carl's middle finger. Why it should be talismanic he'd long since forgotten – he could not recall his father demolishing the telephone with its own receiver, nor himself, dutifully collecting the bits and storing them in his toy box – a small archaeologist of the immediate past.

At dinner – eaten en famille complete with candles, linen napkins and powered cruets – Carl sat sullenly. His downy top lip caught the rays from the spotlights, his gelled hair glistened like seaweed, a pimple – hard and yellow as a nose stud – was in the right position to be one. The odour of hormonal surge and pre-emptive aftershave hung about his sharp shoulders. Conversational sallies from his mother were slapped down with single syllables, Cal's simply allowed to fall. Carl's moodiness might have been within the acceptable range of adolescent disaffection – or way off the dial. It was impossible to judge without a control experiment: another world with different rituals, taboos and family groupings, but the same blond boy.

When Cal, rising from tiramisu, clapped his sort of stepson on the shoulder, bent to kiss the top of Michelle's head and turned to go, a shiver of relief shook the tall room. The Op-Art swirls on the walls dilated – and he was gone to his BMW convertible. Michelle, abandoning her son to the television and the dishes to the morning Pole, trudged upstairs to dissolve her face in bottled alcohol and brush her dry lips with Clarins Moisturizing Lip Balm.

~

There was no forethought on Dave's part. He simply kept ending up here at Mill Hill, up on the Ridgeway, clambering over the fence opposite the National Institute for Medical Research, crossing the nursery-school playground, scaling a second fence, then standing staring towards the Hampstead massif, which rose like an island out of the evening traffic stream on the North Circular. He hadn't intended it – it was the fares that brought him there. His Faredar wasn't working. Instead of detecting *know-nothings wiv deep pockets*, he got *pub-quiz misers*.

At two that afternoon Dave had been grating the cab along Stamford Street towards Waterloo . . . *another bit of fucking metal scraped till it wangs off*. In the steely jam, rain-washed manufacturers' logos shone: PLAXTON, JONCKHEERE, FORD. Windscreen wipers smeared, drivers sneered at pedestrians, cyclists veered to avoid everything. The fare was *one of those cunts* who thought he knew the city, thought he knew the real stories behind the news, thought he knew *the mind of bloody God, 'cause 'e's the Flying-fucking-Eye* . . . and was eager to share it with his paid-for listener. He'd deliberated possible routes. 'I mean, Westminster Bridge is the obvious way' – mulling over traffic flows – 'but there might be an argument for cutting through Covent Garden and avoiding the traffic' – and roadworks – 'there's a lane out going through Admiralty Arch and that means the Mall'll be backed up.' Dave wanted to kill him: *What you don't understand is that I don't bloody care. I just follow the route most likely to get us there with the minimum hassle. I don't make any extra money for sitting in traffic, and besides, I want SHOT OF*

*YOU*. 'It's entirely up to you, sir, if you know a quicker way, I'm only too happy to take it.'

'No, no, driver, you do your thing, you're the professional.' The fare sat back in his seat with a self-satisfied smile that filled the rearview mirror. *Happy now, aren't yer, because you're another fucking control freak who finks 'e's swallered a Trafficmaster.*

Dave dropped the fare off and drove on round the elevated roadway to the front of the station, where stone giantesses mourn the death of its builders on Flanders Field. He ranked up and marched away past Delice de France, Upper Crust, Van Heusen, M&S Simply Food, The Reef, Burger King and Tie Rack, then down into the temple of hiss and piss, where he could wring the neck of his suicidal dick. *What was it Big End used to say? 'I love myself so much when I hold my dick to piss I get a fucking hard-on.'*

Back at the rank Dave's Fairway was holding things up. Two or three trains must have arrived simultaneously, because the fifty-odd cabs were divided among the hundred-odd punters within five minutes. 'North!' the new fare barked without looking at Dave, as if she were crying 'Mush!' to a husky. And when Dave ventured, 'Anywhere more specific, madam?' the fare barked: 'Belsize Park!' Then sat there, her exploratory face pressed to the window as Dave dragged the metal sleigh back through the West End, Euston and Camden Town.

*Dried-up old stick, look at 'er . . . no one would want a crack at that . . .* Dave kept casting glances in the mirror at the hated fare, and, as if responding to this, the woman got out her compact and began dabbing beige dust on a mole. *Got 'er own mirror, eh . . . what's she got to look at innit, only the same fucking face day in, day out. Mindjoo, these old boilers – they've got their own Knowledge, that's true enough.*

The fare wanted Heath Hospital, but was either too grand or too embarrassed to say so until they were roaring down Pond Street, then she ordered him: 'Here!' Dave pulled over outside the Roebuck. The fare tipped generously, then unfolded a gossamer umbrella and flew, like a *fairy-fucking-grandmother*, into the lobby. Dave found himself alone, at four thirty in the afternoon, on the shores of Hampstead. The other points at the end of this run came unbidden: *Anthony Nolan Trust, Armoury Sports Hall, Hampstead Hill Gardens, Hampstead Magistrates Court, Holiday Inn, Keats Museum . . .*

A nervous Japanese woman got into the cab at the Southend Green rank. *No questions asked as to why the detour if we're going to Hendon Central . . . she might as well be in fucking Osaka . . . Osaka . . . tourists . . . flyers . . .* A memory rose up and bumped against the underside of his consciousness . . . *Just before Christmas . . . the nervous City getter on his way out to 'eathrow. 'You can't tell me, Beaky, that it's all off the back of* Bluey *– or whatever that stupid kids' show is called . . .'* His card was still tucked under the clip on the dashboard – so was Sid Gold's. The fare gave a little yelp as Dave arm-wrestled the steering wheel while reading the business card CB & EFN INVESTMENT STRATEGIES, STEPHEN BRICE, CEO EUROPE. *That's it . . . there's stuff there on Devenish . . . If they're going to do it to me – I'll do it to them first . . . Gold'll know someone . . . An investigator . . . a private dick . . .*

Dave dropped *the Jap* at a hotel he'd never noticed before, four semis knocked into one dull frontage. Palms in half-barrels sat on a tarmac apron. A sign flashed RALEIGH COURT in the gathering dusk. She picked up her carrier bags, shouldered her Hello Kitty rucksack and paid what was on the meter. Dave drove on up to Mill Hill, the National Institute for Medical Research calling to him, its copper roof shining over the tiled valley.

Once there Dave took up his position on top of Drivers Hill, and, finding card and mobile phone mysteriously in his hand, he made the call, not expecting anyone to be there at this late hour *. . . least of all a bent fucker like Gold who's gotta be propping up the bar in China White, one hand on a Bellini, the other up a tart's skirt . . .* The wind whooshed in Dave's ear but Gold's 100%-sure-of-itself voice was closer still. He remembered Dave, saying in response to his muttered request, 'No trouble, Dave, I know a geezer, you gotta pen and paper?'

Cal Devenish drove south. The traffic was light enough – a steel spatter on the bluffs of Kingsway. On the south side of Waterloo Bridge, the National Theatre was lit up, *a giant sugar cube soaked with cultural vaccine*. Inside his fellow bourgeoisie sucked sweets and watched Imogen and Ralph play at queens and kings. While not far off, in Brixton, Cal's ex-wife, Saskia, was lying on her crapped-out sofabed, their preposterous granddaughter clamped in her arms. The baby slept, blowing milky bubbles against its grandmother's hammering heart.

'She's done a runner again, Cal,' Saskia had cried that afternoon, a cry Cal heard via the phone as he drove home to Hampstead. He'd frozen for a moment – caught between crushing bergs of work and family – before answering, 'I thought she was on a locked ward?'

'You thought! You . . . thought!' Saskia snorted. 'That's novel!' She was standing, he supposed, in her kitchen. Toast crusts, apple cores, damp clouts, canisters of decadent marjoram and a greasy oven glove lay on the worktop. On the windowsill a miniature mesa of cacti supported a greenfly colony. 'They didn't have her on a section – she's gone!'

'I'll . . . I'll go and find her . . . later . . .' He'd manoeuvred the Beamer on to Hampstead Road. Laurence Corner, the army-surplus shop, was still open. *I ought to pick up a mattock and a water bottle, I'll be needing them . . . later.*

'You do that,' Saskia snapped.

To be fair, Cal thought now, as he turned down York Road, whatever Saskia's lunacies – the shopworn socialism, the maintenance-funded 'creativity', the double-barrels (bi-polar, obsessive-compulsive, manic-depressive, personality disorder) through which she shot at their daughter's pathology – the facts were simple: she'd been a single mother for thirteen years, and now she was a single grandmother. *Some fucker rubbed his legs on Daisy's petals, then buzzed off again.* And she, either hammered by Largactil or ranting on garage forecourts, was in no fit state to care for a baby. *Shit . . . they had to tie her down and knock her out for the delivery.* Even if she'd been sane, *she was only sixteen . . .*

He talked to the duty psychiatrist at St Thomas's, a distant, pharaonic figure. 'Yes, Mr Devenish . . . your daughter, Daisy. I understand your concern.' *But don't share it, obviously.* 'Her GP hadn't been in touch, and the consultant here hadn't made any provision. We had no grounds for holding her against her will.' *Except that she's a fucking loony.* 'She was quite lucid when she left . . . said she was going back' – he consulted a tan transcript – 'to Driscoll House?'

Unwilling to abandon sickroom security, Cal stood for a while by the double doors, looking towards Westminster Bridge. On the lobby floor, in front of the shuttered coffee shop, a ham and tomato sandwich was reduced by scurrying feet to a smear of red, brown and pink.

Heading south down the Old Kent Road, Cal felt mangling hands of anxiety on his neck. He remembered the girl found dead in the fountains at Marlborough Gate. Three days fouling up a tourist attraction – when they dragged her out in her sodden stonewashed jeans she was unidentifiable.

That morning he'd been roused by the whale song of marital farts, semiconscious leviathans calling to one another across a glutinous ocean of duck down. 5 a.m. and fully awake . . . Cal looked at Michelle's profile etched on the pillow beside him by the acid light of a London dawn. *She's holding out on me, I know it. There's something she isn't telling me – it doesn't add up. Her secret is soft – she moulds it to evade detection. It's hidden inside her body – she's a mule . . .*

Low down on the scabrous underbelly of South London, the BMW raced from one shopping parade to the next. From OK Chicken to Perfect Chicken, from Bootiful Chicken to Luvverly Chicken, from Royal Chicken to Chicken Imperium, from Chicken Universe to one forlorn joint in the filthy crotch of Burgess Park that was simply dubbed 'Chicken'. Down here, where men wore nylon snoods, the light industrial premises massed and every public, horizontal thing was planted with metal thorns, Cal felt the turbid threat of the city, which might choose – quite impersonally – to climb into the car at the lights and suggest, at gunpoint, that he step out.

Driscoll House, built in 1913, was Castle Dossula. Vast and four-square, beneath its crenellations ranged scores of loopholes, behind each a rental embrasure. Weekly rates were pegged to the emergency-housing benefit. The security door was propped open with a pallet. Cal made inquiries at a battered plexiglas window. Then he was led along a corridor. Doors opened to either side and faces emerged, pitted, veined and puce. Their owners were drinking fortified wine with Antabuse chasers, and the stop-start strain on their sclerotic hearts was going to kill them stone-dead.

The string-vested seneschal stopped in front of No. 137 and unlocked it with a key from his enormous bunch. Inside were knickers in a twist and jeans draped over a chair; a cheap candle had melted into a Formica tabletop and curled over like a limp dick. 'She wozere,' said the seneschal, ''coz I 'eard 'er carryin' on wiv 'owie.'

'Howie?' Cal queried, although from other Daisy hunts he recognized the name.

'Jock geezer, piggy ring in 'is 'ooter, sells the *Issue*. Collects bottles. Drinks wiv a school dahn at ve Bullring, but 'e azza flop in Mottingham.'

Mottingham was so far out on the outskirts of the city that the avenues the BMW swished along were damp with the sweeter showers of the countryside beyond. At bucolic roundabouts cellophane-wrapped flowers were stacked up to mark the site of fatal collisions. The makeshift shrines were garlanded with plastic gewgaws and papered with scrawled cards; so the prosaic, the accidental, was factored into a Divine Plan for London.

At the address the seneschal had given him Cal found two black teenagers smoking weed and watching a video of a nightmare on another street. A tenner elicited a further address, where '’owie an' ’is bird' had gone to score. At this location – a plyboard warren of bedsits in a venerable Victorian villa – the finder's fee was upped to twenty quid. Finally, at 3.30 a.m., Cal ran her to ground, dry-heaving under a rhododendron bush in the gardens of a derelict pub. The huaraches he'd brought her back from Mexico lay discarded near by. In the silence between his daughter's spasms Cal could hear a nightjar churring, although he thought it was a scooter accelerating along the A20. When he got her into the car, Daisy began to babble about the environment. There was no sign of Howie.

~

'What's the baddest thing in the world, Dad?'

'What did ya say, Tiger?'

'Dad, what's the baddest thing in the world?' Carl stood before Dave in baby elephant pyjama trousers. His front teeth were big white pegs in his chubby six-year-old face. 'Dad, what's the baddest thing in the world?' He repeated himself, and then, because he was a bright kid, never confused like his father by the sheer amorphousness of everything, he supplied his own answer: 'Is it killing yourself?'

Dave Rudman, on his knees in the North London playing field, looked south to where his son *is banged up* . . . He wept and clawed at the grass. He salaamed, head-butting the ground. *Fuck you, earth*

. . . and the blow stove in the roof of a vault full of nastiness. *I was in their garden . . . in their fucking garden . . . I buried it in their garden . . . that mad fucking rant . . . Why did I do it? Why? It put me eleven fucking grand out of pocket, that's why I'm skint – that's why I can't pay Cohen, that's why I'm mushing every fucking hour of the day . . .*

'*What's the baddest thing in the world, Dad?*' Dave imagined six-year-old Carl sitting cross-legged by the mess his father had made, picking up a lolly stick and dabbling it in the mud.

'Worst,' Dave croaked aloud, 'the worst thing in the world is to kill yourself, Tiger, but not if you do it to stop yourself killing someone else.'

~

In the Trophy Room of the Swiss Cottage Sports Centre – group rental £25 per hour, pick up and leave the key at main reception – the Fathers First group did laps in liquid anger, thrashing up and down the lanes, the chlorine of hatred stinging their eyes. 'I'm gonna fucking kill her!' bellowed Billy O'Neil. He was standing in spotless Timberlands, his manicured fists were clenched, the sweat stood out on his tousled brow. 'Calm down, Billy,' Keith Greaves said, 'please calm down.' Billy couldn't hear him – nor could the other premier-division dads. They watched, appalled and yet entranced, as the big man was manipulated by the dextrous fist of rage. Rage that pulled on the strings threaded through all their lives, so they poked their own little fists into others' faces, kicked their feet into kidneys, and slammed car doors so hard the glass disintegrated into *'ackney diamonds*. Dave Rudman's face was in his hands; his fingers sought out the shameful scars of his failed hair transplant. 'Calm down, Billy,' Keith said again – while Dave began to cry.

~

Carl understood that it was part of the whole expensive package. Along with Cal Devenish came Beech House, the Range Rover Vogue, the Tuscan holidays and of course the *poncey fucking school*. Privilege sucked – he longed for his dad. Longed for Dave, who took him out in the cab and showed him parts of the city – Wormwood Scrubs, Lea Bridge, the Honor Oak Reservoir – which the *'ampstead wankers* would never see. In the past three years, as he'd seen Dave less and less, so Carl's idea of his father had come unstuck, detaching itself from both any foundation in the past and the increasingly disturbing reality of the man.

In Carl's view, Dave was a knight of the open road. He knew the city and he knew its people. Dave was as at home up West in a fancy restaurant as he was in Muratori's, the cabbies' King's Cross café. Everyone knew him – cops, bartenders, fellow cabbies, waver-uppers – knew him and respected him. 'Orlright, Tufty!' they sang out as the Fairway squealed to a halt and chip and block got out. So on the fateful day, last October, when Carl came out of the elaborate wrought-iron gates of his new school and there was his dad, hunched down at the wheel of the cab, unshaven, white gunk at the corners of his peeling lips, oily patches under his burnt-out eyes, it was a dreadful shock. 'Cummear, son,' Dave growled, 'cummear.'

Carl's first instinct was to run. Boys in his class had already spotted the odd apparition: a London taxi cab parked in Frognal at four in the afternoon. Not dropping off or picking up, poised five feet from the kerb, but deep in the gutter. Worse still, the Fairway – which, in the days when his father had pride, had never carried any kind of advertising – now sported Supersides. The driver-side one showed a blonde in her bra and knickers tearing a strip from her own inner thigh; below it was the double-entendre PAINLESSLY OFF, PLEASURABLY ON. Puerile eyes sucked this up.

*Why's he cummear? Why . . . ?* Carl was torn between anxiety for his father, who he knew wasn't allowed within half a mile of Beech

House, and anger that he was shaming him in front of the other boys. He hurried over, wrenched open the back door of the cab, slung his school bag in, leaped in after it and called to his father, 'Drive on, cabbie!'

Dave went along with him, saying, 'Where to, guv?' Flustered, Carl replied, 'Savernake Road.' Which was round the corner from Dave's flat. Carl thought they'd go and have a cup of tea together, or kick a ball around on Parliament Fields for half an hour, but his dad was too mad. He drove – *leave on left Frognal. Left Arkwright Road. Right Fitzjohn's Avenue* – and ranted: 'Fucking this and fucking that, fucking coons and fucking Yids, fucking young slappers and fucking old boilers.' It was as if, by impersonating a fare, Carl had exposed himself to the deepest, darkest, most atavistic stream of cabbie consciousness. Too shocked to say anything, Carl sat as his dad's voice crackled over the intercom. At the junction with Roderick Road the cab pulled over. Dave opened the back door and said, 'Op aht, sun.' Carl came forward but before he could say anything, Dave cried, 'No charge on this one!' And roared away.

Carl lay for a long time on the slope of damp grass that stretched up to Parliament Hill. He didn't care about his poncey striped uniform – or anything else. He couldn't cry, but his belly was tight with misery. When at last he'd risen and begun his tramp back through the dusk, the Heath itself was his confidante. He'd reached consciousness on this peculiar island, a couple of square miles of woodland and meadow set down in the lagoon of the city. He wavered from copse to tumulus, from felled old elm to crunchy bracken patch, making his way up to the sandy crossroads, where a single Victorian lamp standard stood, its homely glow illuminating the dark holly hedge that marked the entrance to Kenwood. In touching this roughened trunk and clutching that mossy bole, the lad connected with his past. Kite-flying on blustery days, the kamikaze nylon aircraft diving for the ground; family picnics among the house-high tangle of dead trees felled by the Great Storm of

’87; and in the dead of winter, hurling ice chunks across the frozen surface of Highgate Pond, his woolly paws burning with cold fire.

In the sickening disparity between the affectionate enclosure of his early childhood and the loveless thicket of the present, Carl saw the person he would henceforth be: a young man expelled from Arcadia, an exile, driven out and forced to live on the fringes of society, his only bible a collection of arcana derived from a distant past, a time of loyal chaps and gaudy royalty. Shouldering his school bag, Carl slithered down the hill past the little reservoir and rejoined the path that led up to Well Walk. It was mummy time once more. His clothes were filthy, Michelle would be frantic with worry, he was late for supper at Beech House.

Dave Rudman lined up his pathetic row of male toiletries on the sink surround and resolved to make himself presentable. He washed his remaining hair, he shaved his muddled face, he ironed his trousers and put on a shirt, a tie and the tweed jacket he’d bought to fit in with Michelle’s friends a decade before. She’d laughed at him – they’d laughed at him as well. Big-arsed Sandra, psycho Betty and doormat Jane. Dave could hear their laughter still as he drove down to Paddington. Hear it as he ranked up off Cleveland Terrace, hear it as he walked into the building where Gold’s man had an office. Dave heard it together with Gold’s friendly warning: ‘This guy is good, very good, in fact – he’s the best, but all he’ll say to you is “I don’t handle divorce.”’

‘I don’t handle divorce,’ the Skip Tracer said, picking his nails with a very sharp penknife. He hadn’t even bothered to face Dave while the potential client was stating his business.

‘It isn’t divorce,’ Dave protested to the close-cropped back of his head; ‘we’re divorced already, this is about the kid.’

‘Whatever.’ The Skip Tracer played an absent-minded arpeggio on his computer keyboard. 'Kids, divorce, whatever, I don't do nosebag neither.'

'What?'

'Sniff-sniff, chop-chop.' The Skip Tracer chopped out imaginary lines of cocaine on the desktop. 'YerknowhatImean, barley, rows of, nosebag. Don't touch it, never have, never will. Despise it – despise people that do.'

'I didn't say anything about . . . nosebag.' Dave shifted in his plastic chair and looked uneasily towards the window, where vertical louvres sliced up the nondescript terrace opposite.

'Didn't say – thought.' The Skip Tracer got up, turned around and jumped up so that he was sitting on his desk, a utilitarian steel unit that was pressed against a large map of the Dutch Antilles. He brandished the penknife at Dave. 'I'm quick on the . . . on the . . . quick on the uptake, see. Quick – that's me.' He ran his free hand through his thick grey-blond hair, which was very straight, long at the front and architecturally layered at the back. 'I'm so fast people jump to the conclusion that I'm doing nosebag. You did – didn't you?'

'No, not especially, you do seem a bit wire –'

'Wired, right, wired. Fucking wired, right. Nosebag, that's what you're thinking, right?' *Fucking mental is more like it, I don't get this geezer at all. He looks like a toff, with the Gieves and Hawkes whistle, the braces, the black-bloody-brogues. Chinless as well, gold signet ring, gold cufflinks, but he talks like a bloody space cadet.* 'I don't mind, I can handle it. I don't care what you think.' *Gold said he did mostly financial stuff, chasing money, so that's good for me. Gold said it's all a grey area, this sort of work, and this fellow will do a B & E or a wiretap if he has to – not personal but he has people.* 'I've just got a fast metabolism. See this shirt? Fresh on at lunchtime . . . this morning's' – the Skip Tracer leaped up, went over to a perforated metal cylinder in the corner and plucked up a limp rag – 'in the fucking bin. My cufflinks rust if I wear 'em two days running, 'coz the sweat's just lashing offa me, lashing offa me . . . I'm that fast, see, but it ain't nosebag. Now, what ya got for me?'

'I thought you didn't do kids?' Dave got up, ready to leave.

'A *man's* kiddies is different, daddies is different. Ya see, divorce business is ninety per cent women, ninety per cent. Why? 'Coz they're cats, ain't they, cats . . . curiosity gets 'em every time. Minute hubby's gotta few items on his Mastercard bill he can't square, they wanna know the colour of the bint's pubes he's tomming around with. Gotta know – haveta know. It's not about love, it's not about money, it's not about kiddies – it's just bloody curiosity. You're different – it's your kiddie. Call me sentimental, go on, call me sentimental' – the Skip Tracer skipped over to a grey filing cabinet on top of which were lined up five full bottles of single-malt whisky and yanked from behind them a silver-framed photograph of a teenage girl with a mouth full of orthodontistry – 'but I love my kiddie, wouldn't want to be parted. No way, no way . . . Anyway, Gold says there's a money angle, which is?' He slapped the photograph back down and closed in on Dave, still waggling the penknife.

'This.' Dave handed him the card. 'I had this Brice in the back of my cab; he works for the bank that are handling the buyout of my ex's new bloke's company. His name is Cal Devenish –'

'Oh him!' The Skip Tracer was delighted. 'I've heard of 'im, well, whassthe beef?'

'I heard this bloke on his mobile saying he didn't think Devenish was kosher, thought he was spending more money than he could possibly have –'

'I like it, I like it – liking it, liking it. You wanna know how much he 'az? I'll tell you!'

The Skip Tracer leaped for his desk, yanked up the receiver of one of the four phones on it and punched a string of digits without even looking: 'Channel Devenish, that's right, love, D-E-V-E-N-I-S-H. I dunno, Charlotte Street probably, yeah, yeah . . . Hello, Channel

Devenish? Yeah . . . Barry Forbes here, City Desk at the *Standard*, we're doing a thing on your buyout, can I have a word with the Financial Director . . . and that is? Bob Gubby . . . sure, thanks . . . Mr Gubby? Barry Forbes here from the *Standard*, yeah, yeah, just a short item on the buyout, and, well, *you* actually . . . people are impressed . . . we all know FDs are the real deal makers, juss wanned to check some facts, no time to look up the clips . . . corporate bankers . . . I see, yes . . . in the Haymarket, and they're the seniors? Excellent. One other thing, d'you have a photo? Black and white preferably, bike it over if you could, mark it for my attention and I'll pass it to the picture desk. Barry Forbes, that's right, F-O-R-B-E-S. Brilliant, brilliant . . .' He broke the connection and redialled while hissing at Dave, 'Carrot, see, mug thinks he's gonna be in the evening rag, carrot, give 'em carrot, it's like nosebag for desk jockeys – hello?' he said, returning to the phone, 'Bob Gubby here at Channel Devenish, could I speak to our corporate manager? Mr Hurst, that's right . . . he's at lunch? Well, his secretary will do . . . Hello, Bob Gubby here at Channel Devenish, yes, I know he's at lunch, I just need to check something quickly . . . is that a Barbadian accent? Really, I love Barbados, I was on holiday there last year, no, near Speightstown . . .'

The Skip Tracer's chat-up was like hypnotizing someone with a pendulum: the trick lay in its very obviousness. From the secretary he elicited Cal Devenish's personal bank details: 'We're worried a payment hasn't gone through and everyone's at lunch at this end. Yes . . . a big payment . . . I thought I might have the account number wrong . . . it looks like a five, but it could be an eight . . .' Digit by digit he extracted the account number, without the young woman on the end of the line even realizing that he'd provided her with no accreditation at all except holiday snaps and a false name. 'Carrot, see, big dick Barbadian one!' he snapped at Dave when he'd broken the connection. Then he called Devenish's bank and pretended to be a manager from another branch: 'He's applied for a loan here . . . nothing large, but I felt I ought to check it out . . .' With each call he made, the Skip Tracer morphed astonishingly: from City Editor to Financial Director, from FD to Bank Manager. His voice changed, his accent changed, his wiry body coiled and stretched across the desk. 'I see, really?' He scribbled a number on a pad and chucked it over to Dave while still on the call. 'Well, that is strange, but very rich men can be, can't they? And it's all business for us, no?'

Dave was looking at the number, which had six digits. The Skip Tracer hung up. 'Carrot, see, loan, get it, nosebag, banker nosebag, that is – a loan.'

'He's got over seven hundred grand in his current bloody account!' Dave expostulated.

'£743,485 to be precise,' the Skip Tracer said. 'He's fucking loaded. But I don't do pro bono, my son, no way José, I'm not some fucking ambulance chaser. You'll have to cough up, on the nail, on the nail. And no borrowing to pay me.' He wagged a finger. 'I know those sharks, I know the vig.'

'Aren't you worried about them tracing all of that?' Dave put in. 'All those dodgy calls?'

'Cummear.' The Skip Tracer pulled Dave to his feet and tucked his arm around the bigger man's neck. Dave smelled sweat and aftershave – both of them were lashing off him. 'I'm gonna like you, son. I'm gonna enjoy doing stuff fer you, b'lieve me. B'lieve it. Cummear . . . see the flex, see the phone wire, let's follow it . . .' The Skip Tracer three-legged Dave out the door and in through the open door of the adjoining office. It was empty save for a pile of phone directories and smelled of new carpet tiling. The phone wire snaked across the chequerboard and disappeared into a wall. 'There it goes into its little hole. Company that rents this gaff' – he laid a crooked finger against his tip-tilt nose – 'I've never seen 'em. They'll be one of those nosebag fronts with their name on a plate in an accountant's office on the Isle of Man. Ironically it might be the same bean counter who fronts up for your man Devenish. Geddit?'

~

Dave was renting Chitty Chitty Bang Bang on the full-flat. The open-top, straight-six Bentley was a *pig to handle*, and the wings were mostly useless in Central London. The flying car grunted and squealed at the rank under the heavy steel joists of St Pancras. A fare came flapping out of the greenish aviary of the station, a tall stick of a man, his white beard and black robe giving him a vulturine appearance. 'Where to, guv?' Dave asked him, and the fare replied stiffly, 'Parl-men-till.'

The fare was *a tedious old fucker*, who couldn't forbear from lecturing Dave on London's architecture. Dave hated birds – especially old human ones; he hated their alien stare, their hollow bones, their greasy feathers, their hard, pointed lips. The fare's thesis was simple: the city had ceased to evolve after the Great Fire. The last three hundred and fifty years were only a series of recapitulations, the erection of new–old buildings, tricked out in the styles of lost civilizations. He pointed out the neo-Gothic station frontage, its triplets of lancet windows complete with quatrefoils, its angled and flying buttresses, its iron pinnacles and gabled niches. Despite himself Dave craned to look up and piloted Chitty Chitty Bang Bang into the gulch being excavated for the Channel Tunnel terminal. Luckily, its wings spontaneously unfurled, the huge car swooped back up on to the roadway. The fare was unfazed. He discoursed on the wooden, barrel-vaulted roof of King's Cross, then directed his attention to the neoclassicism of the terraced houses lining Royal College Street – their snub façades alluding to thc possibility of stately porticos, their anorexic pilasters referencing temples long since crumbled. 'Vares nuffing nú unnersun, mì sun.' The fare spoke the broadest of cockney, vowels crushed to death by rumbling lorries on the Mile End Road. 'Doan ask wy ve öl daze wuz bé-er van vese, coz U aynt gó ve nous fer í. Lemme tellya, no geezer az a fukkin clú abaht iz oan tyme, yeah? Ees juss lyke a fukkin sparrer –'

'The sparrows are nearly all gone in London,' Dave put in.

'Eggzackerly!' In the rearview mirror Dave saw the old man's bony digit waggle. 'Eggzackerly, lyke a fukkin sparrer aw a bitta bá-erred cod.'

'They're going inall.'

'Rì agen, gawn, cort inna eevul fukkin net, mayt, an eevul fukkin net vat juss cum aht uv ve fukkin sky.'

Coming up Highgate Road, Dave used the steep slope after the railway bridge to take off, and Chitty Chitty Bang Bang unfurled its wings once more, and soared up over the redbrick, 1930s blocks of Lissenden Gardens. He banked the flying car and came in on a flat approach to the summit of Parliament Hill, touching down on the path with hardly a bump. They rolled to a halt, and the fare got out. Dave searched the dash for a meter but couldn't find one. There was hardly any point in trying, for when he looked again he saw that the old man had done a runner, pelting off down the hill towards the Highgate Ponds, his long black robe streaming behind him. 'I s'pose I'll just have to wipe my mouth on that one,' Dave muttered to himself.

Dawn was silvering the mirrored buildings of the City – further to the east the bridge at Dartford floated above the riverine mist. The streetlights were still on, phosphorescent trails in the oily swell of streets and buildings. Dave felt an aqueous queasiness when he saw the long line of the North Downs to the far south – they were distant islands, uninhabited and uninhabitable. At his back he sensed the ridges of Barnet and then the Chilterns rising up, wooded shores against which London lapped.

Carl and his mother were sitting on one of the benches that looked out over the city. As Dave drew closer, he saw that they were both in their nightwear. He sat down, putting his arm around his son. 'Are you going to do the baddest thing in the world, Dad?' Carl asked, and Dave replied, 'Yes, son, yes, I think I will.'

'How're you going to do it, then?'

Dave looked sideways at Michelle, but her drained face didn't respond. How would he do the baddest thing? There were so many ways. The plunge from Suicide Bridge, drowning in the Serpentine, a shotgun at the West London Shooting Centre. Then there were the things Dave could throw himself beneath: the wheels of a hated fellow cabbie's cab, a police car, *shit* . . . if he timed it right he could probably sever his miserable head with the incisive wheel of a speeding bicycle courier.

The racing bike clattered away over cobbles splattering blood – it had a trachea for a chain. Its clakka-clakka-clakk resolved into the rat-a-tat-tat of the doorknocker. Dave clawed on a balding, black towelling robe and fell down the stairs to the front door. It was a brilliant morning, and the postie – who was a squat African woman with chipmunk cheeks – thrust an envelope and clipboard at him. 'Sign heah, date an' print!' she cried, and when he protested 'Wha?' she reiterated it so forcefully 'Sign heah DATE AN' PRINT YOUR NAME!' that he instantly obeyed. It wasn't until Dave had shut the door and was padding back upstairs while tearing the envelope open that it hit him. He'd been served.

Although the thick, bonded paper was headed with an embossed letterhead Dave didn't recognize, UNDERCROFT, MENDEL AND PARTNERS, 22 VIGO STREET, LONDON W1, the text was clearly addressed to him:

*Dear Mr Rudman*
*In the matter of Carl Rudman we act for our client Ms Michelle Brodie.*
*Following representations from our client we are satisfied that the non-molestation order preventing you from going within half a mile of our client's residence has been breached on two occasions. We have now lodged a temporary injunction for a full exclusion order in the Principal*

*Registry of the Family Division of the High Court, and hereby give notice that until this case is heard any further breach of the existing order will result in an automatic custodial sentence.*

*We also give you notice that pending any appeal on your part, all existing arrangements for visitation to your son, Carl, are held to be cancelled. Should you attempt to contact your son, we will view this as prejudicial and inform the police.*

*If you have any queries regarding this letter, please feel free to telephone me on my direct line, listed above.*

*Yours sincerely,*

*Mitchell Blair*

It was a small letter, but it had unnaturally large teeth. Dave began to cry.

# 7

# *Broken on the Wheel*

## 510–13 AD

The kipper season's wheatie crop had only just been harvested and the Council was still planning the first fowling expedition of the year, when the Hack's party arrived prematurely on Ham. The sight of the Chilmen struck fear into the Hamsters. There were at least thirty of them, all fit, strong chaps armed with shooters and railings, owing fealty to the Lawyer alone. There could be no thought of resisting them, and when Mister Greaves was met on the foreshore by Fred Ridmun wearing his Guvnor's cap, the whole population understood that their coming was no accident. The Geezer made no attempt to hide from the Hack. He was immediately seized and bundled off to the travelodge, where he was confined.

For four days Mister Greaves sat in session and heard the evidence against Symun Dévúsh. One after another the Hamsters scuttled before him to recant and to give evidence of the Geezer's flying behaviour. The weather remained exceptionally fine throughout, a bigwatt foglamp beating down on the island. The Chilmen, despite their disciplined array, were as overawed as any other newcomers to Ham, and they soon began to relax and leave off their carcoats. So it was a considerable surprise to the Hamsters when, at first tariff on the fifth day, they rose to discover that the Hack's pedalo had been pulled back into the water and was being made ready to depart.

– Bring ve fliar dahn, Mister Greaves ordered Fred. 4 Eye an arf mì dads ul B leevin 4 Wyc vis tariff. Ve uvvas ul stä eer 2 mayk shoor vares no maw bovva. Eyel B bakk in free mumfs wiv ve sikkmen. Eye want yaw moto reddy 4 slorta, an ve briks an bubbery an fevvas 4 yaw tikkit. U lot av slungaht viss Geezer, but if vese blokes Eye leev Bhynd katch U ló á í agen vare wil B maw Xeyels!

Cowed, the Hamsters stood and waited in silence as Fred, together with a posse of dävine dads, hustled Symun Dévúsh down from the travelodge and brought him to the jetty.

Far from subduing him, Symun's confinement seemed to have given him new vigour. Kids had smuggled him in extra food and drink, and old Ozmun Bulluk had even slipped him some of the fags the Chilmen had brought. It was while puffing on one of these that the Geezer said farewell to his fares. Before wading out to the pedalo, he turned back to confront the Hamsters, who had gathered on the shore. His gaunt old mummy, Effi, crippled Caff, whom he loved, Fred Ridmun, his mate and his betrayer, the Edduns brothers, Dave and Dick, Fukka Funch with his snub snout and bow legs, old Bettë Brudi, her wrinkled face clenched with pain and sadness. They were all there, from the oldest boiler to the youngest sprog. It was said later that even the motos, led by Runti, filed down from the woods and stood softly lisping their goodbyes, as tears rolled down their pendulous jowls.

Fred Ridmun, fearful of his regained authority being undermined, was disposed to hustle Symun aboard the pedalo without more ado; however Mister Greaves motioned him to allow the Geezer to speak. Symun put one foot up on a pile of bricks, brushed his hair away from his face and, fixing his restless gaze on the Ferbiddun Zön, threw an arm up towards the aching blue screen.

– E oo ayts lyf wil keep í, thass wot í sez in ve Búk, innit?

There was a mutter of acknowledgement from his listeners.

– Wel, Eye doan luv lyf ennymaw wivaht Am, so Eye spose Eye must ayt í.

Another mutter like a response.

– Awl Eye did woz 4 Am, awl Eye evah wannid woz 4 us ló 2 B cumfy.

The mutter swelled into a groan.

– Dave did givus ve nú Búk – U ló no thass ve troof! Ven Eyem gawn . . . by now most of the cab – for that is what they had unwittingly become, the Chilmen included – were openly weeping . . . yul unnerstan vat, an yul C ow fings gesswurs an wurs, coz ve troo Nolidj az bin loss, an ven ve Nolidj iz loss iss ve end uv Am –

This was by no means the end the Geezer intended for his address, but Mister Greaves, apprehending the powerful effect of his words, seized Symun by his shoulder and dragged him bodily through the shallows. Two of the Lawyer's chaps then pulled him into the vessel. The others splashed across and leaped in, then, with a flurry of pedals, the pedalo made fast for the reef. Yet not so swiftly that the Geezer's inflammatory words couldn't still be heard for some time floating over the lagoon, until eventually they became but mangled sounds, a peculiar presentiment of the fate that awaited he who had uttered them.

~

During the three months that the Hack was absent, the Hamsters split once more into mummytime and daddytime. It was a new Breakup, and, bewildered as the kids may have been by the rebuilding of that invisible barrier that divided brother from sister, man from wife, and a child from its own very nature, they knew better than to question it. While some of the mummies and daddies wept as they recalled the long tariffs they had spent ranked up like motos in conjugal bliss, others were heartily glad to have their mutual indifference formalized once more.

Besides, there was work to be done, work that had been neglected during the whirlwind of licence that had been the Geezer's time.

Hard work – all the harder for the unseasonable pedalo fever, the extra mouths to feed, and the Hack's imposition of a substantial ticket. Once again the mummies and opares became beasts of burden. The barrels of moto oil that had been rendered down the previous autumn were brought to the pier, together with truckles of London bricks, bolts of bubbery and sacks of gull feathers. Fred Ridmun and the dävine dads made it clear that there was but one priority alone for the community: the rent must be paid to the Hack.

Away from the Guvnor's hearing, and especially among the boilers, there were those who muttered that, whatever the seriousness of his transgressions, the Geezer had been denied a proper hearing. He himself had not been allowed to speak before the Hack, and this weakened the bonds of fealty between the Hamsters and their Lawyer quite as much as any flying they may have been party to.

It was Mëshell Brudi, out gathering yellowdye flowers near the Mutha's grave, who first saw the returning pedalo. She ran back to the manor and told the other mummies, Ees bak an vairs sumuvva bloke wiv im – nó a Chilman. Eye seen im, sittin up in ve pedalo, big tall bloke wivva wyt barnet! Ees gotta bituv shynë stuff stukkup bì iz mush! This was the first sighting of the new Driver, who was to come to dominate the lives of the Hamsters – dominate them more than their isolation, dominate them more than their peculiar symbiosis with the motos, dominate them, perhaps, even more than the Book itself.

Who was the Driver? No one on Ham ever knew. He never told them his real name – he was always the Driver. He came, like other visitors to the island, out of a void. This much can be said: when he made his landfall on Ham, the Driver was a vigorous man in his early fifties, long and angular of limb, full of beard and severe of countenance. His nose was sharp and prominent, his brows beetling. He did not deign for the pedalo to be tied up to the pier, but splashed overboard and waded ashore, his mirror waggling. He was clad in a full-length black robe, beneath which could be glimpsed black jeans and a black T-shirt of fine London cloth. His trainers – a form of footwear hitherto unknown on Ham – were orange and laced high up on his narrow ankles. In the Hamsters' eyes this raiment gave him the appearance of a giant and savage crow, an impression strengthened as it never altered in any way during the time he was among them. Neither the heat of the summer nor the damp of the kipper seemed to affect the Driver. No one ever saw him disrobe, not even the succession of opares who attended him in his semi.

The deeply credulous Hamsters, still reeling from the deposing of the Geezer, were powerfully impressed by the Driver. Leaving the pedalo to be beached by his retainers, Mister Greaves came over the shingle after him and, seeing the whole population assembled exactly as he had left them three months before, prepared to introduce the alien. The Driver ignored him and turned his back on the peasant gaggle, so that it was his own deep and gravelly voice, speaking not in dialect but the refined accents of Arpee, that rolled over their bowed heads:

– Greetings, good Hamsters! he cried. I am the Driver, and I come to you from the PCO in London. Before news even of this abominable flying reached the Inspectors' Faredar, it had been decided to once again send a circuit driver here, to this remote place, to remind you that Dave sees each and every one of you, daddies and mummies alike, in his mirror.

In later days it was said that as the Driver called over that first time, an unearthly stillness descended upon Ham. The children stopped fidgeting, the motos ceased ruminating. The gulls, crows, ringnecks and flying rats – all, in short, of the aerial flotsam that swirled in the screen above the island – came spiralling down to the bare ground at the bottom of the village, where the tightly clustered birds formed a bizarre, multicoloured carpet of feathers. The winged ants – which were swarming on that muggy summer's day – doodled in to pitter-patter against the back of the Driver's robe, then fell at his feet, writhing in the dust. Even the chafers' legs became motionless, adding to the mounting silence.

Whether any of this actually took place, or it was only the fabulous counterpoint to the tale of the Geezer's final address, is obscure. What is certain is that the Driver had spent the uncomfortable pedalo journey from Wyc – four long days on the open water, four damp nights anchored in densely wooded creeks – hearing the full story of the Geezer's insurrection; and he had concluded, quite rightly, that to establish a rapid ascendancy over the Hamsters it was necessary to employ all the theatricality of his adversary.

Cupped in its grassy bay, the little manor of Ham was a natural amphitheatre. The Driver continued his declamation:

– I have heard all about the disgusting practices that you have indulged in these past months – daddies and mummies consorting in grotesque propinquity – yet I shall not censure you for them any more than your Lawyer already has. I have heard how you abandoned the Knowledge and took up with a vile flyer – yet I shall not punish you for it. I come to bring you the Book! He flourished a huge, leather-bound copy from beneath his robe. See the Wheel! Read the meter! Know that the final tariff is at hand! Leave this place at once, you miserable, perfidious mummies! Sullied by rag and blob – whorish, licentious creatures! Chelle spawn!

He waited while the mummies, opares and children shuffled back to the mummies' gaffs, then rounded on the remaining Hamstermen:

– Do not be mistaken, for I know what happens to dads' minds when they do not honour the Breakup and observe the Changeover. I comprehend how you begin to doubt that Dave forsook the Lost Boy for your own miserable fares. The separate compartments into which Dave has poured all goodness and all badness become once again mingled. The hapless knave begins to think himself dävlike, possessing a freedom to act without the precepts of our faith. He no longer hears Dave speak to him over the intercom – instead mummyness spills into his every thought like piss from a ruptured bladder into the pure milk of burgerkine! The Driver spat as if disgusted by his own figure, then continued: It is for Drivers, queer and untainted by any vile contacts – tittyrub and cunnëlyk – to decide which fares shall for ever hail the cab in vain, and which will ride with Dave to New London!

The Driver fell to his knees.

– Thanks be to Dave! he called.

– 4 pikkin uz up! the Hamstermen responded.

– Let all you dads who have the Knowledge of it kneel down and call over the first run. Forward on left Green Lanes!

– Fawud Green Layns! the dads cried in unison.

– Right Brownswood Road!

– Rì Brahnswúd Röd.

When it was done, and the dads had called over the points, the Driver – to their considerable amazement – went on:

– In the beginning there was Dave's word and Dave's word alone. All that we have comes out of the Book. All that is, all that has been, and all that will come again. You are not the only fares to do a runner, you are not the only ones to breathe the smoky cab of apostasy, you are not the only miserable know-it-alls to look for a shortcut to New London! For three centuries now the Book has been the very rock upon which Ing itself has been built. O yes, a new London has been erected, with wide avenues and grand buildings, with workshops and markets even – yet this is not the city foretold by Dave! This is not New London! For this city has also saunas and spielers, bullrings and cockpits, lewd theatres and pleasure gardens. Only the PCO can build New London, either here on earth or – if Dave so ordains it – beyond the screen!

The Driver lifted the Book up to that screen and cried out:

– I have seen New London! Then he advanced among his terrified listeners, thrusting the heavy volume into the faces of each of the dads in turn, while he continued his rant: I have seen it, and I know it will only be restored by restitution of the pure and original Dävinanity. Let the three cabs be hailed once again here on Ham! Let the twelve dads promulgate the doctrines of Breakup and Changeover! Let no mummy be admitted to your Council lest you be polluted by them!

– For there must be no confusion concerning this matter, he said, striding back to where Mister Greaves stood with the cowed Chilmen and admonishing them with a stabbing finger, there has been a grievous crime perpetrated here against Dave, a crime that can be atoned for only by the most perfect calling over! The Driver fell to the ground and, lifting up handfuls of soil, let the dirt fall upon his head crying:

– Thanks, Dave, for picking us up!

– 4 pikkin uz up, the dads who remembered the correct response dutifully intoned.

– And for not dropping us off.

– Anfer nó droppinus dahn.

~

They prepared fresh straw for the pallet and made ready the medicinal herbs. Sphagnum moss was gathered and dried, for the fibres of this useful plant were both absorbent of moisture while keeping wounds free from infection. The mummies used it for their infants' nappies and to absorb their own menses. Many of them believed that the happy situation of the sphagnum bog at the source of the spring that trickled through the village was a sure sign of Dave's providence. So the sphagnum bed was prepared and garlanded with special Daveworks. To ask for His intercession in a successful birth the Hamsterwomen chose a distinctive, long thin shard of plastic with a narrow slot at one end that gave it the appearance of a flimsy bodkin. These they strung on to long lengths of thread, and hung from the eaves of the gaff where Caff was to be confined so that they twirled in the breeze.

This birth would be special, the first since the Geezer had been deposed. As Caff Ridmun felt new life stirring in her, a fluttering at the sides of her taut womb, the Driver felt a new threat. He had examined both Caff and the Guvnor, and it was beyond doubt that this was the flyer's child. If Caff had a son, he might be another Antidave, ready to spread more poison in the world. The Driver was confronted by a paradox: the service, the ceremony whereby newborn Hamsters were anointed with moto oil, was profoundly antithetical to this rigid Dävist, yet, if he understood the matter rightly, the odds were that Caff's baby would not survive it. The future of Dävinanity on Ham thus depended on toyist superstition.

Caff felt no fear, surrounded by the mummies. She accepted that what would be would be, Dave gave and Dave took away. She gloried in her enlarged body, her marbled tank and engorged breasts. The mummies called the last trimester the moto time, and reverenced the resemblance a Hamsterwoman about to give birth had to their beloved kine. With her withered left leg, Caff could no longer walk more than a few paces. So throughout the blowy autumn days she had sat in the lea of the Dévúsh gaff, her aching back braced against its mossy bricks, and stared out over the sparkling lagoon. With the baby kicking within her, she had never felt before with such intensity her own connection to the land. The foetal shape of Ham encompassed her – while she in turn encompassed this inchoate life.

It was the middle of the third tariff when the birth pains eventually came. There had only been a dipped headlight – and it was long since switched off. Low cloud blanketed the island and from behind it a reddish tinge suffused the screen. Making her way down the stream bed from the Bulluk gaff, Effi Dévúsh came across the Driver, a black-clad and minatory figure. He was muttering in an undertone, but Effi, who had work to do, did not hail him – she knew what he was doing, calling over, countering the wavering paths of Ham with the certainty of his Knowledge.

The Driver remained there until the foglamp was switched on. In all he called over a hundred runs. Such rigour spoke of the deep conflict within him – for did not Dave honour all new life? When at last he heard the bellows of the expectant mummy give way to the reedy cries of the infant, he turned on his heel and lurched along the foreshore to the tumbledown semi of the old Driver. There he fell into a fitful slumber, and dreamed that he flew with Dave over the silvery immensity of New London.

~

In the days following the birth of her son Caff's fatalism foundered on the rocks of love. A savage love for the manikin she cradled, whose twinkling blue eyes and fierce ruff of fine brown hair recalled to all Symun Dévúsh. The other mummies understood this emotion, even if they would not acknowledge it. No infant born on Ham was even named until it had survived its service. It was as if these first eleven days of life were only a final stage of incubation, and the thick coating of moto oil it would then be slathered with was the final membrane through which it must pass into independent life. For inasmuch as a Hamster was born of woman, so he was also born of the island itself.

On the eleventh day, when Effi Dévúsh came with the moto oil and loomed in the doorway of the Dévúsh gaff, Caff, unable to contain herself, began first to whimper and then cry out. Caught between zoolatry and love, she let go of the infant and, dragging her withered leg behind her, crawled into the far corner, where she lay sobbing on the yok flags. Effi, who was attended by two other boilers, ignored her. They went about the ritual with steely efficiency. Her assistants removed the swaddling and held the thrashing limbs, while Effi spread the viscous grease, paying particular attention to the raw wound of the navel. The infant, which at first howled in protest, responded to the mysterious embrocation of the moto oil, struggling less and less, until when it was finally released it lay silent and still in the foglight that streamed through the door, another of Ham's miraculous and shiny fruits.

Outside the Hamsters stood in silence, the dads' shaggy heads bowed, the mummies worrying at their cloakyfings. Now began a time of waiting. If the new infant survived the next blob, it would receive a name. More likely, on the third or fourth day after the service, it would refuse the suck of its mummy's pap, and on the fifth or sixth its tiny pink gums would lock shut. Then the fits would begin – convulsions, which would rack the tiny body with increasing severity – until on the seventh or eighth day it expired. By then, such would be the mite's torment that death would seem a deliverance, even to its own mummy. The Driver stood unregarded among the islanders. Once more he was calling over the runs and the points, for whatever the outcome – torment or release – his faith required above all that he bear witness to the once and future London.

~

To call them cells would have been wrong – they were stalls rather, crudely partitioned with heavy wood beams. Wealthier prisoners, or those who had special influence, were able to secure one of the tiny chambers on the upper gallery, but for those such as him there was only the nightly squabble to get into one of the stalls, then burrow into the stinking straw to find some warmth. Squabbling went on all the time and there were also full-scale fights. The other prisoners had blades and coshes, they spat, kicked and gouged. Symun had never experienced any real violence: the cuffs of the Ham daddies were as mere caresses compared to the savage blows traded here as a matter of course. The first time Symun was attacked, he was so shocked that he relapsed into a vacant stupor, staring at the livid pink impress the kick had left on his leg. Without the coaxing of the prisoner who became his mate, he would have expired then and there, because to survive in this place a dad had to fight.

The Tower was a world in its own right, with its own economy and politics, law and religion. For Symun, this was the only realm he'd ever seen outside of his island home. He was chained in the ferry's hold for the voyage from Wyc. On the rare occasions the gaffer allowed him to exercise on deck he saw distant estates and manors along the coast. When they docked at London, he was taken off and driven through the streets in a sweatbox. If he peered between the irony shutters, he caught glimpses of vast buildings, yet he was unable to comprehend what it was that he was seeing – nothing tallied with the descriptions he had heard, and the tumult was such – of cars, people and beasts – that he recoiled in fear and confusion.

In the Tower, under the tutelage of Terri, a convicted cockney thief, Symun Dévúsh slowly came back to life. The trauma of his birth into this frightening world, where he shared a huge yard with ten times as many men as he'd ever seen before, was followed by a period of infancy. Symun asked questions; Terri supplied the answers. The yard was but one of three in the gaol. There was a smaller one for mummies and a third for alien chaps, who had been taken prisoner in the continuous skirmishing between the King's army and the wild tribes of Jocks and Taffies to the north and the west of the archipelago.

In the dads' yard all the prisoners – regardless of their offence, their sentence, or even if they had been tried or merely remanded – were thrown together: flyers, traitors and murderers alongside petty thieves, debtors and vagabonds. Terri thought there might be as many as a thousand fares confined in the Tower, and each day their numbers were swelled by Londoners, who came from without the walls to ply their trades and even barter for the use of skilled prisoners in their own workshops. Thus there was much commerce in the Tower, which was furnished with its own shops, a bakery, even the services of a notary. For a price a dad might wed in the gaol and lie with his wife. He could engage in his own trade and reap the reward. If imprisoned for debt, he could even fall into debt again, and so be confined in the Tower's own debtors' gaol, a prison within a prison. He could drink and whore, cock fight and game. During the tariffs of foglight the yard was a frenetic arena, and on its beaten earth dads in all manner of strange costumes – suits, striped and checked, jeans tight and flared, tattered cloakyfings and formal robes – strutted and preened like caged birds.

Once he began properly to observe his fellow prisoners Symun was amazed to discover how little religion there was among them. His automatic requests for directions from Dave were met with derision and laughter. One dad, in full view of the warders, squatted down and broke wind, proclaiming: Eye fart on yor polstrë, O Dryva! They took no action against him, but then this dad was not held on a charge of flying. The warders, Symun soon learned, interfered little in the lives of the prisoners, except to take bribes for services given and dole out privileges for those rendered. The prisoners themselves ran the gaol while their gaolers merely looked on – only in the matter of flying were they truly vigilant. The flyers – who numbered a few score – were distinguished by the large, two-spoked wooden wheel they were obliged, on pain of beating, to carry about their necks. Symun Dévúsh had never seen a real wheel before coming to London – to him it was a sacred symbol. Now one hung around his neck, galling him no matter how carefully he moved.

The warders made sure that the flyers were overheard when they spoke, either by themselves or their seeseeteevee men. Should they utter any further word against the writ of the PCO, or the Dävinanity it promulgated, they were summarily punished. The big steering Wheel was brought out into the yard and set upon its column. The flyer was trapped and lashed to its spokes. Then the Wheel was spun and spun, until the unfortunate dad was bleeding from his nose and mouth, and his innards were mangled. Within a blob of arriving at the Tower Symun had seen two flyers die upon the Wheel. Then his own appearances began.

The flyers' appearances took the form of questioning their Knowledge. No flyer could secure his release from gaol by passing his appearances – for once accused of flying you were banished from the cab for ever. However, by calling over the runs and points demanded, he might at least secure a remission. He wouldn't have another appearance for fifty-six more days, during which time he could struggle to improve his Knowledge. If a flyer failed an appearance the consequences were harsh – their next would be in twenty-eight days. A second failure and this was reduced to twenty-one, a third to fourteen. After a fourth failure the flyer went for judgement before the PCO itself, then sentence would be carried out.

The least severe punishment was branding and exile, followed by the cutting out of the tongue and exile. The most severe penalty – which was frequently applied – was death. Dads were wheeled until their brain haemorrhaged, then they were disembowelled. Then, as the poor unfortunate was mindlessly gawping at his guts lying on the ground at his feet, his genitals were cut off and thrust in his mouth. Death came within units. The dead dad's head was then severed and stuck on a spike at the water gate; beneath it a placard was hung that read: VIS MANNE SPEEKS BOLLOX. Mummies – who were not deemed worthy of the Wheel even in death – were burned on the barbie. If they were guilty of evading Changeover, their moribund exhalations were employed in gassing their own children.

All the daddies' executions were held publicly in Leicester Square; the mummies' at Marble Arch. A large enthusiastic crowd would gather to watch and keenly observe the comportment of the condemned; they would lay bets on how long each would take to expire. A common criminal might sway the crowd with his brave demeanour, and the Inspectors would grant him pardon at the foot of the Wheel, but however well a flyer behaved he was doomed.

This much Symun was soon made aware of – yet there was little he could do to prepare himself for his ordeal. He'd had scant opportunity to read the Book since acquiring his phonics. While, like all Hamstermen, he'd been accustomed since boyhood to call over the runs and points, this oral recounting was haphazard and imprecise. In the broad Mokni of Ham the runs were strings of meaningless gibberish – and while Symun knew enough to differentiate one from the other in his own mind, he was by no means certain that he could convince a prejudicial examiner that his was the correct version. It was the same for any cockney or hick – with the consequence that while well-born flyers often survived in the Tower for years, the illiterate were dispatched with great expeditiousness.

Symun's first appearance took place a couple of blobs after he'd arrived in London. He was dragged from the yard by two warders, hauled up the external staircase into the White Tower, then marched along passages, the damp walls of which were green with moss. Finally he was shoved into a chamber where at a table sat the Examiner. His black-robed back was turned, his hair cropped very short at the neck. His eyes hung in his mirror, swollen and veined. He spoke Arpee in a bored monotone:

– Symun Dévúsh of Ham, you are held in the Tower, arraigned on a charge of gross and flying conduct. The testimony of Mister Greaves, my Lawyer of Chil's Hack, is held to account in this matter and acknowledged accordingly. This is your first appearance – he looked down at the A4s on the table in front of him and read – List eighteen, run eleven.

Symun tore his eyes away from the mirror. There was A4 on the walls, covered not with phonics but a curious pattern of leaves. In places it peeled back from the plaster beneath, plaster that had fallen away in powdery chunks to reveal the ancient London brick beneath. Through a high slit-window Symun could see another tower, a crooked edifice mounting to a wonky campanile. Hawks were circling this, riding the smoky exhalations from the fires of the city below. Only the hawks and the leaf pattern were recognized by Symun: the rest of it was a conundrum he could not interpret. The warder who had brought him to the chamber stood against the far wall, his long railing held sloped between his big hands. He stared blankly at Symun.

The Examiner repeated his request:

– List eighteen, run eleven.

Symun took a deep breath and began:

– 4wud Kenzingtun Mal, rì Kenzingtun Chirch Stree, leff Nó-ing-ill, rì Pemrij Röd, fawud Pemrij viwwers –

– Viwwers? the Examiner broke in, viwwers, what pray are those?

Symun gulped:

– Beggin yer pardun, Reervú, thass juss ve wä we sezzit on Am.

– Well, you aren't on Ham now, my good fellow, this is London and in London you speak Arpee, and you call over the runs like a Londoner. I'll give you another fifty-six days to improve your diction before your next appearance. Take him away.

– B-but, Reervú, vass nó rì.

– You what? The Examiner was so incredulous at such impertinence from a flyer that an amused expression lurked at the corners of his severe mouth. Not right, you say? How so?

– 'Iss nó rì 2 eggspekk a dad 2 no vem fings, issit? Eyem sposed 2 B a fliar, nó a Dryva, sew owz a fliar sposed 2 av ve Nolidj? Í doan mayk senss.

The Examiner laughed at this and marked the A4 in front of him. Don't bandy doctrine with me, my fellow. For your impudence

I reduce your next appearance to twenty-eight days. And warder –

– Reervú?

– Give this gaol-yard brief a turn or twenty on the Wheel to make him mind his manners in future.

Terri gave Symun the rind of a fruit unfamiliar to him as they stood waiting under the murky screen. Byte dahn on vis, mayt, the cockney said. Ven ve weel gess goin, U gotta keep yer teef clamped tyt, uvvawyse yul swaller yaw tung an suffercayt . . . thass rì . . . thass rì. Symun only just had time to get the bitter thing between his teeth before the warders led him to the middle of the yard. They laid him down almost tenderly on the square central boss of the Wheel, and Symun felt the raised phonics 'Lti' pressing between his shoulder blades. His arms were lashed to the two padded spokes and his legs stretched and tied to the far rim of the wheel. Orlrì! the Guvnor of the Tower shouted to his subordinates. Ryt an dahn!

To begin with, the big Wheel turned slowly. Symun felt first one pair of hands, then the next, impelling it faster and faster, while prone as he was he could see nothing save the screen above him. The long streak of cloud immediately overhead began to revolve as if there were an axle set in it. He tried to concentrate on its wisps and veils so as to prevent the sickening dizziness. It was impossible – Symun's eyes bulged, the blood pounded in his temples, and the whole glassy panel stretched. He tried to picture Dave behind the screen, looking down on him with stern benevolence, but the figures standing along the balustrade of the upper gallery kept getting in the way. They jeered at the torture being enacted below, their individual mouths merging to become a single elongated O howling derision. The prisoners yelped and shouted: Spin ve fukka! Spinnim! Nausea came breaking over Symun in a wave and crashed into his clenched teeth.

O Dave! Ees onlë gonnan lungdup! cried one of the warders as Symun found himself ascending on his twirling rack, lifting up out of the yard like a sickseed caught by the wind and whirled out over London, over the islands and sounds of Ing, across the sea to where Ham lay, a soft pallet of mossy woodland and neat green field strips. At the blurred edges of his ruptured vision appeared the faces of his loved ones: Caff and Fred, Effi, his mummy, Fukka Funch, the Brudi sisters and Ozzi Bulluk. Symun could feel the rough tongue of a moto lick the puke and gore from his burning face. He dimly entertained the notion – for consciousness was speeding away from him – that the Wheel truly had conducted him back home, and that when it stopped turning everything would be as it had before, before the Ferbiddun Zön, before the Geezer, before the Second Book. Then all was darkness and pain.

~

The Driver addressed all the Hamsters from behind a fence that had been erected around the Shelter.

– See this, he told them, it is a bar the purpose of which is to keep the toyist beast of the field from profaning the sanctity of Dave's Shelter. It has been drawn to my attention – he scanned the faces of his listeners, noting their guileless countenances, their credulous eyes – that before I came among you your kine . . . your motos . . . ranked up here and even entered the Shelter. This is now forbidden. If I cannot wholly detach you from your unsavoury relation with these creatures, I shall nonetheless proscribe the anointing of your infants with their oil. The only true service is the Wheel, and whatever your interpretation of the Book may have been, I say to you now that the moto is excluded from Dave's cab to New London, these beasts being not real and in the view of the PCO toyist!

There was a stifled cry from the Hamsters.

This was not the full extent of the Driver's prohibitions. Rapping and cavorting were forbidden, and the telling of Daveworks was forbidden. There was to be no work at all on the island from first tariff FRI until the end of the second on SAT: for is not the blob-end a higher tariff, with time-and-a-half for calling over the points and the runs? The Driver's impositions were as onerous as his prohibitions: daily calling over for the daddies, while lads were also to attend the Shelter and remain silent. Even the Council was affected – at least ten runs now had to be called over before any business might be conducted.

Fred Ridmun, who had been responsible for the black crow coming to roost on Ham, blanched when he heard this, yet his own Dävinanity was to be still further tested. The Driver saved his most severe remonstrance for last:

– You gossip, you chatter, you flirt and you whisper – don't think I haven't heard you! Daddies to mummies, lads to girls. This is a most revolting congress, and it must cease at once! Dave ordained the Breakup, and the Breakup must be entire! Only at Changeover can there be any communication between noble Dave and perfidious Chelle! O Hamstermen! Speak only of childsupport to your mummies, as it is ordained in the Book!

In response to this tyrannical edict the assembly became greatly perturbed and there was open dissent from the older mummies. However, the Driver's will was not to be flouted; he rose up to his fullest height and glared down on them. They fell silent and slunk away to their own gaffs.

All this took place late in the kipper season, when the screenwash lashed the land and the sea was too rough to venture out upon. During this time the Hamstermen occupied themselves with gentle yet essential tasks – bubbery weaving, moto maintenance and caulking the pedalo. Misinterpreting their layover as sheer idleness, the Driver set the daddies to work at rebuilding his predecessor's semi and laying the foundations for a new Shelter. The old one, built by the previous Driver using prefabricated sections brought from Chil, had long since fallen into disrepair, a leaky and warped vessel for the Knowledge.

The Hamsters had not the art of preserving wooden structures, nor could they build in London brick with mortar. Their own gaffs were of such ancient pedigree that their upkeep was an organic fact rather than a work of construction. The mortar for the last Driver's semi had been imperfectly mixed, and it was already crumbling as thick stalks of buddyspike prised the brickwork apart. The Driver hitched up his robes and led the digging of the foundations for a new one. The younger dads, impressed by his energy and willing to learn new ways that could benefit them, joined him in the undertaking.

Caff Ridmun looked on as the other mummies dragged the truckles of London brick down from the Ferbiddun Zön. She had more intimate concerns: little Carl was three months old, and after much deliberation by the Council he had been given his real dad's name, Dévúsh, for such was the way of the Book. Soon enough he would begin to crawl, then it would be time for him to be paired with a moto.

~

It took several days before Symun Dévúsh could even unclench his teeth, and Terri had to trickle water from a scrap of sponge between his locked jaws. Especially at night, Symun's emaciated body was racked by convulsions, and such was the persistence of the dizziness that he could neither stand nor walk, and soiled himself.

When he was recovered, Symun learned fast. He had to; without a trade or any dosh of his own he had no way of augmenting the miserable slop doled out to the prisoners. Even this had to be fought over, men clawing and biting for a pannikin of cupasoup flavoured with half a raw crybulb. Since his turn upon the Wheel, Symun's strength was declining still faster, and he knew that if he failed his next appearance there was little chance he could survive more than another month in the Tower. Then a curious – and miraculous – thing happened. Terri, who Symun had assumed was only helping him with a view to some as yet undisclosed – and probably vile – advantage, revealed that his motives were quite other: Eye lyke U, dad, he told Symun. 2 tel U ve troof, Eye lyke awl fliars – yer diffrunt. Eye rekkun if U stik arahnd long enuff, yul tel me sumfing incredubbul. Yeah, Eye rekkun U wil. Terri scratched his moulting, carroty hair. He had the ratty features and pox scars of all poor Londoners, his eyes were black stones, rubbed shiny with distrust, yet when he turned them upon Symun they flickered with curiosity and wonder.

Terri got hold of a dog-eared copy of the Book. It was printed on the flimsiest of A4, and entire sections were loose in the binding, but all the runs and the points were there. Every day Symun and Terri called them over together. For Terri, a city urchin reared in the teeming rookeries of London, who'd hardly ever seen the foglight without fog or the burbs beyond the Emtwenny5, this was his getting of an education. Terri knew enough Arpee to correct Symun's Mokni. In return, Symun taught him phonics.

When the warders took Symun for his next appearance, he was dismayed to find a different Examiner waiting in the chamber and shuffling his A4s. This one was a more aggressive character, his yapping voice and queer grimace – part snarl, part grin – at odds with his shiny pate and plump little body. He was tipping so far back in his seat that the back of his head rested on the table. His mirror was skewed, his fingers fiddled nervily with a shiny bauble on a chain. Yet his questions were straightforward enough, and when Symun had called over two runs complete with points, he pronounced himself satisfied:

– Next appearance twenty-eight days! he snapped. Take the prisoner back to the yard.

Terri found Symun employment. It happened by accident. Noticing that the Hamster kept his changingbag always by him – even tying it about his waist when he was wheeled – the cockney asked him if he had anything of value in it. Symun withdrew a curious canister from the bag. It was very flat and exceedingly wide. Then he said, most reluctantly:

– Eye did av sumffing bluddë gúd ineer, but iss gon nah. Awl Eyev got ineer nah iz bitsuv plastik. He opened the canister to reveal a few handfuls of Daveworks.

Terri stared at the stash for a few units and then said:

– Vair ferbiddun eer, U no, ve PeeSeeO sez iss charms, iss majik. Vat doan stop folk nor neevah. Vey buyem on ve sly and wairem unda vair cloves, speshully ve loyahs an luvvies. Eye no a bloke wot smugguls em in from ve stikks. Ee needs elp graydin em.

So it was that Symun Dévúsh, the flyer, found a way to survive in the harsh environment of the Tower. A way to survive – and a drive for survival as well. As long as he could add to his Knowledge and maintain it, he might prevent a reduction in his appearances. He might live.

~

Carl grew into a happy, lively little toddler. As soon as he could break free from his swaddling and crawl off across the rips and linchets, Caff gave him to Gorj to look after. For another two years the moto nursed the human child, letting him suckle her heavy dugs alongside her own mopeds. It was Gorj who picked Carl up and took him over the island. She supervised his first walks along the Layn from the wallows to the Gayt. After that, they went down Winnies to Turnas Wúd, down Bish to the curryings, and even into Norfend to visit the Perg. Carl lay on her broad neck as she waddled along, his little hands twined in her bristles, utterly at peace, lulled in and out of sleep by the big beast's trundling motion.

This had always been the way. The children of Ham were accompanied everywhere by their peculiar nurses, and through the motos' own annual cycle they learned the ways of Ham, its seasons and weather, its flora and fauna. They spoke with the motos' slushy lisp and were physically nurtured by a species untroubled by any taboo. The little kids and the motos wallowed together, slept together in the byres, and even foraged together when the season allowed for those fruits congenial to both species. In kipper the motos chewed away at the trunks and boles of the smoothbarks, deftly pollarding and coppicing them. The Hamsters said: Az ewesful az a moto. In buddout, the motos spied out bees' nests in the woods and brought them down to the village, so that the colony could be settled in a hive. The Hamsters said: Az wyz az a moto. In summer, the motos rooted out the rats and grubbed up the knotweed. The Hamsters said: Az elpful az a moto. Finally, in autumn the motos lay down willingly so that their throats could be cut, then sang beautifully as the lifeblood drained out of them. The Hamsters said: Az dävine az a moto.

~

One by one the flyers who had been imprisoned in the Tower when Symun arrived failed their appearances, were reduced and reduced, until finally they were exiled or executed. Only one defied the process – and through it the PCO – Symun Dévúsh, the carrot-cruncher, the hick from the sticks, who, when he'd arrived at the gaol, had no more conception of the city he found himself in than a worm does of the apple it bores through.

Three long years Symun had been making his appearances. The heavy wheel he wore around his neck had given him two thick callouses on the points of his shoulders. For twenty-seven days the tension gradually increased, until on the morning of the twenty-eighth day he could hold down no food, nor even fag smoke. Then the warders would haul him before the Examiner, he would call over the nominated runs and points, and relief would come for a day or so, until the whole grim go-round began again.

By questioning every flyer who had suffered a reduction, Symun had discovered all the things to avoid. Never answer back to the Examiner; never react to anything that he might do – no matter how outlandish; never appear before the Examiner in slovenly attire, smelling of food or fags. Their failures were turned to his advantage, their maiming kept him whole, their deaths guaranteed his life.

Symun learned other things from his fellow doomed flyers – there was old flying and new flying. There were those flyers who claimed that Dave was still alive and walked among the daddies and mummies of Ing unrecognized, waiting for the time when he could overthrow the PCO. There were others – such as the Plateists – who said that the Book could not be understood without the use of other ancient relics that had been dug from the ground or dragged from the sea. There were those who had lapsed into the crepuscular realms of idolatry, and worshipped twisted hunks of old metal, barely legible signs – even the London bricks themselves. Still more – and these sectaries were strongly represented among the imprisoned flyers – held that Dave was but a bloke in another Book, which had been set down by the true and only God. These heretics failed their appearances with great alacrity and were broken on the Wheel.

By far the most numerous, though, among the flyers were those who held that they might speak with Dave directly through their own intercom, without any intercession by the drivers of the PCO. From talking with these flyers Symun recognized that they, like him, retained a secret mummyself locked inside their breasts – yet accessible.

The flyers came from all over Ing and from every position in society. There were noble lawyers, who through the gift of the King himself had once held estates in the western islands. They were dragged protesting through the huge gates and slung on to the muddy yard, their fine raiment dirty and torn. There were yeoman heretics, sturdy farmers from the burbs surrounding London, who were frogmarched in and stripped to their trainers by the laughing prisoners. And there were barefoot peasants, without money, advantages or connections, who were robbed and abused by all.

For in the Tower the world was turned upside down, and the scallywags of the city became the overlords. Symun, who had the protection of one of these criminal lawyers, was free from molestation and even able to amass a portion of dosh, heavy copper and silver coins that could be exchanged for all manner of goods and services – not least a chamber of his own. When Terri saw that his mate was well established, he encouraged Symun to speak of Ham and the events that had brought him to London. So it was that the Geezer appeared once more among dads.

The news of the prophet spread throughout the Tower. As Symun had correctly surmised, it was not the Knowledge that the Londoners resisted, only the exactions of the heavy-handed PCO. The new message that the Geezer called over was simple, and he now adapted it to be understood by all daddies and mummies, both high and low. Dave's second testament was devoid of the wild language and mystifying gibberish that characterized the Book itself. It was an everyday faith for everyone, which required no one – Driver, Examiner or Inspector – to be an intercom between dad and Dave. It was also a credo that demanded literacy of its adherents, so that they might distinguish between truth and falsity – between the gibberish of the old Book and the clarity of the new one.

So the Geezer picked up fares among the prisoners, and they in turn went out among the Londoners and carried the doctrine forth, written on scraps of A4 or else held in their memory. The agents of the PCO, who had seeseeteevee men everywhere, and who looked for flying and schism with fanatic eyes, were nonetheless caught unawares by the Geezer. They expected such doctrines to be promulgated by their own Drivers and Examiners, men of Knowledge who had taken the wrong turn. Or else they foresaw them arriving from over the sea, from the highlands of the Swiss and the Franks, where the King's enemies resided. That a simple peasant from the most remote portion of the archipelago should have carried the plague of doubt into the very heart of London, into its citadel even, did not occur to them until it was too late.

The Archdriver of the PCO, in formal robes quartered red and white, and blazoned with the device of the Wheel, appeared before the King at the morning getup. When the courtiers had dispersed, the two of them took a turn around Westminster Hall. Scrofulous peasants and pikeys were held back by a detachment of the King's own chaps behind a velvet cord. One mummy of the middling sort held out an infant, and the King did consent to bestow his touch, while a fony presented her with an amulet of the Lost Boy. The King's fool capered, beating upon a drum while he rapped:

A payn in ve nekk
A payn í iz
A payn in ve nekk í iz.

The King was in the full vigour of his middle years, the Archdriver a withered granddad who had to trot to keep up.

– I fear, your majesty, he puffed, that this Geezer is joining forces with other dissenters, in the Institute, in the Inns of Forecourt – perhaps even in the Shelters. This is a most dangerous schism. Fortunately we have an agent in the Institute itself who is close to the sectarians. We will send him into the Tower to act unwittingly as our informant. Others, I am sure, will become turncoats. I am confident we can eliminate these impious daddies and chellish mummies, as we've done in the past.

– We don't want martyrs, the King said, with this flying so widespread martyrs would be much too dangerous. We shall offer those who confess their lives. Their property shall be forfeit, their positions likewise lost. Exile and branding shall be their fate.

– And what of this, this Geezer himself?

– Why, he shall go back to from where he came, or near to it. Anywhere that is suitably remote. Let my Lawyer of Chil decide exactly where, for he must bear responsibility for this matter and take a hand in its resolution.

– A most symmetrical solution, your majesty, said the Archdriver, pressing his clove ball to his pitted old nose. Most symmetrical.

~

The Driver and Mister Greaves stood watching as the sick men of Chil were escorted past them up the stream to the travelodge. The screen wrapped around Ham was dramatically riven, a blue channel sat above the shore, and to the south of this tabular white clouds floated, rank upon rank, while to the north a bruised, magenta mass was banked up over the trees. There would be screenwash before nightfall. The moto slaughter might have to be postponed.

– How do I find you, Reervú? Mister Greaves asked, as he stretched his stiff legs.

– Well enough, the Driver grunted.

– And your fares, how are they?

– As benighted as ever, the Driver sneered, spittle flecking his mirror. Ignorant, venal, idolatrous. They profane this place, which should be an island of the blessed.

– What would you have me do as the representative of my Lawyer of Chil to rectify this?

– I cannot drive any further, Mister Greaves, without that I educate the lads in some way, and so detach them from their contumely association with the filthy motos. I need a teacher, Mister Greaves, that's what I need to cut out their superstition.

I need a surgeon also, I cannot be expected to attend to their spiritual health and their physical being, that much is beyond me.

– A teacher and a surgeon, eh? You don't ask for much! None save those who are most exalted – the Hack made a short bow – would willingly exile themselves in these remote parts. Even if I were able to find you such dads, they would most likely be compromised.

– Compromised, pissed, queer, flyer – I care not, Greaves, I care not. Send me a fellow, and no matter how rebellious he be I feel confident that I shall be able to confine his aspirations in these few clicks. Do you doubt, guv – the old crow leaned over the Hack and bore down on him with his yellow eyes – whose will would prevail?

~

He paused between two streets, and the Examiner reduced him to fourteen days. He stalled at a junction during his next appearance and was ordered to trial. The trial was one in name only. The old testimony of Mister Greaves was all that was required to establish Symun Dévúsh's guilt. No reference was made to his current activities, no defence was allowed. The Chief Examiner sentenced him in ancient Mokni: 2 B browkin on ve Weel. Yaw fingus crakked, yaw 4ed brandid, yaw tung cut aht, an U 2 B Xeyeled.

In the long third tariff before his sentence was to be carried out, the Geezer gathered to his chamber as many of his disciples as could be accommodated and warned them: B bluddë cairful, U lot – ve PeeSeeO ul av U inawl. Dú nuffing, say nuffing, an ven vay brayk me stä ahtuvit. Yet they could not obey him – they loved him too much. When the warders lugged the Wheel out into the yard, the dads touched by the Geezer stood in the heavy screenwash and jeered them. Other warders dragged Symun out, his feet trailing grooves in the churned-up earth. In an echo of his departure from Ham, the Guvnor refused to let him stand or address the prisoners, for fear of his inflammatory words. In the hushed silence while the flyer was lashed to the Wheel, the bitten-off cries of the hawkers without the Tower walls could be clearly heard: Ivers! Marmi! Ockings! Getcha Eterkins cuss-taaard!

This time the big Wheel kept on turning, faster and faster. The Geezer's head whipped round and around, until the vessels of his brain burst and blood flooded into all his memories. The common prisoners pointed out the details of this wheeling with the delight of spectators at a cock fight: Lookatvat, ees swallered iz tung! The Geezer's fares fell to their knees and wept.

It was a long kipper night in London. From door to door of the city the seeseeteevee men of the PCO moved with stealth and efficiency. Scholars, tradesmen, craftsmen, common day labourers and a smattering of lawyers. In all, some two hundred daddies and a handful of mummies were judged to have been tainted by the Geezer's flying. Under torture they all confessed.

They prised Symun Dévúsh's tongue from his gullet and pounded his chest to get him to breathe. Then they stretched the talking member from its root and cut it off. As he gargled in his own blood, they broke his knuckles and all the joints of his fingers with a punishment club. Then they branded him with the F for flyer on his forehead. Finally, as he swooned close to death, he was taken by cab to the Isle of Dogs and bundled aboard a ferry. The vessel lay off in the London roads that night, and in the small units of the first tariff a second exile was brought out to her by the pilot's pedalo.

This queer was unmolested and unchained. He had with him a capacious changingbag and to ward off the kipper cold he wore a heavy, bubbery cloakyfing with an oilskin cape over its shoulders. Soon after he'd come aboard, the gaffer interviewed him in his cabin: Mì awdas R onlë 2 tayk U sarf 2 Wyc, ware U R 2 B landid. Eye no nuffing uv oo U R aw wot U av dun, mayt, so folla ve rools uv mì ferrë an Eyel giv U no aggro. But fukkabaht an Eyel av U, unnerstood? Antonë Böm nodded his head slowly while tugging his prematurely white beard. He assumed others must have suffered far worse fates that long night, and – while not comprehending the cause of it – appreciated his light escape.

For the remainder of that kipper Böm remained at the Bouncy Castle of Wyc. He tutored a few of the Hack's children who were in residence, and he treated the maladies of both chavs and bondsmen as well as he was able. He knew nothing of the prisoner who languished in the dungeon beneath his feet. When buddout came, a pedalo set out from Wyc. It was a light, fast craft, pedalled by the closest and most trustworthy retainers of the Lawyer. It carried a sole passenger and set course for the last finger of land that pointed from the uninhabited island of Barn towards Ham.

Three months later, when the days were stretching to meet the summer solstice, another far larger pedalo headed south. This vessel belonged to Mister Greaves, the Hack of Ham, and was crewed by his dads. It set course first for the Hack's semi at Stanmaw, where trade goods were to be loaded, together with the sick fares of the Shelter. For Ham was its ultimate destination, and on the narrow thwart set in the prow there hunched a plump figure, his spectacles flashing in the switched-on foglamp. The new teacher and surgeon for the Hamsters that the Driver had requested was on his way at last.

# 8

# *The Shmeiss Ponce*

September 1992

The fare was lolling by the Bank of England. The dirty building, with its grooved walls and milled balustrades, was a big copper coin tossed down in the City. He beckoned lazily with an upraised finger, summoning the waiter, and Dave slewed the cab to a halt behind a van disgorging toilet paper. The fare – tall, officer class, sandy-haired, three-pieced – lounged over the road. While he slid into the back, Dave listened to the City itself. Could he hear the aftermath of the awful carnage of the day before? The final gargle as the dregs of fifteen billion pounds were sucked out of its dealing rooms? The sweat and moan of shirt-sleeved, plastic piano players pounding out the blues of ruin? No, there was only the hum of everyday urban vacuity.

'Where to, guv?'

'City of London School, d'you know it?' In the rearview mirror the sandy man's moist face belied his dry manner.

'No problem.'

'Not that . . . um, I'm not . . . I'm picking up my sons there, then we'll double back to Liverpool Street, yah?'

'No problem.' The sandy man blotted himself out with the *Standard . . . Would've pegged 'im as a total getter, but p'raps he's come down a few pegs . . .* Dave almost felt like telling the sandy man how bad things were for the trade. *I can't make the bloody payments, mate, can't make 'em. I've the mortgage on top of that . . . living whatsits . . . the cab costs more than just the loan as well, there's your servicing, your diesel, your bits an' bobs, I'll tell you, some days I'd do better staying at home, least I'd know how much I was down then. We're next in the bloody food chain, mate, that's a fact – you lot push the wrong button, sell short instead of long or whatever, an' it's us lot who catch it.*

When they got down to Queen Victoria Street the sandy man left his fat briefcase in the back – a repository of trust. He took Dave's time – lounging off along one of the walkways leading into the school, which was tied up to the Embankment like a redbrick cruiser. *Domine dirige nos* . . . There was time enough for Dave to read the nameplate on its immobile hull. Time enough for Dave to buff up his resentments and see them shine.

The Fairway no longer shone. When Dave first bought the cab, he lavished his attention on it, laving it, waxing it, shammy-leathering it personally in an autosexual frenzy. It was – he thought – a cool, dark reflection of the man he was. Now it was agony to stroke and rub the black flanks of the thing he'd come to hate, so he took it into the garage where one of Ali Baba's lads gave it a loveless seeing-to.

At the beginning of the year the cabbie had been clearing a minimum of seven hundred pounds every week. *A flat fucking neves, no joke, mate, double-bloody-bubble fer Sundays* . . . Then BCCI collapsed. *Gang of fucking coke heads, it never looked like a bank to me anyway, I remember ferrying those dodgy wallahs to their gaff on the Cromwell Road, all smirk an' no bloody tips* . . . And the unemployment figures cranked up to three million. *No matter, the Tories were still back in come April, rotten bunch, half of them shtupping their secretaries, the other half on the take* . . . Then in June Lloyd's lost two billion. *Granted they were a bunch of dumb toffs – only too happy to take unlimited liability before the shit hit the propellor, but they weren't just Names to me, mate – they were fares* . . . Then only last month the stock market *goes fucking tits-up*. Five billion off shares in a morning and the big bull needed *a fucking Bic round its chops – too late, it's gone an' turned into a bear* . . . Then *Paddies all over the fucking shop in their fertilizer dump trucks. Bomb upside the NatWest Tower, bomb in fucking Victoria Street – I blame . . . my wife . . .*

All of this is only braggadocio, confessed to the windscreen of the cab as if there were still a fare sitting on the tip seat, ear inclined to the sliding window. When it winds down, Dave is left with his diminished self: a big little balding man who's afraid to look at his own sparse brow in the rearview mirror . . . RE-CREATE YOUR HAIRLINE . . . DEVELOPED IN JAPAN – *but why? I've never seen a bald Jap* . . . NEW GENERATIONS STRAND-BY-STRAND REFUSION WITH TECHNO-FUSE CAN RE-CREATE YOUR HAIRLINE AND PROVIDE A TOTALLY NATURAL-LOOKING HEALTHY HEAD OF HAIR. TECHNO-FUSE IS INTEGRATED WITH YOUR SCALP AND THE PROCEDURE CAN BE PERFORMED OVER A PERIOD OF TIME, INVOLVES NO SURGERY AND NO ONE NEED EVER KNOW . . . CALL WIGMORE TRICHOLOGICAL CLINIC NOW. NOW!

The copywriter's medicalese has become Rudman's own private thoughts, a pabulum to chew over: Good News about hair loss. *Perhaps if I did it, she'd fancy me* . . . Because it's all about him, the way Michelle turns away in the bed they still, mysteriously, share and edges to the extreme far side of the mattress, where she rolls herself into a chaste belt of duck down.

The meter went on ticking. *Christ, I'm tired . . . The little runt* was four now, yet it was taking a long time to recover from being woken in the early hours of the morning. When Dave had been doing nights, he'd come in, then drift off, only to be yanked up again by a cry from the slumbrous woodlands. Dave had fought his way through whippy boughs of fatigue to where Carl trampled and snuffled in his cot. Dave had felt stunned as night after night snapped in two or three pieces. *This*, he had realized, *is how soldiers feel in combat* . . . It was then that the ordinary heroism of parenthood struck Dave hard in his selfish face. It was striking him still: *They oughta give you a fucking medal . . . Maclaren buggies lined up by the Cenotaph, spunk-drunk mummies slumped over their handles, bums up to be taken again.* The Prime Minister steps forward – a martial insurance clerk in his steel helmet hair – and pins decorations shaped like feeding bottles, teat-on-teat.

The Sandy Man's lads were two versions of himself: one lanky, stretched on the rack of adolescence, a stipple of happy pimples on his outsized jaw; the other compact, chubby even, a lush blond fringe in his mooncalf eyes. The Sandy Man said, 'On to Liverpool Street, then, cabbie,' and Dave replied, 'No problem,' because he desperately wanted there to be NO PROBLEM. *In the City, if there's one street knocked out by roadworks, then you're edging round for fucking hours . . . Leave on right Queen Victoria Street, forward Threadneedle Street, left Bishopsgate . . .* Dave was convinced this was a mid-week dad: the Sandy Man was too eager to ask questions about new teachers and forms, to pick up on the quick rhythms of lives irretrievably lost for him, the paradiddle of young hearts. *How does it feel,* Dave wanted to ask him, *to be like a nonce, dragging these kids off to your pervy cottage in the sticks For One Night Only?*

Liverpool Street was a *massive bollix* of renovation and construction. The Victorian façade was being torn off, a new one of silky granite slipped on. Inside, a transept of baguette stalls and knicker booths was being laid across the end of the platforms. *In the old Victoria Station there were whole wheeling flocks of scabby pigeons, everything was smoky and sooty, iron pillars shooting up into dingy glass ceiling . . . Dad used to take me down to the Cartoon Cinema . . . Left me in there while he went into the hotel next door for a few shorts . . .*

To get to the set-down Dave had to wrestle the cab down temporary passageways of scaffolding and tarpaulin, humping over rubber sills. The Sandy Man had his twenty out long before they'd stopped. He folded it into a strip that he twined between his clever fingers, then poked the origami earnings at Dave. *Funny the way people handle money, playing with it, touching it up . . . wouldn't do it with any other thing . . .* 'Ain't you got anything smaller, guv?'

'Sorry – but no.' The Sandy Man took his change and the three of them disappeared into the clatter of the station. *Fucking wanker – little tossers . . .* He'd forgotten to tip. Once Dave ranked up, he had a long wait for another fare in the diesel-stinking darkness. He recognized a few faces looming in nearby windows from infrequent trips to cab shelters, or snaffled lunches at the Café Europa in King's Cross – but no one he wanted to talk to. *They'd only wanta moan some . . . Moan-fucking-moan . . .* Magic Tree air fresheners dangled from their rearview mirrors. *All these big blokes, lost in a tiny bloody forest . . .* Dave thought of Benny, his granddad. *I really oughta go and see him.*

CLARINS AT HARVEY NICHOLS pulls Michelle up short. SKINCARE CENTRE. FACE, BUST, BODY AND SUN. TRAINED THERAPISTS. *Yeah, right . . .* Five stormy years of marriage have given her a piratical internal monologue; she stands on the tilting deck of her consciousness wielding a tongue like a cutlass. *Trained bloody slags is more like it. In from Bromley and Selhurst, Traceys and Sharons without an idea in their tiny minds except Darren's cock and she-said he-said . . .* DETOXIFYING FACIAL AND HAND TREATMENT. *Still, I have to admit that sounds good.*

Michelle stopped scanning the *Standard* to look at the scumbled junction of Kentish Town Road and Leighton Road: the neo-Gothic horror of the Assembly Rooms pub, and a daft pavilion with glass roof and cast-iron stanchions beneath which dossers lolled like filthy pashas. Carl was slumped beside her eyeing an apricot. 'C'mon, love,' Michelle said, 'it's nice, it's like a sweetie.' The four-year-old bit into it with frank dubiety, his pretty, freckled features – hers really – screwed up in distaste. 'Iss gusting,' he said and spat. REFRESHING CUP OF HERBAL TEA. *If I don't get out of this shit . . .* She levered the sticky yellow blob off Carl's T-shirt and popped it in her own mouth . . . *I'm gonna do something stupid.* DELICIOUS FRUIT COCKTAIL.

In the two and a half days a week Michelle looked after her son she tried to make sure Carl had a balanced diet – plenty of fruit, no fizzy drinks, green vegetables, brown bread. She had kept abreast of debates about immunization. She had campaigned for the right nursery-school place. It was ironic that now it wasn't quite so bad between her and Dave she felt like leaving more than ever.

*When we were first married, it was alright. I was touched . . . by him* . . . They bought the house on Kingsford Street in Gospel Oak. At National Childbirth Trust classes, held by a woman called Sarona in her endless living room up on the heights of Hampstead, Michelle didn't only learn how to breathe, she found out how to be a different woman. *Dave couldn't partner me, he was working all hours* . . . But Sarona did. *She had perfect style . . . beautiful deportment . . . black trousers, hammered silver jewellery . . . nothing vulgar . . . wispy shawls . . . that very aquiline Persian nose . . . I didn't even know what aquiline meant before that . . . When I went back to work again I had 'it', at last, a . . . seriousness . . . a poise . . . having a kid helped . . . I was grateful to Dave for – for the whole set-up. It doesn't mean they don't put you down or stare at your tits, but once you're a mum their moves are . . . slower, more obvious, sadder.*

The 214 bus shushed to a halt and caught by surprise she dragged Carl on board and paid the fare, snagged the child and collapsed into a seat as the bus thrummed on up Highgate Road. The funfair motion made the little boy laugh, and she cupped his cheek. 'You're gorgeous,' Michelle said. 'My gorgeous – my Gorj.' But then, looking down, Michelle saw that her floral-print skirt had ridden up over the miserable spectacle of razor nicks and stubble on the same leg. GLAMOROUS EVENING MAKE-UP.

*It didn't seem to me . . . I thought I'd suffered enough . . . I could never stand Dave's ham-fisted touch unless I was drunk . . . and when . . . I . . . It . . . He . . . He'd always said he'd had . . . the snip . . . reasonable doubt, isn't that what lawyers call it? I should've told him . . . Dave . . .*

*told them both . . . but I'd made a commitment, hadn't I? Besides* he *was off his fucking rocker by then, booze, charley, Godnosewot . . . what would've been the point? Four completely unhappy people instead of two?* BEAUTY FLASH BALM FOR EVENING'S ENJOYMENT.

*She doesn't know her arse from her elbow . . . Her Hackney from her fucking Ealing . . . She's lived in London all her bloody life and if the tube packed up, the buses stopped running, and there wasn't a cab driver to take her there, she wouldn't know how to get home from work . . . not a clue. No Knowledge whatsoever . . . She went into the hospital in the morning . . . in daylight . . . Made it more clinical . . . Maybe it would've been . . . more . . . brung us closer . . . if it'd been dark . . .* Crushed up in the smoky cabin, Dave lit another filter tip. He grimaced, remembering the jerky shuffle he'd danced with his groaning wife across the swirly linoleum of the delivery room.

The done thing for an eager dad was to hearken to the New Arrival. In the event there wasn't room for Dave in the tangle of tubes and the jive of trained hands. Michelle's face was blanched with fatigue, flattened by agony, all her features wrenched to one side, like those of *a skate or a turbot*. She was that remote from him, Dave thought, deep under the womanly sea. When, at the crucial moment, he did head down to where scratchy brown paper towels were spread ready, he found the gash and the gush – then these other features twisting to confront him. Fucker Finch had said, 'Iss uncanny, yeah, but you'll recognize 'em from the off. Thass what iss bin like wiv awluv mine. I fought "Oh, so iss *you* issit . . ."' But Dave didn't recognize this miraculous, shiny fruit at all; it had fallen from a strange tree.

To be fair, Dave Rudman didn't have any paradigm for the birth of a child. He tried to talk to his father in the final fetid days when Michelle's bump pushed him from the house. 'I was at Tadcaster the day you were born,' Paul remarked, dabbing transcriptase on his pint glass with his wet bottom lip.

'Why?' Dave was nonplussed. 'Did you have some slots up there?'

'No, don't be daft, there was a good card that day, your mother wouldn't've wanted me within a mile of the hospital – she didn't for Sam or Noel neither. I phoned, checked everything was shipshape, then I scooped a monkey on the last two. Reverse forecast – you were a lucky little chap when it come to the gee-gees.'

Fathers – they were always absent, while houses – they endure. Put upon by plaster, MDF and emulsion; ground down by sanders and drills; fiddled with by plumbers and electricians – they come through it all that much more robust. Like so many others, Dave and Michelle had placed their faith in a house: it would be their repository of trust and belief. Dave did his bit and his rewards were fettuccine and salmon bakes, the occasional glass of white wine, a limp hand job on a Saturday morning.

Yet the strange thing was that the more Dave painted, hammered and wired, the more the finished thing was hers – all hers. Michelle had the capacity to psychically invest laminated surfaces, tiles and even the very tiny screws that pinioned towel rings to kitchen units. When she was at home, she was in the house, in every part of it, while he always felt like a lodger.

Strolling up to the ironmonger's at Southend Green, intent on track lighting, Dave noticed an Indian takeaway. The sign over the open door read: PIZZA WORLD AND CURRY WORLD – TWO WORLDS IN ONE. Peering inside, he was taken aback – Faisal, with whom he'd been at school in Woodside Park, was bustling about behind the counter. The nerdy boy who'd set out to become a doctor was sporting collar-length hair, thick sideburns and stained Kameeze. He was sowing the raw dough with rough-cut red peppers and whistling.

They hadn't been friends, and Faisal was wary. Dave was surprised to see him running this ghee shop – and said so. Hadn't he wanted to be a doctor? The other man muttered about family. Death. Duties. After that, whenever it got too tense at home, or the cloacal intensity of it drove him out – mother, mother-in-law, baby, three big hands competing to wipe one small bottom – Dave snuck to Two Worlds, where, on a wonky round table strewn with yellowing tabloids, he ate whatever Faisal set before him. Slowly the two men relaxed into a friendship – an unfocused closeness, as if they were sitting side by side on a riverbank and fishing as a pretext for intimacy.

Dave assumed his new friend was as godless as himself, yet within days of beginning to patronize Two Worlds, he found Faisal on his knees between the two chiller cabinets, making obeisance towards the Holloway Road. Given the glacial pace of male confidence, it took another two years for Dave to discover that Faisal was not simply on nodding terms with the Koran, but a highly advanced believer in the literal truth of the ancient text. As Dave munched his way through Desert Storm, the proprietor of Two Worlds enlightened him as to the totality of his own submission: it was all in the Koran, right down to diagrams of the microcircuitry in each and every warhead. 'You don't really believe that, do you?' Dave twitted him.

'Bloody right I do. It's . . . it's like a blueprint, Dave, that book, it's . . . it's got everything in it that ever has been and ever will be. It's a logical structure: "There is no God but God", that's the first proposition – all the rest follows logically, perfectly, including smart bombs, genetic engineering, the whole bloody lot.'

'Give over, mate! You can't, I mean – you were gonna be a doctor, a scientist, you must understand that some bloke, thousands of years ago, couldn't possibly –'

'Not some bloke, Dave. God.'

When Michelle returned to work, Dave went on a radio circuit. He thought the money would be steadier. It was, but he couldn't stand driving with one ear open to the seedy wheedle of the controller. He couldn't stand the other drivers scalping the jobs, claiming over the radio to be where they manifestly weren't, *as if they're driving a fucking invisible cab*. He got home more irritable than ever, snapping at the merest thing. He switched to nights – it gave him more time with the boy and less with her. Soon Dave hardly saw Michelle at all – their feet dovetailed in the bed for a couple of hours, then she *fucked off* into the West End where she held meetings in *smoked-glass boxes . . . the bitch. Abandoning us both.*

At night Dave worked the mainline stations – Victoria and Paddington mostly. The west of London felt warmer in the winter, better lit, less susceptible to the chill of deep time. The fares were frowsty under the sodium lamps. In the back of the cab they slumped against their luggage, and Dave drove them home to Wembley, Twickenham and Muswell Hill. Or else they were tourists bound for the Bonnington, the Inn on the Park or the Lancaster – gaunt people-barns, where maids flitted through the lobbies, cardboard coffins of dying blooms cradled in their arms. In the wee-wee hours he parked up at an all-night café in Bayswater and sat reading the next day's news, while solider citizens lay abed waiting for it to happen. His fellow night people were exiguous – they wore the faces of forgotten comedians, unfunny and unloved.

Dave took junkies to score in the All Saints Road, tarts to fuck in Mayfair, punters to bet in the Gloucester Road, surgeons to cut in Bloomsbury, sous chefs to chop in Soho. He noticed nothing, retained nothing – glad only to be driving, moving through the whispering streets, feeling the surface beneath his wheels change from smooth to rough to rougher to rutted. In the blank dawns, when Hyde Park seethed with mist, he would find himself rattling through Belgravia, a bony fag stuck in his skull, and seeing the queues of visa applicants – already at this early hour lined up outside the consulates – it occurred to him that *these are the people I dropped off a few hours ago . . . They can't fucking stand it here any more than I can . . . They want out right away . . .*

Michelle click-clacked along Wigmore Street from Oxford Circus tube. She took chilly glances at the steely instruments in the display windows of the medical supply shops. Clamps, forceps, callipers – all were tastefully arranged in front of plastic skeletons. *Anatomy 92* . . . her mind was already on the job. Michelle was the new Exhibitions Executive. Maternity leave or not, the management liked her new NCT style, for she'd honed her natural air of authority. On her first day back she stood in the Ladies applying a second full coating of slap – her freckle-faced days were over. She could hear someone being noisily sick in one of the stalls. A woman emerged. She was greasily emaciated, her woollen suit was a partially sloughed hide, yet her features were oddly fresh and composed. 'You must be Michelle Brodie,' she said, joining Michelle in front of the mirror. 'I'm Gail Farber, I'll be doing the job share with you. They're all wankers here, aren't they?'

Carl – Michelle didn't like the name, it was Dave's choice. When he'd proposed it, she dropped a full mug of Nescafé on a white rug. Then she allowed it, saddling herself with this near homonym only out of a sense of overpowering guilt.

The childcare was a mess. Cath did some days, Dave others. They argued over both possession and abandonment of the baby. At work, flipping through budget forecasts, the figures blurred before Michelle's eyes, then cleared to reveal Carl howling on the floor, cold, naked and forgotten. She heaved with regret for the soft hours of counting tiny toes and patting silky skin.

Michelle didn't want her mother getting too close to the baby – Cath might suss out the secret. So eventually she succumbed to an au pair, hoping that this would impose order on the household. She did, sort of. The au pair was a plump, equable, Friesian girl called Gertrude. She was conscientious, she adored Carl, she didn't go out at night – preferring to low in the converted attic. Gertrude also spent a long time in front of the mirror, using up Michelle's concealer, which sadly, the chatelaine required for herself.

On the two afternoons when Dave looked after Carl he took the baby up on to the Heath. Dave put him in a sling under his bomber jacket, so that all he could see of Carl were metal teeth gnashing those alien features. Whenever he changed Carl, Dave was shocked anew by his skinny shanks . . . *I was a chubby baby, Mum said, Noel and Sam were too . . . These legs . . . I don't like them.* Yet he still loved the boy – he knew he did. He figured they'd recognize each other in time.

The legs extended and the sling was exchanged for a pushchair; so Dave perambulated, calling over to his unrecognizable son . . . *Leave on right Parliament Hill, comply path down to Highgate Ponds, left Highgate Ponds, forward* . . . On the green ridge of the Hampstead massif, where oak and beech screened off the encompassing city, Dave could relax, and hear the swelling chord connecting him to his child. It was enough. On those evenings he talked civilly to his mother-in-law, had a drink ready for his wife when she came home from work. He bathed the baby, and foot-pumped him in his bouncy chair until he was asleep.

Watching Dave tenderly lift her son and bear him away to his cot, Michelle felt that while she could never love her husband, she could at least tolerate him . . . *and that's enough, isn't it?*

~

At last Dave got a fare, and better still he was heading northeast from Liverpool Street to Hackney. Dave dropped him off at Mare Street, then drove down to see his granddad. He parked up and headed up through the clattery core of Homerton Hospital. Rust seeped from metal window frames, there were sweet wrappers on the stairs, and furtive smokers in bathrobes were blowing their lung rot out of the fire doors. *Mister Loverman, Shabba! Always makes me think about sex, this gaff, fuck my way out of death, only natural, innit.* A dirty pearl of cotton wool lay on a nacreous tile.

Beside Benny Cohen's bed there was a bowl of curving, penile bananas. *Mister Loverman* . . . And Dave's great-aunt, who used to be a plain Rachel but was now *Gladys. Weird to change your name at all but to change it to Gladys, that's fucking loony.* She wore a thick overcoat and sagging stockings. Her feet were huge in basketball boots, her fleshy nose twitched in the gloom of the ward, dowsing for misery. 'Oh, David, David!' She collapsed on his leather chest. Dave felt bones and smelled mothballs. *She's two steps from being a bag lady.* He remembered her dismally neat maisonette in Leytonstone, the pathetic little drawers in her shoddy kitchen units, each one full to the brim with neatly folded brown-paper bags. She had eight cats. 'Your grandfather's going to cross over soon, David, cross over the Jordan.' . . . *Which Jordan?* He was looking at her shoes. *Michael? Which holy rollers was it she's mixed up in?*

He thought back to his wedding. Aunt Gladys had brought Benny over in a minicab from the East End. At the reception, held up West in a poncey restaurant none of them had liked, Aunt Gladys had buttonholed the guests, forcing on them leaflets headed 'Jews for Jesus'. Dave overheard her telling Dave Quinn, 'It's alright to follow the Redeemer even if you are one of the Chosen People, even if you've been bar mitzvahed. Don't believe the blood libel, my child, for we can all atone for His Sacrifice, we can all be anointed with his chrism and his love.' Dave was touched when Quinn – whom he always thought of as basically a moral-free zone – patted Gladys's shaky hand and said, 'Thank you, missus, I'll make sure I give it a good read.' Then tucked the leaflet away in his suit pocket.

A nurse bustled into the ward and advanced to the nubbin of life on the bed. First she checked the silvery nipple of her watch, then she adjusted the spigots that were attached to Benny's tubes. He stirred – his head was nut brown, wrinkled as a walnut. It looked as if it had been parboiled, coated in tar, then impaled on a cigarette. 'Shmeiss ponce,' Benny croaked.

'You what, Granddad?' But that was all – the old man's eyes were shut again.

Dave turned away. Outside the filmy window was a bit of Hackney Marsh, seagulls scrummed above a rugby pitch. Gladys joined him. 'I bin talkin' to 'im, readin' to 'im.' She withdrew a purple-bound volume from her coat; a golden angel blowing a stylized golden trumpet was embossed on its cover.

'You still with . . . with . . .' Dave couldn't bear to say it. '. . . that lot?'

'I'm fifty-five years of age,' Gladys lied, 'an' at long last after all me searching I've come 'ome to the true Church. I know now that Jews fer Jesus, well, it was justa way in, so to speak. Now I've made me choice, I'm a Saint, I eggsept the Doctrines and the Covenants.'

'A Saint?' Dave queried.

'A member of the Church of the Latter-Day Saints, what you gentiles call the Mormons.'

'Bloody hell!' Dave expostulated and then again, 'Bloody hell!'

'There's no need to blaspheme, David, no need at all. P'raps if you'd had Christ Jesus in your life, fings wouldn't've got to this pass.'

'Whaddya mean by that?' Dave glared into Gladys's mad blue eyes. 'What's my mum been saying?'

'Only that . . . well . . . it isn't my place.' Gladys folded pious hands on her book and held it in front of her belly.

'No, go on, it is your place, obviously.'

'Well, only that you and your 'Chelle ain't that happy – and I know it can't be good in the cabs eever what wiv this resesshun an' that . . .'

Dave drove back across town to Gospel Oak. He clonked through Dalston, past the burnt-out hulk of the Four Aces. *What was that black geezer's name? Went in the nick there with a shooter – blew his fucking head off . . . Least Benny's dying in a private cubicle thing. With curtains . . . curtains, cubicles . . . shmeiss ponce . . . thass it! The steam baths – that's what Benny was on about . . . the Porchester out west, that's where him an' his mates used to hang out . . . playing cards, snarfin' cheese sarnies and bowls of jelly and custard . . . Fat men . . . all with gold jewellery . . . rings . . . ID bracelets . . . they all smoked too . . . King Edward cigars . . . pipes, fags . . . I remember the shmeiss ponce . . . little fellow . . . Lewis Levy, who bilked his turn with the shmeiss. I'm too 'ot – that's what he whined, I'm gonna 'ave a seizure . . . The others'd watch him scarper through the steam room, then when he'd gone they'd dump on 'im . . . fucking runt, fucking shmo, fucking chancer, dodgy little cunt, shmeiss ponce!*

The cabbies used their ire to withstand the steam's sting as they rubbed away the filth of the job, the city pigment drilled into their skins like a tattoo of the *A–Z*. *They talked, bloody hell how they talked . . . There was one mate of Benny's, Roy Voss – he knew it all, how many hansoms and growlers there used to be, when they got rid of 'em . . . sold 'em off for firewood . . . he knew all the kinds of cabs there's been on the roads . . . never grew tired of recounting bits of cabbing lore, it was like . . . I dunno . . . it was like the cabbing was some sorta secret government or sumffing running the whole bloody country . . . Benny and the others used to take the piss.*

When Dave Rudman got home that night wanting food and sympathy, Michelle announced that she was going out and so was the au pair. 'I'm meeting up with Sandra, we're going to see Pavarotti.'

'What, she got tickets?'

'No, course not. We're gonna have a few drinks and watch him on that screen thingy in Covent Garden. You don't mind, do you? It's not as if you're making that much at the moment, so I –'

'So you what? What?!' Dave tousled his son's hair with an angry hand, then stalked up the little stairs. Over the next hour, as Michelle got ready, the argument flared and guttered.

They did good rowing, Dave and Michelle. When she was pregnant with Carl he'd hit her, once. Her body had always assailed him with ambivalence – he wanted to possess it and yet he was also repelled. Her marbled belly, her engorged breasts – it shamed him the way they tipped him into revulsion. After the blow had been struck Michelle waited patiently, until he was maudlin and self-piteous, then hit him back, much harder. 'You never,' she'd screamed, 'ever lay a finger on me again or I'll fucking have you . . .' Her red hair fizzed round her freckled face. '. . . I'll have you put away!'

On this particular evening they argued about who did what in the house. 'You never change a lightbulb.' 'So, you never stack the dishwasher.' It was really an argument about money, so they moved on to 'You never pay a bill.' 'I can't, I can't! So what if you do clear more than me – you do fuck-all for your money, I graft!' Still, the arguments about money – pressing as they were, with the overdraft screaming red and the living expenses rising inexorably – were really arguments about sex, so they argued about that instead. The arguments about sex cut to the bone of their already lean self-regard, they couldn't even be had aloud – they were too threatening to Dave and Michelle's self-assembled world. So the sex arguments were soundless howls. *I hate your clumsy cock and your slobbery mouth . . . Your pathetic wobbly belly makes me sick . . . . Why can't you be even a little tender to me . . . ?*

*I've had so many better, happier lovers than you . . . . The au-fucking-pair would have me in a sec! Maybe that's the way it should be – me and Gertie and the boy. She looks after him and gives me the occasional fucking gobble – which is more than you're ever bloody up for . . . You! You know nothing about women . . . nothing at all . . . You pant and grunt . . . You're a pig – not a man . . .*

After Michelle had gone, Dave bathed Carl and immersed the child in his own tantrum. 'I wen' swimmin',' his son said.

'What?' Dave snapped.

'I wen' swimmin' . . . swimmin', swimmin' . . . swimmin' . . .' Carl swivelled round in the soapy water, as his humped back capsized blue boats and yellow ducks. 'I swimmin' – swimmin'!' A wave broke over the side of the bath and soaked Dave's trainers, then swamped the floor. 'Stop it!' he shouted, but the little boy went on chanting, 'Lookitme I swimmin', I swimmin'!' Until Dave lashed out and left three livid fingerprints on Carl's shoulder blade. *One* . . . *Two* . . . *Three* . . . There was silence for three beats, the child awed by the cataclysm of adult rage, then, 'Waaaa!' It was the first time Dave had hit the boy – it wasn't to be the last.

'I'm sorry, Boysie, I'm sorry,' he whimpered, pressing his brutish face into the good smell of skin and soap.

In the morning Dave could hardly rise, he was so mired in shame. He shook as he made Carl eggy soldiers and watched the child bayonet his face with them. Carl didn't bear a grudge – but it wasn't his forgiveness Dave needed. 'Wouldja phone in for me, love?' Michelle croaked when Dave brought her a cup of tea. 'Say I'm sick. I've gotta dreadful pain in my neck.'

'You are sick,' Dave stated flatly – then he asked, 'Did 'e do it, then?'

'You what, love?'

'Did he do it, Pavarotti, did he do Nessun whatsit, y'know, the World Cup song?'

'Oh . . . oh yeah, yeah, he did, as an encore.'

*Sleep no more* . . . Dave took Carl to nursery, went for a full English and a dump and a read of the paper, then picked him up again. He'd decided to take the victim swimming at a pool down at the Elephant and Castle, which had flumes and a wave machine. It was the right kind of penance. Dave hated public pools, hated their atmosphere of institutional rot and medicalized exercise, their chemical reek and plugholes clotted with the hairs of the multitude. He slung the cab down through Euston and along the wide trench of Gower Street. *Bloody peculiar* . . . He looked in the mirror at his passenger, whose car seat was strapped into the back of the cab. *But when he's with me it's like I'm drifting again . . . It's like I thought the job would be . . . just driving, just drifting through town . . . no worries . . .*

Carl paddled in between green, frog-shaped floats, his orange water-wings pinioning him to the surface. His father circled him like a remorseful yet sportive shark, closing in with an outstretched arm to sweep the child into hilarity. 'I swimmin', Daddy . . . I swimmin' . . . Lookitme!' Dave persuaded the surly lifeguard to switch on the wave machine. Chlorine combers boiled up in the deep end and came hissing towards them. Carl bobbed, squealing with delight. The waves broke on the tiled foreshore under a prismatic neon sun. His father rose and sank, troubled by an uncomfortable intimation. The agitated water was cupped in a stony outcrop of the two-thousand-year-old city: London, a porous slab of rock through which a million rivulets percolated – sewers, conduits, entombed rivers. High up in the brick escarpments and masonry pinnacles, basins, baths and toilets slopped. The fern-fringed plunge pools in health spas, the jacuzzis of the rich bubbling beside Millionaire's Row, the reservoirs in the Lea Valley, the O-ring itself – a mighty orbital motorway of fluid coursing beneath the tarmac plain. With each automated surge Dave felt the future seething, the present boiling, the past churning.

When Dave got back to the cab and strapped Carl in, he found a message from Gary Finch on his pager . . . *stupid little doo-da, only got it 'cause 'chelle was pregnant* . . . and when he called him the tubby man was in some distress. 'Come over east, willya, Tufty, I need to 'ave a chat. I'm plotted up wiv Big End in the Globe.'

Michelle's period had come that morning, and dumping the used applicator in the bin, and the wrapping in the toilet bowl, she wondered whether all her ill feeling had given birth to this papery curl. 'Are you going out working, love?' He was still love – but it was a love that would dissolve with the next Alka-Seltzer.

'Yeah, yeah, but first I'm going over east to have a bite with Gary and Big End.'

'What?'

'You heard.'

'I didn't mean . . . it's just that . . . just that –'

'Mum! Mum! MumMumMumMumMum –' Carl was tugging his mother's sleeve and his need was insistent – now and for ever, need without end. Dave left. *I know what she means . . . I hardly see any of 'em any more . . . my mates . . . my friends . . . That's what it does . . . being . . . being* . . . Unhappily married. What could they do? To confide in anyone was to invite a dangerous sympathy: 'Oh, yes, isn't he/she awful, I've always thought that, you should leave him/her . . .' and so the miserably bound remain lashed together on their island of desertion while friendships cruise away. Yet even unhappiness can be a kind of intimacy.

~

When Dave arrived at the pub he found Fucker and Big End with a fair few pint glasses on the tabletop in front of them. Big End got up without asking what Dave wanted and went to the bar, where an amiable, doughy blonde had long since replaced Mrs Hedges. Big End looked like a mutant – with the empty wrinkled arms of his overalls hanging down his back. Dave spied his tool grip and spirit level propped in a corner of the bar and envied him for the honest simplicity of his tools. *Fucker looks dreadful* . . . And he did, his natural perm ruined by sweat, his pouchy clown's face drooping with dolour. His fat belly heaved against the table, green Fred Perry shirt riding up to reveal his furry gut. 'What's up?' Dave asked, pulling up a stool.

'Iss Debbie, she's only gone and fucked off wiv the kids.'

'What, did she find out about wasserface, that other bird you got on the go?'

'Nah, she's known about Karen fer ages, they was pregnant at the same time with Jason an' Kylie. Nah, iss this other one she's found aht abaht.'

'Another one?' Dave took the pint Big End handed him and tossed off a third of it. 'What issit with you, Fucker?'

'I dunno, I s'pose iss jus' me nature, innit.' He smiled ruefully and took a swallow of his own drink. There were no such things as jokes now.

'So, wotchew want me for, Fucker, to commiserate or what?'

'Nah, don't be lemon – I know where they are an' that, I wanna go an' get 'em back.'

'I don't like the sound of that, mate,' Dave said. 'You've gotta talk it through with Debbie, don't do anyfing hasty.'

'That's what I been saying,' Big End put in. ''E's gotta talk it frough, if I got troubles with my women I talk it frough.'

'Oh, yeah,' Dave half rounded on Big End, 'how many baby-mamas is it you've got now?'

'Depends,' Big End grinned, 'ooze countin'.'

'But you don' live wiv any of 'em, do you?'

'Well . . . no, not eggzackly, but they 'cept that iss different in the black co-munity.'

'Yeah, right.' Dave turned back to Fucker. 'So why me?'

'You've got front an' that, Tufty, also you got the cab.'

'Where's your cab, then?'

'I 'ad to let it go, mate, couldn't make the payments. I bin doing site work wiv Big End, way fings are on ve job I may let go of my licence an' go permi'. I tell you I'm fucked – you gotta help me. If I don' 'ave those kids in me life I've got nuffing. Nuffing.'

They sat in the Globe drinking for another hour or so. By the time Dave had downed two more pints he was prepared to go with

Fucker to check on Debbie and the two kids as long as he didn't make a scene. Then, with the two unlikely fares in the back of the cab, Dave felt drunk at the wheel and regretted the whole thing. *I could lose my licence if the OB gives me a tug . . . What am I doing?*

The flat where Debbie had taken refuge with little Jason and littler Amber was in a council block at the top of Brick Lane. It was an old LCC building, redbrick with external balconies and tiled staircases. They left the cab on a meter next to a shop advertising a closing down sale of glass slippers, plastic bead waterfalls and mock braziers with trompe l'œil tissue-paper flames. Furtive Bengalis darted into the Friday afternoon strollers, pressing flyers on them: 'Lunch Special, All You Can Eat, £2.95.' 'I could murder a curry,' said Big End.

The plan was that Dave would knock on the door while the other two kept out of sight. When Debbie's mate Berenice answered, he'd explain that he was a friend of Gary and he needed to speak with Debbie. When she emerged so would her husband, and hopefully there'd be a resolution. It didn't work out that way. Berenice was suspicious from the off – she only opened the door a crack. A fat, mixed-race girl in puce tracksuit bottoms stretched tight over a double belly, she goggled at Dave, taking in through the six-inch gap the whole disreputable length of him – or so he assumed. Behind her daytime TV smouldered in a dim, smoky room. 'Bwoy, she ain't even here so you can't talk wiv 'er.'

'I'm sure she is,' Dave wheedled. 'Gary – her old man – told me she was. Look, don't you think it would be better if they sorted this out? It can't be good for the kids.'

'Wotchew knowabout kids? Wotchew know? You push them out, yeah?' She slapped her bellies and they shivered. 'You push them out of your cock?'

'No –'

He was going to try to answer her question, but Debbie forestalled him by wrenching the door open – she must have been standing behind Berenice the whole time – and letting fly: 'Oo you fronting up for, Tufty, issit that wanker? Issit?' Then Fucker came barrelling out of the recess by the rubbish chute, and charged at the door like a pocket bull elephant, howling, 'Jase! Amber! Iss Daddy! Iss Daddy! I come fer yer!'

The mêlée quickly became an ugly stand-off: all five adults were jammed inside the main room of the flat. In the bedroom to the right, Dave could see a bunch of kids cowering behind a bunk bed. Fucker grabbed a thin baby from a bouncy chair and held it against his chest, its little heels drumming on his heaving stomach. Berenice began bellowing, 'Gimme 'im! Gimme 'im! Gimme 'im!' again and again, while Fucker screamed, 'Back off! Back off!' Debbie had collapsed on to the floor, and all Dave Rudman could think of was *very black roots growing out*, in the perverse way that dramatic events force trivia on those involved.

It was left to Big End to do something effective. He strode over to Fucker, relieved him of the infant, handed it back to its mother, then dragged the chubby man out on to the walkway. 'I'll 'ave the fucking raddiks on you, bwoy, you see I won't!' Berenice screamed while Debbie sobbed. Dave tried to calm the situation, tamping the women down with outstretched hands, but Big End came back in and dragged him out as well. When they had regrouped by the cab, Big End put his arms round the two other men's shoulders and said, 'Right, then! 'Owzabout that curry?'

Ten minutes later they were sitting in the Lahore Kebab House on Henriques Street at a rice-bedizened, sauce-smeared table. Fucker had picked up a half bottle of Scotch, and, unmindful of religious sensibilities, the three men passed it between them, taking hefty swigs. Meaty blobs speared by airy cutlery met numb lips. Dave stared woozily at the thickening traffic: the scabrous Transits bumping in from the A13, Canvey Island and all points east; the grumbling dump trucks, anfractuous scrap metal spilling over their grooved sides; the executive landaus with *expense-account arses spread on their buttery upholstery . . . This . . . this is the real East End*, where the soaring towers of the City, prestressed with adrenalin, collapse into the tat and veg of Brick Lane and Petticoat Lane. Here, in this parched badlands, the alien minarets of the new mosque pricked the grey heavens. Across the Commercial Road the rag traders' showrooms were like hot houses pressed from within by multicoloured flowers of brocade, lace and cotton.

A full cab-tariff band later, Dave's heart changed down and struggled to pull his clapped-out consciousness into the dim light of the spieler. He noticed that Big End was gone – and acknowledged he'd been so for some time.

'Heh-heh,' said one of the old faces who was playing blackjack with Fucker, 'wadjew give 'im, whizz or wot?'

'Whizz,' Fucker said. He was at ease with these men, whose mortal clay was fired with venality.

'Heh-heh, hit me, you cunt.' The dealer – a terrifying rail of a man in a zip-up nylon windcheater – chucked the old face a card. 'Busted. Orlright, I'm ahtuvere.' He got up, a bandy-legged little man, who for all that exuded palpable menace. 'Wherejoo 'eaded, Freddie?' the Dealer asked, tipping back on his chair.

'Gants Hill,' Freddie spat. 'I'm minted an' I'm putting a monkey on wiv Basset fer Tony Thornton to whip that prancing nigger Eubank.'

'As you do,' Fucker put in, but Freddie paid him no mind, only shrugged on his blazer and adjusted his display handkerchief, smoothing the two snowy linen fangs. He departed through red velveteen curtains with a puff of dust.

For the next hour or two Dave lay slumped on the narrow vinyl banquette, while Fucker played cards and described his sexual conquests to the rail with gynaecological precision. *They call me*

*Mister Loverman. They call me Mister Loverman . . .* Other men came in through the curtains and sat down for a hand or two. They were all of a kind – lazy and dangerous – their patter reduced to staccato machismo. There was much talk of 'stinky little drummers', 'going out there' and 'doing a bit of work'. 'Orlright, is 'e?' They jerked their dagger-thumbs at Dave, and Fucker vouched for him. ''Im? 'E's a cabbie, we used to be butter boys togevver.'

Gary – Fucker – Finch. He came across the waiting room of the Public Carriage Office on Penton Street the day Dave went to put in his application. He put out his hand to be shaken, and when Dave reached for it jerked it away and sent it burrowing into his own curly mop. That was Fucker, a tubby little chap laughing at his own japes and practical jokes. The inflated condom, the deflated back tyre, the prank phone call – when he was a lad it was endearing, then as he got older it grew staler. What stunts, Dave wondered, would he be pulling in middle age?

With its old kitchen-unit bar, nicotine ceiling and snooker-hall lampshade, the spieler was outside of time and even space. Dave thought they might be in a cellar – but he couldn't be sure. When he went to squirt half-digested curry into a shattered commode, he staggered along a dank corridor. To one side there was exposed brickwork, on the other stacks of plastic-wrapped toilet rolls. But there was no paper in the kharzi, unless he tore another strip from the poster of Sam Fox in string-bikini bottoms. Someone had already ripped off her left breast.

Dave felt drunk, sick and wired all at once. His heart kept thumping him in his conscience. *I'm no kind of father at all . . . I'm nothing . . . If I was gone tomorrow he'd never know . . . He'd never remember the hours spent in the Playzone, the two of us squirming in the plastic balls . . . That fever he had . . . The smell of it . . . Eggy water spilt on a hot ring . . . Pushing him up from Falloden Way to my mum's pulling ivy from a fence . . . Laughing . . . At Brighton he said 'Jewels' and tried to scoop up the sunlight on the sea . . . Trudging across the Serpentine in a pedalo . . . His feet barely reaching the pedals . . . Is this the sea, Daddy, the really sea? There's no point in going home now . . . Too late.*

Later still they were in a strip club and a skinny girl was thrusting her green Spandex crotch in Dave's face. He could see her stubble – she his. Boy George bragged, 'I know all there is to know about the crying game.' Fucker chose this moment to be coherent: 'You 'eard about Phil Eddings, then?'

'You what? You . . . what?'

'Phil, U erred wot 'appened?'

'No.'

'Oh, c'mon, you're fucking jarring me now, Tufty.'

'I tell you, Fucker, I HAVEN'T HEARD!' The stripper reared away from him.

'Not so loud, son,' Fucker took Dave gently by the scruff as a heavy in a black Harrington unbuckled his meaty arms and came towards them. 'No bovver, mate,' said Fucker, fending him off. 'We wuz leavin' anyway.'

In the street – which was the brooding clash of Hackney Road and Old Street – they leaned against each other like discarded milk crates. A tramp came striding by, his certain tread and modern backpack contradicting his boots, which were *shot to shit* . . . uppers and soles with no heels or toes. 'What, then?' Dave burped. 'What about Phil?'

''E . . .'e . . .' Fucker gasped it out: ''E only went and topped 'imself.'

In the minicab Fucker elaborated. 'Like me, Phil couldn't make the payments. 'E did a runner, posted the keys in the door an' took off. But 'ere's a fing.' Fucker's two ham hands held Dave's shoulder. 'They caught up wiv 'im. Skip tracers, they call 'em, you surface – they track you down. Dirty fucking work. Dirty. Finance company were gonna take the cab offa 'im, so he went to a shark. Shark upped the vig, sent round the chaps, didn't get Phil – found 'is girl, Lottie.'

'Don't know her.' *How could I? Haven't seen Phil in five years . . . Never will now . . .*

'They roughed 'er up pretty bad, she's a straight-goer azitappens, nurse or sumfing. Anyway Phil blamed 'imself big time – fought of offing the shark, got a shooter inall – but in the end 'e did the business on 'imself.'

'With the gun?' *For some reason it matters . . .*

''No, 'ung 'imself.' Fucker stared out through gems of rain towards the river and beyond it the Greenwich peninsula. 'Oi, mate,' he said addressing the bullet head of the driver, 'you should've taken the first turn down Westferry, you've gone all round the fucking 'ouses.'

'Pliz?' Thick lips parted in the rearview mirror.

'Oh, it don't matta . . . it don't fucking matta . . . I tell you, Tufty, it's the dog I feel sorry for, the poor little fing was stuck wiv 'is body for free days, see the bird 'ad fucked off . . . trauma an' vat . . . When they found Phil the dog 'ad gnawed 'is legs just to survive.'

The cab pulled into the kerb and Fucker levered himself out. 'Dog, dogs,' he was muttering, 'funny that, 'coz we're on the Isle of bloody Dogs and goin' t'see some.' Dave paid the minicab, while his friend continued, 'Not that they are, really. Seriously, my Carol is a good little sort –'

'But a brass, right? No offence –'

'None taken. Yeah, she's a brass, but it's not like that wiv me an' 'er, it's more of a friendship, mostly we don' even shag, we juss 'ave a little cuddle.'

'A cuddle?' Dave couldn't help but laugh.

'Nah, nah, don' get me wrong, Tufty, thass not what's lined up fer you, there's free of 'em working 'ere, all nice girls, cummon nah.' With artful dabs Fucker guided Dave towards the house, which was a bog-standard Millwall semi. Further south were the pseudo-warehouses stacked with apartments, while up towards Limehouse No. 1 Canada Square towered over the now purely ornamental docks. Yet here Millwall remained, a low-rise grid of ordinary aspiration.

The three girls sat round a muted telly rolling joints and drinking Diet Coke. In their catalogue peignoirs and mail-order harem pants they looked like teenagers playing at being tarts. However, there was nothing playful about Carol – a brunette as tall as Dave, with rigid hair and blurred features, who rose up from the sofa and bore Fucker off to another room. Soon enough Dave could hear her *creating, which leaves me with* Yasmin, to whom he'd been introduced and who now rose up as well. *Jesus! She's a big girl, you don't get many of 'em to the pound* . . . The schoolboy joked because the man felt disgusted with himself – and disgusted by her. *Goods Way in the 80s . . . recession tarts . . . The other lads would 'ave 'em in the back . . . get a polish, then drive 'em to their dealers . . . I never did, though* . . . It seemed much worse because she was Asian. The crow hair, the bluey-brown shadows under her eyes, *the sortuv sideburns those Pakki birds have*. Perversely, he felt concerned for her disgrace. *Can't be any going back up north now . . . not after this* . . . Faisal popped up, admonishing them both with a stiff finger. *Allah Akbar* . . .

*All those ice-cream scoops of brown flesh . . . I can't touch 'em* . . . Yasmin seemed to have no such reservations. She escorted Dave upstairs to a room where damp carpet off-cuts surrounded an avocado jacuzzi. 'Tek yer things off, loov, an' 'op in, ahl give yer oondercarriage a good old soapin',' she sung-said, while sliding from the harem pants to reveal the grim webbing of a suspender belt.

'It . . . it wasn't . . . what I –'

'C'mon, loov, don't be shy like.' Yasmin propped one huge haunch on the rim of the jacuzzi and dabbled the flub-a-dub-dub of the water with electric-blue talons. 'Wassermatter, don'choo fancy me?' Dave recoiled . . . *I don't fancy you at all . . . I can't do this* . . .

*Rubbed by her . . . Rubbed by someone you don't wanna rub in return . . . like a . . . like a bloody shmeiss ponce!*

He couldn't find a cab until he was back up by Westferry Road. 'You're lucky, my son.' The driver wore a Hawaiian shirt decorated with the Miami skyline. 'That dahn there, thass bandit cuntry. You don't wanna be dahn there before sun-up.' His saviour had *more fucking rabbit than Watership Down* and went on and on about football: Platt, Juventus, Spurs' chances in the new season. Dave moved to the tip-down seat and stared at the cabbie's shirt so that one city supplanted the other. The tide of booze and speed was subsiding; in its wake were mudflats of gloopy wakefulness.

In Gospel Oak he turned the key and admitted himself to Michelle's face.

'It's your granddad . . . it's Benny . . .' She didn't need to say any more – Dave sobbed, heaved, then buckled. She caught him in the sternum with her sharp little shoulder. He lurched upstairs to the bathroom, with her close behind. He tore open his own crazy face and fumbled in the potted pathos of the family medicaments – Calpol, Milk of Magnesia, Rennies, Band-Aids – for the ancient Valium he knew was there. Then he burrowed into her hollow and finally, with the analgesic sounds of Carl waking in his ears, and a mouthful of chalk, Dave Rudman slept.

~

The funeral was way up in Edmonton. Thinking back to his early childhood and the colourful cavalcade that surrounded Benny Cohen, Dave was appalled by the few old crocks who managed to make it to the cemetery. Two crotchety cabs drew up at the cemetery gates and disgorged eight or nine bent little men, the desiccated, salty residuum left behind after all those Saturday afternoons sweating in the Turkish baths. A couple of them could barely walk and felt their way forward to the anatomical wound of

Benny's grave with rubber-tipped sticks, as if probing the gravel for unexploded death bombs.

Dave drove his mother and father from East Finchley. His sister, Samantha, tipped up from Golders Green in a dark green Jaguar XJS. Michelle stayed at home in Gospel Oak with Carl. Noel was in Aberystwyth refusing his medication. Annette Rudman resolutely refused to grieve. Dave wondered if her hatred of cabbing alone could be responsible – or was there some other more vital failure that she perceived in both her father and her eldest son?

A hack rabbi retained by the cemetery brayed Kaddish in the chilly prayer hall. When he stepped away from the podium, Aunt Gladys came swishing up in a stiff billow of black nylon. Dave was grateful to her – even if she disturbed the piss-poor congregation with her purple-bound book, there was at least passion in her reading: 'O 'ow grate the goodness of our God, oo prepareff a way fer our escape from this awful monster; yea, that monster, deff an' 'ell, which I call the deff of the body, an' also the deff of the spirit.' Later, as they sat scraping chopped liver from paper plates in the front room of the house on Heath View, he thanked her. Benny's former colleagues nattered, salad cream smudging their moustaches, but they talked more about the roadworks on the North Circular than they did about him.

Benny's death changed Dave the way a father's should, for, like so many families, the Rudmans were wrongly geared, the slow maturation of this generation and the speedy ageing of the last leaving them out of sync. In his grief Dave saw clearly the beauty of his son and the massive forbearance of his wife. He apologized, he curbed his resentment – he did what was necessary to save the marriage for the next few years, so that when it failed it could do so spectacularly. They let go of the bovine au pair. Dave dropped her at Euston and off she clopped on pointy hoofs, fresh meat for an unsavoury boyfriend in Droitwich.

Carl became Dave's main fare. It made sense: Michelle was

earning four times what he could. *Leave on left Fitzjohn's Avenue . . . Comply Finchley Road . . . Comply Avenue Road . . . Left Adelaide Road* . . . Dave drove Carl to swimming pools where they squirmed in the urinary waters. *Leave on left Kensington Gore . . . Right Queen's Gate . . . Left Cromwell Road.* He drove the kid to museums, where they goggled at animatronic dinosaurs. He drove him to playground after playground, where they swung and slid and see-sawed. Boarding the roundabout, Dave pushed it with one foot on the rubberized surround – 'eek-eek, eek-eek, eek-eek', building up speed until the little boy was screaming with intoxication. Feeling his blood pound in his temples, Dave leaned back and watched as the clouds overhead revolved on the axis that was him.

Yes, he was at the centre of it all, and the Knowledge was Dave's Kaddish for his grandfather as well as his son's birthright. It named the God of the city, and prayed that His Kingdom be established, a New London, run by run, point by point. 'I'm sorry for your loss,' people said, but how could Benny Cohen, of all people, have got lost? It was inconceivable to Dave that even when dead his granddad would be disorientated.

~

In the dark of winter Dave succumbed to depression, a winding down, the numb indifference of a mind that couldn't stumble . . . to . . . the . . . next . . . thought. Each morning the comb had a full head of hair, while this *dumb slaphead* looked back at Dave from the mirror. 'Get out,' Michelle urged him. 'Go do something – anything. See your mates, get pissed – I don't care.' Yet Dave couldn't; instead he watched TV, or hobbled up Fleet Road to Two Worlds, where he sat reading the *Daily Express* while Faisal dished up curry. Every week or so Aunt Gladys called: 'Come dahn the Tabbanakcle wiv me,' she urged. 'It'll make you feel better.' Eventually, to get her off his back, he did.

He picked her up in Leytonstone early on a wintry Sunday morning, and they drove across town to South Kensington with the Fairway's wipers sucking bits of road from the aqueous city. Gladys sat bolt upright in the middle of the rear seat – she wanted to go back twice to check that the cats were alright, but Dave wouldn't let her. He must have passed the Mormon Tabernacle a thousand times or more since he got his badge – Exhibition Road was on the tourist loop – but he'd never noticed its elegant golden spire or smooth stone façade.

They were late and the service had begun, so they stood waiting in a vestibule decorated with a panorama of Mormon life. A Nordic baby was born and raised. He studied, married, was gifted with his own baby. The family grew as the Mormon did construction work, then more work – now white collar. In old age the snowy-haired Saint, fulfilled, instructed a granddaughter, before dying a peaceful death on white pillows. The soft hands of a sky god reached down to gather him up. The Mormon go-round was lived out in a city of wide boulevards and spacious, modern dwellings. The Mormon Knowledge was a simple grid pattern, while beyond the 'burbs green hills rose to bluey mountains. Heaven was a ski resort in the Rockies.

An apple-cheeked Mormon youth came over to where Dave and Gladys stood and offered them each a plate of white bread chunks and a tiny beaker of water. If this was the Saints' sacrament, their Saviour's body was bland, his blood tasteless. When the double doors to the church eventually swung open and the latecomers were admitted, they found seats among frumpy Mormon families. The men's suits were a shade too antiquated, the women's dresses three inches too long. The children were very well scrubbed.

From a blond wood lectern, under the exposed engine of organ pipes, a big-framed man with a blond crewcut and the solid, leisurely hands of an engineer was preaching a sermon on marriage and family values. 'As a man and a woman's spirit are ee-tur-naal,' he nasalled, 'so may the family's spirit become ee-tur-naal through obedience to the laws and principles.' Tall windows sliced with vertical louvres illumined the gently smiling Elders. The preacher continued: 'One of the most beautiful of the principles is marriage "for time and eternity", through this sacred covenant and principle wo-orthy couples may be joined together not just 'til death but for-evah.' Strange things were happening in the back alleys of Dave Rudman's consciousness. He stared around at the detoxified Mormons and gulped down his own tarry cud. *No booze, no fags, no coffee or tea . . . They look good on it . . .* He noted that the children were neither sinisterly attentive nor disrespectfully unruly. *They're listening* . . . He glanced sideways at Gladys: she was wholly absorbed in the service, her eyes clear, her expression bright – among the Saints her dowdiness was not out of place. *She has found something, she's not kidding* . . .

The preacher held up a D of metal. 'This is a caa-raa-bin-eer,' he drawled. 'One of ma hobbies is mountaineering and I use these little things all the time to attach ma-self to a rope. Through the power of the priesthood, families can be linked and then sealed. The only people who can unlock them are you and me. If we don't honour our co-mitt-ments, we unlock them; if we don't take our troubles to our bishop, we unlock them; if we don't tithe or attend church meetings, we unlock them.' He cast the metal metaphor to one side, and it fell on a desk with a 'clack'. 'Observe family prayer,' said the devout mountaineer, 'observe a family home evening and family scripture study and our links will remain sealed.'

They sang a hymn without organ accompaniment, and the women kept time by raising their forearms up and down . . . *yanking slot machines*. Dave thought back to the one or two church services he'd attended with his father. Paul Rudman had dragged his three children along to suburban churches with sparse congregations out of a perverse need to acquaint them with a faith that he lacked but had been born into. *Blokes in white dresses sortuv singing . . . and wandering about* . . . Stifling boredom, fidgeting so intense that, aged nine, Dave had thought his entire hand would disappear up his nose. On the rare occasions Benny had taken him to shul it had been different yet the same. *A beardie-weirdo in black robes banging on in Hebrew*, while the Jewish men discussed the price of fish. He wasn't as bored – but the religion was a pointless drone, faith muzak.

The preacher introduced the missionaries, neatly pressed young men and women who smiled and bobbed. 'These are but a few of the 60,000 of our brothers and sisters who are carrying the good news of Joseph Smith's revelation . . .' *Joseph Smith, that's the geezer who found the book. Except it wasn't a book, was it* . . . Dave clawed in his memory. *No, it was golden tablets and he dug 'em up. Great stack of metal fucking tablets that he copied out before this angel took 'em back. 'Coz it stands to reason that no one but Smithy ever clapped eyes on the things. What a load of cobblers – still, you gotta give this lot credit for being getters . . .*

They wouldn't get Dave Rudman, though. After the service and the announcements the congregation split into groups for scriptural study. Dave had had enough. He arranged to pick Gladys up in an hour and drove down to South Kensington. He left the cab on a rank and went into Dino's. Here he ate a pizza and drank a Coke. *Religion . . . any fucking religion whatever . . . it ain't for me . . .*

# 9
## *The Lawyer of Chil*

Kipper 523–4 AD

Heaving up from the fierce grip of the frothy surge, streaming freezing curry water, the motos suckered on to slick stone with their flanges, and their fingers and toes scrabbled for purchase. In that moment, poised between elements, they looked more at home in the heavy swell. Then they were wading in the shallows, mounting the jumble of shattered crete and twisted irony which was Nimar.

The first two beasts were slung about their thick necks with changingbags, moto oil tanks and evian skins. As they shook the water from their bristly coats, these banged and batted their jonckheeres. The second pair of motos were yet more encumbered, for clinging to their folds with white hands were drenched scraps of humanity, the fugitives, the flyers. Antonë Böm and his pupil Carl Dévúsh. They slithered off and dropped to the ground. The northeast wind honed its knife edge on their exposed flesh. The thick coat of moto oil they'd both slathered on before setting off from Ham had preserved them from the worst of the cold – without it they would have been dead. The northern sound was far colder than the placid waters of the lagoon, and half a tariff in the heaving, open water had frozen them to the marrow. Man and lad were too stunned by their passage to speak, and it was the motos who, gathering round, licked them with their leathery tongues and so roused them to self-preservation. G-g-get yer kit orf, Carl urged Antonë, get í orf!

Peeled, one was a whittled sapling, the other a warty puffball –

their genitals were as small as motos'. Bloke and boy slapped at one another with open hands, bringing blood to the surface of their skin in pinkish blooms. Then they lay down on a flat crete slab and were bracketed by Sweetë and Hunnë. The floppy dugs and sagging tanks of the motos enfolded the two humans and the heat surged from them.

When they were dry Carl and Böm draped themselves in cloaky-fings pulled from their bundles and thankfully still dry. Antonë got out his lighter, and with kindling gathered from the underbrush beyond the outcropping Carl started a fire between the rocks. They spread out their jeans and carcoats to steam in its heat. Arncha wurryd baht vat ló seein ve smoke? Carl asked. No, his mentor replied, you know as well as I that it will take the dads a long time before they decide on any course of action, and with the Driver injured they will not have his direction to rely on.

While pursuit exercised Carl, the Beastlyman bothered him still more. Antonë had a bottle of jack and some fags – Carl was amazed to see such luxuries, yet even while swigging and puffing, he cast fearful eyes towards the teetering piles of brick and twisted limbs of irony, expecting the Beastlyman's head to pop up, his mouth gaping, his stump of tongue waggling, uttering his dreadful gargling cries. But there was no sound save for the plash of the waves and no movement except the gulls skimming by and surveying the intruders with their yellow eyes.

The motos were quite unmoved by their transition beyond Ham. Comfy in their cosy child-worlds, they had little recollection of the traumatic past and no thought for the hazardous future. When Carl was convinced that the Beastlyman was absent, he told them they might forage what they pleased. They picked their way between the rocks into the undergrowth, where they browsed spiky chrissy-leaf and waxy rhodies. Nerved up by fags, warmed by the booze, Carl told Antonë of his anxieties. How might they go on from here? Where would they go – and, more importantly, who would they be? Ignorant that he was, even Carl knew that no gafferless dad might travel at liberty in Ing.

Böm had, it transpired, given all these matters considerable thought:

– We must march by night, avoiding all human habitation – for the motos would terrify and amaze any Chilmen we met, and they would alert the Lawyer's chaps. We must disguise ourselves – I shall be a stalker, returning from the southern isles where I've been bringing the Wheel to ignorant folk. You will be my butterboy, on your way to London to make your final appearances. See here – he pulled the appropriate robes, mirrors and trainers from his changingbag – I've got the right clobber.

Carl fingered the garments reluctantly – the soft, cotton pile felt alien after Ham bubbery. The mirror he let fall to the ground with a shudder. Eye – Eye doan fink –

– Carl, Carl! Böm said, grasping his hand, we must do this chellish thing, we must! Otherwise we have no hope of travelling unmolested – this is a far harsher climate than that of Ham! Your mummy and granny risked their all by sewing us this stuff – when we reach the mainland of Chil, we must wear it. And Carl, from now on we speak in Arpee only, even between ourselves. In this way our imposture may – Dave grant us – become more natural.

Antonë showed Carl the A2Z and the traficmaster he'd managed to get hold of. I have determined on this route, he said, however, there are two further stretches of open water before we reach the main island of Chil. Once we're across them, perilous as they are, the real dangers begin. They sat, contemplating the way ahead while staring across the sound at Ham. Dave powered up his demister – 1, 2, 3 – and the clouds swept up into a screen that tinted first grey, then mauve, then violet, before night fell like a black cloth cast over the world. They kept the fire banked up against the cold night air and coaxed the motos to lie so that their bodies would block the clefts in the surrounding rocks. They chewed on curried moto meat washed down with jack and evian. Eventually, exhausted as much by foreboding as by the crossing, Carl and Antonë fell into an uneasy slumber.

Carl woke at first tariff – the foglamp was coming on in a banded screen. Long shadows striped the rubble, and the ubiquitous gulls were perched on bricks, crete – even the sleeping motos. Carl sat up and the rime on his duvet crackled. The noise startled the Beastlyman, whose hairy head hung above the rocks. He gargled, Graaarghlraarr. Carl shot upright. Tonë! he cried, iss im! Böm roused at once, and together they confronted the grim apparition. The Beastlyman was still wilder than Carl remembered, the greasy hanks of his hair strung with shells and bones, his cloakyfing a rag, his emaciated body covered in welts and bruises. W-ware2 guv, Carl said hesitantly. The Beastlyman gargled again – Hurrarghrerh – then swarmed over the rocks and fell on Sweetë's neck. His hands went to her neck folds, and his battered, weathered face butted the moto's pink muzzle. Instinctively, Carl started up and pulled the skinny wretch off the moped. The Beastlyman grovelled before the lad, a stick of arm thrown across his fanatic eyes. Gedderwä U! Carl cried. Gedderwä U, Beestlimun! The starveling scuttled into the bushes. When the commotion of the seafowl had died down, Sweetë could be heard lisping, Eeth nó beethlimun – eeth nithemun.

They packed up their changingbags, filled a moto bladder with fresh evian and, loading the motos, made ready to leave Nimar. As they were on the point of moving off, the Beastlyman came back and tried to gain their attention by darting at them, then away towards a mound of rubble that Carl realized was his gaff. The fugitives ignored him until eventually the Beastlyman came right up to Carl, grabbing his arm he tried to pull him in the direction of his hovel. I wouldn't go with him, Antonë said, you don't know what he might have in there.

Carl, beset by curiosity, was on the verge of ignoring this injunction, when the Beastlyman let go of his arm and darted across to where Antonë stood, inscribing phonics. The Beastlyman tried to grab both notebook and biro. That's enough! Böm cried, pushing him away. We must go, Carl, now. We must go in good order, and you must speak Arpee. If we don't go now we are doomed! With that he slapped Hunnë's withers and the moto started, then clambered over the rocks. Sighing heavily, Carl hearkened to this manifest good sense. He slung the changingbags around Tyga's neck, grabbed his neck folds and followed on behind. So it was that the journey to London began, in haste and in sadness: the Beastlyman left lying at Nimar, gulls lunging down to peck at him, his black mouth open, his red nubbin of tongue struggling to form the most significant words.

The underbrush of Barn was far thicker than the most impenetrable portions of the Perg and Norfend. The fugitives found themselves driven back by dense pricklebush, whippystalk and rhodies. They heard rats scuttling away at their approach, and the gulls followed them from Nimar, harrying the motos. To cut a trail was impossible without sharp tools, which they lacked. The motos, especially Sweetë and Hunnë, could be coaxed into taking the lead, but after a few hundred paces their muzzles were scratched and bleeding. So the party kept to the shoreline, blundering westwards on narrow beaches of stony rubble. When these disappeared, they were forced to take to the water, the humans once more astride the motos' broad backs.

They were fortunate with the weather – the day was cold but clear. They could see back to Ham, and after a tariff both Böm and Carl accepted – with considerable relief – that there would be no pursuit. The Hamstermen might well have set out by pedalo to accost the fugitives at Nimar; however, they feared the hinterland of Barn and would not venture much beyond the fowling grounds.

Carl, in himself, was torn between the fear of this unknown place and wonderment. Alien species of tree and shrub jostled the shoreline. The dwarfish smoothbarks, silverbarks and crinkleleafs, familiar from Ham, were interspersed with larger trees with deeply grooved, ash-grey trunks and others that were like glossier, greener versions of the pines at Wallötop. There were also flitting birds Carl had never seen before, smaller than crows or flying rats, less garish than ringnecks. They were brown, mottled, red-breasted – their piping and trilling filled the screen. He pressed Antonë to identify these exotics, but the Londoner was unequal to the task.

The coastline described a curve away from Nimar, so that, looking back after a few clicks, Carl was presented with a great sweep of a scene: the wild main they were traversing and, in the distance, beyond more open water, the hills of Chil itself, where swathes of woodland glinted under the foglamp. In the last couple of tariffs he had walked, splashed and ridden several times the length of his homeland, yet Carl seemed not to have moved at all. Truly, he thought, the world was a vast place.

The following morning they crossed from Barn to an islet midway in the seething channel. It was a rough passage: the wind was up, and the motos were tossed about by the waves. This time the humans had stripped, applied a coat of moto oil, dressed, then slathered on a second coat. They arrived less discommoded than their mounts. Without their regular mud wallows, the motos' skin dried out and cracked, while the curry-water immersions accelerated this process. Hunnë in particular was beginning to suffer. Scratches on her muzzle were infected and ran with gleet, her hand and feet flanges were ragged and bleeding. She was off her forage. Hunnë was the shyest of all four, needing constant cuddles and reassurance. Carl wept for her, and wept also for himself, for three days out from Ham it was Changeover day.

Antonë, observing how well the motos swam and the small flaps of flesh that stoppered their nostrils, while a transparent membrane protected their deep-set eyes, was driven, as ever, to speculate: Could it be, he mused as Carl tended to Hunnë, that Dave in his infinite wisdom meant for these beasts to undergo such inundations?

Might they be antediluvian creatures, survivals from before the MadeinChina?

They rested for a single night on the islet, and were sorely tried by the rats that infested the place. The three stronger motos were able to catch considerable numbers, while these meaty chips were refused by Hunnë. The following day at foglamp on, the convoy carved a passage through the dancing green swell to Chil.

Here they abandoned their Ham cloakyfings, T-shirts and jeans, and donned the robes and trainers. Böm showed Carl how to fasten them, and strap the mirror arm to his brow, so the lad might see behind at a glance. From now on, he said, we talk only in Arpee, we call over the points and the runs, we speak often and always of Dave, we revile all mummies. Do this now, and if we meet with Chilmen we will not be surprised.

With a knife Böm hacked off his beard – and to Carl his pitted, bleeding face was alien, disturbing even. No Driver on this estate wears a beard, Böm explained. He spread out the A2Z on the flat bole of a felled smoothbark. This is our route – he tapped the oiled parchment – we're to the northeast of Wyc, between the manors of Hemel and Ban, only a few clicks – by my reckoning – from the start of the Emwun, the great trading route. We can walk this track by night, then lay up in the woods by day. When we get here, to the northern coast, we will have to get a berth on a ferry over to Cot, for it will be too far to swim the motos. I have dosh – enough both to pay for our passage and discourage any questioning.

Carl understood by this that Antonë did not expect the motos to leave Chil with them. In his mummyless funk he fell on poor Hunnë's bristly neck. Lad and moto wept copiously. Enough! Böm cried. It's foglight, this isn't the settled part of Chil, yet this woodland is not empty, there are barbecuers, huntsmen and stray settlements. We must be careful, lay up in the day, hide the motos, then go on when it's dark.

The first three nights went according to plan. The weather had closed in, and the screenwash was insistent. Although they had no headlight or dashboard to guide them, the Emwun was embanked and paved with pulverized crete that gleamed even in the blackout. Böm took the lead, scoping for bother, then came the motos, and lastly Carl, who followed up right didgy, slapping slack withers to get the motos on. Long before lampon they herded the motos off the track and sunk them in the undergrowth. Then they ate some of their declining stocks of takeaway and took a swig of evian before turning in for the wan day's troubled sleep. There was no question of lighting a fire.

On the third morning, as they ate their meagre repast, Böm held up the evian skin and shook it. You hear that, Carl? he said. We're running out. There's no evian right on the Emwun; we'll have to scout around today and see if we can find some. We'll take it in turns. You lay up with the motos and I'll look up north, then we'll swop over and you do west of the Emwun. If we keep on like this, staying dead quiet and going bloody carefully, we should find a bit of wet.

Antonë was gone for ten or so units, then returned empty-handed, so Carl set off. It was the first time he had been into the Chil woods. Once he left the track behind, Carl found that this huge expanse of trees consisted almost entirely of smoothbarks – rank upon rank of them, neither coppiced nor pollarded. There was no underbrush, and the stately, columnar trunks marched away from him, up slope and down slough, their roots sunk in damp leaf fall. Carl stared down avenues half the length of Ham and, desperate lest he lose his way, he circumvented trees in his path, knocking off wet shrooms that smeared his robe with white pap.

After a while Carl found himself in a glade, in the middle of which was a bog – there was no clear evian but the deep choccy-blue sludge would be perfect for moto wallowing. Suddenly there was a movement by a dead brack stand, and Carl realized there had been a creature there all along. He twitched and off it sprang, showing a white scut as it crashed through the leaf fall. Carl ran all the way back to where Antonë stood nervously scanning. What's up! he said, and Carl told him about the beast. Munchjack, Böm sighed, bloody good eating, although not for us. This makes it certain – this is the Lawyer's forest. If his chaps found us here, we'd most likely be killed.

Carl told him about the wallow, and even though Böm was worried, he let Carl take the motos to it, one at a time, so they could moisturize. The last one to go was Sweetë, who was always so calm and trusting. Carl led her into the glade and sank her in the wallow, where she shlupped. He took up position, his back against a tree, and lost himself in the blue screen seen through a puzzle of twigs and boughs. A fat bird exploded from a branch and whirred away, little shitballs bombing from its behind. Carl shot up to see Sweetë's baby-blue eyes staring at the irony tip of a drawn arrow. This creature wasn't a munchjack but a lad the same age as Carl. He was done up in a richly embroidered carcoat, and sported a cockpiece, high-topped trainers and a baseball cap. The lad's long barnet reached to his shoulders in luxuriant curls. Carl had never seen this sort of gear before – only heard of it. He'd never seen a bow and arrow either, but knew this was what the lad had aimed straight at the moto. The lad was so afeared he didn't even notice Carl, so terrified that when the wallowing moto lisped, Alwì, mayt? he turned tail, dropped his weapon and ran screaming through the wood.

It was not long before Carl heard the blare of horns, the thud of hooves and the sound of many blokes shouting. He cried to Sweetë: Geddahn, baybs! Geddahn in ve wallö, rì dahn so az onlë yer ootah iss up fer breevin! Then he shinnied up a tree sharpish. No sooner was he concealed than the clearing was full of dads on jeejees, lads on foot and dogs yapping in a furry muscle tussle. The hunt spread out round the wallow, the dads with railings drawn, the lads with arrows strung, the dogs snuffling. The whole posse scoped out the dank water. Carl, horrified, watched as one lazy bubble grew, then popped. Despite his ghastly predicament he was entranced by the hunt. The dads wore bright scarlet leather carcoats and black leather jeans. Their raiment and their jeejees were hung with all manner of irony devices, while most had a dead munchjack slung across their saddles. Their barnets were oiled and teased, they were clean-shaven and had motorage eyes. The lads were puffed out, their shorts muddy, their cockpieces skewed, their breath smoky in the slant, second-tariff foglight. They leaned heavily on their long bows.

As for the jeejees and the dogs – never had Carl conceived that these toyist beasts would have such terrible beauty. With every jerk of the jeejees' foam-flecked muzzles he fancied they must break the spell that held them in thrall to the huntsmen, rear up, pitch the dads to the ground and gallop away. Carl thought the dogs must also be enchanted, for, despite their sharp teeth, savage eyes and slathering jaws, they ran hither and thither avoiding the most obvious prey – slow-witted lads who, armed or not, would be no match for the pack of them.

– Where's this monster, then, Fred? said the biggest dad on the tallest jeejee.

Fred, the lad, was scrabbling round looking for his abandoned bow and arrow. He straightened up at once and bowed down low.

– Mì Lawd, he said, Eye sore í rì ear, í woz gross, lyke a big baybee joynd wiv a bäcön. An í spoak 2 me. Eye swear í, í sed orlrì, mayt.

The Lawyer thought for a while, then he addressed the whole company:

– Yeah, it's a moto alright, the vile and toyist monster. I don't know how it's got off Ham, but we must find it and dispatch it.

The dogs were now snuffling in a furious agitation at the boggy edge of the wallow. Then the pack sang out, Ow-wow-wow-wow! and fused into a single undulation of fur and muscle. They've gotta scent of it, shouted one of the dads, and the whole posse grabbed their reins and wheeled their jeejees to follow the dogs. Horns blared, the dads cried, Nyaaair! Nyaaair! And, as quickly as they had arrived, the whole gaily caparisoned hunt streamed out of the clearing and back towards the Emwun.

Another shiny black bubble grew on the dark mirror of the wallow. It was Sweetë – still breathing, still alive. The wind rose, and leaves skittered on the forest floor. Strung from the branch in front of Carl's face a spider's web glistened with jewels of moisture.

Carl waited until the foglamp was dipping before he climbed down from the tree, and every time Sweetë stirred in the wallow he snapped at her to stay sunk. Finally, they headed back towards the Emwun, the boy with his hand buried deep in the moto's chilled folds, hoping by this stimulus to comfort and warm her. Carl expected the worst – and that was what Dave set before them. The bushes were torn up and trampled down, blood was sprayed on leaf and bough. Champ's guts were spilled out on the ground, and there was a trail of more blood and offal along the track. Eye wan mì mummy, Carl keened over the gelid mess. Sweetë shed heavy tears on Champ's lifeless eyes, she nuzzled his slack withers, then nonchalantly – yet reverently – began to lap at the cavity the Lawyer of Chil's chaps had hacked with their railings.

Böm emerged from the hollow smoothbark where he'd taken refuge and gave his pupil a hug.

– Yaw alyv! Carl exclaimed.

– Indeed, Böm said grimly. Still, we won't live much longer unless we get going. He jerked a thumb at the dead moto. They've taken Hunnë's carcass with them – they had ropes. I reckon they'll tow her to Luton; the Lawyer has a travelodge there. No doubt they'll return for Champ at foglamp on, so say your goodbyes.

– Wot abaht Tyga?

– I dunno, Böm said, shaking his head, he got away in the mêlée, probably not far, though. We'd best assume that he's dead – these hunting dogs will have sniffed him out.

– So vat woz ve Loyah uv Chil, woz í?

– Quite so. Böm pursed his plump lips. I would know him anywhere. He is a boorish, grasping fellow – as was his dad before him. Truly, Ham has been protected from his grievous depredations by the good offices of Mister Greaves.

They siphoned Champ for his oil as best they could and tore flesh strips from his flanks and buttocks. Antonë had found a stream heading northwest, so, with Sweetë hung about with evian skins and oil tanks, they splashed off along it. They kept going throughout that night and for the first tariff of the next day. Eventually, confident that the Lawyer of Chil's dogs had lost the scent, they rested for a tariff before leaving the stream and heading into the woodland. A dipped headlight switched on in a demisted screen, filtering some radiance down on to the forest floor. Despite this, it was awkward progress for the reduced party. The well-spaced smoothbarks ceded to scrubby crinkleleafs, and even urging Sweetë on all they could manage was a crawl. Carl did his best not to show his distress, but the dead motos preyed on him. Vay diddun eevun gé 2 go 2 Dave, he said to his companion. Böm snapped: Arpee, Carl! Arpee! Then slogged on, head down. Piqued, Carl turned sarcastic eyes on his retreating back. Böm was, he thought, a lyttul bloke lost inna grate forest.

On the third day after their fateful encounter with the Lawyer of Chil's hunt, the travellers came upon a descending slope of dead brack. So happy were they to be on clearer ground that they didn't even notice the thinning woodland, until emerging on to open ground. It was a bare field, the wet clods freshly broken, and in the middle of it were the team of Chilmen who'd done the breaking, gathered by a ropey old nag harnessed to a harrow of irony spikes. There were five of these dads, and, although they appeared pretty knackered, they closed on Carl and Antonë with alacrity. Wot ve fukk! said one, goggling at Sweetë. One of the others had been on Ham many years before and recognized the moto. This dad took charge: U ló, tayk vese 2 dahn ve manna sharpish. Eyel dryv ve moto. He grabbed Sweetë's neck folds, and she snuffled: Pleethe, pleethe.

Through sombre, sodden kipper fields the party trod, gathering in their train a mess of dogs and sprogs. They passed a landfill where gulls and crows mobbed over a stinking midden. Although Carl had seen the sick fares of Chil come every year to Ham, he was shocked to find that these dads were quite as windy. Their threads were in filthy tatters, their limbs were scraggy, their tanks swollen. Lots of the kids had Dfishunt legs and many of the dads weepy goitres. Antonë walked by Carl's side and whispered instruction: Leave the chitchat to me. Then he could not forbear from a little pedagogy: See there, those birds grubbing in the dirt, that's pieces and those are roastducks, and over there, through the silverbark screen, that's their manor.

They passed by a small enclosure. In it, on bare and pocked earth, was a creature the size of a small moped with a conical snout and tiny eyes. Carl recoiled from this as they passed by, while Antonë muttered: That's a bacon. Sweetë poked her head over the palings and addressed it, lisping: Alwì, mayt? And Böm could not forbear from laughing, for the toyist bacon only snuffled.

The Chilmen's manor, although far bigger than Ham's, was laid out on the same plan, with two rows of semis set on each side of a stream. Instead of a travelodge at the top end, there was a larger, two-storey semi, and behind that a low, green Shelter nicely knocked up from fine 2by4s. There were ten dads' semis and ten mummies', all of them built in the bëthan style from heavy 2 by 4s painted black and rough plaster daubed white. There were diamond-paned windows of real glass and wooden doors. Manifestly this had at one time been a prosperous manor, but now the fences of the front yards were broken and the windows shattered. As the party moved up the dads' side of the stream, they came out with their opares to gawp at the moto and prod its bloody withers. Pleethe, lisped Sweetë, pleethe doan.

The Guvnor was waiting for them outside the big semi. His carcoat was flung open, revealing a bare chest heavily tattooed with wheels and phonics. He sported a baseball cap and a heavy gold earring, and his pouchy face was covered in grey stubble. Despite his cocky manner, he had the look of a dad from whom fat and muscle had melted away. His eyes were famished and dull, his hands shook. With him was a Driver, a timorous little man, his chubbynut head lost in the folds of his black robe. It was he who spoke first, in prissy and correct Arpee:

– Well, well, a moto, if I'm not mistaken. Presumably this is the one missing from the rank that our Lawyer raised on the Emwun south four days since. We will need to send to Hemel for some chaps so that these – he cast a sceptical eye over Antonë's and Carl's torn and filthy robes – ah, stalkers and their moto can be taken into custody.

The Guvnor took a different view:

– Eye doan giv a toss abaht ve Loyah fer nah, he said. Iss a pizzaDlivree from Dave sofaraz Eyem concerned. U 2 – he stabbed his thumb at Böm and Carl – can slorta viss monsta an ven render í dahn. Mì dad ear sez iss gúd eton, an we aynt ad no oil ear in yonks. Ven weel and djoo ovah 2 ve foritees. Nah! he spat, tayk vair stuff, vair A2Z, vair trafikmasta, vair grub an wotevah. Vay aynt goin noware.

That night Carl was banged up in one of the dads' semis, while Antonë was confined to the Shelter. A few opares fed the kids and put them to bed. The kids were very aggro – spitting, cursing and even shrieking. However, the dads didn't pay them any mind: they had Böm's supply of jack and fags, and were fuddled on the floor. The next day was Changeover at Risbro – which was the manor's name – so Carl was moved over to the mummies' semis. Any joy to be had from this arrangement was short lived. There was no mushy cuddlespeak or mummyish petting for Carl. These were strange bints – all raggy and skinny. They took him in and used him roughly, pushing up their cloakyfings and sticking his face on their tits in a gross manner. We doan av no luvvin an we aynt gó enuff lyttuluns uv R oan 2 luv, they told him. So weel mayk dú wiv U.

It was true – there were very few kids for a manor of Risbro's size. Carl counted thirty-odd mummies in all, but there were only five opares and a handful of kids. Wunce we bin up ve duff, an old boiler explained to Carl, weer untuchabubble! Untuchabubble! Í doan matta if we av a kiddë aw nó – untuchabubble! Chellish! R dads R ve wurs inawl uv Ing.

At night they made him go from one of the mummies' semis to the next. No sooner was he settled in a box bed than some greasy-skinned old boiler plumped in beside him, reached under his T-shirt and jollied him up so she could mount on top, slop-slop. Carl felt nothing save shame after these couplings – his first – but if he tried to wriggle away the entire semi would rise up against him.

By day Carl was allowed out to do the miserable graft of slaughtering Sweetë. With Carl acting as gaffer the older lads knocked up a crude gibbet, gathered seasoned crinkleleaf chips for the smoking fire and forayed in the woods for a suitable hollow log.

The Driver of Risbro, 76534, was impressed by the breadth of Antonë Böm's Knowledge, even if he didn't believe the other queer's claim to be a stalker. The Driver was far from being a learned bloke; he was almost as ignorant as his fares, yet here in the remote hinterland of Chil what strength of character he possessed was roused in condemnation of the Lawyer.

The two spent the half-blob until next Changeover discussing the finer points of the Knowledge as they related to the parlous condition of the manor. In truth, 76534 told Böm, the Guvnor's appropriation of the moto is understandable. Here we are, our fields entirely surrounded by the Lawyer's forest, yet we are forbidden to gather any of the fruits thereof save a scant allowance of timber.

The munchjack and bambi grub up our crops when they're fresh in the field, yet if a Risbroman so much as lays a hand on these beasts the Guvnor must send him to Wyc, where he's sold into chavery. It is the same for the fez and the snip, the whirrcock and the grouse – all are to be found hereabouts in abundance, while my fares make do with a few pork scratchings and chicken pieces – rat flesh even. Yet where in the Book does it make mention of any of this? Where does it say that mums and dads should live in such bondage? Yes – he sighed and took a pull on one of Böm's fags – there's scant regard for the finer points of the Knowledge here in Risbro, or throughout the rest of Chil.

Carl slit Sweetë's throat under a cloudy screen. Smoke from the Risbro semis mingled with the rags of mist that snagged in the brooding trees. The dogs wouldn't lay off the dying moto and darted in to nip at Sweetë even as her blood coursed. The dogs terrified Carl. With their teeth and claws they were like big rats, and in common with rats they were always hungry. Yet even so the lairy Risbro lads kicked and punched them unmercifully. At the corner of the home field there was a gibbet from which dangled four or five dog carcasses. Crows flapped down and lazily pecked at these until stoned by the kids. When they were well hung, the dogs were cut down and their meagre flesh tried for fat.

Yeth 2 pway, yeth 2 pway, yeth 2 pway wiv U awl ve day. Yeth 2 Runti, yeth 2 Champ, yeth 2 Hunnë an Tyga 2 . . . The lifeblood flowed out of the moped in a haunting, sing-song rhyme: Yeth 2 Am, luverlë Am, yeth 2 Am, bootiful Am. Bì-bì, Cawl, bì-bì, Tonë . . . Sniggering and catcalling, the Risbro lads hauled on the ropes and Sweetë was winched up. She moaned, her jonckheeres twitched, her jowls flopped into her staring eyes, then she was gone, rising up into the tortured sky of this Daveforsaken clearing. Carl wept as he called over the slaughter run.

It took a blob to smoke all of Sweetë's flesh, render her blubber and try out her fat. Carl was in no hurry, for he understood that when the last tank of moto oil was sealed, his and Antonë's fate would be as well.

That night the Risbromen returned from the resurfacing work they'd been doing on the Emwun. They came with a car, although only the Guvnor was allowed to sit atop it and whip up the spavined jeejees. It was the first wheeled vehicle that Carl had ever seen, and he was transfixed by its curiously fluid motion. It moved as if it were a pedalo rising and falling on a sea of mud.

When Carl had changed over, he was told to join the lads and dads who were gathered in the Shelter. Böm was there – although of 76534 there was no sign. The Shelter was well equipped by Ham standards, with an irony urn, a large micro, a blackboard and bits of printed London cloth hung over the tiny windows. Carl had already given belly meat and offal to the opares, and they'd made bangers for the dads. These were frying in a huge pan together with chopped crybulbs. The smell of sizzling moto oil and fag smoke filled the air, and the Risbromen's gaunt faces were like skulls in the flickering lectric light. Carl shrank into a corner, trying to make himself as inconspicuous as possible, but the Guvnor called to him.

– Yeah, he said, U dunna gúd job wiv viss moto, boy, an thass jususswel, coz we gotta graft lyke fukkin Paddies on vat Emwun if we wanna survyv ve kipper. Ve Loyahs Hack tayks a grayt big waduv R arvest B4 ve cölsnaps, an we aynt per-mí-éd 2 flog ve ress til buddowt.

The other dads gobbled their assent through mouthfuls of meat.

– Ayntí ve troof, said a tall fellow with greasy black hair. Vey go arfta ve lore abydin an lé awlsorts uv culluds gé awä wiv fukkin murda.

– Weer lukkë 2 gé a warkup lyke U 2, said the Guvnor. Lars cölsnap we ad 4 blokes flogged, 4 fukkin chavs, ayn vat rì?

The other dads groaned and chawed.

– And what d'you imagine the Lawyer will give you when you hand us over? Böm asked.

– Mebë a munkee, mebë a wunna – Eye dunno. The Guvnor spat in the fire under the urn. Mayn fing iz weel gé sum. Í aynt nuffing pursnul – bleev me, iz juss everyfing iz dosh rahnd viss wä an we aynt evah gó enuff.

Carl wondered why Böm didn't offer the Guvnor some of the dosh he was carrying; heavy brown coins, which he kept wrapped up in a piece of moto skin and tucked in his girdle. Böm, however, said nothing further, only blinked myopically at the leering, sated Risbromen, who were puffing on their purloined fags.

– What if we tell the Lawyer's chaps that it was you who stole the moto? Carl heard himself saying. What'll happen then?

– Wot fukkin moto! The Guvnor reached across the table and cuffed Carl in the face. We dunno nuffing abaht í, vairizit? Iss gawn, ve meet iz curried an iddun, ve oyl iz stashed, eevun ve boans iz awl smashed up. Nah, doanchoo fukk wiv me, U lyttul cunt, sooninuff Eyel Bcummin 2 fukk wiv U!

These past days the opares had been fattening Carl up, feeding him Sweetë's sweetmeats, her finest belly meat, and letting him drink as much gubbins as he could hold down. Ure a plump enuff peece, one of the Risbromen had said on the night before they left for the Emwun. Weel fá-én U up sum mor B4 we giv U a röstin! Remembering this, Carl shrank down on the bench, his face stinging, his stomach fluid. Antonë glared at him from the other side of the table. As from a long way off dibbles of the Risbromen's jawing reached his hot ears: We put vem speed bumps in ve röd an ooze í bovverin? Uss. Í doan bovva ve pikeys an ve culluds – vey aynt gó no cars, vey juss go rahn, but R axles R fukked . . . Carl fell into a fitful sleep, then woke to the ugly grumble of a run called over by many drunk dads: Leffbìforrud vebrorway, bare rì crouchenill, rì ornsëlayn, leff azlevil röd, rì saynjonzwä. He collected himself and stumbled from the Shelter with the dads calling after him: B luckë, mì sun!

~

The weather snapped so cold that Risbro was blanketed by powdery rime. Frost twinkled on the bare boughs of the woodland, and icicles hung from the eaves of the semis. The dogs took refuge in the landfill, digging down for whatever warmth they could garner. The community retreated to its bëthan semis, and there, dads and mums alike, they overindulged in their own watery booze. Carl realized that the dads meant to have him the night before the next Changeover, and he readied himself as best he could. The night before that, as he lay sleepless in the box bed with a couple of the lairy lads, Böm appeared with a stump of letric that threw sharp shadows on the toshed walls. The dads lay higgledy-piggledy on the floor and the hearth, snuffling like bacon and hugging each other for warmth. Don't worry, Antonë said, they've had a skinful, they're mullered. They don't think we'll make a run for it without takeaway or evian – but I've sorted all that.

Outside the screen was clear, the dashboard shone, and there was a full-beam headlight. They slithered across the ringing streak of the frozen stream, then slipped between the mummies' semis and made for the woods. A skulking dog growled but didn't bark. Two hundred paces on, Böm stopped and delved at the roots of a stumpy old crinkleleaf, then pulled up a changingbag. It's all here, he whispered to Carl. A2Z, traficmaster, a takeaway and a warm cloakyfing for both of us. Now come on.

All that night they trudged through the crispycrunch woodland. The smoothbarks of the Lawyer's forest marched forward to meet them, and they hurried down the long avenues where the night birds chirred and the wind soughed. Halfway through the third tariff the headlight dipped below the trees; it was another four stumbled clicks before the foglamp switched on, sending lemon-yellow beams into the escapees' eyes. Then there came a marvellous sight: the smoothbarks fell away, overtoppling in a great mess of torn-up roots and boughs. Beyond this tangled barrier the sea unfurled, rucking up green and white under the gathering day. Soaring gulls stabbed at the froth-mantled waves. They stopped for a takeaway, then, after examining the A2Z, Böm guided them along the coast, and eventually down to a cretey bay, where there was a pedalo pulled up on the rubble beach.

What's this, Tonë? Carl asked, disbelieving such good fortune. The grub, the cloakyfings – now this pedalo, owdjoo sort it?

– It was the Driver, Böm replied, dumping their gear in the little craft. 76534. I did a number on him. He was at school with me in the Smoke, and he's a good bloke – he didn't want us handed over to the Lawyer.

– What'll happen to him when the Risbromen find out?

– What can they do? He's their Driver. The penalties for laying a hand on him or any other dävine are most severe – a fact our current circumstance cannot fail to remind you of. So we must make haste – you see out there? He pointed towards the dun smear of land on the horizon. That's Cot, and up there to the northeast is Junction 14 where the ferries take on cargo for London. If we can get out into the sea lanes, we may, perhaps, persuade a gaffer to take us on board. Chil is a wild estate, the Lawyer owing but formal allegiance to the King. However, Cot is a different matter! It is densely settled with many large estates and populous manors. Our disguises would not bear scrutiny there for long.

They made the small craft as ready as they could.

– Tonë, Carl said as they were on the point of casting off, don't you wonder what happened to Tyga? The Risbromen didn't say nuffing about im and they must have eard sumfing when they was ganging up on the Emwun.

– I know. Böm paused in his work and gave the matter the full weight of his consideration. It is strange, yet I fear Tyga's fate was most probably the same as the others', rendered down for his oil – if not by another manor, then by some of the wild barbecuers who haunt the forest. It's tough, Carl – he took the lad by the scruff and looked him full in the face – all we can hope for is that his fare is with Dave.

They shoved off and took to the pedals. There was an offshore current that grabbed the frail vessel and sent it rapidly south. They redoubled their efforts, and Carl, leaning back into the stroke, lost himself in the screen, the wheeling seafowl, the rushing wind that resounded with their cries – and a deeper slushier bellow, the bellow of a distressed moto. He stopped pedalling and gasped, appalled yet delighted, for there, nosing through the tangled tree-fall along the shoreline came, adorably snuffling, the muzzle of the lost moto.

As soon as they neared the shore Carl scrambled from the pedalo, sloshed through the icy water and fell on Tyga's neck. Lad and moto cooed and baby-talked to one another, while Böm looked on, scratching his chin in confusion. The moto was painfully thin, his hide torn and bloody. He had two arrows buried in his left armpit and his hand flanges were ragged. Tyga could say nothing of what had happened to him, only lisp a few disjointed phrases: Bad daddies, bad daddies, ith cowld – no fowage, hep me, Cawl, hep me! Carl, with his hands buried in the moto's neck folds, drew him into the tangle of felled trees. There he scrabbled for what fodder he could find – redberries, bits of shroom – and pressed them to Tyga's loose lips. Vare wur ve bad daddies, Tyga? he asked. Vare we loss U? Tyga only groaned. Either he couldn't comprehend the question, or was too traumatized to answer it.

Böm put a stop to these inquiries. We've got to go. Got to. Look, here's the rope, tie it round Tyga's neck and he can swim behind the pedalo. Carl did as he was told. The odd flotilla cast off, but this time Böm pedalled alone, while Carl sat in the stern coaxing the wounded moto. As they headed into the open water, the coastline came into view, and Carl could see twenty clicks in each direction. Here and there the woodland was broken by deep bays where smoke curled from hidden chimneys, and a few small pedalos like their own bobbed on the waves. Don't worry, Böm called from the bow, they're putting down traps for sea rats and suchlike. If we keep straight out to the north, they won't be bothering us. He checked the traficmaster, the angle of the foglamp, and bent once more to the pedals.

Out in the channel, once again the current plucked and pulled at their tiny craft. Gulls swung down and mobbed them, their crap splattering, their beaks digging at poor Tyga's vulnerable muzzle. Carl, screaming, struck out at them, but they only wheeled away, then swooped down once more. Böm kept pulling and pulling at the pedals as the waves broke over the prow. Eventually, exhausted, he shipped them and called to Carl.

– It's no good, the current's too strong, we're making no headway. We'll have to let it take us.

– W-where to, guv?

– If it keeps on like this, right to the shores of Cot, but we'll cross the sea lanes before that. I don't know, perhaps if Dave wills it we'll run into a ferry there.

They brought Tyga alongside and lashed him to the thwarts. Antonë tried steering with a pedal while Tyga flailed as best he could – even so, the craft spun from the hard barge and wet jam of the open sea. For unit after unit the gulls harried them, while Carl dripped evian into Tyga's cracked lips, for he feared the moto was about to expire, so sickly did he look, his eyes raw and weeping and his gasps shuddery and spume-laden. The foglamp sunk down into the swell while in the east storm clouds boiled up. The wind rose and the gulls fled for land. It looks bloody awful, Antonë cried above the howl. We're shipping water, if we don't make land soon we're done for. You'd best call over a run or two and ask Dave to pick you up!

With the foglamp fast dipping and the wind rushing and the moto groaning and the pedalo foundering on a liquid precipice, Carl saw a black patch of land cut from the sea by its fading, scissor beams. They lashed the stubborn water with their pedals while Tyga's limbs churned below the surface, they veered, yawed and finally gained the inside edge of a groyne. Then, in the dead water, they came in upon a shingle beach, where a tall dad stood, his arms upraised against the bilious screen. He was clad in a bizarre tunic of metal plates. These were inscribed with discordant phonics: W821 TBL, X911 VCF, R404 BNB.

Welcome to Bril, the tall dad sang in a voice that rang out above the wind's rush and push. He made an obeisance, while behind him the long grass swished in the gathering night. Welcome dad and lad – welcome moto. To Carl's astonishment the dad clanked down towards them and, untying the ropes, placed an expert hand in Tyga's neck folds, and so guided him up out of the water. Behind the dad Carl saw sharp squares of light. There was a semi – they were safe. He pulled his drenched cloakyfing tight around him, shivered, took a step up the beach, staggered and fell headlong. Purple dusk plunged to blackest night.

Carl awoke to find himself lying on a snowy sofabed of unearthly softness and luxuriance. Way up above him the dashboard winked in a smoky firmament. Turning his head, Carl saw a long table, beyond which, in a grate the size of a Hamster gaff, a mighty fire roared – entire tree trunks propped on elaborately wrought andironies. Caught by this shifting pattern of light, the bent, bald-wigged heads of many daddies and mummies could be seen by the bemused lad. They were seated at long tables and appeared to be having a curry. Opares floated along the aisles, pannikins cradled in their arms. Then he realized that what he had taken for the screen was in fact the roof of a giant semi, from the rafters of which hung many letrics. Awed, he struggled to rise, and, perhaps hearing the motion, one of the daddies came over to him. It was Antonë.

– Hush now, he said. Don't try to get up just yet. Here, have some of this. He held out a dish slopping with warm oatie.

– B-but where are we?

– In the Shelter of the Plateists of Bril. Do not be alarmed, they won't harm us, they are dävine queers – not Drivers, not even mummies and dads.

– Where's Tyga, is he OK?

– He's being well looked after. They have quartered him in the barn conversion with their own burgerkine. They will not harm him any more than us. Now eat this and have a slug of jack – he held out a bottle – you need it.

Böm returned to his place at table. The booze burned Carl's throat and thrilled his belly. He gobbled up the oatie. His wet clothes had been taken from him, and he was naked underneath the fine cloth counterpane. The big Shelter was warmer than the semis of Risbro – yet not so much so that Carl couldn't feel the draughts. He snuggled down and bent his ear to hear the chatter that floated from the long table; however, of this he could make little sense, save for the occasional place name – Farin, Chip, Swïn – which he recognized from the cross-examinations the Hamstermen gave Mister Greaves.

The dävine queers all wore the same tunics as the man who had met them on the shore. In the lectric the heavy irony plates shone in an unearthly fashion, as if generating their own light, and when their wearers moved the tunics clinked and clanked. Both the men and women sported the bald wigs of Inspectors, and their lean faces had an intensity that Carl found disquieting, despite Antonë's assurances.

When the curry had been scraped, the queer at the far end of the table from the big fire stood. Silence fell and, raising his arms, he addressed the Supreme Driver:

– Ta very much, Dave, for the grub!

– Ta very much! the other queers chimed in.

– Ta very much for the plates!

– Ta very much!

– Ta very much for Antonë and Carl, who come to us fleeing from the PCO!

– Ta very much!

– Ta very much for our Shelter here at Bril!

– Ta very much! And so it went on for what seemed to Carl to be at least half a tariff, the big bloke crying out thanks and the others chorusing assent. Carl nodded off, and when Antonë came to the sofabed, he found the lad curled up in the foetal shape of his beloved Ham. The tension that had scored and blanched Carl's naturally rubicund face was smoothed by sleep for the first time in blobs. It was with considerable reluctance that Böm gently shook him awake.

– What are Plateists? Carl whispered, for, while most of the queers had by now left the building, a few still clanked about the place clearing the pannikins.

– A good question, Antonë replied. He adjusted his spectacles – which somehow he had managed to hang on to through the stormy passage from Chil – and goggled at his young pupil. The Plateists are, as you see, queers who sport the Plateist ephod, the more plates they sport the closer they are to Dave.

– Are the plates Daveworks?

– Of a very special kind, gathered a long time ago from the ancient folkways, the Emwun, Emfaw, Emfawti, Emfive and Emsiks. Which is why you find such Plateist manors as still exist near to these routes. Here at Bril we cannot be more than a few clicks from the Emfawti.

– You have always known of such queers, then?

– Oh, yes, Böm laughed. When I was a lad I dreamed of running away to become a Plateist. You see, like me – or the Drivers – the Plateists are all queers, men and women who have no thought of being mummies or daddies. They live together in perfect accord, yet with no congress between them. In truth, they do not hold with that understanding of the Book at all – they owe no allegiance to King Dave or to the PCO, they live not in mummytime or daddytime but in their own time. They say they love one another the way all did before the Breakup.

– Then what do Plateists think the Book means? Do they call over the runs and the points? Do they believe New London will be built? Do they think Dave will come again?

– Come again! Böm laughed even more uproariously. So far as the Plateists are concerned, Dave is already here among us, each one of us is in Dave's cab and Dave is in ours. No, no, their understanding of the Book is very ancient, perhaps the oldest there is. See their plates? Well, each Plateist takes those letters and numbers and uses them to divine Dave's word from a series of calculations, the numbers referring to the pages of the Book, the letters to particular lines and verses. Each Plateist writes their own commentary according to these rules of interpretation and this is added to the great scriptoria of the Order. In former times, before Ing arose in its present form, the Plateists had mighty Shelters at Stok and Nott, Lank and Mank, large estates grew up around them of perhaps five hundred or a thousand queers, all of them scratching away with their biros, and decorating their scripts with elaborate doodles.

– So, what happened?

– When the dynasty of King Dave arose and the PCO was established in London, they rightly saw the Plateists as a threat. The Plateists' estates were raided, their Shelters pulled down, their lands confiscated, and many of the peaceable queers were slaughtered. Countless Plateist A4s were burned and the remaining fares driven to the furthest parts of the King's dominion. Now only a few Plateist manors remain, here at Bril, at Barf, at Bäzin and a few more to the far west that I do not know the names of –

Böm broke off, for one of the remaining Plateists had clanked over to them.

– The Shelter has been cleared for the night, he said. You can kip here if you wish; however, it would be more seemly if you removed yourselves to the men's dorm.

– Alright, mate, Böm said, rising from the edge of the sofabed where he'd been sitting. Come on now, Carl.

– And be so good as to remember, the Plateist continued as he guided them out into the cold night and towards a low building some paces off, you will be required to reach your decision during the first tariff. Such has been determined by the plates.

Decision? Carl asked when the Plateist had left them alone in the dorm. What does he mean?

– Well. Böm settled himself down on the pallet he'd been allocated. He means whether we go to New London or stay here with them.

– Stay? You mean become a Plateist?

– There could be worse fates for two such as us. The manor here at Bril may be a shadow of its former self, yet the community has endured. The order has its stronghold here and estates beyond at Farin. There are even some Plateist lands left on Cot itself that the Lawyer has, as yet, been unable to sequestrate.

Böm spoke casually concerning this prospect, as if it were of no great importance.

– Bu-but Carl stuttered, what of my dad, Tonë, what about 'im? Woss this all bin abaht if we don't make it to London? You must be taking the piss!

– Of course, of course. Böm reached out a hand, a soft, white appendage that fluttered in the gloom. He patted Carl's shoulder. Don't worry, lad, we're going on to New London. Queer as I am, I have no more tank for the Plateists' initiation rite than I did when it first became known to me – and I'm sure you won't either.

– Initiation rite?

– More of a chop than a rite, really, so far as these folk are concerned. Böm settled down on his pallet and yawned insouciantly. The Plateists view all dads as raging burgerkine, all mummies as complacent, lustful milchers, so, if you wish to join their order you must be gelded.

# 10

# *The Riddle*

August 2002

A cormorant came flying downriver between the two central piers of the Thames Flood Barrier. Dave Rudman watched its black felt-tip body as it drew a line through the piles of containers and metal-jacketed warehouses on the far bank. Rust-grey, pearl-orange, sky-pink – the jumbled-up squares and oblongs of a shredded colour chart. The bird zigged and zagged to avoid a jetty, then merged with the brown velvet of the Thames where it was cinched by the Woolwich Ferry before draping into Gallions Reach. *A poxy little plane full of poxy little getters* lifted off from the City Airport. Banking, it caught the full force of the afternoon sun and blared white-gold in the sky. Dave sucked on the piebald nipple of a filter tip. His throat grated, and painful sludge oozed over his tongue, then down his gullet. His face felt swollen, his fingers when he plucked the *bung* from his *hole* were *half-cooked sausages splitting at the knuckle and oozing grease.*

It was an oppressive day, the sky so low it threatened to crawl beneath the ground. Gulls were *fucking about*, their 'cooee chew-chew-chew' cries evoking seduction followed by consumption. Towards the visitor centre for the Flood Barrier – a glass rotunda capped with grey concrete – the landscaped lappet of lawn held a picnic party, a spew of kids, all shapes and sizes but mostly *picca-ninnies* in T-shirts, jeans and useless cagoules. *Rishawn, Shinequa and Shemar, dragged down here from Peckham for a sugar rush* . . . They were being fed ice lollies and cans of Coke by a couple of young women. As Dave watched, one of them stooped to snag a sweet wrapper from the grass and he saw a tattoo of the sun rise *out of her fucking arse*. Disgusted – not aroused, merely disgusted – Dave turned away. Down on the walkway beside the safety railings stood his fare, scrawny thighs lost in his baggy khaki shorts. He was chatting with a dude who was festooned with techno bling: a digital camera, a brace of mobile phones, a light meter – it was a necklace of shiny circuitry like the Barrier itself, shrunk then wrapped.

Dave had picked the fare up on Wardour Street. 'I'm a runner,' the lad explained as they scooted along the Embankment to the City. 'We've got two units shooting today.' *Bully for you*. 'One down at the Thames Barrier and one all the way up at Shepperton. I gotta get the rushes from the one down east and take them up west 'coz that's where the director is . . .' He went on gabbling, enthused by his mission, as Dave fed the cab through the ancient jaws of the City, past Billingsgate, up and over Tower Hill, down through Shadwell and Wapping, the Old English syllables as solid and clunky as the Fairway's suspension.

'It's sortuva awfurred film about the Thames. This guy, see, he thinks the river's gonna flood and all the like' – the fare's downy lips twisted in the rearview – 'well, like shit an' that, is gonna come y'know . . . bubbling up to the surface.' He didn't seem to notice that Dave never said anything, only grunted in the appropriate patter gaps. Nor did he notice the state of the cab: the oblong eye of the windscreen lidded with road dirt and squashed flies, the cobwebs festooned on the wing mirrors, the dashboard strewn with the clear plastic triangles of discarded sandwich containers, the floor of the front compartment knee high with rubbish. And Dave – Dave stank.

Mornings now he pulled on whatever soiled rag came to hand from the tangled ball in the corner of the bedroom. He drank thick, sweet dietary supplements while doing watery shits. He couldn't tell any more what was making him feel this dread foreboding, see jagged neon at the periphery of his vision, experience the hand tremor and knock-knee, feel the locked jaw and sore throat, suffer the swollen face and wiener fingers. Was it the Seroxat, the Carbamazepine or the Zopiclone?

Before the final bludgeon of the day hammered Dave into teary unconsciousness, he would uncrumple the patient information leaflets that lay balled on the carpet and read them over. As his tired eyes limped along the parlous print Dave found it impossible to divine whether his *dry mouth, upset stomach, diarrhoea, constipation, vomiting, sweating, drowsiness, weakness, insomnia, loss of appetite, rash, itching, swelling, dizziness, faintness, muscle spasms and sudden mood changes* were the symptoms of his depression, the effects of the medication or its side-effects. The drugs had become collaborators with the disease, and together they had carved up the cabbie's mind into zones of delusory influence.

It was all coming to a head – Dave knew that. The annual vehicle inspection was pending, the cab needed servicing, his own badge would have to be renewed, and the meter had to be recalibrated in line with the new tariff bands. It all meant paper work, officialdom, meeting with those *lairy, racial gits* . . . his fellow drivers. The PCO would have his badge, they'd fuck him over, they'd *break him on the wheel and tear his fucking tongue out.*

*A muthafucking giant speed-knitting a chain mail scarf* . . . changed into the whirr of a passing motorbike, as Dave Rudman surfaced from his reverie long enough to clock the wavering mirage of Canary Wharf, before the black rat scuttled down into the Limehouse Tunnel. *Where's Carl? Where are you, mate? Who're you with?* Dave pictured him at the mercy of devilish nonces, shooting up smack with scuzzy junkies, getting the shit beaten out of him *by a bunch of faceless fucking bruvvers, their hoodies pulled down over their mad yellow eyes* . . . Or maybe Carl had left London altogether and was heading north up the M1 *like a tramp or a pikey, all his worldlies tied up in a . . . inna . . . changing bag . . .* What if Dave had found his son, seen his glistening face jump from the pedestrian millrace of London's streets – what would he do then? *I'd give him a fucking clump – that's what I'd do, the grief he's put me through . . . the grief . . .*

In his distress the cabbie found it difficult to hang on to mobile phones. He threw them out the Fairway's window if he was driving and a conversation with a lawyer, mediator or assessor became too contentious. If he was standing, he dropped them to the pavement and ground out the butt-ends of talk. Three or four had ended up like this: pay-as-you-throw. But now he was the Skip Tracer's client Dave hung on to his mobile – because the detective, while refusing a meet, called often, as if he and Dave were gossipy teenagers.

On the mobile, which Dave crammed to his ear as the cab shuddered at the lights in Chiswick, Cheam or Chorleywood, the Skip Tracer's queer rap sounded still stranger: 'Could be nosebag.'

'What?'

'Your man – I say he could be doing nosebag. He's done it before ain't 'e, he's got form. Could explain the dosh sloshing round his accounts.'

'I thought you were gonna do some traces, find out if it was him who ramped up the share price before his company was bought out –'

'Tricky, son, tricky. Don't get me wrong – I'm on the case. But he's sold the bizzo now, so it's aynchun wotsit.'

'History.'

'Whassat?'

'Ancient history.'

'Yeah, yeah, knowwhatyoumean. His-tory. Hor-sey. Horse. Stable. Bolted. I'll spin his bins, though – see what we come up with. But nosebag – that's another matter. He can't be messing with your kiddie if he's wearing a nosebag. Get me?'

The calls came at odd hours and in peculiar places – when Dave was eating at Two Worlds, or as he sat in the automated car wash, the nylon conifers whirling past the Fairway's windows: 'Freddy's done his bins.' The Skip Tracer always began without any preamble or pleasantry.

'Whaddya mean?'

'Freddy, top bin man, a fox he is – a fucking fox. Slunk up to Hampstead, spun your man's bins. Slunk down to Charlotte Street, spun Channel Devenish inall. No one's seen 'im, no one knows 'im, 'e don't exist. Got everything, got the shreddies.'

'Shreddies?'

'Stuff that's been through the shredder – top product, that. Top product. Nosebag for us.'

'But what . . . what can you do with stuff that's been shredded?'

'Betty. Sweaty Betty. Top shreddies girl, is Betty. Don't matter how they shred it – vertical, horizontal, fucking zigzag – same difference to her. She just loves it! Does it like a fiddly little jigsaw. Beautiful to watch, really – you should see it. Not her mindjoo – not her. She's skinny as a fucking parking meter – got, I dunno, got anoxia –'

'Anorexia.'

'Whatever. Still, bit of a headfuck – sweat lashes offa her when she's working. Hence the moniker.'

Dealing with the Skip Tracer, Dave Rudman got the impression that he was only the smallest piece in a citywide jigsaw of horrendous fiddliness. Sitting under the Dutch Antilles in his office suite in Belgravia, the Skip Tracer spent the morning feeding the pages of the *A–Z* into the shredder and watching the papery spaghetti curl up and over. Then he changed his shirt and spent all afternoon putting London together again, breaking off only to make these preposterous calls: 'Got a tail on your man. Only a small team 'coz he's a know-nothing. A steerer, a sweeper, hands-free, no bovva, find out what he's up to – best way.'

'Are you serious?'

'Never seriouser, wassermatter you got frostbite have you, son? Tippy-toes plopping off? Been at the nosebag 'ave you – warned you 'bout that.'

'B-but the money, your fee – the tail's fee, Sweaty Betty's bloody fee – I can't afford all this.' There was a sound like a waste disposal being activated in the ether – so loud and sudden that Dave held the mobile inches away from his ear. When it stopped he realized that it had been the Skip Tracer laughing. 'Fee? I'm not bothered about the fee now, son, I told you from the off where there's daddies and kiddies involved . . . I dunno . . . call me sentimental . . . call me sentimental . . . GO ON – DO IT!'

'You're sentimental.'

'Maybe, maybe, scenty-mental like a fucking comedown, son. Race over, nosebag ripped off, trotting round the paddock, feeling fucking awful. Sweat all foamy on me flanks. I dunno . . . I dunno . . . just don't go borrowing on me, son, don't do that. The vig'll kill yer.'

'Like it did Phil Eddings.'

'You say something, bruv?' The kid in the back of the cab hunched right forward and stuck his fluffy snout through the hatch. Dave resisted the urge to scream, 'Bruv? Bruv! Whothefuckareyou-calling bruv?!' Because there was a long way to go to Shepperton and thirty-odd quid already on the meter. Dave's reverie had swept him downriver and now it was driving him back up. They were snarled up by roadworks in Greenwich, trapped exactly at the point where time begins – the Maritime Museum to one side, the Royal Naval College to the other. In the town centre the masts of the *Cutty Sark* lifted a tracery of rigging into the haze of exhaust fumes, while in the roadway stood *a dumb fucking paddy with a big green lollipop sign* that bellowed 'GO', while forty metres further on, past the clumsy incision the gangers had cut in the tarmac, a second man stood with a 'STOP' sign. *Jobs for the boyos . . . and mine – 'as 'e gotta summer job?*

~

Whatever his father's anxieties Carl was having a pedestrian summer. Michelle had taken him away for a week to a white-tiled compound on the shores of the Med. Here the boy mooched by the pool, or straddled a bulgy, inflatable beast that bobbed on the dilute chlorine. It was the summer when he shed his baby names – or rather, Michelle stopped calling him Sweety, Honey, Bunny or Gorgeous. She addressed him, curtly, as Carl, and when the waiters weren't looking allowed him surreptitious sips from her fruit-choked cocktails.

When they got back to London and his mother's days were taken up, Carl ranged over the Heath or trekked down to the West End, where he snuck into the lobbies of the smart hotels, sitting for whole afternoons unregarded on divans, filching smoked salmon sandwiches from cast-off plates.

Sunk in his own sebaceous ooze, growing like a human weed, his head spinning when he rose too fast – Carl had no conscious mind for mummies or daddies of any stripe or hue. With limp passivity he'd accepted that he could no longer see Dave. *What good is that wanker to me anyway?* And yet he couldn't stop tracking every black cab he saw, checking to see if the driver's window framed that battered head and those bat ears.

The only drama came one evening when Michelle was out at a Kenwood open-air concert – Chablis in a plastic sleeve, deli sandwiches, music on the half-shell. The phone rang at Beech House, and Carl answered the extension upstairs. It was Saskia, Cal's ex. It often was. Cal got on the line, and, although he'd replaced the receiver, Carl could hear him even from way upstairs, because Cal was shouting: 'What the fuck –! Couldn't you have –? Where is she –? Now –?' Bitten-off yelps of anguish. Without quite understanding why he did so, the lad padded back down the carpeted sweep of stairs to hang over the banisters. When Cal came off the phone, he started, aware of eyes at his back.

Turning, he saw *her* son with an expression on his half-Rudman face that seemed, to Cal, oddly familiar – like déjà vu incarnate. On impulse he said, 'It's my daughter, Daisy, she's been arrested again. She's down at some police station in South London, I've got to bail her out – d'you want to come with me?'

They rode in Cal's Beamer through the night-time city. Men stood on every street corner wearing England football shirts printed with the number 10: fat Beckhams, thin Beckhams, young Beckhams, black Beckhams. Scores of unsuitable substitutes for a never-ending game. It wasn't the football chitchat, the complicity of the car ride, or even the grown-up stuff at the police station that did it. They rode over to her mother's flat with Daisy gurning in the passenger seat while Carl kept his head down in the back. It was one short exchange as they rolled home at 1 a.m. up Haverstock Hill. 'It must be tough,' Cal said, 'your dad being . . . I dunno . . . so disturbed.' And Carl said, 'It must be tough on you too – with Daisy.' That was it, a bond forged in the maddening furnace of summertime London.

~

Where was Carl? Where was Dave: the cabbing was all tangled up – the city itself was ductile in the furnace, it warped and curled, becoming overwrought. His Faredar tricked by human chaff, Dave found himself breaking rules, heading south, dropping off *some fucking rude boy* on the Railton Road. Then, backing into a tight space in back of Brixton Market, the chrome bumper of the Fairway kissed the rubber bumper of a mustard Vauxhall Carlton. Dave clambered out of the cab and, more out of reflex than because he felt responsible, went to examine the rear. No dink – no mark even. When he straightened up, he was surrounded by *bredren in their saggy-arsed tracksuits and LA Raiders jackets, yellow gold on their fingers and in their teeth. Mad golliwog hair* . . . Along Electric Avenue, outside the butchers', there were counters piled high with pigs' trotters. One of the men took a step forward, his hair was shaved suede-close, he had a sock puppet's stubbly muzzle. 'Tax, mun,' he said, poking a stiff little trotter right into Dave's chest.

'You what?' Dave was incredulous. The little man pointed at the bumper of the Carlton. 'You fe damage me moto, mun, issall bashedup an vat. Seen.' There was a collective sucking of cheeks, 'tchuk', and a murmur of assent. 'Twenny pahnd,' said the little man. Dave's mobile rang.

'It could be nosebag,' began the Skip Tracer, 'but there's definitely a bird.'

'You what?'

'Your man, I've 'ad that team on him an' they've come up trumps, seems 'e's aht an' abaht all the time, up west, down souf, in and out of fucking crack houses, pubs, clubs, knocking shops, squats – there's no kind of lowlife he won't stoop for, but 'e's always picking up the same bird. Pretty thing – young enough to be his daughter.'

'Twenny pahnd,' the crash victim reiterated. He was standing right up against Dave now, his face almost resting on the bigger man's sternum. His fellow revenue men had closed in as well – a barrier of bloodshot eyes which blocked out the entrance to the Reliance Arcade. Over one man's velour shoulder Dave could see women sitting at little tables in the nail parlour, their taloned hands splayed for the manicurists. He took the phone away from his ear and mouthed, 'I'm on the phone', and such was the obeah of this that his taxers fell back, muttering 'foufou, mun' and 'raasclaat'.

'Perhaps it is his daughter,' Dave said to the Skip Tracer. 'He has got one, y'know.'

'Oh, no, no, no, that I do not think. My team saw them in a very compromising clinch, her tongue right down 'is fucking throat. Oh, no, no, no. This changes everything, right, yes, because I don't think your ex is gonna be too happy wiv this – do you? Might have a bit of a debt-tree mental effect on the old happy home. Gotta go, my son – sweat's lashing offa me.' It was lashing off Dave as well. *I can feel cold drips on my ribs, what the fuck am I doing here? This is bandit country*. It was, because, despite the solid Baptist ladies trundling bags as big as pantechnicons, and the Saturday afternoon shoppers, no one even noticed the extortion being practised on the cabbie. 'Twenny pahnd.' The little man persisted – and Dave just gave it to him. But once he was back in the cab and heading to safety down the Brixton Road, the humiliation welled up and overflowed.

~

On the midget location where his hit show *Blackie* was being filmed, Cal Devenish accepted a cup of sparkling mineral water from one of the gofers and stood sipping it in the shadow thrown by the catering truck. *I'm paranoid . . . spend too much time round miniature cameras and you're bound to think you're being watched . . . and yet . . . and yet . . . what if someone had seen that* occasion when Daisy, caught in a dizzying fugue of mania and rising up, up, up and over the rooftops of Shoreditch, had grabbed her father's head in both hands and slammed her mad mouth into his. *I pushed her away – threw her away from me . . . It was disgusting . . . repellent . . . she tasted of me* . . . Yet she'd hung on to him, they'd teetered, slammed into a wheelie bin with a hollow 'boom'. Cal had been desperate to get her out of the foul alley, into the car and away to safety, so for one minute of yawning perdition . . . *I responded, I kissed her back . . . I felt that bolt in her tongue with mine . . . her hands on me . . . mine on her . . .* When the clinch was finally broken she was calmed, and he could lead her to the car. Then, emerging into the flambéed sodium of Great Eastern Street, Cal saw a back that moved away . . . *too fast.* That was all, the ordinary back hadn't done anything, it was merely that it *accelerated too fast, got away too quickly . . . got away with it.*

~

Even in sleep Dave Rudman couldn't escape. His mobile vibrated on the bedside table, *hungry rats' claws drumming on tree bark.* He groped and drew it down into the darkness of the undercovers, into his man reek. 'Meet me at Wagamama in Canary Wharf,' said the Skip Tracer.

'B-but why?' Dave gagged.

'Why not?' the Skip Tracer snapped.

'It's . . . it's Sunday.'

'Sunday? Sunday! Whaddo I care about fucking Sunday, only bloke who can't get out of his crib on a Sunday is one oozebin doing nosebag on a Saturday night – 'ave you?'

'No, 'course snot.'

'Right, see you there innanour.'

It was a flashback to the mid 1980s when the vast development was a deserted, newly built ruin. The whole of Canada Square couldn't have had more than thirty people drifting across it. Dave ranked up at the foot of No. 1 and sauntered through the precinct. Au Bon Pain was shuttered up – Starbucks as well. In the tiny ornamental garden a languid Somali tweezered leaves from the lawn with a grabber, while a brushed steel fountain plashed to itself. The designer vents from the tube lines below sent waste pages soaring like gulls up the glass sides of the HSBC building.

Dave crossed to the shopping centre on the far side, descended, then mounted a theatrical staircase into Wagamama, which was an aircraft-carrier flight deck of an eatery. The open-plan kitchen full of hiss, steam and clatter gave on to long wooden tables and benches laid out with the simplicity of ruled lines. Dave ignored the girl in the Mao tunic who asked him, 'Is it just you, sir?' because the place was all but empty, and he could see the Skip Tracer sitting in the far corner by the window that looked out over the shopping mall, a big bowl steaming in front of his pink, boyish face. 'Look at this Jap food,' he said when Dave sat down opposite him, 'noodles, dumplings, veggie-fucking-tubbles.' He poked at it with his chopsticks. 'Issa little world in that bowl, innit just.' The Skip Tracer was wearing a heavy, three-piece, herringbone suit and a lilac silk shirt. Beneath the table mirror-shined shoes tapped on the tiling. His queer features – the ski-jump nose, the parboiled brows – were sharply defined by his razor-cut fringe. He was unshaven and the sweat was lashing off him, dripping down through the steam into the bowl like rain from low cloud.

'I saw a dwarf on the way over,' the Skip Tracer said. 'I only mention it 'coz she was stacked, man. Stacked.' Dave ordered a beer. 'Aren't you gonna eat, son?' the Skip Tracer snapped. 'You gotta eat, else people'll think you're on –'

'I don't care what people think.'

'Please yourself.' The Skip Tracer wasn't himself; he kept darting little glances away to each side of them. He dipped at the noodles with his wooden bill, yet never raised one to his mouth. His bitten-off statements lacked their usual emphasis – he was no longer the candour man, the sincerity daddy.

Eventually he gave a deep sigh and, mopping his brow with a yard of white cotton handkerchief, said, 'It's gone tits up, mate. Tits up. Thought I could help you – but I can't. Devenish . . . Devenish . . . well, turns out it was 'izdorta. Surprised – you could've fucked me up the Gary. She's mental, mental, mentally –'

'Ill? I could've told you that.'

'Well, you'll understand, then. Call me sentimental, but I can't be doing with that. Not gonna hound the man – wouldn't be effical.'

'There's still the money angle – his company. We know he fiddled the Channel Devenish buyout, don't you remember? The geezer in my cab. What about all the leg work you did, the bins, the shreddies, the calls – all of that?' Dave was close to tears.

'Good work, sound work, not gonna knock it – my people are professionals. Few corners cut, zoom-zoom.' The Skip Tracer zoomed his hand under Dave's nose. 'Still, at the end of the day there's gotta be a point . . . when –'

'When what? What?'

'When you call – well, when you call it the end of the day.'

Finally, Dave allowed his own eyes to leave the Skip Tracer's face and follow the direction of his darting eyes. Two tables away sat a girl of twelve or thirteen. She was wearing a bright pink tracksuit with a red spangly heart embroidered on the back. Her thick blonde hair was tied back in a pink scrunchie. She was working at a colouring book with an elongated novelty pencil, on the end of which wavered a pink flashing heart. She looked up as Dave gazed at her and smiled, her braces a zipper in the soft, oval bag of her face. It was the girl in the photo on the filing cabinet in Belgravia. Dave's eyes swivelled to the Skip Tracer. 'Yours, is she?'

'Yeah, yeah, obviously, only get her for the afternoon. Problems – difficulties, court order thingy – you'll appreciate that. 'Er mum's a lawyer, as it 'appens – got me by the bollocks. Alright, love?' he called over to the girl. 'Won't be long now, then we'll go shopping.' He turned back to Dave. 'Colouring,' he said, jerking a thumb at the girl and speaking in an uncharacteristic undertone. 'Bit babyish, but makes 'er feel, I dunno, secure.'

'Have they got to you in some way?' Dave's eyes bored into the Skip Tracer's. 'Is that it? Have they got something on you?'

'Nah, nah, you're paranoid, you are, son. If I didn't know better I'd say you were –'

'Whatever. I'm fed up with this, I'm fed up with you.' Dave got up abruptly and began making his way between the tables towards the exit. The Skip Tracer called after him: 'Just a sec, Rudman!' It was the first time he'd ever called Dave by name.

Dave came back to the table. 'What? What is it?'

'Bill, my son.' The Skip Tracer passed him an envelope. 'All there, shitshape, tits fashion.'

'You wha- you. You said not to worry about the money.'

'There's worrying about money and there's paying it, son, two different things entirely. And remember what I said,' he called to Dave's retreating back. 'Don't go to those sharks, matey, the vig'll fucking kill yer.'

~

That following Tuesday, as usual, Dave Rudman went to his Fathers First meeting in the Trophy Room of the Swiss Cottage Sports Centre. He went even though he'd spent the last two days in bed, Zopicloned into inanition. It was a mistake – he couldn't meet anyone's eyes. The venue didn't seem right – it looked like the inside of a cabbies' shelter, the glowing trophy cabinet a steely urn, a ghostly table rising up between the men's knees, on it a plastic cloth patterned with plastic fruit. 'Those fucking coloureds,' said Daniel Brooke; 'they don't pay no bleeding road tax, no insurance, whassit all abaht, eh?'

'An' those speed bumps,' Keith Greaves put in. 'I tell yer my wishbones is shot t'shit.'

'Shot t'shit,' some of the other dads chorused.

'What's going on?' Dave asked Fucker Finch. 'Are these blokes dads or drivers?'

'Snap ahtuvit, Tufty,' Fucker said, shaking Dave's shoulder. 'You look bloody awful, mate. Where you bin all weekend? I woz calling you.'

'Bin sleeping,' Dave muttered. 'Bin laden – laden wiv dreams.'

Daniel Brooke stood up to address the group. He was sporting an outsized black T-shirt that draped down almost to his knees. On the front there was a big white fist. 'This is the new T-shirt, chaps – hot off the press. I hope you like it, there are six sizes, this is the XXXL I'm modelling, a little on the large size for a slender fellow such as myself.' He gave them a twirl and across the back of the shirt ballooned the white letters FIGHTING FATHERS. 'Hold on, hold on, Dan.' Keith Greaves was on his feet. 'That's not what we agreed, that's not the logo we all voted for – and you know it. It's far too aggressive.'

'This is not the only Fathers First group, Keith – you know that.'

'I tell you what I do know,' Greaves said, shaking with rage. 'I know you've been trying to hijack this particular group for ages now. You, you, you're a bloody extremist you are, you're vindictive, you're resentful –'

'You're sounding pretty resentful yourself, Keith,' Daniel Brooke said smoothly, a smile playing round his wet lips.

'We aim to reconcile parents, we aim to forge links – you want to bring the whole thing crashing down! You don't care anything for your own kids at all – it's all about you and your cronies. Why don't you take off and start your own bloody group? Then you can do these direct actions you're always going on about.'

'Maybe I will,' said Daniel. 'Maybe I will do that.'

'D'you know something, Fucker,' Dave whispered to Finch.

'What, Tufty? What?'

'I've written a book.'

~

Dave ran home down Adelaide Road and along England's Lane to Gospel Oak. *Right Haverstock Hill, left Prince of Wales Road, left Queen's Crescent* . . . He puffed over inside his own skull as he ran, staggering to a halt every fifty yards because a stitch had been sewn in his diaphragm and Fanning, the GP, was yanking on it to give his words emphasis: *At your AGE, Mister Rudman . . . a SMOKER . . . with a SEDENTARY OCCUPATION . . . you ought to consider some EXERCISE . . . which would help you with your DEPRESSION. Take some RESPONSIBILITY for your LIFE.* Dave wasn't running for his health, he was running because he could no longer trust himself to drive the cab. He couldn't control this behemoth vehicle, with its chassis of reinforced-steel girders, its pre-stressed concrete bodywork, its York stone carpets and carriagework of herringbone London bricks. When he looked in the rearview he saw that he had more passengers than he was licensed for. Far more – approximately seven million in fact. *They're all back there, the whole population of the fucking city . . . it's gonna kick off . . .*

Back in the flat it was no better. He sat on the side of the bed in his rancid underwear, all his medication held in his cupped hands. *Please, sir, can I have some more, sir?* Not a good idea. Then, on his sausage hands and burger knees, his nose in the greasy carpet, Dave Rudman butted the radiator under the window with a mournful 'clang'. *If only I could see him for a few minutes, half an hour, give him a little cuddle, read him a story* . . . Yet it wasn't Carl that he truly wanted; his desire was for competent arms to hold him, smooth skin to smear on oily love, insulation against the terrifying, heaving green swell of madness. On the floor were pieces of ripped-up card, blood from his cut head spattered across them. Thinking again of *that cunt*, the Skip Tracer, and, for want of anything else to do *until I die*, Dave began to solve the puzzle with the calm ease of a man with a brain that was *scientifically proven to be bigger than normal . . . so full of Knowledge* . . . The lettering steadily emerged from the shreddies – D-R-J-A-N-E-B-E-R-N-A-L-C-O-N-S-U-L – until he'd cracked it. Then he thought: *I better go looking for the lid so I can check the picture on it's the same.*

It wasn't until 3 a.m. that Dave Rudman . . . *comply Pond Street, right access road* . . . finally walked into the reception area of Heath Hospital's Accident and Emergency Department. He showed his painstakingly taped-up jigsaw to the woman at the desk. 'Dr Bernal?' she queried. 'You won't find her here at this time of night.'

'I can wait,' replied the man, who for some reason had a dirty bath towel tied round his head.

'I don't even know what days she comes in,' the receptionist flannelled. 'She's on a rotation.'

'I can wait,' he reiterated, sitting himself down by a Camden Town tart who'd been beaten up by her pimp. 'Give over,' she said through pain-puff lips, and he moved to a different moulded tractor seat. 'You can't –' the receptionist began – then caught herself. He wasn't making any trouble . . . *why not leave the poor bastard alone?*

Dave Rudman waited and waited. He quit his seat only for tea and piss. He filled in the gaps by scanning over and over the same copy of *Take a Break*: 'Sharon Finds a Lump', 'Don't Snip it, Dave', 'Lonely Dad's Last Text – Without Them I am Nothing'. He was the subject of scribbled notes passed from receptionist to receptionist, secretary to secretary. He sat among the victims of street fighting and the casualties of domestic warfare. Patients waiting in queer *déshabillé* for transport to other hospitals were still more refugees, in their outdoor shoes and bathrobes, their raincoats and nighties.

Late on the following day, when he'd been waiting for nearly fourteen hours, Dave Rudman was summoned to the eighth floor and, accompanied by an orderly, rode the lift up. Insanity stank out the confined space like an eggy fart. There was a bird-beaked woman with a pot plant; a limp technician carrying a tray silently chattering with plaster casts of teeth; a yellow-faced girl in a yellow dress eating a yellow aerated cream dessert in a yellow plastic pot – but the stench came from the cabbie.

Even so, Dave wouldn't have been admitted if he hadn't attacked the orderly and clumsily tried to throttle him outside the door of Jane Bernal's office. She stepped out into the pedestrian horror of it: one big white man trying to bang the head of a small Asian one against an institutional wall. 'You fucking terrorist!' Rudman was screaming. 'You wanna cut my fucking head off or what!' A framed watercolour of Betws-y-Coed, allocated by a distant committee, rattled on the brickwork, then fell and shattered at their feet.

Had Dave Rudman been in any state to appreciate it, he would have. Would, perhaps, have been pleased by the whirl of activity his breakdown generated. After thirty milligrams of Chlorpromazine he was lucid enough to give up his keys, his address, Gary Finch's and his parents' phone numbers. A psychiatric social worker was assigned, calls were made, pill pots were collected from the flat in Agincourt Road. A pathetic flight bag was brought up to where cabbie 47304 was ranked up for the next seventy-two hours. Jane Bernal interviewed him, a standard risk assessment: reality testing, cognitive function, a physical once-over that had the functionality of a car service. The gash on his head was sponged and taped by a nurse. But Rudman wasn't interested in any of it; he only wanted to tell her about –

'A book, he says he's written a book.'

'Hmm.' Dr Zack Busner stood by the window in his office, which faced out over the Heath. Gulls were riding the thermals over Whitestone Pond. *What is it with these seafowl?* he wondered. *Have they come inland because they anticipate a deluge? Should we get Maintenance to start building an ark?* 'What sort of book is it, a novel?' He wasn't really concentrating on the conversation, rather trying to dangle a paperclip from the snub nose of an Arawak Indian head carved from pumice, which had been given to him by a grateful Antiguan student. He succeeded for a split-second, then the clip fell, tinkling, into the ventilation duct. 'Damn!' Busner turned from the window.

'No.' Bernal was patient; her colleague was showing his age. The breakup of his second marriage, the suicide of Dr Mukti, his young protégé at St Mungo's – all of it had taken its toll. Looking at Busner's snowy cap of wayward hair and his deeply creased, amphibian features, Jane Bernal could see that he was shooting fast down the senescent rapids. 'It's a revelatory text.'

'Did God tell him to write it – or gods?'

'No, just the one god – except he isn't called that.'

'What's he called, then?' Busner turned from the window and smiled at Jane. She saw she had his attention; as ever her oblique way of introducing a case had drawn him in. 'Dave.'

'No,' Zack laughed. 'Not the patient – the god.'

'Dave, Dave too. Dave – the patient that is – is a taxi driver, and Dave – the god that is – has revealed this text to him. Do you know what the Knowledge is?'

'The Knowledge?'

'It's the encyclopaedic grasp on London streets that a licensed cab driver has to have.'

'So is that it?' Busner plodded to his desk and immured himself behind a pile of buff folders. 'Is that the revelation?'

'In part. My patient, Dave Rudman, says that the 320 routes that make up the Knowledge are a plan for a future London. Between them and the points of interest at each starting point and destination they make a comprehensive verbal map of the city.'

'A city of god . . . or Dave.'

'That's right, a city of Dave, New London.'

'Where is this text?' Busner asked. 'Can I have a look at it?'

'Well.' Jane Bernal drew a chair up to the desk and sat down. 'I don't believe this man literally transcribed his delusion, I believe he committed it to his memory. As you may be aware, brain scans have confirmed that the posterior hippocampus in London cabbies can be considerably enlarged – that's where the book is buried, and there's more to it than just his Knowledge, there's a set of doctrines and covenants as well.'

'That sounds familiar.'

'It is: it's the title of one of the Mormon holy books.'

'Is he a Mormon, then?'

'No, I don't think he's anything much,' Jane sighed, 'except a very ill man.'

'So what are Dave's doctrines and covenants?' As Bernal succumbed to melancholy, Busner became increasingly jolly – nothing pleased him more than a complex delusional apparatus.

'Oh, you know, the usual stuff, how the community should live righteously, the rules for marriage, birth, death, procreation. It's a bundle of proscriptions and injunctions that seem to be derived from the working life of London cabbies, a cock-eyed grasp on a mélange of fundamentalism, but mostly from Rudman's own vindictive misogynism.'

'Vindictive?'

'He's separated from his wife, there's a court order restraining him from seeing his fourteen-year-old son. He's been mixed up with one of those militant fathers' groups. It's all very . . . distressing.'

'Hmm, I see, and his family – does he have any?'

'There are elderly parents living in East Finchley. I've interviewed the mother: she's long since withdrawn from him emotionally, seems traumatized. There's a brother in and out of hospital up in Wales, drug psychosis.'

'The father?'

'Alcoholic.'

'I see.' Busner picked up the Arawak head and began throwing it up in the air and catching it, as if it were an ethnic tennis ball. 'Of course, in the good old days we could have blamed the parents, but now we can go searching for pills to fit the pathology, or a pathology that fits the pills – there are pills, I presume?' Bernal consulted her file. 'Oh, yes, GP called Fanning. Usual story, began him on Seroxat, Rudman had a psychotic episode, Fanning gave him Carbamazepine to buffer it and Zopiclone for the insomnia.

Rudman had another episode and Fanning took him off Seroxat and put him on Dutonin.'

'Ah! Someone's been on a few little junkets to Barcelona courtesy of Big Pharma. So, we take him off all of this and see what's what. And what is what in your opinion, Jane? Schizoid? Borderline? Both?'

'Almost certainly, but the funny thing is – well, the two funny things are – he picked me up late last year at Heathrow in his cab. I was on my way from Canada where I'd been visiting . . . my friend. I thought he was ill at the time, although I couldn't imagine how he was managing to drive a cab if he was schizoid. And then there's his delusion, it's complex, it's durable, but, if you set it to one side, Rudman is altogether lucid. I only got him sectioned because he tried to beat up Raj. He says the book is addressed to his son, that Dave – his god, that is – told him to write it for his son. I think he'd benefit – if you're amenable – from some chats with you.'

'Oh, yes, yes, I think I'd enjoy that – give me the notes. And Jane' – she turned back from the door to see Busner ferreting among the papers on his desk – 'you haven't got a paperclip on you?'

~

Busner did enjoy his chats with Dave Rudman. He enjoyed the first one so much that when Dave's 72-hour section was over, Busner persuaded him to remain at Heath Hospital on a voluntary committal. 'It's highly unorthodox,' he confided to the patient – whom from the outset he'd found a most congenial fellow. 'We don't usually have a bed here for anyone that actually wants one, but my, ah, advanced years mean that the Trust allows me a certain, ah . . . leeway.' This was true: Busner's leeway included a number of intriguing patients who were tucked into odd corners of the eighth floor, like the woman who thought she was growing snakes from her scalp, and for whom Busner arranged a monthly perm at his own expense.

'How does the Book say the family should be organized?' Busner asked Dave, as they sat in his messy office with its Beuys bas-reliefs and vast collection of – mostly fake – antiquities: cuneiform seals and miniature stelae, Acheulian hand axes and jade, Toltec torture knives.

'Erm, well, it's like this.' Rudman searched inside himself for the Book: it was still there, he'd held it all. 'Men and women should live entirely separately. No mixing. Half the week the kids stay with the dads, the other half with the mums.'

'So there is no family as such?'

'No, no, I s'pose not.'

'What happens when the dads are working – they do work, don't they? Who looks after the kids then?'

'Um . . . girls, older girls. Girls who haven't got kids of their own yet, they're like y'know, au pairs.'

'And the older boys?'

'They, they're boning up on the Knowledge, learning the runs and the points.'

'That's men's work, is it?'

'Oh, yeah, you can't be doing with women drivers now, can you?' Dave laughed, and Busner made a note. Schizophrenics seldom laughed when recounting their delusions.

~

During the two months he was at Heath Hospital Dave Rudman occupied an ambiguous position. He was allowed on and off the ward, and also stayed the odd night at his flat, which was only half a mile away. He displayed – even Jane Bernal had to acknowledge – a great sensitivity towards his fellow patients, whose discordant manias, plunging depressions and flamboyant acting up were quite different from his own madness, which seemed almost measured by comparison. The lengthy withdrawal from the antidepressants left the cabbie sleepless and floundering. Plying his weary body, he sought out the fares on the ward. *Leave on right my bed, right aisle, forward door to main corridor, left patients' kitchenette.*

Rudman made the patients' kitchenette into his shelter and stood there at all hours, doling out hot sweet tea to bulimics with bandaged wrists and crack criminals who'd broken into their own psyches, stolen everything worth having and left only coiled turds on the carpet of their own consciousness. Dave guided these unfortunates back to their beds; he helped their twitching fingers with the big brushes and poster-paint pots during the weekly art-therapy sessions. He assisted the old Alzheimer's patients to the toilet and stood in the stinky lobby while they did their solitary business.

Then there was Phyllis. Phyllis with her tumultuous head of black, curly hair, so high and wide it threatened to fall off her head. Phyllis, with her weird, white pancake make-up and her flowing dresses, which she ran up herself from garish African fabrics. Phyllis, who through accident and inclination had fallen through the middle-class safety net into a series of unfortunate, even abusive liaisons. Phyllis, who'd pulled herself together, trained as a chef, and now supported both herself and her father-forsaken son. Phyllis, who came stumping on to the ward with her plump wrists nearly severed by the handles of many plastic bags. Bags full of bananas, newspapers, fruit-juice cartons and books, which she bore to the bedside of her son, Steve, who was full grown now and suicidal. Phyllis and Dave struck up a . . .

'Friendship – you're implying there's more to it than that?' Zack Busner, Jane Bernal, two junior registrars and the ward's psychiatric social worker were gathered for a case meeting.

'I don't know,' Jane continued. 'I shouldn't think there's anything sexual between them – how could there be? He's told me he's impotent – and I believe him. But there's a definite intimacy – and he's very attentive to the son.'

'To Steve?' the social worker put in.

'Yeah,' one of the junior registrars chimed up. 'He spends hours sitting with him, talking to him about' – she wrinkled her nose with amused disbelief – 'cabbing.'

'Cabbing?' Busner saw nothing funny in this. 'Well, why wouldn't he, he is a cabbie after all – as well as a prophet.'

Jane Bernal came back in. 'Phyllis Vance is also helping him sort out his living problems – debts, work and so forth. She asked me to write to the Public Carriage Office on his behalf. He's trying to find out whether he can return to work.'

'Has anyone else been helping him?' Busner asked. 'His family, friends?'

The social worker consulted her notes. 'There was a Gary Finch who came to see him a couple of times,' she said. 'He's looking after Rudman's cab. His sister came once, very uptight woman, not at all sympathetic – other than that no one. His mother never came back after the initial interview.'

'So this Phyllis . . .' Busner ruminated. 'It looks like she's a . . .'

*Good thing. Best thing that's happened to me in years . . . Not that I fancy her . . . none of that* . . . Even Steve, Phyllis's son, felt like *a good thing*. Dave couldn't understand it, but when he saw the young man for the first time, slumped on his bed in the men's ward, his *daft dreadlocks* brushing his knees, the first five inches of his boxer shorts bagging above the waistband of his trousers *like a fucking nappy*, he felt a strange rush of guilt and sympathy. Jane Bernal had been talking to Dave about *stereotypic patterns of thought . . . fear . . . racism . . . woman hating* . . . She thought it would be a good idea if he had *better ideas* . . . Cognitive Behavioural Therapy she called it.

Dave tried out a better idea. 'Orlright, mate?' he said, advancing on the supine figure. 'My name's Dave – I'm like the geezer factor on the ward. I'm a cabbie by trade, see, so I've the knowledge of the gaff, you wanna tea or sumfing, I could show yer ve day room an' vat . . .' Cockney clambered into his mouth alongside nerves – because the lad was looking at him with *zombie eyes*. Dave havered, then sat down on the bed by him. 'What's the matter, son?' he asked.

The matter with Steve was depression so fundamental and so complete that it melted his muscles and coated his mind in a tarmac of despair. Steve threw himself out of windows and beneath the wheels of cars. He hacked at himself with craft knives, he upended paracetamol bottles. His stomach had been pumped more often than he'd filled it. If the revolving door through which he entered Heath Hospital had been attached to a generator, Steve could have provided enough power for his own ECT.

When Phyllis saw that this man, who would be, were he not confined in his tracksuit to the treadmill of the ward, *a typical bloody bigot*, was making an effort with her mixed-race son, she took an interest in him. Over cake at the Hampstead Tearooms his story crumbled out: the cabbing, Carl, Michelle, Cal, Cohen the lawyer, the CSA, CAFCASS, the PCO, the cabbing – always the cabbing. 'Well, if that's what's bothering you so much,' she said, 'the cab, well, we better try to sort it out.' And she smiled with her tiny red bow of a mouth.

Fucker had parked the Fairway up on Agincourt Road a month before – then done nothing more. When Dave saw how filthy it was, the tyres near flat, one wiper bent up like a *broken arm*, he wept. But Phyllis only rolled up the sleeves of her *daft dress* and helped him wash the vehicle until it shone in the citrus autumn sunlight, as much as any black thing could. In the flat, with its airless stew of stale smells and its litter of Final Demands, Phyllis kept her sleeves rolled up and her rubber gloves on. Dave went for rubbish bags and bleach from the shop on the corner. At the end of a stiff afternoon's work the cleared table was neatly tiled with the terrifying letterheads: Mendel & Partners, Transform Services, Transport for London, Halifax Building Society, etcetera, etcetera. Dave Rudman sat down on the bed – which had been made for the first time since the day after he moved in nearly three years before – and wept. Phyllis made no move to comfort him beyond saying, quite calmly, 'We better try to sort this out inall, David – it's time you moved on.'

~

There had been no word of Dave Rudman for six months. No late-night calls leaving threatening messages on Michelle's mobile. No playing at kidnapping – Carl picked up, then dropped off on the borders of Dave's forbidden zone. No contact. If Michelle had hoped that with Dave offstage she and Cal would fall into each other's arms with a pretty duet, she was sadly mistaken. Cal pursued his mad, junky daughter, he ran around after his mad, exploitative television shows. He had no time for her. When he was at Beech House he mostly played computer games with Carl.

Michelle's only consolation was the casual hand she saw Cal rest on his putative stepson's shoulder when Carl had pulled off a particularly deft bit of thumb work. *The loser in all this*, she was forced to conclude, *is me*. She looked from dad to lad and the awful realization dawned in her that to figure out this emotional algebra, she would have to assign a value to X, the secret that had sustained her through years of *fucking brutality . . . abuse even*.

In Vigo Street Mitchell Blair was as dapper in striped shirtsleeves as he had been that April in full fig. He tapped his unnaturally small teeth with his gold propelling pencil. 'This, well . . . business . . . well . . .' Michelle was pleased that the diminutive smoothie was lost for words. 'I fail to understand . . . look . . .' Finally he put together a sentence. 'If you want to proceed along this new avenue you will have to get a DNA test.'

'DNA from who?' she said blankly.

'From whom . . . yes,' he laughed again, 'good question. Well, your son, of course, and then either will do, either of them.'

When she returned to Beech House, remorse seized Michelle, and she called her ex-mother-in-law. Annette Rudman's voice came shuffling towards her down distempered corridors of institutional contempt. 'How is Carl?' she asked without nicety. 'We haven't seen him for over a year now . . . it's not right.'

'I . . . I know Mrs . . . Annette . . . It's not what I want, but you know . . . Dave –'

'Dave's in hospital, Michelle.'

'In hospital?'

'On a psychiatric ward.'

When she tried to hang up after the call, the receiver hit the side of the cradle and fell, bouncing on its spiralling cord, rapping the inlaid phone table. Michelle thought how everyday life was made up of a series of small botched actions, which, although instantly forgotten, nonetheless ruined everything, making it clumsy, paltry and worthless.

The day before Dave Rudman was due to go back to his flat for good, Zack Busner summoned him to his office. Dave found the elderly shrink playing with what looked like a children's toy, a series of brightly coloured plastic tiles that he was arranging and rearranging on a little tray. 'Ever seen one of these before?' Busner asked.

'Can't say I have.' Dave absent-mindedly patted his shirt pocket for cigarette packet and lighter.

'Smoke if you want,' Busner said; 'I approve. Here – here's an ashtray.' He pushed a lump of unglazed clay that had been dumped on him by a grateful obsessive across the desk. 'It's a little thing called the Riddle I put together in the early seventies, absurd really' – Busner clacked the tiles some more – 'but in its day there were thousands sold, people used them to try to look into their own obscure mental processes. You rearrange the tiles into a pattern that you find pleasing or resonant – then consult this' – he took a booklet from a drawer – 'to find out what's going on in your unconscious. Here – here' – the Riddle followed the blob into Dave's hand – 'take it, take it, you might find it useful – I've got a whole self-storage unit in Acton full of them. I only press it on you,' Busner said, tilting back in his chair and peering at Dave over the top of his glasses, 'because you strike me as someone who could do with a great deal more of looking into himself.'

'Maybe,' Dave acknowledged.

'We never quite got to the bottom of what was behind your . . . collapse, did we?'

'No, I s'pose not.'

'The Book, still in here, is it?' Busner tapped his own soaring forehead.

'Oh, yes,' Dave said, looking sheepish, 'but I don't think it's what I thought it was, if you see what I mean.' He sat forward. 'I think it's just, well, just the Knowledge, nothing else. I think all that other malarkey was me falling . . . falling apart.'

'Hmm, well. Good. Tell me, has Dr Bernal arranged for you to see a psychiatrist?'

'Oh, yes . . . yes, she has.' Dave stubbed the blob and took an appointment card from his pocket. 'Some bloke called Boom, is it?'

'Ah,' Busner smiled. 'No, not Boom, *Bohm*, Tony Bohm. Yes, I think you and he will get along splendidly.'

~

Gary Finch called Dave at the flat on Agincourt Road. 'Sprung, then, are you, sprung?'

'I've been discharged, yes.'

'No one need ever, y'know – know.'

'What're you on about?'

'The stigwotsit, the stiggymarta.'

'Stigma, you mean?'

'Thassit – not me, mindjoo, but other people might think you're mental. Still, they won't be getting anything out of me – I was bullied at school, they said I 'ad a touch of the mongs. Lissen, it's Tuesday, come up the meeting tonight?'

'Oh, I dunno –'

'No, come – I tellya it'll be worf it.'

In the Trophy Room everything had changed. Dave realized this as he walked in through the door. No longer were the plastic chairs grouped in an egalitarian circle; instead there were fully tenanted rows of seats all facing a makeshift podium. On this stood Daniel Brooke in his outsized T-shirt. He gave the newcomers a curt nod, but his attention was mostly on a banner he was fixing up over the trophy cabinet together with a Fathers First member Dave didn't recognize. There was no sign of Keith Greaves at all, and the few faces Dave did know were outnumbered by at least twenty new men. The banner was stretched tight; FIGHTING FATHERS it shouted. 'Right!' called Daniel Brooke. 'Settle down, you lot, we've a lot to get through this evening, and I need maximum attention and positivity . . . Gary.' Brooke fixed Fucker, who was still chatting to his neighbour, with a pointed eye. Fucker fell silent.

'I applaud those of you from the old Fathers First group who've had the courage to come with us on this new journey of self-discovery and personal evolution, believe me you won't be disappointed. Keith has his good points, but they're soft ones.' Brooke's eyes kept ranging along the assembled men's faces as he spoke, as if probing them for any softness. 'That touchy-feely stuff may be OK for dads who want to lie down under all the shit they've been dealt out, but that's not what we are. What are we?' He paused and raised his beautifully manicured fist in a swift uppercut.

'We're Fighting Fathers!' the men all bellowed.

'And whadda we want?' Brooke called back.

'Justice now!' the men cried.

The atmosphere of resentful aggression in the room reminded Dave of sour-faced old cabbies moaning on in their shelters. The Fighting Fathers had the distorted mouths and clenched eyes of *some bloody Muslim fanatics burning an American flag* . . .

'Motivation is the key,' Brooke resumed, pacing the little podium. 'Without motivation we cannot hope to have any success with direct action, which is why I'm happy to welcome here this evening a motivational speaker who's going to give it to you straight concerning the Judaeo-Feminist forces lined up against us.' *Judaeo-Feminist?* 'He runs his own, hugely successful data-retrieval business, Transform Services.' *Transform Services?* 'He's a leading light in our brother organization, the Stormfront Nationalist Community. Will you give a big dads' welcome please to Barry Higginbottom!'

A man dramatically bashed open the swing doors and stood in the characterless strip lighting of the Trophy Room. It was the Skip Tracer – and the sweat was lashing off him.

~

'A book, you say?' Anthony Bohm looked at the cabbie through the thick, round lenses of his vintage, wire-rimmed spectacles. When a young man, Bohm had affected the glasses as a badge of maturity – the lenses had been of clear glass. However, with an irony that was not lost on him, as Bohm's career had progressed, so his eyesight had satisfactorily deteriorated, until he acquired the searching gravitas of the genuinely myopic.

'That's right, a book.' Dave looked around at the gloomy room, which was dominated by an enormous duct running across the ceiling, the housing of which was covered by flaking tinfoil. A decade-old flyer hung from bashed chipboard by yellowing tape, proclaiming DON'T DIE OF IGNORANCE. The room was somewhere deep in the basement of St Mungo's, a rundown hospital off the Tottenham Court Road.

This wasn't his and Bohm's first session together – they'd had one up at the Halliwick in Friern Barnet, another down at King's on Denmark Hill. Bohm told Dave that he was seeing him 'on an unofficial basis, it's very much a personal thing between me and Zack Busner', and as the psychiatrist took a series of locum positions around the city, his patient was required to follow. This was no hardship for Dave, who had resumed cabbing as gently as possible, only going out for a couple of hours during the off-peak. He used his weekly sessions as a low-anxiety conduit, picking up fares along the way as he wended to the next rendezvous with the mobile shrink.

'When I was . . . well, y'know, Tone, when I'd lost it,' Dave said, 'I thought there was this book inside me, this book I'd written . . . but now I dunno – I dunno.'

'We've talked about your childhood,' Bohm continued, 'your relationships, your work. I like to think we've built up some trust between us.' He smiled, and his white goatee flicked like a hairy digit. Dave smiled too – anyone with such preposterous facial hair could hardly be malevolent. 'When Doctor, ah, Fanning, prescribed Seroxat for you in 2001 I'm sure he did what he felt was the right thing. However, the facts are that a small minority of patients have bad reactions to the drug – psychoses even. Your book dates from this period. If we can somehow dig it up from your unconscious and, so to speak, read it together, I think it would resolve a lot of your issues.'

Each of these measured remarks had been ticked off by Bohm,

one plump finger pulling back the others. He now held the annotated hand aloft. 'Goodbye until next week,' he said, 'when we'll be meeting' – he consulted a fat little Filofax opened on his hefty thigh – 'at the Bethesda in Bermondsey.'

Dig up the book. Dig it up – search for it in the scrubby desert of his own mind. On the *poxy little colour telly* in the corner of his room, Dave Rudman saw clip after clip, all featuring the same stock characters: UN Inspectors in short-sleeved shirts and sweat-soaked jackets; Baathist apparatchiks in tan fatigues; to one side a gnarled old Bedouin in a *dirty white cloakyfing*. Behind them, on a plain of gravel that faded to a wavering horizon, stood corrugated-iron sheds and hunks of industrial equipment – hoppers, conveyor belts, ducts – all of them streaked with rust and dust. A mechanical digger petted some sand, arid wind plucked at the corners of the Inspectors' clipboards, riffling the computer printouts. *Hard to think of them manufacturing anything there . . . Don't look like they could turn out a bloody widget, let alone nuclear-bloody-weapons* . . . Yet Dave could see, in this taut confrontation, a sinister evocation of his own troubled life. *Buried inside me . . . all that sickening guff . . . poisonous thoughts . . . got to dig it up . . .*

What was he doing with Phyllis? Not that they'd *actually done* anything together. A couple of cuddles on the duffed-up sofa in Dave's flat, a chaste kiss on parting – no tongues. Phyllis wouldn't even invite him out to her place, which was *in the sticks, out by Ongar . . . off the edge of the world* . . . Instead she saw him in Gospel Oak, after visits to Steve in the hospital. Or else Dave drove into town and ranked up in Bow Street. Phyllis worked in Choufleur, a vegetarian restaurant on Russell Street, and, despite the fact that she looked *even freakier* in her voluminous smock and blue-striped apron, a mushroom-cloud hat perched on her curls, Dave couldn't help but recognize the feeling in his chest when she came out from the back entrance to share a B & H with him by the bins as one of *affection, that's it . . . affection . . .*

Slowly, methodically, Phyllis invested what spare affection she had in pushing the cabbie back into the mainstream of life. She persuaded him to contact Cohen, his ex-lawyer, and to begin to probe out the situation with Carl. She helped him to amalgamate his debts, and by taking a new mortgage on the little flat get enough money to start repaying them. Together they wrote letters to the County Court, asking for fresh reports, suggesting that his mental breakdown be taken into consideration. They paid off his arrears and then appealed to the Child Support Agency for a reduction in payments. Then they picked up his paper trail, finding anomalous things, like a bill from a Colindale printer for £9,750. It was dated December of the previous year and had been paid. Along the bottom was stamped: RUSH JOB.

The year whimpered to its end. One day Dave Rudman was by the lights at the top of Lower Regent Street. Limos stretched out beside the Fairway while buses bent around it. First Dave stared at a man holding a sign for a GIANT GOLF SALE. Then he looked at a souvenir stall flogging miniature cabs with Union Jack decals, figurines of tit-headed coppers and tiny red model phone boxes . . . *toyist crap*. Finally, he peered up through the windscreen of the Fairway at the huge electronic signboards covering the buildings of Piccadilly Circus. One showed the Circus itself – the teeming crowds, the enmeshed traffic. Then, without warning, water began to flood between the buildings, a tidal bore that came surging along the rivers of light. Dave was shocked – what could this apocalyptic vision be selling? Then the flooded concourse wavered, fragmented and was replaced by a slogan: DASANI MINERAL WATER, A NEW WAVE IS COMING.

'Excuse me? Excuse me?' The fare was an elderly priest and he wanted to go to Mill Hill. 'St Joseph's College, d'you know it?' Dave did. Who could miss it, with its strange painted bust of Thomas More out front, flesh tones as realistic as those of a *showroom dummy*? The fare was ill disposed to chat – and that suited

Dave fine. He drove up the long, straight thoroughfare from Marble Arch. Then, as the cab passed through Kilburn and Cricklewood, then over the North Circular to Colindale, it began to come back to him. Dropping off the fare at the College, he made change in a cursory fashion, unconcerned by the nugatory tip. Dave drove along the Ridgeway to the Institute and, parking up, retraced his footsteps of the previous year.

*I used to come up here all the time . . . all the time . . . strange to forget it* . . . He looked across the dark valley towards Hampstead. *Yeah . . . came here to look over there . . . over there where he was . . . where he is* . . . Dave found himself on his knees, the damp earth blotting into his jeans. Then it returned to him.

Phyllis took the call on the payphone that was between the kitchen and the toilets. She'd never got the hang of mobiles. 'Phyl,' he said, sounding out of breath, shocked, 'it's Dave.'

'Alright, Dave, you sound like something bad's happened.'

'Well . . . well, it has . . . but a while back . . . Phyllis- Phyl, I've found it . . . I've found the book . . . It's not-not in me, Phyl – it's in the ground, a real bloody book, buried. Fucking buried.'

11

# *The Forbidden Zone*

Kipper 522 AD

It took him almost a year before he could even bear to contemplate the disturbing forms of the motos. Even with myopic eyes downcast, he could not avoid seeing their repulsive hands and feet, which, while human-like, were surrounded by large cartilaginous discs. Their mopeds were a dull pinky-beige colour – as they grew, so they darkened in hue, becoming brownish and brindled. The hides of the fully grown motos reeked of oil. For such large creatures they were horribly adept at concealing themselves, and oftentimes on his peregrinations the teacher would move to place his trainer upon a mossy boulder, only to feel it wobble beneath him. He would start back – the moto, roused, would rear up, and Böm would be confronted by the face of an enormous obese infant, with clear blue eyes hidden in its fleshy folds.

When he saw one come lumbering through the woodland towards him, he took off his eyeglasses and walked swiftly, circumventing its blurred bulk. To touch one of the grotesque anomalies would have caused him such intense revulsion that he feared he would vomit up his curry, should the motos, not sensing his disquiet, cluster about to give him a nuzzle; food, like as not, both cooked in and flavoured with their own oil.

Antonë Böm did become accustomed to the motos in time – and accustomed also to the oddities of the remote community to which he had been exiled. In coming to love Ham and the Hamsters, Böm was, in part, reconciled to that bit of himself that had been isolated during the Changeovers of his own childhood.

As a kid Tonë Böm had run and jumped and played with the others. His dad was a mechanic at the bus garage in Stockwell, responsible for the jeejees that drew the lumbering vehicles through the London streets. Surrounding the dads' block where Böm senior lived were the market gardens of Clapham, which provided London with its fruit and vegetables. Tonë's mum, San, lived in a mummies' block on Brixton Hill, and on Changeover day he'd join the lines of children winding through the orchards back to their dads' gaffs. The older kids carried the little ones when they tired and comforted them when they cried – for in London Changeover came early. When he was small, Tonë, like the rest, soon forgot mummy stuff and his mummyself after the Changeover. Yet as he grew older the consciousness of the different lad he was with his other parent stayed with him, shadowing his mind like a waking dream.

Böm spoke of this to his mates – but they either gave him very odd looks or suggested, in no uncertain terms, that he should speak to a Driver. While only in their early teens, these lads already had eyes for the opares, and they were keen to become dads in their own right. This prospect did not enthuse Tonë at all. He realized he must be queer.

Antonë Böm grew into a plump, shambling young man, quick of eye although slow of speech. His amiable doughy features bore the impress of the pox – which was in nowise unusual for a modern Londoner. He guarded his quizzical, inner eye fiercely, for always he saw the mummies' world in terms of the daddies', the daddies' in terms of the mummies'. He knew that many others did as well; he could detect it behind their closed faces. Yet they had no way to speak of such things, for they were all – dads, mums and queers alike – bound into the immemorial Wheel of Dävinanity, which, with its rituals and precepts, circumscribed their conduct and governed their inmost thoughts from when they arose at first tariff until they lay down as the foglamp dipped.

From when he was very young, Böm displayed the memory and the fixity of mind needed to become a Driver. His mum wanted him to – so did his dad. At nineteen he applied to the PCO and was accepted. Much of a Driver's apprenticeship consisted of calling over in the taxi schools, under the watchful mirrors of fiercely disciplinarian Examiners. The Knowledge Boys also patrolled the streets in their scarlet waterproof robes. They went out in all weathers to memorize such parts of the city as had already been built, and to consult with those Inspectors who were marking out the dävine plan for the next district of New London to be erected.

It was an exciting time to be a Knowledge Boy abroad in the city. Those structures deemed by the PCO to be most integral to New London – and which had been inaugurated at the accession of the King's dad, Dave II, almost forty years before – were now nearing completion. The great stations of King's Cross, Charing Cross, Victoria and Waterloo. The Hilton Hotel and the Houses of Parliament. The Shelters of St Paul's and Westminster Abbey. The NatWest Tower, the Lloyd's Building, the Gherkin and the very Wheel itself – mighty edifices that together expressed the full temporal compass of the dävine revelation.

However, in his second year of doing the Knowledge, when his appearances had been scheduled, Böm had a crisis. It was not one of faith – he still heard Dave over the intercom, albeit indistinctly. It was rather the PCO and the dogma it promulgated from which he detached. He looked at his fellow Knowledge Boys and saw in them only chellish vanity and the desire to exert power. He felt his mummyself recoiling from the brutal inequalities of London life; which meant that while the lawyers, the guildsmen and the Inspectorate lived a life of opulence and ease, there were beggars starving in the streets of Covent Garden.

Böm abandoned the PCO and for a time apprenticed himself to a surgeon in Old Street, who practised at the sign of the Twisted Spine. He providentially discovered that his clumsiness deserted him when it came to the furious, bloody business of the operations. The more agitated the patients became – as their limbs were bound with cloth strips and the surgeon's mate sharpened his knives and saws – the calmer Tonë was. His gaffer said he had the makings of a great surgeon in his own right, but Böm was discouraged by the palpable lack of success their ministrations had. Even a simple operation – such as removing a stone, or amputating a septic finger – would leave three out of four patients dead within tariffs.

Böm left the surgeon and joined the City of London School as an assistant teacher. He found some solace in his contact with lads whose natures were not, as yet, entirely set in the dävist orthodoxy. All this time he continued to live in a young queers' dormitory, keeping himself aloof from their whoring, betting and boozing. He tried also to ignore their rowdy persecution of the Jocks, the Taffies and the Micks – whichever minorities, in short, they could attack sure in the support of the PCO. It was a coarse and uncongenial environment for a young man with an inquiring mind; however, without a patron Böm had no means of escaping it. The best he might hope for would be to use his position as a means of seeking employ in a lawyerly household.

It was at the school that Böm came into contact with the teachings of the Geezer. Another assistant, queer like himself, had a brother who was imprisoned in the Tower, and from this unlikely source came the message Antonë had, without knowing it, been waiting for ever since his last Changeover: the confirmation that he was not alone.

The flyers met in a tiny room above the Whyte Bair boozer off Broadwick Street. The landlawd thought they were a group of literary blokes engaged in the compilation of a volume of dävine raps extolling the unearthly beauty and unutterable pathos of the Lost Boy. In truth, they earnestly studied the words of the Geezer, smuggled out from the gaol on scraps of A4, while endeavouring to contact mummies who might be susceptible to this new faith, which preached the dissolution of the Breakup and direct communication with Dave himself.

For two years their little cab met together to call over the tantalizing fragments of the new Book, to speak of their troubles, to relay their successes and commiserate in their failures to find other potential recusants. None of them ever believed it would last, for the PCO had informants in every place of work, every gaff, every takeaway and boozer. It was only a matter of time. When the seeseeteevee men came to his dormitory in the dead of night, Antonë Böm knew they were there for him. The only surprise was the lightness with which he was punished. He was held in solitary confinement in the Tower a few blobs. Then he was branded on the thigh, rather than on the brow, with the 'F' for flyer. Finally, he was sent forth from the city more as a traveller than as an exile.

We have a peculiar posting for you, Antonë Böm, said the Inspector who examined him. There is a remote part of the kingdom where there is a requirement for your particular skills. We do not think you will be able to make any trouble there. He stamped the molten wax on the exile order with the wheel of his signet ring and called to the warders: Take him down to Canary Wharf; he sails at first light for my Lawyer of Chil's Bouncy Castle at Wyc.

For the first five years of his exile Antonë Böm paid no more attention to Carl Dévúsh than he did to any of the little Hamsters. They were not his concern. Changeover came late on Ham, and the smaller children moved casually between the mummies' and daddies' gaffs – almost experiencing shared parenting. Even after the Changeover, the older kids still remained vitally connected to both parents through the interposition of the motos. Try as the Driver might to stamp out this promiscuity, he was unable. Seeing chellish superstition and toyist practices wherever he looked, the

Driver lived in constant fear of his alien surroundings, a condition he sought to hide from his fares by remaining for the most part confined to the Shelter and his own semi. Out of his sight, and that of the dävine dads, the old ways still continued on Ham.

Nevertheless, from the moment the keel of the Hack's pedalo ground into the shingle of the island and the adipose queer stepped ashore, the Driver moved to ensure his own supremacy. Böm was responsible for teaching the older lads and for tending to injured or sick Hamsters. The Driver had no illusions about his teacher-cum-surgeon – he cordially despised him. This antipathy was fully reciprocated, and, despite the great deal they had in common, the two outsiders had no more commerce with each other than was strictly necessary. The Driver impressed upon him that so long as Böm made the required appearances at the Shelter to call over the runs and points, and so long as he did not taint his instruction with flying, he would be left alone.

Alone in his tiny semi, which had been built by the Hack's chaps using locally quarried brick, to the same pattern as many of the poorer dwellings found elsewhere in King Dave's dominion. The sharp corners were difficult to seal against the curry spray that beset the island's southern shore during buddout and autumn. The roof joists were of poorly seasoned wood that warped. The slate tiles cracked, then fell off; and, having been brought from off the island by Mister Greaves, they were impossible to replace. So while the Hamsters' ancient dwellings remained solid and weatherproof, hunkering down into the green turf, the incomers suffered damp and draughts in the kipper, and the infestations of bugs and chafers in summer.

Böm's semi was tucked at the end of Sid's Slick. This inlet was beyond the headland where the Driver's own semi and the Shelter stood, and immediately beneath the shrub-choked slopes of the Gayt. Who exactly Sid had been it was difficult to discover. Some of the Hamsters claimed that he'd lived within the past few generations, and that the name referred to the fact that he'd fallen into the muddy stream bed and broken his leg. Others, however, told the teacher that Sid was born of a giant and a moto; and that he was a curious chimera who had once wallowed here in the muddy shallows of the lagoon. Whichever the case, the tale of Sid's Slick was but one among a great host of them. Every boulder, copse and crete outcropping on Ham had its own story to divulge. The island was a tapestry of naming, worked over again and again by the thousands of generations who had trod its leafy lanes and grassy paths. Antonë Böm, with his inquiring mind, set himself to map the foetus-shaped island, from the long groynes that projected from the northeastern shores of the Gayt, to the hidden coves and gull-haunted strands beneath the Ferbiddun Zön to the south.

Böm had little experience of rural Ing beyond the burbs of London. Nevertheless, like all visitors to Ham, he felt the otherworldliness of the island. There were no other mammals besides the motos and the occasional rat infestation. There were no bambis, no bugsbunnies, no tree rats – no mice even. Land birds were infrequent, migratory visitors, and the gulls kept to their roosts at the far ends of the island, only occasionally swooping down on to the home fields. With the woodlands managed assiduously by the motos, the field rips carefully manicured by the Hamsters themselves, and even the shrubbery pressed back into neat banks, the gently undulating landscape had the aspect of a stage in a playhouse. Set here and there on the smooth-cropped sward and the mossy floor of the woodland, the humans and their lisping kine became hieratic figures in a tableaux of a gentler, simpler era before King David's dynasty and the inexorable rise of the PCO.

In those first years of exile Böm set himself to compile a description of Ham; he included its flora, fauna and topography, as well as the customs, language and beliefs of its inhabitants. This he set down in the bound notebooks he had brought with him from London. Each night he scratched long into the third tariff by the dim lectric, his biro casting a wavering shadow on the roughly rendered walls of his little semi. It was, thus, to begin with an isolated life – yet he did not find it so. For he was already accustomed to being alone with his secret mummyself.

Being recognized as queer, Böm was free to take his meals with either the mummies or the daddies and was not required to observe the Breakup strictly. Nevertheless, for some time he was circumspect in his intercourse with the Hamsterwomen, until an incident that occurred in the buddout of his third year on Ham brought home to him that excessive caution was unnecessary.

He was out walking with old Effi Dévúsh. Together they strolled through the wind-tossed boughs of Kenwúd and along the spit to the feature known as the Mutha's grave. Here they stood, staring out through the dead heads of the blisterweed, towards the islet, a perfect little tumulus capped by an ingrown copse of pines. Their flat clusters of needles were angled away from the spray in a series of bafflers, their trunks twisted into a strangulated knot. Even at this early season the underbrush was dense. Shil B cummin rahnd ve mahntin ven she cums, Effie rapped. Shil B cummin rahnd ve mahntin ven she cums. Shil B cummin rahnd ve mahntin, cummin rahnd ve mahntin, cummin rahnd ve mahntin ven she cums. Böm was surreptitiously noting down this old rap of the Mutha. The emaciated rapper and her podgy amanuensis were so lost in the haunting air, the sough of the breeze and the vista of heaving waves marching into the distance that they failed to hear the Driver coming up behind them. He spoke – his words sharp and hectoring – and, as Effi whirled to confront him, a lock of her lank, white hair caught the Driver in the face.

He screamed and clawed at his own flesh. Heedless of the blisterweed, he charged straight into the lagoon and plunged his head beneath the water. You touch you – me touch never! he cried. Effi screamed as well and covered her face with her cloakyfing, yet Böm was torn between horror and hilarity; for it had dawned on him that the Driver was not merely careful – as any Driver must be – to avoid contact with a mummy, but terrified to the point of revulsion. The black crow was now dipping his head in a frenzy, the seawater flowing in glaucous cords from his beard and hair.

Eventually, while Effi faded into the woodland, Böm carefully negotiated the blisterweed, waded into the shallows and assisted the Driver back to the shore. The incident was never spoken of again, and this became part of the compact between them: the Driver confined himself still more to the Shelter, to leading the dads and lads in the calling over, to his interference in their Council; while Böm was free to wander the island and commune with the Hamsterwomen.

Effi Dévúsh had borne the brunt of the community's displeasure after the Geezer was deposed. Her grandson, Carl, was the last infant she had been allowed to anoint. Although she still acted as knee woman, as she grew older her skills – which had only ever been rudimentary – became unequal to the task. Apprenticed surgeon or not, of their own accord the Hamsterwomen would never have let Böm be present at a birth. It was he who heard Bella Funch's cries when her baby was being born breech. He ran full tilt into the mummies' gaff where she lay. Eye can elp! he cried. Bleev me, pleez, Eye no wot 2 dú! He did – he eased, coaxed, manipulated and finally yanked the bloody mite into the world. Then he stitched Bella up with neat loops of moto sinew, before applying a poultice of curried sphagnum. She survived – and so did the baby.

It took Böm several more years to gain the mummies' trust, and when he did, he mostly regretted it, for it made a torture garden of his imagined Arcadia. When Böm had arrived, he'd thought the island an idyllic place, for, despite its minatory Driver, Ham was far enough from London for the grip of the PCO to be slack. He understood now that the palisade of blisterweed that guarded the little island wreathed the minds of the Hamsters as well. Böm had seen the bruises and welts on the mummies, their scratched faces and wrists twisted into floppy uselessness. No dad or lad ever spoke of such things – it was as if they could not even recognize that it was they who had done them.

Even so, as the full truth began to come out in dribs and drabs – little gushes of pained recollection – it was only as he had sadly suspected. The beatings and rapes, the dads queuing up to take young opares just changed over, the casual clouts and blows – the dark, mummy-hating underbelly of Dävinanity that Antonë Böm could now recall in the whimpers of his own mummy, as she lay on her sofabed, recúperaytin – as she put it – after another visit from Antonë's own dad.

The secret Knowledge of the Hamsterwomen, which had withstood the Driver's dismal reign by sinking beneath the current of their lives, ran deep within Caff Ridmun. She remembered the time of the Geezer, and lest she ever forget she had only to look into Carl's restless eyes to recall that day at the curryings, the questing hand, the fingertips' progress from mole to mole.

So Caff poured all the love she had into Carl. She snuck into the woods and found him out with Gorj. Lifting the little boy down from the moto's neck, she would then spend whole tariffs with him, walking and talking, reminding him of who the mummies were – that they were not mere chavs, leased to them by Dave in order to do the daddies' bidding, but feeling, hurting fares. Caff told Carl he should never forget his own mummy when the motorage came upon him, and the daddies urged him on, and the young opares cowered in the byres.

When Carl was seven, the summer when Changeover became irrevocable, and for half of every blob he would have to be with the daddies, Caff told him the truth concerning his real dad. Ee woz a grayt dad, she said to the boy, ee spoak wiv Dave an Dave toal im 2 stop alluv vis malarkë, vis mummityme an daddityme, vis Chaynjova. U muss nevah ferget í, nevah. Ear tayk vese. She gave him a necklace of Daveworks that he could hang beneath his T-shirt, special talismans to remind him of the unity of mummies and daddies, before their painful division by the PCO.

~

Antonë Böm was permitted by the Driver only to teach the very phonic of the Book to the lads of Ham. There were five of them in the school the year that Carl changed over and became old enough to join. Lessons were held in the Shelter during the first tariff. After that the lads had to vacate the small wooden shack so that the dads could do their own calling over. Instruction was by rote: Böm called over the run and the points from the Book, then the lads repeated it in unison. Böm would announce a run he had selected at random: List Four, Run Fifty-Four. Leave by forward Kenton Road, left Cassland Road, right Wick Road, right East Cross Route slip, forward East Cross Route. Then the little Hamsters would mangle it into Mokni: Leev bì forrud Kentun Röd, leff Kasslan Röd, rì Wyc Röd . . . and so on, until the run was completed. Then it was the points: Burberry Factory, 29 Chatham Place, WE9 . . . Bubbery Faktri, twennynyn Chá-um Playce, dubbulU ee nyn . . .

For the first two years that Carl sat at Böm's feet there was only this, monotonous repetition. Then, when Carl's younger step-brothers joined the class, Böm split them all into two groups. Henceforth the little ones were quizzed on their Knowledge, while Carl and his mates were taught its application. Böm had A2ZS, drawn up by the PCO, which showed New London in all its growing magnificence.

The city the Book described was a perfect circle nineteen clicks across. Every street and most of the significant buildings had been ordained by Dave. Since the Book's discovery by the founding dad of the House of Dave, in the London burb known as Hampstead, court Drivers had laboured to interpret its dävine plan for the city. As each run was deciphered by these phonicists, so it was laid out. Once surveyed, the principal points were built and occupied, many by the Drivers themselves. In these newly founded Knowledge schools the learned queers debated and refined their understanding of the Book, thus ensuring that yet more buildings might be erected.

There were those sceptics who maintained that New London was not only incomplete but quite wrong. That its winding, muddy lanes and narrow, cluttered alleys bore no more relation to the city of Dave than a child's drawing to what it depicts. Worse, that the buildings themselves were mean travesties, unfit to bear the names of the mighty edifices Dave had inscribed on the irony plates of the Book. Still more critical voices noted how it was that as the PCO had grown and grown over the centuries, London – and beyond it Ing – became increasingly burdened by a religious bureaucracy the sole industry of which was its own perpetuation. However, these voices were stifled by the Doctrines and Covenants of the Book: the exactions of the Breakup and the Changeover, which kept the Inglanders riven inside, and so unable to conceive of any purpose beyond the fulfilment of Dave's prophecies.

Besides, who could gainsay the phenomenal growth and burgeoning prosperity of London, and beyond it of all Ing? In the centuries since the discovery of the Book, the vision it presented of a heavenly world of marvels that might be built here, on earth, had acted as a fruitful stimulus to the Inglanders, allowing them to resurrect the glories of past civilizations with apparent ease, and thus outstrip the haphazard advances of other nations. The Jocks, the Taffies, even the Swizz confederacy far across the sea – all remained mired in barbarism, while in Ing the people were subject to the rule of law. Now, when Inglish privateers encountered the longpedalos of the Nords or the ferries of the Franks on the high seas, the foreigners hove to and made tribute. Could there be any doubt that the dävidic line was dävinely ordained to rule Ing – and beyond it the known world?

The Driver of Ham and many others thought not. These zealots tended to a far stricter and more literal reading of the Book; for them its description of New London was of a city that stood outside time and was never to be built by mere chellish daddies. They pointed to the topographical dissimilarity between the London of King Dave and the New London of the Knowledge. They muttered also about the excesses of the court, where Changeover and Breakup were poorly observed – mummies and daddies openly consorting with one another in the pleasure gardens of Green Park and St James's. They spoke through the intercom and asked Dave for a new wave of Dävinanity to sweep across the land. As yet, these fundamentalist Dävists had made no open breach with the PCO; instead they sought the remoter regions of the King's realm for their missionary work, places where their rigour and zeal had much toyism to contend with.

None of this had troubled Carl Dévúsh, a young lad marooned at the outermost periphery of the dominion; until, that is, Antonë Böm began his more speculative instruction. The lads had committed to memory the Knowledge, the Letter to the Lost Boy and the Doctrines and Covenants. Nevertheless, the complete Holding of the Knowledge required a fare to be not merely conversant in all elements of the Book but capable of interrelating them. This necessitated the so-called Hypotheticals – rhetorical replies to questions that called upon fares to conceive of what Dave Himself would do in a given situation.

Antonë Böm excelled in the posing of Hypotheticals. He would stand by the ceremonial urn at the end of the Shelter and sling them out to the lads seated at the Driver's table: You're driving up Park Lane and you see a prospective fare struggling over the crash barrier. What do you do? What do you think? Name the points, tell me the run? There would be a surly silence, interrupted only by the irritating noise of scrubby hands scratching tousled heads. Then, invariably, it would be Carl Dévúsh who answered: Sloo ve cab ovah 2 ve rì an syd an C if eel mayk í, guv.

Böm, his wet eyes magnified by his eyeglasses, would blink at Carl. His plump hands would go to his tank and tap it. He'd rock on his heels, a buzzing noise coming from his plump lips. Who, he wondered, was this lad with the merry blue eyes and why was his peasant mind so acute? When the Driver came to shoo the teacher and his class out of the Shelter, it seemed only natural for Böm and Carl to find themselves proceeding apart from the rest. Natural too for Carl to go to the dads and suggest tasks that would take him and the teacher roving over the island. Slowly, in the course of these rambles, the queer and his pupil found each other out – discovering that they shared the same inquisitive bent, the same mummyness sealed away in their male breasts.

~

It was early autumn, and the Hack's party had been gone from Ham for two months. The booze and fags they'd brought had been used up. The daddies and mummies were working hard, preparing for the kipper. This year there were four motos to be slaughtered, and the Hack had brought many bales of woolly for the mummies to spin. Soon the screenwash and the demister would come, the leaves would whirl down from the trees, and the Hamsters, confined to their gaffs, would turn in on themselves. It was then, in the dark months, when time lay heavy on their idle, lustful hands, that the worst depredations of the daddies occurred, the beatings and roastings, the rapes and the circlefucks.

Böm preferred to have his curry in the old Bulluk house, where the boilers gathered. One night he looked up from his pannikin to see Caff Ridmun and Effi Dévúsh sitting beside him. He blinked back the tears that always gathered in his eyes when he was in the Hamsters' smoky gaffs and peered at them.

– W-wot iz í, mummies? he stammered, sensing that they had something important to divulge.

– U bin a long tym ear nah, Tonë, innit? Effi began.

– Long enuff – nyn yeers cum nex JUN.

– Anjoo no a ló abaht uz bì nah, innit?

Böm shifted to Arpee:

– I like to imagine that I have studied your ways thoroughly, if that's what you mean, Effi.

– Vares sumffing U av no nolidj uv, sumffing big.

– Oh and what's that? Böm was altogether without guile – he had no thought of trying to gain any advantage over Effi. He had learned to respect these Hamsterwomen, who, despite being treated like beasts of burden by their menfolk, kept the community alive and functioning.

Effi Dévúsh leaned close in, her own eyes were lost in deep wrinkles, her nose was a knife blade, her fingers talons that suddenly swooped on Böm's plump thigh and pulled up the leg of his jeans. He didn't flinch as the welts of the old branding scar were revealed.

– Vare í iz, Effi breathed – and Caff sighed as well. U nevah spoakuv í, didja?

– No, no, I saw no need.

– An ve Dryva – ee sed nuffing neevah.

– No, no, I believe he thinks it will do nothing to further his work among you.

– Av U evah erred tel ov ve Geezer?

Effi and Caff sat back while Böm straightened his clothes. There, their expressions seemed to say – it's out now. The Geezer! Böm was aghast. You mean the dad who said he'd found a second Book, the flyer?

– Ve verrë saym.

– Yes, well . . . Böm said, hanging his head, you could say he's the reason I'm here at all. It was his calling over in London that had me branded.

This intelligence was of no concern to the mummies; the London of which the teacher spoke was a remote – near mythical – realm. When Symun Dévúsh had been taken from them, he was gone for ever.

– Didjoo no, Effi continued, ee woz a sunuv Am, didjoo no vat?

– The Geezer, from here, from this Ham? Böm was incredulous. Surely not?

– Nah, Effi sighed, iss ve troof –

– An mì Carl, Caff broke in, mì Carl . . . ees . . . ees iz lad.

The Geezer. To Antonë Böm it was an age ago and half a world away. He had carried the Geezer's teaching locked up inside of himself, along with his mummyself, for all the dank days of his exile. The tenets of the new faith were as close to his heart as the first time he had heard them from the lips of his fellow teacher at the City of London School: No Breakup or Changeover, mummies and daddies to be with one another, touch one another, speak with one another, care for one another, with all the gentleness of a young opare tending to her infant charge. No PCO, no Knowledge, no Dävinanity – Dave himself disavowed it all, and had seen fit to tell this young, near-illiterate peasant that the first Book had been naught save the ravings of a dävine mind misshapen by anger and hatred.

Dave bore no hatred towards mummies – not even Chelle. He truly wanted His fares to be fulfilled by whatever manner of life that they pursued. He did not wish them to build New London; only to live in the cities and towns that they themselves founded. And if they wanted to speak with Him, to reach up through the screen and touch Him, to sit back, give Him directions and let Him drive them to their destination – then that was what Dave wanted as well. He was there for all daddies and mummies – whatever their estate. He could be reached with the intercom – or even a loud call. No Drivers or Inspectors were needed to intercede – no laborious recitation of arcane Knowledge was required.

It was to this Dave that Antonë Böm called over each night in his mean semi. Settled on a low stool, his arms held out straight in front of him, feeding the Wheel as he opened his heart. Expressing his innermost thoughts and secret yearnings to a perfect and loving Supreme Driver. Often, upon falling silent, he would become aware of that mundane Driver, a scant distance away, who called over to a very different Dave, a savage, hate-filled Dave, who wished nothing for his fares save toil and strife, the Breakup and the Changeover.

No one in London had known precisely where the Geezer had hailed from – the name Ham was whispered, yet this meant nothing, for there were thousands of Hams scattered over the archipelago of Ing. In the time before the dävidic line was established in the city that came to be called London, many of these places were claimants to be the true cradle of the faith. Antonë had never conceived of the Geezer's Book as having a material reality, any more than he had imagined it being found in the same place as the first. Now two kinds of Knowledge joined together in Antonë Böm's mind, two worlds irrupted into each other. If . . . if the Geezer spoke the truth . . . Böm could barely formulate the thoughts . . . Then – then, this . . . this is Ham- Hampstead . . . and that . . . beyond the reef . . . below the lagoon . . . is . . . is London. For did not Dave speak of a mighty flood, a great wave transforming the city's streets into raging rivers?

Böm held the Knowledge of Ham as completely as any native granddad or grannie; it was his Knowledge of the Book that had faded. Its runs and points had been sing-songed into mere sounds by the lads in the Shelter. For tariff after tariff, then blob after blob, and finally year after year. While Böm leaned his weary head on the doorjamb and gazed out to sea, to where the stacks were spray-dashed in the swell, what was it that the lads had chanted? Rì

Wyldwúd Röd. Leff Norfend Wä. Complì Spanyads Layn, Forrud Eef Street . . . The area of dense woodland along the north shore was known as the Wyldwúd. The lane that ran down from the moto wallows between Wess Wúd and Sandi Wúd was called Norf to differentiate it from the Layn that ran along the spine of the island. That these old tracks, worn by the feet of Hamsters and motos, conformed to the runs, conformed to the Knowledge – could it mean anything?

Which had come first: the Knowledge or Ham? Surely it was more likely that the ancient Hamsters had named their rustic tramps after the majestic thoroughfares described in the Book? Yet . . . and yet . . . Forward Heath Street . . . then into the Zön, then left Beech Row . . . and was that where the Book had been disinterred some five hundred years before? If there was an answer to the conundrum it lay in the shrub-choked Ferbiddun Zön. It lay here on Ham.

Antonë Böm did not sleep that night. When the first tariff came and the foglamp was switched on in the east, he was down at the shore pacing back and forth. A rank of motos nosing down from the Layn sighted him. Knowing better than to approach the teacher, they hung back, shrouded by the mist, their slushy calls muffled by the damp air. Alwyt, Tonë, alwyt, they cooed, hoping he had overcome his old revulsion enough to come and pet them. Instead Böm walked on along the shore, past the dim box of the Driver's semi, which seemed to suck solidity out of the nebulous atmosphere, then on around the bay to the manor. All was silent and still, the occasional cooee chew-chew-chew of a gull banking over the beach as mournful as the wail of an abandoned child.

Antonë Böm stood by a stand of blisterweed and regarded the Hamsters' humped and mossy gaffs. It wouldn't be long before the first mummies and opares were up, stoking the fires with fresh wood, heating up cracked wheatie and moto gubbins for the dads and kids. The Hamsterwomen's labours began early and were never done. The boilers and mummies told Böm that before the Driver came there had been little or no violence on Ham. Now he understood – it was the Geezer's fault, the daddies were punishing the mummies for what had happened during the time of the Geezer, and the Driver was inciting them.

Ware2, guv! It was Caff Ridmun who called to him, jerking the teacher away from his thoughts. She'd come out from the Bulluk gaff and was heading over to the spring to fetch evian. 2 Nú Lundun! Böm called back – and in that unit his mind was made up. He would penetrate the Ferbiddun Zön and discover its secrets – whatever the consequences might be.

The screenwash came late that autumn – not until NOV was almost over. The climate on Ham was always temperate, but this year it seemed as if kipper would never arrive. The motos were still sleeping out in the woodland, while fat flies doodled in and out of the shack where the Hamsters made waste of their natural products. The community became uneasy. The oldest of the grannies and granddads told tales of former times, when during such spells freakish waves had reared up out of the Great Lagoon, drenching the home field with curry and destroying the soil's fertility for a generation. On one occasion Ham had been almost completely depopulated. When the Hack arrived from Chil, he found only a few mummies and kids huddled in the empty byres – almost all the Hamstermen had died, some from starvation, others during a desperate fowling trip out to the stacks. The motos too were severely reduced in numbers. Daddies had to be brought forcibly from Chil to settle on the island. It was said that it was then that the decline began, and the Hamsters shrank until they were naught save pygmies compared to their mighty forefathers.

Against a backdrop of flaming autumnal leaves, the Driver called over the Book – while Antonë Böm scurried away from the Shelter as fast as his chubby legs would carry him. Yaw blankin me! Carl Dévúsh called after him. Yaw blankin me, Tonë! The lad ran, his bare feet sure on the slippery turf, and caught up with his mentor.

Oi! Wossup? Ware U goin? Carl's hand was on Antonë's arm, and in its pressure the older man could feel all the weight of the responsibility he sought to avoid, the daddystuff, the daddytime, the need to work and build, to make a better world. He shrugged the hand off, turned from the expectant eyes, walked on hurriedly up to the Layn and went on down into the woodland. Carl was not to be so easily discarded. He followed behind, crying out: Wot ve mummies bin tellin yer, Tonë? Eh, wot vey bin tellin yer? Vey töl U abaht me dad, iz vat í, iz vat í?

Böm blundered in and out of boggy sloughs with no care for the state of his jeans. As the lad pursued him, he became increasingly hysterical – the whirl of speculation about Ham and the agitation in his feelings it provoked sucked him into a vortex of abandonment. Why? he implored aloud. Why O Dave have you dropped me off? He had never wanted it this way: to be queer was bad enough, to be exiled as a flyer worse, now these chellish mummies conspired to place him for ever outside the Shelter. Whippystalks tore at his beard and hair, the wind rose and the yellow leaves flashed against the deep, blue sky – the whole spherical space of Ham was in motion, a flickering between faith and faithlessness. Sweetë, startled by Böm's thrashing through the underbrush, started up from where she'd been lying and trundled off into a thicket. The sight of the moto's vast and brindled flanks set Böm on another course: The motos . . . grotesque mutants . . . slobbering, giant babies . . . are we not all babies, mired in our own ordure, babbling nonsense? Böm sank down in a boggy patch, and his hands drove into the brackish morass. He moaned and brought clutches of the muddy weed up to his face, squeezing the sludge between his fingers. You fucking bitches! he blubbered. You fucking bitches . . . You've taken – you've taken ev-ery-thing!

Carl stood a little way off, his slight figure camouflaged by his bubbery cloakyfing. He looked at Böm with a curious expression, concerned yet almost contemptuous. A fulcrum had been wedged beneath their association – and the balance was tipping in Carl's favour. Eventually he moved towards the teacher, bent down and stared into the muddy face.

– Vey töl djoo, diddun vey?

Böm nodded; there was a smear of blood at the corner of his mouth.

– U no wot cums nex . . . Carl took his shoulder, shook it. U no, Tonë, we gotta go an fynd out. We gotta go intah ve zön . . . U no . . . ware mì dad went . . . We gotta fyndaht ve troof.

– No, Böm said feebly. No, we mustn't . . . we can't.

Two days later, in the middle of the second tariff, Antonë Böm and Carl Dévúsh stood at the brow of Wollötop, where the Layn plunged into the dense undergrowth of the Ferbiddun Zön. At this, the highest point on Ham, the view in all directions was of waves frothing over the reef, as if it were the island itself that was disturbing the sea. Further out to the south, the white caps curled away across the Great Lagoon to the Sentrul Stac; while to the north the deeper sound between Ham and Nimar was like buckled irony plates under the ragged racing clouds.

A chill wind moaned between the pines that guarded the moto wallows, and further along the Layn to the northeast the twisted branches of crinkleleafs scratched at a tinted screen within which pinprick dash lights gleamed. For three full tariffs the storm had lashed Ham, blowing every single leaf from the trees, the screen-wash hosing the paths into muddy chutes. Now the screen was clearing, and the wind scoured Antonë's and Carl's faces. They both carried the Hamsters' heavy mattocks on their shoulders. Böm also had a flaming bundle of oil-soaked reeds, but the brand would shed little light – they were counting on the headlight, which wouldn't dip until well into the third tariff.

– Ready, then? he said.

– Reddë enuff, Carl replied.

Böm hefted his mattock. Come on, then, he said through pursed lips. Let's go.

Within a few paces the quiet of the Zön enfolded them. The hill sloped steeply, and they first slipped, then fell. Struggling on, the pair pushed through a bank of dead pricklebush and found themselves in a gully between high banks over which swarmed the spiky roots of rhodies. Looking up, Carl saw the dark blue rift of the screen fringed by their glossy evergreen leaves. Böm was reverently calling over and over: Forward Heath Street . . . Forward Heath Street . . . Forward Heath Street, as he edged his way deeper in the Zön. He could see a gap in the bank to their left and, thrusting his way into it under the bushy overhang, called back to his companion: Hampstead Square, this should be the last turn-off before we reach Beech Row.

Carl came slithering through the mud to reach Böm's side, and supporting each other they pressed forward. Djoo bleev í? the lad whispered, overawed by the mystery of the place. Djoo bleev viss iz Lundun? Böm cast anxious glances about him at the dark banks. Here and there the soil had crumbled away in the rain, and even through the gloom they could make out the exposed courses of brick. After they'd skidded another hundred paces there came a second gap in the bank to their left. This is it, Böm sighed. If we truly are in Hampstead, then this is Beech Row. Follow me.

Bent double beneath the dense press of the undergrowth, they squeezed into the ditch. After a score of paces they scrambled up the bank to the right. On top the rhodies were quite low, and, upon rising up, they found themselves head and shoulders above the canopy. The headlight was full beam, its silvery letric illuminating the eerie scene. Spreading out below was a lap of land in the hillside; over it shimmered the shiny, purple-black masses of the rhodies, while here and there pinnacles of brick rose up, stark against the night screen.

This mound – Böm indicated the tumulus immediately to their left – must be the gaff. There's Knowledge of this in the Book, Carl. A gull swooped past, coasting on its airy ramp. Böm started and dislodged scree, which pattered down into the ditch behind them. Carl, remembering the granddads' tales of rat colonies in the Ferbiddun Zön, clutched Böm's shoulder. Steady, lad, the teacher calmed him. Be steady.

They clambered down the slope and on to the flat area below the mound. Then Böm began his peculiar search on hands and knees, seeking out first the long-buried remains of the ancient wall, then rising to check its orientation with the mound, then sinking down again. It was eldritch, the queer rustling about in the dark shrubbery, the gulls scooting overhead, the full-beam headlight bearing down on them from the south, smoky cloud roiling across its fly-specked glass. Suddenly Böm's scurrying ceased, and he let out a single, low moan. Carl crashed through the bushes to his side. Böm was kneeling before a gaping pit. The vegetation had encroached on it, the rain had washed down into it – yet still the clay streaks and sand dashes at its edges made the hole appear freshly dug. L-look, Böm stuttered. L-look here . . . and here . . . Where the fill from the pit had been scattered among the rhodies, there were neat piles of Daveworks, twisted bits of irony, bricks and lumps of crete. Th-this is it . . . Böm managed to splutter. This is where the G-geezer, your d-dad dug. This is where he claimed he found the second Book!

– Mebë iss stil vare, said Carl, and, since Böm at first did not acknowledge him, he said it again: Mebë iss stil vare – ve Búk.

– W-what d'you mean?

– Me dad, ee sed Dave túk ve Búk bak, diddunee? Mebë ee ment ee put í bak, bak in viss ole.

– Oh, no, no, surely not – it couldn't be, there's nothing there, look . . . look . . .

They stared down into the pit, and the muddy puddle at the

bottom held the reflections of their two heads outlined against the screen above – as if they were two creatures who had come there to drink, and were now frozen in contemplation of their own, misunderstood image.

– We gotta lúk innit, Carl said after a while. We gotta dig, thass Y we brung vese . . . He held up his mattock. Cummon nah, Tonë, lettus dahn.

As Böm tried to lower the lad carefully into the pit, the sides gave way, and they were both precipitated into the chilly quag. They wallowed there, at first working their mattocks deep into the sludgy pit bottom; then, when that yielded nothing, they sank down, plunged their arms in up to the shoulder and grabbed handfuls of the muck. Finally, exhausted, they abandoned the search and heaved themselves back up the sides of the pit, to lie wet and cold under the dashboard. There's nothing there, Böm gasped. But there was once something – there must have been. This, the very empty pit itself, was enough of a revelation for him; and so, along with its eroding sides, the last vestiges of his loyalty to King Dave and the PCO crumbled away.

~

They came back down through the home field to the manor in the harsh foglight of the first tariff. The pod-shaped gaffs were silent and brooding, for the Hamsterwomen and children had been shut up, while all the Hamstermen were waiting for them at the Council wall. Through the thicket of dead withies Carl could make out the figure of the Driver, standing tall and still as a statue among the crouched figures of the dads and staring at them with his yellow eyes.

He had no need to summon them: cold, soaked, caked with mud, as if they were primordial men, reborn from the very soil of Ham, the two recusants limped towards their destiny. In stony silence the dads watched them approach and in stony silence they listened while the Driver pronounced his anathema:

– Flyers! That's what you are – both of you. Flyers! Digging and delving where you have no business! A branded flyer and a flyer's whelp! The chellish mummies are behind this – of that I've no doubt!

As if it were only another of the Driver's rants, with no more application to him than to any Hamster, Carl Dévúsh felt his attention first wander, then burrow deep inside of himself to that cosy mummyplace where all cares were forgotten. His dad – the Geezer – he had known this escape from the daddytime as well, of that Carl was now certain; and whatever the future might bring, he too would always have this refuge.

## 12

# *The Book of Dave*

October 2000

*Achilles was getting off his plinth; first one big foot then the other tore from its base with a tortured screech. He cut at the rags of mist with his short sword and brandished his shield at the Hilton Hotel. A couple of early-bird tourists who had been posing for a snap in front of the statue – male pecking with camera, female with wings neatly folded – were struck to the ground by one of Achilles's bulldozing greaves, as he clunked by them heading for Apsley House. He did not waver – he had no quarrel with them. He took no issue either with the cars he kicked as he strode across the roadway and on to the traffic island. Seven metres of bronze against two-millimetre thicknesses of steel – there was no contest; in the statue's wake smashed vehicles lay on their sides, their engines racing and groaning.*

*Lit by the rising sun, fingernails of opalescent cloud scratched contrails on the sky. Achilles stood beneath Constitution Arch and beat shield with sword. With a bang, then a spatter of stony fragments, the four horses atop the arch came alive, tossing their leaden heads. The boy holding the traces struggled to control them. Peace, erect in her chariot, her robe coming off her shoulder in rigid folds, flicked the reins and the whole, mighty quadriga rose, banked sharply and came crunching down. Peace threw her laurel wreath like a frisbee, and Achilles caught it on his sword.*

*The other statues on the traffic island were animating: the Iron Duke spurred down his horse, Copenhagen; the bronze figures that attended him – Guard, Dragoon, Fusilier and Highlander – wrenched themselves free from the polished granite and fell in behind their commander-in-chief.*

*On the Royal Regiment of Artillery memorial the dead gunner rose up from under his petrified greatcoat and joined his comrades. Together they unlimbered their stone field gun. David, tall, svelte and naked, shimmied from the Machine Gun Corps memorial – sword in one hand, Bren gun in the other. These terrible figures stood apart, turning to face down Piccadilly, Knightsbridge, Grosvenor Place and Park Lane, undecided what to do now movement had been bestowed upon them. The few pedestrians who were abroad at this early hour scattered like rabbits, tearing between the trees of Green Park, discarding briefcases and umbrellas as they ran, while those drivers not violently impinged on remained oblivious, their heads clamped in their own metal tumult. The company of statues formed up, with Achilles in the van and Peace to the rear. They marched off down Constitution Hill, feet striking sparks as they clanked over the kerbs.*

*All across London, as the statues came to life, they were at first bemused – then only with reluctance purposeful. Clive of India jumped from his plinth and took the stairs down to Horse Guards skipping. Lincoln at first sat down, surprised, then, struggling up from his chair in Parliament Square, crossed over to the menhir bulk of Churchill, took his arm and assisted him to walk. Earl Haig led his mount alongside Montgomery, who was preposterous in his dimpled elephantine trousers. In Knightsbridge, Shackleton and Livingstone stepped out from their niches in the Royal Geographical Society. Golden Albert squeezed between the gilded stanchions of his memorial, and those blowzy ladies Europe, Africa, Asia and America formed a stony crocodile in his train. In Waterloo Place, Scott strolled up and down the pavement, striking a few attitudes, modelling his Burberry outfit.*

*In Chelsea, Thomas More stood up abruptly, his golden nose flashing; while across the river the droopy-eared Buddhas were stirring in their pagoda. Up in Highgate Cemetery the colossal head of Marx wobbled, then rolled downhill over the mounds of freshly dug graves. They were all heading for Trafalgar Square, where five-metre-high Nelson was gingerly shinnying down his own column, while Edith Cavell tripped past*

*St Martin-in-the-Fields, her marble skirts rattling against the pedestrian barriers.*

*Not only human figures were on the move but animals as well: packs of stone dogs and herds of bronze cattle. Guy the Gorilla knuckle-walked out of London Zoo and around the Outer Circle; the dolphins slithered from the lamp-posts along the Thames and flopped into town. Mythical creatures joined the throng closing in on Trafalgar Square: riddling sphinxes, flying griffins and even the ill-conceived Victorian dinosaurs came humping overland from Crystal Palace. The whole mad overwrought bestiary arrived ramping and romping. The Landseer lions rose up to meet them, stretched and soundlessly roared.*

*Multiples of monarchs: doughty Williams, German Georges, dumpy Victorias. Presses of prime ministers, scrums of generals and colonial administrators, flying vees of viceroys, gaggles of writers and artists, cohorts of Christs – from façades and niches, plinths and pediments, crucifixes and crosses, the statues of London tore themselves free, until the whole centre of the city was a heaving hubbub of tramping bronze, clanking cast-iron, grating granite and marble. These graven images, these tin-pot gods! They had no more uniformity of purpose than they did of style, substance or scale – giant warmongers and diminutive deities, they were distorted embodiments of their creators' confused and ever-changing priorities. They didn't mean to cause any damage or distress – but they just did. They left pediments bare and cornices crumpling, domes imploded, porticos and bridges slumped, colonnades collapsed. They didn't mean to hurt the soft little people, but they were so big and hard that skins were split and skulls were crushed wherever they went.*

*Standing on the steps of Nelson's Column, Achilles beat sword on shield, trying to gain the statues' attention. It was pointless – these hunks could make no common cause, they knew nothing, felt nothing – only the rage of eternal sleepers robbed of their repose. Greek gods and goddesses stood about in profile; Saint Thomas à Becket writhed in his death agony; Baden-Powell scouted out the terrain. Slowly – lazily even – the statues began to fight one another. Marble clanged on iron, granite on bronze, as the maddened effigies battled with the incomprehensibility of their own sentience. What were they? Nothing. So sightlessly stared through for so very long that they had no more significance than a dustbin or a postbox – less perhaps.*

*Then there was a diversion – some dumb cabbie had managed to wrestle his vehicle free from the jam on the Charing Cross Road, and now he was trying to turn around in the roadway beneath the National Gallery. He backed and filled, knocking fauns, cherubs and caryatids over like ninepins. Achilles leaped down from his vantage and strode over. He leaned down, and his disproportionately tiny cock rasped along the cab's roof, shattering the 'For Hire' sign . . .*

'Bash! Bash! Bash!' Something was bashing against the driver window of the Fairway. Dave Rudman came to in a flurry of anxiety to find he was parked up on Goods Way behind King's Cross Station. A big cop was knocking on the outside of the window so hard that Dave's head was bouncing off it. As he bent to hit the button, he saw a three-quarters-empty whisky bottle lying on the floor between his trainers. He hooked it out of sight beneath the seat. 'Morning,' the cop said. He was plainclothes; behind him two others were propped against a big estate car, unmarked except for the revolving blue light stuck on its roof. A steely sun was beating down on the gasometers along Battle Bridge Road. 'Funny place to be having a kip.' The cop's face was pink and also unmarked. His grin was wolfish – his full head of silvery hair as neat as the clippers that had cut it.

'I – I, I had a late drop and . . . I . . .' Dave couldn't make any of it work for him: the sentence, the thoughts to build it and the will to power it forward. As he became more conscious, so he became more frighteningly aware of the fag ash and booze reek, his crumpled clothes and stubbly muzzle.

The cop laughed. 'What's your name, son?'

'Um, Dave . . . Dave –'

'Orlright, then, David, here's what you're going to do. You're going to get out of the cab, lock it up, toddle off somewhere and sleep it off. Unnerstan? This is your lucky morning, David – unnerstan?'

'Yeah – yeah . . .'course . . .' Dave struggled up, shut the window, groped for his change bag. He locked the cab under the amused eyes of the cops. *Why aren't they nicking me? Probably from Vice or Drugs, going off shift and can't be arsed with the paperwork* . . . Backlit by the sun coming up over the shoulder of Barnsbury, the three cops had adopted stylized postures: standing to attention, leaning, hands on hips. The dream still banged about in Dave's head as he limped away under their watchful eyes in the direction of York Way. The cops got back in their car and accelerated past him with a cheery wave. At once Dave doubled back towards his cab. *Can't leave it there, onna yellow line . . . haveta move it* . . . As if anticipating this, the cops had done a U-turn at the top of the road. 'Get away from that cab or I swear you're fucking nicked!' the big, smooth-faced cop shouted at him as the car came by, and Dave Rudman recoiled, zapped by the cattle prod of authority. He spent the next couple of hours jangling in a café on the Pentonville Road, waiting until he was sober enough to drive, drinking tea and watching the junkie scum swirl around the drain of the station.

Last night he'd been OK. *Granted, not perfect, but OK* . . . He'd been driving, doing his thing, just another cabbie working the milling, never-ending London crowds. Now what was he? A crushed carrot lying in the gutter, a headless doll, a pissed-upon shadow of a man. Dave had gone out to work around six in the evening, intent on catching the last hour of the commuters. He thought he'd probably work until two or three in the morning, when the clubbers were all settled in – and more importantly Michelle was asleep. It was better to get home when there was no possibility of any interaction, because even the way she turned her head on the pillow could summon up Dave's rage.

For years now their marriage had been broken down. No, not only broken down . . . *nicked by joyriders, ridden into the ground, then torched by the side of the road*. It was the burnt-out shell of a relationship: the foam rubber of comfort fused by angry fire into the crushed bodywork of hearth, home and child. *When, when did we last have a kind word for each other? When've we had a tender moment?* Now that Carl had stopped climbing into their bed for a morning cuddle, they didn't even have this touching by proxy. *Riding her would be like getting on a bicycle made from bones . . . Or my sister . . . Or my mother . . . Her face – so familiar, so fucking strange . . .*

A few years before they had tried stratagems to make the marriage work. They'd gone away for a weekend at a hotel, leaving the boy with Michelle's mother. But once Michelle had had her spa treatments and they'd eaten stodge in the chintzy dining room, they were left even more profoundly alone together in their room, the four-poster bed corpsing them with its stagy insinuation. Michelle read property adverts in *Country Life*. Dave smoked at the window, blowing brown fog into white muslin curtains. They went home early and in silence. They picked up Carl from the flat on Streatham Hill and were grateful for his unceasing eight-year-old twitter, birdsong in their rotten garden.

Dave gave his wife flowers, *because that's what you did . . . wasn't it . . .* when you wanted to speak but couldn't find words? He bought them from roadside stalls, great sprays of lilies and spiky carnation pompoms, proxy Michelles that he laid tenderly on the back shelf of the cab. When he presented them to her, though, they didn't say anything much, only 'Flowers' – a flat, declarative statement of stamens, petals and stalks. Mostly she didn't even bother to arrange them, simply dumped the whole expensive stook in whichever vessel came to hand, a bucket or a waste-paper bin.

It had been easy not to take holidays together: she wanted to go abroad, he was desperate to remain within the orbit of London. Carl grew up with his parents overlapping rather than conjoined. One was always arriving when the other was leaving. They would spend a few hours – or at most days – together, before parting. Since, like all children, Carl had no accurate information on the manner in which other families ordered these things, he had mostly taken this way of life for granted. He was numb anyway – with a deep, dull fear. He didn't ask questions.

No shared holidays and no shared friends. His mother took Carl to meet her girlfriends, their husbands and children. He was an accessory of hers, rather than part of a family. This he sensed, while collecting acorns in suburban gardens, or hunched inside on rainy days watching videos, playing with a favourite toy, while the tipsy hilarity of adults sitting around a messy table washed over him.

His father, by contrast, made a little manikin of Carl. Out in the cab, there were bottles of Coke while Dave drank with Gary Finch and other geezers. There were trips to Carl's sad old doting grandparents in East Finchley – or to the football. But Carl intuited that his father wasn't bothered with the games they attended. He got the tickets through fellow cabbies who were season-ticket holders, then sat in the stand while Carl screamed, looking off into the glittery drapes of rain picked out by the floodlights. Peering up at his dad's face, Carl thought that it was like the advertisements painted on the pitch – only to be viewed obliquely and from a long way off. Up close Dave's features were distorting, becoming more and more unfamiliar.

In Gospel Oak, Carl carved out his own territory: first the estates at the back of their house, then the adventure playground on Parliament Hill, and eventually the Heath itself. He also learned to be the friend who's always asked back to tea, polite, self-effacing, the child these other parents thought they wished they had, not understanding that he was lost, elusive, living on a fantasy island remote from the rest of the world.

The house – which had seemed spacious for a young family – was too small for ill-feeling. Mild irritation could tenant a whole storey. From their bedroom – which was above the kitchen – Dave could hear if Michelle angrily opened the fridge, or even if cheese was frigidly unwrapped. When they rowed they used up the whole house. Screams filled the attic, shouts crammed the living room. Carl at first cowered – then fled. Once he'd gone they said dreadful things. Dave's anger was a secret nuclear programme. For years, in that dark place where his mother indulged him and his father neglected him, warped technicians had slaved to condense his vapoury unlovability, then compress it into a glowing core of hatred. Michelle had her own radioactive secret – fuse them together and you had almost unlimited destructive power.

For the first few years after the rows began Dave stored up huge reserves of rage, then hours or days later he would dump them on Carl. Dave hit the child in secret – a sly clip, an underhand slap delivered with perfect, insane timing, precisely beyond the eye line of its mother. The anger sparked in him, and hand or foot spasmed. The child howled with incomprehension, and the remorse – oh! it was so powerful, like a drug, a moral drug that made Dave behave better for weeks. Perhaps that was why Dave hit the son he loved – in order to discipline himself.

Then one day Carl's primary teacher snagged Dave in the playground and drew his attention to a thick welt on the boy's thin neck. 'I'm not saying anything,' she said when she'd heard out Dave's feeble explanation – but truly she was saying everything.

The rows got worse – far worse. They were hallucinogenic, leaving both of them out of body, watching swirling patterns of mad, red and black hate. The commonplace accusations of inadequacy were no longer enough. Her face pale and pulpy except for when it was sweaty and livid – Michelle said the unsayable: 'He isn't your child anyway! He isn't.' And the silence that ensued hummed – they became aware of the ticking of the electricity meter, a motorbike snarling down Southampton Road. 'You what?' Dave said very quietly. 'Come again?' But Michelle, unable to believe she'd said it at all, crossed her thin arms, her characteristic posture: holding everything in check. She kept on believing she hadn't said it, so that when Dave barged her, his hip ramming her against the kitchen unit – she found it easy to believe this hadn't happened either.

The afternoon before dawn found him on the Goods Way, Dave had picked up a pol with a camera-friendly tie on the South Lambeth Road and dropped him at St Stephen's Gate. Finding himself in Pimlico, he parked the Fairway in Page Street and stalked, like a black pawn, between the chequerboard façades of the estate to the Regency Café. The Regency wasn't a cabbies' caff – but they did come in. There was a bijoux rank round the corner on Horseferry Road. On this particular evening the Gimp was in there – an older bloke Dave remembered from when Benny was still alive. He wasn't one of the steam-bath crowd, but Dave had seen him a few times in the Warwick Avenue shelter. Benny had always said that the Gimp was 'A wrong un, a sly fucker, I've 'eard tell 'e's a tout.' The Gimp had to be seventy-five . . . *if 'e's a day* . . . but he looked alright. Jeans were pulled up tight over a pot belly; he sported a leather jacket and tinted designer glasses.

He called across the café, 'Orlright, Tufty, it is you, son, isn't it, Benny's lad?'

Dave admitted that it was.

'Cummova and join me,' the Gimp said. 'Go-orn, park yer arse.'

He was dabbling his tea, then bringing tiny spoonfuls of it to his sagging old lips . . . *dis-gus-ting* . . . 'Funny thing is,' said the Gimp, poking the teaspoon at Dave, 'I 'ad yer old lady in the cab s'afternoon – leastways I fink it was 'er.'

'Oowdjoo even know it was 'er?' Dave dismissed him with a wave of his smoky hand, but the Gimp was not to be deterred: 'I'm good wiv faces, see, and your granddad once showed me a snap of your wedding. Dead proud, 'e was. An' she's a looker, ain't she – hard to miss wiv that carrot top.' *He is a tout . . . good with faces my arse . . .* 'Picked her up on Southampton Road in Gospel Oak – your manor, is it?'

'Yeah, yeah, it is, as it 'appens.' Dave sounded unconcerned – indifferent even. 'Where'd you drop 'er off, then?'

''ampstead. Probly gone up there to meet a girlfriend in one of them wine bars. She was right dolled up, she was – looked lovely. You're a very lucky feller . . . Nah, my old Vera . . .'

Dave was no longer listening. Sitting there, sucking on his acrid teat and staring at the hideous Gimp sipping his soup-a-cup, Dave was looking instead into the wing mirror of his mind, where all the traffic behind him now appeared much, much larger. *She had every opportunity, I've worked nights for half the time we've been together . . . Why wouldn't she? I know I disgust her . . . After the boy I couldn't . . . I couldn't make her come . . . It was all . . . all slack down there . . .* This was grotesque pleading, for he knew the truth: it wasn't that she was too big for him – he was too small for her. Michelle hadn't meant to; it was a skill she'd sucked up with her mother's formula – belittling a man until he was the size of a toy soldier, then putting him away in a box.

He dredged up the Gimp's real name. 'Where exactly in Hampstead did you drop her off then . . . Ted? I only ask 'coz I said I'd meet her later and . . .' He stopped, realizing he was giving too much away, and the Gimp was looking at him queerly, although all he said was 'Beech Row, up the top end of Heath Street, right outside a big fuck-off gaff –'

'Didduloodoo-didduloodoo.' For once Dave's mobile went off at the right time. It was no one he knew – let alone wished to speak to. He feigned importance, though, and, making his excuses, left thinking, *Cunt'll be dead soon enough.*

At the bottom of the hill, in Gospel Oak, where single cigarettes were sold in the corner shops and kids huffed Evostik in seeping stairwells, Michelle Brodie cohabited with the secret that Carl Rudman was not her husband's child. Yet every time Michelle went up to Hampstead to visit her wealthy lover she thought, *Why tell Cal now – why does he deserve to know what I've lived with for years?* For ten years Michelle's life had been a horror film shot in extreme slow motion. At his birth it was universally acknowledged that the baby was 'the spit of his old man'. Michelle's mother, Cath, said so, Gary Finch said so, Dave's sister, Samantha, said so – even Annette Rudman, when pressed on the matter, conceded that her grandchild bore its father's features. Michelle wasn't so sure: she saw her lover's face cast like a shadow over the baby's pink flesh. She covertly brought her fingers together 'snip-snip', the way that peasants warded off the evil eye. 'Snip-snip', the way Cal Devenish had gestured when she wormed away from him, across the tousled bed in the Ramada Inn in Sheffield, and asked – a little breathlessly – 'Have you gotta condom?' Her blouse lay open, exposing her eager breast – had she ever been more lovely?

'No, no,' he'd guffawed. 'I don't have a condom – I didn't come with the intention of climbing into bed with anyone. But then,' he laughed again and his eyes dissolved into lusty, winey, cokey pools, 'I didn't count on meeting anyone as beautiful as you.' He took her in his arms and kissed her, and even though his breath was, well . . . *rank* . . . she didn't mind because she supposed hers was as well. Then he broke the embrace and held up snipping fingers. 'Snip-snip. You see, I've had the snip. I know, I know . . .' He took a deep shuddery breath. 'I'm young for it. My wife had two very bad miscarriages before the baby and, well, we didn't think . . .' Michelle shushed him with her mouth. She didn't mind – she was too drunk. Sleeping with a married man was bad enough – but to discuss his feelings worse still: better to shush him up, then feed the flexing, velvety limb inside herself.

'Snip-snip'. It became their catch-sound, accompanied by the little manipulation that excised them from any responsibility. Five, ten, twenty? How many times had they met up in motorway motels, or done it on the cold mattresses of the empty, serviced flats that Cal was supposed to be managing for his property-dealing paterfamilias? 'Snip-snip'. Then came the evening at the Hilton – Cal made a fist with his little girl's nappy, punching a hole in Michelle's foamy emotions, and seven hours later Dave Rudman, the sap, crawled into it.

Throughout that autumn the new being erected its little stand inside her: Foetus '87; while Michelle, unwilling to acknowledge what was happening, went on supervising the construction of many other, far larger ones. Ideal Home, The Boat Show, The Motor Show. Up to Birmingham for Office Equipment '87 at the NEC – then back down again. Still Cal didn't call. 'Snip-snip'. She cut him out of her life. It was only when Manning, the fat Exhibitions Executive, stopped looking at her and instead began to sniff, that Michelle was forced to frame the realization I'M PREGNANT in orange, metre-high letters.

It was the first time she had stalled, been checked in her determination to make her life hers and hers alone. This feeling of warm yet tense swelling, the teary identification with everything small and vulnerable, was part of a double incubation: Michelle was giving birth to a secret – and abortion was out of the question. Her childhood had, she felt, been banal, her youth exposed and obvious – now her womanhood would be mysterious.

So Michelle savoured the brutal incomprehension of friends and colleagues. Her girlfriends, exasperated by her refusal to tell them anything – let alone all – included her out. Michelle didn't care – she even revelled in her mother's anger. On Sunday evenings she burrowed down to Brixton on the filthy tube, then was winched up to Streatham on a still filthier bus. Past the *ice rink, where those black girls rapped me on the head with their rings . . . Fucking Irish . . .*

*I cried in the bogs . . . My tutu ruffed up . . . Blood in my hair . . .* Michelle could find comfort even in the stony silence of a chicken tea. Ron at the lager, Cath fretting at the cuffs of her cardie with chipped nails, pressing a damp serviette against her eye with the heel of her hand . . . *Serves her bloody right* . . . Disgrace, so feared, turned out to be . . . a relief. Nothing else bad could ever happen to Michelle. The horse had bolted into the stable. There in the pins-and-needles darkness its little hooves drummed on the taut walls of its stall. Where was this jealous God – this vengeful God? Who could he be? A cabbie who knew about statues and came too quick? A man whose face Michelle couldn't even remember.

Cheryl McArdle, the Personnel Director of LM & Q Associates, Exhibition Organizers, kneaded the prominent mole on her broad cheek; her brown sausage curls tumbled on to her padded shoulders. 'I've secured you six months on three quarters of your salary, will that be enough?' Michelle said, 'Thank you.' Cheryl pointed at the old communion ring that Michelle had got enlarged and now wore on the appropriate finger. 'Nice touch,' she said.

Michelle didn't like this lie. Looking back, years later, as Cal Devenish's features – his low brow and tight, otter ears – swam to the surface of her son's developing face, she realized it was biblical – the one lie had begotten the next. But at the time she thought, *I don't like to deceive my employers . . . He has a right to know . . . It's his child too*. She found herself calling the number scrawled on the taxi receipt. Dave wasn't in, but the guy who answered didn't mind giving her the address. Palmers Green – it was ridiculously distant, a trek so long that in making it Michelle felt the city parch into desert. When the cabbie opened the door, half naked, she nearly laughed – almost puked. His thin hair was tousled and through it she saw the exact pattern of his coming baldness. 'I didn't think,' she said. 'I didn't want . . .' Out of such hesitations whole lives can be stopped in their tracks 'You have a right . . .' She smoothed the contours of the hillock beneath her sheepskin coat and a sloppy grin spread across his face. What did he imagine? *That I'm a plum fare, sweet as a nut?* 'You'd better come in,' Dave said.

'You'd better come in,' Cal Devenish said. 'I'd better,' Michelle replied. Heavy gold cufflinks dangled from the cuffs of his thick white linen shirt. Cal had bought Beech House because there was money sloshing around in his account. Dead dad's money – and income from *Blackie*, his kids' TV programme about a depressed puppy, which had been sold to over three hundred networks worldwide. Cal didn't know what to do with the house that the money he didn't know what to do with had bought. In the tall rooms the plaster mouldings were wire-brushed, the wallpaper stripped away. It was a palimpsest, this house, the past rubbed up out of the surface of the present. There were a few things scattered on the original floorboards: phone directories, a phone, a standard lamp. They pretended she was an estate agent and he a sexy potential buyer, then they made love, in the hall, on the paint-spattered parquet.

~

When Carl was six he'd spend whole mornings diligently tying things up, looping string from the banisters to a chair leg, to a door handle, then propelling toy soldiers along these flimsy pulleys. In his ticking hovel Carl's father began tying events together in his fervid mind, linking all those half-recalled moments when his wife had avoided his eyes even more than usual, got undressed in the bathroom and slid, fully nightgowned, into bed. Dave pulled tight the granny knots that bound this change of plan – 'I got a call from Sandra and decided to go out with her after all, Mum didn't mind sitting' – to a new outfit she'd worn only a week before: 'It was in the sales . . .' 'What fucking sales?' he said out loud. 'What fucking sales do they have in October?'

Dave Rudman wheeled the cab past the National Gallery and

headed north up the Charing Cross Road. Plastic horses plunged from the façade of the Hippodrome, cycle rickshaws were cluttering up the junction at Cambridge Circus. *Rickshaws . . . rickshaws! What is this, fucking Delhi! Soon they'll be burning bloody corpses on the Albert Embankment.* Dave was no longer in hock to guilt – he redeemed his shabby pledge for still more anger. All those hateful digs and savage barges, the slaps, the pinches, palming her face off like a freckled rugby ball – he was absolved of all responsibility for any of it, because *she's been ripping me off . . . taking them off . . . sick . . . I can see her face hot and sweaty . . . Plunging some other bloke's dick in her mouth . . .* He had to stop the cab in Harrington Square and retch out of the half-opened door.

*Forward Southampton Road . . . Right Fleet Road . . . Forward South End Road . . .* It had been a headachey autumn day, the sun hammering its rays into crushed lager cans, embedding these glittering fragments in the city's terrazzo. Now, as the Heath yawned to the right of the cab and Dave saw clouds boiling over Highgate Hill, he had a moment of clarity: *I don't have t'do this . . . the marriage has been over for bloody years . . .* Only infantilism kept him driving on, an angry little boy whose legs weren't long enough for him to reach the brake pedal. *Left Heath Street . . . left Beech Row . . . Points at the end: the Friends' Meeting House, New End School, the Horse and Groom, my wife fucking another man . . .* This was the *fuck-off gaff*, double fronted, two flights of stairs doubling back on themselves to reach a grand front door. He took the stairs six at a time. He looked up to the heavens – cloudy Michelles writhed there, tier upon tier of them. Who was he? Who was this man? For the last decade, every time he looked at his son, Dave Rudman had felt this uncanny jolt – the impact of an unseen object on an unfunny bone. Who was this man? He raised the solid brass question mark and brought it down. 'Bang! Bang! Bang!' In the Family Court the judge beat the fragile bond to bloody mush with his gavel.

They'd been sleeping. She was lying on top of him. His legs were raised, his hands quietly cradled her buttocks. With each 'Bang!' he shlupped out of her, they came awake, parted with a jarring of hipbones, rolled away from each other. 'Jesus Christ!' Michelle cried. 'What the fuck can that be?' But she knew already.

When Cal swung the door open, Dave Rudman looked like an ape man, his arms dangling, his brow bulging. They stared at each other with mounting comprehension. Dave recognized this face, smudged with sleep; it was closely related to one he knew only too well. Over Cal Devenish's bare shoulder Dave could see Michelle doing a thing that in marriage was so workaday – picking up her underwear.

He drove to the Old Globe, he got drunk. He drove drunk back to King's Cross and bought a bottle. A whore tried to toss him off in the back of the cab. He finished the bottle, he slept. He woke – and all over the city the plinths, pediments, columns and niches were quite empty; the Family of Man had fled. When Dave got back to the house it was mid morning. Carl was at school and the only evidence of Michelle was a hairbrush strung with long auburn hairs and a pair of high-topped leather boots. They were empty, broken at the ankle.

~

Big End had married a white girl from Sidcup, and together they'd bought a house in Petts Wood. He hadn't been mucking about, Big End, he had his own joinery business now. The girl was a beautician. Petts Wood, on the leafy southeast borders of London, was as green and quiet as a cemetery. Big End imported some of his kids and threw raucous barbecues that drove his neighbours crazy.

Dave Rudman lay in a spare bedroom stacked with boxes full of moody beauty products: dirty cleansers, hidden concealers, bent foundation creams. He wept and blamed the break-up of his marriage on his baldness. He remembered the oddest week of his life, holed up in a hotel near the Gare Saint-Lazare. He'd cocked up all the arrangements and had to take the Metro out to La Défense every morning for his treatments. In this futuristic city he had Revolutionary Trichofuse. They bored little holes in his scalp and planted tussocks of hair harvested from his groin. The hotel was a smelly warren, and there were tarts bringing back punters at all hours – mostly Japanese. Every night Dave sat staring into the fag-packet-sized mirror for hours at his freshly harrowed pate. He prayed that this would make the difference; after all, he could hardly blame Michelle for not running her fingers through his hair if there was none.

For a few weeks after he got back to London the transplant looked credible. Michelle didn't begrudge him either the time or the money – she understood the naked thrust of vanity, an ambition located in the body alone, a frantic urge for skin to get on, hair to rise to the very top. Then overnight it happened: Dave went to bed still convinced the transplant was a goer and woke up to find that his forehead was a domed groin – he had pubic hair touching his eyebrows. He had to pay out five times as much to get the crinkle-cut hair removed as he'd paid to have it inserted. They filled in the depressions as best they could. He took to wearing a baseball cap.

Now Dave took his hatred out on himself, learning in the muffled little room to quietly bludgeon his head with his fist. 'Bash! Bash! Bash!' The Fairway sat neglected in the road outside, an empty plinth deserted by its statue. Dave still drove every day because he had to, but now he didn't merely neglect the Fairway, he abused it, giving it the sly digs and casual kicks formerly reserved for his family, until the cab's bodywork was dimpled by his animosity.

Only once during the whole protracted disembowelling of their marriage did Dave talk to Michelle about what had happened up in Hampstead. It was April 2001. They were sitting in a sunlit corridor of the Family Division Court at Somerset House. Dust lay heavier than justice on the parquet. Dave was with Rebecca Cohen and the barrister she'd subcontracted to do the talking. Cohen had dyed, caramel hair and a black Jaeger suit. The barrister's striped shirt was escaping from the waistband of his trousers, his yellowing briefs were escaping from their mauve ribbons. He had the florid, old–young face of a man who has witnessed many bad things – none of which has happened to him. Three embrasures along Michelle, tidy as ever, sat with her tag team: Fischbein, a killer newt, and a woman barrister whose downy face glowed. The barristers shuttled between the window seats; their aim was to cut a deal that could be presented to the judge in her chambers. 'It'll save a lot of money,' Cohen said, 'believe me.' The house was chopped up, the maintenance stacked, the child bundled – everything was going in Michelle's favour. She couldn't understand it – why, when he'd caught her in the act, was Dave passively acquiescing to this quickie divorce on the grounds of his bad behaviour?

The barristers were squaring off, trading bits of the Rudmans' lives, when Dave nipped past them and sat down beside her. 'You, him . . .' He was breathless from the tiny sprint; Cohen flapped behind him. Fischbein said, 'You mustn't approach my client directly,' but Michelle waved him away. When they were let alone, Dave said, 'One thing, tell me one thing – and don't fucking lie. D'you love him? Are you going to take Carl and move in with him? That's all I want to know.' Michelle said, 'I don't . . . I can't say . . . I'm sorry, David – truly I am.' While what Dave heard her say was *It was nothing, it meant nothing . . . It's over.* His guilt did the dubbing.

He moved into the flat on Agincourt Road. He thought something iffy must have been going on with the previous tenant, because the gaff reeked of baby oil, and talcum powder puffed from every square inch of the fitted shag carpet. Every other weekend Dave borrowed a vacuum cleaner from old Mrs Prentice who lived beneath him in a nylon housecoat. Glad of the human contact, she also offered him a box full of polishes and sprays. By the time he went to pick Carl up from his school, the gloomy little flat was spick and span, the Arsenal duvet pancake flat on the boy's bed, the video cassettes a neat little office block.

It was Carl's first year at secondary school, and he begged his father not to come near the place. Dave couldn't keep away. The school backed on to the branch line that ran beside Parliament Hill. Beneath its wonky weathervane and crap campanile the older pupils clustered at the gates. They wore Burberry baseball caps and white, nylon-furred parkas. The mouths of these inner-city Inuits spat consonants hard and sharp as teeth, while the girls' adobe skins suggested they'd been renting Mexico by the half-hour. Yet they seemed entirely sure of themselves, while Dave skulked, and when Carl reluctantly detached himself from his peers, they skulked away together.

*Runty . . . Boysie . . .Champ . . . Tiger . . .* These babyish nicknames were no longer applicable to the rootless stripling who flopped along by Dave's side. After the first couple of weekends they spent together, Dave was disabused of the idea that he knew intuitively what to do with the lad. If he didn't put together an exhaustive programme they were thrown back on each other's company – and Dave hadn't a clue what to say to Carl. Already he detected an awful adolescent surliness in him – isolated words roamed aimlessly in the lad's down-turned mouth. Was this payback for those livid marks? Whatever Dave uttered sounded tinny and insincere; he was reduced to the role of chirpy cockney cabbie. They had to talk *fucking football.* And go for endless kick-abouts. Belatedly Dave understood why the gulf between him and his own father had been unbridgeable.

Sunday evenings were the worst – the changeover. Dave couldn't bear to accompany Carl to the front door, so he left him at the mouth of the cul-de-sac; then, punched in the gut by loneliness, he hobbled back to the flat for lamb dhansak and a yanked foreskin. His life, henceforth, would be meted out in takeaway tinfoil pannikins and crispy tissues. There was no one to call – he'd made no investment in life beyond his wife and son; there were no relationships of trust or intimacy. These were interactions he'd only ever witnessed in the rounded oblong of his rearview mirror – the heartfelt confidence, the stuttered confession. These were things that fares said, and intimacy was a mysterious act fares engaged in once he'd dropped them off.

Only Gary Finch refused to let him alone. Fucker Finch – whose long-suffering Debbie had finally given him the push, and whose magic fingers had failed to conjure up another lovely assistant. Fucker was back cabbing – his old man had scraped the money together to front up his insurance and a few months' vehicle rental. Dave ran into him at the kiosk on Chelsea Bridge, where stretch-limo drivers drank midnight teas and watched spectral trains emerge from the cavernous hulk of Battersea Power Station, then jolt their empty, yellow-lit coaches into Victoria.

'Nah, thass the fing, Tufty,' Fucker said when he'd heard Dave's news. 'Vare slime, ain't vay, fuckin' slime, draggin' vare slimey cunts rahnd tahn –'

'I don't want to hear it, Gary,' Dave said – but he did.

'Nah, nah, ears a fing. I bet yaw Chelle is beginning to dick you arahnd, ain't she? Shavin off an our ere, an our vare, makin' it arder and arder fer you t'get kwality time wiv yaw boy – am I right? Caws I am. Iss depressin – thass what it is. Blokes in our situayshun are depressed – weir fuckin mizrubble. Wot av we gotta show fer all vat graft, ay? Fukkawl. I've been lookin' into it, Tufty – there's loads of us single dads out there, an' we're getting organized.'

To shut him up Dave agreed to go to one of these meetings. Fathers First – it sounded innocuous enough. The venue was the Trophy Room at Swiss Cottage Sports Centre. It could have been any self-help group – Weight Watchers or Alcoholics Anonymous; the men who pitched up bore no obvious resemblance to one another, Dave couldn't see the single father's mark on their brows. Gary introduced him to Keith Greaves, a twitchy man whose robust shaven head and thick gold earring were at odds with his craven manner. 'Iss 'is idea,' Gary whispered. ''Im an' that geezer Daniel Brooke over there. They brung it from the States – but they don't eggzackerly see eye-to-eye.' The men squeaked about the lino, getting plastic cups of tea and settling themselves in plastic chairs. The meeting was called to order.

While Keith Greaves tried to direct these troubled men towards 'some positivity – we aren't victims but nor do we seek to make victims of our ex-partners', Dave Rudman considered getting a shotgun certificate, or even just buying *a fucking machete . . . It's in the papers all the time, on the local radio – dads topping kids they can't 'ave. What if Dad had tried to do that to me and Noel and Sam? Driven us off in his Rover to some layby up in the Chilterns or a sports field in Enfield. Stuck a hosepipe on the exhaust and fed it through the back window. Gunned the engine. Fucking foul in there in seconds. Never know how poisonous those fumes are 'til you're in them for ever. Then what? We never would've stood for it – we'd've kicked off, fought to get out, coughing, puking and punching. He could never control the three of us by himself – he was never around enough. Only way he could keep us quiet was at the Five Bells with bottles of pop, bags of crisps, endless yanks on the fucking one-arm bandits. No, he never could've managed it without a mobile* . . . The mobile phone appears, an Excalibur pulled from the stone of the future, its slick screen and nodular buttons glow with a mini-neon intensity. The three kids – the boys in grey shorts, Start-rite sandals, Aertex shirts, the girl in a pleated skirt and ski-pattern cardie – are transfixed by it. Paul Rudman passes it to Samantha. *'This is a phone, darling, and Mummy wants to talk to you . . . I want you to tell her goodbye . . . I want you to tell her that I'm taking you and David and Noel away now . . . for ever . . .' No, he never could've managed it without a mobile, no bloke could, killing the kiddies and yourself – it's an opportunistic crime, innit, and technology's the open door . . .*

*That copper who splattered his two little blonde daughters all over a semi in fucking Maidstone . . . The millionaire who locked his ex up in the fucking cupboard of their Surrey mansion while he did the nippers . . . That Pakki doctor who leaped off a fucking road bridge with his three-month-old son in his arms . . . Shooting sprees at barbecues in the sticks . . . They all juss wanted a one-to-one, didn't they, a chat or a straightener with their old woman . . . same bloody difference.*

He woke in the afternoons to hear the twitter of birds and sirens outside. Parting the curtains, he saw a pigeon fluffed up on the TV aerial. *So many of them flying rats . . . but you never see their kids.* All that summer he drove nights, fearing the monster truck rally of daytime traffic and the jerky crowds of battery chicken people. Molten anger puddled into depression. He had hoped for some explosion of sexual licence – instead his cock went as soft and limp as a snail. Eventually he did go to the doctor – because that's what you did, *didn't you, eat shit?* After all twelve million repeat prescriptions can't be wrong . . . *can they?*

Fanning, the GP, had a consulting room like a teenager's bedroom in a mail-order catalogue: MDF in jig-sawn amoeba shapes, shiny ringbinders, a blood-pressure cuff from Accessorize. Little posters showed happy folk with the treatable maladies. There was a battered cardboard box full of crap toys on the floor – the Fisher-Price logo alone made Dave cry, vinegary tears, sour and reeking. There was only one thing now that wasn't toyist – and that was toys.

Fanning, who wore woven thread around his plump wrist and tan pantaloons fastened with a drawstring, was neither unsympathetic nor unprofessional. He had a good, poseable manner. He heard out Dave's stuttered symptoms: 'C-can't sleep. N-no appetite. P-panicky.' Then rearranged his limbs before asking the appropriate questions. 'Sex? Y-you gotta be j-joking, mate. T-talk about what? T-to who?' Finally, he reached for his pad and prescribed Prozac with a clear conscience. For, while many of the patients who shuffled into his consulting room were emotional malingerers – unwilling to turn up for any of life's feelings – this big, raw-boned fellow was reeling. *He doesn't have either the wit or the imagination to know what's happening.*

The first sign that the pills were working was that the baby oil slithered away – Dave could smell the bacon fat spread on the cooker and the bleach burning in the toilet. When he opened the window, heavy meadow-sweet air blew in from the Heath. Tiny bubbles rushed to the surface of his brown mind in a mounting ebullition; there was a neuropathic fizzle at the tips of his fingers and toes. With reckless levity Dave vaulted pedestrian barriers and stood looking at the rainbow whorls of oil on the wet tarmac.

When Carl came to spend a week with his dad in August, Dave was still gathering momentum. He put the lad in the cab and drove him all over town: down east, up west, to shelters where they listened to old geezers with white, wattled necks pour scorn on 'culluds' and Ken Livingstone's proposed congestion charge. Dave took Carl to see his grandparents – and even to his aunt's house, where Carl played computer games with his cousin Daniel. When they left he was astounded to see his dad give his aunt a kiss. During the hot nights Carl slept soundly if sweatily. At any rate he wasn't aware that Dave hardly lay down but paced from one end of the flat to the other, bopping first one wall and then the other with his brow so that matching niches appeared in the plaster.

Carl thought his father so much improved, so happy and confident, that when it came time for him to pack up his little rucksack and take the short hike back to his mum's, he didn't see any reason why he shouldn't tell the truth: 'Y'know, Dad, she's seeing that bloke again and . . .' He watched, appalled, as Dave's face crumpled, yet he couldn't stop himself. '. . . and she'sputthe'ouseupfersale.'

*She swore . . . She promised . . . She fucking swore . . .* And again: *She swore . . . She promised . . . She fucking swore . . .* This was what Rudman called over as he rammed the Fairway up the M4 to Wales. At last, after all these years, he was going to visit his brother, Noel, in hospital. The cab, howling in overdrive, carried its overwrought driver past Swindon and Bristol, then over the Severn Bridge, a lyre strung with high-tension cables upon which Aeolus played his grandiose airs.

Dave reached Aberystwyth and found a B & B. He drove out to the mental hospital, only to discover that his brother had been discharged three months before. It was then that he stared into the chasm of unloving. *My kid brother . . . I never looked after him.* He backtracked and found Noel's bedsit in a labyrinth of gas meters and fire doors two houses down from his own B & B. His brother – overweight, puffy with medication – was a caricature of himself: Dave Rudman wearing a whole-body fat suit. Noel had big plans. He was going to get a job, ascend a career ladder, source a house and a wife. Only trouble was he couldn't zip up his own flies. Dave wept – while Noel regarded him with consoling eyes. He'd been out in the fungus field for so long now that encounters with people he knew were non-sequential. The two of them were still pelting each other with rowan berries and charging through North End Woods. 'You, you've hurt yourself,' he said. 'Haven't you, Dave?'

The wind, not issuing from the west but coming from within the buildings themselves. The sun catching a chimneystack so that its bricks glowed gold against the sombre London sky. The cab purring noisily down the road, a woman in a headscarf turning, fearful that she was going to be pounced upon by a giant feral cat. The decree nisi, stuck to the doormat like a manila label. 'Welcome,' it said.

Two days later Dave Rudman awoke with an erection so large

and stiff it felt like a tent pole. For long minutes he writhed about under canvas, then rose and stumped to the bathroom. It was mid morning and out of a habit he didn't know he had he snapped on the television. On the furred screen a toyist atrocity was taking place – younger brothers kicking over the building-block tower their older siblings had piled up. It staggered and collapsed. Roiling dust clouds engulfed the camera. Dave Rudman stood looking at it for a while, trying to figure out what it was, then stumped back to the bedroom.

Lying there, the sunlight poking between the drapes and picking out a single wall ornament – diamond battens around an oval mirror – he felt his hearing become sharper and sharper, more and more sensitive, until he could detect the very dust mites groping their way through the weave of the carpet; the 'eek' of a squeegee merchant's sponge a mile away in Camden Town; the 'shissshhh' of a deep-fat fryer in Dalston. Then he could hear It – the still, small, powdery voice of SmithKline Beecham . . . *There is no god but you, Dave, It whispered, and you can be your own prophet . . .*

No Christian god smothering him in cosy-bundle sweet love; no wiseacre Jewish god, rebarbative yet shrewd in his defence; no Muslim god, geometric, elegant, cruel to be kind; no Hindu god-riot of fairground faces and multiple, writhing arms – this was a purely local, contingent deity, a god for the day, who divvied up pay-per-view prophecy: *Peepul* . . . the god looked in his rearview and saw them . . . *chavs, coloureds, fucking pikeys, the Irish, hysterical-bloody-women . . . Peepul, they gotta be kept in line . . . there hasta be orforitë . . . It stands to reason, dunnit . . . There hasta be a Book of Rules . . . A set of instructions you can follow to the letter . . . Like the Knowledge . . . No muckin' abaht . . . twenty lists of sixteen runs – and the 'burbs. No argument. Paddington Green to Askew Road, Albert Bridge to Streatham Common . . . where they hitch up their Freemans skirts . . . nothing but . . . mail-order prossies. If you don't know the shortest way . . . on the cotton . . . then you don't get your badge, you don't make your living . . .*

*Simple as that . . . plain as the nose on my face. If I'm not gonna be allowed to bring up my boy myself, then at least I've gotta be able to tell 'im what's what . . . givvim some fatherly advice . . . That's what I'm gonna do. Eggzackerly.*

It came to him fully formed – a plan and how to execute it. Dave's parents were surprised to see him again so soon – and without Carl. He seemed distracted, beating out a nervous tattoo with his shortbread on his plate. Later on he went into the garage and rooted there. 'Aren't you going to ask him why he's taking that thing away?' Annette Rudman hectored her husband, and Paul grunted 'No.'

It came to him in solid chunks – wrote itself, really. He typed with his index fingers, poking sense into the keyboard of the old Apricot. He hadn't had anything to do with computers since his year at college – but that didn't matter because this machine dated from that time. It came to him when he awoke, in the unproblematic light of day – and for that reason was not to be doubted. It came to him as he sat in his black, terry towelling robe, driving the engine of creation forward with piston keystrokes. Yeah – he was the Driver, a fisher of fares.

He began with the Knowledge. He had held it – now he dropped it, the tangled tarmac viscera fell out of him: Turnpike Lane Station to Malvern Road, Bishopswood Road to Westbury Avenue, Harold Wood to Stratford (via Newbury Park, Gants Hill, Redbridge, Wanstead, the Green Man Roundabout and Leytonstone). And he dumped the shitty points as well: Chapel Market, Angel Station, St Mark's Church, the Craft Council, the Institute of Child Health, the Value Added Tax Tribunal. As he wrote he felt himself ascending, chattering up over the wide river valley. He was the Flying I – he saw all the tailbacks on the Westway, the slow-moving traffic through the Hanger Lane gyratory system, the roadworks on Northumberland Avenue, the shed lorry-load in Kingston Vale. He grasped the metropolis in its entirety, he held in his shaky, nicotine-stained fingers each and every one of the billions of tiny undertakings its inhabitants engaged in, which, taken in sum, added up to chaos.

Yet this was not all. In transcribing his Knowledge Dave Rudman embroidered it. This was no plain cloth word-map, but a rich brocade of parable, chiasmus and homily. *Where to, guv?* he began each run, and when it intersected with a suitable tale he grasped it, then set it down. He kept driving, for out on the night-time streets the map, the territory and prophecy became as one. Whipping beneath the dour façade of the Royal Court Theatre in Sloane Square, he hit the button and began to rant . . . *This plonker clipped me as I was turning into Cliveden Place. I pulls over and gives it to 'im straight: put up or I'll call the Old Bill. He digs deep, comes up wiv fifty nicker. Result – it only cost me a score to patch the cab up. You gotta be sharp in this business, no-wot-eye-meen? The world's out there, through the screen, issall through the screen. It ain't out back, it ain't in the fucking mirror. People are in the mirror* . . . And the fare – some provincial cake-decorator who'd only just quit that self-same theatre – squawked assent through the intercom, bored and a little repulsed, but never suspecting that this was only the tip of a dirty great doctrinal iceberg which that very morning the cabbie had been pounding into an obsolete computer.

Standing on the cobbled forecourt of Charing Cross Station – at the very epicentre of the Knowledge – a fare abused him, daring to question the meter: 'Ten-fucking-quid! A tenner from Camden Town! You're taking the piss!' But the words wailed over the Driver, because the Charing Cross, he happened to know, was a fake, the lions in the Square were fakes, the cars, vans and lorries were . . . *toys – the whole city was toyist* . . . The tin snare drum of the Inn on the Park, the cruet of Westminster Cathedral . . . *Black pepper, sir? All uv it Made in China . . . Made of fucking plastic* . . . and only the Driver knew what was real any more, only the Driver would come again.

A messiah mushing through the two-millennium-old city. A preacher hearkening to his Faredar, and once he has the fare on board, not only subjecting them to his Revelation but also to his unique Doxology. For the Knowledge, once completed, naturally led to a series of Letters to the Lost Boy from the Driver. Epistles, the intent of which was to SET THE RECORD STRAIGHT and tell Carl MAN-TO-MAN what truly happened between his mother THE BITCH and his POOR OLD DAD. *Your mother . . .'chelle . . . when she had you she changed, she became – ha, ha – chellish. She wouldn't give me a fucking look-in – she cut off my fucking balls. I tellya, mate, you're better off never going near fucking women 'cept when they're on the blob . . . On the fucking rag . . . Once they've squeezed one aht they ain't worf dipping yer wick in anyway . . . Better off with the au pair – if Uve got one . . . Or any old tart . . . When they're mummies they ain't got no sense . . . When they get older iss worse still . . . Fucking boilers. When you fink abaht it the queers have got right idea – no fucking Richards – and no bleeding kids neither.*

The Knowledge may have had its glossolalia, but these dribs and drabs of humdrum misogyny flowed together into a mighty Jordan, nothing less than A COMPLETE RE-EVALUATION OF THE WAY MEN AND WOMEN should conduct their lives together. Which, as the Driver saw it, was mostly apart, the mummies crossing over into purdah on the far bank.

The DJ from Crash, having hailed the Fairway by Vauxhall Station long after dawn and relapsed into the stale and ghastly fug, never supposed for a second that when the cabbie's red-rimmed eyes fixed on his via the mirror, and his mouth twisted out the observation 'It'd be better if we never 'ad to shack up wiv 'em in the first place – don't chew agree? Knock 'em up – then fuck off!', this was not a random remark, morning ingloriousness triggered by memories of recent sexual rejection, but rather one proposition among hundreds that made up a comprehensive blueprint for a society in which, once the old world had been swept away by a MIGHTY WAVE, EVERYTHING WOULD BE SPLIT DOWN THE MIDDLE.

'You take my situation,' he urged the drunk doorman, the wayward priest, the absconding cashier, the reluctant whore. 'I only gets to see my lad every other weekend – thass not right. It should oughta be straight down the middle. Straight dahn ve fuckin' middul. If I ad mì way . . .' They let him have his way, turning aside to concentrate on sandbags slumped over men-at-work signs. '. . . it'd be all change on Wednesdays, right across the whole fucking country. Kiddies going from their daddies to their mummies. 'Coz I'm not a monster –'

'I tellya something, guv,' he regaled the MP he was driving back to Kennington from a late division, 'I don't like the trade much myself – most cabbies are ignorant, lairy an' fucking racial.' The pol, full of claret, sighed ambiguously. 'And as for the Public Carriage Office, they've got a fucking monopoly going, what with there only being one vehicle supplier – don't tell me they ain't on the take.' The pol didn't tell him anything, only sighed again, so the Prophet continued. 'But at least they've kept the whole show on the road. There've been licensed cabs in London for four hundred years now. Growlers, Clarences, Hansoms, there's as much bloody tradition in the trade as there is the 'ouses of Parliament – maybe more. The old drivers – they know what's what, they 'ave the Knowledge, like me granddad Benny – straight as a fucking die.

'Tellya what,' he kept on at the man, who was leaning in through the window to pay his fare, lamplight smoothing the nap of his velvet collar, 'p'raps the PCO should run the whole fucking country and your lot should get behind the wheel.' The pol tipped out of weary guilt – he hated the hectoring cabbie so. And when he'd gone the cabbie rested his forehead on the boss of the steering wheel. Rested it there for so long that when, at length, he sat up, he saw the letters 'Lti' stamped on his forehead.

'GOD SAID: MEET ME AT MY HOUSE ON SUNDAY BEFORE LUNCH.' Dave goggled at the placard, his blood seething with a deathly fizz. In the rearview was a trinity of black faces swathed in white muslin. *Members of some fucking nigger sect* . . . whom nonetheless he felt impelled to hector, as he dropped them off at this redbrick barn of a church, on a patch of wasted ground, in a notch of north London estate, 'How the fuck can I do that?' He jerked a thumb at the placard. 'I haven't got a pot to piss in or the time to piss in it. It's alright for you lot, you don't pay any bloody taxes, do you, you don't even pay your fucking road tax, but blokes like me we're on the level, we cough up, we make ourselves known . . .' – and here he parodied an official voice – '. . . to the CSA and they cut our fucking balls off with the child support.' The Coptic worshippers cleared out of the Fairway as fast as they could and tipped out of fear, fumbling coin into the angry white man's sweating hand.

The cabbie drove away rattling with fury. *Not so much as a fucking thank you for picking 'em up – let alone dropping 'em off . . . It's a fucking punishment. I 'ate life so much* . . . And this too made its way into the computer.

Dave stopped making any effort to see Carl at all. His son walked across the Heath and leaned on his dad's buzzer – but Dave wouldn't open the door. He was inside, in the omni-smelling semi-darkness, in his threadbare black bathrobe, clacking away. He'd found the 'contact diary' Rebecca Cohen had urged him to keep in the first months after the separation. This held details of all the time he'd spent with Carl. The boy dragged reluctantly for boating trips on the Serpentine. *Fucking chancer with his pedalos for twenty-fucking-quid an hour . . . same as any other bloody fleet owner . . . trying to rip us off . . . thought we were mugs, fucking tourists*. In the rewrite, Dave's run-in acquired mythic status: the man in the booth was emblematic of every grasping capitalist, his flotilla of fibreglass vessels needed liberating, father and son *pedalled away laughing* through bobbing flocks of inquisitive fowl.

Back and back he went, probing with 26+ tabular tongues the rotten cavities of swimming sessions and football games, children's parties and Sunday-morning matinées. In Dave's warped recollection, the bouncy castle hired by the upper-middle-class parents of five-year-old Carl's slumming schoolfriend became a mighty bastion, inflated with prestige, power *and dosh. Flash it abaht, thass wot wankas lyk vat dú*. Him standing there with a cocktail sausage on a toothpick, made to feel like *an oik by those fucking toffs* while carillons of laughter floated over the impeccably maintained gardens of the Holly Lodge Estate.

Michelle called him up and cajoled him into a meeting. The rendezvous was a pasta and salad joint in Belsize Park. She spent two full hours in front of the mirror, and worked hard on her mascara and eyeshadow to meet the man who'd blackened both her eyes. To begin with it went well enough, true. *He looks fucking dreadful . . . Unshaven . . . greasy hair . . . stained jeans . . .* Still, he didn't talk too loud or throw his arms about. He wouldn't eat, though, and he stared so savagely at her cleavage that Michelle, involuntarily, kept fussing with the lie of her blouse. *Swirls of rainbow dye on the silk.* 'Carl's half-term starts next Friday,' she said, then added, 'He needs you, he wants to see you . . . but not' – this was a mistake – 'like this.' Dave was back on the doorstep of Beech House, watching her pick up her knickers. He was back on the doorstep, looking at his son's face blown up out of all proportion.

'You slag!' Dave swept the plates from the table, a wine-glass stem snapped like a glass bone. He grabbed her cleavage and ripped it. Buttons popped. He slapped her face – once, twice, and he was going for a third when the waiter, whose tofu face suggested he wouldn't say boo to a goose liver, seized him from behind. The police released him that evening – Michelle had refused to press charges. Two days later a restraining order appeared on the mat at Agincourt Road. He was free to contest it – but he didn't. Instead Dave went to Prontaprint and blew up page 45 of the *A–Z* on the photocopier. On to this he drew the mile-diameter circle around Beech House with a thick felt pen. Then he committed this new Knowledge to his mad memory – every street, every point, running round and round it *like that fucking hamster the boy used to have, stuck in its wheel. Silly cow fed it too much . . . Its stomach blew up and it died.* Then he incorporated this new evidence of his MARTYRDOM into the document that was taking shape beneath his fingers, and that he referred to – unconscious of any precedent, devoid of any irony – as THE BOOK.

He typed, he drove, he took the pills religiously. Last thing before oblivion, whisky glugged, lungs tarmacked, he crucified his head on the dirty pillow.

~

There were only two seasons in this hyperboreal city: the brief summer when fatty sun-screen and fallen food fried on the paved tundra, then the long dark winter of drizzle welling up from the concrete permafrost. It was December, and it was done. Dave went up to Colindale to speak to an old acquaintance of his dad who worked at ABC Print, at the end of Annesley Avenue, by the polythene scrap of the Silk Stream, where gulls mournfully circled over the Montrose recreation ground and a knock-kneed old geezer stood in the road mixing mortar on a bit of plyboard.

'On metal you say?' Dick Winterbottom looked quizzically at Dave Rudman. 'Yeah, yeah, we can do that, as it 'appens.' The printer wore a cloth coat the brown of wrapping paper, the baggy skin under his eyes was scaly with age, a roll up pierced his lip like a narwhal's horn. 'Not that it guarantees it'll last for ever – for that you'd aff to dye-stamp it.' Machinery comfortingly clunked and slapped. There were stacks of cardboard, ricks of papery hay, and over it all hung the smell of inky fertilizer. 'You're Paul Rudman's boy – aren'tcha?' Dave looked at the saintly old printer – a headlight was on full beam behind his head.

Dave was up and down to Colindale several times. Winterbottom, quite rightly, thought him crazy – so Dave had to put down a three-grand deposit. He had to pick the metal for the plates that would be pages, he had to select the rings to bind them. He had to correct the proofs himself – and supervise the presses – because no one, repeat NO ONE was to have sight of the copy. 'A one-off like this,' Winterbottom remarked, 'the cost is fee-numb-in-awl. Phenomenal. Sure you don't wanta 'ave us do ten or twenty more – it'll cost yer the same?' But Dave Rudman wanted one – there had to be ONLY ONE. Then, when it was done and he'd taken delivery, he handed the cheque over for the balance and took the film from the press, the computer discs from the setting machine, and any other evidence there was of The Book's production. He found a providential skip, poured petrol on this stuff, flicked a match, got in the motor and drove away.

~

It would have to be by night. He would need equipment: a torch that strapped on to his head, a mattock for the digging, dark clothes and stuff to black up his face. It would have to be a dark night as well, *a moonless night, issa commando raid inter the Ferbiddun Zön*. Dave was far gone now. He could see nothing that wasn't presented to him in the screen; by day he warned potential fares he was coming by *keeping the foglamps on all the fucking time*. By night he transfixed them in the glare of his headlights. A woman could have been raped and battered to death within feet of him – and he never would have noticed. He trapped the hated *fucking flyers* up West and drove them out to Heathrow, past the Moto Services at Heston, ranting all the way, 'Forward', *forward, forward* . . . no longer aware of whether he was speaking aloud or in his mishmash mind.

Michelle considered it nothing short of a miracle that the three of them were managing to get on this well. Granted, the peculiar situation put *stresses on all of us and allowances have to be made for Carl.* Still, Beech House ticked over, and she revelled in the keeping of its moneyed beat. Redecorating was under way, and Michelle had taken a leave of absence from work. In her heart-of-hearts, where ambition was stilled, she knew she wasn't going back. Standing in the bay, at the ebony windowpane, looking out over rain-lacquered gardens at the lap of land that cuddled Hampstead, Michelle could see nothing much besides the questing fingers of TV aerials scratching the rushing night sky.

Behind her in the high-ceilinged rooms, a new reality was taking shape. Carl was up in his computerized crack house, bossing his 'hos'; Cal was taking a bath. A stately pine dominated the drawing room, a heap of boxes contrived by the Harrods specialist gift-wrapping service spread out beneath its shaggy, sagging limbs. *It's a lie . . . another fucking lie . . . Until they know which one of them is the boy's father, it's just another fucking lie* . . . Michelle's head was reflected in the glass – a shapeless pile. *At the flat in Fulham . . . I had those mirrored doors on the fitted cupboards . . . I used to watch blokes make love to me in them . . . Then with Dave crammed in beside me I watched my belly swell. I woke in the middle of the night . . . the night before we were married . . . I started shaking . . . I could see a figure in the dark . . . evil coming off it. I turned to Dave and he was awake already – he'd seen it too. He put on the light – it was only a shapeless pile of clothes on a chair. We both calmed down, then I said, 'We're making a big mistake, you know.' And he said, 'I know.' It was mad, but we were closer – we felt closer then than we did the whole next day. What's that, then – knowing you're making a big mistake but doing it anyway . . . a conspiracy?*

~

The hole was thigh-deep. Deep enough, surely, to withstand the delving of public-school-educated landscape gardeners. Deep enough to remain undisturbed until – by some mysterious signal that Dave could not yet divine – Carl would be informed and excavate it. Dave took the queer ringbinder of metal plates, wrapped it in a plastic bag and placed it in the hole. He dropped a chunk of York paving on top, then shovelled the earth and clay back in with his army-surplus mattock. He stomped with his claggy trainers until the surface was levelled off. He was turning to leave – for it was done – when she saw him.

'Cal!' Michelle shouted. 'There's someone in the garden!' She already knew who this someone was. Cal came running from the bath, spattering bergamot bubbles and slip-sliding on the newly laid marble of the grandiose hall. In the garden Dave turned towards her cry. A flap of curtain was open, and buttery light spread across builders' rubble – barley-sugar twists of reinforced-steel in a fudge of old London bricks and mortar. *Smoked salmon scraps from Greenspan's the deli . . . A Danish pastry ring and the News of the Screws . . . Dad shitting out his hangover in the bog . . . Sunday morning in the 'burbs* . . . He fled.

They saw him as he scattered along Beech Row. They saw him, Cal and Michelle, standing on the front step of their seven-figure lifestyle, and Michelle shook her red head and said, 'Poor Dave, what's he doing? Where's he going to?' Cal put a bare, wet arm around her shoulders.

He was going to the day, because he couldn't hide in the night-time any longer. The darkness was where he'd done it – the darkness was where they might find him. So he fled into the day, through the curtain of drizzle and into the chicane at the bottom of Park Lane, where Achilles was back up on his plinth, fending off the hair-styling wand of the Hilton with his black shield.

# 13

# *New London*

MAR 524 AD

The mainsail, which all that tariff had bellied overhead like the wing of a mighty seafowl, now whipped, snagged, then crumpled. The ferry was going about. Cummon nah, U fukkas! the gaffer shouted down the forward hatch. Out of it burst a ragged company of dads, eleven in all: two coloureds, three pikeys, a Mick and five of the gaffer's own chavs. With their gaffer aiming kicks up their arses, the crew sprang to the rigging and swarmed aloft. The wind was quartering and the sails must be trimmed. The Catford Light had been raised – they would be in London before nightfall.

From where Carl stood by the wheel, he could see all of the *Trophy Room*, this floating wooden island that had been his home for the past three blobs. Tyga was in his cage on the foredeck, the mate was at the wheel. Antonë Böm stood at the bow, his plump hands thrust in his drawstring jeans, his threadbare robes lashed by the stiff breeze. His mirror caught the foglight dancing upon the waves, while tucked beneath his arm was his leather-bound copy of the Book.

The gaffer of the *Trophy Room* had accepted Böm's story without questioning. Stalkers and their butterboys were common enough in the further dominions of King David. Besides, the queer let drop the names of powerful connections in London, and as for the monstrous brindled beast they had with them, the gaffer consented to take it aboard – such freaks fetched a pretty price in the Smoke. It would pay these lowly Drivers' passage to the capital.

The Plateists of Bril had not cavilled at Antonë and Carl's decision

– theirs was a society founded not on coercion but on liberty of conscience. The travellers rested and waited for Tyga's wounds to heal; then, furnished with fresh provisions, they were rowed out into the sea lanes in one of the Plateists' pedalos. Although this craft was far larger than the Hack of Ham's, it still seemed a mere cockleshell bobbing on the waves when the *Trophy Room* came beating up the main of Cot under full sail.

The *Trophy Room*, Carl thought, was a vessel such as the giantess might have ridden in. It creaked and groaned with constant life, it stank of tar, hempen rope and its spicy cargo of fags and booze from the far south, beeswax from Ex and even a few tanks of moto oil freshly loaded at Wyc. Below decks rats scuttled and the alien chavs blubbered with their clipped tongues. There was more irony attached to the *Trophy Room*'s rigging alone than Carl had seen before in his entire life. The gaffer wore a golden cap embroidered with the arms of his getter, and held the course of the ferry by eye and memory, with little recourse to his traficmaster.

The coast of Cot was a panorama that unrolled alongside the ferry. Bëthan semis stood in the hedged fields, their white plaster and black beams sharp against the tawny ground. After the *Trophy Room* had made the northern cape of Cot, these isolated buildings were succeeded by small manors, which clumped together into bigger and bigger settlements. Here the semis were of brick and crete – some of them two storeys high. The Shelters were magnificent; great green halls capable of holding a hundred fares at intercom. On their roofs stood wheel vanes, and the loud chimes that rang out from their slatted speakers carried over the waters.

Having crossed the sound between Cot and Durbi, the *Trophy Room* anchored off Nott to trade. Carl was astonished by Nott Bouncy Castle – and refused for a while to believe that it could be of human construction, rather than a curiously shaped stack. When the crowds piled out from the Bouncy Castle's gates, then came churning in their pedalos across the harbour to the ferry, Carl took refuge with Tyga, snuggling down in his comforting flesh folds. The gaffer threw a tarp over them. While the Nott blokes bargained with the gaffer, Antonë Böm remained below deck, scratching away at his notebooks in the tiny cabin.

The *Trophy Room* lay off Blackheath under a dipped headlight. The Port of London Authority pedalo came out to the ferry with a pilot. They were to proceed upriver at first tariff and berth in St Katharine's Dock. The pedalo returned to the city carrying lettuce from the gaffer to his getter in Lombard Street, and from Antonë Böm to the Lawyer of Blunt at Somerset House, his fuck-offgaff in the Strand.

Neither Antonë nor Carl could sleep that night. They assembled their few, pathetic belongings over and over again, packing and repacking their changingbags.

– You know, Carl, Antonë said, speaking softly, the gaffer will only take one payment from us for our passage and that payment alone. He has made it clear that if we do not give him this – this thing, he will hand us over to the harbour master as soon as the ferry docks.

– I, I understand, Carl replied, tears flowing down his cheeks. He went up on deck. The headlight was a silvery sliver, the dashboard a smear of illumination.

– Paw Tyga. Carl stroked the moto's salty jowls and spoke in comforting Mokni: Iss onlë 4 a lyttul wyl, yeah, an Eyem shor ve gaffa ul lúkarfta U.

Tyga regarded him with tiny trusting eyes. But Eyeth wuwwyed abaht U, Cawl, he lisped. Eyeth wuwwyed abaht U.

The foglamp came on in a screen demisted, and revealed the great earthen rampart of the Emtwenny5. A large, flat-bottomed pedalo came alongside the *Trophy Room*, its crew of Taffy chavs pedalling furiously. The pilot was still in his cabin, so Carl coaxed Tyga into the cargo sling, and he was swung over the side of the ferry and winched down into the well of the smaller vessel. Carl could hardly bear to look at poor Tyga. He thought of all the dangers they'd endured on the journey from Ham, and how at every opportunity the moto had placed his own life at the service of his young gaffer. Now he was being abandoned, almost certainly to a fate even worse than that of his rank.

At first tariff the *Trophy Room* weighed anchor, and, with only a mizzen sail set, she coasted gently on the flood tide into the mouth of the Thames. From the yawning gap between the piers of the Barrier a sleek, black shag came, travelling low over the riffling waves. The pilot took the wheel, the crew hung from the bare rigging, and, while the gaffer and his mates busied themselves below deck, Antonë and Carl went forward and watched as the prospect of the mighty city opened out before their eyes.

Past the Barrier the Thames narrowed so much that Böm was able to point out the principal districts, streets and even the individual buildings of the metropolis to his young companion: the hilltop manors of Millwall and Deptford, the smoky ravines of Greenwich and Hackney. Coaches pulled by teams of ten and even twelve burgakine were rumbling along Silvertown Way in clouds of dust. The Millennium Dome rose up on the southern shore, the long arms of cranes wavered over its bellying sides. Even at this early tariff teams of chavs were swarming up ladders, carrying hods of brick and truckles of mortar, adding to the courses that coiled like a mighty rope.

Carl could find no point of reference in this tumult; for here the trees were but buddyspike stalks rooted in the gaps between buildings, and the flocks of flying rats that wheeled about the roofs of the towering Shelters were as flies to the ordure of burgerkine. The bobbing waterfowl divided by ferry prows; the smoke streamers blowing from scores of chimneystacks on the riverbank; the turbine propellers flashing bigwatt; the hundreds of little pedalos plying from shore to shore; then, when the breeze slacked, a stench – sharp, bitter, unnatural – welled up and stung Carl's eyes.

Antonë called over the runs that pertained to the unfolding view – but this dismayed Carl still more, for, while some of the streets were lined with semis, others were but muddy sloughs edged by yok kerbstones, with a few wooden uprights in place of gaffs yet to be built. Still more were but holloways gouged in the earth by the passage of the multitude. Then, as the *Trophy Room* entered Wapping Reach and the Bermondsey Hills closed in on the southern shore, so the city began to clot, its roads tangling, its streets narrowing, the gaffs – painted bright reds, blues, greens and yellows, their gable ends resplendent with golden wheels – climbed atop each other, three, four and even five storeys high.

Carl could now see the people – so many of them – and, as the ferry passed by the end of a street, it was as if a log had been rolled over to reveal a multitude of scuttlebugs hurrying about their business: lawds and luvvies lolling in their cabs, a pair of jeejees between the shafts; getters in rickshaws; the middling sort in mini-cabs; carrot-crunchers on top of coaches piled high with sacks of wheatie, veg and other comestibles. Chuggers, decaux pasters and squeegee merchants darted hither and thither in the roadway; and everywhere there were gangs of skinny urchins that, startled from their nefarious activities by a seeseeteevee man brandishing a staff, seemed to dance like midges above a puddle, before alighting once more.

As the *Trophy Room* pulled under Tower Bridge and into the Pool of London, Carl saw above the roofs the plunging rim of a mighty Wheel that rode over it all. The glass windows of the cars attached to this awe-inspiring contraption coruscated as if each were a miniature foglamp. It revolves once each tariff, Antonë observed, powered by the Thames. It is in the shape of the Knowledge and it can be viewed from any street in London – truly it is the very mill of the city, its orrery and engine.

The press of ferries increased until bowsprits were passing within a hand's breadth of hulls. The pilot stood stock still at the wheel, crying out commands to which the crew responded with wiry alacrity, trimming the sails so there was but a tiny noserag of canvas straining on the mizzen. The pilot brought the ferry in unerringly, until, with a final flurry of orders, she slid into the slopping basin of St Katharine's Dock.

Hawsers whipped from the shore and crashed on to the deck. The gangplank went down and a posse of coloured dockers scampered up it.

– It's time we bade farewell to the gaffer, Böm said; the harbour master will come aboard soon enough.

– Where to, guv? Carl asked. Where are we goin'?

– A boozer in Stepney known as the Öl Glöb. From the lettuce I received this tariff when the bargees took Tyga, it would appear that my Lawyer of Blunt is disposed to assist us. We are to lie low there for at least the next blob – then he will contact us. He or his mates.

The duo made their way through the fetid lanes beside the Clink and into the precincts of Borough Market. Stepping into Southwark Street, Böm was taken by surprise by the press of traffic. He wondered if there had always been this mad jam of van, truck, car and lorry. For in the decade he'd been away the number of vehicles on the road seemed to have doubled. A veritable river of shit and piss ran down the gutters and the foul cries of the chavs rent the air. Standard sellers and decaux pasters were abroad – and the blizzard of A4 was equally diverting to the returnee. Even in the fastness of Ham, Böm had learned of this printing explosion – the multiplication of presses throughout the cities of Ing until there was a prontaprint on every high street. Still, it was a shock to discover that the cockneys, when not engaged in abusing each other, were to be seen with their ratty features blotted out by phonics.

Ware2, guv? the rickshaw dad snapped. He wore a dirty singlet and tight shorts. His back flesh was flayed, and he had a prodigious goitre. All his muscle was in his rigid arms, which held the shafts, and his splayed legs, which seemed to belong to some better-fed and cared-for creature. The famished eyes that met Carl's spoke of no favours received or tendered, a two-tariff day every day, fighting with elbow and knout to wrest a living from the London streets. The Öl Glöb, Stepney, Böm commanded him as they clambered in, and the dad reared back before throwing his entire meagre weight forward on the ball of one foot. The rickshaw lurched, teetered and rolled into the rumbling cavalcade.

Despite all his looming fears of the city and their fate within its walls, the young Hamster was gripped by the smooth motion of the first wheeled vehicle that he had ever ridden in, and his fancy flew, seeing himself in the not-long-distant future as a mighty Lawd, drawn through the streets in his elegant limmo; a Taffy on the roof, four pairs of jeejees in the shafts and magnificently liveried fonies poised on the bumper.

Although it took the rickshaw a long time to cross London Bridge and trundle through the City, at least they did not suffer the thousand buffets of those who went on foot. The toffs had no fear of the hugger-mugger, preceded as they were by fonies, their staffs raised to smite the riffraff, their didduloodoo cries warning that a getter, a Driver or a Lawd was approaching. What a sight these exalted personages were! The getters wore flowing pinstripe robes, the trains dragging a full metre behind them, and their lobbs were mirror-shiny.

If this was not sufficient to dazzle the little Hamster, there were also the many likenesses of the Supreme Driver himself. Dave was everywhere. Along the span of the Bridge in niches, and occupying plinths and columns in the City, were many stone and irony statues: Dave standing, Dave sitting, Dave driving, his massive arms held out in front of him. He was depicted in His humble raiment of plain leather jacket, jeans and trainers. His cap was tilted back on his pitted forehead. On Ham there had been no such representations, save for the engraving of Dave on the tattered frontispiece of the sole copy of the Book; yet these effigies bore the same bulging, all-seeing eyes, the same full and judgemental lips, the prominent nose like the prow of a capsized pedalo.

All along Leadenhall the gable ends of the gaffs were wooden plaques carved in the semblance of Dave's features, while below them dangled the guild signs: the twisted spine of the Chiropractors, the flaming torch of the letric lighters, the hair-styling wand of the barbers – vivid reminders that even here, in the very citadel of the PCO, the toyist still held sway. As the rickshaw jolted through Aldgate, Carl shrank down in the seat, for above the massive lintel of the gate, impaled on a palisade of spikes, were the rotting heads of traitors. He turned back and saw a kite making a stately circle over the very highest buildings of the City. The bird was etched for a moment against the tetrahedral spire of the NatWest Tower before soaring still higher and disappearing into a glowing cynosure rent in the grey-brown smog.

In the Öl Glöb the floorboards were scattered with booze-sodden rushes, and letrics burned with a guttering flame. Coming in through the door, Carl paused and sniffed the smoky interior. Moto oil, he muttered, and Antonë said, Yes, yes, you'll find it in widespread use here.

– Oi U! the boiler behind the bar broke in. U cummin in 4 a drink, aw wot?

The travellers proceeded along the low room and came face to face with the boiler, who had the corpulent babyish features of an old moto.

– Um . . . err . . . I am Tonë Böm, the teacher said, and my companion is –

– Eye no, Eye no, Eyev erred awl abaht U. Eyem Missus Edjez, iz Lawdships bloke spoke wiv me, sed Ud B cummin. Cuppuluv blokes wot need 2 lay low 4 a wyl, keep ahtuv ve mirra.

Troubled by this loose talk, Carl and Antonë cast suspicious looks at the denizens of the boozer – a slovenly company of mummies in filthy cloakyfings and tracksuits. Their faces were scooped out with want and privation – they coughed and spluttered with the chancre. There were kids playing on the floor at their feet – one little girl's head was blown up like a bladder with some foul distemper. Missus Edjez laughed, a great bosom-heaving chuckle that set all her dewlaps a-jiggling. Vem? Vem! U doan need 2 wurri abaht vem – vare awl abbsolootlë ragarsed! Cummon nah, she continued, Eyel shew U ware yaw kippin, Ūle av no bovva ear at ve Glöb, no sneekë cunts from ve PeeSeeO, no seeseeteevee, nunuvit!

The two travellers followed the garrulous old boiler up a dark winding staircase and along a warped corridor, at the end of which she showed them into a cramped garret under the eaves of the ancient gaff. Missus Edjez left them, and they set down their changingbags on a dropsical sofabed. At long last the journey, which had begun four months ago on the distant shore of Mutt Bä, was over.

The Öl Glöb was a creaking pile of timber beams, bent laths and pitted plaster that rose up – each tilting storey seemingly wider than the next – above a base of crumbling London brick laid in queerly oblique courses. The gables were as high as the masts of the *Trophy Room* and intricately carved with cabs, pedalos, dogs and cats. The topsy-turvy wings of the boozer were so angled that through the diamond-patterned mullions of their garret Carl could see the stock bricks of its massive chimneystack glow gold against the tinted London screen.

The Öl Glöb stood isolated in the strange wilderness of Stepney Green, among deeply rutted roadways lined with two-storey-high hoardings upon which had been painted crude murals of the terraces described in the Book. There were also a few points – the Royal London Hospital, Queen Mary College – likenesses of which had been daubed on to still larger hoardings. The aim of the PCO's Knowledge Boys had been to anticipate the emergent New London:

shiny, three-dimensional, every façade commercially artful. The hoardings and their murals had, however, been completed in the reign of the first King David, and since that time there had been little attempt to fill in the Knowledge of this tumbledown part of the East End. Behind the wooden walls there were expanses of open ground where the ruderals grew both dense and high.

As soon as they were settled in the Öl Glöb and Böm had ensured Carl was provided for, he began to absent himself. He left the boozer early in the first tariff and did not return until after lampoff. Carl kept to the garret during daddytime, for if he did venture downstairs Terri, the old potman, had a way of cornering him and putting to him the most disturbing and intrusive questions: Oo R U? Ware R U from? Y R U ear? Terri was foxy-faced and ginger-haired, his arms twisted and his legs bent. He leered – yet Missus Edjez dismissed Carl's concerns. Im? U doan wanna wurri abaht im, eez an ol lag, bin broak on ve Weel.

At Changeover the mummies and kids who hung out in the bars of the Öl Glöb departed and in their stead came a rough crowd. Dads who worked at the docks, cabbies and puddlers from the steelyard by the Tower. They brought their opares with them – loose girls, little more than common prostitutes, whom the drunken dads openly fondled.

Feeling abandoned and worried, Carl eventually confronted Böm. Why did he go abroad each day? Had he forgotten their revelations on Ham? For was it not a risky business? What news was there from the Lawyer of Blunt? How long would they have to remain cooped up here? And what tried the lad most severely – what about Symun Dévúsh, what about their mission to discover the Geezer's fate? Antonë was both emollient and placatory. He soothed Carl and stroked his hair. Do not worry, I have no position or place and the city is large. I pay no moto tax nor keep any chav, while this tattered robe insulates me from prying eyes. I have been about my old haunts, and I have discovered that there are forces for change at work in London. It reminds me of the months before my exile, when your dad's followers were in the ascendant. This time the revolt against the King and the PCO is an affair of reason and thought conducted by lawds and even luvvies. It is not for us to impose ourselves on my Lawyer of Blunt – we can only hope that he will contact us.

That night Carl dreamed of Ham. He wandered the woods and orchards beneath the moto wallows. The soft breeze filled the air with fluttering blossom, and Runti was resurrected by his side. The moto gently butted Carl's tank with his moist muzzle and slooshed terms of endearment. In sleep Carl groaned as he stroked and rubbed the bristly flanks of the one he loved.

The Lawyer of Blunt's fony came for them the very next day, not long past first tariff. Having gobbled down his starbuck, Carl emerged from the boozer to find four pairs of jeejees, their bridles chinking as they bent their heads to crop the meagre turf. A light mizzle suffused the air, and the jeejees' coats were a sheen of moisture. Still reeling from his homesick reveries, Carl addressed the lead jeejee tenderly and insinuated his hand where its jonckheeres should have been. The jeejee snapped at him and Carl recoiled. The big fony and Antonë laughed heartily. It's not a moto, Carl, Böm said, but a mere toyist beast! Carl took a seat in the limmo, while Böm fetched their changingbags from the garret. As he climbed in, Missus Edjez and Terri, the weaselly potman, appeared at the back door. The Taffy cabbie cracked his whip, and the limmo jolted out of the yard and turned to the right, rattling along the Whitechapel Road towards the towers of the City.

Soon, however, the limmo slowed to walking pace and joined the queue of artics lumbering in from the forbidden zones to the east of the city. These were drawn by large teams of burgerkine, and overloaded with brick, yok and irony for the ever-hungry developers who laboured by day – and when the headlight was on full beam by night as well – to raise New London. Sorrë, guv! the

Taffy cried out. Vares taylbaks on ve Wessway – aw so vaysay. Traffiks jammedup cleerfroo tahn. Then, seeing a gap in the traffic heading into Houndsditch, he cracked his whip and the limmo lurched forward again.

Mindful of his instruction Antonë pointed out to Carl the crowds clustered beside the door to the Royal Exchange waiting for the day's trading to commence. Dosh tossed down in the City, he said, the King's maxed-out credit cards bought and sold in an unseemly scrabble. He gestured towards a group of dads wearing peculiar blue robes. See them gathered there, the blokes in the odd robes? The Swizz League. All the land between here and the river is granted to them by the King. They live apart, eat their own curry, worship in their own Shelter. They have the right to trade free from the moto tax to which the Guilds are subject – their presence here in London is a sore affront to native daddies. See the screwing out they're getting from the Inglish getters. I am told that not a day passes without an affray on the floor of the 'change.

As the limmo rattled on along Cheapside, the enormous green walls of St Paul's Shelter rose up before them, towering above the surrounding gaffs. Antonë could not forbear from pedagogy: My dear Carl, think on this, the tea urn is the biggest in the entire known world, the gingham curtains took a thousand mummies to sew, the Shelter can hold five thousand daddies at a time, it was burned down in the reign of the first King David and then rebuilt. The meter on its roof is the largest in Ing . . . But Carl wasn't listening: his attention was caught by the press of Drivers who were swarming out from the elaborately carved doors. Drivers tall and short, thin and fat. All were richly caparisoned, the peaks of their caps embroidered in silver, their trainers bright white and barred with the colours of their orders. All of them bore the sign of the Wheel worked into their breasts with gold thread, and all of them were calling over. Their massed recitation broke against the gaff fronts in wave after wave of dävine incantation, carrying with it the transcendent Knowledge of the once and future city. As the Drivers moved into the packed streets, they began to move faster and faster until they were almost running. Guided by the pure radiance of their Faredar, their eyes alighted on guilty opares, backsliding daddies and uppity mummies. In their rearview were craven fares, frantically making the sign of the Wheel.

The cabbie gave a blast on the horn and the Lawyer of Blunt's limmo parted the throng on the Strand and sped into the courtyard of Somerset House. Mechanics sprang to the jeejees' bridles. Standing at the top of a wide flight of stairs, waiting to greet them as they clambered out, was a figure at once outlandish and familiar to Antonë and Carl. She was very tall for a mummy. Her barnet was a tight and glossy helmet around her pasty white face. Her mouth was a perfect, carmine oval, and her eyes two black eyeholes. Tinfoil earrings dangled beside the taut tendons of her neck, her black nails were as long as talons, and when she parted her lips her teeth were blood-stained. Her legs were clad in woolly hose and a wispy shawl was around her shoulders.

– W-where to, Luv? Carl uneasily saluted her.

– To New London, she replied, then continued, So Carl Dévúsh, you are with us at last, a Hamster in the Wheel. My sister, the Luvvie Joolee, has sent me lettuce concerning you and your companion – she turned to Böm, who made obeisance. She acknowledged him then, saying, I am the Luvvie Sarona and you are welcome in Somerset House. Now follow me, for there are mummies and daddies who fain would meet with you.

– W-why, Carl whispered to Antonë as they followed the Luvvie's clacking heels through halls, along galleries and between the columns of elegant colonnades, does she wear a mask?

– Mask? Mask? Oh, I see, you mean her slap – this is only such unguents and creams as London luvvies are wont to adorn themselves with. It is customary – a sign of refinement.

Carl thought it no refinement at all but a ridiculous oddity, making of the mummy a stranger to herself. However, he had not time to dwell on this, for his surroundings were so marvellous and unexpected that he struggled to take in their bewildering detail. The archways they passed beneath, the wall panels, the domed ceilings, the very flags of the floor they trod upon – in short, every surface was adorned with painted scenes drawn from the Book. Carl's eyes, attuned to the subtle shades of green and brown that dominated his native Ham, ached with the bombardment of lectric blues, intensified indigos, dayglo oranges and the silvery curlicues that drew the vignettes together into a continuous, dävotional mural. He wanted to touch and prod the tiny figures and little black cabs. He wished he might clamber into this brilliant London and, together with Dave and the Lost Boy, escape the chellish PCO. Carl's head began to swim – and he would have fainted had not Luvvie Sarona pushed through a final set of doors and guided him to a chair, where he gratefully subsided. The floor of the vast chamber that Carl found himself in appeared to be covered with a woodland canopy, as if screen and ground had been reversed. Here and there on this dappled expanse were little posses of mummies and daddies. To begin with, so still were they that Carl assumed these figures weren't living fares but some fresh trickery of the eye. The dads stood with their arms cocked, their hands on their hips, their chests thrown forward to emphasize the snowy expanse of their T-shirts. Their leather jackets curved into great rigid tails like the folded wings of birds. Their white jeans were skintight, their cockpieces upraised, their trainers laced to the knee. The long peaks of their caps were pulled down low and the smoke from their fags boiled there.

The mummies – although far fewer in number – were no less resplendent. Their long legs were sheathed in hose, their skirts were as short and tight as belts, their décolletage plunged to reveal cunningly contrived chokers and gorgets of Daveworks. Their faces were uniformly mask-like, and they peered quizzically at the new arrivals through the heart-shaped lenses of their lorgnettes. A curious stench – at once fruity and spicy – emanated from these mummies and daddies. On the mantel a meter clunked the units with dreadful finality.

Then, quite suddenly, as if this were a prearranged signal, Luvvie Sarona closed the double doors with a 'clack', and the toffs sprang to life. They closed in on Antonë and Carl, their fags poking, their earrings jangling, questions firing from their painted lips. What did they think of London? How had they contrived to get here? Was it true that Carl was the Geezer's son? And Antonë Böm, a learned queer, how had he withstood exile at the very limit of the King's realm? These motos of which the Luvvie Joolee had written – did they indeed speak as lisping children? And, most importantly, what of the second Book – the one the Geezer was reputed to have found on his native island – did they know its whereabouts?

Carl did his best, yet no sooner had he begun to reply to one of his inquisitors than another interposed himself. The gathering was fast degenerating into a mêlée. The peaks of the daddies' caps jabbed at Carl's face, and he was on the verge of swooning, when Luvvie Sarona called them all to order. Daddies! Mummies! she cried. These blokes are weary and have travelled far under the most terrible exactions, there will be, I trust, time aplenty for them to make appearances before you all. For now they must rest, and in due course it is only proper that this young lad be afforded the opportunity to go about the town and learn something of our ways. He comes among us in the figure of the Lost Boy! Let us revere him – for my sister tells me that he also bears more of the Geezer's revelation!

At the mention of the Geezer there was a great commotion. The toffs all fell to their knees and a confused babel arose from them, part calling over, part pleas addressed directly to Dave, exhorting him to tear his eyes from the mirror and confront them. Two of their number – a gawky mummy in a purple skirt and a daddy wearing an eyepatch – were thrust into the centre of this ecstatic circle. The others joined hands and began to chant: Don't breakup! Don't breakup! Don't breakup! Carl looked from ghostly visage to cockpiece, from brandished Daveworks to mouths flecked with spittle. His dazed eyes slid to the arched windows of the chamber, and through the distorting glass he could see a rainbow shimmering against the muddy clouds. Don't breakup! Don't breakup! Don't breakup! the mummies and daddies continued, working themselves into a frenzy. It was all too overwhelming for the peasant lad, and at last he did faint quite away.

~

Carl recovered consciousness in a sumptuous chamber, lying in a high hard sofabed on strangely chilly white material. A shapeless covering lay over him, upon which was the sign of the Wheel. In the pool of light thrown by a tall letric sat Antonë Böm, scratching away at his notebook. Carl lay for a while, staring up at a painted ceiling that depicted Dave in his flowing robes, composing the Book in golden letters. Carl was at once oppressively aware of these opulent surroundings – and curiously divorced from them. He was miserably uncomfortable – he longed for the prick of straw and even the nip of the bug. He wanted to be where he was a lad to every dad, where he wasn't a stranger or an oddity.

– W-wot – wot woz awl vat abaht, ven? Dön braykup an vat?

At the sound of Carl's voice, Antonë looked up. Arpee, Carl, Arpee at all times, Antonë reminded him, then continued, And that, ahem, little ceremonial was conducted because Danëel and Karen Brooke have been caught cohabiting by the Lord Chancellor's Department, yes indeed. Naturally, the Blunts' sect has been under surveillance by trained mediators for many years now – ever since Luvvie Blunt was exiled for the same crime. Böm sighed heavily. These hoorays, Carl, they speak of the Geezer as if it were his calling over that led them into such practices, when the truth is that posh mummies and daddies have always shacked up with each other, daddies even as they left the very Shelter itself, going straight to the mummies of their children, children they freely acknowledged as their own. No, no, it is only since the dävidic line assumed control of the PCO that the writ of State and Shelter have become one, and that the King's political allies have sought to dignify their suppressions with dävine doctrine.

Yet upon whom does this weigh most heavily? Böm rose and began to pace back and forth, pontificating in a manner that so vividly recalled to Carl the days of his childhood, far away in the Shelter at Ham, that he could not prevent himself from smiling. I will tell you upon whom, the poor, the cockneys and the peasants, the Taffies and the Scots – even the chavs, who are mere property to be bought and sold, are subject to the rigours of Breakup and Changeover. I have no cause to disparage my Lawd or Luvvie – they have been our protectors – still, when I see these foppish fellows smiting their perfumed brows and crying out how they are overawed by the tragic vision of the Lost Boy, abroad on the Heath and at the mercy of Nature's savagery . . . well, I confess, lad – I do not know what to think. No, no, indeed I don't.

Carl drifted back to sleep, and when he awoke again the next tariff, the chamber was full of bigwatt foglight. Böm had already risen and was dressed in the tight jeans, frogged T-shirt and full-skirted leather carcoat of a Hack. Come on, come on, he cried, get up, lad, The cabbie has already brought the limmo from the garages, we hardly have time to bolt starbuck before we must be gone for our sightseeing tour. Your threads are over there, he added as an afterthought, indicating a pile set atop a pair of high-topped trainers that were broken at the ankle.

With his top lip scraped raw by a bic and his hair smarmed back under a cap, Carl felt like a little ponce. Antonë, however, assured him he looked the part. What part? Carl asked, and his mentor explained: From now on I am a Hack who holds a mortgage on one of the Blunts' estates, my name is Barrë Iggynbumme, you are my son and your moniker is Sam.

The Taffy was at the reins of the limmo team; he lashed at the jeejees, and as they swept out of the courtyard two fonies leaped on to the rear bumper. From their flub-a-dub-dub through the back window, Carl assumed they were chavs rather than bondsmen. He wanted to ask Antonë about them but the marvellous sights outside the limmo soon captured his attention.

The limmo rollicked along Whitehall and clattered between the precincts of the Royal Palace. Wide courtyards opened out on each side of the roadway. In one of these Carl saw rope-dancers and fire-eaters performing for the amusement of a posse of young dads in screen-blue robes. The King's EyeBeeEms, Böm saw fit to inform him. These striplings are brought into his service to keep the Exchequer's tallies and manage the coinage. Then, between two wings of the Palace, Carl saw a beautiful garden, bursting with unusual blooms arranged in cunning patterns and low walkways overarched with clipped shrubbery. Along one of these sylvan aisles he espied laughing luvvies, tottering along on the highest of heels and accompanied by fools cutting capers and opares wheeling maclarens.

The Palace was so large as to defy comprehension – it spread along the river bank in a thick moraine of yok, crete and London brick. This behemoth building was pierced by a myriad windows and hung about with numerous, precarious wooden staircases. Its sweeping roofs were speared by a forest of smoking chimneys and seeseeteevee masts, while everywhere Carl looked, flapping from high poles, was the King's standard, the golden Wheel folding, then stretching to proclaim the motto of the dävidic line: DAYV GUYD UZ.

On they rolled, into the boggy water meadows beyond Westminster and through the pretty little riverside manors of Millbank and Pimlico. It wasn't until the limmo slowed to a crawl and the cabbie asked them all to climb out and walk, for the King's Road was too steep and too muddy for them to haul up, that Carl emerged from his reverie. There were other cars being drawn up the rutted roadway, while their posh passengers trailed along behind, gingerly lifting their trainers to avoid piles of horse shit and other ordure.

As they joined this workaday cavalcade, Carl asked Antonë:

– What sight is it, exactly, that we're going to see?

Böm was abstracted. Why, we have come here to see this, of course.

They had gained the heights of Chelsea and, looking back, Carl could apprehend for the first time the whole lazy bend of the Thames as it swept through the city. On the far back were the hilltop manors of Kennington and Battersea, while below them and to the east London spread out: a carpet of tiled roofs, pierced by dense thickets of smoking chimneys and redbrick towers. Here and there were golden domes – which to the lad's eyes had the aspect of giant shrooms. With the black bugs of motos trundling through the streets and the flocks of flying rats, crows and ringnecks circling, London seemed Ham-like to Carl, an island of urbanity in the windswept burbs.

~

The following day Carl Dévúsh awoke to discover that the mist had blown in off the burbs during the third tariff and mingled with the sulphurous smoke of the city's thousands of fires to engender a thick particular. This lay as heavy as crete over the malodorous river. The masts of luggers, barges and wherries disappeared into it, while the wärgaffs lining the south bank emerged from it wavering and insubstantial – as if they were but a temporary solidification of the smog and it was the more durable element. The brackish reek of the river water and the richer pong of London's effluvia seeped into the Lawyer of Blunt's fuckoffgaff, and, despite the best efforts of the chavs and poles – who darted hither and thither strewing incense on the fires – the elegant chambers stank as the meanest hovel.

Idle, with time heavy on his hands, and no tank for the rich curry or strange takeaway the Luvvie Sarona pressed upon him, Carl wandered the galleries and halls. He tried to imagine the Hamsters here in London – genial, squat, broad-faced Fukka Funch striding bow-legged among the crowds on the Strand; or his stepdad Fred Ridmun's lanky length poling a pedalo over the colloidal waters of the Thames. It was impossible, though: like the buildings on the far bank, the Hamstermen wavered and dissolved into the smog. They had no place in this ant heap; they could never adjust to this rigid hierarchy of chavs, bondsmen and commoners – which mounted up to the Inspectorate and the King himself. The Hamstermen would have wanted to sit down and discuss it all at great length over booze and fags – and there was no time for that. No time at all.

At first tariff the following day the foglamp was once again bigwatt in a clear screen. The Luvvie Sarona was in the front hall when Carl came down, her changingbag packed, her opares fussing about. It's Changeover, she explained to the lad, and I will be off in the limmo to my brother-in-law's estate in the sticks, while he will return here before third tariff. Dave be with you, lad, I understand that your teacher has a diverting day planned for you!

It was indeed a diverting day – although not in a pleasant way. As soon as they turned out of the ornate gates of Somerset House, with their lawyerly escutcheons and wrought irony spikes, they found themselves in the thick of an hysterical crowd. The Strand was packed with children, opares and mummies, all of them bent under changingbags, all of them attempting to secure the available transport. Cabbies, rickshaw dads, the fonies who had charge of vans and artics – all were bargaining with the desperate mummies in a most savage fashion. Carl saw one huge pikey tear the dosh from a mummy's hand, then bodily throw her and her children on top of his coach, where ten or so other unfortunates were already sprawled.

The keening of the mummies and kids as they were pushed and shoved contrasted grotesquely with the set faces of the few daddies who were abroad, hurrying about their business, and the seesee-teevee men who leered down from their watchtowers. The kiddies must all be changed over and their mummies off the streets before the beginning of the second tariff, Antonë explained; after that the PCO begins to make arrests. Thousands of gaffs are searched every Changeover day. No parent can escape them.

They gained Trafalgar Square, and here the commotion was even greater, for crowds of mummies and children were being forced up on to the steps of Dave's Column – forced by a tight wedge of running dads who were spilling from the mouth of Whitehall. And if the PCO doesn't get them, Antonë said ruefully, then the mob will. The daddies all wore long black T-shirts, their faces were twisted by venom, their mouths gaped, their trainers stamped, they struck out with their fists to the left and right, smiting mummies and kids both. Fukk ve SeeEssA! Fukk ve SeeEssA! they were chanting.

Böm hustled Carl down Northumberland Avenue away from the riot. These dads' groups, he sighed, they are always angry. Their grievances against the Child Support Agency and the Lawd Justice's Department are entirely unreasonable – deranged even. They have no love for child, dad or Dave – yet the King and the PCO, rather than suppressing them, prefer to use them after the fashion of a cat's paw, to strike terror into the populace. Come on, my son, come on – he took Carl by the arm – make sure your cockpiece is prominent, without it you still have the aspect of a boy, and if you were taken for a kiddie . . . He did not complete the ghastly thought, and, while Carl hearkened to him, as they made their escape across the Golden Jubilee Bridge and on to the Southbank, it was not anxiety that he was filled with but a feeling he could not identify, a queasy yet not unpleasant sensation – which had been triggered by a single word from his mentor's plump lips: son.

The pair sauntered along the Southbank and skirting the dävine precincts of the Wheel itself, headed across Victory Gardens and past Waterloo Station. By the time they reached Bedlam, which was the object of their promenade, the crowds had altogether died away, and, save for the occasional hurrying mummy dragging a squealing child, the rutted tracks and rubble-strewn boulevards were almost empty. However, on the steps of this monumental building – the elongated dome of which towered above the mean semis and tumbledown boozers – awaited a posse of lawds and luvvies.

They treat the spectacle of these unfortunates, Antonë explained, somewhat after the fashion of an entertainment. Here are confined lunatics, prodigies and even freaks – all alike and in the most insalubrious conditions. While nominally a charitable foundation, set up by worthy dävines, there is also a hard getter instinct here enshrined, for the warden of the asylum is permitted to run Bedlam as a paying concern. So saying, Böm dropped a coin into the palm of a grovelling fony who bowed, scraped and admitted them.

Antonë and Carl soon detached themselves from the toffs, who were led on ahead by the warden; instead they sauntered along a cavernous wing, beneath a barrel-vaulted ceiling. To each side irony bars formed a dense palisade, and behind them the maddads rocked and raved. They were filthy, they stank of shit and piss. Seeing expectant faces on the far side of the bars, these pitiable figures came shuffling through the rotten straw and addressed Carl with a babble of broken Mokni gibberish: Ware2, guv, ware2! Eye ad vat geezer in ve bakkuv ve cab. Nah, nah iss no bovva an vat . . . Many of them think they are Dave, Antonë observed, and call over after the fashion of Drivers. In my own youth there was only one madgaff in all of London, yet now I am told there are several, and still more are being erected upon the burbs.

They had reached the wing allocated to the mummies – and, if this were possible, these fares were in a still more wretched condition. See how they preen themselves, Antonë whispered, and apply their own shit as if it were slap. The poor things believe themselves to be Chelle and beat their heads against the brick walls to drive out their own evil.

One mummy was slumped right beside the bars. Her skirt had ridden up, and she was masturbating with an expression of utter vacancy on her blurry face. Carl turned away, but Böm responded as he did to any notably unusual phenomenon and continued to expatiate: There are those who say the flyspecks on the foglamp are growing in size and that this accounts for the increase in the numbers of the insane. Others contend that the fullbeam headlight is the cause. Still more blame bad water, or the monstrous size of the city that under the lash of the PCO grows at the pace of a walking dad. However, I . . . I – here he faltered and dropped his voice – I blame the Changeover itself, which latterly has become so rigid that it cleaves in two minds not yet formed. So I wonder if these desperate fares are only those, who, like ourselves, retain that cleavage after the end of Changeover. When I was a young bloke I thought I might go mad; until, that is, I heard the calling over of your dad.

They had caught up again with the warden and his party. This hunched fony, who averted his face from all and ceaselessly grovelled, was telling the toffs: Be not too frettened or afeared, your lawdships, the fings you are about to see are all Dave's critturs juss lyke uz. He withdrew a prodigious bunch of keys from the skirt of his leather carcoat and, unlocking an irony door, ushered them in with great ceremony. From a bracket on a wall the warden took a guttering torch, and then he led them on into the darkness.

In the first chamber they came to a coloured dad who was spread out on the straw. He was quite naked and of immense size. Viss fella iz an Eeefeeopp chavage, my lawds, the warden explained, brought here by ferry froo mennë lands. Eees so chavage vat Eyev putte im in fettas coz givven arf a chanz eed rip yer éds orf! The luvvies gasped and drew back in the way the warden clearly desired. Antonë, however, only whispered in Carl's ear: Arrant nonsense. It is but a coloured chav bought in the market like any other. Granted, he is of prodigious extent, but this our 'ahem' guide has sought to exaggerate. Look closely, all the articles in his cell have been made small – the chair, the table, even the tincan – so as to enhance his stature.

So it was with all of the so-called freaks: the Hairydad, the Monkeydad, the wattled mummy, the Pyrenean Twins – in each case Antonë sought to bring these oddities within the compass of comprehensibility. An nah, the warden cried, Eyev sayvd mì bess til lars. Viss . . . viss fing – he was lost for words – az bin wiv uss onlë a short wyl but iss gotta B ve stranjist bluddë creetur imajinobobble. Nunnuvuz can figga aht wot í iz – dad aw beeste, reel aw – he shuddered – toyist. Í az ve aspekk ov a gyant bäcön, but, az U wil C, mì nöbbul lawds an luvvies, í speeks wiv ve voys uvva –

Carl was no longer listening. He shouldered his way between the toffs, who stood honking on their clove balls, and there, behind bars, his flanks, his tank, his shoulders deeply scored with bloody welts, his jonckheeres tattered with some awful fungus, one of his eyes a bloody mess, and a disturbing nappy wrapped around his hindquarters, was Tyga.

Carl pressed his face between the bars and, weeping, cried out:

– Tyga, O paw Tyga!

The moto shuffled over to him, lisping:

– Ithat oo, Cawl? Ithat oo? Eye wanna go oam nah. Eye wanna go oam 2 Am.

At third tariff, following a mournful curry eaten alone in the sumptuous dining room of Somerset House, Antonë and Carl were back in their own chamber when they heard the sounds of a limmo arriving in the courtyard below. Shortly afterwards, and not proceeded by fony, gaffer or retinue of any sort, the Lawyer of Blunt came to them, sliding diffidently through the door. He was a smallish dad, the skin stretched tight on his close-cropped head. His cheekbones were sharp, his green eyes deeply recessed and fiercely acute. His small hands fidgeted at a bundle of signets and seals that hung on a chain from his neck. His threads were bespoke – yet hardly sumptuous. On receiving him, Antonë and Carl fell to their knees crying, Where to, guv? but he waved for them to rise, stuttering: P-please, my d-dear blokes, no such deference is required, truly – I beseech you.

While Carl sat, sunk in his own sad thoughts of Tyga and his miserable confinement, the Lawyer and the teacher spoke in hushed tones of weighty matters. From his notebook Antonë produced a brief he had been labouring on, the essence of which was a petition requesting information on the fate of Symun Dévúsh. I understand and appreciate your strategy, the Lawyer said; the CSA can prevent no lad from knowing his own dad, no more than any dad be kept from his lad. This much is sacrosanct. Such a course will alert both the King and the PCO to our intentions, yet it may well be that they would prefer to reach a private accommodation – for if we cry it abroad through standards and decauxs it could spark rebellion. To treat with those lawds and commonfolk who oppose the Breakup and the Changeover would be no less than they have done hitherto, and such pragmatism might commend itself to our purposes if it allowed for – and here he sighed deeply – the return of my poor wife from her exile, and the pardon of yourself, Antonë Böm, and your young companion.

This effusion led, quite naturally, to a request by the Lawyer for news of Luvvie Joolee and her sojourn on Ham. So it was that they passed the remaining units of that tariff until the lampon with Antonë and Carl telling tales of the remote island demesne.

With none of them having had any repose, the Lawyer nonetheless proposed that they sally forth once more before the second tariff. I would speak with you concerning your speculative philosophy, he averred to Böm. The doubts you have expressed concerning the origins of the Book engage me powerfully, and I warrant the drive to Hampstead will be a most satisfying backdrop to our discourse. Furthermore – and here, for the first time, Carl apprehended a shadow of anxiety pass across the Lawyer's bony countenance – we will be in the manner of sitting ducks if we remain within doors and the PCO comes a-knocking.

All was as before: the Taffy on the roof rack, the glossy jeejees straining in the shafts, the long black limmo pressing the mob into the gutter. They drove up the Finchley Road and by the time they had passed the Swizz Cottage they were in the sticks. Carl was thrilled to see open field strips and woodlands for the first time in blobs, while up ahead the burbs rose, wave after wave of hevver, streaked purple, lavender and blue, gently steaming under the bigwatt foglamp of buddout. Ringnecks dipped and rose through the shreds of mist while gulls circled overhead. The characteristic London reek – which had filled the lad's nostrils for so long he had become unaware of it – had abated.

How can we conceive of this scene in the time of Dave? the Lawyer mused. Why, in contradiction of the Knowledge itself, we see that these roads out of London are not straight but winding up and over steep hills and down into deep defiles. And where is the great mass of brick and crete that the Book describes? How can it be that here in London itself it has gone so entirely, while in so many other places in the kingdom there are the remains of many ancient gaffs? The Drivers charged with the Book's interpretation cite the MadeinChina – yet they swaddle themselves in ambiguities when it comes to the question of whether this deluge preceded or followed the Age of Dave.

The Lawyer of Blunt would have continued with these flying speculations were it not that the limmo had now gained a spur of burbland and was jolting along a flagged highway towards Beech House itself. As they drew closer, Carl saw a high façade topped with a triangular pediment, twelve-paned windows, irony fencing and two staircases curving up to a grand door on the first storey. Crowds were milling on the beaten earth in front of the dävine semi: Drivers and Inspectors, mendicant stalkers, pilgrims who had struggled on foot up from the city below, and even a handful of outrageous mushers who flapped about in the hevver crying out broken orisons to the Lost Boy. At the very eye of this hurly-burly stood a row of wooden booths, and as the Taffy reined in the jeejees, leaped down and the travellers stepped out, Carl saw that these were tenanted by still more Drivers and that the pilgrims who mobbed them – lawds, luvvies, commoners, even a few chavs – were all sore afflicted.

One after another they presented themselves to the Drivers in the booths, placing before their mirrors a crippled leg, a scrofulous neck, an arm purulent with the discharge of a carbuncle. The Driver called over a run and a few points, sprinkled the diseased or damaged member with a few drops of dävine evian, palmed the supplicant the tinfoil badge, then held out his hand for some dosh. Eyeing the scene critically the Lawyer of Blunt muttered: Such peculation defiles our faith more than any grander exactions of the PCO or even the King. Then, as they worked their way towards Beech House, he wisely remained silent, save for saluting the indulgence sellers: Where to, guv? Where to, guv? Where to . . .

While the common pilgrims had to queue to enter the shrine, the Lawyer and his companions were ushered straight in by an obsequious fony. Beech House was bare and unprepossessing, the chambers stark and without any adornment. In the harsh foglight that streamed through the uncurtained windows, every scuff that tens of thousands of trainers had left on the boards could be seen. At the centre of each room was an eerie tableau of life-sized figures. One showed Dave in his cab; a second, Dave, Chelle and the Lost Boy at the Breakup; a third, Dave burying the Book. The effigies were wax and obviously of considerable antiquity, for they were clad in worn and tatty garments, and their features disfigured by the heat of summer and the chill of kipper. In one of the tableaux the Lost Boy's nose was missing, and the effigy of Chelle had been so assailed with stones and brickbats that one leg had come away from the body and dangled in its sagging hose.

Initially the fony, like his Bedlam counterpart, was disposed to offer a commentary; however, the Lawyer of Blunt soon disabused him of this requirement, and so it was in silence that they at last descended to the inner sanctum of the shrine, down a corkscrewing staircase that bore into the very earth. The fony sparked a letric and by its faint wattage they saw weeping brickwork and the white tendrils of deep, questing roots. The fony could not forbear from affecting a tone of great reverence and informing them that:

– Viss, yer reervús, iz ware íall Bgan 2 fouzand yeers ago, wen Dave berried ve Búk. Eer í lay til ve Kings great-great-granddad – but an umble woolly bloke on ve burbz – duggí up.

Carl looked and all he saw was a yok-flagged pit. It had no resonance, no atmosphere of sanctity. Its revelation was only in its emptiness – a void on to which any idea or belief might be superimposed.

When they were once more without, the Lawyer took the opportunity to point out to his young companion the biggest points of the distant city: the NatWest Tower, the Lloyd's Building; No. 1 Canada Square; the Gherkin and the vast complex of the PCO itself – the dreaded Tower. It squatted by the river, its high walls forming a rough rectangle with a sentinel tower at each corner. In the centre rose the white keep, and from its roof flew the banner of the PCO. Even from twenty clicks away the Tower emanated overbearing power, its flint walls glinting with embedded broken glass and coils of razor wire. Carl looked up to the screen, hoping to see a harbinger of the dävine, but there was only a single gull, its wings flexing in the airy currents, swinging back and forth as if it were suspended from a wire.

They drove back to London in contemplative silence, and the Lawyer of Blunt let them out at Marble Arch; for while he had to go about the town canvassing signatures for Böm's brief and arranging for its deposition at the Lawd Chancellor's Department, it was decided that the other two would take a turn in the Royal hunting park. Dave f-forfend, the Lawyer stammered, b-but should our plans go awry you may soon find yourselves in close confinement.

As the Taffy cabbie whipped up the jeejees and the limmo pulled away in the direction of Selfridges, Böm realized they had made a bad mistake. The noise in the square was loud and mounting, while from the Edgware Road came the sound of chanting. He looked up and saw that the roofs of the buildings were thronged with seeseeteevee men. The chanting grew closer. It was the same horde who had been terrorizing the mummies and opares in Westminster the day before, and now there were far more of them – perhaps as many as two or three hundred dads. As before, they were tightly packed and marching at a run. Their uniform black T-shirts, their high-topped white trainers, their gnashing teeth – it all gave them the aspect of a many-legged, many-headed beast intent on some monstrous and predatory act.

They were preceded by twenty or so mounted Drivers and a platoon of chaps with shooters at the ready. As they came into the square some fanned out to stop the traffic, while another posse escorted a sweatbox towards the Arch itself. O my Dave! Antonë exclaimed. It's an execution, we don't want to get mixed up in this. It was, however, too late for them to escape, for along with the dads and Drivers came the London mob in all its perversity: lawds, bondsmen, tradesdads and chavs. Carl saw the most gussied-up dandies cavorting alongside the filthiest slubberdegullions. From the Queers' Quarter came blokes who looked like Antonë, plump, digit beards, soft hands in their belts. There were opares and mummies mixed up in the ruck, with the ubiquitous urchins darting here and there, snatching at cockpieces, cutting at purses. A great proportion of the crowd were mullered, for the landlawds of the city's numerous boozers, not content with plying their wares to the mob as it processed from the Tower to Marble Arch, had seen fit to join it. There were many little vans bumping along with barrels resting on them from which chasers could be bought for a penny. The stench of jack was overpowering.

Fukk ve SeeEssA! Fukk ve SeeEssA! the angry dads chanted. Some held aloft effigies of mummies lashed to long poles. The cloakyfings of these dummies bulged in a peculiar and obscene fashion as they were thrust up and down. The mob propelled all before them – and Carl and Antonë found themselves in the front row of the spectators, who, trapped between ranks of dads and Drivers, ranged about the arch. The sweatbox had been drawn up to the pale-pink cliff, and a pair of warders roughly extricated a mummy from the inside. She screamed and tried to claw her way back in to where three children could be seen, weeping and beseeching. The warders were having none of this and dragged her up a ramp on to the top of the arch, then over to where a barbecue was erected amid a pile of faggots.

Fukk ve SeeEssA! Fukk ve SeeEssA! The dads sank the poles bearing the effigies in the dusty ground and linked arms. Two hefty chavs in the livery of the PCO stepped forward into the square. One bore an immense drum on his back, which the other beat upon. The defeaning reports of the drum reverberated from the crete frontage of the Odeon, and the crowd began to fall silent, save for a few urchins who were climbing about on the scaffold.

A Driver stepped forward, while behind him a fony unrolled an A4, and once he had it in his mirror the Driver began to read in a deep, stentorian voice that was clearly audible to the whole assembly:

– That you, Sharún Lees, on three separate occasions, did wilfully retain your three kiddies and keep them concealed from their lawful dad; for this heinous malefaction, a profaning of the Book and the Wheel and of Dave Himself, you have been sentenced in the Children and Families Advisory and Support Services Forecourt to be burned and the noxious exhaust of your chellish body piped into your kiddies. Let it be marked, no Changeover –

– No lyf! the crowd bayed.

– No Breakup.

– No Nolidj!

– No Knowledge.

– No Nú Lundun! No Nú Lundun! No Nú Lundun!

Mercifully, the mummy had fainted dead away as the sentence was read. In the sweatbox the kiddies threw themselves against the bars. Another driver stepped forward and began to pour glistening moto oil over the mummy, the barbecue and the faggots. A third came afterwards with a lighter. There was a moment's stillness – then 'Fumf!' The mummy was a writhing, pulsing, fat-spitting firework. Fonies pushed forward a funnel-shaped contrivance attached to a bellows and positioned it so as to suck up the noxious exhaust. It was conducted through a pipe and into the sweatbox, the irony shutters of which were slammed against the whey faces of the children and bolted by attendant Drivers.

'Fumf! Fumf! Fumf!' All through the crowd the dads had set their sinister effigies alight. The cloakyfings went up in a flash, revealing that beneath them were bundles of live cats, tied by their necks to the poles. Their fur fizzed and flashed; they yowled in torment. The dads began their chanting once more: Fukk ve SeeEssA! Fukk ve SeeEssA! Fukk ve SeeEssA! Fukk ve SeeEssA! Carl could not conceive of a more horrific scene, as the pall of meaty smoke rose up over the square in poisonous billows, and the mob eddied and moaned with evil exaltation. A thick musk of excitation emanated from the close-packed bodies around him. The mummy was still writhing – although tongues of white flame were shooting from her eye sockets and mouth. Carl shut his own eyes and resolved not to open them until they could escape this hell on earth.

Then he involuntarily opened them – because he'd received a sharp dig in the nape of his neck. Hanging in his visual field was another pair of eyes – bloodshot, indifferent, very fatigued and framed by the mirror that was dangling right in front of his face. Carl turned to his companion. Antonë also had a mirror positioned before his face and behind him stood a Driver with a drawn blade. The crowd had fallen back on all sides, and a third Driver bearing a badge that showed the Wheel superimposed on the Tower stepped up and unfurled an A4. He began reading in a bored voice:

– Carl Dévúsh and Antonë Böm, I arrest you both in the name of the PCO on charges of bilking, flying and treason. You will accompany us to the Tower.

The crowd, its anarchic hysteria instantly transformed into fearful conformity, drew back to allow a wide gangway, and down this Carl and Antonë were hustled in the direction of Park Lane.

# 14

# *Getting Out from Behind the Wheel*

February 2003

In the sparkling-wine light police tape festooned the traffic lights and the crash barriers – the bunting of a criminally enormous party. A police car, its blue light revolving, siren squawking suppressed whoops, shepherded people along the roadway like a game little terrier. A volute of cloud twisted across the sky, and the cold bit into Dave's neck. He saw the already discarded placards that littered the verge and the scores, then hundreds of demonstrators. Individually they were aimless, yet the whole throng moved with collective determination over the churned-up sand of Rotten Row and towards Speakers' Corner.

Phyllis looked as eccentric as ever, wrapped up in a woollen coat sewn from crocheted panels of scarlet, green and yellow. Her mad curls escaped from beneath the ear flaps of a Laplander's hat, her dolly hands were tucked into matching mittens. She took his cold hand in her woolly pad and squeezed it. 'The turn-out,' she said excitedly, 'it's huge. I knew – but I never thought – so many people.' Dave saw gloomy old pranksters in harlequin tights, Socialist Worker clones in donkey jackets and Doc Martens, laughing crocodiles of British Asian girls down from their northern redoubts, their Muslim Association of Great Britain placards held at jaunty angles. Between these factions, stolidly tramping, in their pastel anoraks and buff fleeces, was a great mass of ordinary punters, who, even to Dave's jaundiced eye, seemed secure in the knowledge that by their *sheer weight of numbers* they could prevent the bombers from taking off and Stop the War!

Through a scraggy barrier of trees and over the balding grass – with every yard they gained the compression of bodies grew greater. 'Palace-stein! Palace-stein! Palace-stein!' *I'm not racial*, Dave admonished himself – yet their fanaticism smelled alien, a dangerous spice, saffron and suicide. A head taller than the crowd, he was borne forward on an undulating carpet of scalps, entire acres of hair combed over by the teeth of the breeze. Up ahead the scene was Babylonian: flags and banners waved, obelisks of speakers loomed on a stage, only the yowl of feedback stopped the subsidence of this era into the last.

All masses – no matter how pacific – contain within their sumps many thousands of litres of adrenalin the motor oil of rage. Dave Rudman felt this potential conflagration slopping about them as he and Phyl were driven forward to the steady, four-stroke beat of a massive Lembeg drum. Then they were trapped against a barrier fence. Through its wide mesh police snappers in blue-checked baseball caps probed their telephoto lenses. A line of stewards sporting fluorescent tabards bearing the legend IN THE NAME OF ALLAH, THE MOST COMPASSIONATE, THE MOST MERCIFUL struggled to keep back the demonstrators, who barked, 'Who let the dogs out?!' before yelping their own reply, 'Bush! Bush!'

Dave felt himself detaching, lifting up into the now lustreless sky where surveillance helicopters chattered and swooped. He felt for Phyllis's mitten – a soft anchor – to ground him, but it was gone. She was gone. He began frantically scanning thousands of faces. *Izzat'er? Izzat? Izzat?* The rant started inside his pock-marked face. *Fucking lefties . . . dumb cunts . . . middle-class tossers . . .* 'Who let the dogs out?! Bush! Bush!' *They don't even know where they fucking are . . . Pakkies down from Bradford . . . The fucking stewards couldn't find their way to Tottenham Court Road . . .* He began shouldering his way back through the whippy limbs of this human scrub, still looking for Phyl but understanding that it was pointless. When he reached a clearing where three whey-faced kiddies were drinking cans of

Mecca-Cola in a shieling of milk crates, he had a moment of clarity. They weren't having sex yet, *but we're like a married couple* . . . at ease in ways both profoundly irritating and comforting; *we aren't having sex*, although he couldn't have said which of them was resisting the slide into that damp pit of guttural obfuscation; *we aren't having sex* – nevertheless he'd agreed to come along on this idiotic march because . . . *I love her.*

~

The air was crinkled up like cellophane by the exhaust fumes. It stank; he stank. He felt the ingrained lubricant of a thousand thousand fill-ups slide between his fingertips and the shaky rim of the wheel. His past was a mirage, glimpsed across the stained forecourt of time. Through the miserable slot of the Fairway's windscreen he could see the glistening skin of the Swiss Re Building, as like some monstrous penis it self-erected over the City. It already had a nickname – the Gherkin – but a proper cockney wouldn't ask for a gherkin and chips, *he'd say wally . . . gissa wally.*

As the cockney wally rose up, it dumbly forced new parallaxes on the earthbound toilers. Dave Rudman had never felt so imprisoned in the wobble boards of the cab's bodywork, so coiled in razor wire, so commanded to KEEP LEFT, GIVE WAY and STOP. The CCTV cameras angled across the box junctions; the traffic wardens like urban Watusi with hand-held computers for spears; the cops in their cars; the PCO in their concrete bunker – every square foot of London was accounted for, taxed and levied. He looked about him at the other cars in the jam. The drivers sat, mobile-phone hands clamped to their aching heads, suffering the neuralgia of ceaseless communication. The radio on the Fairway's dash muttered on: 'Lorry shed its load on the A3 Kingston Bypass . . . stop-start traffic there . . . Lane out on the Marylebone Flyover . . .' Dave had become a cabbie to miss out on the supervisory eyes that made adult working life another fidgety classroom, yet here he was '. . . coming into junctions fifteen and sixteen on the Emtwenny5, that's the Emfaw and the Emfawty, lane and speed restrictions are in force . . .' with the worst guvnor of all – insecurity. Insecurity and the Flying Eye, its rotary eyelid blinking overhead.

Dave pulled into a side street and turned off the ignition. He got out his pills and began to pop the antidepressants out of their plastic blisters. He didn't stop until the gulches of his jeans were choked with little white boulders. Then he opened the door, picked up his change bag, got out and chinked away, scattering dumb Smarties as he went. He didn't look to see if he was parked on a yellow line; he didn't even bother to lock the cab. He didn't care. It was over – he'd grabbed the fat moment. He was free.

As he walked, Dave Rudman looked not up to the sky, nor around him at the brutal buildings, but at the ground, at the tarmac upon which his life had been rolled out. Tarmac blue-black and asphalt dimpled; tarmac folded and humped like a grey-brown blanket; tarmac cratered, bashed and gashed. This was the petrified skin he'd been feeling all his prostituted life, its texture transmitted through rubber tread and steel shock-absorber. Dave felt a compulsion to kneel down on the kerb and bow his head into the gutter – to lick the abrasive surface with his rough old tongue.

Dave licked between Phyllis's shoulder blades and drove his tongue down her grooved back. She shuddered and, grabbing his thigh, pulled it up and over her own so that he half straddled her. In the confusion of their bodies – his hairy shanks, her sweaty thighs, his bow-taut cock, her engorged basketry of cowl and lip – there was clear intent; so that when he penetrated her, they moved into and out of one another with fluid ease, revving and squealing, before arriving quite suddenly.

Dave and Phyl were having sex in her cottage outside Chipping Ongar. They'd had sex the previous evening after a healthy meal of cauliflower cheese. They had woken twice – perhaps three times – in the night to do it again, and now, with the larks crying over the fields outside, they were having sex once more. There was no billing or cooing between them – mouth chanced upon mouth infrequently. She pulled him into her spasmodically, her heels jamming on his hips. He felt the solidity of her – she wasn't blubbery but taut with fat. He plunged and rebounded. No words were spoken – yet neither doubted that they were making love, plenty of honeyed love to be stored for the future in their cells, should there come another time of scarcity when they needed replenishing.

In the late morning Dave walked into the little town to get the Sunday papers. Even in brisk March, with branches still bare, and rain showers moving across the Essex landscape like shading on a drawing, the gathering heat of summer was resounding through the land. He paused by the ancient moat of the long-since-levelled castle and lost himself in the subsurface bloom of duckweed. This would be a special day – they would not fret or worry. Towards evening they might walk across the fields to Good Easter, watching the returning flocks of swifts clench, then relax in the umber sky. The letters had been sent, the calls had been made, the reports had been written. At Phyllis's instigation Dave had taken matters into his own hands. Lawyers – they both agreed – would only sop up money and make things worse, like they always did. Better to make as direct an approach as possible and state – with clarity and humility – that if Carl was at all willing, and his mother would permit it, Dave would like to resume seeing his son.

Dave ranked up by the cop shop on Old Burlington Street and walked down towards the offices of Undercroft Mendel. Since coming off the antidepressants he still felt the elbow-jabs of reckless thoughts – but mostly he felt better. Much better. Even so, he couldn't judge whether his damp palms were a withdrawal symptom or a dread anticipation. The newspaper rattle of pigeons taking flight startled him – and he mounted the steps feeling dizzy, fists clenched in the pockets of his old tweed jacket.

There were no sugar-dusted shortbreads or gold-rimmed coffee cups. There was no propelling pencil or unctuous manner. Instead of tipping back in his chair, Mitchell Blair leaned forward, doodling nervily on a yellow legal pad in unadorned biro. 'The thing is, Mr Rudman . . . at the end of the day' – he picked out demotic phrases from a mental file he maintained for such occasions – 'it isn't down to the Lord Justice, CAFCASS or even the courts' – he glanced towards the reassuringly open door – 'whether or not you resume contact with, er, Carl.'

'With my son, you mean.' Despite the rehearsals he'd been through with Phyl and every internal restraint he'd imposed upon himself, Dave was already warming up.

'Well, that's precisely the issue.' At this, Blair, losing all professional detachment, ducked down behind a barricade of heavy volumes. 'Ms Brodie has raised the matter of Carl's paternity. To be blunt, she doesn't believe that you are his biological father.'

Dave shook his head slowly – a great lummox pole-axed by a low blow. He felt uncomprehending and untidy. He groped automatically for a cigarette, although, even while so doing, he was appalled to hear his voice going on without him: 'Whaddya mean?'

'I mean – that is to say, I can state with some certainty' – Blair was recovering his sang froid, his fiddly features reappeared from behind the leather shield – 'that it has been established that Carl's biological father is, in fact, Mr Devenish.'

'Cal Devenish?' Dave kept on shaking his head. 'But that's impossible – how? When?'

'Mr Rudman.' Blair was now fully composed. He lay back in his chair, the sole of his loafer cleaner than Dave's shirt. The gold propelling pencil was out, the toothy timpani began. 'Ms Brodie had no intent to deceive you – both she and Mr Devenish understood that he was . . . well, he had had a vasectomy. However, these, ah, things can happen. Very rarely – but they do happen. Your ex-wife thought you would be upset, she understands that she owes you a full explanation. Were it not for your er' – he paused, smiling faintly – 'behaviour in the past, she would've been present for this meeting. Instead, she has given me this letter for you' – he placed it on his blotter – 'and should you – quite reasonably – require verification, your own nominated doctor can take both your blood and the boy's. Arrangements can be made for these DNA samples to be independently tested . . .'

By the time Blair had completed his speech, Dave was already on the stairs. He hadn't bothered with Michelle's letter. The phrase that stayed with him – albeit edited – was *take . . . your . . . blood*, for his very blood had been taken from him. Or had it? Checking himself in every reflective surface he passed – brass plates, plate glass, wing mirrors – Dave was forced to concede that this hereditary cap didn't fit at all well. *You suspected all along . . . The dates never made sense . . . never added up . . . She got funnier about it the older he got . . . And Carl, well, he . . . he just doesn't LOOK ANYTHING LIKE YOU.*

~

The fare, chunk of silicone chips soldered to his ear, was going to check out David Blaine. The American illusionist was sealed into a perspex box, which had been dangled from the arm of a crane on the south side of Tower Bridge. The new London Assembly had appeared near by – beamed down from the future so suddenly that its concrete and glass walls bellied with the impact – and all that was left of the park that used to occupy the site was a patch of exposed dirt. Every day a crowd gathered here to bay, catcall, take photos, catapult hamburgers, hold up babies, flash their tits and bums, frolic, gass, guffaw – and generally confirm the truth that, as Blaine's beard grew and his fat evaporated, nothing ever changed in this city: the most grotesque of street theatre always had – and always would – take place within the very shadow of governance.

The Fairway was snarled up in Tooley Street. In front was a white Securicor van with plexiglas windows. *Sweatboxes, that's what they call 'em.* Some crim who used to drink in the Old Globe told Dave all about them – the tiny, individual cells in the bouncing vehicle, no room for the prisoners to stretch their legs, no hand-holds, everything made of plastic. In winter they were like . . . *fucking fridges* . . . but in summer the cons slopped in their own sweat. Still, wasn't the whole of London *an endless bloody sweatbox? Nuffing to hold on to, everyone going somewhere to do nuffing*. The cab limped past the London Dungeon, where a dummy felon hung from a *fucking toyist gibbet*. The fare had run out of friends to call . . . *no wonder* . . . and was scratching his balls.

Tiring of this tax on disorientation, Dave saw a parking place and plonked the cab in it. 'Wossup, mate?' said the fare, who was young with a vulnerable dimple in his chin. 'I'll stroll down there with you,' Dave explained. 'I fancy a gander at this chancer.' They clambered out, and Dave locked up. He asked for a fiver, even though there was twice that on the meter. As they walked along past Hay's Galleria towards HMS *Belfast* Dave wanted to put an arm around the lad's shoulders, because he was another one *young enough to be my son*. But not.

It was a weekday, and the crowd wasn't that big. There were *dossers struck by White Lightning . . . language-school Lolitas* . . . and because it was lunchtime *the Prêt-a-fucking-Manger mob* were ranged along the parapet of Tower Bridge, swigging mineral water and chomping baguettes. In an enclosure immediately beneath Blaine's box snappers and camera crews oscillated to find the best angle. All eyes were raised towards the modern Diogenes, who slumped in a starved torpor, a silvery space blanket serving him for a robe. Everyone bayed for his attention, while he looked deep inside himself, focusing with steely resolve on *major fucking sponsorship deals*.

Dave had lost the ex-fare and was sitting on a bench when he became aware of a wholesale perturbation in the crowd. Eyes were swivelling away from the hunger artist towards the top of the northern tower of the bridge, where an oddly attired group was clambering out on to the parapet. Dave was up on his feet – even at this distance, and outlined against deceptive bends and furbelows of cloud, he could see that the three men were wearing historical costumes: cockade hats, cloaks and doublets. One of them was a dumpy fellow struggling with the end of a long, sausage-shaped bundle. 'Bluddy el!' exclaimed a dosser who was beside Dave. 'Iss isstree cum ter lyf!' The crowd, grasping that something – or somebody – was going to be pitched over the edge, 'ooed' and 'aahed' with sadistic glee. The London Show – in its two thousandth year at the same venue – was hotting up.

The camera crews were wrenching their tripods round to capture the action. From Wapping came the demented whippoorwill of a police siren. A couple of white-hatted Port of London Authority beadles could be seen trying to break into the bottom door of the tower, a police helicopter came chattering upriver, and it occurred to Dave that this could be *the big one, code black* . . . the bundle might be *a fucking missile launcher*. For Tower Bridge was a prime position for an attack by suicidal terrorists on the computerized dealing rooms and electronic vaults of the City.

There was a man close to Dave in the crowd who had a pair of binoculars. 'Please, mate?' Dave requested, then he crammed them to his eyes just as the three players on the roof of the tower heaved their bundle over. A long banner unrolled with a loud 'Thwack!' Dave Rudman absorbed the legend on it at the same time as he recognized the clownish lips and curly hair of the tubby man sporting the red cloak. It was Gary Finch, and he was giving the finger to the circling helicopter. The banner read: WE AREN'T HISTORICAL FIGURES – WE'RE FIGHTING FATHERS, FIGHTING TO SEE THE KIDS WE LOVE. There was the clenched-fist logo, which Dave had last seen in the Trophy Room at the Swiss Cottage Sports Centre.

The Fighting Fathers managed to stay up on Tower Bridge for a long time. When the police stormed the tower, Fucker and one of the others got out along the top cantilever and chained themselves to it. Their companion was arrested immediately – but this was probably intentional, for Barry Higginbottom had taken it upon himself to be the spokesman for Fighting Fathers, and it was he who appeared on the rolling news bulletins for the rest of the day.

Watching him on TV that evening at Agincourt Road, Dave had to concede that the Skip Tracer did a good job. He was interviewed in a well-appointed playroom, against a background of Disney film posters, with colouring books and cuddly toys strewn beneath the rockers of his chair. The Skip Tracer spoke lucidly concerning the inequalities of family law: the presumption that separated and divorced mothers should have care and control of children; the financial burdens placed on separated fathers; the difficulties these fathers had in getting their former partners to comply with court access orders. The Skip Tracer's usual machine-gun delivery was slowed to an emphatic beat, his vowels flew up to buttress his rediscovered consonants. There were no obscenities, no talk of nosebag and the sweat-lash was little more than an earnest sheen.

However, the Skip Tracer's front was then demolished as his schoolboyish fringe and exposed nostrils were supplanted by exterior shots of his detached villa in Redbridge. This – the viewers were told – was equipped with a state-of-the-art security system, comprising CCTV cameras, razor wire and motion-triggered alarms. Quite why such a sensitive, loving man should be so paranoid was then explained by an appropriately nervy reporter on the scene: 'His considerable fortune was amassed during the property crash of the early 1990s, when his agency – employing scores of operatives – tracked down desperate mortgage defaulters . . .'

The irony of such a large house being paid for by the loss of so many other smaller ones was not dwelled on – for there were still more queries, dangling like his own, blond forelock over the Skip Tracer's head. His ex-wife was interviewed and her testimony was damning as to the Skip Tracer's shady financial dealings and his flirtation with the extreme right wing. The former Mrs Higginbottom stopped short of the nosebag, although she did suggest that 'Barry has . . . issues he'd rather not look at. Issues of dependency.' Nevertheless, despite his fickleness when it came to the practicalities of childcare, she supported his right to see their daughter, while maintaining that 'his . . . behaviour in the past means I don't have a lot of confidence . . . in his motives'.

'Why'd she marry the bloke, then?' Phyllis observed tartly. She was sitting in the humpbacked armchair that had become 'hers' and sewing a name tape into a pair of Steve's boxers. Dave grunted – and Phyllis gave him a sharp look. 'You know him, don't you? It isn't only your mate Gary who's mixed up in this, is it?' Dave conceded that he had met Higginbottom at a Fathers First meeting, while neglecting to mention that he'd also consulted him in a professional capacity – let alone that he still owed him.

Dave had finally made his mind up – he was finished. It was over. There had been one or two false starts – the Fairway left by the road temporarily abandoned – but he'd always crawled back. He'd argued his way round the two police cautions on his record when his badge was up for renewal, and he hadn't declared his medical record – so he held on to the job quite as doggedly as it hung on to him. The cab grasped him in its steel fist – and beyond that extended the muscle-bound arm of his Knowledge, its tendons flexing through the city streets. What would he be if he walked away from it for ever? *At my age, with no other training . . . no qualifications.* He saw himself in mid morning on a quiet residential pavement, *a poor, bald fucker delivering leaflets for an Indian takeaway at one-fifty an hour* . . . The squeal of a gate in need of oiling resolved itself into the squeal of brakes, and Dave found himself turning into the Roman Road. *I'm doing it . . . I'm fucking doing it.*

In the lumpy lane beside Ali Baba's garage he found a handful of cabbies waiting their turn to pick up or drop off vehicles. Getting out to join them, Dave, for the first time in years, examined the Fairway, comparing it with the newer TXs parked either side. The *poor old wagon*, with its chrome trim and narrow waist, looked *out of date, like an old Hansom or something.* A foxy-faced fellow whom Dave vaguely recognized came towards him waving a copy of the *Sun* in one hand and a kebab in the other. 'Orlright, Tufty,' he said. 'This is your mate, innit?' He showed Dave the open spread: on one side, with greasy fingerprints on her roasted thighs, was 'Naughty-gal Nikki from Norwich', while on the other there was a grainy black-and-white photo of Gary Finch dressed as Henry VIII. 'Thass Fucker, innit?' reiterated the foxy man, and Dave owned that it was. 'What's 'e doing up there, then?' More finger marks smudged the balustrade Fucker was poised on. 'Thass the Royal Courts, ain't it?' put in a second cabbie who had a fleshy nose clefted like *an arse*.

'It's a protest,' Dave said wearily. 'They dress up as historical figures to protest about fathers' rights.'

'But Enery ve Aytf! 'E didn't eggzackerly myndaht fer iz kids, did 'e!'

'I think the point is' – Dave had reverted to type, speaking his mother's hard-won, didactic English – 'that Henry desperately wanted a son – that he was prepared to go to any lengths to get one. Look at the other blokes with him, they're all dressed as other famous men. He's Prince Albert, that one's Churchill. I think the sort of dads these men were is . . . well, besides the point. They put on these costumes when they climb up on public buildings, cranes, anywhere high up that'll get them attention, and it works, doesn't it?'

'I fink they're two stops short of Dagenham, mate,' said the foxy-faced cabbie, and his mate cackled. 'Yeah, fucking barking!'

Dave had little inclination to defend Fucker – anyway, he was saved by the diddle and doo of his phone. It was Dr Bernal at Heath Hospital. 'The test results are through,' she said without preamble – they both knew what she was talking about. 'Would you like to come up here to discuss them with me?'

'No, that's alright, thanks for sorting it out, Dr Bernal – but you can give it to me straight, I'm ready.'

She sighed. 'Well, they confirm what your ex-wife and her, um, partner have been saying. Dave – Carl . . . he isn't your son – not biologically, that is – he's . . . he's Devenish's.'

Dave removed the phone from his ear and stared at it. It lay in his big, damp palm like an artificial pearl. The teeny voice of Jane Bernal cried to him, 'Dave – Dave? Are you alright?'

He put it to his ear again. 'Yeah, yeah, I'm fine – to be honest I was expecting this. Listen, I can't talk now, I'm tied up, I'll call you later.' He squeezed the phoney spot.

Ali Baba himself was long gone – back to Famagusta to play out his days on a plastic card table, downing shots of raki and gambling away his London wad. Ali's eldest son, Mohammed, had taken over the business. He was a mercurial figure, phases of *'roids, slappers and raves*, interspersed with regular attendance at the Finsbury Park Mosque, and a grim-faced determination to bring about a worldwide uprising of the *umma*. For the last year or so he seemed to have quietened down: he'd dropped the -hammed, and it was plain Mo who stepped forward to meet Dave, scrunging Swarfega between his oily knuckles. Behind him, in the stygian interior of the arch, Kemal's wrinkled lower half hung from the chassis of a brand new TX2. A radio warped R & B round the brick cavern.

With age and responsibility Mo was starting to resemble his old man: he had the same iron-filing hair and waddling gait. 'Wossup, Tufty?' he asked. 'You can't be wantin' anuvver service, you 'ad the wagon in 'ere a couple uv mumfs ago, an' even ven there woz only a few 'undred more on the clock than wot there woz the time before.'

'No.' Dave spoke in his new plain and considered fashion. 'I want to sell the cab.' He held out the keys. 'I'll take what you can give me if you want it for the fleet' – Mo's eyes widened – 'or, if you can find a private buyer, you can take whatever percentage you like.' He dropped the keys into Mo's sticky green palm and without waiting for an answer turned on his heel. From beneath the TX2 there came a resounding chuckle – but Mo called after him, 'I'm not surprised, Tufty – you needing the dosh an' that. To be honest there's been a couple of the chaps over this way looking for you. I didn't say nuffing, but they was Turks, Tufty. Turks, and they looked like the heavy mob.' Dave wasn't listening – he was gone, past the other cabbies, out the end of the alley and into the traffic on Vallance Road, which was coagulating into a scabrous rush hour.

He wandered aimlessly out of town, trudging up through Hackney and London Fields. At the junction of Mare Street and Dalston Lane a ragged company worked the stalled traffic: Romany women in full skirts patterned with tiny bits of mirror wielded squeegees, while their drugged babies lay by a gutted phone booth; a *Big Issue* seller, crying his wares, had the hollow cheeks and lank hair of a prophet – of his own doom; and, preposterously, there was also a fresh-faced chugger, who tried to get the charitable cases thronging the pavements to give their incapacity benefit away. Dave held it all – he knew it all, he moved on into Clapton.

It was a Friday, and the metal exodus was angry and fearful. Flabby arms let crumpled burger wrappers fall from the wound-down windows of cars; a miasma of exhaust fumes hung over the rooftops. The only fresh things Dave could see as he slapped from slab to slab were dog turds. He'd been walking for about an hour when it happened. He found himself by a duck pond that cratered a strip of park, its surface coated with algae as thick and green as emulsion. There were hulking nineteenth-century villas to one side, a primary school and an uglification of 1980s flats to the other. He hadn't been making any conscious effort to lose himself – the idea was ridiculous – and yet he had. He didn't know where he was.

A young woman came limping towards him. She wore a bright blue puffa jacket and her brown ringlets lay hopelessly on her pitted cheeks. She had the broken nails and scuffed trainers of poverty. 'Excuse me, love,' Dave began, 'but you wouldn't happen to know . . .' then he tailed off, because she was looking at him with eyes bruised by utter disorientation. Her dry lips parted and she said, 'Pliz? Pliz?' *She doesn't know where she is . . . She hasn't got a fucking clue . . . She looks like she's been brought here from Massy-fucking-donia smacked out in a van . . . Kept locked up in a gaff near here for months getting fucked stupid . . . Fucked up the cunt – fucked up the Gary . . . She don't know where she is – she don't even know what city she's in . . .* 'Don't worry, love,' he said, 'you don't worry.'

He left her and stumbled down through a new development: tall, narrow townhouses ranged round courtyards choked with cars. There was a kosher deli open and outside it Frummer kids were gathered licking ice lollies. As Dave limped by, they stared at him, their pale blue eyes, velvet skullcaps and corkscrew payess giving them the look of earnest spaniels. Next he found himself on a towpath beside a sluggish reach of brown water.

He was losing it – whole chunks of the city were falling out of him. Kenton and Kingsbury, Kingston and Knightsbridge. He didn't know the name of this canal, or any other, only that it was oozing south, so he turned in the opposite direction and walked north. North past the grassy ramparts of reservoirs guarded by palisades of Giant Hogweed, north, past the tumbledown shacks of shedonists, who'd pitched up on this toxic Limpopo in their bashed barges and cashiered dredgers. He skirted industrial estates where metal tortured itself and ducked under the echoic stages of elevated roadways. He traversed pancake-flat parks where adolescents mooched on mountain bikes, their thin faces lost in the shadows of their hoodies. They moved slowly, so very slowly, their feet only just maintaining purchase on the very outer edge of the pedals.

Towards evening Dave found himself mounting a hill. Up he went through saw-leafed patches of nettles and the whippy stalks of brambles, while Stanmore and Streatham dropped from the back of his hot head to lie gently steaming on the crushed grass behind. He was disembowelled – he was losing it; and as he lost it the crushed plastic bottle of his soul expanded with sudden cracks and pops.

At the crown of the hill the shrubbery gave way to cool shady groves of silver birch and alder. In the middle of a clearing there was a concrete trig' point. Dave turned back to see the city he had lost spreading to the far hills of the south in brick peak after tarmac trough, blood-orange under the dying sun. In the foreground tall towers stood up to the ochre sky, while to the southeast close-stacked blocks were already subsumed to an electric glare. In the mid distance a river streaked silver and beside it a mighty wheel revolved so slowly.

Dave knew none of it – his Knowledge was gone. The city was a nameless conurbation, its street and shop signs, its plaques and placards, plucked then torn away by a tsunami of meltwater that dashed up the estuary. He saw this as clearly as he'd ever seen anything in his life. The screen had been removed from his eyes, the mirror cast away, and he was privileged with a second sight into deep time. The great wave came on, thrusting before it a scurf of beakers, stirrers, spigots, tubes, toy soldiers, disposable razors, computer-disc cases, pill bottles, swizzle sticks, tongue depressors, hypodermic syringes, tin-can webbing, pallet tape, clips, clasps, brackets, plugs, bungs, stoppers, toothbrushes, dentures, Evian bottles, film canisters, widgets, detergent bottles, disposable lighters, poseable figurines of superheros, cutlery, hubcaps, knick-knacks, mountings, hair grips, combs, earphones, Tupperware containers, streetlight protectors – and a myriad other bits of moulded plastic, which minutes later washed up against the hills of Hampstead, Highgate, Harrow and Epping, forming salt-bleached reefs, which would remain there for centuries, the lunar pull of the new lagoon freeing spiny fragments to bob into the cockle-picking hands of *know-nothing carrot-crunchers* who would scrutinize them and be filled with great awe by the notion that anything ever had – or ever would be again – Made in China.

Dave turned and wandered away into the woodland, dipping down into damp hollows where midges swirled, then rising up over root-buttressed ridges overarched by the gnarled limbs of oaks that sawed at the thickening night.

When the ex-driver crossed over the M25 and walked down into Epping, darkness had fallen. White flashes from the exposed rails of the tube station imprinted after-images of the privet-lined paths he trudged along. A public-address system barked 'This is the Central Line service for all stations to West Ruislip', but it meant nothing to Dave. On he went, over humped fields of alien maize, up to another wood of smooth-barked beech where pipistrelles stroked his remaining hair. Some trees had been pollarded, and outlined against the bruised night sky they resembled the knobkerries of giants sunk in the beaten earth.

Coppices stirred, then rattled, as Dave mounted a footbridge over the M11. Out in the middle he stopped and peered down at the streaming traffic, car after van after lorry, their headlights drilling the murk. The windscreens were blank until they shot beneath the parapet, then, momentarily, the drivers' faces were revealed: jaws bunched, eyes white-rimmed with exhaustion. Dave understood now that they would always be pinioned in this moment, while he was free to swim in the entire current of fluvial time.

The moon rose over the coxcomb of a wood, and it looked like a headlight cratered with flyspecks. He reached Phyllis's cottage beyond Chipping Ongar after midnight. He was as ignorant as a baby, and accordingly she gathered him to her breast.

~

Dave Rudman met up with Anthony Bohm in the boardroom of the Chelsea and Westminster Hospital. It was a featureless white box, buried on a subterranean level. Steel-framed windows gave on to the bottom of an atrium, where stripy stones propped up *dildo cactuses*. Bohm sat, his goatee dowsing his regulation psychotherapist's Cornish-pasty shoes. Dave had walked from Sloane Square – Bohm had been tied up on Albert Bridge for hours. A Fighting Father was suspended from one of the cast-iron towers. 'Dressed as Thomas More,' Bohm laughed – an unendearing neigh. 'But why, when he was little more than a domestic tyrant?'

'Location,' Dave explained. 'His house – his statue on the Embankment.'

'Um, quite so – did you say you'd walked here?' Bohm was amazed.

'Yeah, it's all up with me, Tone – the cabbing, that is. I thought it meant, well, everything – it was who I was, but now –'

'I suppose you associate it with the loss – as you see it – of Carl?'

'That's about the size of it, mate. The Knowledge was what I had to pass on. I believed that even before I wrote that mad rant and buried it in their garden – now it seems like a load of bollocks, a load of fucking bollocks.'

As he grew agitated the consonants flaked away from the scalp of his diction: 'Ant, I gotta – I haffta, I gotta go back there. I gotta dig it up. S'pose 'e found it? It'd fuck wiv 'is 'ed. I mean – I know it ain't likely – but what if 'e did?' Bohm refused to be drawn. If Rudman was seeking permission for this peculiar escapade, he was not in the business of granting it. He took a different tack: 'You know one of them, don't you, the Fighting Fathers?'

'Yeah, Fucker – Gary Finch. Daft tosser – he's like a, a tool for them. 'E don't really get it – 'e does what they tell 'im to do. 'E's always the one up on the plinth, or the column or the building, with the Old Bill trying to talk him down.'

Bohm contemplated this – along with his shoe – for quite a while. Dave looked at the gilt-framed portraits on the wall; celebrated and self-important sawbones stared back at him. 'Am I right in thinking,' Bohm said eventually, 'that you see in Gary Finch's fate what might've happened – had things turned out differently – to you?'

~

There were misty haloes around the streetlights, and the parked cars were blistered with raindrops. The night was subdued save for the swish of the occasional vehicle plummeting down Heath Street and the divine booming of jets holding a pattern above London. The long, low villa next to Beech House was entirely dark; its round windows goggled through wisteria lashes at the figure that came padding along the pavement. Steel rods pierced the high garden wall, Acro props were strung with razor wire, a blue alarm light pulsed, a stylized child was obliterated by a black bar. DO NOT PLAY ON THIS SCAFFOLD the sign read. Dave Rudman decided to double back and work his way through the gardens.

It took him over an hour. Every time a cat sneezed or a fox yelped he froze for whole minutes. He was in full possession of his faculties while creeping like a madman through exotic plantations of gunnera and black bamboo, and imported bark chips that shifted under his rubber soles. A green nylon rucksack was slung over his shoulder, in it a mattock he'd bought the day before from an army-surplus shop on the Euston Road. He was going equipped – yet not sufficiently, and he realized what he would find before he hauled over the last wall. And there it was: the York paving, glinting in the diffused light, the non-renewable hardwood decking, solid enough for a man-o'-war. Under it – deep under it – was the Book. *How the fuck*, Dave thought. *How the fuck am I going to get it up?*

Cal Devenish stood at the French windows in the drawing room examining his own jet reflection for signs of guilt. *Not long now . . . Papers all signed – deal all done . . . Share price inflated – the bunce creamed off. Business flogged – the bunce skimmed off again . . .* yet he saw neither satisfaction nor shame in his face – only an intractable weariness, along with other things: a settle big enough for a cardinal to prop his fat behind on; a dormant log-effect gas fire; investment art on the silky wallpaper; and shoved up in the corners of the room the little beige boxes of the alarm system installed to protect it. Cal wondered where his son was; it made a change – he wryly conceded – to wondering where his daughter was.

Now that the truth was free to range the burgundy carpets of Beech House, its elegant chambers resounded with the cackling of a freak who's been told a sick joke. The sympathetic hatch opened between Cal and Carl on the night they sprang Daisy from the nick had been slammed resolutely shut. Carl took to wearing River Island jackets and Burberry baseball caps as nurture wiped the floor with nature. Cal even thought the lad physically resembled the dad who'd changed his nappies and blown his nose. A long streak of fifteen-year-old, his ears stuck out like Rudman's, and like Dave he took the high dive off Hampstead and into the London lagoon. Carl stayed away from Beech House and hung out on the estate down in Gospel Oak – for this Cal was guiltily grateful, because when his new son was in residence, Carl passed on those sly digs and underhand blows he himself had received, years before, from Dave.

Dave Rudman and Cal Devenish – two men sharing the same cab. Cal sat on one of the tip-down seats, and they caromed along the road of life separated by only a few centimetres of foam rubber, vinyl and steel. They were idiotic twins, conjoined in ignorance of each other. 'Snip-snip'. Cal had cut out his conscience as the surgeon snipped his vas deferens – while Dave Rudman forgot his dates. Yet their denials were but tributaries of a far mightier river of masculine unknowing.

Where was Carl? He was upstairs in his hated, modular study-bedroom. He knew his parents thought he was out – and he delighted in allowing their ignorance to shade into anxiety. Except he didn't think of Michelle and Cal as his parents – only 'that fucker' and 'that cunt', the words lubricated by hatred. Carl was upstairs with a Benson & Hedges stuck under his downy top lip and a rolled gold Dunhill lighter – purloined from Cal's desk – in his downy hand. He lit up while striking a defiant pose in front of the mirror, then swished back the curtains and eased up the sash window.

Caught in the searchlight, caught as if he were an escapee *from the nick*, one arm thrown across his eyes, the other brandishing an entrenching tool. Caught *bang to rights*. Dave looked up and saw a neotenous head and a cigarette falling towards him end over end. While Carl saw some *chav or fucking pikey* . . . a shambolic, middle-aged fatso . . . *trying to nick the fucking patio!* A pathetic thief who had his mouth wide open yet couldn't scream. In the red cave Carl saw the wet root of his tongue uselessly gargling. He didn't recognize the man – but he knew who he was. Carl cried out, 'Dad! Dad! There's a beastly man in the back garden!' Even as he taunted one man and conferred a title on the other, he thought, *Beastly – beastly? Where the fuck does that come from?*

They held Dave Rudman overnight at the police station on Rosslyn Hill. The cell he sat in was only a few hundred feet from Heath Hospital, but Dave was in no mood to ponder such narrative circularity, the centrifugal striving of the individual against the widening gyre of history. The magistrate, however, understood Dave and history, although, having his record laid out on the bench in front of her, she viewed it in a different light. While the non-molestation orders that had been imposed on Michelle Brodie's ex-husband may have lapsed, here was the original source material: the violence in the marriage, the breaching of previous orders, the assault in the restaurant, the psychiatric treatment. So it was only reasonable for the magistrate to assume that the victims of this *obvious thug* would be looking for a charge of criminal trespass, perhaps even – given that he had gone equipped with a mattock – *malicious damage and intent to wound?*

When Dave was eventually bailed, there was someone on hand with the same intent. 'What the fuck was that for?!' he exclaimed, rubbing his smarting cheek.

'What was it for?!' Phyllis screeched. 'What was it for? It was for being an irresponsible fucking wanker!' Her wiry curls sparked with anger as she prodded Dave down the wheelchair access ramp for the Highgate Magistrates Court. *What must we look like?* he thought. *Fat old boiler duffing up a bald old git of a drunk* . . . She confronted him on the pavement, her accent flattening into Essex as it did battle with the artics booming past within inches of them. 'Djew fink you ain't got no responsibilities any more – issatit? Izzit?' He shook his head. ''Cause if that's the way you feel you can piss off – and I mean it. There's Carl, there's Steve and there's . . . well,' she hesitated, 'well . . . there's me.'

'Carl?' He didn't mean to provoke her – he was genuinely incredulous. 'Carl? He doesn't even know who I am – I haven't seen him properly in years.'

Phyllis sighed, her exasperation was so profound – it was heavier than the hill they stood upon. Then she was calm again. She took a ball of tissues from the pocket of her denim skirt and screwed it into her eyes, one after the other. 'Let's go and get a cuppa,' she said, taking his arm, 'then you can tell me what the hell you thought you were up to. Somebody needs to do something about this whole balls-up, David, and that somebody isn't you.'

~

Fucker Finch was wearing a floor-length, dirty grey shift, and there were manacles on both his chubby wrists, from which dangled chinking lengths of chain. When Dave came into the empty bar, he was sitting at one of the round glass-topped tables, fiddling with a headache-pill dispenser shaped like a mobile phone. It was late morning, and the whole ground floor of the Charing Cross Hotel – half a French chateau hammered on to the façade of the station – reeked of furniture polish. Contract cleaners in nylon tabards were whipping the carpeting with the flexes of their vacuum cleaners.

'What's all this about?' Dave asked without any preamble.

'This?' Fucker held up the pill phone. 'Iss fer Nuro-whatsit, Nurofen.'

'No, not that, the cloakything.' He took a fold of Fucker's shift between his thumb and forefinger. 'Lovely bit of shmatte by the way.'

Fucker gave a mordant shrug. 'Iss burghers, today, we're men-nabee burghers today.'

'Burgers? Whaddya mean?'

'Burghers, Tufty, the Burghers of Calais, there's a statchew of 'em in that park by Parliament. Plan was fer us to dress up like 'em and chain ourselves to it.'

'Isn't that a bit low level for your mob? I mean, the Old Bill'll cut you off that in seconds.'

'Yeah, I know what you mean, mate' – Fucker necked a couple

of Nurofen with a swallow of lager – 'but we gotta take whatever opportunities present themselves – thass what Barry says. There's a debate in the Commons today what affects all us single dads, an' they'll 'ave every 'igh fing fer miles under surveillance. Me, I get a buzz ahtuv the 'igh ups. Far as I'm concerned – the 'igher the better. When I'm up there it's a big fucking buzz – better than sex, better than charley. I feel, y'know, alive.'

Dave consulted his watch. 'So when you heading over, then? It's gone eleven thirty.'

'Nah, y'don't geddit.' Fucker shook his rubber face. 'I'm surplus to requirements, I am. I pitches up wiv me robe an' manacles an' it only turns out they've got six other fucking burghers in hand already. So 'e mugs me off, don't he.'

'Y'know Fucker – Gary,' Dave spoke as softly and reasonably as he could, 'you want to be careful with that lot, Higginbottom in particular. It could all come on top – you know what he's like.'

Fucker snorted, 'Yeah, yeah, I know what 'e's bloody like. I tellya, Tufty, it's like poetry watching him do all that telly stuff – 'e's got more front than Brighton. I swear, I sometimes fink 'e's 'aving a bubble wiv 'em, 'cause 'e ain't like that wiv me, 'e's juss an ordinary geezer.'

'He's using you, Gary –'

'Oh, yeah? Well, maybe that's the way I want it, it's all up wiv me, Tufty, all I got left is this an' it's a matter of prints-supple – thass wot it is, a matter of prints-supple. Even if I never get to see the kids regular again, least I'll 'ave made me point.'

Dave tried another tack. 'What're you doing for money, then, Gary?'

'Gelt? I'm fucked, mate – I 'ad to let the begging box go. Weren't no point in 'anging on to it anyway – I bin nicked so many times this year they was bound to take me badge.'

'Did you sell it?' Dave asked, thinking of his own old Fairway underneath the arches off Vallance Road.

'Sell it!' Fucker guffawed. 'Nah, I didn't bloody well sell it, my old man was renting it for me on the half-flat, donchew remember? Fing is' – he leaned forward conspiratorially – 'I borrowed a couple of grand on it before I let it go, so now I've gotta give the old manor a bit of a wide.' Fucker swerved his manacles across the table.

From deep inside the station came the mammoth door chimes that precede an announcement; here, at the very epicentre of the Knowledge, a hefty realization was requesting admission. 'They're looking for you, Gary,' Dave confided, 'couple of Turks, heavy mob, they've been round at Ali Baba's – Mo thought they were after me, but it's you they want, innit?'

'I dunno, mate – don't fucking care neever. 'Ow they gonna find me anyway? I'm kipping in a fucking bail hostel over Vauxhall. Barry sees me right for a few quid, an' whenever I go out' – he gave his manacles a shake – 'I'm always in disguise!'

~

Michelle wondered if the woman standing on the doorstep of Beech House was wearing a disguise, because she had the oddest costume on. Whoever she was, she appeared to have carefully selected her clothes with the aim of maximizing what a dumpy figure she had. She wore a short white denim jacket and a long white denim skirt that fell to the ground in a series of distinct tiers, each defined by a tufted cotton ruff. The ensemble was completed by a white denim cloche hat, which crushed her abundant black curls down about her kabuki face, and a white denim shoulder bag as shapeless as a cloud.

Under the bulging blue eyes of this stocky apparition Michelle felt highly conscious of her own Tunturi-turned legs, sheathed in silk and knee-high suede; her own piquant face, made tasty with sweet creams and savoury exfoliants. She was about to lie 'Can

I help you?' when the funny little woman came straight to the point of everything. 'You must be Michelle.' Her voice was common yet clear and confident. 'I'm Phyllis Vance – Dave's girlfriend.' Michelle was deeply shocked. She had no idea that Phyllis, or any Phyllis-type person, existed. Social acuity had never been Michelle Brodie's thing: she had lived her adult life with her gaze at an upward angle; behind and below her lay Cath, Ron, Dave and what she now perceived as the inner-city slum of her marriage, cobbled alleys full of barefoot kids with rickets, fat boilers like Phyllis hanging out laundry to soil in the smutty air.

Phyllis was not remotely intimidated by Beech House or its mistress. She knew women like Michelle only too well – had she desired it, she might have gone that way herself. Every day in Choufleur she stuffed them full of macerated okra and aubergine. From her steamy kitchen she could hear their clipped tongues snipping at their lettuce as they commiserated with one another about their enslavement to Dr Atkins. The only mystery, so far as Phyllis was concerned, was what conceivable reason – save for sheer, mucky moral turpitude – Michelle could have had for being with Dave Rudman. They had the house to themselves – the sunlit drawing room jaggy with taupe swags and eau-de-Nil ruches. To Phyllis's surprise Michelle told her it all. When the penitent is ready the confessor appears, and Phyllis, in her denim surplice, with her unthreatening mass and risible make-up, made Michelle feel very safely superior. She began by conceding that: 'The letter I wrote to Dave, well, it wasn't . . . it wasn't about anything much but me really. I couldn't – I didn't . . .' Then 'snip-snip', she managed to cut away at the sack of lies and out spilled the seedy truth: she had been weak, she had been vain, she had been self-deceiving to begin with – but then a far greater deceiver. 'By the time I could admit to myself the truth that Carl wasn't Dave's at all, well . . .' The arms race was on, the hateful escalation of elbow-dig and low blow. Now Phyllis understood not only how far down her lover had been

– but the extent to which he'd raised himself up. 'He's changed, love,' she explained to Michelle, 'believe me, he has.'

They had a light, bitter lunch of cottage cheese and chicory leaves in the kitchen, and Michelle opened a bottle of Chablis. The view of the tilting garden with its heavy decking levered up incredible news. 'He wrote a book? I can't believe it.' Believe she must, for, as Phyllis explained, despite all the madness surrounding its composition, this was still a true expression of Dave's love for Carl – a love he still felt. 'That's what that idiot was doing in your garden,' said Phyllis, waving a bit of Ryvita. 'He thought he oughta dig it up, get rid of it. He's worried it's gonna be found. Not now – maybe not for ages, but when it is it'll screw Carl up. Apparently' – she shook her head in amazement – 'it's full of the craziest shit.'

By the time Phyllis left for her evening shift in Covent Garden they'd reached an understanding. 'I know this must be very hard for Dave,' Michelle said, 'but Carl still doesn't want to see him. To be – to be honest . . .' *And why the hell not?* . . . 'he doesn't want to see me or Cal either. He – he's got a lot of stuff to work through, and I don't think there's any way we can help him. I don't think he even thinks of any of us as . . . mummies or daddies.'

Cal Devenish got home in time to hear one end of a telephone conversation. On the other end was a Detective Sergeant based at Rosslyn Hill. 'No,' Michelle was saying with winey emphasis, 'no, we have no wish to press any charges at all – we want them dropped, all dropped.' Cal dropped his briefcase on the hall floor and walked towards his partner. 'No,' she went on, 'none of us is prepared to make witness statements, or appear in court should the CPS decide to prosecute. I don't think I'm making myself clear here – we want the charges dropped, he wasn't trying to steal anything, HE WAS TRYING TO GET IT BACK!'

~

It had taken ages for them to get over to Basildon from Chipping Ongar, the bus trundling from estate to village as they worked their way across the Essex badlands. Steve didn't seem to mind – but then he didn't seem to have a mind. He'd had another course of ECT in hospital. The shrink had said, 'It might jolt him back to life,' as if the depressed young man were one of Dr Frankenstein's faulty automata. Instead it had jolted him deeper into catatonia.

Now Phyllis's son sat keeled over on the rubber bench, the cotton dag tails of his frayed jeans sopping up the water on the floor. From without came the reverberating yelps of child bathers. 'C'mon,' Dave said, 'I'll help you into your trunks.' He'd chosen a family changing cubicle for this reason. He let down the wall-mounted nappy-changing table so he could lay Steve's clothes in its plastic depression. Steve wasn't entirely catatonic – he uttered sighs and coughed negatives – the bits of conversation that weren't words. Whatever position Dave placed him in he remained there. He was emaciated – his collarbone so pronounced it could have been grasped like a handle – and the presumptuous dreadlocks he'd sported at Heath Hospital were gone, leaving behind a nubby, scarred scalp.

Dave held and even stroked Steve's pitiful thighs, as he coaxed first one foot and then the other into zooty surfer's trunks. Then he led the ill young man through the footbath to the pool area and conducted him down into the chlorine broth. Outside the undulating windows that swam the length of the pool Dave could see a shopping arcade with ordinary life going on in it: pensioners pushed by wheeled baskets, seagulls scrapping over the yellowy rinds of white bread, a young mother struggling with the harness of a baby buggy. Steve fell forward into the migrainous waters, and Dave, panicking, lunged for him and held him up from beneath his belly. Steve's feet kicked out into Dave's nylon crotch, and the first words he'd spoken all morning blurted out: 'I'm swimming!' he spluttered, 'I'm swimming!' Dave Rudman began to cry and for the first time in a decade the tears weren't for himself.

~

It was a fortnight before Mo finally came back to Dave with an offer: five grand. Although it was almost half what Dave could have got if he had taken the trouble to arrange a private sale, he accepted. He wanted rid of it and he needed the money. Once the lawyer's bills had been paid off there was *fuck all* left from the sale of his flat. When Dave went down to Bethnal Green to pick up the money, there was the Fairway – a stupid, bulbous creature with a radiator grin. Its engine purred, its bumper nuzzled him, it demanded affection – it wanted another twenty-odd years of creepy, inter-specific cuddles. Dave was repelled.

Mo had more bad news: 'Those geezers 'ave bin by again. I told 'em what you said about Finchy, but they weren't 'aving nunnuvit. Said they didn't borrow 'im 'iz money. You pozzitiv you shouldn't be giving 'em summuv this?' Dave shook his head and took the wad of cash. It would give him a few months' respite, and pay for the three of them to take a little holiday, if, that is, Steve was up to it.

The Turks called by Dave's old flat in Agincourt Road as well. Mrs Prentice offered them a cup of tea, because they were well-spoken and she was a trusting soul. They accepted, because subterfuge was integral to their job performance and they enjoyed it in a sick way. She had nothing to tell them, though – her former neighbour had left no forwarding address.

~

The evenings were long at Phyllis's cottage, there was no television, and Dave found it hard to settle to any reading. It was a tiny weatherboard box cast down in the corner of a ten-acre wheat field, and hidden from the world by the dip and swell of an ancient holloway. At dawn, the low-angled sun revealed pod-shaped depressions left behind by some lost village in the dew-soaked stubble. A few roses clambered over the bottle-bottom glass of the window-panes, starlings nesting in the chimney scratched and chirred.

On the weekends Steve came home he would sit at the kitchen table drawing in felt tip on rolls of shelf-lining paper. His drawings were always of elaborate demons – many-headed, multi-armed, their fur green and spiky, their eyes purplish swirls. 'Better out than in,' his mother said, 'and that goes for you too, David.'

'You what?' The cottage was quiet save for the squeak of Steve's felt tips and the 'pop-pop' of a moth caught in a lampshade. There was no way he could have misheard her.

'It's time you wrote to Carl,' she continued. 'You've got to, you have to tell him the truth about all that mad bollocks you buried in their garden.'

'What for?' he snorted. 'I mean to say, what am I gonna do with this . . . I dunno . . . this letter if I do write it? Send it him, or bury it as well?'

'Whatever,' she countered. 'That's not the point, the important thing is you can't let all that stuff you wrote when you were off your' – she checked herself – 'when you were ill to be the final word. It's bad enough that it's there at all, up on that hill, cast in bloody metal, screaming' – she made a foray into the unmapped territory of metaphor – 'screaming at the future.'

They didn't make love when Steve was at the cottage; he slept on the other side of a plaster-and-lath wall as thin as matchboard. Dave, unable to sleep, thought back to when Carl was a toddler and he, back from a night's driving, would lie in the pre-dawn grey glimmer, desperate for repose but with the road still rearing up in front of him. There would be a creak, the stolid thump of little feet coming across the landing, the insinuation of a head. Dave felt no love on these occasions, only colossal irritation at the prospect of little toenails scratching his thighs. Now, years later, a sense of loss welled up in him, sweet and cloying as honey. The child hadn't been a part of him at all – he was from another species, half human, half something else. He had been engineered only to be loved and then sacrificed, his corpse rendered down for whatever psychic balm it might provide. Eventually, Dave slept, then woke in the pre-dawn of the present, with Steve stretched out beside him on the mattress.

He went into the village and bought three A4-sized, narrow-feint notebooks from the newsagents. They were the sort he remembered from childhood, the covers obliquely striped in shades of blue, the stripes wefted with what looked like massively magnified bits of bacteriological goo. Dave stared deep into the cover – another familiar thing that was, it transpired, altogether strange. Beside the shelves of stationery were racks of newspapers. On the cover of the *Sport* the gusset of a soap starlet's exposed panties was circled and enlarged; on the cover of the *Daily Mail* Gary Finch was being brought down from the Clifton Suspension Bridge, a distant pygmy in top hat, cravat and frock coat. His police escort made it seem he'd only succeeded in engineering another failure. Behind him a banner hung from the parapet: FIGHTING FATHERS – BUILDING RELATIONSHIPS.

Dave and Phyl sat at the kitchen table, the notebooks in front of them on the plastic cloth. 'It's like the Knowledge,' she said. 'It's like what you've told me about when you were a Knowledge Boy – you know it's all there in your head, so you've got to call it over, don't you?' He did: he left on the right, then went into the tortuous pattern of mad DOCTRINES and madder COVENANTS. He summoned it up, the hellish DESIGN FOR LIVING he'd tried to foist on his LOST BOY. Each lunatic run across the mental metropolis was pulled out of him and coiled on the table to be picked over by the two of them, between ceaselessly refilled mugs of tea. Phyllis, in these mornings before she set out for the city, her white mask still in a pot in the bathroom, her ruddy features earnestly starred with burst blood vessels, helped Dave to recant. 'No,' she insisted, 'that's not right – you know you don't believe that, you know that's wrong. I don't care what went down between you and Michelle – you don't treat me like that, and now you've got to make things right. It doesn't matter what she did then – it's what you do now that counts.'

A new Book took shape. As Dave trudged along the laborious biro furrows, he turned up a new EPISTLE TO THE SON, which told the lad to RESPECT MEN AND WOMEN BOTH, to strive always for RESPONSIBILITY, to understand that WE MAKE OUR OWN CHOICES IN LIFE, and that BLAMING OTHERS is not an option. Children NEED BOTH THEIR MOTHERS AND THEIR FATHERS, yet if their union does not last there should be no CONFLICT, no tug of HATE. The new Book's composition was evidence of this harmoniousness, for its true author was Phyllis quite as much as Dave. And as for the KNOWLEDGE itself – the mad bigotry of the London cabbie, his aggressive loneliness, his poisonous arrogance, his fearful racism – that too, that had to go. What profiteth a man who can call over all the POINTS and RUNS, if he still does not know where he truly is? This extraordinary document took shape in the little weatherboard cottage, while outside valetudinarian bumble bees veered across the field under a hard rain of ultraviolet rays. Although their thoughts lay in a proximate future, yet the Book became inflected with a STOICISM worthy of Roman citizens hearing the barbarians at the gate, or Sumerian scribes setting down their monumental ataraxy. Between the narrow feint the new Book whispered: the ice caps may melt, the jungles shrivel, the prairies frazzle, the family of humankind may have, at best, three or four more generations before the BREAKUP, before they find themselves sundered from the MUMMY EARTH and compelled to lie down on a crunchy sofabed of a billion animal skeletons, yet there can be no EXCUSE for not trying to DO YOUR BEST and live right. Put a BRICK IN THE CISTERN, clean the ugly smear of motor oil from beneath your TRAINERS and walk away from the city. Abandon it, lose it, let it fall from your mind, for there cannot be – not now, not ever – a new London.

When they were done the two notebooks were filled and it was properly autumn. The harrows came chattering across the great field, tearing up the earth with their steely argument.

## 15

# *The Moto Slaughter*

JUN 524 AD

The reception area was a long, sunlit corridor on the third floor of the Forecourts of Justice. Every few paces there were deep embrasures and through their windows Carl could see the workaday traffic of the Strand, its deep gorge full of bustling folk and trotting jeejees. Beyond this the high-gabled roofs of the ancient wooden gaffs tumbled down to the tangle of jetties and walkways on the quaggy bank of the Thames.

Foglight streamed through the panes of these windows, picking out every pock and liver spot on the brief's lined sullen face. Carl was closeted with this peculiar-looking bloke in one embrasure, while, three embrasures along, Antonë and his brief – a skinny fellow with a pronounced goitre – were in deep consultation. Both briefs were imposingly attired in thick woollen tracksuits and knee-high trainers. Their cockpieces were tasselled and their formal bald wigs gave them the guise – in Carl's eyes – of granddads at the Council of Ham. This was reassuring to him – while nothing else was.

The corridor bustled with warders, seeseeteevee men, Drivers and Inspectors. From time to time a fony would didduloodoo and a brief would hustle his client towards one of the forecourts. Carl's own brief hadn't deigned to introduce himself, merely droning, Ware2, guv, before shuffling his A4s and continuing:

– I've been engaged by the Lawyer of Blunt to represent you . . . as part of your defence he has given me a petition of inquiry regarding your dad – he glanced at a sheet – Symun Dévúsh, is that correct? Carl nodded. Let me tell you right away, said the brief, at last regarding his client with weary eyes, that just as any stay-of-appearance has been denied in your case by the Chief Examiner, so I believe he will reject this petition. As I'm sure you have the wit to realize, objects in the mirror –

– May appear larger than they are, hurrying-up Böm supplied the end of the well-known tag. Yet what need have we of caution now? I suspect the Examiner will have proofs of our guilt aplenty and no need of magnifying them. If we show any restraint it can only be with a view to furthering the interests of the Lawyer of Blunt and his claque, and at this perilous junction I fear we have diverged from their lane.

Carl's brief spat his gum on to the crete floor but made no other response.

A fony coming right up to them didduloodooed, and they rose and were led into the forecourt. It took a while for Carl's eyes to adjust to the gloom, and then he was gripped by awe. The forecourt was a great chamber, many metres high and lit only by a few dim letrics dangling from lengths of chain. A window set high above the Examiners' bench admitted a single beam of foglight that lanced down into the inspection pit. Here, in formal array, stood the Inspectors in their brightly coloured formal robes, some quartered scarlet and white, others striped yellow and green, still more checked like Shelter drapes. Above their bald-wigged heads mounted the bench itself, tier upon tier of elaborately coffered dark wood with platforms let into it at regular intervals, so that the wigs of the Examiners who occupied them were as the whitish blooms of a pyramidal shinynut tree.

At the very apex of this was the Chief Examiner's seat, above which hung the shield of the dävidic line. This mighty escutcheon was party per cross in argent and gules, blazoned in the first quarter with the Cab of Dave, below it with the Rampant Wally, in the upper-right quarter with the Toyist Cab of the Lost Boy and below that with the Pink Chelle of Perfidy. Beneath this on a carved scroll was the Royal motto: DAVE GUYD UZ.

It was only once they had been ushered to the dock that Carl began to look around the forecourt. It was surrounded on all sides by three tiers of galleries, and within each were perhaps four or five rows of benches, all of them packed with spectators. The highest gallery to the right of the inspection pit was boxed off apart from a long, slitted grille behind which there was considerable agitation and the occasional flash of eyes. Hides, Antonë whispered, bird hides. All the luvvies will be in there, justice in New London is accorded a great spectacle. Carl was amazed to note that the queer ran a hand through his white hair and smoothed his filthy T-shirt. If justice was a spectacle, then Böm was determined to play his part to the hilt.

As his eyes grew accustomed to the gloom, Carl began to pick out individual faces from the mass of gawpers. They were all there – every fare he'd picked up in London had done a runner on him. The gaffer of the *Trophy Room*; the Lawyer of Blunt and his fony Tom; Terri, the creepy old potman from the Öld Glöb; and even the grovelling warden from Bedlam. Some of the toffs from Somerset House were there – and, although he couldn't see them, Carl didn't doubt that Missus Edjez and the Luvvie Sarona would be in the hide; nor did he imagine them to be any different from the other spectators, all of whom were noisily chewing gum, taking swigs from evian bottles and craning forward to point out this or that to their neighbours.

Geddup! Stannup! the court fony cried out. The hubbub died away, and the entire assembly rose as the Chief Examiner swept through a door at the back of the forecourt. Carl was shocked by how young he was – a thick blond fringe of hair escaped from beneath his bald wig. He wore a long robe of three distinct tiers – the breast was red, the waist orange, the trailing skirts green – the panels separated by cotton ruffs. As the fony assisted him to mount the steep ladder to the top of the bench, Carl noted the Chief Examiner's smooth skin and tip-tilted nose. The forecourt was cool in contrast with the hot, dusty streets outside; yet, despite this, sweat wormed from beneath the Chief Examiner's bald wig and formed shiny patches on his exposed neck.

At last, settled on his bench, the Chief Examiner called the forecourt to order:

– Where to, guv? His voice was deep and strong – it reached to every corner despite his back being turned.

– To New London! the Examiners, Inspectors, briefs, fonies, spectators – and even the accused – all bellowed back.

With that the trial of Antonë Böm and Carl Dévúsh for the most grievous flying began.

For the first tariff Carl did his best to concentrate on what was happening; yet, by the end of the second, despite the mortal importance of the proceedings, his mind began to wander – wander back to Ham. Antonë had said this would be a toyist trial, that they were naught save plastic figures played with by the Law. In truth, Carl found it difficult to conceive of how any trial conducted in London could be anything besides toyist, given the empty rituals practised by briefs, Inspectors and Examiners. Some speeches had to be made in Arpee, others in Mokni; some depositions could only be read in the Examiners' mirrors, others might be directly perused. On frequent occasions the Inspectors and briefs were required to mount the bench and confer with one or another Examiner on matters of procedure. The Chief Examiner had a fony on hand whose express function was to mop the sweat from his bonce with a mansize; despite this it was necessary for the forecourt to rise at least three times each tariff so that he could retire and change his T-shirt. The sweat, Antonë whispered, must be lashing off him.

The first day of the trial had a carnival atmosphere; the spectators never stopped their chattering and rustling. If Carl made the mistake of meeting the gaze of someone he recognized in the galleries, they wouldn't hesitate to call out to him. With each successive day the crowd thinned out, while the smoke from the letrics grew darker and denser, for as was customary their moto oil was not changed. Soots floated down into the inspection pit, and a deepening and ominous silence welled up, as, with their audience departed, the forecourt officials began to hiss their obscurantism in sibilant legalese.

At the end of each day the accused were taken from the forecourt, chained and bundled into a sweatbox, which was then drawn with much lurching and crashing along Cheapside to the Tower. Through the barred hatch Carl saw down the narrow alleys that wound into the rookeries. Here, bowlegged Dfishunt kids played on the mucky cobbles, while fat boilers hung their laundry out in the smutty atmosphere. Squalid as the scene was, Carl still wished he might be one of their number – that he'd never grown out of the Changeover. He bitterly recalled the thrill of his first car journey in London, how the easy progress of the Lawyer of Blunt's limmo had, for a time, smoothed out his life's bumpy course.

At night, in the Tower, Carl and Antonë huddled together in the soiled straw of a stall they shared with twenty or more other prisoners. Despite the terrifying human dregs who sprawled about them, Antonë continued to exhibit a most phlegmatic disposition, and endeavoured to instruct Carl on the finer points of each day's proceedings:

– Don't listen to what the briefs or Inspectors say, he stressed, watch instead the way they move about the forecourt. The Law is the very engine of Dave's cab. Here the secular and sacred aspects of the Knowledge gear one into the other, each functionary is a part of that engine, his robe patterned so as to resemble cog, wheel and alternator. In their revolutions from inspection pit to bench is to be seen the drive shaft of the Knowledge, which extends from the Forecourts of Justice into the city, the burbs and even the sticks beyond.

The Tower was not a place that either Antonë or Carl could have survived in for long. Its population had swelled mightily in the years since Symun was held there, and the continual skirmishing on the far borders of Ing added Taffies and Scots to the burgeoning numbers of cockney crims. No matter whether they were captives or offenders, most of these dads were given only the most cursory of legal examinations before being snipped, chained and sent off in gangs to be chavs on lawyerly estates in the sticks.

On their arrival in the Tower, Antonë had expected provision to have been made for them by the Lawyer of Blunt – however, there was none. Instead their London finery was stripped from their backs in front of the laughing warders. The following morning they had to attend forecourt in the dirty T-shirts and cut-off jeans offered to them by the lowliest of their fellows. On returning late in the third tariff, they were close to despair, having failed even to wrest a pannikin of oatie from the mêlée, when a new protector made himself known. He was foxy-faced and ginger-haired; his teeth were blackened and snaggled. Terri the potman from the Öl Glöb extended his squamous hand to them.

Carl didn't know which was more shocking: that this bloke, whom he'd seen in the forecourt gallery that first tariff, was now within the Tower, or that the other inmates, who had been harassing them, fell back as Terri came forward, bowing low to him, and near pressing their faces into the dust of the yard. Seeing the state they were in, Terri went first to one of the little stalls where the wealthier prisoners snacked and bought them some takeaway. As they snaffled this down, both Antonë and Carl fired questions at the potman: How did he get here? Who was he? Why was he prepared to help them? He refused to answer, only laid a scaly finger against his sharp nose and said, Awl in gúd tym. Awl in gúd tym.

The trial lasted a full blob, and each first tariff when the dipped headlight was still in the screen and the dashboard twinkled in the east out by the Emtwenny5, Carl, having no pot to piss in, would clamber up to the battlements, where the prisoners made void of their natural waste products. There was London spread out before him: the peaked roofs of its majestic Shelters, the lofty masts of the ferries moored in its docks and basins; the smoking chimneys and stilled wheelvanes; the flying rats swooping about the long knife edges of the mock terraces. Carl had eyes for none of this. Rather, he was transfixed by the cages hanging above Traitors' Gate; in them were dads convicted of treason – some had once been noble Lawyers, now they were torpid skeletons, their yellow skin stretched drum-tight over their ribs, and scraps of cloth their only robes.

Carl lifted his face up to the screen and called over, for despite every evidence of suffering he could not abandon the belief that Dave was above it all, wise and benevolent. He still hoped that when his own torment was ended, and he found himself witless from the wheeling, branded and his tongue snipped, he would rise up there, over the cloudy wipers, another Lost Boy gone for all eternity to be with his true dad.

On the fifth day, at the second tariff when the Chief Examiner was back from his sixth recess, he came to consider the admissibility of the Lawyer of Blunt's petition. Until then arguments and counter-arguments had been concerned entirely with whether it might even be presented to the forecourt. Carl's brief, advancing across the inspection pit, addressed the Chief Examiner in formal Arpee:

– Reervú, my client has been maintained in an ignorance entire of his own dad's fate. I put it to the forecourt that he cannot be held to account for any crimes he may have committed in pursuit of this Knowledge.

There followed two full tariffs of whispering, the briefs, Inspectors and Examiners all hanging precipitately, in clusters, from the top bench. Eventually the Chief Examiner rose and boomed:

– Enough! Shut it! I cannot be expected to weigh these arguments in such circumstances. I shall adjourn to my chambers, you, you, you and you follow me!

They were gone yet another tariff, and when they filed back in Antonë guessed the answer even before the Chief Examiner regained his lofty perch:

– No lad may be denied knowledge of his dad, he barked, and nor shall you be, Carl Dévúsh. However, your crimes are of such an extent and so singular, your flying so high and fast, that no mitigation can be allowed for them. Petition denied!

A great acclamation went up from the galleries, where the diehard spectators were mostly those who desired to see the full weight of the Law descend upon the malefactors. Above this, Carl heard the Lawyer of Blunt clearly exclaim: O my Dave! Now all is lost! He spoke too soon – there was, for him, far more to be lost. Inspector after Inspector now hitched up his robes to climb up from the pit to the bench and make his depositions. Statements had been taken from witnesses to every stage of Antonë and Carl's journeying – toffs in the Lawyer's own circle were turncoats, Missus Edjez had been broken by torture, the gaffer of the *Trophy Room* had had his say – and it transpired that no run out to the sticks had been too long for the Inspectors to undertake. The Plateists of Bril had been examined, and seeseeteevee men had been to Chil and even Ham itself, for the words of Mister Greaves and the Driver were read out in open forecourt.

The evidence of flying was overwhelming, not merely against the accused but also the Lawyer of Blunt. If he had been hoping to escape the censure of the Public Carriage Office by reason of his status or connections, then he was rudely mistaken. To the accompaniment of loud didduloodoos double doors were opened into the inspection pit and a cab was lugged in. Carl gasped, for through its barred windows he could see a sharp, commanding profile, a pendant earring, a clawed hand and a bloody gash where an eye should be. It was the Exile – the Luvvie Joolee Blunt herself. Seeing his wife so arraigned, the Lawyer made haste to quit the gallery. Sturdy chaps seized him and the few remaining members of his circle. The Chief Examiner's voice boomed out over the forecourt:

– No daddy or mummy may defy the Changeover! He gestured at the cab: The evidence of this contemptible wretch has been extracted under torture. All over London – he rose and his mirror flashed – the members of your chellish conspiracy are at this very moment being arrested! Take these flyers to the Tower!

Once the Blunts and their followers had been removed the Chief Examiner turned his attention on Carl and Antonë. He pushed his mirror away from his face and confronted them with his sweaty and distorted sneer. Judgement was nigh:

– Az 2 U 2 – the harsh Mokni consonants cut like knives through the thickening atmosphere of the forecourt – U lì, U cheet, U R trayters, U R fliars. U raze up ve toyist an drag dahn ve dävyn! He drew a scrap of black cloth from a fold of his robe and slapped it on to his bald wig. He parted his robe so that the sign of the Wheel was clearly visible on the sweaty breast of his T-shirt. He drew himself up to his full height and pronounced terrifying anathema on them:

– U wil B taykun bakk 2 ve Towa an brökun on ve Weel. Yaw tungs wil B cú aht. U wil B brandid an ung aht 2 dye inna box! Tayk em dahn! Ware2, guv? he bellowed.

– 2 Nú Lundun, the forecourt responded in a subdued fashion.

When the sweatbox door was yanked open, booze reek surged into its boiling confines. It was only the middle of the second tariff, but the warders at the Tower were already mullered. They left Böm chained in the sweatbox, then lashed and kicked Carl along narrow brick corridors and up spiral stone staircases, until they reached a cell high up in the white keep. There they taunted him while swigging their jack. Yaw juss annuva lyttul mummy, cried the ringleader, a burly bloke with thick, black stubble, an thass wy Eyem gonna fukk U up ve garri. He grabbed Carl's mop of hair and banged his head against the wall.

Oodoo U luv, mummy?! he yelled. Oodoo U luv?!

Carl, through blood and tears, screamed back, Dave, Eye luv Dave!

Mercifully, by the time the third warder stepped forward and undid the heavy wheel-shaped buckle of his belt, Carl Dévúsh had lost consciousness.

He regained it to the sound of a peculiar neighing sound. Looking up from where he lay on the stinking straw, he saw Antonë's bare, bulbous chin trembling in the gloom. The teacher was sobbing. Seeing that Carl was awake, he crawled over to him, his fetters chinking, and, taking the lad's battered head, cradled it against his tank. They stayed like that for a long while, Carl drifting in and out of the hateful present. He was a toddler once more, beneath him was the broad, bristly back of old Gorj rising and falling as they bumbled through the woodlands of beloved Ham.

Midway through the third tariff the heavy bolt rasped and the cell door was yanked open. Looking up, Carl and Antonë saw familiar foxy features nose into the cell – it was Terri. Blymee, he exclaimed, seeing them huddled on the floor, dishevelled and filthy, U R fukkedup orlrì! He had a bottle of jack, and, even though the fumes made Carl retch, Terri forced him to take a swig. Then he did vomit. O Dave! Terri cried, ees onlì gon an lunged up, iss gonna stink in ere! Böm glanced nervously towards the open door. Noticing this, Terri gave a bitter laugh:

– Vat ló? Veyv ad vair legovah an nah vair sleepin.

– But what if we were to –

– Escayp? Terri laughed again. Ardlee lyklee – ware woodjoo go 2? U R gafferless, U av no Lawd aw Dryva, no estayt aw manna aw Shelta. Evree standard an decco in ve ole cittee as yer böts on í – ware woodjoo scayp 2?

Pulling himself to his feet and brushing the soiled straw from his clothes, Antonë confronted the sinister little dad:

– Who are you? he demanded. Just tell us, who are you?

– Oo am Eye? Terri cackled again. Oo am Eye? Thass gúd, thass veri gúd. Eyl tel U oo Eye am – tel U in pertikular. He fixed his gaze on Carl. C viss? He pulled a thong from his T-shirt. From it dangled a Davework identical to the toyist one that Salli Brudi had found by the giant's house on Ham. It spun in the dim light that came from the cell door. Eym yaw öl mans fare, thass oo Eye am. Terri's eyes shone. Eym ve Geezers bloke 100%. Eye woz wivvim ere, Eye sayvd im from ve Weel az long az Eye cúd, an wen . . . an wen . . . he said, faltering, wen vay tookim Eye kepp ve fayf.

– But why? Böm expostulated. Why, dad? Why did you tell us none of this until now? He stepped forward threateningly, but Carl's croaky voice stopped him:

– U, U say vey tookim, Terri – tookim ware, ware2, guv?

– Wy oam, ovcaws, oam 2 iz manna. To Terri it seemed the most natural thing in the world. Bak 2 Am, thass ware vey tookim.

Carl and Antonë looked at each other first in shock, then in wonderment and finally in shameful despair. The pathetic figure with his matted hair clambering over the rocks of Nimar to get a cuddle from the motos. The red cave of mouth, the stump of tongue struggling to form the most significant of words.

– Ve Beestlimun! Carl gasped. Í woz ve Beestlimun awl ve tym, an we woz rì vare wivvim . . . an vey, ve dads, vey nú, vey awlways nú!

– Caws vey nú! Terri snorted. Caws vey nú, vey ad ve powa, mí sun, an powa iz nolidj.

Now Böm did advance and grab the potman's arm:

– The Book, Terri, the Book given to Symun Dévúsh by Dave, the Book he called over – the Book he said Dave took back. Do you know of it? Do you think it ever existed, did you see it? Tell us, dad, tell us!

Terri shook himself free and said:

– Eyel tel yer, ee ad a chaynjyngbag, yaw dad, ee awlways kepp í wivvim – sepp 4 iz peerunces, ven Eye kepp í 4 im.

– Did you look in it?

– Nah, nah, Eye nevah did, coz í wurnt abaht ve Búk, í woz abaht im. Ee woz a grayt bloak, yaw dad, ee ad reel bottul. Ee nevah Btrayd no 1, nó eevun wen vey . . . wen vey ad im on ve Weel . . . The tough old cockney couldn't go on; he took a slug of jack to mask his intense emotion, for he was crying.

Carl was crying as well. Eyel nevah av ve bottul ee did – Eye no vat. Eym skard, Eym skard uv ve Weel – ítul brayk me . . .

Terri shuffled through the straw and laid an arm on the lad's shoulders:

– Doan U wurri abaht vat, mì sun, he said. U aynt gonna B on no bluddë Weel. Eyev gó í awl sawtid – yaw goin oam inall.

Terri had, it transpired, followed the fugitives every step of their way in the capital. He was no potman: he was an embezzler and an angler, he ran a gang of headlight cursers, and he had made a small fortune in barratry. He was one of a select group of dads who, from deep in the waste lands of the East End, defied the authority of the Public Carriage Office. Terri saw no anomaly between his lawlessness and the teaching of the Geezer – for he served neither lawyer nor Driver, only Dave-beyond-the-screen. So when Carl and Antonë bombarded him with questions – How would they escape the Tower and evade the seeseeteevee men? How would they be able to leave London, let alone journey back to Ham? – he was quick to silence them:

– Simma dahn! he said, raising his hands. Eyev payd ve scroos, Eyev payd ve seeseeteevee men, Eyev payd ve gaffer uv a privateer inall. Ees layin off Tilbury 2nyt an ee sayls fer ve Swizz mayne at furst foglamp wivva commishun from ve King imself, 2 ava crakk at vair traydin pedalos. Eel ava cuppuluv xtra passinjas on bawd, a cuppuluv Inspektahs wiv a mös unUshul creetyur –

– Tyga! Carl cried. Cannit B trú?

It was. Terri had sought out the warden at Bedlam and paid him generously for the freakish beast.

– Yaw dad, he explained to Carl, ee toll me abaht ve motos, an ee sed vey eld ve kë. Ee sed vey woz dävyn creetyurs, appi an surcúre lyke kiddees wúd av bin wivaht ve Braykup an ve Chaynjova. Ee sed wotevah Ls appened, az longaz vair wur motos on Am vair woz stil oap fur ve wurld.

As he struggled out of the filthy cloakyfing and into the Inspector's robes Terri presented him with, Carl began to sob again. He was cursing himself for a fool, thinking of how he had travelled all this way to find a father who had been there all the time. There all the time, on the far side of the sound, looking towards Ham. Perhaps even in his shattered mind Symun Dévúsh had been seeking for the son he'd never even known he'd had, while Carl, even when he'd come face to face with his dad, had failed to recognize him.

Böm's thoughts were upon other things, for even in the midst of flight his speculative mind had got the better of him and he was drifting inside of himself to where he could hear the second Book screaming from the rocks of Nimar. If it's still there . . . Böm was thinking . . . if it's still there it might yet have the power to shake the PCO to the very core. It might explain us to ourselves . . . Ingland – even the world entire . . . For in these turbulent times is there not a rabid curiosity for such things, and would not even the most dävine Dävists be forced thereby into a novel apperception of history? A second Book could prove beyond any doubt that Ham was the cradle of our faith . . . Undermine the pretended claims of the dävidic line . . . Circumscribe the very turning circle of the PCO itself . . .

There were misty halos around the few letrics along the Ratcliffe Highway. Behind the fences parked cars were blistered with drizzle.

Carl and Antonë's flight from the Tower had been effected without a hitch. As they slipped along the corridors and down the staircases, the warders turned their faces to the walls. As they crossed the central ward, heading for the side gate on to Tower Bridge Approach, Terri's chaps fell in with them – the heavy mob, their trainers slapping on the yok flags like hard hands on taut flesh.

At South Dock, under the blank face of No. 1 Canada Square, there was a pedalo waiting for them. The posse formed a protective circle around the fugitives, who exchanged hurried embraces with their saviour.

– Wot wil appen 2 U? Carl asked, but the wily cockney only laughed:

– Nevah U mynd, Eyev lastid viss long in Lundun, Eye rekkun Eyel stä ve disstunce.

– Fanks 4 evryfyng! Carl called across the widening watery gulf – but he could not have said whether Terri heard him, for the ebb tide had already caught the frail craft and they were being swept around the Greenwich peninsula beneath the massive curved walls of the Millennium Dome. Within units the Barrier was in sight and the pedalo, like the common shag flying close to the swell that Carl had seen upon his arrival in London, shot between the two central pontoons and out into the Thames estuary. Ahead the foglamp was switching on, its beam dabbing the racing waters with bloody smears, while behind New London – with all its madness and cruelty – sank in their wake.

The *Fairway* was a three-masted ferry built for speed with long, clean lines. It was armed with twenty shooters for the cut and run of combat on the high seas. The crew were the usual band of rapscallions – chavs, pikeys, coloureds and gafferless dads. Mercifully many of them had been snipped, so even if they could mouth off among themselves, they were prevented from asking the odd pair of Inspectors awkward questions. The gaffer, a hard-faced dad with a wooden leg and long jet-black hair, played along with Carl and Antonë's imposture. He's a freebooter, Böm explained when they were alone in their cabin, he owes no more fealty to the King than you or I.

The *Fairway* lay off Tilbury another day until the wind was in the right quarter and the tide was on the turn. Then it weighed anchor and slipped downstream. This was a hastier, more purposeful voyage than the long slog the *Trophy Room* had made up from Bril. With a strong northeasterly wind bellying the privateer's sails, the prevailing westerly currents could do little to hamper it; and with every timber creaking and rope straining, the *Fairway* carved a deep, white path through the booze-dark sea. The ferry shot along the coastline of Durbi; Nott Bouncy Castle was raised at first tariff on the third day out from London, and the long, low island of Chil sighted before the foglamp dipped at the end of the second.

Antonë Böm spent the short voyage below decks, still immersed in his speculations, covering page after page of his notebook with inky grooves. His fingers were numb, his mental capacities exhausted. The escape was no relief for him, no life after life, but an antechamber that debouched into yet more tense anticipation. By contrast Carl had been returned to the encompassing present, the snuggled-up, cuddled-down now. For on the foredeck stood a large cage, and in it, wounded and wary, was Tyga. To begin with it was bad between them. Upon their reunion Tyga had rejected Carl – a thing the lad had never even heard of a moto doing. Tyga curled his thick top lip and flared his nose flanges. His eyelids dipped, he rolled over on the straw and, in so doing, showed the criss-cross scars of the beatings he had received at the Bedlam freak show.

It took several tariffs of gentle coaxing, Carl moving slowly closer and closer, until he could stroke Tyga's jonckheeres, and then the tale emerged in sibilant phrases: U leff me . . . Eye hayt U . . . Heeth thwapped me . . . Hith thingee . . . Eye wath thor . . . the broken-off narrative of vile abuse. The sly kicks and pokes that the chav lads set to tend to the moto had administered gained in frequency and intensity, until the horrific night when the warden had come in and thrust the bottle of jack halfway down Tyga's throat. Then, when the moto was mullered, his arms and legs buckled, the warden used him in dreadful ways.

Carl held the moto's huge head in the cage, which was redolent of the beast's sweet shit. They were surrounded by the creak of the *Fairway*'s rigging, the snap of its sails, the groan of timbers caulked with moto oil. As they gently rocked into reconciliation, Carl felt the hardening muscles of his arms. His hand strayed to his top lip, where last year's transparent down was hardening into stubble. He looked down and in the parting of his Inspector's robe saw the wiry hairs that were creeping up from his wally to his navel. Seven months they had been gone from Ham – the other three motos were dead and Carl was, he realized, irrevocably changed. He held Tyga's head with fierce love as the world turned about the still point of the ferry. Soon Carl would be a dad – there was no stopping it.

The lights of the dashboard twinkled serenely in a screen free of London smog or the orange glow of its countless letrics. The JUN night was warm yet the sea still chilly – and when Tyga's hands and feet dabbled in the water, he struggled, twisting in the offloading sling. Carl was alongside in the *Fairway*'s pedalo. He stroked Tyga's jonckheeres and calmed him, whispering: Cummon, Tyga, nó long nah, Ure goin oam, gonna C yaw wallö mayts, gonna B on Am.

They splashed ashore in a narrow inlet, and the pedalo's crew slung their evian skins and changingbags after them, before shoving off without any further ceremony and heading back to the *Fairway*. The privateer came about with a cracking of canvas and under a headlight so vast and bigwatt that all its flyspecks were clearly visible. Then it beat off up the sound, heading for the open sea and the mysteries of Úro. The two blokes were left standing by their moto, so near to their journey's end yet utterly abandoned.

They slept that night on the rocky foreshore and were awoken past first tariff by the foglamp burning down on them. Carl cracked open his stinging eyes and saw a few clicks away across the waves the green crown of the isle-driven-by-Dave. Despite all their travails his heart seemed to accelerate, until with a surge it broke from his chest and flew up to join a whiff of golden cloud floating in the pink screen of morning.

They took two tariffs to work their way along the rugged coast. The rocks were even bigger here than those they'd encountered on the westward flight from Nimar – great piles of brick and yok, whole jagged clumps of crete. There were many twisted prongs of irony, and spikes of other corroded metalwork lay treacherous in the shallows. Tyga, denied proper wallowing in Bedlam, had never really recovered from the journey to London. His fresh wounds smarted in the seawater, and his old wounds reopened as he bucketed along. Yet he bore it all with great fortitude – it was enough that he was going home. Carl, for his part, tried to comfort the moto, wading out into the water again and again to cuddle him. But whatever intimacy they had recovered on the *Fairway* Tyga had repudiated; again and again the moto flipped Carl off with a shake of his massive shoulders, and, turning his pathetic, scarred muzzle seawards he plodded on.

At the beginning of the third tariff, with the foglamp dipping in the screen, they rounded yet another promontory and came, quite suddenly, upon Nimar. The gulls were in tumult. It was the breeding season and the ferociously cawing blackwings and oilgulls were fighting to preserve their nesting sites from bonkergulls that dived down from above to harry them. There was nothing unusual about this dense mobbing, the ever-mutating fractals of wing and beak. Nevertheless, as the travellers drew closer to this feathery riot, Carl saw a sinister focus to their botheration, where the concentration of seafowl was so great that their sharp wings cut the air into wedges of white, grey and black.

The gulls were fighting over the yellowing strips of flesh that they tore from a corpse – the corpse of the Beastlyman, for it could be no other. Carl started forward screaming and striking at the gulls, and a humming vortex opened up. One oilgull poised, webbed feet on gory eye sockets, pulling a slack goo away from the corpse's exposed, mulish teeth. This, this was his dad . . . this tattered puppet, manipulated by a bird with a tendon in its beak. Nó U! Carl cried. Nó U Beestlimun! And Tyga hearkened to his call, letting out a bellow of motorage as he charged over the rocks scattering the gulls. He stood at Carl's side looking down and lisping: Ith not a beethlimun, ith a nithemun.

To cover up his confusion and his own grief for the Geezer he'd revered, Antonë Böm took refuge in surgical detachment. I would say that he cannot have expired much more than a tariff before we arrived, he pronounced as they shifted bricks to furnish a safe tomb for the dead dad. Then, remembering the way he had failed to recognize his Geezer, Antonë said falteringly, I'm so very sorry, Carl, so very sorry. The lad was, however, almost serene as he dropped a flag on to his dad's face. He reached a hand out to Antonë, so that they stood hand in hand as, through some spasm of dying faith, they called over the funeral run:

– Leave on left Homerton High Street, forward Urswick Road . . .

And the point at the beginning:

– Homerton Hospital.

And the point at the end:

– Jewish Federation Cemetery.

– Djoo no wot kyld im? Carl asked as they went over to the Geezer's hovel of a gaff. Woz í wunnuv vose wankas, he said, gesturing towards Ham.

– I doubt it, Carl, Antonë replied. It is naught save the saddest happenstance. For long years now he had been here, in pain, in hunger, tormented by memories of grievous handling, and still routinely abused by those who had once embraced him. That we should have arrived too late to save him . . . well, even so, perhaps there was some dävine mercy in it, for our own future is so uncertain.

They found Symun Dévúsh's changingbag easily enough. The battered old moto-hide satchel was lying in his hovel on a pallet of gull feathers and rags. Carl lifted it up and heard the pitter-purling of hundreds of tiny bits of plastic. He reached inside and withdrew a strange discoid container of metal, metal mottled with the verdigris of age yet unrusted. I have seen such artefacts before, Antonë said, they are exceedingly rare. See how perfect the circle is, how skilfully milled as if by a metermaker. If you find the seam betwixt the top and bottom you may open it up. Carl did so. Peering inside, all he could see were Daveworks, a shingly mound that he combed with his hesitant fingers. Nuffing, Carl said eventually, no Búk, no nuffing. His voice was as lacklustre as the box from before the MadeinChina, and for the first time Antonë heard his young companion speak with an accent of despair.

It was an odd flotilla that breasted the current towards Ham. The humans held fast to the evian skins, and with the changingbags lashed about Tyga's thick neck they positioned themselves so as to contribute their churning feet to the moto's more efficient motions. In the gathering darkness and the open water, both Antonë and Carl were gripped by the same nightmarish vision: the Driver, his face a mush of decay, rising revivified from the ground where he had been lying dead these past seven months.

The foglamp had been switched off when they at last came ashore, to discover that the current had pushed them some way along the coast to the curryings at Goff. The headlight was driving up over the woodland, illuminating every stately tree and twisted shrub. Despite this, they would be safe for now – no Hamster or moto would be abroad until first tariff. They could even risk a fire to dry their wet robes. While Antonë plied his lighter, Carl went forward with Tyga and watched with pleasure as he foraged smoothbark nuts and acorns, the motos' favourite snack.

Home – Carl was home. The old rutted lane of Stel curved up through the woodland to the Layn and the Gayt field beyond. A scant few paces and Carl would find himself standing on the southern shore at Sid's Slick by Antonë's old gaff. Home, apprehensible, recognizable, graspable home – every criss-crossing greenspike, bending sawleaf and feathery frond of brack spelled HOME as clearly as if the phonics had been inscribed upon them. For a few units, as Carl abandoned himself to the cool green embrace of the woodland, he dared to imagine that the Hamsters might greet him with open arms the following day. That they might embrace him as if he were the Lost Boy come among them.

The humans picked at the greasy takeaway the Guvnor of the *Fairway* had slung at them, while Tyga, gorged on his native fodder, fell asleep. His huge body curled up to provide a living windbreak for their little encampment. The flames from the fire shot up into the screen as the driftwood burned with vivid licks of green and blue flame. Repose did not come readily for Carl and Antonë – yet the chitchat flowed easily enough between them. So they ranged in speech back and forth, from Ham, to Chil, to London, then to Ham once more, recalling the sights they had seen and the adventures they had had. In this dark time the queer and the stripling found themselves most completely engrafted, until at last, with only a few units to go before Dave switched on the foglamp, they slumbered.

Acting with entire accord, the two blokes urged the moto on into the deep undergrowth of the Gayt. They had awoken late and scrambled to break camp and quit the curryings before the Hamsterwomen were abroad gathering kale and samphire. It had been agreed that Antonë and Tyga would hide up in the Gayt while Carl – with his more intimate knowledge of the island – went forth to discover how things stood in the tiny commonwealth. Beyond that they had no other plan, or at least none that either was prepared to confide to the other, for Antonë also had fantasies of confronting the Hamstermen with their deception and how poorly they had used Symun Dévúsh.

Broad, flat moto hands and feet displaced clods of earth and clumps of brick that rolled down the ravelin. Slowly yet unerringly Tyga discovered a gap in the dyke and pushed a path deep into the crackling rhodie boughs. After a couple of hundred paces they discovered a tiny clearing in the undergrowth, and here Carl bade Tyga lie down. The moto didn't want to – he was agitated, he kept lumbering in a tight turning circle, his broad flanks sweeping the two humans into the bushes.

– Doan go, doan go, he implored Carl, Eyeth fwytunned, Eyeth fwytunned.

Carl tried to soothe him:

– Iss onlë 4 a lyttul wyl, juss so Eye can fynd aht woss wot.

Yet it wasn't until Antonë closed in on the moto, took his huge head in his arms and stroked Tyga's agitated wattles that the beast could be quietened:

– I'll cuddle you until Carl gets back, I'll get you a snack. You'll see, we'll have a great time. Turning to Carl, he continued:

– Don't worry about him, I'm sure he'll settle down as soon as you've gone.

Carl decided to make for the point where the Layn debouched into the moto wallows. As he tramped through the dense scrub of Turnas Wúd, then the dells and clearings of Norfend, an uncanny sensation gathered in the small of his back. After Nimar, after London, after the burbs and the forests he had seen on their trek across Chil, these, the playing grounds of his boyhood, were eerily still. There was no rat-scuttle, bunny-hop or tree-rat-scratch. No flying rats coo-burbled in the crinkleleafs. He took his smart trainers off the better to feel his homeland – yet even beneath bare feet the bark chips and leaf fall felt desiccated and lifeless.

Then it struck him – by this time in the tariff the motos should be filling the woods with their deep lowing, the reedy cries of their young mushers and infant charges piercing the leafy canopy. The crackling thud of flanged moto feet and the mechanical rasping of moto molars was so integral to Ham that without it, it was as if the very life force had been stilled. Carl shuddered, even though every tree and bough was familiar to him, yet this was no more Ham than the painted hoardings of Stepney Green were the proud buildings of New London foretold in the Book.

Lost in this reverie, Carl nearly tumbled over a figure that was bowed down between two mossy smoothbarks, grovelling in the earth with a mattock. It started up and ran – he couldn't tell if it was mummy or daddy, so swathed was it in a cloakyfing. Before he had time to consider what he was doing, Carl found himself running in hot pursuit, smashing through brack and sawleaf. The figure was making for the Layn – soon they would be exposed to whatever watchers there were down below in the manor. Carl put on a spurt and the pelting wraith tripped on a root and fell headlong into a boggy slough. Fell, sprawled and twisted so that the cloakyfing was torn away from the freckled face of:

– Salli! Salli! Carl cried, Ware2, luv? Ware2?

She didn't answer his salutation – only glared up at him, her pale eyes brimming with the dull hatred of a toyist beast.

Carl stared at Salli. Her cheeks were hollow, her neck scrawny, there was a film over her frightened eyes. The cloakyfing was wound round her emaciated body like a shroud on a living skeleton. The Beastlyman swam up again in Carl's fevered fancy – was this a vision? Were he and Salli in the breaker's yard already, was she about to rise up and hail Dave? The cloakyfing was wound so tightly, Carl hadn't seen such a cover-up even with the London mummies. He bent down to offer her his open hand, and she spat in his face:

– Wanka! she cried, then, Fukkin wanka!

He knelt down beside her to show he was no threat, and she cowered, then spat at him again.

– Doan tuch me! she said cowering, Eyem a boylar nah!

– A boylar? Carl was incredulous. Waddya meen? Owzat?

– Lyke Eye say – Eyem a boylar, aniss yaw fukkin fawlt. U fink yaw awl dävyn but U aynt – iss mummies wot mayd U juss lyke we mayd vat fukkin kweer – wurs lukk!

Misunderstanding her ire, Carl began a halting explanation as to why he and Antonë had left the island. He told Salli of their hardships on the way to London and what they had discovered there, then, as he told of his dead dad on the rocks of Nimar, Carl became more and more agitated – he so needed her to comprehend the shifting sands of belief that quaked beneath them, yet the only potent image he could call upon was one at the very core of Dävinanity.

– I-iss . . . iss lyke viss, Salli, he stammered. Ewe C Eyem lyke ve Loss Boy – ewe C wot Eye meen? Ve Loss Boy –

– U! U aynt no Loss Boy! She spat again. Ure a wanka juss lyke enni uvva dad – juss lyke ve dads wot nokked me up.

– Wen?! Wen diddí appen!? Mummy shame and daddy jealousy curdled in his hammering chest.

– O ajez ago, she laughed bitterly, B4 U leff Am. Eye dunno oo í woz, if thass yaw nex kwestchun – coz sew mennë ovem ad a krakkat me – up ve kunt, up ve garri, U no ow í –

– Stop! Carl shouted. Stop í! Then, groping for some new fact to dispel this sickening image, he asked, An ve baybee, wot appened 2 í?

– Ded, offcaws, stoan fukkin ded – an me, Eye aint got no fukkin woom no maw neevah. Vair woz no neewoman coz yaw nan woz ded inall, an U, U took Tonë wiv U wen U went, diddun U!

Salli Brudi was wailing by now and clawing at her hollow cheeks. Carl reached for her – and once more she recoiled.

Wossup wiv U! she snarled. U gó motoräj aw sumffing? U wanna ava krakkat me inall? Wel go on, ven. She tore at her cloakyfing, tore frantically until she ripped it apart to expose a breast lying slack on her corrugated ribcage. Go on! Fukkin av me! Fukkin av me!

Carl – appalled and repelled – shuffled backwards, rose, turned tail and ran away through the woods, plunging into dense patches of pricklebush and whippystalk. He ran along the margin of the Gayt field, then crashed on, tripping over crete rubble and brick piles, ripping the flesh from his knees and elbows. It wasn't until he'd floundered into the deepest portion of the zön, where the ancient tumuli brooded beneath their bushy covering, that he collapsed to the ground. A crow, disturbed from its roost in an old crinkleleaf throttled by ivy, cawed once and, leisurely whipping the hot air with its oily wings, lifted into the screen. Carl registered neither this nor any other phenomena – he was lost. Lost in tears, lost in grief for Salli, for himself and for Ham.

~

Carl's robe was tattered and bloodied when he finally found his way back to Antonë and Tyga. He lay on the ground and babbled. Antonë gave him a shot of jack, then, after Tyga had thoroughly licked Carl's wounds, the one-time surgeon dressed them with poultices of selfheal. It wasn't until the third tariff was well advanced that the young dad had recovered himself enough to recount what had happened. Böm meditatively stroked the bum of his chin where his goatee used to be until he had heard everything, then he said:

– What is the matter here? Did Salli speak of the Driver or of the other Hamsters?

– Nah, Carl replied, she sed nuffing, but Eye tellya, maytë, iss bad wotevah í iz. Vey gotta awl B banged up in ve manna . . . Vey gotta B.

They spent a fitful night in the clearing, Tyga rousing up many times and waking the two equally nervy humans. At lampon they took stock. Both were in agreement – there was nothing for it, they would have to see what was going down on their manor. After a few miserable spoonfuls of oatie and another slug of jack, they coaxed Tyga up and began their laborious progress; avoiding the easy tracks and keeping to the woodland, they worked their way round to where the dyke dividing the Gayt from the home field joined the Layn.

Fortunately mist had blown in off the lagoon during the night. Even so, as they crept along behind the dyke, they were painfully aware that only its earthen bulk separated them from the full glare of publicity. Carl urged Tyga to keep his belly pressed to the ground, while he and Antonë also went on all fours. It took them many units to reach the point of closest proximity to the manor. Then, with a final soothing caress of Tyga's jonckheeres, Carl instructed the moto to lie still in a furrow, while he and Antonë scrambled up the bank and peeked over.

The scene below impressed itself on Carl Dévúsh with nightmarish immediacy. The Hamsters' manor was gone. Gone like it had never been there before – every brick, flag, rope and thatch bundle of the ancient structures had been removed, leaving behind only seven pod-shaped depressions in the turf to show where the gaffs had once hunkered down. Some hundred paces away, lined up across the little headland that interrupted the smooth curve of

Manna Bä, there was a new manor: ten sharp-cornered, four-square semis with gabled roofs. Their bottom halves were of the reddest brick, their tops rendered in white plaster between black beams. Bëfan semis, Carl gasped, Ees mayd em bild bëfan semis. The bëthan semis were laid out in two straight lines of five, divided not by the merry twinkle of running evian but by a severe brick wall that rose up taller than two dads.

It wasn't only bëthan semis that the Hamsters had been building – nor their old gaffs they'd been demolishing. With a shock Böm saw that his own little semi at Sid's Slick was gone – as was the old Shelter. In their stead was a new place of calling over, impossibly large and commanding for this isolate place. It was perhaps thirty paces long and three storeys high. It stood very near the shore, and beside its raw, unpainted sides the stands of blisterweed looked as small as burgerparsley.

There was an even more shocking piece of new construction a few paces beyond this: a huge stockade of rough-hewn crinkleleaf stakes had been hammered into the sod. Inside it the bristly backs of the island's entire moto population were ranked up. Carl counted twenty-three motos together with seventeen mopeds. The motos were restive – snorting and butting against their enclosure – yet, as was the creatures' way when afeared, they made no utterance. Alongside this vile pen there stood the stark rectangle of an elongated moto gibbet – far larger even than that which was customary for the autumn slaughter.

As the two returnees watched, a posse of Hamstermen emerged from one of the semis on the daddy side of the wall and, carefully skirting the mummies' side, made their way over to the Shelter. They carried slopping cans of green paint and were under the direction of:

– A Dryva! Carl blurted out.

However, it wasn't the Driver himself – this one was short and dumpy; his robes were cut in the London fashion, his trainers were high and his mirror dangled from a golden rod. As the work posse reached the new Shelter, it was met by more Drivers who came out from inside, together with a large gang of off-islanders – alien chavs, a posse of Chilmen, and the Lawyer of Chil's chaps. Such a swarm of dads Carl had never known to be on Ham before. It was no wonder Salli looked to be starving – they must be eating all the Hamsters' curried preserves.

Then the Hamsters' own Driver appeared. He limped from his semi leaning heavily upon a staff. Set beside the bustling incomers, he was a diminished figure – bent over, his white hair greasy and unkempt. Fred Ridmun, together with Mister Greaves, emerged from the doorway behind him, and, following the Driver towards the gibbet, Fred called out: Peet! Bert! Billi! The lads detached from the milling crowd and came over. Carl had grown up with these three, and, like him, they had suddenly reached dadhood. They carried themselves erect in a sharp jabber of knees and elbows – yet from the way they also shuffled their bare feet and spat their gum juice in the dirt, it was clear that this was to be no welcome task.

Carl realized what was going to happen even before the first moto was prodded out from the pen and came waddling across to where the Guvnor, the Hack and the Driver stood. Awluvem, he groaned. Vare gonna slorta awluvem! For once speechless, Antonë gave Carl's shoulder a squeeze. Billi Brudi, who'd been guiding Lyttulmun by his jonckheeres, now kicked the beast on the back of his leading arm, so he sank down and rolled over on the ground. With no preamble Fred Ridmun unsheathed his blade – clearly, this was to be no ritual killing, no joyfully anticipated collision between men and motos. Billi did not kneel to caress the moto – nor did the Guvnor call over the slaughter run; instead he lunged down and plunged the knife in with a savage dig, as if to proclaim by action alone that this was guilty work. Lyttulmun, frightened and in pain, began to thrash about. Tyga, smelling his wallow mate's blood on the breeze, reared up from behind the dyke, and Carl had to tear himself away from the gory spectacle below so as to calm him and get him to lie down again.

When Carl resumed his place at the top of the dyke, Lyttulmun had been tied and dragged across the dusty ground to the gibbet. Here a gang of chavs were straining to winch him up. The next moto had already been selected from the pen, and, as if cowed by Lyttulmun's bellows, she lay submissively, awaiting the Guvnor's blade. One of the London Circuit Drivers came over and turned so that he could watch the abomination die in his mirror. Execrations floated over the wind-smudged wheatie field:

– Bluddë toyist beest! cried one of the blood-spattered chavs beneath the gibbet. Oo duz ee fink ee iz!

Then, quite abruptly, the focus of the action shifted. The Driver struck out with his black arm and screeched: Trap that flyer! Carl followed his quavering finger to where a squat dad had broken from the crowd by the new Shelter and was zigzagging towards the gibbet. Two or three chaps tried in vain to catch the bloke, but in their cumbersome flakjackets, with their railings drawn, they were too clumsy to arrest Gari Funch before he reached the first upright and, with the nimbleness of a true stack-jumper, clambered straight up it.

Gari Funch gained the cross beam and stood upright on it, one foot on each side of the rope from which the dying Lyttulmun hung. Chavs, chaps and Chilmen came running up and made a circle of upturned faces. B4 U kil annuva 1, Gari roared, yaw gonna aff 2 kil me furs! The Drivers and Hamstermen had joined the audience, the former with their backs turned, the latter with their heads bowed. Wivaht ve motos, Gari continued, his fat lips blubbery with emotion, vare aynt no Am ennëwä, so U may az wel tayk me aht inall! Cummon U fukkas – bringiton!

Ees rì, Carl said to Antonë, thass wot ve Dryva wonz, wivaht ve motos vares no Am, an ve PeeSeeO doan wan no Am atall. Carl gathered himself together and stood up on the top of the dyke, fully exposing himself. He took in the whole deranged panorama below: the trapped motos now snorting and lowing in their pen, the saddened Hamsters gathered beneath the gibbet, the steely agents of the PCO. He felt a hatch inside his mind slide open and at long last he heard over the intercom the crackling, unearthly voice of Dave:

– All you have done, the Supreme Driver intoned, all your dad ever did, was to speed the destruction of your beloved island. Be that as it may – you must not blame yourself, my son, for that destruction would have come anyway, sooner or later. You have seen New London! You have witnessed the mighty currents of change that course through its smoky gaffs and muddy alleyways. The Public Carriage Office has no need of motos – nor of the truth. They require only the Book and the Wheel, the Drivers and the Inspectors, the King and his servile lawyers!

The oracular Arpee fell silent – the intercom clicked off. The crowd surrounding the gibbet had caught sight of Carl. At first one or two of the Hamstermen gestured and cried out, then more and more – Drivers, chaps, chavs and Chilmen – turned from Funch to confront this strange apparition. Hearkening to the acclamation, from the bëthan gaffs on the near side of the wall, hidden in their cloakyfings, came the mummies of Ham, cowed and terrified. Carl took a deep breath. He needed no intercom to tell him this: that if it hadn't been Dave who so blighted the world, it would've been some other god – Jeebus or Joey or Ali – with his own savage edicts. The only recrimination that Carl allowed himself was to mourn this foolish quest for a dad he'd never known – when right at hand there had always been a bloke who was prepared to be a true father to him. He held out his hand and helped Antonë Böm to stand upright.

– U – U – he struggled to say.

– Eye no, Eye no, Böm replied in comforting Mokni. Eye no.

– U, Uve awlways bin a dad 2 me, Tonë, nah cummon, me öl mayt.

The steady easterly had pushed the cloud up in a massy white bank above the Ferbiddun Zön, so that all of Ham was revealed, a green foetus floating in its amniotic lagoon. It was in bigwatt splendour that the three ill-assorted figures – the slim young dad, the portly queer and the shambling moto – made their way down to the manor and whatever fate awaited them.

## 16

# *Made in China*

October 2003

Dave Rudman didn't go into town much – and when he did, he took the tube. He walked the six miles from Chipping Ongar to Epping, then got on the train. In mid morning, on a weekday, the tube was the emptiest of places. The ex-cabbie sat alone on the snazzy seats; the rubberized floor at his feet was scattered with flakes of discarded newsprint – the dandruff of current affairs.

With a slappety-clack the train accelerated through sprawling housing estates and satellite towns cluttered with toyist developments – hair-dryer civic centres and filing-tray multi-storey car parks. Slowly at first, then with more and more crashes and bashes, until it reached a crescendo of steel squealing upon steel and threw itself beneath Mile End. The tunnel was at first just cut-and-cover, so that plashes of daylight fell on the soot-blackened walls and worming high-tension cables. Then the train buried still deeper into the scabrous crust of the city – through bloody orange, shitty brown and black bile, down to the London clay. At Bank, Dave took the escalator up to ground level and emerged, a blinking fieldmouse, into the stony kernel of it all. He discovered himself under the pediment of the old Stock Exchange, with getters and secretaries coursing past, greenish flickers on the grey-glass screens of the buildings. Above him an energetic statue of General Smuts struck out for Holborn . . .

. . . Yet never got anywhere: his bush hat and cravat were no protection against the smirch of exhaust on his bronze back. Turning his own back on the Bank of England, Dave would sidle down to the river, then idle over one of the bridges. He would only recover any sense of where he was when, leaning over the parapet, he saw the stern of a sightseeing boat disappear beneath it, its wake a foaming gash in the beery water. Straightening up, swivelling – the London diorama pivoted about him: the toothpick steeples and cruet cupolas of the remaining Wren churches, the steel braces and concrete Karnak of Broadgate and the Barbican, the AstroTurf lawns and inflated, latex walls of the Tower, the brass doorknob of the Monument. Downriver a flock of pigeons clattered over the prettified wharves on the south bank, where graduate stevedores in blue striped aprons loaded *boudin noir* into the holds of German financial engineers.

All day Dave Rudman walked hither and thither. Newly ignorant of London, he attached himself to flocks of tourists, and together with them followed the shepherd's staff of a raised umbrella to where he might listen to a Walloon explanation of St Paul's. Or else he drifted over to South Kensington and sauntered through the museums, slowly absorbing the perverse stratigraphy that had arranged these fossils in horizontal bands, interspersed with gift shops and cafés. Returning to daylight after aeons, Dave threw his head back and allowed the vivid sense of estrangement – which had haunted him all that long hot summer – to beat down anew.

One afternoon Dave was browsing the bookstalls under Waterloo Bridge – *Shell Touring Guide to Anglesey . . . The Houseboats of Srinigar . . . Theatrical Design in the Thirties* – when the usual eddies of cinephiles, skateboarders and tourists channelled, then flowed steadily, upstream towards the Millennium Wheel. The London mob, so assured of its own theatricality that it gave parts to screevers, classical-music underachievers and dossers senatorially draped with sleeping-bag togas. Dave was stoically disposed to ignore them – until the trestle table of books was kicked in the leg and collapsed. Then, ever so wearily, it occurred to him: *They're running scared . . . It's a bomb – an attack . . . Everyone's been waiting for it – lad in the paper shop, he said don't go into town today . . . I've got responsibilities . . . to Phyl, to Steve – to Carl even* . . . He began hobbling along with the crowd, intending to peel away across Jubilee Gardens – for quite suddenly Dave was completely orientated.

Coming out from under Hungerford Bridge, he realized how wrong he'd been – this was a rush to another's danger, another spectacular revival that London had been waiting centuries for. Dave's head fell back on his neck and he was part of the ring of upturned faces. The Millennium Wheel arced overhead, a bracelet on a puffy wrist of cloud. Usually it moved so slowly that in capturing its ponderous progress blood rushed to spectators' temples, and they staggered, feeling the dizzying revolution of the globe beneath their feet. But it had stopped.

The mob had also achieved a critical, lowing mass – there was no way forward or back, serried info-boards blocked off Jubilee Gardens with a screed on history and renovation. The crowd was already unattractive . . . *soon they'll get ugly*. They smelled of sugar and hydrolysed corn syrup, Marlboro Lights and pirated Calvin Klein. On the terrace of County Hall a party of schoolchildren from Lille bounced up and down in cradles of rubber webbing. Police in Kevlar jackets armed with submachine guns shoved their way down the steps off Westminster Bridge – the crowd parted with an anguished, polyphonic moan.

The Wheel had stopped moving. *Whadda they call it now . . . the London Eye?* He remembered his one revolution with Gary and little Jason – the boy in his Spiderman costume, spreadeagled against the clear glass of the pod. As they rose up in a smooth parabola, London popped up beneath them, the cardboard ministries and papery monuments unfolding into three dimensions of doubtful solidity. Dave had felt an express lift of nausea shoot up his gullet. *The only way I could stop myself from puking or screaming was by calling it over, picking out a cab on Lambeth Bridge and bunging myself in the driver's seat and driving it out to Picketts Lock or Willesden, Camberwell or Wanstead Flats . . . the Days Inn in Hounslow . . .*

There was another tiny costumed figure spreadeagled against the sky. *Like son – like father* . . . Hearing the crackle of the police loudhailers, as they forced the ghouls through a gap in the fence and back over the parched grass towards the Shell Centre, Dave Rudman wondered whether *Fucker's doing it now, calling it over, the points and the runs . . . trying to give himself an, an identity . . . convince himself he's not just another nutter* . . . Because that's what the man next to Dave was saying to his mate:

'Look at that fucking nutter willya!'

'Ow djoo fink ee manijed 2 gé ahtuv ve capsúl?' the other one spat.

Dave was wondering this too, because, rather than heading around the Wheel's rim – which was equipped with a safety ladder – Fucker was a third of the way along a spoke that tended towards the hub at a sixty-degree angle. He inched up caterpillar-like, dragging his rolled-up cocoon behind him. There was a second insect struggling to exit the capsule Finch must have been riding in, but for some reason only his top half had emerged through the escape hatch. *Has he lost his bottle?* Or were enraged tourists grabbing on to his costumed legs? Slapstick in the sky. The police were furious – yet surely they realized that these stupid men were no more terrorists . . . *than I am?* Surely they wouldn't shoot with their snub muzzles that swung from the retreating crowd up to the Wheel? Surely they would wait for *I dunno . . . whadda they call 'em?* trained negotiators. Breathless, Dave Rudman was about to turn away when the bug on the white stalk staggered, yanked from behind by his lopsided burden, and fell.

Gary Finch had taken the fall slowly – almost leisurely. Had he been unconscious – or experiencing a dizzy high at pulling off the Big One? Perhaps his clownish mind had been gripped by the absurdity of it all – or perhaps he felt a final release from the Lord

Chancellor's Department and the lawyers, the mediators and the Child Support Agency? For weeks after, night after night in the sweaty bed, deep down in the coiled mattress, Dave revisited each bone-powdering crunch and flesh-cleaving impact. There was so much blood when Gary hit the balustrade – a screen-washer spray that arced high enough for the individual drops to fall among the leaves of the stunted plane trees and glitter there *like berries*. While Finch's body was a travesty, the stuffing knocked out of it, broken on the Wheel.

Phyllis didn't tell Dave about the two Turks who came into Choufleur a month or so after Fucker Finch had died. What was the point – Dave's mate was dead now, why drag still more of his pain and messy bewilderment into their lives? Besides, Dave was so sunk down inside himself; Phyllis tried to regard him as a bear with a bothered head, resting up in their little cottage on the edge of the woods. Much of the time this was a fairytale – Dave was down so far, almost back where she'd first encountered him, limping from the day room to the men's toilet in his black bathrobe so he could wring a few drops of piss from his drugged bladder. *Still this*, she hoped, *this is genuine grief, isn't it? Best not send him back to the shrink.*

Anyway, the Turks had been civil enough. She didn't doubt that they were chaps, the heavy mob – but they weren't going to get heavy with her. The talker – a burly bloke with black stubble running all the way up to the racoon rings beneath his feral eyes – wore a navy-blue blazer with brass buttons. He spoke with sudden flicks of his hands, shaking the weighty Rolex on his hairy wrist, showing off his manicure. 'Pliz?' he queried after every reply Phyllis made. 'Pliz?' They were standing out in the road, beside the plate-glass window of the Theatre Museum. In it there was a dummy Harlequin wearing a golden mask and a patterned bodystocking – diamonds of lilac, mauve and citrine. She explained to the Turks that Gary Finch was dead. 'You might've read it in the papers – he fell, fell from the wheel, the big wheel?' She made a big wheel shape with her outstretched arms. 'Pliz?' the main Turk said – and his sidekick jabbered at the Royal Opera House, the earpiece of his mobile phone like a nanobot about to crawl into his hairy ear.

Phyllis couldn't exactly dump anyone in it – she didn't know Gary's ex, his dad or his other mates, and she wasn't going to ask Dave. *If I did know 'em I'd tell . . . it's their fucking problem – not mine, not Dave's.* Her boss came out to see what the bother was, and even though he was an innocuous man, effeminate, with glossy chestnut hair, silk shirt and high-waisted trousers, the Turks still took this as their cue to leave. Phyllis noticed that they were driving an old London cab. It had dirty patches where its supersides and official plates had been removed. She turned towards the staff entrance of the restaurant – then looked back to see the two blokes standing by their strange old motor.

~

Winter was a long time in arriving that year. The earth refused to relinquish its heat, no winds came and the leaves, declining to exit the trees, remained there limp and furled. Waking from shameful dreams in which all his past liaisons – including his marriage – took on a fantastical, honeyed hue, Dave Rudman would stagger down the stairs to the kitchen, where pensionable flies drowsed on the rough-adzed windowsills. Death had never felt so close before – not even in the fibrillating heart of his madness. Death's dust coated every surface, and he felt a frantic irritation with pernickety manual tasks – flicking at the waxed cardboard spout of a milk carton – that he was certain would haunt him for ever. Dave trudged across the cloying fields and watched the local farmer harrowing, a mob of seagulls in the tractor's banded wake. He'd had the occasional pint in the local pub with the farmer – and he raised his arm in ordinary acknowledgement.

At last the chill arrived and sought them out with numbing fingers. Phyllis and Dave had stopped making the love that bared their souls – instead they rolled their padded selves into bathrobes before bed and cuddled up to hot-water bottles. For even if winter baulked, the cottage remained impossible to heat. Steve was back in hospital. Money was short.

Gary's dad had wanted to give him a cabbie's send-off. There was even – and Dave thought this *a little strong* – a wreath in the shape of a steering wheel on top of the shiny black coffin. On the day the weather had been mercilessly hot, Debbie had brought Jason and Amber in beach wear – heliotrope shorts, garish singlets, tatty trainers. Even given the shit Gary had put her through, Dave still thought this *a bit much*. He was surprised to see a decent crowd pitch up at the crematorium – even if he hardly recognized any of them besides Big End and Dave Quinn.

It dawned on him, as a concealed speaker hissed a fugue, that the men of child-bruising age, in newly pressed suits and self-shined shoes, weren't cabbies at all – or even builders – but Fighting Fathers. Fighting Fathers who fidgeted like children and then, when the officiating priest offered everyone a chance to say 'a few words', spewed forth many and inappropriate ones, about how Gary had been 'a martyr to the Cause'. Debbie and the kids seemed bemused, while Gary's dad and mum were lost in teary contemplation of the coffin, which stood on the roller road to nowhere, waiting to drop off its fare.

Turning to look along the row of mourners, Dave saw a familiar profile etched against another – a juxtaposition that made both faces more fleshy. It was a profile he'd been expecting to see – the arrogant flick of surfer hair, the ski-jump nose, the pink glisten of well-irrigated skin. 'Gary was a man who loved his kids more than anything else,' the voice at the lectern was saying; 'he put them before everything, and when he died he was climbing that wheel for little Jason and Amber.' Little Jason was as big as his dad now *and I swear he's stoned*. The Fighting Father cleared his throat and consulted the text he'd prepared on the back of an envelope. 'I'm sorry, Dave,' Phyllis hissed, 'but I can't take any more of this – I'm going.'

Dave left with her. Outside the chapel of rest the hearse was reversing on the gravel. It was a brand new TX2 that had been chopped in half and the bodywork extended. Hand in hand, Dave and Phyllis near skipped down the avenue of dwarf cypresses – it was a little moment of levity before the burden of it all descended on them. Looking back, Dave saw that the Skip Tracer had come outside and was standing in the porch, blotting his face with a brilliant mauve handkerchief. Dave thought he might call after them; instead all he did was smile – a tight little grimace – and raise his hand for a valedictory chop.

Dave Rudman never saw a London taxi cab again without thinking of that hearse, obscene and elongated. He never saw a cab again without picturing its passenger as a cadaver and its driver as a sullen undertaker.

When Christmas was past Dave took the two exercise books that had lain abandoned on top of a bookcase in the snug sitting room. He put them in a Jiffy bag he'd bought at the newsagents in Chipping Ongar. He wrote a letter to accompany them on their journey to the stranger who used to be his son. *Bloody odd – I know, mate . . . might as well hear it from me. At the end of the day – you can throw these away – or keep them . . . It's up to you . . . Don't want to lay anything on you – I quite understand . . . it's difficult to explain . . .* So he didn't, only signed off: *I'm sorry – truly I am . . .* because at long last he truly was.

The daffodils stalked from the copses in January – the apple blossom burst before the end of February. Winter, outgunned, retreated before the creeping, vegetative barrage. When the clouds rolled back, the sun had the switched-on intensity of a sunlamp, its ultraviolet rays frazzling the new shoots. Towards Harlow big cock chimneys belched out smoke, and in the lanes exhaust fumes lay in swathes, like the contrails of permanently grounded aircraft.

The cab-sale money was gone, and Dave looked for an earner. Driving a minicab was *only logical*. He applied to a couple of local outfits, and for the first time in months switched on his mobile phone. There was a text message waiting for him that announced itself with a sterile chirrup. It was from Carl: 'Thanks 4 the lettuce.'

Dave drove Macedonians to pull potatoes and Poles to wrench onions. The unwelcome guest workers dossed down fifteen to a labourer's cottage – or even in corrugated-iron barns on the farms. They clubbed together to hire Dave, so he could take them to the supermarket, where they bought gut-rot booze. He needed little knowledge for these A-to-B runs, no gazetteer imprinted on his cerebellum, no immemorial arrogance. So Dave drove stubbly old people to daycare centres and hairy housewives to be waxed. He picked kids up from school because some mum had rolled over her 4wd, then endured their torment behind his back. He drove City getters back from the tube terminus at Epping to their peculiar gated communities – crescents of modern semis, double-glazed, red-roofed, and marooned in fifty-acre fields of oilseed rape, so bright yellow that they jaundiced the sky above.

'Support price is good,' the farmer, Fred Redmond, explained; except that to the minicab driver's ears his words sounded like 'Suppawt prys iss gúd,' because Redmond spoke an earthy Essex dialect. 'Folk are always moanin' on abaht the fucking E E Yew, but I tellya, Dave, wivaht the subsidë awl this land would be owned by wun bluddë corporation or annuva.' Not that Redmond was nostalgic about the past; he had a grown-up son who was a computer programmer in Toronto. 'And good-bluddë-luck to 'im.' Nor did he view himself as some noble steward of the native sod: 'Thass awl bollix, I've grubbedup 'edjez an' sprayed pestyside wiv the bess uv 'em.'

Even so, at first on short limps back from the pub – for Fred had a gammy leg – and then on longer stumps over fields and through woods, the farmer – seemingly inadvertently – began to instruct the ex-cabbie in the naming of the parts.

At first it was the crops – the wind-dimpled expanses of young wheat, the feathery rows of barley, the rattling stooks of alien maize. Then, as they wandered further, Fred Redmond deciphered the groves of crinkle-leafed oaks with their understorey of spiky green broom, saw-leafed nettles and ferny bracken. Before he moved *out to the sticks*, Dave would have been hard pressed to tell a silver birch from an ash. Now he discovered himself affectionately stroking the smooth bark of beeches and grateful for the whippy stalks of brambles, pricking him through his jeans into attention.

The pretty, yellow-gold furze flowers reminded Dave of posh, overprotected offspring, guarded by savage thorny fences. When Dave commented on this, Fred drew his attention to rampaging banks of blackthorn – 'Fukkin pest – but good fer keepin' off cattle' – before leading him down to the River Roding, a weedy rill that rived his own land, and showing him the mighty umbels of the Giant Hogweed growing on its shady banks. 'Iss tock-sick,' the farmer explained, 'weird bluddë poison – í doan bovver U when U rubbub against the stems – onlë layter when iss exposed to sunlyt.' Fred was charged with forcibly deporting these ecological migrants who'd muscled in from the Caucasus in the past quarter-century, but, as he put it: 'MAFF don't givva toss az long az the kiddies don't get 'urt. Beesyds – less I ware a fukkin space suit I get burned sumffing chronic cuttin' í dahn.' He pulled up a moleskin trouser leg to show Dave the white patches where his leathery skin had swelled with gleet, then burst.

'Annuva fing,' Redmond continued as they trudged on through the meadows, the dew of late morning soaking them to the crotch while blackbirds gorged in the hawthorn, 'iss served me well, the 'ogweed, iss lyke a letric fence – keeps folk offa my piggery.' Not that there were many folk to be seen. It never stopped impinging on Dave that, despite the squawk of televisions from behind leylandii and the ever-present roar of Japanese engines, once he stepped from the road there it was, the land, undulant and encompassing, with shimmery poplars shading the river beds and damp alders trailing their limp, phallic catkins.

Dave took to walking across to Redmond's piggery so he could commune with the pinky-tan beasts that grubbed in the dust or slumbered in their iron humpies. Looking at them from behind a taut, ticking strand of volts, he would allow himself to see, what? Some humanity in their eyes, sunk deep in their fleshy snouts – some delicacy too in their arched legs and high-heeled trotters. They would come snuffling up to him, and even though he knew he shouldn't – that such sentiments were inapposite for the bacon of the near future – he found himself addressing them with the baby names he'd once bestowed on Carl: 'Little Man' and 'Champ', 'Runty' and 'Tiger'. When he turned away the hogs ambled off, back to their muddy wallows.

As the summer days stretched out, Phyllis registered the change in Dave's state of mind. *Letting him get over it* had, she thought, been the right approach. He began to shave regularly, bought her bottles of the sweet German wine she liked and brought her bunches of wild flowers back from his rambles. One night in July they made love for the first time in three months; then spent, the two of them lying like beached porpoises on the salty mattress, she dared to murmur, 'It was prob'ly better that way for him.'

'Better in what way?' He nuzzled up to her, a hand fanning over the broken blood vessels that gathered, like tributaries, in the sunken valley at the small of her back. 'Better' – she hunkered up and pulled a pillow underneath her breasts – 'before those Turks caught up with him – the heavy mob that was after him for the cab debt.' She feared she'd said too much, because Dave rolled away from her and reached for his cigarettes on the bedside table. 'Them?' He spat fresh smoke and a rare gob of cabbie nous. 'They wouldn't've done much to him, duffed 'im up a bit maybe – broke 'is nose. They want their money same as everyone else – dead blokes ain't great earners.'

Was Phyllis too old for it? The thought had occurred to Dave when they started sleeping together, and she waved away the condoms with their ludicrous packaging of a chastely smiling youthful duo. *She didn't say she was on the pill*, only that it wasn't necessary. *She still has her period, though* . . . it was irregular, that much he noticed – now that he was noticing things again, things outside of himself. *Best not push it* . . . Not that there was time – they were out of time – more that *I gotta . . . accept what's happened . . . I'm gonna be one of those blokes what doesn't have kids – not ever*. He couldn't forbear from connecting this realization with his behaviour towards Carl. *It's payback time* . . . even though he couldn't understand who he'd borrowed from. There was no *cosmic fucking loanshark* that he believed in. Not like *Aunt Gladys squeaking across the Mormon basketball court in her sneakers . . . Devenish an' his ill-gotten dosh* . . . Michelle even *with 'er creams an' slap . . . They're all worshipping sumffing . . . like those fucking nutters totalling themselves in Bagdad . . . It's only that they want a heaven here, on earth.*

At the back of the moat that half circled the old castle mound, a meadow unfolded and reached along to a little kids playground tucked in the far corner of a cricket pitch. Sitting on a bench sacred to the memory of a former Redmond, Dave Rudman meditatively stroked the bare ground left behind by his botched hair transplant. Dense thickets of furze and brambles extended along the edges of the field, and from these rabbits came hesitantly hip-hopping – first ones and twos, then, when this advance guard detected no danger, threes and fours. A brace of crows staggered to the ground near by, and the rabbits retreated. A bird scarer half a mile away went off with a flat 'bang', and the crows limped aloft. The rabbits came sniffing back. In the lolloping, furtive boogie of the animals, their ear-flick and paw scratch, Dave divined soft answers to the hard questions that assailed him.

After watching the rabbits for ten minutes or so, as the sun tugged up to its zenith, Dave noticed a sinister focus to their botheration – a glistening scrap on the turf that had also attracted a twister of flies. Strolling over from the bench, he found the broken necklace of vertebrae on its offal display cushion; other trinkets – the skull with semiprecious eyes, the ribcage like a gory tiara – lay a few paces off, surrounded by the parched shot of rabbit droppings. *Don't push it . . . Let her come to you . . . She's 'ad enough drama in her life.*

A shadow fell across the dead rabbit and Dave looked up to find Fred Redmond standing there with a shotgun broken over his bare arm. 'You . . . did you?' Dave didn't want to sound like a townie bleeding heart. 'Nah.' Redmond was offhand. 'Cooduv bin a fox – feral cá eevun. Eyem nó in ve abbit uv dissembowlin em. Still,' he continued, guiding Dave to the far side of the field with his free arm, 'vare a bluddë menniss, vay ar, lookí ve way awl viss bank eer iz riddulled wiv vare burrös – vayl av ve ole pitch subsydin if we doan keep em dahn. U shud cumaht lampin wiv me wun nyt – gimme an and.'

Dave wasn't keen on the idea at all. But Phyllis said, 'Why don't you? It's the company he's after – since his wife died he's been on his own a lot. Besides, he's been a good neighbour to me and Steve over the years – not like some of the others round here. He's come over and done bits and bobs in the cottage – it'd be good if we could do something for him in return.'

~

They waited for a moonless, overcast night. Fred had an old car foglamp mounted on the back of his pick-up. 'Awl U gotta do iz aim ve beem an Eyel andul ve shoota.' They lurched along green lanes and rutted farm tracks. Fred swerved the pick-up off the road into areas of heath, where the fire-frazzled stumps of furze bushes stuck up in defensive palisades. They stopped, got out, went round and clambered up. Dazzled by the spotlight, Dave looked away into the bruised pink flesh of after-images, blinked a few times, then saw the rabbits, mute and curious, come nosing into the killing cone.

It bothered him much less than he thought it would. It helped that Fred handled the weapon with studious, unflashy movements: aiming, firing, breaking, ejecting, reloading – a piece worker on a cat-food production line. The rabbits' eyes shone in the big wattage, the gun reported, the dust and cordite smoke cleared to reveal another brown bump. They packed it in close to three in the morning; the back of the pick-up was lumpy with little corpses. 'What'll you do with 'em?' Dave asked, hoping for utilitarian news, rabbit stew canned and exported to starving Africans. 'Lanfil,' Fred snapped. 'Up bì Arlo.'

'U shud C ve playce,' he resumed half an hour later when they were back at the cottage and companionably gulping sweetly burning Jack Daniels. 'Iss lyke ve surfiss uv ve moon, Uje pyls uv rubbish, Uje mobs uv gulls cummin from ve C. Eye tellya, Dave,' Fred said, relighting his mouse turd of a roll-up and blowing a thin thread of smoke into the tassels of the lampshade, 'Eye sumtyms fink iss awl gon arsy-versy, yernowoteyemeen? Ve C az cumminta ve lan – ve lan az gon aht 2 C.'

*The past has become our future and in the future lie all our yesterdays* . . . Was it a stale aphorism freshly baked, or an ancient pop song dimly recalled? Dave could not have said.

They went out often after that – the old farmer, the reddish-brown hide on his neck creviced like sun-baked mud; and the ex-cabbie, potbelly and arm wattles melting off him in the sweat of their night-time exertions. Another unlikely duo – a dad in search of a lad, a lad wandering fields hazy blue with memories. Fred acquired his own tea mug at the cottage, his own chair and cap hook. They would sit up well past dawn – not exactly getting drunk, although certainly not staying sober. Phyllis didn't mind, Dave came to her in the dewy period before she arose to go to the city. Came to her lean and lovelorn, gently athletic.

One night in mid August they came back from the lamping and got *fucking lashed*. Dave was relieved Fred didn't become maudlin, only tight-lipped, little dribs of sadness escaping with his fag smoke. Yet they both exposed their mummy selves that night, Fred regretting the lack of understanding he had shown to his son: 'Eye wannid im on ve lan – vares bin Ridmuns eerabaht fer sentries,' while Dave regretted everything – and nothing – all at once, for surely *it's only a tosser who says he regrets nothing at all – it means he remembers nothing . . . be-because to remember is to regret.*

Too pissed to drive, Fred tottered off about six in the morning. Dave came out to see him on his way. The old farmer's boots left crushed swathes in the unmown grass, each with its own scattering of mashed flower heads – dandelions, buttercups and daisies – twisted like wreaths. Fred forgot his shotgun, which was leaned up against the bellying plaster by the front door – as commonplace as an umbrella. Seeing it when she came down at seven, Phyl went back upstairs and gently shook Dave awake. 'Fred's left his gun in the house,' she said. 'Do make sure he comes over and gets it, we don't want any bother.' Dave grunted, 'Yeah, yeah, no bother, love, I'll get on it.' She felt his cheek against hers – as pocky as a newly surfaced road. She inhaled his shitty whisky breath and tousled his sweaty tonsure. He flumped back into the bed – she turned, went downstairs and drank a cup of rosehip tea standing at the draining board. She fetched her handbag, looked at the shotgun once more, then shut the door carefully, listening for the latch to fall. She set off across the fields, on her way to catch the bus from Chipping Ongar to Epping.

~

As the Fairway bucketed northeast up the M11 the two men inside were engaged in two different conversations. Rifak, who was driving, had his slick earpiece-and-mic combo inserted, and so was able to carry on his row with Janice while holding the rattling old cab steady in the slow lane. Mustafa, by contrast, lay almost prone on the back seat, one of his new Gucci loafers – of which he was inordinately proud – pressed against the window. Mustafa spoke in Turkish, Rifak in crumbly English. Both men were smoking, and their consonants cut like scimitars through the silky blue swags and furbelows.

'Ewer runnin abaht tahn givvinit larj!' Rifak spat. He was in thrall to this woman, who was – his colleague thought – nothing special, only another cockney whore who got her tits out in a pub on the Mile End Road every Sunday lunchtime, so she could pick up a few quid from the dissolute boozers. However, Rifak, having stuck his cock in her arse, her mouth and latterly her cunt, before slapping her about a bit, was now convinced that he possessed her more than he even possessed his wife. His wife was a similarly abused girl, flown in from Central Anatolia and confined to the hejab and a flat above an upholsterer on the Lower Clapton Road. Here she had endured two murderous pregnancies in rapid succession, stuffing her frightened face with honey cakes, while receiving the hushed sympathy of other mummies.

By contrast Mustafa's phone conversation was measured and – he felt – subtle. Their boss, who lived behind redbrick walls in Cobham, liked to have situation reports – and Mustafa was happy to oblige. He held the razor-thin mobile so that it shaved his hairy ear, and spoke eloquently of how this account was being pursued while that one had been closed. His Knowledge was comprehensive, the entire conurbation – its grids of overpriced, semi-detached hutches, and sclerotic arteries clogged with superfluous travel agencies – resolved into sums owed and the dizzying interest rates charged on them. In Mustafa's inner eye, he saw the city laid out as a diorama, the mounting sums rising in fluorescent plumes of digits from unsuccessful beauty salons and the serviced apartments where Toyota Lexus drivers fiddled with Romanian tarts.

They pulled off at Junction 7 and had breakfast in the Little Chef. During his seventeen years in London Mustafa had acquired a taste for slopping up runny egg yolks and the juice of grilled tomatoes with a scoop of bread. While performing these expert manipulations, he lectured Rifak on what a fool he was making of himself. Of the job in hand there was nothing to be said. It was routine.

By the time they had paid their bill and walked out to the car park, the sun was pummelling its way through the overcast sky. Ten or twenty wasps swayed by an overflowing bin, alighting on ketchup-smeared paper to feed. The two Turks got back in the cab, drove up to the roundabout and took the A414 for Chipping Ongar. Peering through the windscreen, Mustafa still found the monochrome fields and shaved copses lush and unsettling. He regretted the two sausages, the two rashers of bacon, the two fried eggs, the two grilled tomatoes, the two axe heads of fried potato mush, the two bits of toast. His belly gurgled like a nearly empty fuel tank.

~

Dave Rudman was sitting at the drop-leaf table in the tiny front room of the cottage reading yesterday's paper. There was an article on the vacant fourth plinth in Trafalgar Square, rubbishing the proposals for the arty sculptures that might be poised there. The paper editorialized that this prime position should only be afforded to the image of a mighty national hero. *Gary – Fucker Finch dressed as 'enry the Eighth . . . pigeons shitting on his doublet . . . Fighting Fathers banner in his bronze-bloody-hands . . .* Dave had a biro in his hand and annotated the newspaper, scrawling in the blank linchets between rips of text and photos: EMPTY, I'VE HAD ENOUGH. TAKING THE PLUNGE.

Then he heard a cab come grunting down the lane and squeal to a halt. *Can't be a mate – they'd've called . . . An' it's too far for a fare* . . . The small crystalline facts he had ignored tinkled and shattered. He knew who it was even before he saw their hot cheeks pumped up with blood. *It was me they were looking for all along . . . Looking at Ali Baba's . . . Looking at Phyl's work . . . it was them as called Mum and Dad inall* . . . Dave was forced to conclude that *I wanted this to 'appen*, and, more defiantly, *I was justified – why should I pay that cunt back, why? I was off my bleedin' rocker* . . . Yet there were also his own words, echoing around the M25, all the way from the hackneyed past: *You never owe a Turk. Never.*

Over the foam shoulder pads of the Turks the wheatfield swelled, the ashes shimmered, the crows circled and the clouds – impacted upon by incomparably many puffs of causation – arranged themselves into greyish-blond sweeps of cirrus, cumulus blobs of tip-tilt nose and receding chin. In the core of it all was a ragged hole through which the Skip Tracer intoned, 'Juss don't go borrowing on me, son – don't do that. The vig'll kill you.'

Dave made to shut the door and the lead Turk stuck his foot in it. He knew they were only there to put the frighteners on him, *smack me about a bit . . . so why am I reaching for Fred's gun? Why? P'raps I've simply 'ad enuff?* Through the crack between the door and its hinge Mustafa saw Dave grab the shotgun. He ducked back, leaving Rifak exposed as the ex-cabbie levelled twin barrels at his gut. 'Get the fuck ahtuv –' Dave began to say. He didn't finish because the Turk threw himself forward, knocking the gun aside, and grabbed for his throat.

For a while there was a mercilessly inefficient struggle, neither one gaining an advantage – so that when Rifak did manage to get hold of the shotgun, it was with that element of shocked surprise with which a younger brother wrests a toy from his older sibling. Still in the giddy grip of his accomplishment, Rifak pulled both triggers – really just to see what might happen – and smoky flame tore a big chunk out of Dave's middle. Such a big chunk that for the moments before he fell a visible notch could be seen in Dave's side between his hip and his ribcage. Then he did fall, and, despite the liberal scarlet splashes, streaks and even blobs that rendered a chair, the newspaper, his cigarette packet and lighter, and one of Phyllis's darning mushrooms objects at once challenging and messy, Dave nevertheless found himself to be *lunging up fresh blood*.

Mustafa began the clean-up while the shotgun's report still echoed through the environs like the angry slamming of a giant car door. A quarter mile off Fred Redmond's sleep was perturbed by the after-echo. He stirred, thinking, *Eye sware vat man puts vat byrdskara on urlia an urlia evri bluddë mawnin*. The flock of crows lifted off from the ash plantation – oily rags flapping in the thickening sunlight. Mustafa calmly snapped on rubber gloves, took the shotgun from the stunned Rifak, wiped it down with a shirt-tail pulled from his crocodile-skin belt, kneeled and, taking the dying man's hands carefully in his own, arranged everything so that Dave held the trigger guard and the stock, while the gory muzzle was rammed in his chest cavity. Straightening up, Mustafa turned to Rifak. 'I tellya one fing,' he said in cockney, 'I'm not goin' dahn fer vis one, you div. They come lookin' – I'm pointin'. Now get in the fucking cab.'

As the Fairway pulled off up the lane with Mustafa driving, he adjusted the rearview mirror, so that he could check that the ex-cabbie truly was dying.

Dave was – and his entire life was passing before him. Not the significant or profound parts of it – his mother's love, Carl's birth, getting his badge, a priceless fuck – but the prosaica: the flicked spout of a milk carton; cash-point queues; the sweet rack in a video-rental outlet; a television programme about Flemish canals; warped furniture piled in front of a matchbox terraced house in Erith; the dirty 'tester' on a hospital wall; the loose chain on his moped when he was a Knowledge Boy; the name plaque reading

JONCKHEERE on the bodywork of a coach juddering at a traffic light; the Hammersmith roundabout; a computer-generated phone call telling him he'd won a prize; a rolled-up ball of silver paper – but most of all, the fares. The fares, the endless succession of fares – their cropped faces in the mirror: male, female, old, young, white, brown, yellow, black (although it had to be conceded far fewer of these); their eyes wary, hesitant, bored, angry, screwed up with laughter, closed in a gob-stopping snog; their skin stretched and slack, lined and scored; their mouths purse-lipped, clenched, half open, sour goo on their mulish teeth. The fares, picking their noses, dabbing at their eyes and peering at him with self-satisfaction, confident in their own small nugget of Knowledge, which he, groaning, was forced to extract from them: *Where to, guv? Where to, luv? Where to . . . ? Where to . . . ? Where to . . . ?*

Death itself Dave Rudman remained in ignorance of – he was a tourist, standing beside a large monument, staring bemusedly at the map that showed its location. True, as a dark crescent eclipsed his view of the sun, so he struggled to avoid unconsciousness, backpedalling into the present. His heart stopped, his legs pushed feebly against the doorjamb, his hands convulsed and his hips jerked – yet he couldn't hang on and expired like that, in quizzical pain.

~

The funeral was held at Willingale, a quiet little village a few miles away, deeper into the fastness of north Essex. Willingale – if it was remarked upon at all – was known for its two churches, which stood adjacent to one another, in a single churchyard overlooked by a sentinel yew and many massy beeches. One of these churches was Gothic enough – it had flinty walls and stepped buttresses that mounted to a castellated tower; the other, older edifice was a plain stone barn, with a shingled roof topped off by the characteristic vernacular campanile of Essex – a clapboard hutch rising to a tapered point. The yarn thereabouts was that the second church had been built by a wealthy lady who had fallen out with her sister over who took precedence in the pews of the first. The locals – credulous peasants that they were – had got it quite wrong; as anyone with the slightest architectural knowledge could have told them – and frequently had – Willingale's two churches were separated from one another by two hundred years in time, if only a hundred or so yards in space.

No one – not even Phyllis Vance – seriously doubted that Dave Rudman had taken his own life: the heavy history of depression, the toxic jungle of his brain chemistry, the loss of both son and career, the opportunity, the scrawled notes in the margins of the newspaper: EMPTY, I'VE HAD ENOUGH. TAKING THE PLUNGE. These were, if not incontrovertible truths, at any rate telling clues in the absence of any others. There were no others – the Turks, their cab, their breakfast at the Little Chef – no one had noticed any of this, while in Clapton, Fatima bore the consequences of the crime: more bruises on arms and legs, Rifak in a raki-sodden, self-piteous heap.

Even so, Phyllis Vance had enough canniness to introduce doubts into the mind of the local coroner, so many doubts that the death certificate laconically recorded the end of Dave's wayward journey through life with a further 'misadventure'.

If it bothered Phyllis that her lover was to be interred in Willingale – so near to and yet so remote from his native city – she showed no sign of it. In death she was more proprietorial of Dave Rudman than she had ever been during his life – she needed him near to her and Steve. Not that she was off-putting when it came to Michelle and Carl – she wanted them at the funeral more than anyone else; there to observe how properly it had all been arranged, and how skilfully she had talked round the priest – a circuit vicar who passed through Willingale once a month like a tardy rural bus service – into committing this recent and most unobservant of his parishioners.

For the fractured Devenish family – who had driven from London respectively silent, stunned and surly in their opulently padded seats – this voyage in their brand-new Volkswagen Touareg was way off road. Michelle, irretrievably lost in her memories of how *it all went wrong*, lacked even the spirit to argue with Cal when, bedevilled by nerves, he took wrong turning after wrong turning. In the back, immersed in a soundscape injected straight into his brain by a computer, Carl smirked, then winced. He couldn't tell which of them he hated more – his slutty mummy, his unreal real daddy, or the *stupid fucking cabbie who'd blown his bollocks off*. There were painful blisters full of nicotinic fluid on the insides of Carl's skinny arms, for at night, at the open window of his bedroom, looking out over the light lagoon of the city, he touched the furious tip of a cigarette to his own flesh, desperate to discover if he could feel anything at all any more.

When they finally drew up outside the two churches of Willingale, the September day, which had been brooding all morning, began to arrange itself in the purpling drapery of a coming downpour, unfurling great swags of cumulonimbus on to the shushed land. Stepping down from the high vehicle, Michelle found herself aptly diminished and was able, in all humility, to approach the similarly shrunken figures of Paul and Annette Rudman, who stood by the lychgate with their daughter, Sam, uncertain of what they should do or feel. Michelle tore away the fine embroidered cloth to show them her cropped, ginger head. *They ought to . . . They have a right . . . I wish they'd under- . . .* Chopped-off intimations of her own shame accompanied her silent obeisance. Cal hung back, while Carl advanced and applied his lips to the strange faces of his former granddad and granny.

It was a measure of the dissipation of the Church's doctrine – its moral authority knocked over as casually as a drunk topples a beer glass – that a suicide's funeral was to be held in the more youthful of these senescent buildings. But then, self-murder and the mildewed hassocks, the musty drapes, the tarnished communion rail, the worm-holy rood screen, the foxed flyleaves of the prayer books – it all sat well together. After all, the Church had murdered itself, as with every decade more and more depressed dubiousness crept into its synods and convocations, until, speaking in tongues, it beat its own skull in at the back of the vestry. Divorcees and devil-worshippers, schismatics, sodomites and self-murderers – they were all the same for the impotent figures who stood in the pulpit and peered down at pitiful congregations, their numbers winnowed out by satellite television and interest-free credit. 'Dearly beloved,' they intoned – and meant it, because if they expected anyone to pitch up at all, they had to go round to their parishioners' houses and help them on with their underpants.

Clear across the flat lands of Essex the spires stabbed up at the sky, abandoned launch pads from which the soul ships had long since blasted off. Inside them, clad in laughably obsolete uniforms – frilly laboratory coats, army surplices – the priests did kitchen-garden juju with corn dollies and ewers full of sour water. They were marionettes and mime artists, fifth-rate impressionists at the end of the world pier, officiating over a state cult for which the state no longer had any use.

Michelle stood at the back behind a ragtag bunch of mourners who could have comfortably been accommodated in three London cabs. She recognized none of them besides immediate family. Not Anthony Bohm and Jane Bernal, nor Mo from the taxi garage. Faisal was a stranger to her – and Fred Redmond a terrible sight, guilt-stricken almost to the point of expiring. Nonetheless, in her ignorance Michelle realized that *this was where I came in*. An involuntary hand went to her head, and she felt the impoverished frass of middle-aged hair thin on her scalp. She conjured up the cavernous, suburban Catholic churches of her childhood, where Cath Brodie wept, rent her British Home Stores garments, and even banged her head on the flags. Michelle recalled the lubricious sanctity and smelly mysticism of these venues. *At least . . . at least it was dark in there*, while here was bright and desiccated, the priest's hands were as papery as the pages he turned, his voice rustled out: 'We brought nothing into this world and it is certain we carry nothing out. The Lord gave and the Lord hath taken away; blessed be the name of the Lord . . .' Phyllis was weeping softly – Annette Rudman looked straight ahead through the battleship-grey legs of a medieval knight imprisoned in a glass slide. Through force of habit her husband checked his watch and made a wager with himself on the length of the sermon.

'When thou with rebukes dost chasten man for sin . . . thou makest his beauty to consume away, like as it were a moth fretting a garment: every man therefore is but vanity.' Michelle Brodie smoothed black silk over her leg. *All my life – my adult life – I thought the secret lay in birth . . . but all along the secret was that we're going to die*. In that moment, with the priest starting to say a few uplifting words about a man he'd never known, all the suppleness left Michelle, body and mind slackened, and she exhaled deeply. She felt her age – and she looked it as well.

~

At the graveside Carl looked anywhere save at that earthy trench. He eyed a little posse of local kids who were lounging in the road on their BMX bikes . . . *fucking chavs*. Their baggy jeans rode up over their skinny shanks as they hobby-horsed up and down, scooting fallen beech mast and immature chestnuts with their trainers. Carl felt his top lip – the transparent down of the year before was hardening into stubble. 'Man that is born of woman . . .' *dad that is born of mum* '. . . hath but a short time to live . . .' *is fucking dead you mean!* Yet there was a sincerity in these words that not even an adolescent could sneer away, no matter how desultory the hireling's delivery: 'Our Father, who art in heaven, Hallowed be thy name, Thy Kingdom come, Thy will be done, On earth as it is in heaven . . .' Right at hand was a man who was prepared to be a father to Carl, and, intuiting that now was the right time, Cal laid a paternal hand on his shoulder.

~

Cal Devenish had a whole pile of old 35-mm film canisters that he kept in the detached garage of Beech House. They were mementoes of the time in his life when he'd imagined he might – despite every evidence to the contrary – become an inspired auteur, decanting his miraculous vision of the world on to celluloid. Stoner Cal worshipped the neophyte Greek goddess Media at college and, funded by indulgent Daddy, he persuaded friends to act as his crew. Together they'd shot a few thousand feet of wooden acting and recorded Cal's cardboard words. To give him some small credit, when Cal had seen the first week's rushes he was consumed by shame and canned the whole shoot. Cal threw away the stock, keeping only the cans for biros, paper clips and plastic oddments.

'Y'know,' Cal said to his son as they sat side by side on a wrought-iron bench in the garden, 'when you read over this stuff' – he chonked together the exercise books – 'you've gotta admit that Dave was on to something.' He'd fetched one of the old film canisters from the garage, and now Carl laid the two books inside the shallow tray and eased the lid on. Cal helped him seal it with a long strip of gaffer tape.

Michelle had allowed the digging of a hole beyond the teak decking that separated the lawn from the big bed where, when spring came, mail-order blooms would be planted. There were limits – even to honouring the dead. The son placed the film canister in the moist, friable earth – then the father covered it. Short of digging up the other book – the one the dead cabbie swore he'd buried there – this was what they both felt he probably would have wanted. Michelle stayed inside. She sat at the kitchen worktop, coffee cup cold on the marble slab, her fists ground so hard into her eye sockets that a belated eternity ring Cal had given her drew blood.

Carl didn't feel Dave's presence in the sigh of the autumnal wind through alder, birch or poplar. The London that spread out below them might have been impressive to a visitor – to a native it was mundane. Later father and son went out, the two intent on escaping the *bad vibe*. There in the road, pulled over to the kerb, was a Knowledge Boy on a scooter; or rather, a Knowledge Man, because when he pushed his full-face crash helmet up on his head to speak to them Carl saw that he was older than Dave would have been – had he lived – for another decade. 'Oi, guv,' he said, addressing Cal, 'can I get froo to Well Walk dahn vis way?' Cal looked uncomprehending – but Carl, whose Knowledge was far fresher, patiently explained to the *sad old loser* that he'd have to work his way back round via New End and Christ Church Hill. 'Ve streets on vis manna iss awl tangled up lyke bluddë spaghetti,' the wizened Knowledge Boy said, before he farted off on his bike.

They were walking down Heath Street when Cal asked, 'Have you ever considered it – doing the Knowledge, I mean?' Carl didn't reply immediately – not out of surliness, only because it often took a while for messages from the outside world to make it over the high wall, to where he crouched, hidden inside his secret mummyself. Eventually he climbed up and over to the daddy side and replied, 'Nah, t'be honest I'm kind of interested in being a lawyer – there's gotta be more of a future in it.'

# *Arpee–English*
# *With Some Alternative Mokni Orthographies*

## *A*

| | |
|---|---|
| A2Z (A–Z, AtoZ, aytoozed) | map or plan |
| A4 | paper |
| access<br>(akksess, axes) | another term for daddytime (the half of the week spent with fathers) |
| Arpee | court or sophisticated speech (as opposed to Mokni) |
| artic<br>(artik, artyk) | large wagon for carrying goods |

## *B*

| | |
|---|---|
| bacon<br>(bäcön, baycun, baykun) | pigs, swine |
| bambi | deer |
| barbecue (1)<br>(barbieQ) | charcoal |
| barbecuers | charcoal burners |
| barbecue (2) | stake<br>(as in 'burnt at') |

| | |
|---|---|
| barnconversion<br>(barnconverzshun) | barn |
| barnet<br>(barnit) | hair or hairstyle |
| bëthan semis<br>(bëfan semis, beefansemis) | vernacular architecture of Chil |
| bigwatt | bright, bright sunlight or the sun itself |
| bints | women (derog.) |
| biro | quill pen |
| blackwing<br>(blakwyng) | gannet |
| blisterpack<br>(blistapak) | packet (for tobacco) |
| blisterweed<br>(blistaweed) | Giant Hogweed |
| blob | week |
| boiler<br>(boylar, boyla) | grandmother, or any woman past childbearing age |
| bonce | head |
| bonkergulls<br>(bonkaguls) | Great Skua |
| booze | alcohol (gen.) |
| brack<br>(brak) | bracken |

| | |
|---|---|
| Breakup<br>(Braykup) | the time in the distant past when the promulgation of Dävinanity led to the separation of the sexes |
| brick<br>(brik, Lundunbrik) | building material |
| brief<br>(breef) | denotes both an advocate and a lawyer's petition |
| bubbery | any tweed or rough woollen cloth |
| bubble | to lie |
| buddout<br>(buddowt) | spring |
| buddyspike | buddleia |
| bugsbunny<br>(bugzbunnë) | rabbit |
| burbs<br>(burbz) | moors and/or the hinterland of a city or town |
| burgerkine<br>(burgakine, burgakyn) | cattle, cows |
| burgerparsley<br>(burgaparsley, burgaparzlë) | cowparsley |

## *C*

| | |
|---|---|
| cab (1) | five fares (in Dävinanity three 'cabs', or fifteen fares, are required to form a Shelter, or congregation) |

| | |
|---|---|
| cab (2) | gig or two- or four-wheeler |
| calling over<br>(caulinova, caulinovah) | praying aloud or preaching |
| car<br>(ka) | cart |
| carcoat | characteristic Inglish garment for dads, usu. made from woolly, bubbery or shishskin |
| changebag<br>(chaynjbag) | purse or wallet |
| Changeover<br>(Chaynjova, Chaynjovah) | mid blob, the WED when children pass from daddies to mummies, or the SUN when they return |
| changingbag<br>(chaynjyngbag) | valise or portmanteau |
| chaps | the armed retainers of a Lawyer or any other armed men |
| chav | slave |
| chellish | evil, bad, deceiving, wanton, licentious, venal |
| childsupport<br>(chyldesuppawt) | bride price |
| choppa | formation of seabirds that will rescue a birder falling from a stack |
| chrissyleaf<br>(crissëleafe) | holly |

| | |
|---|---|
| click<br>(klik) | <br>unit of distance in Ing: one is equal to a thousand of a dad's paces |
| cloakyfing | variously: the plaid (worn in remote areas); or berka (worn in urban ones). Characteristic garment of Inglish mummies and invested with religious significance as a protection against chellish immodesty; also worn by daddies in cold weather |
| crete<br>(creet, kreet) | <br>concrete (usu. shattered) |
| crinkleleaf<br>(crinkuleafe, krinkuleef) | <br>oak |
| cockpiece<br>(cokpeece, kokpiss) | <br>codpiece |
| coloureds<br>(culluds, kulluds) | <br>any dark-skinned person or alien |
| crybulbs | onions |
| cupasoup<br>(cupasúp) | <br>broth or soup |
| curry (1)<br>(curri, kurri) | <br>hot meal |
| curry (2) | salt |
| currying | salting (preserving food) |
| curryings | pasturage subject to tidal inundation |

## *D*

| | |
|---|---|
| dad | man |
| daddytime (dadditym) | the half of blob spent with daddies |
| dashboard (dashbawd) | the Milky Way |
| Dave's curry | ceremonial meal |
| Daveworks (dävwurks) | plastic fragments deposited in the sea by Dave at the MadeinChina. Worn by Inglanders as charms and talismans, periodically proscribed by the PCO |
| Dävinanity | established religion of Ing |
| dävine (dävyn) | divine, holy, or a dad who has such qualities |
| Dävist (Däyvist) | one who observes Dävinanity |
| dävitude | godliness |
| decaux (deccos) | advertisements or handbills |
| demister (dëmista) | wind (esp. that clears clouds) |
| Dfishunt | malnourished |
| dire (dyr) | dreadful or awful |

| | |
|---|---|
| Driver (Dryva, Drivah) | priest |
| *Also*: | |
| Circuit Drivers (Sirkit Dryvas) | appointed by the PCO for missionary work |
| Examiners | judges in consistory courts |
| Inspectors (Inspekturs, Inspektahs) | bishops, deans, any members of the PCO hierarchy |
| Knowledge Boys (Nolidj Boys) | trainee Drivers who have made their London appearances but not yet for the burbs |
| mushers (1) | traditional holy men |
| stalkers (storkas, stawkas) | mendicant friars |
| dry-vys | violets |
| duvet (doovay, dúvä) | blanket or other bed covering |

## *E*

| | |
|---|---|
| Emtwenny5 | City wall (of London) |
| estate (esstayt) | town |
| evian | spring or spring water |

## *F*

| | |
|---|---|
| fags<br>(fagz) | tobacco (can be in the form of snuff, chewing tobacco (*see* gum) or loose for pipes, cigarettes or cheroots) |
| fare | a soul (also used to denote believer in Dave) |
| Faredar<br>(Fayredar) | mystical power to locate the believer |
| ferry<br>(ferrë) | seagoing vessel, ship |
| fez | pheasant |
| fireweed<br>(fyrweed) | rosebay willowherb |
| flyer<br>(fliar, flyar) | heretic |
| flying | heresy |
| (The) Flying I | Holy Ghost, immanent and omniscient avatar of Dave |
| flying rat | pigeon |
| foglamp | sun (can be full beam (foolbeem), dipped, etc.) |
| fony | beadle or footman |
| fridge<br>(frydg) | conical drystone building used for storing food |

| | |
|---|---|
| fuckoffgaff | lawyerly palace |

## G

| | |
|---|---|
| gaff | house (primitive) |
| gaffer<br>(gaffa) | head servant or butler; also captain of a ferry |
| garri | anus |
| geezer | literally 'disguised one'; homespun prophet |
| getter, getters<br>(getta, gettaz) | brokers, traders, businessmen |
| gherkin<br>(girkyn) | penis |
| greenspike<br>(grënspyke) | hawthorn |
| groovebark<br>(grúvbarc) | ash tree |
| gubbins | catholicon made from a decoction of moto oil; served with all curries on Ham and used as a specific against the pedalo fever |
| gum | chewing tobacco |
| guvnor<br>(guvnaw) | boss, leader, any immediate superior |

## *H*

| | |
|---|---|
| Hack | tacksman (cadet member of aristocratic house who manages lands for the Lawyer, collects rents, etc.) |
| headlight (édlite, édlyt) | moon (can be full beam, dipped, etc.) |
| *Also*: | |
| lightoff (lytoff) | moon set |
| lighton (lyton) | moon rise |
| hoodie (hoody) | characteristic garment of the London poor |

## *I*

| | |
|---|---|
| Ing, Ingland (Inglan, Ingerland) | England |
| intercom (interkom) | the dävine voice heard by the fare, or his prayer to Dave |
| irony (ironi) | metal |

## *J*

| | |
|---|---|
| jack<br>(jak) | aquavit, distilled alcohol |
| JAN, FEB, MAR, APR, etc. | months of the year |
| jeans | thick britches of bubbery or flax |
| jeejee | horse |
| jeepee | doctor or surgeon |
| jonckheeres | wattles beneath the muzzle of a moto containing highly sensitive mucous membranes; possible evidence for marine period of moto evolution |

## *K*

| | |
|---|---|
| kipper | winter |
| knee woman | midwife and wise woman |

## *L*

| | |
|---|---|
| lairy<br>(lairë) | insolent |
| lamp | sun |
| *Also*:<br>lampoff | sunset |
| lampon | sunrise |

| | |
|---|---|
| Lawyer<br>(Loyah, Lawd) | used exclusively to denote dads who have large land holdings |
| letric<br>(lettrik, lectric) | oil lamp, or light thrown by one |
| lettuce | letters (correspondence) |
| lezza | childless woman |
| lighter<br>(lyta) | tinder, flint and steel |
| limmo | brougham or landau |
| London cloth<br>(Lundun cloff) | cotton |
| luvvie<br>(love, luv) | noblewoman's title and female honorific |

## *M*

| | |
|---|---|
| MadeinChina<br>(MaydinChyna) | creation |
| manor<br>(manna) | village |
| mansize<br>(mansys) | handkerchief |
| marl | marble |
| micro<br>(mykro) | sacred ark, kept in the Shelter, in which the Book is housed |

| Mokni | Inglish dialect |
|---|---|
| moped | infant moto |
| moto (1) | large, viviparous, omnivorous, mammalian creature native to Ham and found nowhere else. Used by the Hamsters as a source of meat and oil alone. The moto has the functional intelligence of a two-and-a-half-year-old human child |
| moto (2) | collective term employed in New London to describe wheeled transport. Here are kinds of motos: |
| 4dubbulUdee | wagon |
| artic (artik, artyk) | wagon |
| cab (2) | gig or two- or four-wheeler |
| car (ka) | cart |
| coach | coach (usually drawn by four or more jeejees) |
| limmo | brougham or landau |
| mummies | women of childbearing age |
| mummytime (mummitym) | the half-week (blob) children spend with mummies |
| munchjack | muntjac |

| | |
|---|---|
| musher (1) | traditional holyman |
| musher (2) | child of Ham assigned to look after motos |

## *O*

| | |
|---|---|
| oatie (otie, otey) | porridge |
| oilgull (oylgul) | fulmar |
| opares | women from adolescence until they become mummies; they are exempt from Changeover and perform childcare duties for the daddies during daddytime |

## *P*

| | |
|---|---|
| PCO (PeeSeeO) | priestly hierarchy, the established Shelter of Ing |
| pedalers | oarsmen |
| pedalo | small boat |
| pedalo fever | illness brought by visitors to remote communities |
| pedals | oars |
| phonics (fonix) | letters (of alphabet) |

| | |
|---|---|
| pieces<br>(peesiz) | chicken |
| pizzaDlivree | manna |
| prettybeaks<br>(prittibeeks) | puffins |
| pricklebush<br>(prikkulboosh) | furze or gorse |

## *Q*

| | |
|---|---|
| queer<br>(kweer, kweah) | childless man |

## *R*

| | |
|---|---|
| railing<br>(rayling) | spear |
| Reervú | holiness or excellency |
| rhodies<br>(roadies) | rhododendrons |
| roastduck<br>(rozdukk) | duck |

## *S*

| | |
|---|---|
| sawleaf<br>(sorleafe) | nettles |
| screen | sky |

| | |
|---|---|
| screenwash | rain |
| seeseeteeveeman | watchman, agent or spy in the employ of the PCO |
| semis | modern houses (i.e., built in brick courses with mortar) |
| Shelter | both the physical place of worship in Dävinanity and the quorum of dads required for a congregation |
| shish | lamb |
| shitter (shitta) | latrine or earth closet |
| shooter (shoota) | arquebus |
| sickseed (sycseed) | sycamore |
| silverbark | silver birch |
| smoothbark (smoovbark, smoovbarc, smúvbarc) | beech tree |
| snip | snipe |
| sofabed | bed (as opposed to simple pallet) |
| sound (sahnd) | good (appropriate) |
| squishprims | primroses |
| standard | broadsheet |

| | |
|---|---|
| starbuck, starbucks (stabuk, stabbuk, fúlinglish) | breakfast |
| sticks (stikks, styx) | the countryside or provinces |

## *T*

| | |
|---|---|
| 2by4s | beams (wooden) |
| T-shirt (teeshyrt) | simple shift of either London cloth or bubbery |
| takeaway (taykawai) | light meal eaten on the go, or any form of cold provisions |
| tank | belly or stomach |
| tariff | |
| first | 6 a.m.–2 p.m. |
| second | 2 p.m.–10 p.m. |
| third | 10 p.m.–6 a.m. |
| ticket (tikkit) | fine or any levy |
| tincan | drinking cup |
| toyist | fake, unreal or taboo |
| traficmaster (trafikmasta) | compass |

## *U*

| | |
|---|---|
| units | minutes |
| Utree | yew tree |

## *W*

| | |
|---|---|
| wheatie (weety, weeti) | both bread and wheat (the crop) |
| whippystalk (wippistawk, wippistalk, wippëstork) | brambles |
| whirrcock (würkok) | woodcock |
| woolly (vooli) | sheep |

## *Y*

| | |
|---|---|
| yok | York stone (usu. in flags) |